The Enchanter
Merlin

BY THE SAME AUTHOR

Ahasuerus

The Enchanter
Merlin

by
Edgar Quinet

translated, annotated and introduced by
Brian Stableford

A Black Coat Press Book

Visit our website at www.blackcoatpress.com

TABLE OF CONTENTS

Introduction

Merlin l'enchanteur by Edgar Quinet, here translated as *The Enchanter Merlin*, was originally published in two volumes in 1860 by Michel Lévy. It was reprinted in 1878 as volumes XVI and XVII of the author's collected works, published by Hachette; that version was reprinted several times. Quinet had begun writing it in 1853, and it represented the core of his endeavor for seven years while he was living in exile, first in Brussels and then, after 1858, in Switzerland. He had been banished from his native land following Louis Napoléon's 1851 coup, because he had previously held an administrative position in the Republican government established in 1848.

Many of the Republicans banished by the self-proclaimed emperor returned to France after a relatively brief absence, when an amnesty was offered by the new régime. They included such prominent literary men as Eugène Sue, Alexandre Dumas and P.-J. Hetzel, but Quinet, like Victor Hugo, refused to return while the Second Empire remained standing. When he completed the book, however, there was still no end in sight; he had no way of knowing that the Franco-Prussian War would eventually bring it down in 1870. In consequence, and inevitably—especially on the part of a writer who inserted himself into his fiction as much as Quinet did—*Merlin l'enchanteur* is deeply impregnated with the sensation and desperation of his exile, as well as the hopes and ideas that assisted him to bear it.

The Bibliothèque Nationale, which purchased the manuscript of the novel in 2005, captions its advertisement for that purchase with the statement that the novel constitutes "the only fictional rewriting devoted to Merlin in France during the 19th century," and claims that, on that basis alone, it is of great importance in the history of the myth, as well as the author's biography. We are now so accustomed to the popularity and familiarity of fiction of this kind that it is difficult to imagine a time when it seemed so extraordinary as to be bizarre, but that was the case when Quinet conceived the project of writing his fictional "biography" of Merlin. Nor was the situation in England much different at the time, even though the mythology of King Arthur's reign and his court was not only more familiar in 1860 but was beginning to take on something of the appearance of a "national epic," by virtue of the reprinting, earlier in the century, of Thomas Malory's *Morte d'Arthur*, albeit in abridged versions and under different titles.

Morte d'Arthur had not always been a popular work, although it had the distinction of being one of the earliest English printed books when William Caxton produce an edition in 1485—reportedly with some reluctance, because he did not believe that King Arthur had ever existed, and needed to be persuaded of the contrary. Wynkyn de Worde had produced a second edition a decade later, but there was no subsequent one throughout the 16th century. William Shakespeare and Edmund Spenser both knew of its existence, but their references to the myth of Arthur and Merlin are fleeting, and Shakespeare did not seize upon it as he did upon two other mythical Dark Age kings, Lear and Cymbeline, in order to exploit its tragic potential. The work's resurfacing in the early 19th century was, therefore, something of a Renaissance, and the employment of the stories it contains as a form of imaginative capital was to change dramatically in the last decades of the century.

Although the members of the British Romantic Movement had mostly steered clear of Arthuriana in their heyday, save for Thomas Love Peacock's delightful but neglected prose romance *The Misfortunes of Elphin* (1829), Alfred, Lord Tennyson's "Morte d'Arthur" (1842) was extended over the next four decades into the verse epic *The Idylls of the King*, which cemented both the popularity and cultural status of Malory's account as a kind of formative myth of England, with the heroic Arthur as a central role model whose spirit was echoed in such modern national heroes as the Duke of Wellington.

In early 19th-century France, of course, the situation of the myths of Arthur and Merlin seemed quite different, most importantly because they did not seem to be British at all, let alone quintessentially British, Malory being virtually unknown there. One of the key elements of the French Romantic Movement, however, of whom Quinet was a key member, was the quest to rediscover and revitalize mythical and folkloristic materials, which several adherents of the movement saw as vitally important to a proper understanding of both history and human psychology. Just as the German Romantics, with whom Quiet had familiarized himself during a long sojourn in Germany in the late 1820s, were seeking in their own myth and folklore for an essential *volksgeist* [spirit of the people] which they were attempting to celebrate and revitalize in *kunstmärchen* [art folktales], Quinet deliberately went in search in something similar when he had occasion to examine various manuscripts of 12th century romances, many of which had never been printed and only a handful of which could qualify as well-known.

Quinet searched that material for the "soul" of the then-embryonic French nation, and discovered his own version of it. Typically, however, he did not discover it in what would have seemed to almost anyone else to be the logical place, in *La Chanson de Roland* and its rich spinoff of tales of Charlemagne's heroic knights, but in Arthuriana. From his viewpoint, however, as a Frenchman and a pacifist, Arthur could not be the key symbol in that nexus of tales, because Arthur had been a king in England, and a warrior; the symbol that Quinet thought it appropriate—and, indeed, necessary—to represent as the putative soul of France was the far more mercurial figure of Merlin. *Merlin l'enchanteur* is, in a sense, intended to be the ultimate quintessentially French *kunstmärchen*—but, like Tennyson's *Idylls*, it was a long time in gestation.

Quinet's initial study of verse and prose romances, based on his original research, was published as *Rapport à M. le Ministre des travaux publics, sur les épopées françaises du 12ème siècle, restées jusqu'à ce jour en manuscript* (1831) and reprinted in the *Oeuvres complètes* as "Les Épopées françaises inédites du 12ème siècle" [Unpublished French Epics of the 12th Century]. The assertions he made with therein regard to the nature of early French romances, and their importance to an understanding of French history and national psychology, were reiterated and strengthened in chapters IX-XIV of his *Histoire de la poésie* (1837), which was reprinted along with the earlier essay in vol. IX of the *Oeuvres complètes*. He remarked in the preface that he added to the essay in the *Oeuvres complètes* that it had been the first work that brought him to public attention, by virtue of the "strange tempest" of "violent anger" that it unleashed against him.

It now seems strange that such an esoteric essay could have unleashed a storm of controversy, and even more strange that the violent reaction was provoked by assertions that are now broadly taken for granted, but Quinet's membership of the Romantic Movement put him in automatic opposition to "Classicist" scholars, just as it did to "Classicist" litterateurs, and there was a reaction ready to burst forth at the slightest provocation, even something as trivial as his assertion that the prose romances had been preceded by the verse romances. The contention that really brought scholarly wrath down on his head, however, was the idea that the French romances had appropriated material generously from "Celtic" [i.e. Welsh] sources.

That assertion too now seems utterly uncontroversial—and, indeed, incontrovertible—but in 1831, at least in the intellectual arena in which Quinet was working, it was a matter of some dispute, and by the time he published his *Histoire de la poésie* it was the focus of intense and rather intemperate argument, the brunt of which was born by another historian and folklorist associated with the Romantic Movement, Théodore Hersart, Vicomte de La Villemarqué. Hersart was a native of Brittany and was intensely interested in Breton history, folklore and culture. He made little distinction between Bretons and Britons, and regarded Medieval Bretagne as having had far closer links with Grande Bretagne, especially with Cornouailles [Cornwall] and Cambrie [Cambria, i.e. Wales] than with most of the regions that were subsequently gathered into France—with the possible exception of neighboring Normandy.

Hersart caused controversy when he published a collection entitled *Barzaz Breiz* [Breton Ballads, in Breton] in 1839, which ostensibly rendered many traditional Breton ballads into modern French, tacitly claiming much of French folklore for his native province. He was widely accused of falsifying the material, at least in the translation process, and probably by some outright fakery, but the collection nevertheless proved very popular. He followed it up with a two-volume collection of *Contes populaires des ancient Bretons* [Popular Tales of the Ancient Bretons] (1842), which is an anthology of four Medieval romances adapted into modern prose, beginning with *Perceval*, in a version that includes one of the several long continuation of Chrétien de Troyes' original *Conte du Graal*—one of the most important Arthurian tales of the period. The collection is prefaced by a long essay examining the key elements of the Arthurian mythos, with separate essays on Arthur, Merlin and Lancelot, treating them as inventions that had arrived in Grande Bretagne from continental Bretagne, and had been initially developed there in a specifically Cambrian context before being reimported to France.

Hersart apparently began working on a much more elaborate version of that essay almost immediately, and, to all appearances, on his own prose epic summarizing the entire "tradition," but it took him too long, and by the time his *Myrdhinn, ou l'enchanteur Merlin: son histoire, ses oeuvres, son influence* [Myrdhinn, or the Enchanter Merlin: His History, His Works and His Influence] was ready for publication, it was 1862, and he had been comprehensively upstaged, as he wryly noted in his introduction. Although the book is ostensibly non-fiction, its longest section by far, "Myrdhinn, personne romanesque" [Myrdhinn, Romantic Character] is presented in narrative form, and could easily have been issued separately as a work of fiction, although it remained, even in its own day, so obscure that it is unsurprising that the Bibliothèque Nationale's caption-writer ignored it when promoting Quinet's work.

How well Quinet knew Hersart is unclear, and he certainly cannot have had much contact with him while in exile, so such similarities as there are between their two versions of Merlin's biography—and the differences are much more obvious—are probably due almost entirely to the common sources on which they drew, but there are a few passages where the overlap is very striking, most remarkably those dealing with the Council in Hell that prompts the Devil to sire Merlin, as described in *Merlin* in 1860 and *Myrdhinn* in 1862, although both passages must have been written many years earlier.

In Britain, not unnaturally, the attempt to "reclaim" Arthurian folklore from its early literary deployments in France has focused entirely on Wales rather than Brittany, and probably with justification, but the British Arthurians, from Malory onwards, like Quinet and Hersart, have always been more interested in myth creation than historical clarification, even though some of them might not have been entirely conscious of the fact. Whatever the actually evolutionary pattern of the oral folklore that provided the seeds the Arthurian mythos might have been, there is no doubt at all that its growth and flowering was primarily a literary process, and that much of what is now taken for granted (in Britain at least) as "Celtic folklore" relating to the Arthurian mythos was imaginatively projected "backwards" from French literary sources in a period when much of the British Isles was under the sway of the "Norman Conquest."

Modern literary works based on the stories of Arthur and Merlin, especially when they represent explicit, earnest and artistic endeavors in myth-creation, as Quinet's, Hersart's and Tennyson's do, thus have very complex historical roots, at which it is worth looking more closely if the specific features of Quinet's *Merlin* are to be better understood. Because the original seeds of Quinet's endeavor were drawn from the 12th century manuscripts he studied in order to make his 1931 report, it is undoubtedly helpful to look a little more closely at the content of those manuscripts of the genre of "romances" to which they belonged.

The word "romance," in both French and English, is ultimately derived from the Old French *romanz*, whose approximate meaning was "vernacular," and which was initially used to refer to documents translated from Latin. By the 12th century, however, the term and its evolving derivatives were more frequently and more particularly used with reference to a nascent genre of poetry and prose fiction that had moved on from translations of Latin epic poetry to prolific original composition. Just as the translations had referred to what was by then a distant mythologized past, the imitations and pastiches also looked back nostalgically to a whole series of mythologized distant pasts.

The best-known of the verse romances of which 12th century copies survive is *La Chanson de Roland*, which describes the ambush in the Pyrenees of a company of Charlemagne's knights returning from fighting Moors in Spain. Another cycle of poems referring back to the same era is the "Guillaume cycle" featuring Guillaume d'Orange, of which no 12th century manuscripts survive, but which presumably dates from the same era and has slightly better connections with actual history. Other early examples of the burgeoning genre included the story of verse *Floire et Blanchefleur*, about the love of a pagan prince for a Christian captive, and several versions of the story of Tristan's highly problematic love for Iseult, the intended bride of his liege-lord King Mark of Cornwall, of which two substantial—but still fragmentary—12th century texts survive, as well as numerous later manuscripts.

One version of the story of Tristan and Iseult that has not survived is known to have been written by Chrétien de Troyes, who became the most popular of the late 12th century writers of romance, and was also the most inventive. He was the great pioneer of romances featuring the court of King Arthur, beginning with *Erec et Enede*, which focuses on the conflict of conscience the knight Erec experiences as he tries to reconcile the demands of his chivalric ideals, which summon him to errant adventure, and those of his love for his wife, which incline him to stay at home. *Le Chevalier de la Charrette*, also known as *Lancelot*, tells the story of the much sharper conflict generated by the knight's deeply problematic love for Arthur's wife, Guenièvre. It became far better known than *Le Chevalier au Lion*, also known as *Yvain*, a story of moral progress and redemption whose hero loses the love of his life but eventually recovers her after a period of madness in the wilderness.

All three of those completed works were eventually outshone, however—at least in terms of modern pseudoscholarship—by Chrétien's unfinished allegory

Le Conte du Graal, also known as *Perceval*, which was apparently intended as a further story of progress and redemption with a more definite Christian decoding, but whose incompleteness left it with an intriguing aspect of mystery, further supplemented by confusion caused by the fact that it was bundled together for posthumous publication with another unfinished work, featuring the adventures of the knight Gauvain.

Although the particular popularity of Chrétien de Troyes was undoubtedly a major factor in establishing Arthurian romance as a core topic of the genre, contemporary politics also played a leading part, many of the key events of the period being the slowly-unfolding consequences of the event that subsequently made 1066 the best-known date in British history, when William I defeated his Saxon rival for the English throne, Harold, at the Battle of Hastings. The wealthiest and most powerful woman in Western Europe throughout the latter half of the 12th century was Eleanor of Aquitaine, who first married Louis VI of France but almost immediately after the annulment of that marriage, in 1152, married Henry, Duke of Normandy, who became Henry II of England two years later. The sons she bore Henry included the future kings Richard Coeur-de-Lion and John.

Eleanor's court was undoubtedly an important source of patronage for writers and performers of romances, especially the epic-imitating *chansons de geste*, and her concerns undoubtedly help to shape the substance of the genre. Many subsequent historians credited her with the importation of an important element of southern "troubadour culture" into the chivalric romances of Northern France, hence generating the stories of problematic love that played a central role in the genre from Tristan and Iseult onwards. Although her personal role might have been exaggerated, the effective fusion of the Duchy of Aquitaine with Normandy undoubtedly formed the practical background to the amalgamation, as well as assisting its symbolization. The confusion of influences, however, extended much further than that central marriage.

The conquering Normans, who had originated as invaders from Scandinavia, were pillars of the feudal political system, glorified in romance by the retrospective extrapolation of the contemporary hierarchy of kings, barons and knights into imaginary pasts, where it could be more easily credited with imaginary virtues. Much of that mythology was, as Hersart de La Villemarqué argued, borrowed from the Normans' neighbors in northern France, the Bretons, who were already taking a nostalgic delight in the twelfth century in looking back to lost glory days of heroic *preux chevaliers* [gallant knights]. Meanwhile, the rulers of large parts of both France and England had long been descended from invaders—the Franks and the Saxons—who had partly displaced and partly absorbed previous cultures, loosely describable as Gauls and Celts, which had been previously conquered, at least briefly by the Roman Empire. In consequence, the mythological pasts cooked up in France and England in the 12th century were blessed with a rich complexity and confusion of inherited and improvised materials.

Literary romance was an inherently syncretic genre, tacitly celebrating the kind of blending obtained by conquest and reorganization that was inherent in the actual history of feudalism as well as the flattering ideological image that romancers tried to construct. Central to that syncretic process was the fundamental marriage of the Breton/Norman "chivalric romance" glorifying knightly prowess in combat with the Provençal/Aquitanian "courtly romance," which offered idealized depictions of intimate relationships. The writers were also willing, and often enthusiastic, to embrace other local folklores and superstitions, and to gather them into their generalized melting-pot—always, of course, with the proviso that threats originating from such dubious imaginative apparatus could not withstand the ideological forces of Christian faith and knightly heroism. It is against this background that the mythology of Arthur and Merlin was invented. Although Chrétien de Troyes was the principal literary progenitor of the Arthurian subgenre of romance, he was not the inventor of its substance, and he made no contribution to the development of the myth of Merlin, who was almost entirely the brainchild of a writer nowadays known as Geoffrey of Monmouth.

Galfridus Monumentensis, as he referred to himself in Latin, lived in the first half of the 12th century, and might well have been born in the Welsh marshes, although there is no evidence that he could speak or read the Welsh language. Most of his adult career was spent in Oxford, where he was probably associated with one of the teaching institutions that subsequently evolved into a university—the first in England—in 1167, when Henry II banned English students from attending the University of Paris. Although he was appointed Bishop of St. Asaph in 1152 there is no evidence that Geoffrey visited the see in question before his death, not long thereafter. The first of his works to survive is known as the *Prophetiae Merlini* [Prophecies of Merlin], in which the prophet Merlin is asked by an English king, Vortigern, to interpret a dream in which a red dragon is defeated in a fight by a white dragon. Merlin interprets it as an allegory of the defeat of the Britons by Saxon invaders—a prophecy whose accuracy, like that of almost all accurate prophecies, comes from having been made after the fact. Other "prophecies" cited in the text have the same advantage, which doubtless helped make the work popular, providing an entirely illusory "basis" for a few gnomic remarks related to events as-yet-untranspired.

Geoffrey subsequently included the substance of that brief early text in a much more elaborate *Historia Regum Britanniae* [History of the Kings of Britain], dating from the late 1130s, which relates the supposed history of Britain from its first settlement by refugees from Troy to the death of a king named Cadwallader in the 7th century. Other 12th century writers, who referred to Geoffrey's work, including William of Newburgh and Giraldus Cambrensis, were extremely scathing about its lack of accuracy, regarding it as a romance in disguise, but time lends a certain gloss to documents, and many later scholars took it more seriously. It does, in fact, draw upon the very few earlier "histories" that existed at the time, but it transforms their material very considerably, and is best regarded as one of the great classics of genre of "scholarly fantasy": works of imaginative fiction that pose as non-fiction, often contriving by that imposture to impose upon the reader's credibility to a far greater extent than responsible writers of fiction generally feel entitled to do.

Some of the material in Geoffrey's history is appropriated from *De Excidio et Conquestu Britanniae* [On the Ruination and Conquest of Britain], a polemic written in the 6th century by a monk named Gildas, complaining about the sad state into which Britain has fallen since the Romans pulled out. The rather bizarre text is heavily swathed in flamboyant rhetoric and imagery borrowed from prophecies featured in the Biblical books of *Daniel* add *Revelation*, including a symbolic dragon, but it also includes a account of a victory of Briton forces over invading Saxons won by one Aurelianus Ambrosianus. Gildas was himself mythologized by two highly fanciful (and contradictory) accounts of his life, the second of which was written in the mid-twelfth century by Caradoc of Llancarfan, whom Geoffrey cites at one point and with whom he might have been acquainted.

Geoffrey's principal source for his history, however, was the *Historia Brittonum*, apparently written in the 9th century, although the oldest surviving manuscripts date from the twelfth; it is sometimes attributed to Nennius because a preface with that name attached appears in some versions, although it was obviously not part of the original work. The history contained therein begins with the fictitious settlement of the British isles by refugees from Troy, and its subsequent rule by a descendant of Aeneas named Brutus, who was appropriated by Geoffrey. One of its passages concerns a king named Vortigern, who allows the Saxons to settle in England, and who also recruits a magically-talented youth named Ambrosius to solve a problem involving subterranean dragons—the obvious source for the materials of Geoffrey's *Prophetiae Merlini*, which are further elaborated in his *Historia*, where Ambrosius is said to be an alternative name for Merlin.

By that means, Gildas' Aurelianus Ambrosius and the earlier *Historia*'s Ambrosius are rather awkwardly fused by Geoffrey into the character of Merlin. It is, however, not with Vortigern that Geoffrey's Merlin is primarily associated but a different Saxon-fighting king, Arthur, who is credited with winning a whole series of victories against the invaders. Manuscript references to Arthur prior to Geoffrey's are very thin on the ground, and are mostly made in passing, as if to someone whose name is assumed to familiar, thus strengthening the hypothesis—although it remains a hypothesis—that he was a significant figure in Welsh folklore long before the eleventh century. If so, that would also explain why there is absolutely no mention of him in any chronicles of the period produced in England. If Arthur was well-known in Welsh oral folklore, that proba-

14

bly helped the character to take wing, throwing the many other kings cited by Geoffrey entirely the shade, and would certainly help to explain why Geoffrey associated him with Merlin, whose name and prophetic abilities are clearly adapted from that of a character featured in several Welsh poems, Myrddin Wyllt (the suffix means "Wild" or "Mad").

Myrddin, who was supposed have lived in the 6th century, was said to have been so traumatized by his patron's death in battle that he went to live wild in the woods for the rest of his life, occasionally harassed by his patron's killer, but receiving in the process an alleged gift for prophecy. The oldest surviving text referring to him is the 10th century *Armes Prydain* [Prophecy of Britain], the obvious model for Geoffrey's *Prophetiae Merlin*. Geoffrey might have introduced the *l* into Merlin's name simply for the sake of variety, although the philologist Gaston Paris (writing some time after Quinet) has suggested that he did not want to Latinize the name as Merdin because his readers might have linked it with the Latin *merda* [faeces]—the root of the French *merde*, which is frequently used as an offensive obscenity. Geoffrey's invention of Merlin was the principal factor in the speculative attribution to him of a third Latin work featuring the character, the poem *Vita Merlini* [Life of Merlin]; although its depiction is much closer to the image of Myrddin Wyllt than the Merlin of the *Historia*, it does refer to the madman's previous acquaintance with both Vortigern and Arthur.

The earliest French Arthuriana, including Chrétien de Troyes' romances, do not make much of the association between Arthur and Merlin, but later ones did, to the extent that he soon became intimately entwined with such obviously-French additions as Lancelot, Gauvain and the Holy Grail—sufficiently, in Quinet's estimation based on the romances he studied, to be representable as a symbol of French cultural identity and a presiding spirit of the evolving nation of France. Merlin's apparent Welsh origins are, of course, deliberately blurred by Quinet, taking his cue from later 12th century writers as well as from Hersart: a tactic supported by Quinet's refusal in his own romance to make any substantial distinction between Bretons and Britons, thus effectively making Wales (and Cornwall) an extension of Brittany, and hence of at least part of France.

Geoffrey's *Historia*, written in Latin, was notionally readable throughout Christendom, but its popularity among the laity in France was greatly assisted by a rapid adaptation into French verse, the *Roman de Brut* (1155), credited to Henry II's court chronicler Wace. Wace's version amplified the Arthurian component considerably and added several new details thereto, including the Round Table and the prophecy of Arthur's future return from the isle of Avalon. Wace treats that additional material as fanciful folklore rather than history, but the distinction was unimportant to the romancers who borrowed from him. Marie de France, also a member of Henry II's court, must have known Wace, and his work is the source of the Arthurian material she incorporated into some of her *Lais*, written in the 1160s and 1170s. Wace was also a key source for a further scholarly fantasy based on Geoffrey's *Historia*, entitled *Brut* and produced around the year 1200 by Layamon, which not only elaborates the story of Arthur but those of Lear and Cymbeline, thus providing the basis for two of Shakespeare's plays.

After Chrétien de Troyes' death in 1185, and especially after the posthumous publication of *Le Conte du Graal*, imitations of his works became commonplace, including several continuations of the unfinished works, the grail story attracting particular interest. By the end of the 12th century, the monks of Glastonbury had claimed that they had discovered the tombs of Arthur and his wife, and they went on to produce their own version of the grail story. That claim was apparently familiar to Robert de Boron, who is known to have produced three Arthurian significant texts in verse during the 1190s, *Joseph d'Arimathie, Merlin* and *Perceval*, although only the first and fragments of the second survive. The fragments of Boron's poem indicate, however, that it was the source of a prose adaptation known as the *Estoire de Merlin* or the *Prose Merlin*, which became an important source not merely for Quinet but many other writers. It is sometimes credited to Boron, although there is no evidence that he wrote it.

The *Prose Merlin* helped popularize the notion, obliquely mentioned by Geoffrey, that Merlin was sired by an incubus on a virgin, with a view to his becoming the Antichrist, and it also introduced his teacher Blaise and several other significant motifs borrowed by Quinet, although Quinet studiously ignores its heavy emphasis on Merlin's shapeshifting abilities. The *Prose Merlin*'s importance was further amplified by the fact that it was integrated into a series generally known as the "Vulgate Cycle," apparently dating from 1220-1230, which included works apparently based on Robert de Boron's other two titles, as well as a sequel to the *Prose Merlin* entitled *Suite de Merlin*.

The *Prose Merlin* also introduced the character of Viviane, with whom Merlin falls in love. The character was, however, to be greatly elaborated in the *Suite de Merlin*, in which she puts an end to his career by using the magic he has taught her to imprison him permanently, and further complicated in an imitative "Post-Vulgate Cycle" of 1230-1240. Initially a huntress, in later works she became the more ethereal Lady of the Lake, and her name began a process of extensive variation that produced, among others, Niniane, Nimue, Elaine and Evienne, some of which are probably due to careless copyists. Although Quinet's primary interest was in 12th century texts, it was in the 13th century, with such linked cycles as these, that Arthurian romance really took off on a large scale, and much of the material used in his *Merlin* is taken from 13th century sources. Few of the writers who developed the Arthurian mythos in France after Chrétien are known by name, but they allegedly included Wauchier de Danain, Manessier and Gerbert de Montreuil, all of whom were credited with producing continuations of the *Conte du Graal* in the early decades of the century, and Raoul de Houdenc, who wrote two long poems featuring Gauvain in the

1220s, and might have played some part in influencing the substance of *Merlin l'enchanteur* by virtue of his subsequent authorship to *Le Songe d'enfer*, an account of an allegorical voyage to Hell far in advance of Dante's.

It was also in the early 13th century that the Arthurian mythos began to spread more widely in Europe, most spectacularly in Wolfram von Eschenbach *Parzifal* (c1210), which expanded Chrétien de Troyes' *Conte du graal* vastly, although it claims to be based on an entirely different source—obviously hypocritically, although that has not deterred scholars from searching for the work in question. Its adaptation into the evolving English language was more belated, and decidedly eccentric, in the enigmatic 14th century poem *Sir Gawain and the Green Knight*. Malory's 15th century *Le Morte D'Arthur* is heavily dependent on the Vulgate cycle, especially the *Suite de Merlin*, but develops the material in a fashion that is very much his own. Quinet, however, although he was certainly well aware of the *Suite de Merlin*, preferred the *Prose Merlin* as a key source—and his development of the material was even more distinctive and adventurous, not only because he was writing in a very different era and with a very different political agenda, but because of the intensely personal elements that he imported into his version of Merlin's story.

The most striking thing about *Merlin l'enchanteur*, especially from an English point of view, is the radical de-emphasization of the character of Arthur, to the point that he is not even called Arthur, his name being deliberately varied as Arthus. He is, of course, indispensable to the story, and he retains his status as the ultimate model of benevolent kingship, but he remains in the background for by far the greater part of the story, only appearing in the narrative foreground occasionally and briefly until he dies—or, rather, goes into a long suspended animation. Indeed, he is far more prominent in the story after that incident than before it, because he is always far more important as an idea than an active individual. Although he has a reputation as a warrior, we never see him strike a single blow—nor does any of his knights, whose presence is even more fugitive; Lancelot and Perceval are only mentioned in passing and Gauvain only appears on stage once, in very peculiar circumstances.

That relative absence reflects and embodies the fact that the central concept of Quinet's version of the Arthurian Mythos is not heroism but what he terms "justice." Arthur is a great king, in this view, not because he slays Saxons but precisely because he is rigorously opposed to anyone slaying anyone, wanting everyone to live in peace and harmony, and to be happy—a utopian state of affairs that cannot be achieved by violence, but which Merlin's magic contrives, for a while. Merlin is, however, deeply committed to the notion that the end in question ought to be achievable without the necessity of magic, by the force of human desire and will alone, and it is the perverse failure of human beings not only to achieve it, but even to desire it, that provides one of the two determining features of his bleak character and his anguished sentiments. The other determining feature of that mental trouble, in Quinet's epic, is his relationship with Viviane.

That Bibliothèque Nationale's advertisement for the manuscript summarizes the story of *Merlin l'enchanteur*, a trifle brutally but not unreasonably, as an account of Merlin's "perfect love" with Viviane, cruelly interrupted by a fatal separation. Although Viviane is off stage for the bulk of the narrative, her absence provides the essential context for everything that Merlin does and feels during his travels and exploits, and their peculiar correspondence provides more narrative energy than any of his actions. The text was initially published with a sets of brief endnotes by the author, mostly serving to indicate which elements of the story were "in the tradition," but the second edition of 1878 and reprints thereof contain a second set of notes added by "Madame Edgar Quinet"—his second wife, Hermione, who edited several posthumous volumes of his work and wrote her own commentary in order to identify some of the links between the story and Quinet's own life story. Hermione's notes are, however, limited in their analysis by their tendency to gloss over the fact that many of those links reflect the importance of Quinet's relationship with his first wife, Minna.

Minna had died in March 1851, before the coup, and Quinet married Hermione, the daughter of the Rumanian writer and political activist Gheorghe Asachi, during the first year of his exile, in 1852. He and Hermione were, therefore, together for the entire period during which he was writing *Merlin l'enchanteur*. Given that circumstance, the character of Viviane, insofar as she reflects aspects of Quinet's life story, must be a composite, embodying elements of both his wives, although the plot, where the authority of the "tradition" only equips Merlin with one passionate love-affair, does not permit that to become obvious within the text. It might also be as well to bear in mind that Hermione must have read *Merlin l'enchanteur* while it was in progress, and that Quinet must have written it with that consciousness, which surely affected the references in the text that relate to Minna as well as those to that relate to Hermione.

Merlin l'enchanteur was only Quinet's second significant work of prose fiction, although the earlier one, *Ahasvérus* (1834; tr. as *Ahasuerus*),[1] had been preceded by a kind of preliminary sketch of its central motif, and it was his last. In between, he had written two verse epics, *Napoléon* (1835) and *Prométhée* [Prometheus] (1838). Although he undoubtedly identified with his own version of Prometheus, just as he had earlier identified with the Wandering Jew while writing the earlier prose epic, his poetry is considerably more distanced than his prose, so the two major prose works form a pair, not merely in reworking myths in a fashion that is quite unparalleled in its scope and ambition, but also in the intricacy and fervor in which the author's own sentiments are interwoven with

---

[1] The Introduction to the Black Coat Press translation of *Ahasuerus* (2013, ISBN 9781612272146) contains a broader synoptic account of Quinet's life and career, which there is no need to repeat in full here.

his cosmic themes. It is significant, in comparing the two, that *Ahasvérus* was written before Quinet married Minna, at a time when he was far from sure that he would be able to do so, and that the entire work is thus figuratively located within one of the periods represented in the latter novel by Merlin and Viviane's estrangement.

The principal reason why Quinet thought that his separation from Minna might be permanent following a disastrous return to Germany in 1831 was that her family, who had welcomed him previously, had turned against him, her father having died and Minna having recently acquired two brothers-in-law who were extreme Lutherans highly disapproving of French freethinkers; on their instructions she broke off the relationship. The rupture lasted throughout his subsequent trip to Italy, and was not repaired until late in 1934, not long before their marriage. That rupture is clearly mirrored in the rupture between Merlin and Viviane in *Merlin l'enchanteur*—in which Merlin and Viviane's relationship is necessarily far from perfect—and it is significant in this context that the first edition of *Ahasvérus* carried a dedication to another woman, which was removed from all editions published subsequent to the marriage. The transfiguration of the relationship in the second novel would have been bound in any case to be markedly different from the transfiguration represented in the earlier novel by the similarly remarkable relationship between Ahasvérus and Rachel, but the presence of Hermione's observing eye must also have colored the spectrum of those differences in a more vivid fashion.

It would, however, be misleading to read *Merlin l'enchanteur* simply as a complicated transfigurative love story, just as it would be a mistake to read *Ahasvérus* that way, viewing its extraordinary macrocosmic embellishments merely as a narcissistic magnification of microcosmic issues. If, for Quinet, the personal and the political were so intimately bound up as to be inextricable, it was not because he was inclined to a species of quasi-solipsism, but because he saw similar underlying principles, causes and conflicts active in himself and the world. The cosmic issues that he addresses in both *Ahasvérus* and *Merlin l'enchanteur* are taken very seriously, in their own right, and it is that seriousness rather than any exaggerated self-awareness or self-importance that drives and produces their unparalleled scope and originality.

There is a sense in which the imaginative scope of *Ahasvérus* left no scope for further melodramatic inflation, in that God's "Last" Judgment is not only appealed but successfully overturned, with the result that Ahasvérus is not only redeemed from his tedious punishment but gets to choose the form and conditions of his redemption, while God withers and dies in future irrelevance. That was a conclusion whose imaginative reach could not be exceeded, and the conclusion of *Merlin l'enchanteur* wisely does not try—but that does not mean that the novel does not attempt to explore imaginative realms untouched in *Ahasvérus*, or in any other work of imaginative fiction produced before or after.

In fact, *Merlin l'enchanteur* boldly embraces the one cosmic archetype deliberately omitted from account in *Ahasvérus*—the Devil—and deals with him, and with the Hell whose king he is, in a suitably extravagant symbolic fashion. Typically, however, Quinet casually sidesteps precedent; when Merlin first goes to Hell to meet his father, he is offered a tour by Virgil, who is hanging around with a very long wait in prospect before Dante turns up to exploit his services, but he treats the invitation lightly and his observations of Hell are skimpy in the extreme. Nor does he cast more than a sidelong glance at Heaven, and ignores the very possibility of Purgatory. Instead, he takes an elaborate extended tour of Limbo, conversing not with the regretful spirits of the dead but with the embryonic spirits of the not-yet-born: an experience that gives him, and the reader, a new and unique perspective, not only on the nature of life and the history of the world to come, but also on his long and equally idiosyncratic relationship with the spirits of the ruins, and with the tomb itself, as he eventually has to experience it. That shift in perspective is not labored in the commentary provided by the narrative voice, but it is nevertheless crucial to the work's epic quality and the uniqueness of its essay in myth creation.

Modern readers, especially those familiar with other narrative reconfigurations of the Arthurian mythos, might well find *Merlin l'enchanteur* a trifle lacking in action. Popular fiction thrives so heavily on violence, almost to the point of a consistent and extreme sadism, that is by no means lacking even in modern love stories, that the very idea of pacifist fiction can seem alien as well as tedious to habitual readers, who are unwilling to entertain it even as an intriguing exercise in contrast. One of the things that Quinet's narrative asks of its readers, in fact, is to consider that aspect of themselves, and what it might indicate about them. It is very much a book written by an exile, but it is a narrative of an exile far more profound than a casual banishment by a despicable usurper: an exile, in fact, that cuts far deeper than the political, almost to amount to an estrangement from the human condition, if not the human race.

Paradoxical as it might seem, that is a sensation with which a not-inconsiderable minority of people can easily associate themselves and sympathize, and those readers, at least—most of them are, inevitably, inveterate readers—will find that very few books can speak to them as intimately and as interestingly as this one, because rather than in spite of the fact that it is a narrative that revels in its own paradoxicality. That is evident from the very beginning of the extant version, because Quinet took the trouble to write a second preface for the book, flatly contradicting the preface he had attached to the first, which his editor wisely juxtaposed with it in the *Oeuvres complètes*. He had already indulged a similar paradoxicality in the conclusion, by continuing to provide further text after having declared the story finished. At both narrative poles, however, the form and content of the work alike make it very obvious that *Merlin l'enchanteur* is, fundamentally, a book about uncertainty and the essential impossibility of certainty, on both a personal and a cosmic scale.

This translation was made from copies of the version contained in volumes XVI and XVII of Quinet's *Oeuvres complètes*, published by Hachette. I have not reproduced either Quinet's notes or Hermione's notes in full, the first being rather vague, mostly reporting that certain elements of the story are "in the tradition" without giving specific references, while the second frequently include long quotations of dubious relevance and eulogies that make no substantial contribution to the understanding of the text. I have, however, integrated the material that I consider to be useful into my own footnotes, crediting the sources of the information more specifically whenever I am able to do so.

Brian Stableford

UNPUBLISHED PREFACE[2]

I once had a starling that came from Bohemia. It was a magical bird. For as long as I was occupied with Merlin it stayed with me. While I wrote, it flew over my head or perched on the edge of my table. If I stopped, it began its chirping, which filled an entire arbor. An accomplished artiste, it mingled striking thrusts of the bow with its songs, after which it assumed a voice in a lower register, and made wise speeches in clearly-articulated human language. Then it looked at me with its great dark profound eyes and said: "Write!"

It would never have imagined that the pages it whispered in my ear were a grimoire of metaphysics and science. It took them simply for the summer song of prisoner in his cage, suspended from the vault of heaven. As for thinking that they were an academic thesis, it would rather have shed its plumage, colored violet and orange, with a gold and azure sheen. Anyone daring to contradict it on this point would immediately have received a sharp peck, whose mark would still be visible.

One day, someone took advantage of my absence to ask the bird whether this work did not contain memoirs and details of my intimate life. It took it upon itself to respond discreetly that its master was doubtless too clever to seek his poetry in a void, that everything here was real, drawn from the truth and sown with bloody plumes torn still raw from the natal nest.

They persisted. It replied that in the tomb of Merlin it recognized its master, buried alive with everything that he loved most, but that he could not say any more and did not want to reveal the deepest secrets of the house. Besides which, it found once again in Merlin the familiar echo of the birdsong of forests and ideas freely born in the open air, under the vault of heaven. That was sufficient; why ask more questions?

For as long as the composition of this work lasted, there was not a single day when the starling thought of flying away, although it was left at liberty. Every new page showed it vast horizons, hidden springs and hawthorn bushes. It played in my thoughts, as in the bosom of nature, and did not seem to desire anything else. Incredibly, though, on the day the book was finished and I put it away, our guest—our faithful, inseparable companion, our starling—flew out through the open window. I saw it fly away, as rapid as an arrow, in splendid daylight.

---

[2] This preface was added to the version of the work contained in the *Oeuvres complètes*, having evidently been written three years after the publication of the first edition but not previously used.

At first I could not believe my eyes; I called it back; I ran after it. It was futile. I never saw it again. Although an entire village was put on its track, no one was able to give me any news of it.

Reader, if you want this work to serve as a nest on a stormy day, follow the advice of a bird of heaven. Don't rack your brains, any more than it did, searching for enigmas. Don't imagine monsters to which the author never gave a thought. Make yourself, for a while, an airborne soul; read with the heart what was written with the heart. Pick up the good grain that I have put into these pages, and when you have nourished your fantasy, you will feel your wings, and you will be able to take flight toward a higher and clearer sky. Then you can forget me, if you wish; for all of you are birds, and never think of anything but forgetting or leaving.

Veytaux, canton of Vaud,
1863.

PREFACE TO THE FIRST EDITION

Dare I say that I am attempting herein to open new routes to the imagination? If that is too great an ambition, I ought to accuse myself of it in the very first line.

The plan of this work was made nearly thirty years ago. I was thoroughly imbued with the traditions of our ancient French poetry, then unpublished. I thought that one might still be able to renew the French imagination in its national sources. That idea never left me. Merlin, the first patron of France, became mine.

What I conceived in youth I have executed in maturity. Perhaps it is for that reason that more than one joyful thought concludes in a grave tone. However, all things considered, serenity holds sway; the initial hope was not vanquished.

For an epoch that prefers improvisation to anything else, I fear dooming myself in the mind of the reader by confessing how much time, how many scruples and various cares I have put into a purely literary work. Begun in Belgium at the end of 1853, Merlin was finished in Switzerland at the beginning of 1860. During that long interval, I scarcely ceased—in the midst of very different occupations, it is true—to return to the work on which I ought to be judged, for I have not put as much of myself into any other.

The legend of the human soul until death, and beyond death: that is my subject. There is none greater. I will perhaps be excused for having employed so many days in it if I add that Milton wanted to devote his life to it.

To reconcile all legends by combining them into one alone; to find in the human heart the intimate thread of all popular and national traditions; to bind them into a single serene action, reconnecting the discordant worlds that the imagination of peoples has enchanted: that is what I have dared to attempt.

A true theory of the world would be one that took account of all the facts of the physical order. A true literary conception would be one that found the harmony of all the facts of the ideal or imaginary world, and combined them in a single drama vast enough to contain them all effortlessly.

We have before us a great lyre whose strings have been slackened and falsified by time; it is a matter of retuning them.

Why should the French, who created the vastest inventions in the Middle Ages, no longer be capable of doing so? Why should they resign themselves to creating nothing but fragments? Whence comes that condemnation? What is its basis? Why should the century pass without even attempting the great paths on which the imaginations of the majority of other peoples are engaged? Why that exception for the French? The public, it is said, is too enfeebled, too corrupted, too worn out; it can no longer bear or follow great compositions; it lacks the breath to travel extended horizons. What do we know? Let's try.

The tradition of Merlin, which plunges into our primal origins, has extended from the Middle Ages to our days, reflecting the colors of every age. I have taken up that common foundation, and I have developed it with the same freedom as my predecessors.

This is the soul of French tradition: everything France possesses with which to augment herself, rejuvenate herself and revivify herself with a new sap. What I have said toward the end of my work is no vain ornament of the imagination. It is in all verity that I leave the reader the branch that has made me penetrate the world of Merlin.

You, who are reading me, take possession in your turn of the hazel-branch that I am handing to you. Take the fruits that I have abandoned voluntarily on the branch, in order to leave you the pleasure of picking them yourself. Take, above all, this work, to which I owe so many serene and regretted days, which has given me the strength to live, and to communicate with others as with myself.

I separate myself from it with difficulty, as if from a comforter.

Edgar Quinet
Veytaux, canton of Vaud,
26 June 1860.

THE ENCHANTER MERLIN

BOOK ONE: HOW MERLIN, BY LOVING, BECAME A GREAT ENCHANTER

PROLOGUE

I

And I too am searching for a man, a hero! Let him come, let him stand before me; I promise to march after him on the road of justice.

All that I ask is that he should be very real, and even a strong inclination toward the material would not be superfluous, so many people of our day being confused by ideal creatures. In attaching myself to a historic individual, I do not have to answer for his virtue of his vices.

Like the Florentine during the Black Death—and today the disease is no longer only afflicting the body but the immortal soul too—may I not also, in a circle of friends, in the shadow of an olive-tree, on the edge of a crystalline spring, my forehead circled by an oak-branch, my hands full of flowers, listen to hundreds of stories, until the burden of the burning day diminishes and night brings repose, if not forgetfulness, to my heart?[3]

Blue birds the color of time, chimeras with silken wings, vagabond unicorns, who never sleep, who help a man to get through the sterile hours, either because you amuse the waiting and appease the dolor, or because you sow a torch of glow-worms beneath the footsteps if the man whose route is tenebrous, can you not find me a hero?

On the other hand, I can invoke only you, the wisest, the best-loved, the most accredited, the most powerful of the Muses, O Routine, who render all enterprises facile: I shall consult only you. Come, guide me, on foot along the beaten track, by the side of which grow the vulgar flowers easiest to pick. Take me away from the summits that give one vertigo; I have lived there for too long in mist and storms. Put a brake on me if I forget myself to the point of straying from the banal highway, followed by the human herd. Open their hearts and ears for me! They yield proudly to your slightest desires.

---

[3] "The Florentine" is Giovanni Boccaccio, author of the *Decameron*.

The one I was seeking is found. Yes he is, Reader, and you'll believe me if I swear to you that the choice has not been purely voluntary, but was imposed upon me by the hero himself. For you need to know that, since my early youth, the individual in question has never ceased to haunt my dreams, to obsess my wakefulness, as if he were depending on me to give him life for a second time. I repeat that he has been knocking relentlessly at my door, like a revenant to whom I have the power to return to the light of day; and in his plaints and moans, he begged me to recall him to the memory of forgetful earth, promising me that in return he would cause to pass before me, without overwhelming me, the slow cortege of evil days. He promised to diminish for me the cares of the present, if I would consent to reawaken for him the magic of the past in its glory.

I have obeyed.

His name, his parentage, his genealogy, whether it was noble or plebeian—that is what I ought to begin by telling you; I'm not unaware that that is the first rule. But a false shame retains me, for you are the great slave of words; I fear that, on the name alone, you might form a false idea of my enterprise, and go away without wanting to listen to me. On the other hand, when the sequence of events brings him on to the stage, the opportunity to argue will be gone; he will have become a *fait accompli*. You will accept him as such, with ordinary docility. That is what experience has taught me, although rhetoric denies it.

Now, without deliberation, help me to transport you from the very start to the threshold of the inferno, with which I assume you are familiar, and even into the heart of the abode of eternal dolor. Not that I belong to the satanic school—as you shall soon see—but because the truth commands me to set that first scene. History speaks; tradition commands; it is necessary to follow it.

I shall begin. Listen.

II

Have you ever seen a deliberative assembly divided into a host of parties, each of which is trying to defeat all the others? If you have witnessed that spectacle for a day, or a minute, you have not forgotten it. You know, then, that everyone sets a trap beneath everything he says. There, nothing is more perilous than a smile, because it is the messenger of fraud, and fraud drags death in its wake. Silence is also deceptive, but it is only momentary; it immediately gives way to immense sniggering, the echo of all the filthy, subterranean minds that moral darkness attracts as a funereal lantern attracts the swarm of night-flying moths.

If you have seen that spectacle, you can already picture the aspect of Hell at the moment this story begins. You can imagine the stupid bewilderment of the crowd, proud of being fooled majestically; the oratory precautions, gentle doves that are suddenly transformed into serpents; speeches in which every word sti-

28

fles thought; intelligence no longer serving any other purpose than to hollow out, spiral after spiral, the ever-new creation of Falsehood.

Everyone was busy with that toil. Every mouth was giving birth to lies, and in the middle of an inextricable discussion, interrupted by the hissing of snakes, the Word of Hell was consummate. Every fraudulent word, as it emerged envenomed from a demon's mouth, evoked a demonic creature that rose up as if to an abysmal summons.

All the petty powers were avidly disputing the floor at every moment, forgetful that they had eternity before them; it seemed to them that if they missed, for a single second, the opportunity to make their strident voices resound, it would secure the empire of evil forever.

In that chaos of voices, only one voice was silent, and that was the most powerful; it was hidden there, like a boa constrictor beneath a hive of buzzing bees. Coiled up and mute, it had almost been forgotten. More than one yapping tongue, deafening itself, was beginning to scorn that taciturn king, when, with a prodigious leap, it launched itself from its lair; unfurling its coils in the vast confines of the abyss, it raised one of its heads above every group.

Silence abruptly fell, and this is what it said:

"Your discussions charm me, because they lead nowhere. You are the true kings of sophism. I listen delightedly to your speeches, which dry up thought in souls. Know that I would never have thought of interrupting you if necessity— the sole god that we recognize—had not demanded it of me. Thus far, you have counterfeited masterfully the creation on high. Beneath every heaven you have set an abyss, beneath every joy a dolor, and I congratulate you for it. But is the imitation complete? Have you demonstrated that Hell is as knowledgeable and as profound as Paradise? Have you copied the classical Heavens, without omitting anything that they contain? In sum, as the Heavens have unfurled, have you unfurled Hell?"

"Yes, certainly, we have done that," replied the swarm of the subterranean worlds.

"My dear friends," the king of Hell continued, "fatuity has blinded you. The most beautiful work of what they call Providence, you haven't even tried to imitate."

"What is that work?" cried the accursed.

"What!" their leader replied. "You don't even suspect? The immaculate angel of the Annunciation has descended from Heaven to announce to the Virgin of Judea that Christ will be born of her womb. Have you attempted anything similar? You haven't even thought of it; your imitative minds haven't dared to risk that model. Believe me, you're degenerating."

"What shall I do to prove that I am still worthy of you?" roared the ancient abyss.

"An easy thing, if one dares to attempt it. Nothing simpler: you need an infernal Christ, born of a virgin."

All of them shouted at the same time, in a thousand different tones: "That's true! Narrow minds that we are! Why didn't we think of it? Yes, like Heaven, we need a Christ born of a virgin."

Then the king of Hell went on: "Who among you will go to earth to play the role of the angel in regard to Mary?"

At this point a universal roar replied; an inextinguishable desire for love rose up from the very hearts of those who had never loved.

With that, it continued: "You put too much passion into my cause. Truly, you're emotional. That bears too much resemblance to life. It's good taste here not to acclaim so loudly. Lukewarm, insipid, evasive words—that's what I prefer. One could say 'infernal' without ceasing to be polite. I'll go myself.[4] In Hell, I alone am sufficiently advanced to counterfeit angelic power."

III

In what era did this story take place? It's impossible for me to reply to such a question. If you want a rigorous date, I can do no more than leave this page blank and abandon my narrative. However, I shall say, following the example of the ancients—what better authority is there?—that it was before the harvest. The ears of corn were still green; they gave off the odor of smut on the edge of the wood. I shall also say that the day was mild and temperate. It might have been a morning in the month of May, or perhaps June. A sparse warm rain had refreshed the stifling air of the meadows; it had almost dried up, except in the calices of the wild roses and the flesh leaves of the oak-trees. Only a few gilded clouds on the borders were carrying away, I know not where, in red tatters, some ancient belated and fugitive go—for all the pagan gods had not yet quit the earth. The cross was unsteady in the place where it was most firmly planted; the world, not knowing yet whether it belonged to Jupiter or Christ, adorned itself with its most beautiful radiance. Its breath resembled ambrosia, as if to say to ancient voluptuousness: "Don't worry; whatever happens, I'll remain faithful to you."

A forest extends into the distance, from ravine to ravine, from mountain to mountain, where more than one city lies dormant beneath the moss. In the mid-

---

[4] Quinet adds a note at this point to say that this assertion is "in the tradition"—and, indeed, there is a very similar passage in Hersart de la Villemarqué's own romance in the 1862 *Myrdhinn*, likewise derived from the *Prose Merlin*. However, Hermione also adds a note to the chapter saying that "this first scene in Hell is none other than the memory of a session of the Legislative Assembly on the eve of the *coup d'état*, of inextricable arguments between two camps of Reaction, each of which was attempting to damn the other. 'In that chaos, only one voice was silent'—that of Louis Bonaparte: 'a boa serpent who enlaced France in his coils.' That prediction of Edgar Quinet's dates from October 1848."

dle of the forest, on a vast lawn, on the bank of a torrent, what do you see? A monastery, doubtless the first to have been raised in this part of Gaul.

The wall is high, carpeted with ivy, higher than the hill that surrounds it on all sides. If you could climb to the top of the mountain, you would see at your feet the closed chapel, the open tomb, hollowed out in advance, the courtyard, the garden strewn with brambles and wild sorrel, a solitary stork walking along a path bordered with mallow.

What! Not a single human figure!

Is the monastery inhabited? The door has never been opened; no prayer has ever been heard therein, nor the sound of any bell; a saint has walled herself up in that holy place. She is the daughter of a king who was gripped by earthly ennui in her cradle. Her soft virginal breath purifies the world from afar. She has sworn never to have any husband than Jesus Christ. No oath was ever more sincere.

Today, a knight arrives, at the gallop of his black Saxon hack, a golden helmet on his head and a red cloak on his shoulders. He knocks on the monastery door.

"Open up," he says. "I'm a wounded penitent; I bring news from Calvary, I've recently saluted Bethlehem and Nazareth. I shall perish, my sister, if you delay any longer. Remember the good Samaritan." And he points to gaping wounds; he clutches a crucifix to his bosom.

The walled-up door is unsealed; the knight enters through the debris.

Night has fallen; a night of Erebus, dense and furrowed by lightning. The innocent, holy virgin throws herself down on her bed, whiter than hawthorn blossom, and goes to sleep, her head on her arm. Agitated and unquiet, however, she has forgotten to make the sign of the cross at the foot of the crucifix. Hell is alert and has seen it! It has said: "That's good; she's mine!"

Night has fallen. The young woman has remained saintly. There she is, asleep. But great God, what sleep, and what dreams! In the depths of the woods, what blazing sighs! In the clouds, what tears! In the heavens, what an inferno!

The night has passed. The day is fine and radiant. The saint awakes; her guest has gone. She falls to her knees, veils her face, and drowns in her tears. Oh saints, protect her from any gaze. Burning tears on the flagstones, prayers, vows, macerations, abstinences, cilices—what does it take, then, to efface a dream?

Her guest has gone. Jets of red flame are attached to the four feet of the foaming horse. The grass of the valleys dries up in the distance; the forest is aglow with the reflection of a blaze.

IV

A few years have passed—five or six, at the most. The hero of this story has been born. He has been born, but for him there have been no tears, no screams, no sobs, no breast-feeding and no weaning. His mother dared not even offer him her breast in secret. She called him Merlin.

The day after the day he came into the world, she took him in her arms, sadly, and wept.

"Don't weep, Mother," the new-born said to her, in a man's voice, opening his eyes.

Frightened and delighted by the prodigy, his mother lets him fall at her feet. He gets up safe and sound, smiling, and emerges from his swaddling-clothes.

"I'll comfort you, Mother."

"You're my shame."

"I'll be your glory."

"You're scaring me, my child!"

With that, leaving his linen behind, he starts striding back and forth in front of her, an open book in his hand. His eyes are glued to it, pensively.

"Who taught you to read, Merlin?"

"I already knew before I was born."

"Why, dear child, nail your eyes to that tome so soon? Wait, my son, until you become a man."

"Become a man, dear Mother, like all the rest? Is it worth the trouble? My life to come, I assure you, will be more astonishing than my birth."

Such was the first advertisement that the mother of my hero received of her son's destiny. Nevertheless, wise and prudent, she feared being mistaken. How many times premature flashes of intelligence have been followed by imbecile darkness! How many times infant prodigies have been seen to become nonentities for the rest of their lives! I've known several myself, which I could cite without overmuch embarrassment.

That was the danger for Merlin, if her mother was deceiving herself. There were moments—as we shall see—when he gave the impression of being an infant god.

Nothing is truer—but what would it have taken to give birth to an opposite idea? A game of dice, of quoits, a kite, a drum, or a little bell, and the marvel of Heaven would be no more than a paltry homunculus.

To help nature in one direction, and fight it in another, was a great task for a young woman like Séraphine, almost always alone, devoid of advice, who scarcely dared bear the name of mother.

V

One day he was playing downstairs with knucklebones when his mother, gazing intently at the knight in the golden helmet, said to him: "Advise me, Seigneur. This child, I swear to you, was born without a father. He's a prodigy, the son of a dream. Even if his education cost me eternal life, I wouldn't want to spare anything. What plan should I follow? What direction?"

"You're right," said the knight, raising his red cloak over his face. "Let's talk about it at leisure."

During this dialogue, Merlin, while pretending to play, listened.

"First of all," the mother continued, "I'd sacrifice all I possess to initiate him into Christianity. I've already vowed him to the Virgin Mary. That's why he's wearing a blue robe."

"That's good, Séraphine. If you'll take my advice, though, you won't neglect to instruct him in paganism. Its gods, believe me, aren't as dead as people pretend. They have an infinite fondness for those who don't deny them in times of ill-fortune."

"But Merlin might be the foremost of monks," replied the mother, timidly.

"It would be a hundred times better for him to be the last of the druids."

"But truly, what can be set above the Christian Heaven?"

"Many things. Personally, for example, I prefer the pagan Elysium, without a doubt."

"Isn't it necessary to direct Merlin toward spiritual matters?"

"Believe me, don't exalt him so soon; it's necessary not to neglect the material too much."

"Oh, Seigneur, if all my wishes came true, he'd find happiness in the contemplative life."

"What are you saying? It's the active life that will suit him: business, war, the foundation of all nobility, that's at least one goal of existence."

"O celestial ignorance! If only you could accompany him until his final day!"

"I hope, on the contrary, that he'll bite into the fruit of science."

During this dialogue, Merlin listened in anguish, torn between the two forces that were attracting him to the two opposed extremities of the world. His mother looked at him benevolently. The stranger fascinated him with a serpentine gaze. But neither was more astonished than the other when the child, interrogated as to what he wanted to become, replied in a voice as forceful as a giant's, while stamping his foot: "I want to be an enchanter!"

VI

What was the cause of such an indiscreet response? Doubtless the difference of opinions, sentiments, beliefs and religion between the father and the mother; add to that the deadly habit, transmitted all the way to us, of talking in front of children as if they don't understand us. While we imagine ourselves to be alone, those little intelligences drink deep draughts of the poison that pours from our lips. You think that they're entirely occupied in chasing a fly, but we're imprinting on their ingenuous souls the wrinkles of an anticipated old age, for which there is no longer any remedy.

No one in the world experienced more cruelly than my hero the consequences of that custom. After the fatal conversation between his mother and the knight, you would no longer have recognized him. Two spirits were incarnate in him, arguing over him. What's astonishing about that? Incontestably, he bore a strong resemblance to his mother. It was from her that he got his beauty, his forehead, his eyes, his ingenuous mouth, his eyebrows like those of a Madonna, and, with regard to the internal, his piety, his desire for sanctity, his moral life—or, to put it better, his soul, almost in its entirety.

Nevertheless, he had a few distant traits of his father: for example, curiosity, an inexorable memory, impatience, and a horror of restraint.

Via his mother, he was tightly attached to Heaven; via his father, to Hell.

Via one, he soared in the future; via the other, he was the serf of the present, the slave of the past.

God or Satan, which would emerge victorious within him? A cruel question, which already made his life a torment, at an age that, for others, is golden.

Sometimes he thought he heard the extinct voices of all the pagan gods wandering on the heath, which said to him: "Merlin! Merlin! Remain faithful to us! Only build us a little house of heather; we will promise you happiness."

As soon as he set to work, though, another voice rose up to his left, which said to him: "What are you doing, Marlin? It's a cross that it's necessary to plant! Look at the flowers! They have all converted this morning; now they are taking the form of the cross; look at the clover in your garden."

Then Merlin picked a bouquet; he counted the clover leaves: one, two, three. He stopped, in amazement. His reason was half-vanquished; it only remained for his pride to submit. And, God be praised, he would have done it without reserve! But immediately, the pagan gods made one last effort, setting him a hot of ambushes.

They whispered in his ear: "Is it the time to abandon us, then, when no one any longer gives us honey-cakes? Merlin! Look at the ram crossing your path; he still wears the horns of Jupiter-Ammon on his head!"

Merlin was forcefully shaken again; he whispered to himself: "Since the ram still wears horns in imitation of Jupiter, how can one doubt that Jupiter leads the flock of the worlds?"

To this reasoning Merlin added his natural generosity. He would willingly have doomed himself for such modest gods.

And that is enough to understand how unhappy he was, torn between those two powers. He could no longer find any peace. At a time when the earth was full of calamities, there was, I dare say, no one who suffered more than Merlin. Thus, his early adolescence was spent in tears.

VII

As his melancholy increased and nothing could cure him of it—he had suffocations and palpitations of the heart that robbed him of sleep—his mother thought about sending him away to complete his education with the wisest man of the epoch. His name was Taliesin.

Whether he was a druid or a Christian no one knew exactly. Some affirmed that he was one or the other. He lived in a wood in which he had built himself a hut, near which herds of aurochs that he had domesticated ruminated in peace. Oak trees graying with age, covered in mistletoe, hid him with their shade. Picture a man seventy years of age, of tall stature, with a clear complexion and scarlet hair, under which shone two sky blue eyes and a physiognomy both robust and mystical in its entirety.

As soon as Merlin had confided the cause of his torments to him, Taliesin interrupted him, generously.

"Oh, my son," he said to him, "You've doubtless been sent to be my heir. An entire world is perishing with me. If you're the one who is to announce the new world, I'll tell you who I am. You alone will have known me!"

With these words, he took Merlin by the hand and, having led him to the densest part of the forest; he sat him down beside him on the moss and continued in these terms:

"I haven't always been a hermit in this forest. Old age hasn't always weighed down my footsteps. At your age, my son, I was a commander of men, and even of the army of the stars, which have forgotten me and mock me now."

"The army of the stars!" exclaimed Merlin, dazzled. "You're an enchanter then, Father?"

"What! You doubt it too, my son?" the old man replied, bitterly. "Listen to me. Several faults doomed me; I want to forearm you against them. When young I was, like you, very modest. People took me at my word; because I was modest, they concluded that I had reason to be, and soon, I had lost half my authority in helping them. They left me to follow the prideful, who trampled them underfoot. Don't do as I did!

"I had another setback. For a long time I thought that the truth, once expressed, would be resplendent of its own accord. I thought then that its light would pierce the darkness by itself. So, scarcely had I found one truth than I went in search of another. In that indefatigable race toward enlightenment, I thought that the world was following me breathlessly.

"Let my example be a lesson to you! It's said that your generation is even harder of hearing than ours. When you've published a truth, repeat it; when you're repeated it, say it again. You'll learn in your turn how much more rebellious the human head is than the heart. It's a hundred times easier for us—enchanters, that is—to change earth and Heaven in the blink of an eye than to get a new idea into those heads of stone.

"Of all the faiths that display right and justice, people reject the dazzling light as if it were a poisoned arrow. How many days, years, centuries does it take before their eyes adapt to the splendor of the truth? Then they bless what they cursed, and curse what they blessed—but it's always too late.

"One more piece of advice, my son. People are convinced that a person can only do one thing. Personally, I've been a bard and an enchanter, and that's what completed my damnation. Always do the same thing, my child, and they'll believe that you do it well. Be careful at the outset; if you begin by smiling, they'll demand that you keep you princely smile on your face to the tomb and beyond. If you begin weeping, they'll demand tears until the end. Such as I have known them, they surely still are!"

"Can it be?" exclaimed Merlin.

"Yes, my son. I foresee that you'll be hated, especially by the wicked."

"Why is that?"

"Because you won't be their dupe. They're accustomed to regard honest men as their natural prey, and when, by chance, one refuses to be, the wicked experience an authentic indignation, for they believe themselves to defrauded of their most reliable and most legitimate property. Imagine the wolf, if a lamb denied its right to kill it."

Merlin collected the enchanter's words submissively, but he thought that old age had rendered him misanthropic. He opened his ears to the sage's advice, but in secret, he closed his heart to it.

"What should I do, if I must be your successor?" he asked.

"Do you know the twenty-five thousand verses of the Triads?"[5] the old man replied.

"No," said Merlin. And he perceived then, for the first time, how ignorant he was, and that a few vague notions and general aspirations, to which his knowledge was reduced, were very little without a knowledge of facts. He made a vow to become as knowledgeable as Tailesin.

From that day onwards no one encountered him without seeing a book in his hand.

"Go and tell the world in what isolation I'm dying," Taliesin said then. "The death of the smallest bird, or the smallest insect buzzing in the wood, makes more noise than mine. Watch and learn, my son."

Then, becoming more excited as his end approached, already illuminated by the light of the tomb, he added, with an incomparable majesty:

---

[5] The reference is to the so-called *Trioedd Ynys Prydein* [The Triads of the Island of Britain], collections of which are contained in various 13th and 14th century manuscripts, although the notion that they are detached fragments of a monolithic work assembling the wisdom of the Welsh bards, as is tacitly assumed here, is dubious. They include fragments of Arthurian mythology appropriated from Anglo-Norman sources as well as Celtic materials.

"I was at God's right hand when he created the world. I was walking in Eden at the moment when the word of malediction emerged from Satan's mouth. I was the first bard, my son, and my first abode was the region of the stars. I was with my Lord in the highest sphere, when Lucifer fell into the infernal depths. I have carried my banner before Alexander. I knew the name of the stars of the North and the South. I have been to the throne of the All-Highest in the Milky Way; I was in Canaan when Absalom was killed. I have transported the Holy Spirit in the valley of Hebron. I was a master in the company of Elijah and Enoch I was present at the crucifixion of the son of God. I was the original architect of Nimrod's tower. I am a marvel whose origin is unknown. I was in the Ark with Noah and Alpha. I have seen the annihilation of Sodom and Gomorrah. I was in Africa before the foundation of Rome, and I have taken shelter in what remains of Troy. I covered Moses with the waters of the Jordan. I was in the crib with my Lord. I have suffered hunger for the son of the Virgin. I have been a bard, a harpist on the white mountain. I have sat upon the white throne of the ecliptic. Now I am Taliesin."[6]

With these words, the old man yielded his soul. Merlin buried him with his own hands beneath immense mossy stones, which a dozen men of our day would not be able to move.

I have often seen that tomb, when, in my youth, I too went to read enchanted books on enchanted days on the hill that is known today as the Corne d'Arthus,[7] because of the debris of an old wall that crowns it. The immense forest has disappeared. At least the ax has respected the weeping fir-trees atop the sepulcher.

---

[6] Quinet adds a note saying that this speech is a literal translation of "a fragment of Gallic poetry." Hermione's notes comment that this chapter and the surrounding ones reflect Quinet's "adolescent sentiments, poetic reveries [and] the influences that presided over his education," and claims that Taliesin "recalls the scholar Kreuzer;" it is not obvious to whom she is referring, although either of the famous violinists named Kreutzer might be considered as a bard of sorts.

[7] La Corne d'Artus—which Quinet's alternative spelling makes more approximate to "Arthur's Horn" is a hill in Beaubery, in Burgundy, at the top of which is what was long imagined to be a Druid monument, although more recent belief asserts that it is the ruins of one of the towers of a castle built by Artus, one of the original overlords of the Charolais. The young Quinet's familiarity with the enigmatic artefact presumably occasioned his later decision to call his mythical king Arthus, and might well have helped formulate the notion of "the spirits of the ruins" that he subsequently refined in Greece.

VIII

The twenty-five thousand verses of the Triads were only the start. Merlin, the son of his father in that respect, learned all of Virgil and the Sibyl by heart, to which he added the Church Fathers, a collection of whom he found in the home of his mother's confessor, a hermit named Blasius;[8] thus mingling with neither choice nor prudence, profane and sacred, pagan and Christian, dolmens and chapels, adoring everything, mistrusting everything, lies and truth alike.

One day, as he took his leave, Blasius said to him: "Take care, Merlin. The true God will punish you with chaos. Don't compile the gospel of Hell, my child."

It is evident from that how far his education had already gone astray. And who could blame him? He had no guide but his instinct, except for a little elementary white magic. He inflated himself with vain science; the poison did not take long to become manifest.

Drunk on so much new knowledge, Merlin sensed extraordinary thoughts rising within him. His heart beat with such violence that he seemed to be choking; his humor became chagrined; he torment all those surrounding him with his caprices.

It's the spirit oppressing him, his mother thought.

He found nothing satisfactory in himself or in others. *So much the better*, Merlin said to himself. *I can see that the enchantment is commencing*. And he plunged back into his old books.

One day, his unhealthy soul was ready to burst. He was on the heath confining his residence. The pools let out an occasional sob. "The moment has come to exercise my power!" he shouted, enthusiastically. "The universe is silent, awaiting its prophet."

And he assembled in his mind everything that science had taught him.

"To be sure, I sense in my heart the wherewithal to tilt a world. The moment is solemn. My soul commands the earth. Spirits of the skies, the woods, the waters, flowers and metals, do you recognize me as your master? Spirits who are stifling, imprisoned in the ardent veins of stones, sylphs who intoxicate yourselves on dew in the carved cups of acorns, fays with diaphanous wings steeped in the rainbow, elves who dance on cobwebs to the high-pitched song of the robin and the wren, undines who bathe in the foam of the eleventh wave, come salute your king! Today is his coronation!"

---

[8] This Blasius, Merlin's teacher in the *Prose Merlin*, has no connection with the St. Blaise whose legend is featured in Voragine's *Legenda Aurea*, who was not a hermit and has no connection with France, nor with the more obscure St. Blasius of Brittinis, who was a hermit but has no connection with Britain or Brittany—although it is not impossible that the author of the *Prose Merlin* might have thought that he did, and borrowed his name in consequence.

He only heard the echo of his own voice; that echo seemed to him to be mocking laughter. He went on: "What! I don't have the power to curb a blade of grass to my intelligence?" And he looked angrily at a joyful meadow daisy, which was smiling although he was crushing it with his gaze.

An earthworm passed by, replete with mud. Merlin shouted at it: "Stop, slave, soul of clay!" It was in vain; the worm mocked the great Enchanter.

The disgust for books that gripped our hero then is easily imaginable. He threw them away. He lapsed into bleak contemplation, which, on the part of anyone else, would have been called idleness.

IX

On a beautiful spring morning, Merlin was wandering over the deserted hills. Whichever way he directed his footsteps, he always found himself in the middle of the same immense circle that a great magician traced and retraced around him, on the horizon, with heaths, rocks, woods meadows, yellowing wheat-fields and blue-tinted summits. Here and there, a slender fir-tree pierced the blue sky like the head of a spear, at the limit of vision, like a black eyelash on the edge of a huge eyelid. Melancholy, unknown desires, an aspiration toward the distant hills, drew a sigh from Merlin. Weary of pursuing the inaccessible horizon, he stopped beside a spring; his tears fell drop by drop into the water. Out of spite, he threw stones into it, and followed with his eyes, for hours on end, the ripples succeeding one another over the surface of the water.

"My life," he said to himself, "is more vain than those vain circles, which amuse me momentarily and disappear forever. What am I doing here? Alas, I'm only a shadow myself. I aspire to everything, but cannot grasp anything."

Then, soon passing from humility to pride, he abandoned himself to the belief that this world was not worthy of him, that the Creator had made a mistake in casting him down on this indigent earth, because he was made for a better universe. But these surges of vanity did not last long. Fundamentally, Merlin was good, simple and devoid of pretention; his suffering was all the keener for it.

As he was floating in these cruel thoughts, he heard a concert of voices in the heart of the forest, and the singular idea occurred to him that those sweet and honeyed voices were emerging from flowers. Soon, reflection told him that flowers cannot talk, much less sing. He lay down in the fresh and odorous grass, and thought he could hear a chorus of cicadas, from which he disentangled, approximately, the following:

"All of you who live in the forests and make them resonate with your early-morning voices, disperse in the heather, in the sonorous stubble; go announce that Viviane is awake, and that the soft flash of her eyes has rejuvenated the earth.

"Vigilant sentinels, who nourish yourselves with dew, go, awaken the idle bees everywhere. Say, publish and announce that the grass has grown during the night, that the winter chill has fled, that the spring dawn has anticipated the sky-lark.

"Command everything that lives to put on its spring garments. Fly, publicize the new season. Climb the summits, hop down into the profound valleys; evoke with your strident hymn in the cavernous trunks of oaks, in the gaping fissures in the rocks, in the furrows of the earth, the deaf insects that roam in the middle of the night and the nightingale that has fallen silent on the branch.

"Disperse through the ravines of the impenetrable forests. With your feet and your wings, aid the first buds to blossom. Deploy the buds at the tips of branches greening the hawthorn and the precocious chestnut.

"For us, who have sung the last chorus on the steps of the temple of Sunium,[9] we salute today the new spring in the heather of Gaul. None among us knows what is in preparation, but the earth truly has an odor of incense.

"We rise with a start in the night, and we wander over the sacred moss to collect the golden herb before dawn.

"Here, here is our radiant mistress who signals to us, imposing silence upon us. We must fall silent; now it is for the gods to speak."

Merlin reflected once again that cicadas can neither speak nor sing. He even laughed at his credulity. *What is it about this universe?* he thought. *What continual trap is extended for my senses? I won't be so easily duped.* That said, he lent his ears more attentively; no sound could any longer be heard.

Soon, Merlin burst into sobs. His heart overwhelmed by isolation, he shouted with all his might: "Am I alone in this immensity? You to whom I'm calling, where are you?"

A voice replied, quite distinctly: "Where are you?" as if it were emerging from a rock.

That breathless response troubled Merlin at first. Then he understood that his voice had struck the rock, and that it was nothing but the very vulgar phenomenon of an echo.

After a moment of ecstasy, that discovery covered him in confusion. "Deadly science!" he said. "So that's what I owe you: disenchantment! If I had conserved my initial ignorance, I would believe that the stones were moved by my trouble. I would not die thinking that no other spirit had responded to mine."

And he fell back into his desolate contemplation. Meanwhile, he raised his eyes to the crest of the mountain, which was covered in black fir-trees, and saw—or thought he saw—a woman sitting at the foot of a tree. She seemed to him to be radiant, plunged like him into an eternal reverie. Flocks of birds

---

[9] The temple to Poseidon on Cape Sounion, Latinized as Sunium; Lord Byron carved his name into one of the surviving stones, and Quinet probably saw the signature when he visited the ruins.

emerged from the wood, in order to come and feed from her hands. Her dress was the same shade of green as the forest; her forehead was white and polished, like the stone of summits washed by continual storms. Her eyes were the violet hue of the fields.

Why would wild birds come to feed from the hand of the daughter of a king? Had the forests been seen to give their mantle of verdure to anyone at all? It was nothing but poetic imagery confused with everyday life. Merlin concluded than ennui and isolation had rendered him visionary, that the women he perceived from afar was merely morning mist—and it must be admitted, in fact, that the country was heavily wooded thereabouts, and that the multitudinous exhalations of plants produced vaporous phantoms that might have deceived an intelligence less shrewd than his.

That evening, Merlin went home head bowed, very pensive. He knew that it was a matter of dreams and phantoms; he promised himself to give them no credit; and yet, in spite of himself, his mind was full of both delight and a vague fear. He resembled an Aeolian harp, one string of which has been brushed by a spirit. It resonates for a long time after the instrument has been plunged into its somber sheath, under lock and key.

Unable to sleep, he reflected for a long time on his fortune; two sketchy triads, a few vague prophecies and a multitude of dreams—were those his only possessions? He knew how highly the young women of the region prized wealth, not only in gold but in brilliance. And the parents were even worse. Who would want to give him their daughter? If he did not marry some fay or beauty of the woods, therefore, was he condemned in advance to the almost eternal celibacy of men of his art? That thought was heart-rending.

The night passed in those reflections. The day surprised him with them again: a sad, misty, gray day, but which might yet become radiant if a breath of air dispersed the mist, already traversed here and there by opal and crimson haloes.

X

O Amour! Never—no, never—have I profaned your name. You know that. Never have I mocked your power. Never have I caused you to descend needlessly from your celestial abode, like a *deus ex machina* for unraveling a drama. I would have preferred not to summon you here, for no mouth is sufficiently divine to pronounce your name; to call you in a human voice is already to profane you. But it's necessary that you spread over this moment at least one of your rays, pagan or Christian, since you are the only one of the ancient gods who is still alive, as in the primal days of Uranus and Saturn.

The next day, before dawn, Merlin was in the same place, beside the same rock. He had never yet been able to look at a mountain peak without shivering, especially if that summit was covered in sparse trees. Through the clusters of

41

shadows, illuminated by distant splendors, he embraced I don't know what apparition, which he called happiness—a vain superstition, from which a better-directed education would have protected him. But the harm was done; it was too late to cure him.

Merlin looked up at the mountain, and what was his amazement, his anguish, when he saw on the same mound, at the foot of the same pine tree, the same figure that he had seen the day before.

It was neither a mist nor a phantom, but a young woman who really existed, since she was holding a golden comb and tranquilly combing her long hair, which streamed down to her feet and enveloped her like the sparkling radiance of the morning.

When she had finished, she went to a spring and, looking at herself in its waters, picked up and braided her tresses around her head, with an ingenuous coquetry that redoubled her beauty. Then she came down the mountain in a straight line and advanced toward Merlin, whose astonishment rendered him motionless.

"You called to me yesterday," she said, "but you didn't wait. I'm here. What do you want?"

Merlin was too nonplussed to reply. He lowered his eyes. Then, raising them again, he encountered a long, immense, placid gaze, like the one I perceived one day when leaning over the source of a glacier, seeking the reflection of the Alpine sky.

If Merlin had dared to speak, he would have said: "I feel that I'm dying and being born simultaneously." Then he would have added: "Who are you? Who are your parents? How do you come to be in this solitude? Where are you from?" For, at the same time as his heart was beating forcefully, a singular curiosity was oppressing him. But he dared not, or could not, say anything that was on the tip of his tongue. You would have thought that he had been changed into a stone statue.

"I'll speak, since you want to be silent," the young woman said. "My name is Viviane; my godmother is Diana of Sicily[10]—do you know her? I come here to collect the golden herb."

These words rendered Merlin capable of speech. "You're a child of the earth, like me, then?"

"Let's simply talk," Viviane replied. "Let's go visit the flowers."

"You haven't descended from the clouds, then? You're not a dream?"

---

[10] The reference is to the ancient Temple of Artemis [Diana in the Roman mythology] near Cefalu in Sicily. Viviane is credited with the celestial huntress Diana as a "godmother" on the warrant of the *Prose Merlin*, in which she is a huntress rather than the ethereal Lady of the Lake that she subsequently became in the *Suite de Merlin* and later texts, but Quinet's Viviane does no hunting.

Viviane put a finger to her lips, and said to him, severely: "Let's leave dreams to the night; they're cold and resemble death. Look, the sun's rising! The cicadas are humping, the bees buzzing. It's time to rejoice, with the bees, with the insects, with the sun that's shining on our heads."

As she spoke, she took Merlin's hand and led him along paths that only she knew, through the dense woods. As they went along, she gave him accounts of the plants that they were treading underfoot.

Merlin picked flowers; he wanted to give them to her.

"What are you doing?" she said. "You're hurting me. They're my sisters. When you tear their stems, you're wounding me." And she showed him a drop of dark red blood shining on her cheek.

What a loving heart! Merlin thought. He would dearly have liked to wash away that drop of blood with his tears.

The brighter the daylight became, the more dazzling Viviane's beauty became. The moment came when, beneath the splendor of the day, all the sounds of the earth died away. The birds fell silent; even the ephemera, normally so active, imitated that silence. Then Viviane began to sing in a spring-like voice, enthusiastic and yet rhythmic, a hymn like nothing that Merlin or any other man had ever heard.

The day passed in that enchantment.

As the shadows of the evening elongated at the feet of the mountains, Viviane's ecstasy and inspiration diminished. She was gripped by a weakness, a mortal sadness. "What's happening to me?" she said "I think that I'm going to die with the day. Why is that sinister silence massing over the earth? Already the sad night-bird in beginning to sing. Listen, listen—how it's calling me with its lamentable voice! Will this be my final hour?" And her lips became chilly and pale, making it impossible for her to continue. "There's one word that might save me," she said, "but do you know that word?"

"Yes," Merlin murmured. "I know it. I love you."

"Ah! I defy the darkness!" said Viviane. "I'm sure of living at least until tomorrow."

Reader, if you're wondering who Viviane is, some maintain that she's the last daughter of the waters, the last of the druidesses; others say that she's simply a young woman more beautiful than your own beloved. Personally, I don't know whether, in accordance with the formal rules, a historian should ever mingle his judgment with his story. I'll continue.

XI

They walked together along the sea shore.[11]

---

[11] Herrmione's notes record that these lines were written at Blankenberghe, near Ostend, in July 1852—thus predating the date that Quinet gave as the com-

Their soles scarcely left an imprint in the silvery sand; and while they talked, the curious waves coming from the open sea broke at their feet, covering them with sea-shells, and seeming to say: "Take me for your witness."

"Who are you, then?" asked Merlin. "When we walk in the meadows, your gaze is softer than the lily-of-the-valley and the jonquil opening to the dew. Now, your gaze is deeper than the Ocean."

"Have I asked you who you are? Viviane replied, shivering. "Oh, Merlin, you're making me suffer. It's not sufficient, then, to know that I love you? Your thoughts aren't all enclosed, like mine, in the moment where we are? For me, this moment is eternity. Oh, if you only knew how to love!"

Then she added: "Who am I? I've forgotten. Why remind myself? Ask, if you want, the reeds and the eagles. Perhaps they know. For myself, I can't say."

Two tears ran from her eyelids; at the same time, the last star shining on the sky suddenly went out, like an overturned candle; the flowers bent over and buckled. A long moan was audible in the forest, which rolled over the waves.

How Merlin repented of what he had said! He accused himself internally of having afflicted with an indiscreet question the person for whom he would have died, Doubtless she was the daughter of a queen who had forgotten her throne for him. Was it necessary to make her remember? Perhaps their conditions would separate them forever. Perhaps she was engaged to some king, or some knight at Arthus' court? What could the silver ring be that she wore on her finger, if not an engagement ring?

All those ideas, and a thousand others as cruel, traversed Merlin's heart and mind momentarily; like her, he began to weep silently.

Scarcely had she perceived those tears than she conceived a hectic joy, not of malevolence, but of delight. And, passing from one extreme to the other, she showed Merlin that she was the most frolicsome person in the world, the most cheerful that had ever been seen. Everything immediately began to smile with her.

"You command the universe, then?" said Merlin.

"Of course! What's astonishing about that? I love. With that word, everything is easy."

"But I love too," Merlin replied, going pale. "I love, and not a single blade of grass obeys me!"

"You're mistaken. Since we've wept together, you have the same power as me. Just try. Here's my ring. What would you like?"

"That your name be written in the vault of heaven!" said Merlin, taking the silver ring.

"Well, look!"

---

mencement of the book. Other pre-existent fragments might well have been incorporated into it as it developed; its composition might not have been strictly linear, although Hermione's notes give no indication of any shuffling of the text.

At those words, the sky opened like a book; written there in letters of gold by seven stars, was: VIVIANE.

Thus Merlin, who felt that he was loved, and by loving, became an Enchanter. From that moment on, everything that his eyes encountered was ensorcelled. Beneath his feet, the dew changed into diamonds; he only needed to touch something for it to become immortal. From every object, as from a lyre, emerged a sacred hymn that intoxicated him. As soon as Merlin and Viviane appeared in the woods, in a marvelous cadence, ladies immediately appeared, and demoiselles and red-clad heroes, accompanying them and holding them by the hand. Some danced, others sang, and their voices were so sweet that they might have believed that they were listening to angels. The refrain went:

All is divine!
Love will commence!
Then comes decline:
Dolor immense!

Flowers were born at their feet, which bloomed in the breath of the melody; they had as many iridescent leaves around their calices as there were lines in the chorus of the song.

Arbors of clematis extended over Merlin's head in places where there had only been bare and brutal rock before. Viviane's relatives and the neighboring populations were astonished to encounter that company, to hear that music in things. They recounted what they had seen, exaggerating it, in the most distant cantons.

From mouth to mouth, from kingdom to kingdom, the rumor soon spread all over the world that a great Enchanter had just appeared on earth.

XII

Where is the place in which that first enchantment of Merlin by Viviane occurred? Bretons, it was in Brittany, in the bushy wood of Broceliande; Welshmen, it was in Cornwall; Provençals, in the Crau of Provence. Reader, if you care to believe me, you will think, as I do, that the place that still retains today the trace of those enchantments is the one where I have spent a good part, if not the best part, of my life. Picture impenetrable forests, filled with dormant pools, that I could just as well call lakes, whose banks are reddened by the first and last rays of daylight. Less than a league away, at sunrise, is a curtain of mountains, still humble, it's true, but behind which are the Alps, sacred virgins, taking shelter to put on their mantles of ice; between the forest and the mountain, a plain of pebbles, worn away at the edges by Merlin when he played quoits ion the grass with his companions, which the villagers still call the Crau today. All is peace, silence, gentleness and mystery there. How many times have

I heard Merlin and Vivian conversing in low voices, in the month of May, in the clumps of sweet-brier or flowering gorse or wild gillyflowers? I could show you a thousand paths traces by their footsteps, and which, abandoned and neglected, covered with fern-leaves, no longer lead anywhere but deserted heaths.

It might be objected that Merlin and Viviane were walking on the sea shore, and that there is no trace of it in that region, but that objection has no force, since it is easy to reply that the sea has withdrawn, that the plain has risen, that the mountain has lowered, that the pools are the remnants of vanished oceans.

If you pass that way—may heaven preserve you, first of all, from the fever and magical dreams that tremble beneath the willows at the water's edge, but only after midsummer!—look at those places, so ingenuous and so solitary, at those fields of thatched cottages, those placid horizons, which I filled with my winged visions by myself. Whisper my name to them; they have not forgotten it!

I can, if you wish, indicate to you the place, the very place, where Merlin and Viviane were sitting when the prodigy occurred. It's the place where you find a heap of stones on an eminence in the meadowland, the remains of a dwelling for which you would search in vain for any other vestige. Knock on the foot of the debris of that threshold hidden beneath the nettles and the hazelnut bushes; voices will emerge more melodious than those of the stones of Memnon the Egyptian.

And that's too much on that subject. Let's get on.

BOOK TWO: MERLIN ENCHANTS PARIS, AND THE LAND OF FRANCE

I

As soon as Merlin's renown was established, there was an immense crowd of people around him who came to ask him to enchant their ways. The first who presented themselves at his threshold at daybreak were kings, dukes, counts and barons. Among them were distinguishable, in the first rank, King Arthus, his ally Hoel of Armorica, Ossian in a cloud, Mark of Cornwall, Queen Genièvre, the blonde Yseult, King Lear, followed by an innumerable court, and the long-haired Pharamond, dragging an entire iron people after him.[12]

King Arthus spoke for all of them. He bowed and said:

"Merlin, wisest of men, if you are not a god, it is to you that we want to hold out our scepters and our crowns. Will you enchant them, in order that people will be submissive to us, for if force alone is mixed up in it, they will always be ready to revolt? But when a charm is attached to the yoke, they bear it joyfully; everything is easy for them and for us."

Merlin, who had never seen himself in such a solemn assembly, was troubled at first; he seemed very emotional, but he soon mastered himself. He took the thirty crowns from Arthus; after having touched them and mingled his enchantments with them, he returned them to the kings, but not without having offered sage advice with them. He wanted to attach headbands to some of them with his own hands, with chains of diamond, and to anoint them with dew. He did that, in particular, for the great Arthus, for Pharamond, and for the Erl King, because they were the chiefs of races.[13]

---

[12] Hoel of Armorica, or Hoel I Mawr, is depicted in Geoffrey of Monmouth's imaginary history of Britain as a cousin of Arthur, who helps him repel the Saxon threat to Britain. Pharamond was a legendary Frankish king who allegedly reigned at the beginning of the fifth century; he is first mentioned in an 8th-century text, the *Liber Historiae Francorum*, which constructs an imaginary history for the Franks, much as Geoffrey invented one for England.

[13] *Le Roi des Aulnes* [The Erl King, or King of the Alders] is the title of the French translation of J. W. Goethe's ballad *Der Erlkönig* (1782), although the erl king in the poem is a supernatural being, barely glimpsed, which assaults a child being carried home by his father, and this reference is to the mythical prototype. Shakespeare based Lear and Macbeth on names mentioned in documentary sources, although the former is fictitious; similarly, Ossian is almost entire-

"You see," he said, "I love, and it's for that reason that I received my magical power, If I didn't love, in spite of the science that I learned from Taliesin, I couldn't do anything more than anyone else. I've told you my secret; it's up to you to do likewise. Let your peoples be to you what Viviane is for me."

"That is what we will do," said Arthus.

"You promise?"

"We swear."

All those surrounding King Arthus began repeating after him, with their hands held high: "We swear."

To confirm the oath of the lords, the troop of knights saluted with their swords.

"Give me your swords too," said the Enchanter. "I can see that they are thirsty for blood. I will sate them."

Having taken the sword in his hands, he baptized them one after another; to the best-tempered he gave the name of Durandal.[14]

"I return them to you sharper," he added, "in order that you might cut the knot of justice. But if you make use of them for any other purpose, they will turn against your own hearts of their own accord. If you will only meditate violence in advance, the blood that is not yet shed will stain the blade to the hilt; it will cry out against you until the earth opens up."

Only one blade remained in his hands; it was that of the long-haired Pharamond.

The Enchanter looked for a long time at the blue-tinted blade, after which he shouted, as if the words were inadequate to his thought:

"O France, at least see what I am doing for you! How many times, jeering and forgetful race, you will sicken me with this blade I have forged myself! It will grow from one age to the next, every sharper, until the point will touch the pillars of Hercules, and I can already feel the profound wound in my heart. Why, France, do you sicken me with this blade that I have sharpened myself? Your children will be dazzled by the sparks of iron and steel that spring from it; they will intoxicate themselves with that iron dew; they will forget the innocent light of day."

Then a voice that seemed to emerge from a dense fog cried out to him: "What will be my sword, my crown? Shall I leave here with empty hands?"

"Who are you, whom I can scarcely discern, so heavy with frost in the mantle wrapped around you?" Merlin asked.

---

ly the belated literary creation of James Macpherson, only faintly pre-echoed legendary material mentioning an Irish bard named Oisin.

[14] Roland's sword in the relevant cycle of romances. Hermione notes that this episode of the swords reflects Quinet's regret in 1852 that France was still fascinated by "the Napoleonic tradition."

"The daughters of the clouds call me Ossian," replied the one who lived in an eternal mist—and he let his snowy beard fall upon the invisible harp; it rendered a sound like the breath of a dying man.

"Ossian, king of the mists, what need have you of a sword?" retorted Merlin. "You will reign, like me, not by the blade but by the harp. Of all the kingdoms, that is the only one that iron cannot shake. Every chord will raise columns of diamonds around you, and you will make your abode in the green emerald grotto, where I myself will bring you presents."

At these words, the old man fell silent, appeased, his tears mingling on his cheeks with the silvery evening dew.

As they were about to withdraw, a lord of the isles, a tall clan chieftain, strode forward from the crowd surrounding him.

"Look, Merlin, my lordly crown is not solid on my head. I can feel it tottering. Reattach my headband yourself, or I feel that I shall perish."

Merlin replied: "It's your own fault, Macbeth. Why are you already lending an ear to the woman who whispers to you with a homicidal joy? Look at your sword. There is one that is sweating blood. Macbeth, you have already meditated murder!"

Seeing himself revealed in the depths of the future, Macbeth kept silent, and went away to wander on the heath. But all eyes remained fixed on his sword, which was dripping a crimson dew. Several others were betrayed at the same time by a similar sign.

II

As clusters of jasmine and lilac agitate in the first light of dawn, and a matinal perfume is emitted therefrom, which no other hour of the day can match, so the lips of the queens, chatelaines and the women who came after them agitated and murmured at Merlin's approach. Expectation, hope and curiosity colored with rosy tints the aurora of more than one virginal cheek.

Not content with what he had just done, Merlin picked up a cup, full of a beverage that he had prepared with his own hands with tufts of golden herb.

"This," he said to the women, "is a love potion. Whoever drinks it will love you until death. It's no longer the worn-out cup of the old goddess. It's a new, unknown, painful charm full of dreams and divine sadness, which holds the heart in the clouds and causes the face to pale under blinding tears. The world has never seen its like."

"Taste it yourself first," said the blonde Yseult.

The Enchanter put the beverage to his lips. He drank it first, in long draughts—and after him, Viviane, and then all of those who formed a cortege.

But several of them—Genièvre, Arthus' wife, Blanchefleur, Isaure and the beautiful Enide—cried with one voice: "How bitter the taste is, Seigneur!"[15]

Turning to Queen Genièvre, the Enchanter said to her: "You will gain an eternal memory therefrom; but for every one that will survive, how many will be swallowed by eternal silence, along with their lovers?—and their lot will be no less worthy of envy."

With that, he sent them away with a smile. They went, from one people to another, to pour the cup of the new love upon the lips of men; and a vague plaint, mingled with a vague hope, emerged from all things. The swords quivered in the hands of the knights. Even the men of stone, in their marble niches, began to pale and bow their heads. Each of them was dreaming of a lady of stone beneath the vault of the heavens.

Meanwhile, the kings, the lords and the clan chieftains had withdrawn, banners at the head. Arthus had the good grace to throw to the people a handful or two of medallions bearing his effigy, and the people, on seeing the cortege go by, fell to their knees. They said:

"Oh, the good lords enchanted by Merlin! Look: stars are shining on their foreheads.

"Oh, the good masters! May they live long, and may the sons of our sons be submissive to them, as we are!"

Such was Merlin's second prodigy. The masters and the servants, the kings and the peoples, had a similar amity for one another.

III

After having hesitated a great deal, the peoples, murmuring, heads bowed, foreheads full of redness, eyes half-closed, painting, crawling, dragging themselves on their limbs in the manner of some Polyphemus, came to kneel before Merlin, and the earth was then very muddy.

"Get up, please," he said to them.

They had to be begged for some time to stand up, for they did not dare to show themselves to the Enchanter on their feet. They thought that they would be lacking in respect if they were standing up like him.

"Give us some spells too," they said to him, finally, but in their regional dialects, and in voices so humble, so stammering, so plaintive and so inarticulate

---

[15] The name Blanchefleur is featured in several different romances, but this one is presumably Perceval's beloved in Chrétien de Troyes' *Conte du graal*. Isaure is also featured more than once, the name being best remembered in Quinet's day by virtue of its attachment to Clémence Isaure, the legendary figurehead of the Floral Games of Toulouse, the supposed ideal of the Medieval troubadours. Enide is the heroine of the first of Chrétien's romances, *Erec et Enide*.

that Merlin was obliged to lower his head and cup his hand over his ear in order to hear them.

"We haven't dared attempt anything for so long because we haven't been anointed by your hand."

"Good God!" he replied. "Why didn't you come first, with the kings, the dukes and the barons? I wouldn't have refused you anything—not even their crowns."

"How could we have dared?" said the peoples, kneeling down again and crawling.

But Merlin, taking them by the hand, raised them from the ground for a second time.

They stammered: "They are made to reign, we to serve. Merely give us the crumbs from their tables."

"Not only the crumbs," Merlin retorted, "but the feast, gladly, insofar as it intoxicates them. Who made you so humble, then? You resemble the ocean in Brittany. When it is afraid it stammers like you, holding its breath, in the sea-weed; then, as soon as it thinks itself stronger, it inundates its shores. I should like to see some noble confidence in you, instead of this earthworm language that conceals tempests of which even you are unaware."

There were peoples there from all lands, from Italy, France, Spain, England, Poland, Hungary, Germany and Switzerland; there were also Rumanians. To the Lombards he gave a Milanese viper to bite the Germanic hunter in the heel; to the French a Gallic skylark that sings in the storm; to the English a leopard crouching in ambush; to the Venetians a lion with a golden mouth that roared on the towers; to the Spaniards a unicorn; to the Portuguese a dolphin; to the Germans a tortoise; to the Austrians a hyena; to the Swiss a Bernese bear; to the Poles a white eagle; to the Hungarians and unbroken horse from Tartary; to the Greeks a sea-hawk; to the men from Rumania an aurochs. Each of those domesticated animals was educated in magic, and licked the Enchanter's hand.

"Follow them," said Merlin. "They know the best way, which I have taught them myself. Take care, however, not to fall far below the least of them, for most of you are still touching the confines of their blind empire. How many I can see among you who are thinking, at this very moment, of selling their birthright, like the shaggy Esau, for a bowl of lentils.

"You would rather be flattered than served. I, on the contrary, will serve you and not flatter you. That is why I too shall have my Passion, by your fault. How many times you will deny me, before the soldiers, and before the judge! You will also deny me before the servant. As I think that, I'm torn between anger, disgust, pity and shame—but it's still the pity that holds sway."

Scarcely had the peoples found themselves alone than they excited their magical guides in a thousand ways to bite one another; then the strongest wanted to despoil the weakest; they attacked one another, and there was a moment of horrible confusion, because they were all imitating the howling of beasts of prey, to the point of being mistaken for them.

They tore at one another furiously, as if they themselves had claws, talons, horns, fangs, tusks, forked tongues, glittering scales and raptorial beaks. Fortunately, the animals conserved the greatest self-composure in that melee. The example of their wisdom made the men blush, who finally calmed down. By then they were almost all enchained and kept out of sight by one or other of the sacred animals, which held them beneath their paws, yawning.

IV

Love had not produced its usual effect on Merlin; it had not rendered him idle. On the contrary; Merlin never ceased visiting the neighboring countries in order to do good. Every path was good to him, provided that his eyes encountered Viviane there. For her part, she could not lose sight of him for fear of dying. As they traveled together, the arid earth was covered with verdure. One might have thought that worlds were being born beneath their feet.

One day—an immortal moment!—at sunrise, they arrived on the bank of a river with green-tinted tranquil waters, which snaked along a bed cluttered with grasses and reeds, through a forest of oaks, birches and beeches. Its two banks were covered with shadow and mystery; the place seemed uninhabited, save for motionless herons on the edge of marshes and a few green woodpeckers, which, upright against the trunks of old oaks, were waiting for oracular voices to emerge from the heartwood of the centenarian trees.

Anyone who has lost his way in the forests of America has encountered solitudes as profound, without being able to tell whether they remained the domain of savage beasts or were the cradle of a nascent people. Did the place harbor birds' nests, insects, an anthill or an empire? Who could tell? All of human wisdom could not decide between the empire and the anthill.

In the middle of the river, our voyagers perceived a lush wooded islet bordered by poplars, which were piercing a thick fog. It had the elongated form of a ship whose prow was cleaving the watercourse. As they drew nearer to it they could not hear any sound, except for the clucking of a fowl and the cries of a flock of frightened sparrows, which alighted noisily in a flowering apple-tree. At that sound, Merlin turned his head; the mist with which the earth was enveloped had just cleared at the first breeze of the day; it allowed the sight of a small village of thatched cottages, gathered in the center of the islet beneath a quivering clump of alders. The smoke of the huts was vanishing in the blue air, along with the morning vapor that beautiful autumn sunlight was dissipating.

"What a pleasant spot!" exclaimed the Enchanter. "How I'd like to go there!"

As it happened, there was a woodcutter close by who had just finished chopping his quota of branches and was preparing to climb into a boat; he had already detached the hempen rope by which it was moored to the bank.

"Take us with you," Merlin shouted.

"Gladly," said the peasant.

Merlin and Viviane sat down, smiling, in the boat, on the heaped-up branches.

"What is this river?" Merlin asked.

"The Seine."

"And that village?"

"Lutèce."

V

An enclosure of palisades, sharpened for protection against the nocturnal terror of unknown forests; a wooden tower for the watchman whose trumpet had announced the daybreak; a few mossy fishermen's cabins with large roofs; thorny hedges; nets suspended from the overhanging thatch; wandering geese squawking under Merlin's feet as he crossed the open spaces; here and there a grim yarn-spinner on her threshold with a child suspended from her breast; a fisherman weaving a wicker basket; a laborer driving his two semi-tamed oxen into the byre; an odor of strewn straw and fuming stables, fish gaping in the sunlight, perhaps also vines or elderberries; the barking of shepherds' dogs, the bells of herds, the plash of oars, the cries of boatmen, and, in the distance, the sonorous howl of a wolf-cub in the forest of the Louvre—yes, that was Lutèce!

Before landing, Merlin contemplated at his leisure, on the two banks, the deserted places, the profound, sacred forest from which surged in those days the shady summits of Montmartre, Saint-Cloud and Mont-Valérien, like the shaggy heads of black bison rising above the pasturage, damp with the water of invisible springs.

The grassy plain, a kind of European savannah, unfurled in the distance, endlessly, limitlessly, patched with gold here and there or brightened mat white by the reflection of a dormant pool into which the sunlight plunged, illuminating dazzling fires beneath the lustrous foliage of oaks. The wind that passed over the slender crowns of the birches extracted something like the whimper of a new-born from them. A single path, scarcely traced, frequented by large snakes, traversed the plain like an emerald robe from the village all the way to Montmartre. Through the thickness of the shadow, hills of chalk and plaster whitened in the distance, dirtied, crumbled and torn by the rain of storms, like sepulchers opened by a crack, vomiting the bones of a world of giants into the cradle of a people.

In the places where Saint-Roch, Saint-Merry, Saint-Germain and Saint-Sulpice now stand, wheeling in the air in rapid, hectic flight, were multitudes of hawks, buzzards, kites, and even seagulls and stray ospreys that traveled up the

Seine in those days. All were soaring together, with piercing cries, above the cadaver of some red deer died of old age, buried in the densest part of the wood in the undergrowth, which the wolves were beginning to tear apart. Above that sea of verdure, the Montagne Sainte-Geneviève, itself enveloped at its summit by a garland of forests like a mural crown, gazed at Montmartre and seemed to be saying: "Will human feet ever tread upon us?"

On entering the woodcutter's enclosure, Merlin admired two fig-trees enveloped with straw, which had been acclimatized by dint of artistry; he immediately took from that a good augury for the future of that hamlet. Then he redirected his gaze to the waters of the river, on which a flock of swans had just settled among the flowering water-lilies, which resembled a clutch of eggs hatched during the night.

"No place has ever inspired me like this one," he said. "I feel outside myself in contemplating these virgin solitudes, where the great Arthus has not yet ridden. Queen Genièvre has not once sat on the edge of that indolent river. What is happening beneath those dense shadows, where I can hear ephemera buzzing and green woodpeckers hammering the trunks of trees. I love this earth more than any other. I would like to see a happy people here, submissive to the king of justice."

"Do you not have the power of enchantments?" said Viviane.

"Oh, if I have that power, now is the moment to prove it. I bless this earth, where your feet repose, this place from which you are smiling at me; I bless this river, which reflects your face; I bless these banks and the unknown heaths that no one has visited. But such a profound solitude saddens me; this earth calls for humans. What can I do to assemble them here?"

"Desire it," said Viviane.

"By my love, I wish it!" Merlin exclaimed.

"Let it be done according to your will."

VI

The next day, at dawn, Merlin, still half-asleep, heard something like the buzzing of a swarm; he thought that it was the ephemera awakening in the garden. The sound only increased, however; he ran to the window and perceived that a swarm of humans had assembled in haste, and was covering the horizon. They were already busy building huts and houses, even cloisters and bastilles. But they did not have any plan; they were working at hazard, not perceiving one another.

Scarcely had Merlin recovered from his astonishment than he learned that the wisest of those people wanted to salute him and wish him welcome. As soon as they came in, Merlin invited them to sit down on a trunk in the corner of the hut.

Without seeming to have much understanding, they said to him, with a hint of conceit: "We are the sages of this country. Would you care to tell us what your nature is, your essence? Is it double or simple? Do you have faculties?"

"Yes, undoubtedly," said Merlin, precipitately.

"If that's the case, how many do you have?"

Bewildered by that tone, suspended half-way between seriousness and irony, Merlin replied, modestly, and also because those words always came to his lips first: "First of all, I have the faculty of loving."

Some of them burst out laughing; the others immediately went on: "Aren't you bringing us any new dogma? We're quite disgusted with the old ones. What do you think about the accord between dogma and philosophy?"

"I assume," Merlin replied, that you're talking about the philosopher's stone?"

Without giving him time to finish, the sages went on: "What is your solution to the problem of destiny? Your means of enriching the human species in a morning? For you must sense that it's quite pointless to build the smallest edifice here, if you don't bring us the ultimate verity of all matters first."

"Nothing is more certain," put in one of the sages. "For myself, I can say that I'm in touch with the truth, but I haven't yet grasped it in its entirety. Until then, believe me, neither sow nor build; until I've finished my Treatise on happiness, it would be a waste of effort."

"In sum, Merlin," they continued, in chorus, in a nervous voice taut with impatience, "bring us the final solution, or you can't expect us to stay here in the mud of Lutèce any longer. Speak, then!"

The worthy Merlin, who was beginning to be stunned by so many precipitate questions, asked for a few moments to think. He apologized because he was not used to improvisation.

At that reply, the sages cried out, angrily: "You see! The wretch! He's reflecting! He doesn't have the solution that cuts through all difficulties, present and future. No, he doesn't have it. Look—he's still thinking about what he ought to say! No, never since remote antiquity has anyone seen such slowness of mind. Honestly, where does he come from? In his place, we'd already have resolved the problems of twenty worlds."

Merlin listened calmly to that torrent of impertinence, to which he replied, gravely: "Alas, impatience befits ephemera, so I shan't reproach you. You're only rough drafts, as yet, and already, I see, you're very curious, and somewhat sarcastic. Perhaps, for you, that's the source of great things. Just be careful of being too refined, because I foresee that you might get caught up in your subtleties, as if in spiders' webs. That, I warn you in advance, is your principal danger; you carry it within yourselves. Beware that intelligence doesn't lead to a complete lack of it. Your objective, in brief, is good sense—don't stray from it, I beg you. If you lose the appetite for pure light, even I won't recognize you any longer. Don't strive for darkness; don't be jealous of moles."

In the same tone, he added a great deal of advice about the conduct to adopt for nascent peoples, and, as he did not mingle any bitterness with it, his simple and modest language ended up winning the hearts of his audience. They had come with a secret desire to mock him; they went away full of respect for his science. A large number, in fact, who did not believe in enchanters, had only decided to visit him in order to poke fun at his enchantments; even those, vanquished by what they had heard, said to him as they withdrew: "Master, enchant our ways."

And the good Merlin, without retaining any rancor, traced circles around them that promised them peace, prosperity and liberty, on the sole condition that they followed his advice. He spread spells over them by the handful.

"I give them to you gladly," he said, "because I love you, without yet knowing why. But please, be modest! Don't go boasting about being Merlin's favorites, the only ones, the Benjamins, the elite, the incomparable, the conductors of worlds, without doing anything to merit those titles. The wise will mock you and you'll excite the hatred of all the rest against me."

VII

The next day, he went with them to the place where the Louvre is today. In those days, there were no carts rolling or anvils resounding in the vicinity, nor people murmuring like the sea, but magpies were chattering in the trees, wolves were howling in their lairs and otters were prowling in the marshes.

Merlin and his cortege were stopped at first by a herd of aurochs, which had been grazing in the area since the origin of the world. The enchanter took a hazel-branch and dispersed the wild cattle; they fled lowing. Afterwards, he came back to his companions.

"Master," they said to him, on seeing him again, "Draw us the plan of a new city here."

"Gladly."

"But do it today, before nightfall; tomorrow will be too late."

"What! Always so impatient!" Merlin replied. Bending down, however, he drew on the ground the plan of the new city, and gave it the name of Paris, instead of that of Lutèce, which it had previously had. In addition, he laid its foundations, blessed the first stone, traced the walls, marked out the portals, rounded the bastions, baptized the streets and chose the paving-stones—in brief, he wanted to make a city of light, the hostelry of the world.

After having crossed the river again in a small boat, as he was clearing a path not far from the Thermes, a blackbird taking off from the undergrowth uttered a screech. At that screech, the Enchanter looked up. At the entrance to the clearing he saw a shepherdess who was spinning with her distaff while guarding a flock of sheep. Her long-haired dog was beside her, lying on the new grass and licking her feet.

"Who's that?" Merlin asked the person nearest to him.

"What? Don't you know here? That's Geneviève the shepherdess."

Then Merlin went over to her, and saw that she was weeping, because she had lost two new-born lambs that morning, the best in the flock, which had gone astray in the vines, perhaps in the Thermes or the thickets with which the place was covered then. Firstly, he helped her to look for them, and then consoled her with these words:

"Don't cry, Geneviève. I'll look after your sheepfold. Your ewes will grow so well that the fold won't be able to contain them, and they'll jump over the barrier that you've made out of reeds. Your flock will fill all the surrounding area, as far as the eye can see. It will leave wisps of its fleeces on the most distant hedges, and chilly nations will make white woolen tunics therefrom, against the winter cold.

"For as long as it covers the country freely, the worlds will blossom in hope. Unfortunately, no one will want to follow its guidance; everyone will think himself the ram with the silver horn, and will march alone, head held high, along the bramble path, without looking back to see if the flock is following. And when your flock is tied up, by the neck, in the fold, the earth will also be tied in the night without a dawn. The mute word will reenter the hearts of men, and the poison will accumulate there. Your song will no longer be heard in the wood, nor your pipe, but the sniggering of goats and the wicked. After you, Geneviève, will come the harsh shepherds who will make use, not of the crook but of the knife."[16]

Speaking thus, they arrived with the shepherdess at the entrance to her hut, situated on the top of the hill; its roof was covered in thatch and moss, intermingled with white bindweed, which hung down over the paltry wall. A little black bread, ewe's milk in an earthenware bowl, a few clusters of hazelnuts still attached to the branch, medlars in a basket made of the pith of rushes and elder—that was the maiden's treasure; she covered it with a straw mat.

Having eaten and dunk at their leisure, our guests withdrew. As they were on the threshold, they turned back once again, and saw a nimbus shining around Geneviève's head. That glory, still expanding from circle to circle, girdled the entire horizon with a sacred band of red, opal and incarnadine, from Meudon to Nanterre, from Nanterre to Suresnes, from Suresnes to Saint-Denis. There was no one there who did not display the greatest astonishment, except for Merlin. He seemed to be pleased by it, as if by his own handiwork; he only smiled.

The dog uttered a long howl.

---

[16] This depiction of St. Geneviève, the patron saint of Paris, carefully ignores her supposed prowess in battle, to which other versions of her legend call attention.

VIII

Nothing was to be seen then in the surrounding area but good people sowing justice and reaping joy. Abundance entered by a hundred gates, with overflowing carts, and peace through twenty more. No one coveted anything, having everything in profusion: money, food, clothes, rest, and even sufficient love! Vanity was yet to appear; no one would have sold his soul for a word, a coin, a rag, and scarcely for a treasure!

In basin of sculpted marble, full to the brim, flowed the virginal Seine, to which the deer of Montmartre and Vincennes came to drink, pell-mell with the people, the gentlefolk, the barons and the kings. Montmartre had sunk, the marshes had been raised. Suresnes produced the wine of Candia. The old city gleamed, like an ivory boat on a silver river. On the heights of the towers of Notre-Dame, which had no wrinkles on its forehead as yet, one could read: *Hic Regnum Merlini.*

Having found a skylark's nest, not far from the Seine, he built a bastille, which he surrounded with a surplus of moats and drawbridges.

"Who will live in this fortress?" people asked him. "We cannot see here a roof for vagrants, a convent for monks or a keep for the king!"

"The most beautiful of new-borns," Merlin replied. "But you must be a better fortress for her."

"And who is this new-born?"

"Liberty," said the Enchanter. "She has only to be born. Listen to her, weeping and wailing! Be careful that no one tricks her nurse. Good people, here is the layette woven by my hands and marked with my name." At the same time, he handed the keys, which were sculpted and studded in pure gold.

"Liberty?" they replied. "It's a nice name. We've never seen her, or met her, or touched her. How will we recognize her?"

"By this linen cloth and this bracelet of fine gold."

Wicked individuals, having heard, were the only ones to profit from these words. They went into the country to search for a stray child, hairy and hideous—some son, I believe, of Caliban. After having dressed him in linen cloth and put a fine gold bracelet on his arm, they smuggled him into the enclosure by night, instead of the new-born announced by Merlin. Her, they took into the woods in order to leave her to perish—and the people did not perceive the difference. They nourished the substitute infant with their sweat, as they would have pampered the true one, and perhaps even better.

"It's strange," they sometimes said, "how he bites his nurse." The most honest dare not say any more; it would take centuries to realize that the child was counterfeit.

58

IX

While the walls, the towers, the bastilles, the belfries and the steeples, still enveloped by their scaffolding, emerged confusedly from an ocean of mist, as one sees a host of masts of frigates, corvettes, caravels and brigantines rise up in a port, groaning, from the dormant gulf, Merlin took the greatest pleasure in the world from walking outside the nascent city. His mind soared above that social chaos. A great dazed crowd never failed to follow him through the countryside, which was then fallow.

As he was always hanging on Viviane's words and smiles, he walked with an odd gait, at hazard. When Viviane stopped, he set up a stone in the form of a boundary-marker, on which she sat down and recovered her breath. At other times, he took a little golden knife with a mother-of-pearl handle from the pocket of his doublet, and distractedly made a broad scratch in the ground.

"What are you doing, wise Merlin?" asked one of the men who was following him.

"I'm dividing up the fields," he replied. "I'm giving them to you. These are as many heritages that I've marked out in the earth with Viviane's dagger. Everywhere she wanted to sit down, I've placed a boundary marker. Fortunate is the place that her feet have touched! Respect it!"

Then he showed each of those who were following him the share that he had allocated to him. But the greater number cried out: "Why have you made the portions so unequal?" And they pointed to their fields, capriciously divided and randomly variegated, without any wisdom seeming to have presided over the division.

Merlin bowed his head. He searched for a reply. He felt that with more reflection, he might well have done otherwise. Was he ruled, then, by Viviane's caprice? Might the excess of love have led him to injustice? That was what he was asking himself, silently. Extraordinarily, he had the courage to express himself overtly.

"How can one hold to the rigor of geometry when the heart is astir?"

Everyone agreed that it would be difficult.

After such a frank confession, Merlin continued. He said that the best enchanters had not succeeded any better than him in establishing the equality of property, as witness Moses, Joseph the Egyptian, Pythagoras, Orpheus, Numa Pompilius and all the rest; that it was the usual snag of people of his art; that what doomed republics were false ideas as much as evil princes; that he wanted to found his on granite and not on clouds; and besides, one risked a great deal by trying to do everything at the same time.

For his part, he was proud of his discretion, of the known reason of those who listened to him; he wanted to attach himself to the people not by vain chimerical bait but by veritable benefits, the sole mark by which once could distinguish good enchanters from evil ones. To which he added that, if all the shares had been equal, they would soon have ceased to be, but that he could not be intervening all the time in new distributions of the land, which would not leave him a moment of leisure. Furthermore, if anyone was at fault, he accepted all the blame himself, instantly demanding that no one should be held responsible but him.

His final word was that the damage was easy enough to repair.

"Easy!" cried the crowd. "What do you mean, Merlin?"

The worthy Merlin indicated the best remedies, but none of them satisfied him fully. They always lacked something, principally in their institutions of credit. He did not know how to please the debtors and the creditors at the same time. To be sure, he would have liked it to be possible, to everyone's satisfaction, to lend without being out of pocket, to borrow without repaying, to produce without laboring, to labor without sweating, to enjoy without consuming, to live without nourishment, to die without weakening, to resuscitate without dying. That would have been ideal, so far as he was concerned, but to realize that at a stroke would be difficult. For the first time, he felt seriously embarrassed.

"Oh," he cried, in the end, "love will repair the fault of love! The man whose field is insufficient or sterile will be aided by the others. No one surely, will want to leave him in difficulty."

"God preserve us!" they replied, in unison.

"Wait," said Merlin, again. "To the man who has the smallest share, I leave Viviane's golden knife. See how it shines. Everywhere it plunges in, abundance will spring forth."

X

Scarcely had he returned to the city than an innumerable host of artisans presented themselves at his threshold. They had heard that the fields had been divided up.

"What remains for us? You've given everything to them," they said to Merlin.

Then Merlin had them pass before him one by one.

"Don't judge me so lightly. This is what I've reserved for you."

Then, as they filed past, he handed them the primary tools of each profession. For some it was the vagabond shuttle, to others the toothed rasp; to this one the drill, or the awl, or the mallet, to that one the plane or the workbench, to others the pruner or the chisel.

These tools, unknown until that day, caused a great admiration in the audience, and as Merlin handed them out he informed them of their usage. He also showed them that Viviane had hidden treasures under each of those modest implements.

Everyone was in a hurry to make use of them, for, although they had not long assembled, time was beginning to weigh upon them. They set to work joyfully and forgot the initial surge of ill-humor that they had experienced in the morning at the news of the division of heritages. In addition, as soon as they were weary, Viviane mopped their foreheads with a flap of her own veil. No worries harassed them, and, trusting in Merlin's words, they waited patiently for the marvels that each tool concealed.

Then came one last artisan, empty-handed, named Fantasus.

"Who are you?" said Merlin. "What is your estate?"

"Poet," Fantasus replied.

"Are you sure of that?"

"I think so."

"What reason do you have for thinking so?"

"These are my reasons: I'm discontented with everything I see and everything I hear; I curse this nascent city; I don't care about the ancient; I'm melancholy and irritable; I only like what doesn't exist, and execrate everything that does; I make myself the center of the globe—if there really is a globe—and am only interested in my own history. Are those not the marks that reveal the true poet?"

Merlin saw that he was dealing with a mind even more prideful than poetic; he refrained, however, from wounding him, for he recognized an authentic dolor in that pride. He tried to show him that the supreme poetry is also the supreme reason.

"What we need to do," he added, "is restore common sense. You have a few ideas hereabouts, but three-quarters of them are false. Attach yourself to the small number that are true."

"But what about the future?" Fantasus put in, excitedly.

"The future, I can talk about," Merlin replied calmly, "since I'm its messenger. Well, Fantasus, be sure that it won't arrive in the world with as much fuss as you suppose. It isn't always on the tripod, as you imagine. It isn't always in the burning bush, nor on the mountain in the midst of lightning flashes. Believe me, my friend, more often than not, it comes without anyone noticing. It slips in, it arrives, it's there, it reigns, and all without the pomp and thunderclap that you imagine."

"That's utterly wretched!" retorted Fantasus, indignantly. "Is that, then, the poet, the diviner, of whom I've heard so much talk? Great gods, what a pity! What a disappointment, as soon as one approaches prophets! What do you take me for, wanting me to be swallowed by such a city?"

With that, he went away, full of wrath—but no one followed him.

XI

The crowd of sages who had stayed behind then cried: "Merlin, give us the final word of your doctrine today."

"Listen," replied the Enchanter gravely, "From everything I see here, I can tell that you're still only rough drafts. Harsh proof has shown you that you're a hundred times more leaden in thought than you think you are. You're scarcely born, and already your minds have rusted with regard to all sorts of higher things. The time hasn't yet come for me to unveil to you my final thought. How could you tolerate the glare, you who can't even spell out the runes written in letters twenty cubits high on the rocks?"

He taught them then an elementary, pygmy religion, which might nevertheless save them. It was neither paganism nor druidism, nor was it the purest orthodoxy. It was a page of the eternal Gospel, written in all languages in the flowers, in the rocks, in the veins of crystal, in the faces of stars, and even in the hearts of children. Those who did not know the ABC were astonished to be able to read that book fluently. There were exemplars of it everywhere, displayed on the earth. Negligently, they were left there to be spelled out by the vilest insects.

"Certainly," Merlin said to them, "it's a very modest step, but it's infinitely superior to the one where you are. It's said that your forefathers scaled the heavens. You do the opposite, and crawl in the abyss. Several of you have told me that you expect a new dogma to impose itself on the universe. Good people, I tell you that you've been duped by your old ideas. The new dogma has come and you haven't seen it. You're waiting for the Messiah? The Messiah is in front of you and you don't know him; his name is Liberty. Please don't imitate the peasant who sits down on the bank until the river has passed by. Do you know his story? The dark river did not weary of flowing; it amassed its waves; it growled like an angry man. The peasant found himself swallowed up among the reeds, with his bundle and his flock. Doubtless hunger, cold, frost, and the long wait and the false hope too, had already killed him by the time the great waters reached him."

Such were the speeches that he gave them, but that language did not please any of them. They would rather have perished a hundred times over than recognize what they lacked. Seeing that they could not reach Merlin's height at the first bound, they preferred to plunge back, head first, into their most ancient and sordid superstitions. They formed associations to weave wicker baskets, in which they burned prophets. Their self-respect was greatly soothed by that, and they devoted themselves intently to the affairs of Heaven.

XII

"Be our king!" said the people to Merlin, every time they encountered him.

"God preserve me from that!" he replied. "I make kings, and wouldn't like to be one. But be patient; I'll give you the most handsome of kings, young, well-built, obliging, better than you imagine. You'll thank me for him."

He had, in fact, warned the king of the just, Arthus, to be ready to receive the most beautiful of kingdoms. Arthus was waiting with all his court in the shade of the bushy woods of Vincennes. It was Merlin that opened the gates for him and handed him the keys of the city on a silver platter. He also presented him with an embroidered and deployed flag that could shade the entire tiny people if necessary. Clad in a sable cloak, the king of the just, riding a bay palfrey shod with gold and caparisoned with silk, made his entrance to the city to the sound of bells and oliphants. He confessed that he had never seen a kingdom garnished with people he liked so much.

"Paris! Paris!" he repeated, in a low voice. "It's the best of my thirty crowns. I owe it to you, Merlin; you'll advise me." But he did not feel at ease on seeing the crowd respond to him with acclamations that rose up to the clouds.

Crowned at Notre-Dame, he visited the Louvre, the Bastille and Geneviève's cabin; everything seemed to his liking.

Merlin said to him, as he extended the hand of justice to him: "If you find fault with anything, my king, say so. These people are very new, but they're inconstant, lighter of heart than the lightest leaf. I'm apprehensive of some disturbance, but I think I'll be able to correct it."

"By the Son of Mary," Arthus replied, "don't do anything, Merlin—you'll annoy me. Everything is going well, emerging from your hands. These people please me as they are: lively, cheerful, almost child-like, and easily amused. Don't touch them, for God's sake—you might make them worse."

"As you please, Sire."

Night had fallen. The king slept at the Louvre, Perceval at the Marais, Tristan in Les Halles, Blasius in the cloister at Cluny, Yvain in the Boucheries tower. Arthus' porter, Gleouloued of the wide hands, bolted the door and posted the watchmen. The prefect of the palace, Owenn,[17] lodged in the Thermes. After the trumpets had sounded, silence extended over the city and the river.

XIII

The night was black. When Merlin found himself alone, still full of what he had just said, done and heard, he felt divination awakening within him. What presentiments filed his mind then! How he found himself oppressed by the weight of future centuries, seeing in advance the nations linked to their crimes, without wanting to detach themselves therefrom. He was the only prophet of his time who sought the truth and not illusion.

As he measured the faults, the frivolity, the vanity, the hardening and the ingratitude of the people he loved, he wanted to try to soften them with his

---

[17] Owenn is the leading character of *Owenn, ou la dame de la fontaine* [Owenn; or The Lady of the Spring], one of the romances included by Hersart de La Villemarché in *Contes populaires des ancient Bretons*. The name is more usually rendered Owain. The same romance features the character that Quinet names as Gleouloued, known in Welsh documents as Glewlwyd Gafaelfawr.

songs, like a lullaby casting its spell into the cradle of a newborn. Perhaps he also thought that a note, a sincere sigh, or a word, might ward off the future. Most of all, he wanted to mingle with the winged words of the poet the education of the sage, for he hoped thus to make it enter, through the gate of song, into the heart of the sleeping nations. He took up his harp. At the first chord, the towers and keeps trembled all the way to their foundations. His thoughts overflowed; they broke the rhythm and cadence like a dyke.

Merlin allowed his first prophecy to fall from his lips.

"There are three roads, three abodes, three kingdoms, three worlds, and I am the guide through those three lives.

"I do not prophesy by the flight of the bird, by the blade of the oar, by the orb of the shield. My runes are written in my heart.

"Others make their enchantments with the hazel-branch, with simples collected in the forests. My enchantments are in my soul.

"All have announced dolors, plagues, famines; for my part, I announce joys, benedictions, smiles.

"I say to winter: 'There will be a spring," to tears, 'There will be a smile,' to injustice, a judge, to malady, a cure, to death, a rebirth.

"I too have lived in tears; the world was indifferent to me distress. All my hopes changed into the points of swords to transpierce me,

"I have cried: 'Is there nowhere a place for justice, for hope, for love?' I was ready to perish when I saw myself saved.

"Now, I say: 'When iniquity has covered all the earth, if justice has been able to hide in the shadow of a blade of grass, that will be enough for it to grow and perfume the three worlds."

The prophet interrupted himself momentarily and pricked up his ears. He heard the sound of a leaf falling on the edge of the river. But the people were profoundly asleep, like new-borns.

Then he resumed, in these terms:

"If only I had a hundred scribes around me! The earth would hear the scraping of their pens in the silence of the consternated worlds.

"I gaze at the stars that heap up soundlessly above my head. They inform me of the routes of kingdoms across the mute generations.

"Speak! How many sparks does it require to remake the widow's hearth? How many men to remake the human race? How many grains of wheat to save the dough? How many of the just to save justice? You who have replied to me, be the seed that will repopulate the devastated field of hope!

"Shall I no longer see a human face blossom in gentle pity? Is the speech of the flame that nourished all those who listened to it extinct forever? Will women always have a gaze as harsh as men? Pity, beauty, love, will you never return?

"They pass beside one another hard, pitiless and grim. They have only to glimpse one another momentarily upon the earth, and they flee! Or, if they

64

speak, the words are brief, cold and sordid, like the rusty voice of copper in a miser's hand.

"The wicked! They have made my life an island, separated from their iniquities. They have hollowed out an insurmountable precipice all around; their insulting voices can scarcely reach me. They have put guardians around that abyss; an entire army watches over its bounds to prevent me from approaching them; but all of their precautions protect me from them. If only they could raise a wall of steel in order that their thoughts, on rampant wings, could not reach me!

"Yes, they have made my life a sacred isle. Far from here are the vain dolors, the deceptive hopes, the servile desires and the black regrets. Only alight here, you flocks of white swans departed from eternal shores. Teach my soul incorruptible whiteness!

"In whatever place injustice resides, close at hand or far away, through the ages, through the darkness, I see it! I recognize it by its shadow; I understand it by its breath; I follow it by the odor of blood. Present, absent, hidden, disguised, mute or resounding, it robs me of sleep.

"I see it through the thickness of mountains and heaped-up lies. If it hid at the bottom of the sea, I would still see it through the murky, jaundiced waves, on its throne of algae and hair-like grass. Above all, I can recognize it through the honeyed smile of a hypocritical face. Let it disappear from the earth, or I shall fall upon it!"

At that moment a cloud veiled the disk of the moon over the treetops. Darkness extended everywhere.

Merlin went on:

"The night is amassing around me! Oh, how profound and full of ambushes is the night of the soul! The sepulchral darkness of subterranean places is nothing by comparison. In spite of the darkness, I await the dawn. If the dawn does not come, I shall await the daylight in its glory; if the daylight deceives me too, I shall see the uncreated splendor of the following day. In a slave universe, I shall live and I shall die free.

"O world, I defy you! You will extend indifference over me, and then malevolence, and then disgust, aversion, denial, exile, bloody words, like a shroud perforated by the corners of the sepulcher in a desert heath. After that, you will add the silence heavier than stone. Then you will weave over my lips the web of forgetfulness, more subtle than the spider's; you will then sit down upon my cold remains. And when you have finished your work, you will keep me buried and you will say, shaking your head: 'He is dead, the diviner, the dreamer, the hollow dream!'—and then I shall raise myself up on to my elbow, with a burst of laughter; I will call you by your name. The gentle words of hope, long retained, will emerge from my mouth, in waves as urgent as the snow. And you, you will respond to me with hatred, with derision, with insults, with calumny, with blasphemy, with the sword, with death. You will go a little further, full of wrath, to hollow me out another abyss with your fingernails; I shall obligingly allow myself to be swallowed up, without fear, for I shall laugh at your impotence to keep me imprisoned; I shall emerge almost immediately to mock.

"Why should I no longer dare to smile? I have proven my heart in the darkness. I have felt it, like a faithful armor, which rust cannot corrode.

"Those who loved me love me still. I have not known treason—or, at least, it has come from those who cannot offend me.

"When the sea of servitude has risen and has covered the earth, I have rediscovered the route of serene thought. I am sitting on a sheer peak with the companion of my eternal life; I have driven back with my foot the Ocean vomited by Hell.

"The vulture called to its chicks and all the birds of the air. It said to them: 'Today is the day that you shall take your nourishment from the free human heart and the flesh of innocent peoples.' And it brushed with its livid wing the pale forehead of nations. I have driven it away to its lair with a cry; since that moment, fear has vanished from the human heart. The earth, widow of the sky, has taken back her bridal garland."

There Merlin stopped and pricked up his ears again, but his voice found not a single echo. It passed over the face of the nations as if over desiccated bones.

Dawn was beginning to appear. Merlin perceived in the distance the peoples who were keeping still, as one sees stone dolmens rising in a deserted landscape, whitening in the night. None tried to respond, none took a step toward him.

One figure alone, paler than all the rest, approached him and said to him, weeping: "Don't speak to them anymore; they're deaf, for they've been turned to stone. I alone have heard you; I alone know who you are. I too know justice and hope, but I am dead!"

"Console yourself, poor soul in mourning," the prophet replied. "Whether or not they've been turned to stone, I don't know; I'm beginning to believe it, on seeing them so mute and so hard, but I'm patient; I can wait until they open the hearts and their ears again."

XIV

Merlin discovered in the future the entire destiny of the people who had just blossomed around the hamlet of Lutèce. He described the most imminent dangers point by point, and also marked out the means of avoiding them. From all that, he formed a set of instructions that he gave in a sacred volume to the principal individuals of the city, with the express responsibility of explaining them to the ignorant—who, unfortunately, were numerous in the region.

From that moment on, that book of Prophecies has not ceased to be consulted in cases of public calamity, but fatality determined that it would only ever be consulted after the event, when Merlin's wisdom arrived too late to remedy the evil.

"At least," the sages said, then, "we know exactly why we're perishing."

"That's true," replied the indiscreet, "but why didn't you open the book a day sooner?"

"We'll remember that another time," said the sages.

The opportunity recurred the following years; the book was forgotten again.

Such was the character of the people. Who could correct them, since Merlin had been unable to do so?

XV

Prophet, king, poet, enchanter, bard, son of a saint and an incubus—how many different characters my hero has! Not only, like other heroes, has he a double divine and human nature; he also has a touch of the infernal, softened, corrected and tempered but not destroyed by science. Small at the moment when he seems largest; when I seek him in the clouds he is on earth; an incredible difficulty for his historian, that diversity of tones, of language, of conditions!

What pen would be winged enough to follow him in his course through the three worlds? And it's not enough to depict him in his public life; it's necessary to show him in the hearth, in the intimacy of his private life. That's where the difficulty lies. The lesser danger, with such a hero, is going astray and being precipitated a hundred times a day, by passing too abruptly from heaven to earth, from earth to Hell, from the sublime to the familiar, from the tragic to the comic.

I'll give you proof of it. What did Merlin think, would you say, of the women of Lutèce? What became of his art and his science with them? What was his facial expression, his bearing? I ought to say, if I don't want to leave an unforgivable lacuna in that regard. Let us lower the tone, then; it's time to furl the wings. The classics open the way to me here, as witness the two twins, spoiled children of the gods, who were living in Olympus one day, and the next in the miserable hamlet of Therapnes.[18]

Take this confession as you wish: Merlin was afraid of the women of Lutèce. Their soft voices, like mocking birds, disconcerted him at first. He listened, without daring to speak, to that human twittering between earth and sky, without knowing whether it was art of nature. Their smile also scared him, because that smile, brushing everything, seemed to challenge everything.

Merlin did not know how to act with them, and felt disarmed as well as mistrustful. He was incapable of playing with the sacred words like a viol player improvising a prelude on the viol of love. Was it because his heart was so full

---

[18] Castor and Pollux.

that he could neither imagine anything, nor want anything, not covet anything? I don't say that. In a full soul, there always remains at least enough room for a drop of poison. A word fallen at hazard from a playful mouth dug into his heart, all day long, as a drop of joyful water will hollow out a rock.

He knew a thousand stories that he believed to be charming, a thousand confidences of streams with pebbles on the bank, a thousand ingenuous secrets of flowers, stones, elves, and even stars—but those stories, to his great astonishment, did not interest the most beautiful of beauties at all, to whom he told them for preference. What a humiliation it was to see the slightest anecdote from any passer-by preferred a hundred times to all the sparking secrets of the errant stars, which he knew so well. That was his first disappointment.

One thing astonished him even more. The young women laughed wholeheartedly and made fun of his enchantments as soon as his back was turned. That seemed to him, not without reason, a great ingratitude. *For after all*, he said to himself, *they profit from them. Whence comes, I ask you, if not from Merlin, that* je ne sais quoi *more powerful than the girdle of the ancient goddess? They do not have her Greek profile, but nevertheless, they have her humor, her taste, her cheerful Attic knowingness. Who taught it to them? There they are, scarcely emerged from the woods, having only two or three garments at the most, and already they seem to be queens among queens. Who taught them, if it wasn't me, the power of a ribbon, a strip of fabric, a flower in the hair, the magic of a glance, of a half-pronounced word, of slightly parted lips—less than that, of a silence? I taught them all of that, so that they could mock me.*

Full of those ideas, he did not hesitate to open up to the most beautiful, named Isaline.[19]

"Don't be offended, Merlin," Isaline said to him. "We've only just made our entrance; we're already laughing at everything in this region, at what we love as well as what we hate, the rose and the thorn, liberty and slavery, the cradle and the tomb, and even love. Sometimes—rarely, fortunately—in the midst of those games, those smiles, a profound thought slips into the heart and raps itself in its folds. Then the poison is more subtle, more venomous, I swear, than in any other land."

"That's some consolation," Merlin replied.

Isaline had cheeks that were a trifle pale for her jet-black hair, a mouth full of amorous malice, a high, angelic forehead, a figure as supple as meadow-grass and, better than that, the largest, daintiest, most mischievous, most profound, most serious, most ingenuous and most reflective dark eyes that were ever seen on earth. When Merlin saw those large velvety eyes for the first time, he thought

---

[19] Hermione's notes say that the portrait of Isaline is "taken from life" but does not reveal the model's identity, and Quinet might not have told her; she observes that this entire section reflects Quinet's memories of his arrival in Paris in 1820 and his subsequent reactions to the city.

he was seeing the luminous source of all magic. He drank them in at his leisure, slowly and conscientiously. Was it not the starry flame in which every enchanter ought to bathe?

By dint of intelligence, Isaline understood Merlin's imagination, or at least let him think so. She had no taste for what we would now call nature, art, poetry or reverie; she would have traded all the stars in the sky for a single diamond from the lapidary's boutique, all legends for one telling gibe, all the harmonious lowing of the distant sea for one whispered conversation in private with a friend, by the fireside. Although society—or what we understand by it, at least—did not exist as yet, she had divined it.

What we have learned about the tide of the passions would have been antipathetic to her, but that was unknown to both the men and the women of her time. Nor would she have been able to bear our systems of theology transported into amour, our mysticism, our bombast, or even our good qualities—if they exist—acquired at the price of grace. She was grace itself; she cursed as an impiety everything lacking it.

Just as she belonged to ancient France, she belonged to the old school, preferring prose to poetry. She would have been a Classicist if there had been Romantics in her lifetime. Don't ask what she would have thought about enjambment in verse or realism; such questions didn't exist in her era.

Thus, she seemed frivolous; in reality, she wasn't; there was even a little routine in her way of being. She resembled the sea, mobile on the surface and immutable in the depths. But she would have rejected that comparison as too ambitious. I've already said that she would have preferred the clarity and simplicity of the eighteenth century to all our lyricism.

The sound of her voice resembled...please, don't ask me what. I don't know of anything that bears the slightest resemblance to it, except one, that I no longer hear and can't talk about. That one, if I heard it, would immediately make me feel homesick—and that's precisely why I want to avoid it throughout the course of this work. Let's pass on!

Was she married, yes or no? I can't say for sure. I think she was. In any case, it made no difference. Perhaps she was separated? Perhaps her husband was on a long voyage, for distraction. Perhaps he was busy with commerce or the crusades? Perhaps he was dead? Not that she wasn't good, and aware of her duties, but, all things considered, nothing about her announced the hindrance of a servile, obsequious linkage. If she had a restraint, she forged it voluntarily, every day, with her own reason.

Was she religious? Yes, she was, but not as we understand it nowadays. She didn't wear her devotion like a mantle. She didn't talk about the Gospel, the Holy Fathers, or any of the commandments, at table, at a dance, a concert, in the woods or at the Opera. She only talked about them in church, and then in hushed tones. She didn't deploy her most sacred thoughts like a fan. On the contrary, she shut them away, withheld them, like a well, in order to drink therefrom on difficult days. The rest of the time, she was cheerful, playful, detesting hypocrisy like ugliness itself, never mingling the sacred and the profane. She even made fun of the Triads. That was wrong, I know; once again, it was a product of her time, not her individuality. Don't ask her time for the virtues of ours. Let's at least respect historical color.

With so many differences and so few resemblances, how were Merlin and Isaline able to understand one another for a single day? They were both young, and both had grace. That, I think, is the first link that was able to bring them together.

Doubtless Merlin thought he was only amusing himself, or at least distracting himself from his sublime endeavors; he didn't know that conversation can be simultaneously an art, a game, a drama and a combat. He felt caressed, mocked, admired, challenged, lacerated and cured, all at the same time. As I say, he didn't have the slightest idea of the art of playing with the heartstrings without breaking them; at first he was amused, then dazzled, then stunned.

Sometimes he experienced a burning anguish, as if all his beautiful azure palaces were about to dissipate at the first breath from that laughing mouth, and he remained suspended from that smile, between life and death. All his magical kingdoms were then at the mercy of a mocking word that might fall without warning from Isaline's lips like a raindrop on a soap bubble. That anguish, in which his life was at stake, was, however, full of indescribable delights.

Merlin, the child of legends, knew very well what could be done with enthusiasm, genius and prophetic inspiration. No one could have taught him anything in that regard. But wit, something new to him, astonished him to the highest degree. He was obliged to admit that no one knew anything similar in the court of Brittany or in the three Bardic kingdoms. Sometimes he compared the effect that he obtained to that of lightning in a forest of resinous fir-trees, ready to catch fire, sometimes to the blade or the sparkling edge of a sword with a diamond hilt in the hands of a virgin, but most often to a fire-follet drawing a traveler toward a crystal palace in which a feast is laid out.

"Leave your fire-follet and your feast there," Isaline said. "Get back to the diamonds!"

Disconcerted, Merlin brought the conversation back to what he knew best: the blue sky, infinite space, the mysterious region of the ecliptic.

Without rising to those heights, Isaline replied with a good deal of sense by talking about the earth.

When would they see his sister Ganieda?[20] Was the city of Loel as nice as Paris? What was said about the king of the Orkneys? Who was, in his opinion,

---

[20] Ganieda is named as Merlin's twin sister in Geoffrey of Monmouth's *Vita Merlini*, and plays a major role in the narrative section of Hersart's *Myrdhinn*, but it is perhaps surprising to find her mentioned here, as Quinet's Merlin has no siblings. The name is adapted into the Welsh Gwenddydd when cited as

the most beautiful of beauties? Was it Enide with the azure robe, Lady Yguerne[21] or Tegaf with the golden breast[22]—or even Queen Genièvre?

Thos simple words resonated like as many pearls in a silver bowl.

Again, even more troubled, he talked about the three lives, the three felicities.

"Three felicities!" Isaline exclaimed, half laughing, half weeping. "If I could only know one!"

Oh, first winged divagations of two hearts, pursuing one another and fleeing from one another in the transparent morning air! Let's not hope to describe them to you. With so much divergence of ideas, how could their minds ever reach one another? They kept long silences. At least their eyes spoke, and thought they understood one another. Merlin no longer knew where he was; he found himself delighted in Isaline's presence; he took her by the hand, and his prophetic lips resounded, choked, allowed weak sighs to escape, certain presages of dolor and felicity.

I repeat that it was, of course, only a game. And yet Merlin's heart was bleeding. It was only a childish game, and yet the heart and the mind came together, colliding, breaking, lighting up. And what sparks sprang forth from that impact of two such different hearts!

Did Merlin forget Viviane, then? It would be madness to think so, an impiety to say so. No, certainly, he did not forget her. He knew what a difference there is between an ideal person and an exceedingly positive person, however charming. But in the end, he could not help noticing for the first time that there are different sorts of beauty on the earth. Viviane's was certainly prodigious, celestial, uranian, almost supernatural; nevertheless, Isaline's was not to be scorned.

Was my hero eclectic, then? What a question! We are too accustomed to spoiling the best of things by means of pedantic terms.

It happened that one day, at a feast in Arthur's court, Viviane found herself in the same company as Isaline. Immediately, she lacked air, she thought she was about to die a thousand times. Everything that emerged from Isaline's

---

Myrddin's sister in a poem contained in the *Red Book of Hergest*, which dates from at least two hundred years later, although enthusiasts for the Celtic origin of the Arthurian mythos would argue that both must have been drawing on earlier Welsh sources.

[21] I have left this name as Quinet renders it, although Geoffrey of Monmouth renders it as Igerna, Malory as Ygrayne and other sources as Igraine; she was Arthur's mother.

[22] Again I have retained Quinet's idiosyncratic spelling, although other sources render the name as Tegau or Tegau Eyfron [Tegau Golden-Breast]. She is mentioned in the Triads as the wife of Caradoc, one of the knights of the Round Table, whose fidelity is subjected to various tests, which she passes.

mouth struck Viviane like an arrow. If she had not hastened to leave, she would surely have died.

When Merlin caught up with her, he found her in tears. She had just discovered that Merlin did not have the fixity of the stars. One might have thought that it was their first quarrel, the first ripple on their silvery lake, until then as smooth as a mirror. At least no one witnessed it. A few brief words, a few precipitate steps, a broken alabaster cup, then a momentary silence, and after that a sigh, a sob, and almost immediately a furtive reconciliation, sealed with tears— that was all that anyone head. It was also the unique denouement of the story.

Perhaps it would have been better not to say anything about it? I'm beginning to think so. But could I, then, conceal Viviane's first tears?

Certainly, it was a fault on Merlin's part, although it didn't exceed the limits of a simple conversation, such as the best of men permit themselves every day a thousand times and more, without criticizing one another. I would have liked my hero to be perfect, so that he might serve as a model to all the generations to come, for him never to have turned his gaze away for an instant from the pure ideal to look at a real creature, even in a conversation. That's what I would have liked! But since he was unable to maintain himself at that height, I ought to say so—and may I not have any other confession of that sort to make!

In any case, Reader, don't worry! Expiation will have its hour. You'll be content. If the hero leaves something to be desired, the moral of the work will be all the more perfect for it.

BOOK THREE: THE WORLD OF THE HAPPY;
MERLIN SEARCHES FOR HIS FATHER

I

What a joy it is to open the door to beloved guests a long time awaited![23] There is nothing sweeter beneath the vault of heaven. How the walls smile at the newcomers! How the angle of the roof reddens with a warm ray of sunlight! How the cricket on the hearth repeats its song, especially if an ingenuous, modest but beautiful young woman fills the old abandoned hall with her merry laughter! Even after the guests have gone, the echo of their footsteps still cheers up the shiny stone of the threshold.

Such were the sentiments that Merlin left everywhere he went. For himself, he experienced things quite differently. Experience had shown him that he was not born for the noise of cities. With his science, as he was little accustomed to society, nothing was easier for people than to make him suffer. He took everything they said seriously, often heart-broken by a word or a glance to which others would not have attached any importance. He dug too deeply into that which it was necessary to skim. That is the malady of the solitary.

At the same time, seeing that, in spite of his advice, the people were not following the right path, the prophet became sad. *Tristis fit vates.*[24] A black misanthropy took possession of him; he would have liked to flee to the depths of the woods.

"Oh!" he exclaimed, several times a day, sighing. "Reality is too bitter. Scarcely have I touched it than it has wounded me mortally in the heart. Where are the solitudes populated with beings with which I wanted to fill the world?"

"I know where they exist," Viviane replied.

"What? They're not dreams?"

---

[23] Hermione comments that many of the Books making up the novel commence with an "invocation" unconnected with the subject but designed to fix the memory of some event occurring at the time of writing; this greeting was allegedly offered to a "charming young woman, Marie de Guelle, since dead in the prime of life" who visited Quinet and Minna in Veytaux on the day he began this section. That implies a long gap in composition between the earlier sections of the narrative, compiled in 1852 or 1853, and the text from now on, dating from the late 1850s, though not necessarily written in the order in which they appear in the text.

[24] Approximately "sadness makes the seer". Although the phrase is not a quotation, a similar observation appears in the *Vita Merlini*.

"When you see them, Merlin, perhaps you'll believe your eyes. Let's just leave this mocking habitation where you inflicted my first dolor. It's stifling here. Let's go breathe in my domains."

Scarcely were they out of the town than the silence of the heaths and the spectacle of the work in the fields restored Merlin's serenity of mind. On the seventh day they reached a forest that some believes to be that of the Ardennes, but which was really that of Dombes, where I spent the first half of my life in almost continual enchantment.

A few chimeras with shining eyes, which I rediscovered myself in the same place, under the tall ferns; here and there, unicorns tranquilly sharpening their horns, salamanders with golden abdomens, ibises, phoenixes, starlings with black and white patches, halcyons, pelicans, ichneumons, and especially blue birds, the color of time, welcomed our voyagers as they entered. Add to that numerous horses whose stirrups resonated noisily against the trunks of magical trees. There was Bayard, the horse of the four sons of Aymon;[25] there was Roland's Brigliadoro; there was Valentine, browsing the hornbeams while waiting for Charlemagne.[26] They all whinnied as Merlin approached, as if they could already feel the spur of chivalry.

A storm that had threatened during the night had dispersed in the morning, growling. Mild, warm air and a pure blue sky, the first breath of spring in everything: it seemed that nature wanted to add her enchantment to the day.

Merlin's curiosity was at its height. He darted long glances around him. He would have liked to divine, as always, the meaning of words before they had been pronounced.

Solemnly, Viviane said: "We're getting close; let's speak softly. The world, ever blind, has believed until now that poets find the radiant, aerial, charming winged creatures with which they populate the universe in the hollows of their fantasy. To hear them, they have only to draw upon the waves of their genius freely to donate an immortality to their visions that they would be only too glad to possess themselves. That is what they have persuaded people, so easily duped, to believe. You too, Merlin—yes you, the sage—have allowed yourself to be abused on that point. You too believe in errant phantoms that haunt the heads of poets.

---

[25] *Quatre Fils Aymon* (The Four Sons of Aymon] is a 12th century verse romance, part of the Charlemagnian cycle, that exists in several versions, and which formed the basis of a 14th century prose romance. It appears to have been one of the most popular of all the works in the genre.

[26] Brigliadoro and Valentine are really the same horse, the former being the rendering in Ludovico Ariosto's *Orlando Furioso* of a name that had gone through various transitions but probably began as the French Veillantif [vigilant], that being the name given in the earliest version of the *Chanson de Roland*.

"O injustice! Must it be, then, that the most beautiful, the most sublime, the most durable existences pass for the pure inventions of a few good talkers? Will the individuals that I know best and esteem the most be treated as phantoms for a long time yet? If that's the case, what will we soon be ourselves? Won't there be some poet vain enough to swear that he's invented both of us in a moment of caprice? Believe me, Merlin, it's time that these lies ceased and ephemera no longer contest life with immortals! Know this, then: the individuals reputed to be visions, creations and dreams of a few princes or artisans of speech with gilded tongues, live just as you and I do. They are all gathered in this very place, beneath this shade, merely waiting for the poet to come and call them by their names and bring them out of their obscurity."

"Can that be?"

"Look!"

"Which way?"

"Listen! Listen!"

From the edge of the wood a refrain then emerged, the echo of fine days, muffled by the branches:

All is divine!
Love will commence!
Then comes decline:
Dolor immense!

Merlin, seeking to discover where those familiar voices were coming from, discovered, sitting on the new grass, in the shadow of oak trees as old as the earth, the same radiant groups of individuals that he had encountered in the first hour of his felicity. Foreheads circled with garlands of wild roses and narcissi, they seemed to be living in expectation of some great event.

The sunlight, veiled by the foliage, was playing at their feet in a thousand webs of shadow and light.

"Oh!" Merlin exclaimed. "Here, then, are those melodious people who disappeared too quickly for my liking! I've found them again. It seems to me that they neither hunger nor thirst, nor suffer any earthly cares. Yes, these are what I'm looking for, and by whom I'd like to be remembered."

"You will be," said Viviane. "They're made to love forever. They're the winged, harmonious people that the poets, artisans of lies, pretend to have invented, because they lend them a few garments to clothe them when they emerge from the forest."

At the sight of Viviane, the women stood up and welcomed her as their queen, but a vivid blush colored their faces when Merlin spoke to them. Their incomparable beauty increased to such a point that Viviane was almost jealous. Already she was repenting of having brought the Enchanter to this place.

"Who are you?" he asked, without seeking to hide his delight.

They replied one after another, in various tones:

"I'm Titania."

"And I'm Angelica."[27]

"And I'm Juliet of Verona."

"And I'm Desdemona of Venice."

"And I'm Ophelia."

"And I'm Clorinda."[28]

"And I'm Julie."[29]

Merlin turned toward another group of women, each of whom, their eyes fixed, their lips parted and quivering, could have depicted the spirit of expectation. They said to him:

"I'm Chimène!"[30]

"And I'm Erminia!"[31]

"And I'm Clarissa!"[32]

"And I'm Virginie."[33]

Yet others tried to speak; they were all so impatient to identify themselves that not all of them could find a opportunity to pronounce their names. Then they fell silent with a sigh.

"Why are you sighing?" said Merlin. "What do you want from me?"

"We're waiting for the man who will give us liberty and speech. Is it you? Be our king!"

Titania recounted then how she had been chained by a sylph to a sprig of rosemary. She uttered faint moans; Merlin hastened to set her free. She immediately started running over the flowers without curbing them. Griselidis[34] and the

---

[27] Angelica is a princess in the *Orlando Furioso* and its predecessor, Boiardo's *Orlando Innamorato*, pursued by both Orlando [Roland] and Rinaldo [Renaud, one of the four sons of Aymon].

[28] Clorinda is the warrior-maiden in Torquato Tasso's *Gerusalemme liberata* [Jerusalem Delivered] (1581)

[29] The eponymous heroine of Jean-Jacques Rousseau's *Julie, or the Nouvelle Héloïse* (1761).

[30] Chimène is the leading female character in Pierre Corneille's *Le Cid* (1637), who became the title character in Antonio Sacchini's operatic version of 1783.

[31] The original has "Herminie," which is the title of an 1811 poem by Fidèle Delcroix based on the character of Erminia in Tasso's *Gerusalemme Liberata*, who must be the intended reference.

[32] The eponymous heroine of Samuel Richardson's 1748 novel, very popular in France.

[33] From Bernardin de Saint-Pierre's novel *Paul et Virginie* (1788)

[34] Charles Perrault's version of the name of the heroine of a tale first published in Boccaccio's *Decameron*, known in numerous English adaptations as "patient Griselda."

Gioconda, who were standing in the shadow of a beautiful Italian pine, ran to join her in procession, an all of them, holding hands, began to dance around our Enchanter. You might have taken them for the matinal hours dancing around the Prince of Day at his awakening, or for beautiful grape-gatherers around the kind of the vintage—for they seemed intoxicated, not on grapes but on innocent hope. As they moved they wove a hat of flowers for Merlin, which they set on his head. The good Merlin wore it, smiling. Viviane took slight umbrage; she remained silent. Merlin was also mute, with admiration. He would have liked to ask: "Are they really my subjects?" but he did not dare.

A little further on, beyond a summit strewn with mossy stones, he discovered groups of men in vast clearings, without being able to discern whether the noise that he heard in that place was the murmur of a stream, the whisper of foliage or the conversation of those unknown individuals. In order to find out, he increased his pace.

Having reached them, he asked: "Who are you?"

They replied, one after another:

"I'm Roland."

"And I'm Hamlet."

"And I'm Tancred."[35]

"And I'm Alceste."[36]

"And I'm Lara."[37]

"An I'm Don Quixote."

"And I'm Othello."

"And I'm Saint-Preux."[38]

"And is it you who have come to open the door to the real world to us?"

"No," said Merlin. "I've quarreled with that world. What else do you expect from me?"

"Give us strength and immortality."

"Give us grace first!" cried the women, extending their hands toward him, having followed him so silently that he had not even heard the sound of their footfalls.

Merlin immediately lavished upon them, without bargaining, all the gifts of his art. He had never heaped anyone with such munificence. When the men saw what a great fuss Merlin was making of the ideal beauties that were so close to them, they began to look at them for the first time, and, far from disdaining them, as they had done until then, they began to be seriously smitten with them.

---

[35] In Tasso's *Gerusalemme Liberata*.

[36] The protagonist of Molière's *Le Misanthrope* (1666), not to be confused with the heroine of two operas based on Euripides' *Alcestis*.

[37] In Lord Byron's narrative poem (1814).

[38] Julie's counterpart in the Rousseau novel.

Oberon became engaged to Titania that day, Medoro to Angelica, Romeo to Juliet, the Sire de Saluces to Griselidis; they were never apart thereafter.

If he could have, at that moment, Merlin would probably have taken them all across the invisible boundary that separated them from the real world, all the more so since the circle in question was only traced by an autumnal thread of spidersilk. He consoled them by telling them how cruel that world is, and how everything there is poisoned. They would not be able to take a step there without tearing themselves on the brambles of the path.

"Enjoy," he said. "Enjoy the conditions that you have created in these retreats, in the embalmed shade of these magical trees. Don't be too desirous of emerging. Later, poets will come, who will give you the publicity and the tumult, alas, that they call glory. Passion, wrath, hatred, jealousy—they can only lend you what they possess. Dread that you might then regret your original obscurity."

At the same time, he delighted his eyes and his mind with the spectacle of an immaculate world in which everything was peace, beauty, bounty and harmony. All the people he met in that solitude were a hundred times more beautiful than the poets who later pretended to have imagined them had claimed.

"Charming daughters," said Merlin, dazzled by so many marvels, "be your own society; believe me, it's the only one worthy to receive you!"

But the enchantresses continued: "O good Merlin, take us into the cities, into the dwellings of men. It's so sad to mirror oneself all alone in the springs of the forest! We shall only believe in our beauty if we see it reflected in the eyes of people."

"You want that!" said Merlin. "Have you really thought about it? In emerging from your obscurity, you'll lose at least half of your primal beauty?"

But they replied: "What's the point of our beauty if no one sees it?"

Then Merlin conversed with each of them individually. He tried, for a thousand excellent reasons, to prove to them all that they had to lose by emerging from that primal innocence, which was for them the innocence of Eden. He enabled Desdemona to glimpse from afar the sad pillow of Othello, Erminia the indigent hut of the shepherd, Clorinda the sword sated on her blood, Griselidis the dozen ordeals, Marguerite the pool into which she would plunge her child, Ophelia the pale garland of cornflowers that would deck her crazed head, Juliet the cruel agony in the tomb in Verona, Angelica her flight without respite or mercy, Veleda the sickle,[39] Julie the sheer rock of Chillon, Virginie the wreck of the *Saint-Géran*, Clarissa infamy.

Only a few were moved by those words.

---

[39] Veleda (or Velleda) was a Germanic priestess involved in the Batavian revolt against the Romans in the 1st century A.D., but this reference is surely to the equivalent character in the 1795 novel *Velleda* by the German Romantic novelist and folklorist Benedikte Naubert (née Christiana Hebenstreit)..

"Is it true," said Desdemona to Othello, "that I shall suffer that cruel death at your hands? If you wish it, let it be so; I shan't go back on my word."

At those words, Othello made an effort to smile, as if it were a game; deep down, from that moment on, he felt a commencement of anguish; he begged the Enchanter to answer for him to his beloved.

"Is it true," murmured Griselidis, in her turn, "that I shall suffer for you, my lord, everything the Enchanter says? No matter; if I had to endure a hundred times more, I would not take back my ring."

With that, the Sire de Saluces implored Merlin to vouch for him, but the Enchanter refused.

Addressing himself once again to the women who formed his cortege, he said: "That is what is reserved for you, as soon as you let the burning thoughts that men nourish into your virgin souls. That is what they call the real world—as if yours were imaginary! Today, you live in eternal peace. Do you really want to exchange that for eternal anguish?"

"What is this peace?" replied the daughters of incorruptible amour. "This calm is death; we're weary of our serenity."

"Beware of summoning and unleashing tempests in your souls!"

"Well, yes, we summon them, we invoke them, the unknown tempests full of thunder and lightning. They weigh upon us less than this ancient repose in which you have found us. Are we flowers of the woods to vegetate like them? We're weary, Merlin, of competing with the radiant stars in the long summer nights. This Eden without a serpent, without a tempter, is tedious."

Erminia, Juliet and Ophelia addressed him intimately, in chorus: "Give us tempests, you who speak so well." And they took his hands.

"You want that, insensate maidens!" said Merlin. "Well, it's you who'll have made your destiny. I shall soon awaken the bards who, with a thousand flattering words and cadences, will draw you to the thresholds of brilliant dwellings, where you'll be lulled day and night by the rhythm of their songs; people will call them poets. They'll teach you soft, honeyed words. But as soon as you entrust yourselves to them, they'll bewitch you; you'll no longer belong to yourselves; that will be your fall from Eden."

"Let them come!" said crowd of accomplished beings who filled the forest.

"When they come," Merlin said, "and it might not be long delayed, at least don't forget my final advice. I'm lending you my power; your siren voices will speak everywhere; you'll stir the hearts of peoples. As soon as your tongues are untied, spread wisdom over the earth. Publish the truth; sow justice; praise liberty. When you speak of love, let it be while blushing."

Such were the supreme commandments that he gave to the people as he left them. He added very few laws to them, only a handful of extremely flexible, extremely broad regulations adapted to the genius of each of them. The first was beauty, which he did not permit to be neglected in any circumstances of life, under any pretext, neither in tears, nor in laughter; the second was pleasure, the third serenity. Almost anything was permissible against ennui, easy to recognize at a distance by its leaden wings. Nothing that resembled toil; an air of festival, or at least of ease; no contention, no hindrance or fatigue. No artifice, but much artistry; no make-up, and yet a lily-white complexion. Even in irons, it was necessary to seem free.

To these commandments, the women relied with ecstatic cries; the men bowed, hand on heart, and promised without objection what Merlin wished.

Then strange forms trailed at his feet, veritable monsters that could not raise themselves from the ground. Caliban was the first, Adamastor[40] the second, Morgant[41] the third; all of them were hairy, gigantic and hideous. Without speaking, their paws joined, they dared to cling on to the hem of his robe, asking him to enable them to enter real life.

Merlin considered them for some time, with a horror mingled with pity.

"What?" he said to them. "You also desire real existence? Have you never seen yourselves in the mirror of a spring? What good would more life do you? Made as you seem to be, deformed at pleasure, don't aspire to more glory! Keep your posterity to yourselves. Who could love you?"

But the monsters stuck to his heels like beggars that no refusal can discourage. They growled dully, and could only reply: "Oh! Oh! Oh!" so persistently that in order to escape them, Merlin gave them a nod of the head that meant: "Hope anyway, then!"

Caliban rejoiced in his heart in thinking about his posterity. Adamastor stopped, stupidly expectant; he resembled a rugged rock overhanging a gulf.

Merlin was about to withdraw when a strong odor of tar reached him, mingled with dense smoke. He investigated. In a little inlet strewn with seaweed, two individuals, in the midst of numerous tools, such as hammers, nails, saws, ropes, axes, a few pints of fresh water and rum, were caulking the inverted hull of a boat with oakum and moss.

Robinson Crusoe and Gulliver were their names; both of them were busy, very discreet and even more modest; they dared not come closer. Merlin advanced cheerfully; he learned from their own mouths what an immoderate desire they had to sail for strange lands. They could hardly wait for the boat to be finished; they thought they might die of impatience.

Everything that he could reasonably do to dissuade them from their project, Merlin did; he warned, he scolded, he begged, he implored.

What would they gain from this distant voyage? Were they so sure of avoiding shipwreck? Anyway, it was a very bad time; there was no talk of anything but disasters that year. Then again, after all, what would they see? Peoples scarcely born, already degenerate and disfigured. If curiosity was driving our

---

[40] The sea-monster in Luis de Camões' epic *Os Lusiadas* (1572).

[41] The protagonist of the chivalric romance *Morgant le Géant*, who becomes Roland's squire, heroic in spite of his size and violent inclinations

two friends, what need was there to go so far? Could they not enter into themselves? They would find unknown abysses, tempests and even sandy deserts in the depths of their heart, as easily as beyond the Indian sea.

All that was said gently and sympathetically, not in the tone of a master.

Robinson and Gulliver did not give an inch, and Merlin did not persist. He wanted them to follow their whim, not his. After a few items of advice about climates, trade winds, monsoons, currents and tides he gave them two little compasses, the first that were ever used, and two maps, one of Lilliput for Gulliver and one of the desert island for Robinson. You would have seen therein not merely the general disposition of the land but also, distinctly marked, the landing-points, the creeks, the cliffs, the inlets—in brief, everything that might help avoid a shipwreck, or even render it profitable. After which he took his leave of our two adventurers, wishing them *bon voyage*.

Personally, he withdrew with a contented heart, his mind more satisfied with that day than any other. Nevertheless, he was careful to advise those who were following him not to try to cross the barrier.

Some of them disobeyed him, too impatient to enter the real world. Roland, Hamlet, Don Quixote and Manfred[42] hurried after him. What did they have to fear from the thread of spider-silk that served as a fence?

Scarcely had they touched it than they fell backwards. And from that day on they were inclined to vertigo. It was the first intrusion of grief into the world of the happy, but the sadness was only momentary.

II

It was then the month of May. Vigorous messengers, sent in all directions, published the news that the wedding of the nightingale and the rose, so long deferred, would be celebrated that year.[43] Everyone was ordered to take part in the procession. The earth had already put on its bridal gown.

As chance would have it, the messengers encountered Merlin as he emerged from the forest.

"We were looking for you, Seigneur; come to where the fiancés are waiting for you. Without you, the celebration would be a wake. There will be kings, counts, barons, gentlemen, and especially poor people. Be the priest, the prince and the poet, at the same time.

"Don't refuse them," said Viviane. "They're my godmother's people."

"Let's go," said Merlin, following them through the flowery groves.

---

[42] The eponymous protagonist of Lord Byron's poem (1816-17).

[43] Hermione's notes refer the story of the rose and the nightingale to "a Persian legend…that embodies the most serious thoughts on marriage." The allegorical folktale in question is the basis of much Sufi poetry and art, although it is now best-known in English by courtesy of Oscar Wilde's mock-cynical adaptation.

At that moment he would have liked to lend his happiness to the whole word. He was therefore not sorry to put an end by means of legitimate marriage to the tearful sighs of the nightingale, which had often woken him with a start in the night and touched him with compassion for such a grand amour.

From the depths of the Orient many queens arrived; they all brought cassolettes full of incense. Poets from Persia also came, each of them having composed an epithalamium. Serenades, aubades and ballads filled the first half of May, well into the night. There was a truce between nations; no slaughter, only the occasional quarrel if one preferred the voice of the fiancé, the other the virginal silence of his beloved. In any case, everyone, delightedly relaxed, confessed that no wedding had ever attracted such a great cortege of princes and joyful peoples. All the glory of that reverted to Merlin.

He took the opportunity to invite to the fête all the couples who, without being aware of it, were made for one another: all those who had a secret relationship of heart, mind or taste, sometimes of facial appearance, whom nature had destined for one another.

What did he ask of them? Only one thing: sincerity. In return, he promised to remove the obstacles that might separate them: differences of condition or birth, misunderstandings, family prejudices, the stubbornness of parents or guardians, fortune on one side and lack of it on the other. Even quarrels, provided that they were only matters of vexation, ceded to Merlin.

Gathering them from all points of the earth, he asked them whether they accepted one another mutually as spouses—to which they replied: "Yes."

Without further ado, he celebrated with equal magnificence the wedding of the nightingale and the rose and those of an innumerable host of couples, including the Sleeping Beauty and her knight, Madame de Vergy and the Sire de Coucy,[44] Erec de Nantes and Enide, Perceval le Gallois and Blanchefleur, Antar the Negro and his cousin Ablla,[45] Marko the Serb and Rosanda,[46] emirs and almas, Aladdin and the Sultana, several fairies, as many princes, twenty shepherdesses and twenty kings. No one had any need to produce birth-certificates or other identity papers; everyone's assets were assumed to be the same.

The musicians gathered for one marriage served for the others. To begin with, there were a thousand wrens, two thousand turtle-doves, three thousand reed-warblers and as many woodlarks. Seventy greenfinches and chaffinches, and as many siskins, uttered their mordant, piercing notes at intervals, after eve-

---

[44] The central characters of *Le Roman du chatelaine de Coucy et de la dame du Fayel*, subsequently adapted by Boccaccio and others.

[45] The central characters in a legend recounted by Alphonse de Lamartine in *A Pilgrimage to the Holy Land* (1835).

[46] Prince Marko, King of Serbia in the late 14th century, is the hero of much Serbian epic poetry, in which Rosanda occasionally features as a love interest,

ry sigh; the bass parts were sustained by fifty waxwings and fifty centenarian rooks.

The first betrothals of souls, marriages of minds, inexplicable sympathies, natural kinships, alliances, impulses, the consanguinity of two hearts that, without knowing one another, ran, flew and precipitated themselves toward one another; chains of flowers, or rather diamonds; voiceless conversations, the language of gazes, mute consents, interior smiles, the first gifts of the morning, invisible contracts, sealed by dew in the hands of the Enchanter, were initiated that day.

As for the ceremony, Merlin wanted to put a certain solemnity into it. The most important thing was his speech to all the couples gathered before him. He completed it with these words:

"Go, be happy! I bless you. Under all titles—bard, diviner, prophet, king, enchanter—I say to you, there is no terrestrial felicity outside legitimate marriage, such as I have just celebrated by solemn rites. Outside of that, not one assured hour; pleasures ever frightened, for which it is necessary to blush repeatedly, the soul unquiet and tormented; and what joy, I ask you but the impious, fraudulent sharing of oneself?

"Avoid, then, those pretended espousals in which one vaguely takes the clouds as witnesses, a sure means of breaking your word. Take a serious witness, all of you, before God and men. Let the oak be taken as a witness by the reeds, the green woodpecker by the robin, the hooded crow by the swallow, the centenarian deer by the cicadas, the bard by humans, Merlin by the bards. Words of bronze are required to enchain ephemera."

By way of conclusion, he added: "Nightingale, be faithful to the rose! And you who are listening to me, kings, shepherds, humans and homunculi, remember that Merlin has signed the contract."

To these words he added considerable presents: robes of white wool for the priests, a hundred gold necklaces for the virgins, a hundred new pairs of trousers for the poor folk.

When the celebrations were over, Merlin sent the favored couples away, who went hither and yon, singing his praises, hoping that those he had united would never be divided by fate.

But how many of those diamond chains have been broken pitilessly! How many of those souls married legitimately by Merlin at the outset have been divorced by hazard, by birth, by prejudice, by avarice, by avidity for gold, by the cruelty of parents! Some of those spouses spend the rest of their lives searching for one another without ever finding one another; others encounter one another when it is no longer permissible for them to love one another, or, if they do, it is their damnation! Others, even more wretched, have forgotten that they were ever married and that the contract is still in the enchanter's hands. Hence the ennui, the sadness, the insipidity of human things. Everything is forgotten there, even felicity, even despair.

At least the nightingale has never forgotten that he espoused the rose.

III

All the flowers of the fête had not yet all faded, and all the singers had not yet quenched their thirst, when the sound of trumpets and oliphants, mingled with the clash of blades and battleaxes, shook the doors of the hall—which were fortunately made of oak-wood armored with bronze.

"Hola!" cried Merlin. "The reckless! Who invited them? It wasn't me. They've arrived early. I was expecting them, but not until winter."

A valet named Gui de Nanteuil[47] enquired in the street as to the origin of the tumult. They learned from him of the imminent arrival of the barbarians. Wearied by the journey, poorly nourished and ill-clad, they were announcing themselves from afar, in advance, in the form of a few marauders, in order that people might have time to prepare a refuge.

At the moment when that news was reported to Merlin, he was sitting down, holding a silver goblet in his right hand filled with red wine, about to raise it to his lips. Suddenly, he changed his mind. He deposited the cup, still full, on the edge of the table, and radiantly, taking advice from his hospitable good humor, he stood up.

"Let's go to meet them," he said, "to compliment them on their coming, to feed them, to assist them, for I suspect that they're hungry, in body and in mind."

He had, in fact, heard much good said about barbarians, and he put his greatest hope in them, believing, perhaps a little inconsiderately, that they were coming at the right time to regenerate the people, who were, in truth, already somewhat worn out. He was counting on buying the amity of those people with some gift of his art, in addition to which he would not be sorry to step himself once again in the sacred waters of legend.

These reasons caused him to march at dawn until he reached the great waters, the Moselle or the Meuse, or, according to others, the Rhine.

There, a barbarian, a giant—the first he had seen with his eyes—was in the middle of the river. On his shoulders he was carrying a new-born child, and the child was holding a glob in his hand, and playing with it. The waves rose, and the giant stopped; the water came up to his knees. Bent over, panting under his burden, he uttered confused cries, which the rocks repeated: "Help me! Help! I'm carrying the world on my shoulders!"

At that cry of alarm, and anchorite, the sole inhabitant of the region, emerged from his hermitage, a torch in his hand. He recognized the child who was crushing the giant's shoulders: it was Christ!

---

[47] The eponymous protagonist of a fragmentary *chanson de geste* newly discovered when Quinet wrote the novel.

Shining like a beacon in the night, the new-born had leaned over; he had taken a little water in the palm of his hand, which he poured over the giant's head to baptize him.[48]

Merlin saw everything from the bank, and was filled with an extraordinary emotion. Trembling, scarcely breathing, he fell to his knees when the giant deposited the child on the verdant bank.

That is what people called the conversion of Merlin; he had been moved, astonished, amazed, one might have thought that he was convinced; he ended up imagining that he was, permanently.

As the people arrived from the depths of their forests, one after another, all white with frost and bristling with icicles, Merlin imitated what he had just seen. He bent down and filled the palm of his hand with water, after which, he poured it over the heads of the nations, which looked at him with a savage expression, not knowing whether they wanted to smile at him or tear him to pieces. As for him, he was not afraid.

On the contrary, he covered their bare shoulders with a few bearskins that he had brought with him; he put his own socks, still new, on their feet; he refreshed them with a few cordials and a little beer. He put around their neck an amber necklace that Isaline had given him and even wanted to make them a few huts of leaves, so cold were the nights.

"No, Merlin," the barbaric nations said to him, with a grim expression. "First, let us shelter the God who brought us here."

"That's true," said Merlin, confused to receive that great lesson from those semi-naked people.

Then, living in the clearings, only thinking about the greenwood, only drinking dew, he invented the ogival arch and, to please them, made a forest with stone foliage, populated by granite birds, sown with marble or porphyry flowers, sometimes emeralds, everywhere profound, immense and gloomy.

That pleased them all; everyone wanted to have a plan in his hand. Our hero's strength was sufficient to that labor, so naturally great and generous was his heart when nothing got in his way. You would have seen him, singing and whistling, hammer in hand, until well into the night, transporting black mossy rocks, with which he embroidered cathedrals.

Architect, mason, carpenter, sculptor, decorator, he wrought iron, festooned stone, dentellate wood, illuminated the vermilion and ultramarine windows. As he did not embrace anything coldly, and everything in him was enthusiasm and passion, he was no longer occupied with anything but columns, colonnettes, naves, aisles, arches, imitating in granite the lacework of the veils of Queen Genièvre or Isaline. More than once, Viviane got into a bad mood, and hid his tools—but always in vain.

---

[48] The legend of St. Christopher, as Hermione points out in her notes.

A host of animals followed him, breathlessly: green salamanders, black Kylburn dragons,[49] wooden men, wyverns, gorgades with goatish bodies; he commanded them to crouch down in silence for eternity at the tops of capitals, which he made incontinently. Others received orders to sustain the coving of naves with their backs and their contracted feet. A few were even obliged to crawl, vertiginously, to the tips of steeples.

The trefoil flower in Marlin's garden had been one of the reasons for his change of creed. That was enough to make him put stone trefoils everywhere in his constructions—after which he gave them, by means of a final effort, that he had given his previous works, the power of enchantment that captured human hearts unawares.

Unfortunately, Merlin was fickle; his faith was less profound than he thought, and that is why his grandiose architecture is nevertheless delicate and unsteady. Sometimes, it even happened that Merlin, before having completed a temple, had changed faith. How embarrassed was he then! I leave it to you to imagine. It was impossible for him to complete what he had begun, as witness Cologne cathedral, which Merlin had started full of faith, the day after encountering Christ, but which he left in the state in which one can see it today, with the crane hoisted over the wall. Twenty times, the worthy Merlin, who dreaded more than anything afflicting a soul, solicited by the Teutons, wanted to resume the interrupted work; twenty times he was obliged to renounce the task, which he had ceased to comprehend.

Have I mentioned that Merlin, with all his great qualities, was capricious? I make no excuses for that, but what earns him considerable pardon is that he was honest.

IV

Explain this eccentricity if you can!

At the same time as he was building colossal churches—who would have thought it?—his secret desire, his supreme ambition, was to visit Hell. Personally, I think that an unhealthy curiosity, a feverish desire for contrasts, or rather, an unreflective filial instinct, was driving him in that direction. On his travels, he never encountered a cavern, a cleft in a rock or a rift in the ground without stopping and wondering whether it might not be the route to infernal worlds. More

---

[49] The text contains several references of "Kylburn dragons," but the original reference from which the phrase is derived, which probably involves a variant spelling, has proved evasive; there does not seem to be any determinable connection between Kilbourn Priory and a dragon, nor any connection between the white and red dragons symbolic of England and Wales to any place with a similar name.

often than not, people looked at him in astonishment, but that did not discourage him.

"I don't know," he said, ingenuously, "what attracts me in spite of myself toward those desolate regions. Others before me have been driven to visit them by curiosity or by some poetic convenience or other. For myself, it seems that it's a strict duty at least to make a brief pilgrimage to those places. If I dared, I'd confess that I feel a kind of homesickness every time I think about them."

He was understating the case. Truthfully, he ought to have admitted that the thought, the desire, the dread and the vague hope of meeting his father again was at the bottom of all his aspirations toward the abyss.

Viviane did not know that secret. She helped Merlin to accomplish his desire, and even wanted to keep it as a surprise until the end—which she did with a great deal of skill, under the pretext of undertaking a pilgrimage to the sacred isle of Avalon. It only required a short journey to reach a port named the Bay of the Dead. From there, opportunities were frequent.

No delay; they embark. Can you see them, already far from the shore. Personally, I can see them distinctly, and the boat, of rather mediocre appearance, and the mast and the passengers, just where there is a wisp of foam. But what can it signify that there is neither a sail nor oars, nor a pennant nor a tiller?

The boatmen do not say a word.

"Are they mute?"

"They're dead," Viviane replies.

The sea becomes black, throwing her long sniggers into the distance.

The passengers are mute too, and although they are numerous the boat seems empty, so slightly does it skim the surface of the water, where it leaves no wake.

An osprey with an enormous wingspan hovers over the travelers as if over its fodder. The lightning is less prompt to precipitate from the clouds. Merlin ducks down and straightens up again. Frightened by having found a living being where it was seeking a dead one, the bird of prey brushes the Enchanter with its wing, utters a screech, loses a feather and disappears over the horizon. Everyone has remained motionless.

The crossing has lasted a day. No one has shouted: "Land!"

They land near St. Patrick's cavern. Preceded by Viviane, Merlin advances toward the paternal domain, which opens there in a spiral. A momentary anguish grips him when he sets foot on the threshold.

"Are you with me?"

"Yes."

And, sensing love stir within him, he enters Hell. He would like to confront it without delay.

V

Scarcely have they crossed the threshold than a man dressed in a toga, carrying a shepherd's crook crowned with ears of wheat, places himself in the middle of the path.

"Are you, who advance without fear, the Florentine I'm waiting for?" he exclaims. "Is it you who will sing of the Inferno, Purgatory and Paradise? If so, tell me, that I may accompany you."

"O good Virgil," Merlin replies, the time of the one for whom you're waiting has not yet come. I'm not the Florentine, but it would not be just to disdain me, for I too am an enchanter, like you. Make the journey to the inferno with us; it will be easier afterwards to show the way to the one whose guide you have to be."

"If you're not the Florentine, you must be the Enchanter Merlin?"

"You're right, Virgil; I'm Merlin."

Immediately, they both attempted to embrace one another, and, having not been able to do so, they looked at one another with an infinite tenderness. Then Virgil said: "Don't hope, brother, to remain in eternal dolor long enough to bring peace to it. This isn't your domain. Another will take possession of these regions. Do you understand that his formidable *terza rimas* have been forged here in advance, on the infernal anvil? Don't try to steal them from him. You're the prophet of happy days in future worlds. The regions that you need to visit, I don't know."

"Let me, please, contemplate eternal anguish once. As the price of that vision, I'll rejuvenate your antique, Elysian verses, which only specters babble today."

"What! My sweet language is only that of shades now?"

"I shall resuscitate it; it will resonate again on the lips of people in gentler, crimsoned words mingled with honey."

Tempted by these caresses, Virgil smiled. "I'll do what no one has commanded me to do. Pass more rapidly than the lightning."

"Yes, more rapidly than hope in the hearts of the accursed."

And as they advanced, they seemed to be migratory birds who knew they route, without ever having traveled it before. The wise Merlin explained everything they encountered without difficulty.

"The slightest shadows are better known to you than to me," said Virgil. "Have you been this way before?"

"Never," Merlin replied—and he continued to astonish his guide with his precise knowledge of the smallest abyss. How different his explanations were, moreover, from those that were given later! At every torture he encountered, he said: "I can imagine a greater torture."

"What is it?"

"Seeking Viviane and not finding her."

"Be careful, brother, of evoking your torment. Everyone here creates and forges his own."

And as Merlin and Viviane took one another by the hand as they walked, their joy was so profound that Hell itself was moved and quivered. It could not annihilate their felicity. On the contrary, it was reflected around them. On seeing those happy souls pass by, the damned felt appeased; they said: "O blessed souls, what, then, is your felicity, since it expands around us? Here at last is a moment without pain. It's the first since we've been resident in this abode!"

Merlin stopped, and said: "Whoever you may be, such great torments will come to an end."

"What are you saying?" said the tortured souls. "How can there be an end to malediction? Never has anything similar been pronounced in this abyss. Do you believe what you say, or is it only to console us?"

"I believe it," said Merlin, weeping.

"What! You're weeping! There will be a time of forgiveness?"

"Yes, if you can still love something."

There was such a great bounty in Merlin that even the souls of bronze were unable to resist him. It seemed that they were about to melt, like metal when it begins to liquefy under a greater heat.

That moment was an interval of hope that spread through all the regions of Hell. Even Astaroth, Asmodeus, Mephistopheles, Cagnazzo and Malacoda began to sob,[50] and, approaching Merlin, said to him something that they had learned on earth: "Knight, let's change the subject!"

Then, rejecting hope themselves, they made use of their most dangerous weapon, sniggering irony, to disconcert Merlin. They were all sure that by a false shame, a vain human respect, he would surrender himself.

But they did not know him! Merlin's best quality, after bounty, was to defy mockery when following a conviction. Far from defeating him, the mockery of the demons only made him bolder. He continued to breathe hope everywhere.

However, anxiety began for him when he sought the king of Hell. At every step, he hoped and dreaded to perceive him.

Suddenly, at a bend in the path, he saw him in front of him, on his throne.

What a moment! Their eyes met...

Was it really the knight who had concerned himself with his infancy? There was no doubt about it: the same red cloak corroded at the edges; the same spurs of flame; the same golden helmet—except that he had taken it off momentarily in order to breathe more easily. He was allowing his blazing red hair to float free in the air.

At that sight, nature speaks; it screams; Merlin has recognized his father.

---

[50] Cagnazzo and Malacoda are both demons invented by Dante in order to play minor roles in the *Inferno*.

Dread and a certain horror, mingled with an ancient respect, shame, spite, the worm of anguish and the terrors of Hell oppress him simultaneously. He feels as if he is burning and freezing. He dare not advance nor recoil, nor speak, nor remain silent.

His father sees his disturbance, and hastens to take advantage of it.

"There you are, my dear son!" the master of Hell says to him, holding out a hand from which sparks are spurting. "Come here, into my arms, that I might hug you, my son, to my breast. Come, I tell you. Sit down beside me, on this old family seat. Get away, my faithful, make room, make room at the hearth! Today the prodigal son has returned! All my wealth is his—good fire, good shelter, and the rest."

Immediately, the vast boilers fill up as if in readiness for an infernal festival. The dormant brands in the hearth reignite. The subterranean forests crackle, releasing burning rivers of coal and there is not a black Kobold on the blood-colored banks, armed with a fang in the guise of an oar, who does not raise a cheer to Merlin, as to the favorite son of the house.

Then his father, approaching Viviane, says: "Plague, Merlin—a pretty girl! She's doubtless my daughter-in-law. What eyes! What a mouth, my darling! What pink lips! What a figure! She won't disdain the paternal house? Dear friends, your wedding will take place here this very evening, for it seems to me, Merlin, that you've put it off too long. I mean by that that you're giving purchase to the criticism of society."

In the meantime, Merlin had fallen into a dull stupor. He seemed insensible. It was the first time that his relationship with Hell had been solemnly published, and the abysm taken as witnesses. Until then, he had had a vague, confused presentiment, but the secret had not yet emerged from any mortal mouth. So, obstinate in doubt, he murmured: "You, my father? Me, your son? You're mistaken, Seigneur..."

"Don't stifle nature, my child! She speaks to you more clearly than I do myself."

"But still, what are the signs?"

"Do you know this hank of hair?"

"It might be false."

"Gently, strong mind! And this bracelet, on which is engraved your monogram with that of Séraphine?"

"I'd like other signs."

"I put them in your cradle."

"What happened to them?"

"You've kept them all."

"Where?"

"There, in your heart. Look into the depths, and you'll see me yourself."

"I'm not, like you, Seigneur, of royal blood."

"Don't be so modest. You resemble me, my son, feature for feature. Here is my face, my attitude, my stature, such as I was at your age—and it's even better within; it's there that you keep the imprints of my lineage and my blazon. The same vagabond whimsy, the same curiosity, the same impossibility of remaining serious, the same spurs of the flesh, just as sharp…you know them, eh? Those intimate resemblances don't deceive me, my dear; I got them directly from our forefathers."

"But one thing distinguishes me from you and your family."

"What's that, pray, my son?"

"Hope."

"Oh yes! Wait until tomorrow. You'll lose it as I lost it; it falls out for us like hair. There will remain to you, as to us, the bald opportunity that you won't be able to grasp, for century after century—so give in!"

"I can't submit so quickly."

"You can't submit? Precisely: I was, I am and always will be the same."

"I don't know what I ought to fear or desire."

"Like me! Come on, prodigal son, let's embrace!"

"Not yet."

"Believe me, then."

"I can't believe."

"That's it! Like me, I tell you, like all of us here. Trust in the evidence."

"I still doubt."

"Exactly. That's my family's trait, doubt! But open your eyes."

"I see nothing but darkness."

"Well said! There, my son, finally, is that great sign, darkness; recognize your father by that."

"If that's the way it is, Father, convert."

"It's too soon, my son."

"Look at him, Viviane—you'll vanquish him with your gaze."

As he pronounced these words, Merlin felt his entrails stir for such a great sinner. He was about to put his hand in the one that was offered to him, and that would doubtless have done for our hero, when Viviane saved him.

"Let's flee," she said. "His wickedness holds sway over my power."

With those words, she drew the prophet away. He followed her, but not without dolor; more than once, he looked back.

The evils that he had seen accompanied him, and still weighed upon him. The anguish tearing him increased when he heard his father cry out, in an almost extinct voice: "Son of Hell, you're betraying Hell! How have you been bought? Do you intend, then, to be the Judas of Satan?"

And the echo of the abysms, beneath the accursed vaults, repeated: "Your old father is too fond of you, Merlin; it's us who'll pay for his weakness."

At those roars Merlin stopped; eternal dolor tempted him. What if he were to retrace his steps? Why not? He would see his father again, beg him, hug him in his arms. Why had he left him so quickly, with no word of farewell? He could carry him on his shoulders, as Aenes did Anchises, out of the eternal blaze of the city of lamentation...

Already, he had turned round, and he was meditating plunging back into the accursed regions, when his two companions blocked the way to him.

"Leave the past, which you can't remake, prophet," said Viviane. "The future alone is yours. Listen to the wailing of the new worlds that are calling to you. Do you want to disappoint their infantile expectation?"

Virgil showed him the radiant carved doors of Paradise.

"No, not yet, good Virgil," said Merlin. "What would I do in the accomplished dwelling of the just? They're happy, what need to they have of me? Let's see instead, as this one advises, the wellspring of things, the commencement of beings and all those awaiting life in the cradle of future worlds, for that's where my domain is."

With those words, the two enchanters parted, weeping.

The wise Merlin had been the first to bring a ray of hope and pity into Hell. It was, to be sure, only momentary, but the tortured would never forget it.

BOOK FOUR: THE CONDUCTOR OF THE THREE LIVES

I

Beloved dead that I have known alive on earth, and who have disappeared so soon from the world, leaving us the tears!

Beautiful winged, matinal souls, who, borne away by too great a curiosity toward eternal things, have departed before the day and have left me in darkness!

Souls detached from the mud, you who know the roads I want to attempt, the mere thought of which would frighten me, if I did not have you for a cortege!

You who lives on the sheer peaks of the invisible, who one touch with your feet the immaculate essence of things!

If your memory is present to me at every hour; if in sadness and in joy I seek you as my light;

You who have been, who will be in the life eternal; Be my guides to that place where all paths traced by humans stop; conduct my eyes that I might see, through the darkness of the centuries, what no eye has seen, what no eye can see without you.

As at the foot of the Bernese mountains where the rock looms up, where the universe is closed, the guide conducts the pilgrim over snows contemporary with the first day, and prevents him from missing his way, in the same way, sustain me through the still-immaculate abyss where Merlin is taking me. For his greatest desire is to fray a path for humans through the unfrequented regions; and now he has resolved to visit the vast limbo into which no one has penetrated with him.[51]

Indecisive, formless noises, like the whimpering of the abyss, welcome him at the entrance to those places where the pale and unknown roots of all things intersect. It is not day and it is not night. There is neither sun nor moon nor stars in the sky, but only nebulae that powder and snake in the meanders of the Milky Way, without being able to give birth to the aurora. You might think that worlds were being formed in secret, and babbling in the somber workshop.

To begin with, in the densest part of the Alpine labyrinth, toward Glaris, there is a long avenue of pyramidal mountains, on pedestals of black marble, which touch the heavens; and as one advances, they become higher and prouder.

---

[51] Hermione's notes record that in 1858, when this passage was written, she and Quinet were living in the valley of the Linth at the foot of icy peaks, which provided the imagery for the entrance of the domains of Limbo

At their feet, brown forests of maples extend, like the furry bearskin rugs, where cascades dance and leap to the sound of avalanches. Higher up, fir-trees rise, and the slope is already so steep that they seem to be rooted in one another's crowns. After them the coarse grass, grazed by the chamois, and then the bald rock. There hang the low glaciers, like the udders of heifers trailing in the long grass. In the distance, beyond the black chaos, stands the bare, dented, dazzling skeleton of a snowy peak, the icy throne of death. There, by some mouth, the Linth precipitates, and its taurean roar is stifled in the gulf before rising in the meadows. Take away that anticipatory vision of the inferno of ice.

Pale clouds punctuated with black coil around the sharpest peak like a collar of down-feathers around the neck of a vulture, but the wind moves them on; then they envelop the great specter of stone and snow from head to toe; they are torn apart again, allowing a glimpse of the spike that emerges into an aerial gulf of dark azure.

It is there that the earth is cleft from Heaven to Hell. A cold, unknown breath rises from the horrible crevasse: the breath of subterranean worlds; with it, you feel vertigo. Between the two pale, damp, vertical walls, a bridge lost in the cloud, narrower than the edge of a razor, stands out against the black face of the sky. How can I pass over it without falling?

On the far side, the realm of Limbo commences, a vast, incorruptible, snow-white country, like an unwritten page, which contains the premises of all existence. That domain is ruled by a pastor. Armed with a crook, he commands the troop of beings awaiting life. From his point of view, he prevents the impatient worlds from hastening toward the light before their day has come.

Have you see a cowherd conduction his herd in May over the reddening Alp to the sound of nocturnal bells? Without a host, without a companion, he lives in the clouds. Such is the pastor of Limbo. Devoid of parents, of a spouse, of any posterity, separated from the living, he resides in the source of things.

At that moment, with his back to the rock, in front of a brushwood fire, he was murmuring a strange song, faint and ungraspable, and no one knew whether it was to awaken or send to sleep the worlds nascent in the cradle of Limbo. As he was utterly pensive, occupied with those cradle-songs, Merlin was able to approach him fearlessly, and he said to him: "You who retain in Limbo the creatures and forms promised to life, cease your song and show me the granaries of abundance where the eternally-renewed seeds of nascent worlds are buried, with the treasures of the hail and the autumnal rain, and those of celestial anger. Tell me also where the light resides."

The pastor of Limbo would have liked to hide the amassed treasure of future things and the promises of life confided to his protection, but his surprise was so great that he did not raise any objection. Having put his flute into his basket, he picked up his crook and pointed at his distant domains. Then he opened the first barrier, the joists of which were shaky, mingled with thorns, as in the Roman countryside.

While they both advanced, a colored vapor iridescent with a thousand gleams, surrounded them. It was lighter than the mist that rises from the meadow-grass.

"Whence comes that red mist, O shepherd? It is not the daughter of the rain and the dew."

"No," replied the pastor of Limbo. "That light vapor you see rising beneath your feet is the luminous dust of future worlds."

"What! Every nascent universe is merely smoke? And am I the child of that vapor? Is that also what forms the gods with gilded faces?"

"Don't worry about the gods! I'll show you later where they're born, for I'm their guardian too. Just be wary of dissipating a world with your breath without knowing it."

At that response, Merlin, half-lost in that dawn of life, held back the words that were pressing upon his lips. However, he could not help saying: "I sense, O pastor of Limbo, that my heart is stronger than the myriads of nascent worlds. What! So weak! So wretched! So similar to nothingness! Where, then, can pride be born? Whence comes wisdom? Where is the commencement of love? And where is hope born?"

"I've already told you: in that radiant mist."

And, having both become more pensive, they traversed the vestibule of Limbo in silence.

At the place where the way narrowed, in the middle of the steep path, there was an old man who was holding a book on his knees; bent over, he was writing relentlessly on the pages that were still blank, without seeming to take any notice of those who were approaching, nor of the abysms open to either side.

For some time Merlin considered him, in the hope of seeing him raise his head; but the stain beneath the scribe's rapid pen grew, and it scratched without ever pausing.

"O eternal scribe," the prophet asked him, "what are you writing with so much haste on those pages which you're desperate to fill? I don't see anyone dictating to you."

The scribe replied: "Pass by without pausing, as they all do. I'm writing here the divine name of every being, and every thing, as they come to life, in order that their number can be counted, and no creature, however tiny it might be, can escape the science of the Eternal. Be wary of stealing even one from him, for I too know the count." Then, angrily, looking at him askance, he added: "It's wrong of the shepherd to have let you come so far. Another more powerful than me will reproach him for it."

"You see, prophet," murmured the shepherd, drawing Merlin away. "You see what I endure for you. At least keep my secret."

II

Beyond the vestibule, on the threshold of Limbo, giants were lying who seemed to be guarding it, although they were asleep. Lying down randomly, here and there, they had left gaps between them and it was by that tortuous path that it was necessary to find a route.

The shepherd touched those who were sleeping thus before his fold with his scepter.

"They are," he continued, "the future days waiting for the morning breeze to come and caress their hair—for that will be the signal that they have to get up. Then they'll stand upright, their faces illuminated by the light of dawn, and they won't remain eternally naked and hairless as you see them now. But some will dress themselves in a reddening dawn, others in cloud the color of ash, charged with thunder and lightning, which will hang down to their belts. Diadems dotted with stars will crown their heads. Until then, it's necessary that they all remain equally drowsy with the sleep of Limbo. They can scarcely dream of their splendor to come."

"And the females sleeping alongside them, who are they?"

"Their faithful companions the nights. Heads supported on their elbows, they wait, in a sterile vision, to be wedded to the future days."

Vast reservoirs opened up at that point, the innumerable larders where the premises of things were gathered, sketches of plants and animals that no human eye has ever seen, and the substance of future worlds which are only a desire as yet.

As flocks of pigeons take off in the morning, when the laborer enters the field where he has left the plow standing the interrupted furrow, and fly around his head, so immense sketchy flying reptiles, still attached to the primitive mud, rose up and beat the air with their viscous wings at Merlin's approach. There were lizards a hundred cubits long, with golden underbellies, which, mouths open, barred his way with a dull sound of scales and abandoned carapaces. Others, more gigantic, with serpent's necks and teats from which their young were suspended, were sharpening their tusks on the trunks of colossal ferns. Mammoth was with them. But these innumerable creatures, gripped by fear, retreated in confusion into their stables; in their stead, others appeared, stranger still, half-formed, which fled in their turn. There was a hierarchy between them, for they arranged themselves obediently, the most imperfect before the best. Finally came Leviathan and Behemoth, but they did not flee before the face of the prophet; they dared to remain.

For a long time, Merlin contemplated that mystery of beings born without parents; he saw them emerge fully armed from the ample bosom of the earth. Then he exclaimed: "No, never, neither under the trees of the fays of Brittany, nor in the Sabbat swarming with salamanders and dragons, on the wooded heights of the Hartz, nor on the edges of ensorcelled springs in the forest of Ardennes, nor in the stony Crau of Provence or Bresse, has such a company been found in my path. Are they all enchanted? But by whom? What magician has evoked them? Is it you? Give me the secret word by means of which one makes them appear and disappear, in order that I too might augment my domain."

"I, who am their shepherd, don't know that magic word. That word comes from higher up. Don't pause any longer."

And they passed on.

III

As a fishing-bird glides through a storm at the surface of the sea, seeking with its eyes for its prey through the thickness of the waves, uttering raucous cries, so Merlin, on the surface of things, sought souls everywhere. To seize them, he would have plunged into the ocean of being.

That is why, after having visited the premises of things, ashamed of touching nothing but vain shadows, he stopped and said:

"O conductor of Limbo, it's very little to have seen the treasures of the hail, the rain and the thunder; it's very little to have visited, in the stables, the whimpering herd of beings as yet unformed, half-attached to the glebe of nothingness. Tell me now from where the souls of the beings that arrive on earth are taken. What do they do before seeing the light of day? In what hidden retreat do you keep them, assembled and veiled?"

"You're the only one," replied the pastor, "who has ever asked me that question. You shall be the only one for whom it will be answered."

Then he led him to the most secret place in his domain. A wall of jagged rocks, cut into zigzags, sculpted by thunderbolts, like petrified lightning on the face of the Pennine Alps, separated that place from all the others.

It was there that the embryonic souls that had not yet lived encountered one another, on barely-traced paths. Those larvae were wandering hither and yon, driven by an infantile inquietude, for they had not yet had a cradle. They were all consumed by an immoderate desire to cross the portals of life for the first time. What would they not have given to enjoy the sunlight an hour sooner? What vain projects might they be nourishing?

They were waiting for the century, the year, and the moment to come for them to put on a body of clay, and for a great voice to command them to mingle in their turn with the choir of the living. Until then, a curiosity full of anguish held them in an eternal insomnia. The principal dolor of those who wander in limbo is that they have no names as yet; they seek themselves confusedly in the depths of nameless darkness, and they sense the oppression of nothingness day and night.

At that moment, some of them, prouder than the rest, were shaking the bronze doors that still separated them from the daylight, moaning.

"Why are you so pitiless?" said Merlin to the pastor. "Listen to them wailing, desirous of life. Why refuse to let them out a day sooner from the Limbo in which you keep them imprisoned? What does a day matter to you, who possess centuries?"

"I only possess vain shadows." Saying these words, the pastor touched the bronze doors; they were the portals of life. "Go in," he added. "You who know the language of Heaven, give each of them the name you wish, in order that they might be called by it; it will please them, coming from you."

And he prepared to withdraw.

On seeing his guide move away, however, Merlin was afraid.

"Why are you abandoning me? I don't know the way."

"It's up to you to find it."

"At least Viviane led me by the hand."

"No—whoever passes through these doors has only himself for a guide."

And, like a miser surprised with his hidden treasure, the pastor of Limbo went away, sad and anxious. He went to count the sketchy shadows again, the vain things that were under his guard—for he feared, in his heart, that the prophet might have stolen the best of them from him.

IV

As soon as Merlin had entered, those who were nearest to the threshold fled. They seemed to dissipate permanently. But soon, their immoderate desire for the light brought them back to the threshold of the living.

"Who are you?" he demanded then, of the first he perceived—and he was already thinking of giving them a name.

At that question, they all turned their eyes inwards and seemed to be searching themselves, nonplussed and desolate. None was able to reply.

"Why are you hastening toward these closed doors? Merlin asked, again. "There must be more than one among you who will repent of being born."

None of the souls whimpering in Limbo understood that language. Then he approached one of those that seemed most impatient to live.

"Why," he asked, "are you running thus toward the terrestrial light, you who surpass the others by a foot? You will shed tears that will not be wiped away after ten centuries."

As they all assembled around him, like a brood beneath the wing of a fowl, waiting for another word, he added: "The darkness does not know you yet, but the world will call you Charlemagne."

At that name, the first that had been produced in that region, astonishment and stupor passed over the pale lips of those who were listening.

The colossus replied, in a child-like voice: "Here I am!" For he believed that he had been evoked; full of haste to tread the morning dew, he murmured, in a language of limbo that was still awkward: "Come on! Come on, Barons! Oyez, Oliphant! Let's go where day breaks! If I wait for dusk, I'll be shamed!"

Those who were later to be his dozen peers and his barons were enveloped in steel; they repeated in their turn: "Come on! Come on!" And they went toward the spark that sprang from Durandal.

Merlin stopped them with these words: "Peace, Emperor and Barons! Your hour approaches; be patient! When it arrives, I'm the one who will invite you to the sword, even if I'm in my tomb. I'll make your gilded helms and bucklers myself, and your broadswords of polished steel; you will only have to take them."

The great Charles, seeing that his hope was still vain, became child-like again, and wept.

Several others, hands together, asked the prophet: "Is it nearly time for us to be born?"

He replied to them: "Sleep your larval slumber. Your hour is still distant."

At these words, as if a verdant forest were shedding all its foliage, to the very last leaf, at the first blast of the cold November wind, the souls felt that their premature hopes and joys were being stripped away in an instant They went away, looking down at their feet; then they crouched down on the ground, saying: "We have not had a cradle; why have we had a sepulcher?"

One alone, the most superb, remained standing, and that one began to trample all the others pitilessly in order to reach the sun of the living first. The prophet blocked his way.

"Do you think you already reign, you who are still a larva? What are you pursuing with so much anger? All the others here seem to count for nothing in your eyes. Whence comes that pride? Tell me—what are you searching for? What do you want?"

"A name!" replied the proud soul, weakening, in a voice fainter that that of reeds.

"Only a name?" said the Enchanter. "It's me who will give you yours. You can gorge yourself on it here in advance, at your leisure, so fully that all glory will seem faded by the time you taste it."

And as, without hearing anything, the unknown continued to cleave through the crowd, colliding with the vague nascent shadows, the prophet went on: "Stop, Napoléon! Do you hope to defraud the Eternal in the count of your days? Your vain desires will not enable you to arrive one day sooner in the sunlight of the living. On the contrary, you will delay the rising of your star. Have you such a thirst to dominate and enslave that you cannot be patient during the call of the centuries? Does a day, a year, seem to you to be important? Go! Continue to sharpen your blade."

Then the whimpering soul, which still lacked the power of speech, having raised its eyes, turned back, full of disdain, to face the void; it went a long way through the multitude to put on and lose itself in its swaddling-clothes again, which seemed a shroud. The sound of a blade being sharpened on a stone became audible in the distance, and the feet of armies passing far away, and bearing chains.

Another soul knocked angrily at the portals of life; that one, without speaking, seemed to be saying: "I'll break the hinges; I'll get in by means of my own strength."

Merlin turned toward it and said: "Your impatience too is veritably too great, Maximilien.[52] Why are you hastening to the point of losing your breath? Do you know what's waiting for you on the far side of that door? Do you know? A sea of blood, in which you'll struggle in vain to avoid drowning, for your memory will remain plunged within it; it will do you no good to call yourself the incorruptible. The cry of men will be so opposed to you that every lie, even the vilest, will prevail against your word. See, now, whether you want to advance or retreat."

On hearing these words, the soul that was to terrify the world hesitated, and began to tremble; it veiled its face with its hand and recoiled from the sun of the living. Then, with a gesture of pride, it appeared to say, as it drew away, looking back over its shoulder: "I shall have my day, though."

Not far from there was a marshy, leaden shore where the north wind whistled eternally in the mist. In the midst of uprooted seaweed, a spirit was standing on a narrow dune, in spite of the storm that had curbed all those around it. No word had ever emerged from its lips since the beginning of things. Several had questioned it in order to discover its secret, but its tongue had not yet loosened. None in the innumerable multitude of larvae knew its thought.

The prophet approached it in order to tempt it.

"Tell me your secret and I will conduct you today toward the light of the world. What are you planning here? What are you preparing?"

The figure he had addressed put a finger to its lips and refused to speak.

"O fecund silence, which will give birth to a people!" said the prophet, in a whisper. "Rightly will the world call you Taciturn.[53] How many nations lavish speech in vain, while you will create a world on the waters without pronouncing a word!"

He stopped and fell silent himself. He took pleasure in seeing a great design germinating in the depths of a free soul, in the silence of things.

At that moment, Merlin discovered, hidden in the densest part of the crowd, a soul that scarcely dared to raise its eyes to look at him, so naked did it feel, and yet it sheltered under his cloak.

Now that soul, Reader, was mine.

---

[52] Maximilien de Robespierre.
[53] William the Silent (1533-1584)—Guillaume le Taciturne in French—founder of the house of Orange and leader of the Dutch revolt against the Spanish that began the Eighty Years' War.

The Enchanter lowered his head toward it, looked at it kindly, and said to it:

"You who are hiding under my cloak, I shall not call by your name, but I will tell you where you will be born and what your life will be. Your cradle will be near the weeping women who veil themselves with marble around the great sepulcher of Brou.[54] To say where your tomb will be is more difficult. I fear that it will not repose in the fatherland. O deserted valleys of the Ain, heaths, subterranean lakes, forests, solitary pools, humble heather of Certines—how many times your heart will hasten in that direction, and almost always in vain!

"You will adore justice; it will be refused to you. You will sense the truth on your lips, but—cruel circumstance!—you will be unable to publish it. Every day you will await liberty; it will not come for you, but you will retain the hope for others. You will want to begin the reign of eternity in time, of heaven on earth; in that enterprise, many will weary of marching with you. Why will you put so little honey in the cup that you present to others? Do you not know that flattery leads them? You know it, but you disdain to make use of the science.

"It is a rude task to swim upstream in a torrent, without paying court to the passing wave. But you won't complain; on the contrary, you'll be astonished that bread will not be lacking for a single day in the desert that you have chosen. Books, solitudes, reveries, the woods, the soft music of the speech of masters, those will be your principal joys. Love also will not quit your heart, even when mortal life is close to quitting it. But you will repent of every hour that you allow the wicked to sleep, when words changed into a blade might awaken them.

"In the end, the long exile will come, and your own people will no longer know you. You will leave behind you two tombs, you will go in search of a third. There will be a great silence around you; you will often mistake it for that of death. You will wake up in the night, believing that you have been nailed into your coffin while sleeping. However, you will go on to the end, your head held high, without knowing the yoke; that will make you love the proof.

"You will sense forgetfulness passing over your face, like a forerunner of the eternal night, but at the moment when the burden becomes too heavy for you to bear, a better soul than yours will come to your aid; it will stand next to you, like invincible hope; it will hide from you the abandonment of almost all the rest."

Merlin had already passed by, but the soul to which he had addressed these words was still listening. It seemed to the latter, before having lived, that its life had already run its course; it became so pale that it could no longer distinguish the night, and searched by its side for the one who would console it.

---

[54] The church of Brou, where Quinet was born, contains the tomb of Marguerite de Bourbon, wife of Philippe II; beneath the tomb are the small figures of four "pleureuses" [weeping women] generally considered to be exceptional examples of the art of sculpture.

"Is she the one who will survive?" it wanted to ask, but it lacked the strength to pronounce the words. Invisible tears blinded it before it could attempt to speak; increasingly troubled, it hid in the prophet's shadow, and followed him silently, at an uneven pace, through the primal darkness.

V

Beyond the first labyrinth of limbo a plain extends, similar to the great desert of Arabia. In the middle of the desert, a figure was lying asleep under a tent. At the noise of the pilgrim's footsteps, the sleeping soul awoke, but not sufficiently to walk toward the person who was coming to visit it.

"Why are you late waking up, voluptuous soul?" the Enchanted exclaimed, as soon as he perceived it. "You're doing the opposite of others who would like to hasten the appointed hour. You're forgetting here, in the midst of your dreams, that your time is approaching."

At these words the soul shivered and came to a half-standing position at the entrance to the tent.

"Get up, Mohammed," the Enchanter went on, "if you don't want the century that is summoning you to pass. Gird your loins for the combat of life. You'll also need your scimitar."

The soul completed its awakening. It made the gesture of a man buckling an invisible sword to his waist. All made way for it silently as it advanced, envying its imminent appearance in the light of the world. It walked without sadness and without joy, as a matter of necessity, to the bronze doors, which opened noisily to let it pass.

Meanwhile, all the souls enclosed in Limbo looked at one another, murmuring. Those who were standing furthest apart said: "Why has that one been favored? He does not have the sign of Christ on his forehead; nor does he have the blood of Christ imprinted in his rare words. Since when are the enemies of the Eternal preferred? Will his disciples and his believers always be rejected before birth, into insurmountable oblivion?"

The one that seemed to be speaking at that moment for all the rest was clad from head to toe in the manner of a monk. Only its head emerged from the hood that was tipped back, and its neck was swollen with anger. The horror of what it had just seen passed like a shadow over its face.

The Enchanter said to it: "Save your anger, Luther, for other battles. You too ought to gird yourself in advance, but not with a scimitar. Truly, more than one century is yet required to polish the blade of intelligence. If you expend the divine fury here before its time, what will you do when it's necessary to turn Rome upside down in its house of stone?"

"Rome!" replied the one that had difficulty in adjourning the vengeance of God, as an archer has difficulty retained an arrow in a taut bowstring. "Rome!

What name are you pronouncing there? I'm hearing it for the first time, and already I want to annihilate it!"

"Be patient for a little longer. All indignation is fecund when it is amassed slowly in the depths of the heart. Then it bursts forth; it disperses profane altars; it librates the captive God of men. But if it is squandered inconsiderately, it only attracts the ridicule of the world. Retain your violence, then, until you encounter the violence of the earth. This is the sojourn of peace. No one will put your taurean Germanic head under the yoke here. Go, and don't point your horns at those who pass before you again."

At these severe words the anger of the superb soul faded away in a moment. It bowed a mystical face, which nevertheless radiated the laughter of the victorious, all the way to the ground. But no one saw it as it moved away into the distance, so simultaneously fearful was its triumphant step. It went to sit down alone and apart in some ruins, and opened a Bible with golden pages, which was resplendent in the pale twilight. Every time it turned a page in the book, the noise it made was audible across the abyss. All the souls shivered at the same time.

A little further on, the pilgrim arrived at the place where a vast sea extends, the motionless waves of which never rise up in any season, in any tempest, nor are they brushed by any breeze—to the extent that one might mistake that ocean for solid ground, if its bed were not blue-tinted. On the edge of the gulf, two souls were walking side by side, which seemed to belong to the same family and to speak the same language, so familiarly were they speaking to one another, and without mistrust. One was veiled, the other was speaking with its face uncovered. The first seemed to be seeking a passage that the second could not indicate to it; they looked alternately at the sky and the water; both made visible their sadness at feeling such a great desire within themselves, with such utter impotence.

When the prophet passed them, the more anxious soul came toward him, and, as if it were continuing a conversation already begun, pointed to the ocean and said: "Will you show me the way?"

"What way?" asked the prophet. "Tel me what you're looking for."

"A world."

Then, drawing nearer to the soul, and seeing that it was veiled, he said: "There's darkness enough here, without adding that of the shroud folded over your face."

With its right hand, the one to whom he was speaking drew aside the Genoese mantle that enveloped it and allowed its face to be seen.

Merlin said to it: "I know you now and I'll show you the way. It's you who will bear Christ on your shoulders across the Atlantic Ocean, and for that they will call you Christopher Columbus. Sharpen your mind's eye here, in order that they might be keener than those of the hawk and the sea-eagle, for it will be necessary for you to discern a world through the breadth of the ocean.

"See this blue gulf here, circled by jagged mountains that rise into the clouds; such is the one where your cradle will float. But the port from which you will depart for the great voyage will be humbler, and without you, its name would remain unknown.

"When the great day comes and the sail is hoisted, steer your vessel when it emerges from the Pillars of Hercules toward the place where the stars set. Never change course, in spite of appearances. Don't listen to the winds or to human murmurs. Only consult the migrating birds; they know the way. Refrain from attempting to find a better one."

The one to which he was speaking remained as motionless as stone; it was fully occupied in engraving within itself the words that it had just heard. It learned them by rote, repeating them with its own lips. Then, bowing its head like a man who has received an order and is promising to obey, it said: "I'll remember the way." And it went down to the beach; it stayed there in a contemplation so profound that it seemed to be counting the number of the waves.

Then its companion, which had remained mute, seeing that it was alone with the prophet, was gripped by a divine terror; it tried to escape, its hair and beard bristling, over the precipices that opened beneath its feet.

But the Enchanter followed it closely, immediately crying: "Shy soul, why do you flee by these steep paths? Do you think that I don't know how to walk across the abysses too? Is it thus that you flee inspiration when it swoops down upon you like a falcon? Or are you afraid of seeing the daylight too soon? Fear not, I bring you peace."

Soothed by this language, the shy soul stopped. Merlin said to it: "There! I recognized you more rapidly than your companion, although you have veiled your face to me too. Why are you running away from me, you whom men will call Michelangelo?"

On hearing its name for the first time, the indomitable soul smiled, for that name pleased it; it took pleasure in repeating it.

"Are you too in a hurry to be born?" asked the Enchanter.

"No," replied the sad and already terrible voice of the one who was meditating Moses.

"Take advantage of the days and centuries that are left to you to prepare at leisure the beautiful forms that you will show to the world. There is also clay in Limbo with which to knead beautiful bodies; there'll be no lack of mud. Sketch your divine works in advance in this vast studio, in the depths of your thoughts, and prevent yourself from arriving in the daylight empty-handed—for human life on earth is shorter than you imagine. If you don't begin your work here in Limbo, you won't have time to finish it in the sunlight. You'll have to leave your figures buried in the stone, for lack of another day. How you will regret then the time consumed in vain things before having lived!"

Vast Limbo exhaled a sigh.

The prophet continued: "Do you hear that groan? Don't imitate it. Fill your memory with the images and faces that populate this abode. Look that way, at the gigantic night that lies dormant over the earth, its head on its elbow; owls and fireflies are fluttering around it. Wouldn't you think it was made of stone, it's so still? Contemplate, in this direction, the livid daylight, parent of years, ancestor of centuries not yet risen, and yet indignant at the darkness. Remember both of them when you're on earth. The living will be afraid of the visions you bring from Limbo.

At these words, the one who had seemed so recalcitrant bowed majestically; as if time were already pressing, he bent down to the ground, humid with invisible tears. He picked up mud, with which he formed strange figures, images of colossal shadows passing in the night, while stammering with a superhuman smile: "These will form my cortege."

BOOK FIVE: LIMBO

I

Already, the place where the second labyrinth of Limbo ended was whitening on the edge of the horizon. The Enchanter could see the end of his journey, when other souls, more hidden and more enveloped than the others, suddenly showed themselves to him—and I, who had followed the least of his footsteps this far, without daring to open my mouth, became more attentive than before. From the words with which he greeted the new souls flocking to his passage, I thought I understood that they were to rise to the earth after me, when I had quit the world of the living.

Curiosity pricked me then with its sharpest needle. I felt consumed by the desire to know their names and what they would do on earth when I was no longer there. And I, who had scarcely dared look at the prophet a moment before, suddenly carried away by a desire stronger than humility, drew nearer to him and said:

"Oh, for pity's sake, tell me the names of those who will live after me and will tread the earth when I am in my tomb."

"Who told you what it is to die, and how the tomb is made," the prophet replied, "you who have not yet seen the light of day?"

"Please let me approach those who will live after me. At least lift the flap of their cloaks so that I can see their faces. May I not at least salute them with my eyes? In advance, I feel full of love and respect for them, as if they might warm my bones with their breath. Who is that one coming first, who is the tallest? With how much assurance he walks! And that other one, turning in my direction? Both attract me equally with different forces. Look, they'd like to summon me—they're signaling to me. Oh, show me their faces! Only tell me their names, their fatherland. Are they of my country, my race, my language, or will they do honor to a foreign land? Tell me..."

But the one who had been so indulgent thus far interrupted me severely.

"All curiosity is not good!" he told me. "Isn't it sufficient to have seen them pass by? What you take for their lowered visors are the veils of bronze that cover the future. Know only that they will not put all their joy into the blade, and that they will dry up the tears that you see assemble here in the eyes of multitudes. What do their names matter, and the syllables that form them? Names deceive easily. Learn in advance to look at things."

While I retired, rendered confused and tremulous by that vision beyond the cradle and the tomb, he penetrated serenely into the further regions of Limbo.

II

Have you ever seen the torrent of Ain, at the place where the sharp rock advances to close its passage?

You might think that the torrent was vanquished, and that it had no option but to retrace its course, backwards, toward its source. On the contrary, however; it advances more proudly, after having looked more closely, into its blue-tinted gulfs, at the rock that wants to enchain it. That place is like the one where the valley of Limbo curves and closes to impede the passage of those who aspire to life. The narrow gorge suddenly opens out broadly, like a vast maremma.

"Who is this coming toward us?" said two souls embracing amorously on the edge of a gulf. "Is he coming to summon one of us to life and separate us?"

They both trembled simultaneously, each of them became paler as Merlin approached.

He addressed the young virgin soul that was even more bewildered than its companion, saying: "Why are you afraid?"

The amorous soul replied to him: "Eternal love holds us in this embrace above the storm. It has been thus since we have been inhabiting this place. I tremble now to remain forgotten in this abode, when you summon to the light of the living the one whom I cannot yet name. I'm afraid of remaining alone here, lost and astray, without my companion. Tell me whether you've come to search for him, to take him, without me before me, to where we desire to live together. After we have been betrothed in Limbo, will we be parted by time on earth? Shall we see the light of day together, or will he see it without me, while I remain imprisoned in this place, with those who have never lived?"

"Console yourself, amorous soul," Merlin replied. "You will not be disunited. The same time will be granted to both of you to traverse life. Together you shall see the same spring, the same days, the same years, the same sunlight. Together you shall savor rapid youth; together you shall pick the same flowers, together you shall see them wither. One will not be retained in this pale abode while the other is warmed by the amorous rays of terrestrial daylight."

A glint of joy illuminated the faces of those who loved one another in Limbo. The young female went on: "One thing still saddens me; I don't know what to call the one thanks to whom I live before the cradle."

"Call him Abelard," the prophet replied.

"And me—what name should I call her?" asked the spirit that had kept silent thus far.

"Call her Héloïse."

When the two amorous souls had heard their names, an infinite joy appeared in their gaze. It seemed that they had just encountered one another for the first time. For a long time they repeated to one another, delightedly, the names that were for them an anticipatory revelation of the life awaited. The soft whispering of the two spirits continued even when a stronger voice made itself heard

in the distance, toward the place where the plain gave way to a mountain bristling with rocks.

They followed the Enchanter as far as the entrance of the valley, but on
seeing in the distance a young female advancing through the landscape, they
both stopped at the same time and left him, saying: "It's not permissible for us to
go any further. The one who is approaching would disapprove of our desire for
love."

With those words, they ran away.

Without having heard them, the one that had scared them continued walking, picking cornflowers from the long grass. Everything about her appearance
was humble and rustic, except for her gaze, which cut through Limbo.

Why are they afraid of her? the Enchanter thought.

When he was closer, although a fast-flowing stream still separated them,
he recognized the other without difficulty. None of the other souls that he had
encountered thus far touched his so deeply, to the point that he was close to
tears.

"Jeanne," he said, "do you know where you're bound?"

"I know."

"And how hot the pyre is?"

"I know."

Meanwhile, she crossed over the stream on a tree-trunk that was set there
like the rustic bridges that villagers throw over streams in Champagne when the
rain has swollen them. Two spirits were walking beside her, to her right and her
left, whispering into her ears.

Having perceived them, the Enchanter exclaimed: "Jeanne, why are you
thus accompanied, on this path where all the others are walking alone?"

Before she could reply, the Archangel Michael, who was to her right, said
to her in a low voice: "Beware, virgin, of the one who is coming toward you; he
has already mingled with the living, but neither I nor the one who is to your left
have ever seen him in our celestial abode. He is not of our legion."

"You have not met me yet," said the Enchanter. "In spite of that, I belong,
as you do, to the Eternal."

At these words, the shepherdess, having realized that he had seen the two
spirits at her sides, was filled with a joy that she had not yet experienced.

"You, at least, have seen them," she said to him. "You have heard their
voices when they whisper in my ear. You will not be like those who insist that
they are dreams. But since you have already seen the sun and traversed life, tell
me what I ought to know about it, and what path I ought to follow. For these are
learned in the ways of Heaven, but they are scornful of the world and the messengers who arrive there."

"With companions like those for guides," the prophet replied, "I have nothing to teach you. However, since you question me, I shall speak. The village
where you will see the light for the first time is already covered in thatch,

Jeanne. The swallows are already nesting there; the chicks are chirping under the roof near your birthplace, not far from the magical tree."

"Will I not arrive too late?" asked the shepherdess. "That is my only fear."

"Fear not, shepherdess. You will appear at the hour of the battle; you will lose no time in finding the oriflamme and the sword."

"How shall I carry the blade, who can scarcely carry this crook? How shall I tame a warhorse, who trembles at every passing shadow?"

"You'll learn here, in this night of limbo. The archangel who walks beside you will teach you the virtues of the sword. Look, he is leading his black charger by the bridle; you will tame it in the darkness. When you arrive among men, you will come fully armed. Thus the good Achilles was raised before you in Limbo by the wise centaur."

He was going to continue, but he lost his voice when he saw a company of spirits on a path on the edge of any abyss, who all had crowns on their heads. They were walking in single file, mutely, so that they did not appear to know one another.

The shepherdess and her companions had stopped to watch that company pass by, which was advancing majestically. When at least half of them had disappeared, the virgin cried out at the sight of one of the crowned pilgrims: "There he is! It's him—the king!"

The Enchanter said to her: "Yes, Jeanne, you've recognized him, your Charles; form his cortege; march to his advent."

Then the shepherdess started walking alongside the one she had greeted; she seemed, as she accompanied him, to be protecting him against the darkness.

Meanwhile, the august troop continued passing by. The Enchanter stood motionless, counting how many there still were. One of the kings, who was walking with difficulty, stopped and, emerging from the crowd, with an expression more amicable than the others, said: "You, the only one who has seen the sun, tell me whether life is as light as it seems to us here. Tell me what kinds of incense the people are preparing for us, and the red cloth they are weaving for the kings. Tell me whether my felicity is more assured than that of the others. Our eyes enclose more than one invisible tear. Will those tears ever flow? This crown weighs upon me in Limbo; will it be lighter in the world of the living?"

"King," the prophet replied, "you only need to know one thing: accustom yourself to tears; they will flow later. Above all, remember, if you can, those who are marching so rapidly before you to escape justice; tell them to change direction, for the path they're following is bad. They'll leave a burdensome heritage. See, already, what anger is amassing behind them!"

The one to whom he was speaking seemed nonplussed. He was frightened by his solitude. He would have liked to call back though who were marching ahead of him, but they were all in a hurry to draw away. Each of them dreaded remaining the last.

"Your companions are cruel to you," said the prophet, sadly. "They have made peril for you; will they retrace their steps thereafter to defend you?"

"What peril?" asked the spirit wearing the crown, anxiously.

"Beware of the anger of the people."

"I've already seen mutinous larvae here; I know how they can be tamed with a smile."

"It's not always like that on earth."

"Tell me how to tame unchained peoples on earth."

"No one knows that secret, except those who have no need of it. Sometimes, the people are more flexible than grass; they crawl; that is their joy. Trample them, crush them; they will love you more for it—and that is what happens more often than not. Sometimes they sleep like lions huddled in the reeds; release the bit then, and they will be scornful of you; tighten it again and they will curse you; caress them, and they will tear you apart. Whatever you do, they will doom you."

"What have I to fear? The eternally-awaited day will not be taken from me. If the hours are counted by the crowd, they are inexhaustible for kings."

"Disillusion yourself, Louis, who will be called the sixteenth. It would cost you too much to know the truth, until the hour when you feel the trenchant blade strike you. Why are you pressing me to pronounce the words that I want to hold back? It behooves you more than anyone to praise the duration of the terrestrial day. It's you who will teach others how brief joys are, how heavy shadows are, and what poison abounds in the finest cup. They will tie your hands because you will be the most debonair. They will punish you with iron. Your head will seek in vain to rejoin the trunk, although it is not you who will have committed the crime, but those who precede you and whom you see in the distance, marching indifferently before the bloody dawn."

As he finished speaking, the one who was listening to him shivered. He took the hand of a child who was following him and who said, weeping: "Where are you taking me, Father?"

Then he let the entire cortege pass and brought up the rear, looking to see whether anyone was coming after him, like a man following a crowd who is afraid of arriving. At every step he turns round, stops and sighs—but dare he turn back?

III

The last of the file was no more than a slingshot away when the feeble, uncertain twilight began to glimmer. The light was slightly paler than at the hour and season of the year when a host of falling stars pierces the mantle of the night. By that light, however, here and there on both sides of the valley, fragments of towers, buildings and walls were visible: pale cities begun and abandoned, without anyone knowing whose hand had secretly laid their foundations.

110

There were also blanched ruins; they began suddenly to crumble; no one could say who had built them.

Among those ruins, a spirit advanced with head held high, which seemed to disdain them. He was not a king, but he was more superb than the kings. Like a laborer spurring on a herd of cattle, in order to get them to the table before a storm bursts, he was urging breathless people on with the spur of his words, who desired to stop and graze at every step. As soon as he saw that the crowd was dulled by its hard labor, however, he urged it on again with his goad; in order to avoid it, the herd ran blindly on without looking back.

On the wrinkled face of the stranger, you might have thought you recognized the ancient traces of thunderbolts, with the marks of the bitumen of Gomorrah. You might have thought that he had already traversed the subterranean flames, and had retained more than one scar therefrom. But that was not the case. His pride alone demonstrated that he had never been defeated. He was emerging like the rest from the native profundities of inviolate limbo.

When he was close to the prophet, whom it was impossible to pass without being seen, he did not lower his head like the others. On the contrary, he straightened up and, looking at the crumbling towers, said to him: "Who made these ruins?"

"You know who rendered them irreparable, but you've already forgotten, Mirabeau!"

The latter, without pausing, went on: "Which way did those I'm pursuing go? I've lost track of them because of marching too hastily in their wake."

"Those you're pursuing have taken the path at the foot of that rock; you'll soon catch up with them. They're walking slowly; the last, especially, is weighed down by the burden of his crown."

On hearing these words, like a hunter unmuzzling his pack of hounds, the arrogant soul unleashed the mob, which began howling under his blazing words.

"They're here!" he cried. "Run! Forward! Howl! Don't let the prey escape!"

And the pack went on, mouths agape, over the desiccated grass.

"Why do you press them thus, in Limbo, so quickly that they lose their breath? Afterwards, you'll have to restrain them, for fear that they'll escape you, and you'll no longer have the leash, because you'll have broken it yourself. As for them, they'll be so breathless that they'll run out of strength as well as breath, when they arrive in the sunlight. Instead of pursuing their route in glory, they'll lie down, tongues hanging out, beneath the feet of the wicked."

"I already know," replied the arrogant soul, "what their love is worth, and how it changes into hatred. Since I've been walking them in this royal void, I've learned to lead them where it pleases me. Trust in my word to attend to them and rule them. On seeing how vain they are, and how little they weigh, I'm learning here, in advance, to scorn them all. That's my crown."

"You have your feet in Hell, you who speak in the clouds," retorted the prophet. "Look at your hands! How gold has dirtied them! Why are they soiled when your heart is so noble? If I could wash them here with my tears, I would do it in advance, for I don't know yet whether I ought to crown you or curse you. By rejecting you, I dread dishonoring the light of the world, and yet, it's certain that you're holding in your right hand gold that doesn't come from noble labor. If others don't know it, I can see it from here. Pass on; I'll keep quiet for now. I can neither forget you nor hate you."

At these words, the disdainful soul opened his hands, from which a rain of gold fell, and replied, sniggering: "Do you take me for Judas? That was to pay my fare."

Then, standing up more proudly than before, he shook his immense hair and rejoined his companions, who seemed more like his subjects.

IV

When the pilgrim of the three worlds turned his head, he saw something like a swarm of larvae escaping from a hive, or rather, a great assembled nation, that was advancing from the depths of the night, singing in the manner of those leaving on a journey: "Liberty! Cherished liberty!"

They were all afloat in a sublime delight, as if they had already take possession of the light, for they believed themselves to be emancipated of the darkness because justice lived within them and scintillated in their faces. Cold Limbo was momentarily warmed by the presence of so many palpitating souls.

The prophet said to them: "It's certainly a fine thing to launch yourselves at the first bound toward justice, but perseverance is necessary, even for larvae to become human beings, and only the outcome will show what that ardor is worth. I greatly fear that those who demand the light might get a taste for darkness as soon as they glimpse it. Just as it is glorious to be the first to enter into justice, so it is shameful to renounce it as soon as it draws near. Later, we shall count those who have persevered; how many will there be then?

"All of us!" cried the crowd.

Scarcely had the words resonated than terror chilled the lips of those who had pronounced it, and several of those generations of larvae were blown along by the wind of fear, paler, more mute and more vain than the rest. They murmured very softly, for fear of being overheard: "Let's get further away from the daylight. Here come the twelve!"

Then, raising his eyes, the prophet saw twelve men with long hair, each of whom held a double-edged sword; and a tricolor standard, blue, white and red was floating over their heroic heads. As they marched, their shadow grew longer, but the multitude was as fearful of that shadow as the swords themselves. At the head of the twelve he recognized the one that he had found when he first entered and whom he had called Maximilien.

He said to him: "See what fear you have caused them! And the sons of their sons will tremble with that same fear. There are some turning back in the night. How do you know whether they won't want to get out of it now? Hide the blade of your sword, then, if you want them to come back and pass on."

As all the birds hide when the kite in soaring in the clouds, and the countryside seems dead, so all the spirits called to life fell silent, so much did they dread being seen in the azure-tinted light of the blade. For a long time, the prophet sought them himself without being able to discover them. In the end, he found them here and there, crouching on the ground, refusing in advance the gift of daylight.

"That's not the route, sordid souls who seek to sell yourselves before having lived," he said to them. "Why are you going back into the darkness? Why are you rejecting the golden light? Do you want to dishonor the dust of the ancestors? Where do you want to retreat? The void is behind you. It's poor and meager; it won't buy you anything. Whether the fear is true of hypocritical, it's necessary nevertheless to go on and enter into life. And you who are the palest, Maximilien Robespierre, if it's you who guards the threshold, lower your sword. Open the way for them. Go on! As if they weren't sufficiently afraid already!"

They obeyed, but not all of them. There were two who refused to kiss the blade. In that fashion, they attracted the following speech:

"You who are the youngest, Saint-Just, it's true, then, that that you're also the most implacable? You hold your head too straight. As for you, Billaud-Varenne, be careful of the homicidal maremma of Sinnamary.[55] For the dead that you will heap up on this side of the ocean will traverse it with dry feet. They will go to search for you in the shade of the mangroves, where you will have no companions and defenders but the parrots of the forest that will perch on your shoulder."

Twice the timid crowd hesitated; twice it sought an exit in order to turn back and re-enter the night devoid of dawn. If it had been able to get back it would have done so that same day. How it regretted then the native darkness in which it had slept the slumber of clay! How it repented having sought the pale clarity of Limbo! For at that moment, Death loomed up above its heavy shield at the extremities of the horizon, twenty cubits taller than the human ocean at its feet, and began to snigger on seeing that they all belonged to it equally.

Then the prophet struck the crowd angrily with his hazel-branch. All of them hastened tumultuously toward life, fearfully, turning away their eyes—but there was no reasoning with the rod.

---

[55] Jacques Nicolas Billaud-Varenne, one of the principal architects of the Terror, was sentenced to be transported to French Guiana in 1795 when the Convention turned against him; the coastal town of Sinnamary was one of the earliest settlements founded there.

V

On the other side of a stream that seemed to be the source of the Ocean, a single soul was standing apart. From the height of the bank it had contemplated the civil tempest without changing expression. Vast savannahs extended around it. Without fear, as without anger, it advanced in a modest fashion, although it seemed to fill a world on its own.

"Who are you, whom the fall of a world has left unmoved, and who seems to be inhabiting a new world on your own?" the Enchanter shouted to him. "You're still too far away for me to be able to greet you by name."

The two marched toward one another, around the humble source of the Ocean. When they were near enough to touch, the prophet had recognized a long time before the spirit to which he had spoken.

"Why," he said, "does it not depend on me to advance the hour when you would see the light, honor of the unknown world that still sleeps beneath the Ocean? I would not let you wander any longer here in this mute twilight, which resembles death so closely. I would lead you by the hand when I climb up to the earth again. The terrestrial light would thank me for showing it Washington."

Then, touching him, he added: "O liberty, which I have not yet seen and have already loved so much, it's you, serene soul, who will forge its cradle! You will see how sweet it is and how wretched is the man who has not known it! Better for him to remain buried forever in this desolate limbo where the sun never shines. Don't become sad in advance, preferred soul, if your name is not the one that resounds most loudly in the human mouth. Oh, if you trampled them underfoot, you who had the strength to do it, how they would fête you! If you put your pleasure into binding them in herds, charging them with irons, how they would revere your memory! They would praise it to the clouds; all their mouths would be full of hymns to you. If you crushed them, you would be their demigod. But, while able to enslave them, you will respect them, and they will only ever have partial praise for you."

"For whom, then, will they reserve their love and the full measure of glory?" stammered the astonished soul.

"I've already told you: for those who scorn them, and sow behind them the dust in which slaves are born: those who call themselves Alexander, Caesar..."

"Don't name the third," the free soul replied. "I know it already; I know how heavy his yoke is, even in this place where everything is so light. Just tell me what I most desire to know. What will my country be, and my people? Name the land that will receive me. Under what sky shall I see the light? What do you call it?"

"The land where you will see daylight for the first time is still unknown in the depths of the seas. It does not have its name as yet in human mouths. Only the Eternal knows it and sees it across the green-tinted Ocean. Already the insect is working day and night, though, to raise its coral temples."

114

For the first time, a somber sadness spread over the impassive face of the one who was to be Washington. He cried, in amazement: "What! The land where I am to be born has not yet emerged from the waves? It has no human inhabitants yet? They have not built dwellings there or heard the sound of their speech? It is, then, the prey of winds, of tempests, perhaps reptiles and wild beasts? Or instead, undoubtedly, it will never be, and my destiny is to float here in eternal expectation, without finding anywhere to rest on a shore that is not itself a mere dream. All the others have a fatherland; they await it in advance. All are sure there, on seeing the light, of finding the ancestral land that will smile at them from the cradle on. I alone here have no ancestors, nor parents, nor a dwelling ready on the shore of the living. I alone will find no clay to make myself a mortal body."

At these words, the soul of bronze bowed his head and began to moan.

As a master simultaneously scolds and consoles a child who has hurt his hand by virtue of excessive impatience, and who thinks himself near to dying for having seen his red blood flow for the first time, the prophet replied:

"Is it for you to moan, when you seem made of bronze? By your tears alone I see, whimpering soul, that you're not yet entirely finished and retain something of Limbo. If there's anyone here who ought to rejoice, it's you— because, for your cradle you shall have a world, and no serpents will take you by surprise there. While you taste the premises of eternal justice here, the land that will be your fatherland is covered in secret with savannahs and forests. When your heart is ready for the great combat, the soil will also be ready to drink the blood of oppressors. On seeing you, it will say: 'I'm free!' Already the wind is blowing over the virginal crowns of tamarinds newly emerged from the depths of gulfs; the seed is sown of the tree whose bark will make your cradle. Already the great rivers have hollowed out the bed of peoples. The cataract is roaring like a herd in search of its pastor. Let's be quiet, and you might perhaps hear it."

Thus the prophet consoled the soul, naked as yet, which was frightened that it might not find mud to make itself a mortal body. Then the latter became indignant that someone had seen him weeping and despairing. Resuming his visage of bronze, the said: "They already have a fatherland. I shall make mine."

And without saying anything more, he continued his pilgrimage toward the light.

VI

In that part of Limbo something was happening more extraordinary than all those I have recounted so far. There was no one who did not turn his head to make sure that it was not a dream.

After the crowd of pale larvae marched a black people, slower and sadder, as if laden with invisible chains. Those negro souls were the color of night and their hair was wooly. Their teeth shone in their mouths like a necklace of white pearls, so that they seemed to be smiling even when they wanted to weep. The trace of a bloody whip was on their ebony shoulders, and they did what none of the spirits that the pilgrim had encountered had done: they fell on their knees at his feet, seeming to say to him: "Deliver us from this burden, which we cannot bear."

At that moment, the blow of a club resounded in the darkness. No one saw the arm lifted, nor who the murderer was, but the man who had been struck fell like a dead man at the prophet's feet.

"What hand struck this innocent man?" he cried. "Is injustice already born in his place, and death with it? Does crime already have its cradle here? Are there already Cains in Limbo?"

All were fearful, but no one replied, for none knew as yet what death was. Only one groan was heard below the ground, in the place where the seeds of invisible things were hidden. The moan emerged from millions of warm and panting breasts. The Enchanter than saw that white men had laden the black men with a thousand heavy burdens that kept them bent down to the ground; and that servitude, before birth, was no less cruel than the one the light of the world illuminates. For it was pitiful to see those fragile souls dragging themselves along, exhausted, in the semi-darkness, toward the doors of life—and the saddest thing of all within them was hope.

"Will the desired light soon arrive," they said, "in order that we might put down these burdens that are crushing us and preventing us from holding up our heads? Oh, we long to see the sweet light, where all servitude ceases and where the black man will be the equal, the brother, of the white, in the terrestrial hut. Our sole dread is to remain here, buried in this place, under the shackles with which they have, as you can see, charged our shoulders."

On hearing them, the prophet sighed; he dared not tell them the truth. Turning toward a more robust soul that was passing by, however, the only one whose head was raised, he said to him:

"You who are the first among black men, you can bear this word, for you have the shoulders of Atlas. You are truly made of stone, Toussaint L'Ouverture, if gentle pity does not grip you on seeing the ingenuousness of your people. They believe that life will liberate them from harsh servitude. Oh, how disappointed they will be, as soon as they see the light! How they will regret Limbo, where, thanks to the darkness, they often escape the master's gaze. I cannot tell them what awaits them; they would lose courage; I can already see their knees flexing under the load. But I say this to you, in order that not everyone will fall simultaneously into the ambush of the cradle."

Toussaint L'Ouverture shook his head and replied: "That's enough—they're listening! Don't say any more."

A little further on, Merlin encountered another company of bound souls; these were white and seemed to be natural slaves, for they had no masters. They were, however, crawling as if they had felt the whip.

"Why are you crawling already, servile souls?" Merlin asked them. "You have no masters yet! Who keeps you curbed thus? Is it the memory of having lived badly in times I do not know? Are you deserters from Heaven? Get up— look at things from your full height!"

But without making any effort to obey, they looked at him as if they had not understood. Then Merlin lifted a few of them to their feet, he told them to look at the sky, which they had not yet glimpsed. They tried to smile at those azure plains, but as soon as Merlin had passed on, they fell back, embracing the muddy ground again, which their feet had kneaded.

VII

At that place, something like the sound of dead leaves rose up under the prophet's feet. It was a multitude of larvae curled up on the ground, who were trying to laugh. They were the most wretched of all.

"Why are you striving to laugh?" he asked them, making a detour for fear of treading on them. "Nothing is sadder than your joy."

"We're laughing at your promises of life," replied the inhabitants of the pale valley. Why, prophet, are you playing games with the poor larvae? We shall never believe that there's a real life and a sun that rises, beyond the vast limbo. More than once, that rumor has been spread among us, and it has always been found to be a lie. Leave us, larvae that we are, to enjoy the realm of larvae in peace. We don't want any other."

Merlin exhausted himself trying to persuade the crowd that beyond the abode in which they were plunged, half-formed, there was a sun of life that warmed creatures with its gaze as they entered the world. Were they made to remain forever confined to such a sad place? It was only, in truth, a preparation for a better life, a sketch of the universe, a Propylaea barely ajar—or, rather, a prison. Did they not feel the human growing within the homunculi they were? The future days could be read in advance in their faces.

He spoke, with all the force of conviction he could muster, of the splendor of things beyond the cradle.

The blind souls replied: "You're a bard and a poet, Merlin; you live in gilded fantasies. For us, who do not have your wings, reasoning is required. Has anyone ever come back from this pretended world of the living? Until then, we shall call it the world of dreams."

More sad than indignant, Merlin invoked his own testimony. Was that not experience, then?

"Look," he said, "blind people that you are! Come nearer, touch me! This hazel-branch I cut in Brittany, in the land of the living. I've come from there, I tell you. Here is its dust, still whitening my feet. What more do you need? Please, friends, brothers, don't close off the future out of vanity. Believe in life at least to be obliging; if not, you'll remain here, vain, frivolous, devoid of renown, seeds gone astray, sown in death."

At this speech, accompanied by pleas and even a few tears, the spirits, hardened by the contradiction itself, were content to murmur enviously: "All that is visions, Merlin. It's not us who'll be taken in. We're serious larvae. It's another trick; we know that. There's nothing beyond Limbo but eternal darkness. We don't believe in the cradle."

How Merlin regretted then not having Viviane for a witness!

She wouldn't have any need to speak, he said to himself. *Merely by seeing her, they'd believe in life, in the dawn, in perfume, in the woodland songs of spring, the promises of the year in flower, the sparkling gaze of daylight. For myself, it's true, I possess existence, but I often lack the art of convincing others.*

He drew away at a slow pace, often turning his head and sighing. But he could not blame himself if so many beings called to immortal life remained forever stuck, imprisoned in formless darkness, for want to belief.

Soon, the cold sniggering of those who doubted life dies away by degrees. The larvae, deprived of hope and even of desire, lapsed, one after another, shaking their heads, into the silence contemporaneous with death.

BOOK SIX: LIMBO CONTINUED

I

The air had become still. There was not a breath of air, nor any voice to be head. Already, the nebulae were letting rays that were less pale fall at the feet of the leafless trees. The escarpments of the mountains became similar to the region where the Jura raises its towers and boulevards to form a belt for France, and although the slopes were black, the peaks were flamboyant with the red gleams of an invisible sun.

No path led to the summits, where several people were standing who seemed to have wandered away from the crowd passing by beneath their feet. Perhaps the eagles had lent their wings to those solitaries. They seemed to be occupied with the dreams of a sacred sleep. All of them, with one exception, had retained the serenity of the nascent world in their facial expressions.

"Have you lost the path of the living?" the prophet shouted to them. "Or have you forgotten to live, you who are taking the place of the eagles?"

His voice was lost in the air; the solitude became greater.

The conductor of the three lives searched to discover where the rock was least harsh, but did not find any beaten track. Helping himself then, with the wings of the mind, he made a path for himself, and went to join those who were inhabiting the summits, much as the shepherd leaves the wilting low valleys in summer and takes his flocks on to Mont Rose, where they drink the virginal snow.

The first he met stamped his foot as soon as he had the opportunity to speak and said: "Tell me whether it moves?"

"Yes, it moves, Galileo! Have no fear of vertigo."

At that response the spirit, radiant with joy, tried to stammer on the edge of the gulf: "Brothers, it moves!" But his voice scarcely passed his lips. He was ashamed of that, and his divine joy was mingled with dolor. He would have liked to hide his confusion behind his companions.

"Don't flee the light, Galileo," said the prophet, holding him back. "That's how all science is acquired. A little dolor is mingled with every new enlightenment; you'll experience that yourself when you come into the world. Make an apprenticeship here in the pale light of Limbo, before contemplating the sun. Otherwise, you won't be able to support it in its glory."

He was about to continue when one of the solitaries approached him from behind, believing that he had not been noticed—but his shadow betrayed him. Out of dread or surprise, he dropped the globe and compasses that he had been holding in his hand, to while away the idleness of the hours, since the commencement of things.

At that sound, the prophet turned round severely. He picked up the compasses and opened them to their full extent, and, bending down over the globe, he placed the sharp point at the necessary spot, saying: "It's here, Newton, that it's necessary to put the finger and trace the circle to enclose the vast heavens. Be careful never to forget it! Don't let yourself be diverted any longer by passing matters."

Meanwhile, he had arrived at the summit brushed by the rays of an invisible sun, and he saw, close at hand in that dawn, a spirit that seemed to be drifting, full of anxiety, like a migratory bird that soars for a long time high in the sky, interrogating all the points of the horizon with its eyes, before finding the route to the natal nest and launching itself forward with rapidly-beating wings.

"Are you their chief?" he said to him. "What brought you so high on these uninhabited peaks? Was it the birds in the sky?"

"I don't know," the spirit replied, "what brought me to this place, or where I came from, or where I'm going. That's why you see me so pensive."

"What are you searching for?"

"The Eternal."

At these words, as a lapidary divines beneath the brute stone the diamond that ought to sparkle with a thousand fires, the eyes of the prophet recognized the spirit beneath the humble swaddling-clothes that still covered him. He greeted him with these words:

"O sweet Bretagne, it's true, then, that I'm looking at one of your long-haired children! This one will be born on the same terrain as me.[56] He'll drink the water of the same river as me; he'll speak the same language. Hail, source of all wisdom! In Bretagne they'll call you René; for everyone else you'll be Descartes. But how far off the day is when you'll shine through the veils that hide you here!"

As he finished this speech, the thought of the sweet homeland made him forget where he was. He held out his hands to the one to whom he was speaking. But the Breton soul moved away and said, fearfully: "Am I not a breath, a vapor, a nothing?"

"No," the Enchanter told him. "You're an immortal spirit of my family." And, drawing him closer, he tried to embrace him.

The spirit remained astonished for some time by that first grip of life; then, parting the long unkempt hair that fell over his forehead, he said: "If it's true that I'm to have the same cradle as you, tell me where these larvae, sketched like

---

[56] Descartes was not actually born in Brittany, but his father was a member of the Parlement de Bretagne at Rennes. This is the first time that Merlin insists on his Breton origins, the account given in Book One having been deliberately vague about the location of his birthplace.

me are going—these shadows, these mute individuals who never come back and whose number never diminishes, What abode is great enough to receive them all? See how they march in silence, insouciantly, with their heads tilted, without looking back. What hand is pushing them? What hand is pulling them? Where are they coming from, so confident and yet so timid? How, weak as they are, are they going along this rude road?"

"It's you, René, who will serve as their guide."

"O master! How shall I be their guide if I remain lost, like them, among vain things. Which is the best way? Where does the light separate itself from the darkness? Where does the dream end? Where does wakefulness begin? I cannot walk as all those around me do, taking the night for counsel."

On hearing him speak thus, the prophet took pity on that immortal spirit; he led him by the hand, as a guide leads a blind man, making him touch each of the objects around him one after another. He taught him thus to distinguish the random gleams of Limbo, the vain errant fireflies, from the flame that springs internally from the tiniest spirit. When he saw that he was reassured, he gave him a thread that he took care to attach to one of the roots that penetrated to the center of the earth.

"Have no fear that it will break," he said to him. "I've woven it myself; it will guide you easily, you and your companions, through the labyrinth of eternal things."

The one who had been lost a moment before seized the thread avidly ad started marching among the abysms, in such a way that his feet hardly touched the ground; and, turning round, he saw the flock of the spirits that were coming after him increasing.

A new ambition gripped him then.

"O Master," he added, "since you love me, conduct me toward the source of things. I can hear it, dully, not far from here. Show me the dust from which sparkling worlds are born. Teach me to weigh in my hands those shaggy globes that I perceive here by accident—for they, at least, when they pass by, do not refuse their light to our Limbo. Enable me to taste the premises of that terrestrial daylight, which knows neither darkness nor shadow. I shan't publish before time the glory of the heavens, if you entrust it to me. I'll put my finger over my mouth. No one shall know the splendor of the visible universe prematurely. They'll flock around me; they'll ask me, as they're accustomed to do where I know what lies beyond the gates of Limbo, but I'll reply: *I don't know*."

"Restrain your curiosity, René!" the prophet replied, with an almost-divine majesty. "Dread allowing yourself to be consumed before time by everything that glitters, as you see a nocturnal moth hurling itself ecstatically into the burning naphtha source. What do the changing skies matter that your eyes can't yet see? Content yourself today with the immutable, and seize the invisible at your leisure. What have you, who fear so much being deceived, to do with the deceptive promises of waves and seas?

"If you're not yet oppressed by the burden of the senses, know that you'll enjoy them further on, while criticizing limbo. How much wiser you would be to take advantage here of the silence of things, and the matinal meditation of the nascent universe, to converse freely, one to one, a pure spirit with unveiled spirit! Later, the vestment of flesh will weigh upon you heavily; your efforts to get rid of it will be in vain. The visible world will distract you with its illusory fêtes. It will disguise the ingenuous soul with tatters. It will envelop you and hold you captive with its sounds, its colors, its perfumes and its vain splendors. What toil it will be then, René, to recover within the nudity of the stainless soul that first inviolate dawn of Limbo! I don't know whether you'll ever succeed.

"You will want to make the universe fall silent around you, in order only to listen to your own thoughts, but the smallest cicada will resist you with its obstinate song. The buzzing of flies will cover the voice of infinity. You'll put your hands over your eyes to flee the deceptive light of the terrestrial day; it will rise up between the truth and you to cast the eternal light into shadow.

"Do you not see how the forms around you are attenuated here, how the colors are obligingly effaced, how the pale nebulosities close their eyelids in order that your thoughts might gleam alone and unrivaled? Don't wait any longer, then, for the body, in growing, to come to oppress the mind. Don't call out any longer in your impatience for the vain tumult of things. More often than not, it disperses the best ideas."

"Can I not at least converse today with humans?" murmured René.

"Be glad to converse with the larvae; they seem to honor you. The people of my time have descended too far from the summits. They won't understand you."

These words filled the one that the prophet had called René with the melancholy of sages. He would have liked to ask whether, after Limbo, it would be necessary to pass through other Limbos, whether the novitiate of darkness would soon be complete, and when the true rebirth would come, no longer in an uncertain and deceptive corpuscle but in the splendor and the plenitude of the eternal sun. Already armed with courage, he was about to open his mouth, when a chorus of larvae was heard in the distance.

When he heard that, the master stopped him with a gesture of the hand and said to him: "Can you hear, unquiet soul? Come with me to meet those who are singing so sweetly *Gloria in excelsis Deo.*"

René followed him, and looked behind him at a spirit who was holding a cup in his hand and walking as if intoxicated, but not by wine. "That's my disciple," he said. "Shall I wake him up so that he can come with us?"

"No," said the prophet. "Of all of you who inhabit this region, that's the most serene soul, and the only one I envy. I know him; he doesn't need anyone. His pilgrimage is finished before having begun. Before life, as afterwards, nothing has changed for him. Because of that, you will call him Benedict Spinoza. Come on, let's go. He's drained his cup; he's drunk on the Eternal."

II

The mountain was divided on one side by a horizontal band of white vapor, so that the frowning black summit seemed to be floating on the cloud; you might have thought that it was a celestial hill floating in mid-air.

Who were those descending the rocky slope singing, while fireflies sowed a fiery dust in the atmosphere? Momentarily, they plunged into the cloud; then they came through it and reappeared under the awning of mist. Pale and pensive, some put their hands together to pray; others carried white hawthorn branches stripped of their bark, tied together in the form of a cross.

It was a great population of mystical souls amorous of tears, intoxicated by terror, who were going in search of divine voluptuousness. They had at the angelic Doctor[57] at their head, and in scattered groups, Saint Bernard, Joachim of Fiore, Catherine of Siena, St. Theresa, and you too, Adam the Pole, whom I have seen with my own eyes and loved with a faithful heart during your pilgrimage on earth—too brief, alas, not for your glory, but for the consolation of your captive people.[58]

All of them, wandering together over the landscape, were coming to meet the children who had died unbaptized, who were returning to the depths of limbo in bewilderment. The crowd had surrounded the new-borns who had barely glimpsed the light. Everyone was interrogating them with gestures and gazes, trying to discover what they had seen and heard beyond the cradle.

"Did you visit sacred Jerusalem?" they said to them. "Did you see the Lord?"

But like a flock of birds emerged too soon from the roost, in haste to return to it, having been surprised by the bird-catcher, they returned, weeping and wailing, to the most secret place from which they had been taken. If they stammered anything, it was: "Mother, where are you? Father, why have you expelled me from the cradle into limbo?"

In the distance, an invisible bell was tolling a knell, and that knell resembled one that I once heard in Rome in the gardens of the Palatine hill, in the evening, when the laity came out to bury their dead.

Then the spirits of the mystic crowd lost themselves in a thousand confused thoughts. They could not understand why the new-borns had come back among them, for none of them understood what it is to die.

At that moment, they encountered the conductor of spirits at a bend in the wooded path. The one who would one day be St. Bernard said to him: "You don't resemble any of us, for you're already clad in a body and you appear to

---

[57] Thomas Aquinas.

[58] The poet and political activist Adam Mickiewicz (1798-1855), a central figure of Polish Romanticism.

know life, by virtue of having experienced it. Doubtless you're a messenger of the divine Sion, and are bringing us news of the cross. Why have you come back, like those who can only babble? Why have they fled the daylight so soon? What has made them so pale?"

"They're dead," the prophet replied.

"What is dead?" asked the crowd, whose members, without knowing why, began to shiver. That word was soon on the lips of all those who populated Limbo. A secret anxiety agitated the virginal souls; the first mourning extended among them.

"You've seen the Lord at the portals of life," they said, "and the roses of Sion strewn on the threshold."

"I've seen the tomb beside the cradle everywhere," the pilgrim of the three worlds replied. "All enter and emerge weeping and wailing."

"The dwelling of eternal love is prepared in the stainless city; have you not lived therein?"

"I have seen the gnashing of teeth by those who speak of love, and the swords in their hands."

"At least the heavens remain."

"I have seen the heavens change. The gods wither like leaves; like them, they strew the parvis of the eternal portals."

At these words, the mystic souls went away, confused; they veiled themselves for the first time; their sadness was unconsolable; it seemed that life and death were both lacking for them. Adam the Pole was the last to linger, very pensively. He turned round to say to those who were following him: "His words are harsh, but they are merited. Churchmen, you are the Pharisees who have doomed the cross."

III

The ringing of the bell was already fading away in the air when, in its stead, a soft chirping became audible, like the chorus of young nightingales in a nest in a cypress, awakening at dusk. Those who were interrupting the silence of the nascent world were the winged population of souls who nourish themselves on beautiful sounds, and search the universe for the music of things. They would one day be called Guido of Arezzo, Palestrina, Pergolese, Mozart and Beethoven. At the moment, sad and thoughtful, they were lending their ears to the muted, inarticulate sounds traversing Limbo, like those who are searching for something and cannot find it. Each of them carried a viol in his hand, but each of those viols had but one bronze string, and they did not know where to find the ones that were missing, of which they had a presentiment.

From time to time, one of them drew a note from his instrument that resembled a sigh; immediately, the others repeated that sigh—after which, discouraged, with heads bowed, they fell back into eternal silence.

124

When the pilgrim passed by, the boldest among them—the one that was to be Beethoven—separated from his companions.

"O bard," he said, "tell me how the wind moans over the surface of the sea. What is the titillation of nascent light? What have you heard in the silence of deserts? How does soft human speech resonate in the hearts of the living? What is the sound of a breaking heart? What does the sight of a soul occupied in contemplating the nascent daylight resemble? How does a person belated in the night moan?"

Without making any reply, the master took the viol. He drew a chord from it that made the hearts of those who were listening quiver. They all tried to imitate it. Having been unable to succeed, however, their eyes were veiled by sadness. Of all those inhabiting limbo they were, if not the most miserable, at least the most filled with desires. Their laments seemed to be the best part of their art.

IV

At the master's sweet music, the larvae crowded around him—and I, who had so far been walking behind him, was more prompt this time than all the rest. The sweetness of those chords intoxicated me so much that I had never felt a greater desire to emerge from limbo, nor a greater audacity to attempt the paths that had not yet been frayed. Remembering the reply he had made to me, I asked him for another.

"If these chords touch your heart," I said to him, "as you can see that they stir Limbo, have pity on me and give me the response that I have been seeking since I have been following in your footsteps. Tell me, before emerging from this place—for if I'm not mistaken, you're preparing to leave—who among these will be the companions who will make the pilgrimage of life with me. Teach me to know them I advance. Lead my heart toward them; show me their faces in advance."

The master replied to me with the following words, which were imprinted on my thoughts so firmly that I can still hear them: "Your request is less ambitious now; that is why I want to answer it. Come, follow me. I shall introduce you to those you will have for companions under the sun of the living."

Having said that, he led me from one group to another through the crowd, and he said to me, pointing out ingenuous and smiling souls, the oldest of which had not reached adolescence:

"These are the first you will encounter in terrestrial life, on the torrential banks of the Ain, and the majority will follow you no more than half way along the route. See how the sweet beverage of childhood rejoices them in advance! But their joy will be brief, and that separation will be your first. See how they find their vain amusement in Limbo! They are unaware of their premature end.

"Look now at those who will traverse radiant youth with you. How sweet their embrace will be to you! How promptly your heart will go out to them!

How many hopes and projects will be common to you! How many sweet secrets will bind you with magical chains! Few of these will conserve the flame until the final hour. Time, absence, the road that each one has before him, will disperse their thoughts. But they will not betray you—except one, perhaps, and even for that one, it will be weakness and not perfidy."

At the same time, he told me their names; I was about to hurl myself toward them, already sensing the sweet flame of amity, which, at first, so closely resembles love, when he stopped me by saying: "Look this way, and prepare your heart. Here is the one you will love in the first hour of youth, and the blow will be so heavy that you will almost fall."

"Who is she?"

"You'll know soon enough, when you receive life. Come, let's pass on."

And he continued to speak to me thus: "This is the first one who will teach you what it is to die—for you will live along time without knowing; she is the one who will give you the light."

"Stop, Master!" I said to him. "She won't live as long as me, then? Oh, you've rendered life cruel before I've tasted it. You've introduced me to the poison before my lips have touched the cup. I fear now that that word might come back to me when I'm under the sun, and corrupt all the joys for which I hope."

The master continued: "Here are those you will bury with your own hands. There are three, and among them the palest is a saint. See how little they suspect the final hour! How they bathe their eyes in yours! How sweet the promise of life is to them! But you, who know how brief it will be, weep and moan!"

Seeing that the dolor with which he had just filled me was stronger than me—for my vision darkened and I was obliged to lean on him in order not to fall—the master tried to console me. He continued in these terms:

"Get up! Look at the one who will travel with you longest and who, from the first day to the last, will give you the strongest friendship.[59] He is not your brother, but he will be more than your brother. Several will try to divide you, but they will only serve to unite your more solidly. O peace! O strength! O repose! O sweetness of two souls united in combat and justice! Look at him. He is carrying in his hands the tablets, blank as yet, on which he will inscribe the history of France. He is conversing with the one who will be called Vico."

I took a step toward him and was about to call out to him, but the master held me back.

"It's not yet time," he said. Others are arriving whom you will only know in bad times. They will not follow the same path as you through the hours of youth, but when adversity comes, it will unite you all. See how proudly they are marching, and how the storm has not curbed their heads. The world is insulting them, because it sees them disarmed.

---

[59] Jules Michelet.

126

"They are alone; they fall silent, because they are forbidden to speak. Their mouths are sealed, but their thought is shining on their foreheads. See how their children, following them on the austere road, are racked by hunger, and how they weep as they walk! See how their wives toil over linen, groaning in the night in order to smile by day! See how they are refused shelter because they want to bring justice in with them, and how they are rejected from one threshold to another, without anyone crying: Pity! See how they nourish themselves with hope and are indulgent to the people who have forgotten them! You will be one of them. Like them, you will live on hope, but you will not have the same softness of heart, and your indulgence will not be as great."

They were his last words. As he finished, I envisaged with piety those who would one day traverse terrestrial life at the same time as me. I hastened toward them, as if they had already formed an eternal society with me, but they seemed astonished. Not knowing my secret, they passed on without turning their heads or giving me any sign. That first apprenticeship in life was bitter for me.

Soon, they drew away, and it seemed to me that my life was fleeing as I tried to grasp it. I remained, as on the day after a fête, among ruins. The impression of that existence, which had passed over me, lighter than a shadow, is still present as I write these lines.

I wanted to cry out: "Friends! Brothers! Companions! Stop!" but speech failed me; they all continued on their way in silence, without looking back. Only one, whose consciousness shone like a diamond, stopped and said to me: "Go on! I'll follow you."

Seeing then that that first intuition of life had passed, without return, I lost myself, annihilating myself in the sentiment of the brevity of all things—for I had only had the complete sentiment of existence for as long as the pilgrim of the three worlds was speaking to me. For as long as he was speaking, I had felt fully alive; I thought that I was liberated from oblivion. As soon as he stopped speaking to me, I ceased to believe in myself; I fell back into the depths of limbo. As he drew away, the anticipatory consciousness of existence faded in my heart.

At that moment, a terrible cry of "Merlin! Merlin!" pierced Heaven, Hell and Limbo.

That voice reached the prophet. He ran, for he feared that he might find the door closed. Was it not already too late to see once again the one who was calling to him from Viviane's Heaven?

When I heard him, from afar, crossing the threshold of Limbo with great strides, never to enter it again, and closing the sacred portals behind him, I mingled with the host of indifferent larvae, groaning. The promise of life no longer seemed to me to be anything but a lure. I mocked myself for having believed it so easily. I looked at the one who was accompanying me and I said to her: "Where is your hope? The world has passed. You remain to me."

And the spectacle of everything that was not her foundered, irredeemably.

V

Whence came, Reader, that formidable cry that had made our hero's heart tremble? I cannot omit telling you that. By a strange, truly providential coincidence, in the interval when Merlin paused in the idleness of limbo, the king of the abyss had taken advantage of the Enchanter's absence to abduct his mother, Séraphine, from the place where she was doing penance. He had dragged Merlin's mother away by force. Already he was approaching the black shaft, seeking to give his abduction the classical appearance of a free descent into Hell.

"Come, dear Séraphine," he said to her. "You have not aged an hour. Come into my fortress."

"Let me be!" cried Merlin's mother. "Get out! You won't abuse me any more with false promises. I know who you are. I know you. I hate you. You've doomed me already; once was too much. Your words are serpents. O night, cover me! Defend me!"

"Why flee from me, Séraphine?" replied Merlin's father. "I'm not asking you for anything, my dear—absolutely nothing. Only give me your hand, nothing but your hand. No? Well, I'll content myself with kissing the hem of your robe, the edge of your wimple."

"Get away, dog of Hell!"

"You drive me away in vain. The dog will lie down at your feet. He will let himself be insulted, beaten, whipped; he will lick the hand that strikes him. Then, O my love, know a little of the whim of the lion who spares you, being able to devour you."

"O Death, deliver me!"

"What are you afraid of, Séraphine? A descent into Hell? But nothing is more frequent among the living. Only remember prudent Ulysses, pious Aeneas, Orpheus, Telemachus, Hercules the Strong, Psyche—none ever repented of that mark of confidence."

"Vile serpent! Down! Crawl!"

"What, Séraphine, insults? Why? Call me, if you wish, Iblis, like the dark-eyed women of the Orient. Tell me, my angel, has a child not sealed our marriage? What is there more sacred on the earth? Is it not a valid, respectable marriage? I only want to legitimate our child by a solemn union. Where is our son, Séraphine? What have you done with him? My beloved child, where is he? Oh, it's taken me a long time to find and finally enjoy, in all conscience, the holy name of father!"

"I'm no longer what I was—repentance has changed me. Holy waters have ashes away my sin."

"Do you call a sin the most authentic marriage to which darkness has served as witness? Don't dishonor our beautiful days. If you've changed, I haven't; I never will. Come!"

128

"No! No!"

"Come on, darling, don't oblige me to use force. I'd be in despair, but I'd do it, in the sacred interest of my son. I can't leave him to rot, dishonored, in bastardy. I need to give him my family name, honorably. Whenever there's some incompatibility, everything must give way to the interest of the children. Come on, no more procrastination—come! Suffer this gentle violence. It originates from the sincerest love, dear angel!"

"Will no one come to my aid? O Death! O Night! O Merlin!"

It was the last cry that had just reached the ears of our Enchanter. He launched himself forward to bar the way to the abductor, and found himself face to face with him; he was already about to recall Virgil and ask his advice, when the abductor reflected that the place was badly chosen for a wrestling match. If victorious, his victory would only be partial in that subterranean location; if vanquished, all of Hell would be witness to his defeat—so he immediately decided to avoid combat, certain of finding a more propitious opportunity at a later date.

Séraphine had thrown her arms around her son's neck and was hugging him.

"Oh my son, my Merlin!" she cried. "Will you let me descend among the damned? You're strong; you're more powerful than Hell. Protect me."

Before Merlin had pronounced a single word, the sniggering Beelzebub had raised his voice:

"Welcome, my dear son! This is just a lovers' quarrel—don't worry about it. O joy, O transports! The father, the mother and the son, all together at last! What a spectacle! Dear child, contribute to the union of your parents. Arbitrate between them; your wisdom is precocious. Tell me, isn't it necessary for the mother of a family to live with her spouse? Isn't it the simplest of duties? Why, then, pray, defy opinion unnecessarily, with no serious reason? If I've ever discontented or annoyed your mother, I repent of it. Well, what more can one want? If I've sometimes been in a surly mood, that's largely due to the pain your absence has caused me. The vivacity of character, the impetuosity of temperament, a few minor faults, a few inequalities, a few words slipped out in a moment of displeasure, irritable nerves with the north wind blows, perhaps too much ardor in the manner of my love-making, an overly-delicate sensibility, but never a serious defect—can't that be forgiven? Come on, dear son of my loins, sit down here, closer, between the two of us. Make my peace with your mother. Bring her back to the paternal hearth. The family! The family! My dear, that's the supreme wealth!"

During this speech, Séraphine was clinging to her son and trembling in every limb.

"That's her response," said Merlin. "Don't hope to vanquish her by force."

"Force!" his father interjected. "Why, my son, who's thinking of making use of that? Have I ever employed any arms in her regard than those of pure love? Persuasion, sighs, winks, kobold music, moonlight conversations, reveries, tales of my long insomnias, my sufferings, my distant wars, from which I never brought back a single scar—that's what my arms have been! She rejects me! She leaves me to stew in my burning solitude! Well, since she wishes it, I'll bury myself here all alone. I shall suffer, alas! I can suffer! She wants it; I consent to it. Nothing remains to me but the desert hearth. Let her spend happy days on earth! Let her lend her ears to the aubades and serenades of young men, while I, here..."

Would you believe that Merlin, at these words, thought for a moment of advising his mother to immolate herself for such a great exile? He did not say anything, thank God! But his heart was stirred by what he had just heard. He could not help finding some nobility in that language.

"Come on," the incubus added, "since your hour hasn't come, I'll release my prey again, although I have the right to seize it. Think about your father, Merlin—and you Séraphine, at least don't forget that you have a husband."

With these words, the incubus plunged into his dark realm. Merlin, Séraphine and Viviane went back across the dismal threshold in silence and saw the light again. Séraphine returned incontinently to her convent, whose door she walled up for a second time. Viviane did not leave Merlin's side. Merlin had not found his father as odious as he had been depicted.

After all, he said to himself, *he's my father. And who knows whether there was not at the start, some fault on the other side?*

Thus was avoided, that day, the combat between the father and the son. But open warfare, for having been delayed, could not fail to burst forth eventually.

VI

Merlin had not taken a hundred steps outside Hell when he encountered a pauper covered in rags. It was the first he had seen in the world. He contemplated him at fist as a marvel, and then felt troubled and gave him his purse.

Fifty paces further on, a pauper more wretched than the first was lying by the roadside; Merlin gave him his cloak. The pauper pointed out that his feet were bare; Merlin took off his shoes and gave them to him, adding his hat and his sky blue doublet.

He took another fifty steps and encountered a third pauper. It was a handsome young man who had found nothing to do with his hands and was eaten away by anger. Merlin apologized for having nothing to give him.

Immediately, the indignant young man raised his head and cried: "That's the rich all over! Hard, pitiless, miserly! They never have anything when it's a matter of giving. Curse them all!" And he continued his invective.

"I see, my friend," Merlin put in, "that poverty hasn't taken away your pride."

130

Then, approaching a chatelaine who was passing by on horseback, with a falcon on her wrist, he said to her: "I bring you a great joy."

"What?" asked the lady, stopping.

"A unique opportunity to give away your horse and your falcon."

"To whom?"

"To this wretch."

"You're mad, Merlin, I think," said the lady, darting a disdainful glance at the pauper. "What are you thinking?"

"Oh, Madame," said Merlin, "I've just come back from Hell; I didn't see anything there more terrible than what I see at this moment: impassivity, harshness and avarice on the face of an angel."

That response caused the lady to look into herself; she remembered that she had a heart; above all, she was ashamed of having been caught frowning with pursed lips, as if she had wrinkles.

She darted a more expansive glance at the wretch. Her astonishment was unequaled when she saw that he was a man, and that a wretch could have dark eyes and curly hair. She leapt lightly to the ground and handed her horse and falcon to Merlin.

"Here," she said. "I'm giving them to him."

That gesture melted the young man's heart like wax; poverty alone had distorted it. He immediately improvised lines of poetry born of his emotion, and, in his gratitude, he was already head-over-heels in love. They were the first lines that had ever been composed in that land and in that language.

The lady's name was Gabrielle, which inspired the young poet with the idea of comparing her to a gazelle, in order to have time to arrange his thoughts. That chance resonance made both of them smile. That was the origin of rhyme among the people of that land.

Astonished and even more delighted by that new, rhythmic language, of which she had had no inkling, the lady was prompted to a thousand reveries.

"What honeyed language," she said. "I've never heard anything like it in my castle. Is it the language of the poor?"

"No, Madame," said Merlin. "It's the language of love; I ought to have invented it."

With that, he told her that those lines were the most beautiful that had been composed, and how she had occasioned the miracle.

When she returned to her castle, the lady was gripped by a great ennui.

"Talk to me in verse, then," she said to the host of courtiers who wanted to be loved.

No one understood. They all seemed coarse and rude to her by comparison with what she had heard. She listened from the top of her tower; she could still hear the song of her servant in the valley. From that day on, one gave, the other received; both were replete.

That prodigy was one of the greatest that Merlin wrought. He reconciled the rich with the poor, and invented poetry at the same time.

VII

What was Merlin's recompense for spreading so many benefits through the world?

His recompense was this: in one of the places he had enchanted, he had built a dwelling at his whim. You would not have found it large enough or sumptuous enough for you, but it was exactly proportionate to his desires. Perhaps the main body of the building would have been too severe, had it not been cheered up at the two sides by two wings with Roman arches, each supported by twelve columns, in memory of the twelve knights. Around these columns wound garlands of honeysuckle and wild vines. A wooden gallery and an iron balustrade connected the two wings. Oh, how often they resonated under joyful or thoughtful footsteps!

Above it there was an orchard of sacred apple trees that always bore fruits and flowers; below it a gently-sloping garden, a trifle wild, planted with linden trees. Sometimes, a muffled groan emerged from the dormant waters, but the blue-tits put an end to it by twittering and fluttering in eccentric short hops, like dancing spirits, from tree to tree.

Every year, in that region, there were a certain number of serene, gilded, red-tinted days, such as are not seen anywhere else in the world, but they did not last long, scarcely beyond the month of May. As soon as June, the honeyed breath of nenuphar lilies and mallow expanded into the air, causing you to breathe melancholy itself. There was a softness, a languor and tears in everything, like presages of a soft sepulcher. What an indescribable, mystic, angelic, incorporeal odor emerged from the extenuated plants then! There was nothing of this world about it. I think the pacifying breath of the dead was exhaled with the myrrh of long hedges of hazelnuts and raspberry bushes, through the curtains of the clayey earth, and that breath passed through your hair.

The mystery was especially profound around the dormant pools into which the great oaks dipped their feet, shivering. A ruin, an old tower, emerged from the middle of the deep water, but no one was nearby; there was no boat to land there, no one to indicate the way. In the calices of water-borne flowers, sparkling white sylphs danced rounds, chasing one another hither and yon, and the airborne down of thistles was carried away by the breeze. It was there that the foxglove opened its large flowers, gaping like the mouths of serpents around a caduceus.

Motionless on the edge of a distant oat-field stood a heron, the hieroglyph of a world of dreams. Never was the screech of an axle heard in the clearings, never a herald in the depths of the forest. Sometimes there was a conflagration of dry grass, which no one had lit and no one thought of putting out.

Assuredly, the place could have been better chosen, but so what! Merlin had put his heart into it from the first day. He never disavowed it.

When he went to stroll in his garden, the bees, either because they were visiting the cornflowers in the neighboring hayfields, or the strawberry flowers, or the opium poppies, or because they preferred to settle on the new buds of the hawthorn, formed a chorus as he passed by, and cried out in their high-pitched voices: "Honor and glory to Merlin!"

With their matinal voices the bees woke up the other creatures, which said, all together: "Let nothing ever trouble the betrothal of Merlin and Viviane! Their happiness spreads over is. The future of the world is attached to their love. May no cloud ever come between them, for that cloud would cast its shadow over the earth, and the tempest would engender reptiles.

"The serenity of the heavens envelops everything. Viviane's breath expands over the wild roses hidden in the heather, and Merlin's wisdom fills the buzzing towns.

"We thought that we would not see the spring again, for the chill of death kept us enclosed in hollow trees or subterranean dwellings. The snow covered us with a shroud and the universe seemed dead. But when Viviane exhaled, a sacred breath penetrated our profound retreats. A quiver of life makes itself felt all the way to the heart of the oaks, when the footsteps of Viviane and Merlin have trodden the daisies in the meadows.

"Butterflies, sleeping the slumber of the dead in your white cocoons of silk, listen to the trump of the cicadas announcing the resurrection to the four winds! Quit your shrouds! Emerge from the sepulchers that you have woven for yourselves. Resuscitate, iridescent troupe, light souls! Winged flowers, do not scorn the flowers because they remain enchained to the earth, where you refuse to alight.

"Come, all of you who have a voice that the echo loves to repeat! Awaken, cicadas, to the eternal song! Bees who mingle murmur with toil; nightingales, inhabitants of bushy clearings; damsel-flies with azure corsages that hover over the sources of streams! Say, without wearying: *There is nothing as beautiful on earth as Viviane; there is nothing as wise as Merlin. May this moment last forever!*"

Plunged in a mute reverie, the good Merlin listened to the choir, under the linden-trees that were then in flower. Pensively, he held Viviane's hand in his, while drops of water fell from the vaults of grottoes into the profound source.

BOOK SEVEN: THE FORTUNE

I

Passing hour, pause! Let this day, this moment, never end![60]

Why do you flee, rapid dawns, sunlight, fiery days? Who hurries you? Nocturnal perfumes, morning breezes, buzzing bees, where are you going? It's here, it's here, that lies the emerald frontier at which it's necessary to stop.

You stop too, passing waves, vagabond stars! And you, my heart, don't hope for a better hour!

Beautiful rosy dawn, don't hasten toward noon; it will consume you. Splendid noon, don't hasten toward the paling dusk; and you, constellated dusk, don't rush toward the tenebrous night.

Giant shadows, don't grow any more at the foot of the serene mountains! All you spirits, the soul of things, don't go beyond this azure hour.

They had rediscovered the Eden of our first ancestors; they had brought back Paradise to earth. Their eyes were attached to one another; they drank an invisible philter, which descended from the clouds, for inexhaustible hours. They loved everything they saw, for everything, and every creature, was filled with their love. They must have thought that benevolent eternity had commenced for them.

Nothing informed them of the succession of the hours and the moments. Every instant seemed to be the first that they had ever encountered; at the same time they had the sentiment of always having loved one another. How could that have been the case? I only know that it was.

Forget that I compared their happiness to that of our first ancestors! My heroes were happier than the inhabitants of Eden. For Adam and Eve had a third party perpetually between them: a divine host that held them in a respect bordering on dread. Sometimes, too, the serpent coiled around the tree, hissing, suddenly chilled their gazes and their voices. Their love was more cosmogonic, more religious, than that of Merlin and Viviane, but it was assuredly less passionate.

Merlin and Viviane did not encounter any divine stroller, or archangel with golden wings, or serpent with a woman's head. They only encountered, saw, heard and sought out one another—and perhaps, in that, they were egotists. No

---

[60] Hermione's notes record that this line was written in the valley of the Linth, and subtly suggests that this passage is a transfiguration of the life that she and Quinet shared there, surely identifying herself more completely with Viviane, at this point in the story, than is justified.

superhuman law stopped them at bends in the path when they were picking the fruits with which heir garden was filled. No apprehension, no threat, no flaming sword. They did not converse with the animals because they had no need to speak to them. A gesture of the hand or the eyes was sufficient for them to be obeyed.

They did not sing the morning hymn to the Elohim, but life there was a continuous hymn, addressed to one another. Doubtless they were not overly deified, especially the early morning hours when they were both dazzled by one another after the darkness. That was their fault. You shall see how they expiated it.

How many times our first ancestors must have been saddened by the desire of disobedience, the presentiment of the irrevocable fall! They desired what was forbidden to them; in their felicity there was already a commencement of dolor. It was not so with Merlin and Viviane. Either by virtue of blindness or ignorance, they had no notion of the fall.

What am I saying? They had an entirely contrary sentiment. After every caress they found one another embellished, and the world with them. In addition, they had no vain curiosity; they believed that they possessed everything as soon as their hands were interlaced. No muffled anxiety of mind and soul ever tormented the wise Merlin when his lips were glued to Viviane's. He thought then that he knew everything. What did it matter to him if the storm made the thorny branches of the tree of knowledge quiver above his head?

Sometimes my hero extended love as far as superstition. Fragments of rock that ten men of our day could not have lifted were child's play for him. He stood them on top of one another and formed an altar of them, an eternal monument to felicity. Oh, if he had known how perishable felicity was, he would have made edifices of clay, not granite. When the stones were standing he took Viviane in his arms and helped her to climb on top of them. Viviane leapt about like a wild mountain goat, and smiled at the Enchanter.

As for him, ever serious, he contemplated her silently, and adored her.

When you encounter one of those mysterious dolmens somewhere in the middle of a heath, say boldly: "The powerful Merlin moved these stones." Love sees everything, knows everything, and explains everything.

Did they never quarrel? Were they the same all the time. Did they never pronounce a word they wished they had held back? If they did, I think that it was very rare, two or three times a year at the most, and then the caprice—for those rare misunderstandings don't merit any other name—only lasted a moment. I would rather have said a second, if those moments had not been so many eternities.

Afterwards, a sacred tear scarcely moistened the eyelid, and that tear produced the effect of dew in a burning landscape. No trace of it remained in the heart, which felt, on the contrary, renewed. Suspended momentarily, life resumed its precipitate flow. It was like an almost ungraspable dissonance that a skillful artist throws into the weave of his melodies in order to heighten their value. For we are such imperfect beings that good only pleases us on condition that it is mixed with a tiny flaw.

Furthermore, each of them conserved their own character even in those difficult moments. Viviane, more fickle, also recovered more rapidly. She was never seen so serene as when one of those clouds had just passed over her face. Merlin had a more even humor; by way of compensation, when he fell, it was more heavily and he had more difficulty getting up again. A more terrestrial pride chained him to his fault. But when he was able to vanquish himself, how he was able to humiliate himself! He begged for pardon passionately, as if he had committed a crime. It would, indeed, have been an unpardonable crime to spoil the greatest felicity that there will ever be on earth.

They did not only nourish themselves on the fruit of the trees, or slake their thirst uniquely with the water of the streams. A few faithful servants prepared modest but appropriate meals for them; dairy products, honey, eggs from their poultry-yard, saffroned cakes, a little game and a little claret wine from the nearby coast was sufficient.

Few people visited them. Everyone feared being importunate. A few old harpists were always welcome in Merlin and Viviane's dwelling. As for them, they only sought the marvelous beings that we have encountered with them in the forest of Dombes. Those they visited regularly twice a week. The comparison they made between those purely ideal existences and their own, so replete, had a great deal to do with the pleasure they obtained in their company. "How happy I am to have received the entire gift of life!" exclaimed Merlin, every time they came back from one of those visits.

How did they pass their days? Nothing was more regular. In the mornings they read the magic book together. That was their principal occupation. Merlin, resting his head on Viviane's shoulder and putting his arms around her, read the sacred words in a low voice. As they fell from his mouth, they spread happy fates far and wide over the blossoming worlds, for the rest of the day. Was there a cloud somewhere in the sky or on a darkening forehead? It disappeared immediately; a gently dewy light penetrated human hearts. Everything in the distance felt rejuvenated, without even knowing to whom they owed that breath of unexpected felicity.

After that, they sang, not great savant hymns or laborious canticles, but petty tunes that they had adapted to their two voices; and the nightingales, the siskins emerging from meadows, reed-beds, rose-bushes and clumps of gladioli came and competed with them, sometimes drowning out their songs.

At the fall of dusk, they were often seen riding on black horses through the narrow clearings or the flowering wheat-fields. They preferred to go on foot, however, because their hands could more easily intertwine like ivy.

What did they talk about? Their subjects of conversation were very various. First of all, themselves, and then themselves again; after that, the stars, the unknown worlds, Sirius, Saturn, the cornflower in the furrow, the music of the spheres; doubtless also sacred politics, ideal justice, the felicity of all future beings; the joy of the nations that would take them for guides, or only for counselors; liberty given without avarice to whoever wanted it; at other times, sleep and a few dreams with a little glory; then a hank of hair, a ribbon, a cobweb, the forgotten book of magic, open to the rain under a linden tree; then their little world again, the song of the cricket, their garden; all that punctuated by kisses and bursts of merriment, as if a playful spirit were laughing next to them in the grassy tufts of the meadow.

Every spring they sent messengers abroad, to search as far away as Libya for strange animals, which they amused themselves by taming with a mere glance. When those savage beasts had become gentler than lambs, they gave the smaller ones to their neighbors. They could not bear anything around them that reminded them of the cares and miseries of humans. Their poultry-yard was guarded by a beautiful bird that served as a shepherd. As for the buffalo, they introduced the first among us. Its black face frightened Viviane at first, and she refused to go near it. Merlin made her ashamed of hr fear. From that day on, she could get the monsters to follow her like a flock of ewes. Nothing was more charming than to see her playing with one of them while leading it by its horn the color of ebony.

They also liked to sow strange plants whose seeds were brought to them by bluebirds that they had trained for that purpose. As soon as the bird came back from its voyage it perched on Viviane's shoulder, shaking its wings. Viviane kissed the beautiful messenger, which flew off again joyfully. Often, before it departed, she gave it a breadcrumb from her lips; after which, picking up the precious seeds, she went to sow it in the garden. Thus it was that jasmine, lilac and acacia, not to mention a host of climbing plants, all appropriate to forming amorous bowers, were eventually brought together from all the corners of the earth in Merlin's garden; he never refused their seed to anyone who asked for it.

What else did they do? It has been said that they played chess. They soon gave up; Viviane did not like it when she lost. The wise Merlin was not always wise enough to let her win. Then again, they found that the game prevented them from dreaming about one another. They abandoned it for other dreams that they invented every day. There were often words that only had meaning for them, inconsequential murmurs, a human twittering or cooing, more melodious than the twittering of warblers and blue-tits in the branches of the willows.

How quickly days thus filled came to an end! And they did not prolong them artificially with the blinding light of lamps. They did not disturb the order marked by nature, but meekly followed the counsel of the skies. After having lived during the day like the woodland birds, they went to bed like them, or very nearly, an hour after the sun had disappeared. Long feverish late nights never paled their cheeks. Why should they refuse salutary sleep? They knew that the next day would rise for them more beautiful than the day before.

II

They loved one another and they were happy; I can assure you of that. The monuments of their felicity are innumerable; you cannot take a step without encountering them in our heather. What is wrong with people, if such testimony is not sufficient for them? What thoughts, what memories, what sentiments have ever left such imprints? The rocks themselves speak. We believe in the pyramids because they inform us of death; can we not believe in the dolmens because they inform us of the eternal happiness of two individuals? Come on, skeptics, doubters of everything, is it necessary to doubt what is written before our eyes in exclamation marks of granite twenty cubits high?

Yes, they were happy, as I said—but they ceased to be, and that is where the difficulty commences for me. It's easy to write alongside one another words as discordant as paradise and hell. Experience enables you immediately to understand such opposed states, felicity in the morning, despair in the evening. That is seen, and will be seen. But to bring those things into accord on the same page, to pass harmoniously from an excess of good to a excess of evil, from smiles to tears, to explain everything, to smooth everything out, to reconcile everything—that is the most difficult part of my task.

Why demand, anyway, that a book written by a terrestrial hand should be more harmonious and better connected than the book of destiny? That one doesn't give reasons for any changes; it doesn't manage any transitions. Everything therein is abrupt and unexpected. Turn the page, and heaven and earth have changed their face. The most intoxicating passage finishes with a cry of pain. And the cause, the motive, where are they?

No condemnation weighed upon their heads, No archangel armed with a flaming sword expelled Merlin and Viviane shamefully from their Eden. If they had wanted to, they would have been able to remain in the paradise; perhaps they would still be there.

But no! They alone banished themselves from it; they alone forbade the return. They wanted it; no one else is responsible for what followed.

Were they weary of unalloyed happiness? They had never loved one another more. Was it the effort of a long reflection? Anyone who would have said to them "You will seek one another tomorrow and will not find one another" would have transpierced them with his words. Was it a caprice, a whim, a test, a moment of bad temper, a flash of pride that they were unable to vanquish, a dispute over a game of chess? Look, seek, examine yourself, or, rather, have the patience to wait. I can assure you in advance that the cause will be found proportional to the effect.

That day, Viviane, had put on her best clothes, as if for a solemn occasion. When Merlin came in he found her up, striding back and forth with her arms

138

folded. Her immobile eyes were armed with a strange resolution—but the good Merlin did not notice that at first.

However, she stopped abruptly in the middle of the arbor and, without looking at him, in a voice that sprang forth like a torrent after which everything is dried up irredeemably, she uttered these precipitate words:

"Merlin, it's necessary for us to separate."

Merlin began to smile, and his lips remained petrified for some time. He conserved the impression of past felicity in the first grip of an infinite dolor, for his eyes had settled upon her and he had encountered one of those gazes of bronze that chill the words in the depths of the heart.

Doubtless he should have thrown himself down at her feet, bathed them with tears, but his eyes were dry. Perhaps dolor had dried up his heart, ordinarily so open and so expansive; perhaps indignation had hardened it momentarily. Perhaps, too, pride, that serpent that delights in our ruin, reared up at that moment in his soul. Through the confused, disorderly words that pressed upon his lips, without being able to burst through, he had the misfortune to reply:

"Yes, I'll go."

He was wrong a thousand times over. But it was still no more than a childish game, an extravagance such as the best often commit, a word that he could have effaced immediately with another. It would only have required one tear, on convulsive clutch of the hand. But he was obstinate in that speech, solely because he had pronounced it and had not had the strength to hold it back while it was still half-formed on his lips.

Then, Viviane's increasingly inflexible gaze completed his doom.

He throws himself on his dolor as a man throws himself on his sword and pierces his breast with it, without being able to draw it out again. The more resolution and coldness Viviane shows, the angrier Merlin gets. In the end, he almost storms out.

He goes down the steps that he will never climb again. Oh, why does he not come back? Why does he not fall beneath Viviane's feet? Why, at least, does he not turn his head once toward the open window? Their voices might have been able to respond to one another, their eyes to meet. Soon, in a few moments, they will be lost to one another.

Has the wise Merlin gone insane, then? He draws away with long strides. So long as he thinks he is visible, I don't know what blind anger sustains him. Doubtless some interior demon has just slipped into his. Without seeing, without hearing, an infernal force aids him to destroy himself. But as soon as he has passed a certain clump of trees and is certain that he cannot be observed, all that artificial strength abandons him immediately. His body collapses and trembles. A mortal sweat inundates his face; one more step and he lets himself fall by the side of the path, his eyes staring, his head slumped over his chest.

No one hears his sobs. They remain locked in his bosom.

O passer-by, look at the great Enchanter, who, scarcely a moment ago, lent his smile to everything. What remains of him? Is he a man or a child? Who would not pity him? But who could even recognize him?

Incapable at that moment of any reflection, Merlin nevertheless felt that a part of his power had been irreparably destroyed. But he did not seek to explain what had happened. In any case, no words would have been adequate to express what he was experiencing. A world crumbling, a void hollowed out all the way to the utmost depths of Hell, a chaos where there as a Heaven—all of that would only have given the slightest indication of what it was necessary to say. The most probable thing is that he had lost the gift of enchantment, but that was the thing he cared about least, for the moment.

What does it matter to him if the disillusioned world loses its magic, if a bleak gray veil extends over half the earth, if all the roses wither at the same time? In the egotism of dolor, he is only occupied with what he has lost himself. He seeks a gaze that he no longer encounters; he holds his breath to listen for light footsteps, the sound of which does not reach him. Above all, he feels his heart weighing in his breast like a stone, and he is silent.

But what my hero does not say, I must say in his stead, in the interest of those who seek the instruction in this story. They have seen in this chapter that there are exceedingly brief words, or rather syllables, whose consequences are irreparable. They will learn here to die a hundred times rather than pronounce them. A little further on they will see that a resentment, an unjust remark, a lovers' quarrel, a rancor, a grain of darnel in the good wheat, can have the most disastrous consequences for the economy of the world.

If my heroes had only petty personal interests at stake, if their lives had not been mingled at all with universal life, I would not bother to report their disputes to the readers, who, I suppose, have their own troubles to occupy them.[61]

III

The stars were fading, and the sun was about to rise when Merlin opened his eyes. He perceived that he was in the enchanted forest, where he was accustomed to visit the ideal creatures whose king he was. His first impulse, on recognizing that location, was not without tenderness, for he believed momentarily that he was relieved of the crushing weight of real existence, and that he was

---

[61] The only comment made by Hermione's notes on this chapter is: "Legend demands the rupture of Merlin and Viviane, as does the interest of the story." She comments immediately thereafter that in the account of the pilgrimages, "autobiography reappears." In one of the volumes of biography that she published after Quinet's death, however, she quotes this scene as a figurative reflection of Quinet's rupture with Minna in 1831.

140

about to be confused with those imaginary individuals and to float with them between reality and the void.

As glad as he had been before to be in entire possession of existence, he would then have been to be nothing but a specter, a larva. Already he was swearing to himself never to emerge again from the company of the airy individuals he had known in the depths of those forests. For a long time he searched, and called out, but in vain. All the celestial forms that had once come running to him of their own accord had disappeared. None responded to his voice. He heard in the distance, however, the sound of an ax in a clump of old mossy oaks. He ran in that direction.

"Is that you," he cried, "happy spirits, who have not yet tasted the cruel beverage of real life? Come, surround me, hide me, don't let me leave this blessed enclosure again!" On coming closer, he was astonished to encounter, instead of the accustomed residents, a half-dressed peasant, who had come early that morning to obtain his provision of firewood on the sly, for fear of foresters.

He was a serf from the hamlet of Ripes. Tall of stature—or, rather, gigantic—his unkempt hair falling over his shoulders, his face shaven, resembling a cyclops but nevertheless human, his blue eyes wide, his nose like a bird's beak, a trifle thin, he walked heavily, because, apart from the fact that he was wearing clogs, the cold fever had gripped him all that year. He still had a somewhat swollen spleen.

"What's your name?" Merlin asked him.

"Jacques Bonhomme Populus,"[62] replied the rustic. "I know who you are—you're the enchanter Merlin."

Without paying any attention to that reply, Merlin continued: "Since you live in this forest, take me to the marvelous beings who make their dwelling here. Where are they? I can't find them this morning."

"Who are you talking about? No one other than me has ever lived in this forest."

Merlin explained to Jacques that it was a matter of individuals clad in red and gold, who neither ate nor drank, and lived in constant expectation. Jacques Bonhomme, already shaken by those words—for no one in the world was more credulous than him—tried momentarily to remember whether he had ever encountered individuals similar to those Merlin described. In spite of his good will, he could not succeed in remembering a single one. All he had heard were whispers in the densest part of the forest at daybreak and dusk.

"That's them," said Merlin.

"Oh, as for their voices, I've heard them clearly," Jacques went on. "It's as if I'd seen them."

"Exactly!" exclaimed Merlin.

---

[62] "Jacques Bonhomme" is generalized nickname for French peasants, used to belittle them; the Latin *populus* means "the people."

Reciprocally encouraged by these remarks, they both set off again in search of the happy people, and as the wood was not very large, they had looked in every corner of it before dark, but they had not found the slightest trace of those they sought. With that, Merlin understood, not without bitterness, that he had lost the gift of seeing the invisible world, and that he had descended by at least one step from the emparadised realm in which he had lived before.

IV

The next day, the sun was very hot; toward midday they were sitting in the shade of a large beech-tree, waiting for the heat to die down. Merlin was almost exhausted, but Jacques' ingenuousness did not displease him, and they felt irresistibly drawn to one another.

A long time before daybreak, Jacques had been mulling over a thought that he dared not express. He ended up voicing it anyway, on seeing the Merlin's generosity and simplicity, which even despair had not been able to alter.

"Ah!" Jacques murmured, crossing his hands. "If Monseigneur Merlin would please tell my fortune..."

"I'd like that," Merlin replied, and immediately took Jacques Bonhomme's hand in his.

It was a broad, bony, red-tinted hand made for handling and bending iron. After having considered it attentively, the Enchanter obligingly spoke as follows:

"The first thing that appears to me in these lines, Jacques Bonhomme, is that you'll have a numerous posterity."

"Good!"

"More numerous than that of Abraham."

"And the second thing?" asked Jacques.

"The second thing is that you'll often be duped."

"But not always?"

"Wait, my son! Not always, but often, and for a long time," Merlin repeated, gravely emphasizing every syllable. "You'll change masters frequently."

"Will I sometimes be my own?"

"Rarely."

Jacques Bonhomme's broad face darkened.

"Don't be discouraged, my son. There are better signs."

"What are they?" asked the bewildered rustic.

In a kind of exaltation, which increased as he went on, Merlin continued: "To begin with, plagues, blood-sweats, tears, iron, jails and dungeons; a somber manor for the master, a little straw and dolor for you."

"That's a long list, Seigneur Merlin. Will it never end?"

"Yes, it will end. Your armies will cover the earth; they will carry justice with them; they will sow glory."

"My armies! Do you think so, Monsieur? Where are they, my armies? I only have five goats and two cows."

"The isles, I tell you, will be submissive to you, and the continents will roar beneath your feet."

"After all, why shouldn't I, too, be a chief of archers? Why shouldn't I wear armor, like the others? Yes, I'll wear it, word of an honest man; we won't tolerate the strongest beating the weakest; you can take my word for it, *Montjoie et Saint Denis!*[63] I can't wait for the battle. The dust is already enveloping me and blinding me. Some advice, Monsieur Enchanter! Let's suppose for a moment that that big oak is the enemy. My troops are with me, this is my iron-tipped baton. What do I do now? Where do I place myself to strike hardest? To the right or the left? Where shall I begin the attack? I'm already in the skirmish."

Merlin let Jacques Bonhomme vent himself, as he was already in the grip of the excitement of battle. Then he reprimanded him gently, as follows:

"On seeing how the mere word *war* intoxicates you with a fine folly, I fear that you might drink far more than necessary from that cup. If you allow yourself to be dazzled so easily by the clash of swords, how will you ever get out of servitude? You resemble a bear that one leads by a sparkling iron ring passed through its nose, to the sound of a tambourine. To be sure, I have no anxiety about your courage in the killing-field that you'll call fields of glory, but I don't know whether you'll show the same courage in matters of intellect."

"The same!" Jacques put in.

"Know, Jacques Bonhomme," Merlin went on, severely, "that it's necessary never to interrupt enchanters when they're speaking. If you do, unless they're as clairvoyant as I'm fortunate to be, they lose the thread of their thought, and those who interrogate them impatiently remain forever lost in an inextricable tangle from which it's impossible to escape. Realize the danger you're running because of your own fault, and try to refrain another time."

Jacques swallowed the words that were on the tip of his tongue.

"Now give me that hand," Merlin continued, increasingly carried away by the wings of divination. "Rejoice, Jacques Bonhomme! I see you clearly here, marching to the conquest of the Lord's tomb. What a cohort of peoples you're drawing after you, my lad! Yes, it's really you who's carrying the banner. But by these three wrinkles I recognize that you'll have great difficulties to endure in order to take Jerusalem: hunger, thirst, the desert, and numerous wounds."

---

[63] The traditional battle-cry of French armies, usually omitting the "et"; its origin is unclear, but St. Denis became the second patron saint of Paris, and its kings were buried in his basilica there. Brewer's *Dictionary of Phrase and Fable* claims that *Montjoie* in a corruption of *Mont Jovis*, that being the name of mounds used are direction-markers, dismissing the alternative explanation that it derived from "*mon joie*" [my hope], but who knows?

"Never mind that, Monsieur. Let's go on—I'm with you. The city's very strong, then?"

"Strong enough."

"Surrounded by high walls?"

"Yes."

"Can they be scaled?"

"With difficulty."

"It's necessary to use ambushes, then. How many souls are in the city?"

"Nearly a million."

"So much the better; we'll starve them out. After that, will I take the city?"

"Undoubtedly you'll take it."

"That's good. I'll stay there as the overlord of the land."

"Don't delude yourself, my poor Jacques. It will be necessary to leave."

"What? I'll leave? But in fact, what's the point of staying there. Haven't I taken the city in order to be able to say, when I come back to the village: *I've been there.* And everyone will look at me, amazed, and say: *There's Jacques! It's really him; he's come back from the holy tomb. He was the first to climb into the breach of Calvary.* Let's see, in truth, what more will I be able to I want when we receive here, under this tree, the key to the city on a silver platter? Continue, I beg you."

"Listen, Jacques. Here I see your tall son; he will harness to the same yoke of law the rich and the poor. Wait—I can read his name. You'll call him Marcel."

"Yes, Seigneur, but you shall be his godfather."

"Gladly," said the Enchanter. After a momentary pause, he continued: "What do I see in the palm of this hand? A plain, yes, a village, a bare wood, and under the enchanted tree, a shepherdess. There she is, taking the banner and armor. She's the one who will lead your army, Jacques Bonhomme; you'll only have to follow her along the right path. Can you see her on that bridge, clad in iron, with a white plume, on her palfrey? Where is she going? The hand that led the flock is now guiding men of war. All of them kneel before her. Do you see her?"

At this point, Jacques Bonhomme could not help bursting forth; as he had been asked a question, he thought that it was the moment to reply. He exclaimed: "A shepherdess, Seigneur, you say? Yes, I see her, in my mind's eye. I'll wager that she's one of my sisters, Jeanne or Jacqueline. Which? I think it's Jeanne. Oh, no man's as good at her at putting two oxen under the yoke. Courageous, too, gentle, obedient, scornful of the young gallants. God knows that if she told me to go into the fire, I'd go, sure of not singeing a hair."

Not listening, Merlin kept silent. At his final words, the oaks and pines of the forest had resonated and leaned toward one another, as if the soil of France were responding to them. Merlin sensed that he had not lost all of his powers of enchantment at a stroke. He rediscovered a little hope in his heart.

144

"Here's something extraordinary, which has never happened before in my life as an enchanter. In this line, my poor Jacques, I lose sight of you. You become so small, so poor, that you disappear. A little while ago, I could only see you. You filled the cities and the kingdoms with your rumors. You resembled the sea swollen by the tempest. Now, only two or three men are disposed on the land, and you've disappeared. There you are, weaker, more wretched, more downcast than the scarab searching for its nourishment in filth. In the end, I can no longer see you at all. What a strange destiny yours is!"

"Doubtless, Monsieur, at that moment I'm asleep on the straw, or in a furrow, or under the table, which occasionally happens to me. But fear not: I'll wake up; just look for me for a moment—there, for instance, where I move my little finger. You'll find me again."

"Indeed," said the Enchanter, after a long examination. "I've found you; you've woken up. But, O horror, my friend! You have a dagger in your hand. Who is pursuing you crying: 'Long live the masses!'? How you've changed! What are you doing with your pike? Good God, stop! Is that really you, murdering that honest man on a street corner, on Saint Bartholomew's Day? Cover your face, Jacques Bonhomme, and weep!"

"Why should I veil myself, Monsieur? Assuredly, that isn't me, or any Jacques. My family is well-known. Oh, if I'd done something like that, I wouldn't want to raise my eyes from the ground again. In war, when the bugle has sounded and warned the enemy, that's different. Yes, indeed! But at night, in a back street—get away! That's not me, I swear. Look harder."

The Enchanter went on: "How changed you are! That's no longer Jacques Bonhomme—it's Monsieur Jacques. It's no longer a serf, barefoot in a smock. What! Lace, and a wig that hangs down to your waist; an arrogant and disdainful expression! Where have you made that fortune, Monsieur Jacques? Why are you looking down from so high at the world at your feet? Don't you recognize your forefathers any longer?"

"Again, Monsieur, that's not me. Someone's disguised himself in my place. Me, disown my forefathers? I'm not proud—everyone knows that. It's not my fault."

"Indeed, Jacques, here you are again, small, humble. You're crawling, Jacques Bonhomme; I recognize you in that. It's really you! The master has whistled, the basset hound appears, ear to the ground. Go on, run! Flush out the game for the hunter. But no, that's no longer you. You've changed again. Who are, you, then, Jacques Bonhomme? Merlin is weary. Merlin is exhausted from chasing you. You flee, you change your form, determination, face, heart and color as he tries to grasp you. I heft you humble and gentle; here you are, superb again, your head lost in the clouds! Why are you breaking what you have built? The sea, the winds, the reeds are models of constancy by comparison with you, Jacques Bonhomme. Just now, I saw you with my own eye building those keeps; why are you now rushing to demolish them? What are you doing to those towers and turrets? Oh, so much blood, poor Jacques! More blood! Look at your hands! How many times will you be reproached for that, even by your own? How will you wash them? You'll be tracked by means of that blood. How will you bring justice out of that fiery source?"

"Justice will wash me, Monsieur. I'm Jacques Bonhomme, and haven't done any of what I'm accused of doing."

"You, so mild, so human, how are you able to be so pitiless?"

"It must be the case. Monsieur, that I was deceived that day, or driven to extremes. I'm not, believe me, a sea or a reed, but an honest man who only demands his due. Oh, perhaps I was driven to lose my temper. Perhaps someone made me false promises that day, refused me what was my right, or stole my cattle and my goats! For that's true, Monsieur—for those animals, I'd no longer know myself."

"That's enough," said the Enchanter. "Let's not talk about it anymore. Demand your due, my friend; nothing is more just—but try, as much as possible, not to employ violence, which is the means of the wicked rather than the good."

"I'm damned then, Monsieur?" exclaimed Jacques, and began to weep.

Merlin immediately consoled him, saying: "Remember, my friend, that nothing is yet lost. Everything I've said only concerns the future, and not what has happened."

"That's true," said Jacques, as if falling from the clouds.

"It's up to you to belie the oracle, in everything injurious to your renown."

"I intend to do that, Monsieur."

"How will you go about it?"

"In truth, Monsieur, I'll learn to read, and I'll ask Monsieur the Enchanter to lend me one of his books, for it's a great deal to have even one in the cottage and to look at it from time to time."

"Nothing is more true," said the Enchanter, "but be careful not to hurt your brain. For perfectly honest men who have read enchanted books, Jacques Bonhomme, have been known to become ensorcelled themselves, to the extent that they can no longer tell their right hand from the left."

With those words, Merlin gave Jacques the book of his prophecies. "Here," he said. "Nothing like that can happen to you."

Jacques Bonhomme accepted the book, kissed it, and said: "How will it all end, Seigneur Merlin?"

"Well," Merlin replied.

"I'm beginning to believe so."

"There's no doubt about it," said Merlin.

And they continued to get excited. Increasingly carried away by the genius of divination, the Enchanter was no longer worrying at all about whether Jacques had understood him. Jacques did not make any effort to understand Merlin. Moving from one ecstasy to the next, they both found themselves at opposite poles of the intellectual world. They replied to one another without

146

caring whether they understood one another. But what did it matter? Their tongues were disparate, but their hearts were in perfect accord.

"The dust of the ancestors will be renewed!" cried Merlin.

"Great God!" said Jacques. "There'll be a fine feast!"

"The land will be flowing with rivers of milk!"

"Adieu, my goats and my cows!"

"The mountains of Gaul will distill the honey of Greece."

"We'll no longer have to labor to sow, to sow in order to harvest."

"You'll rise up with me into the Milky Way, at you'll take your seat at the highest point of the ecliptic."

"Yes, certainly; I'll sit down beneath you at the helm of the cart, like a good servant."

"No, not beneath me," Merlin interjected, indulgently, "but in the midst of the shining radiance of justice."

"Oh yes!" relied Jacques Bonhomme. "On the straight road that leads to Heaven."

"The isles of Cambria and Cornwall will quiver with joy. The worlds will be as white as swans."

"And the swallows will arrive at Christmas."

"Arise, infinite hopes, immaculate auroras, sublime thoughts that draw the heavens as the horses draw the cart!"

"Get out of bed, idle servants, it's broad daylight!"

"Universe, put on your joyful adornment!"

"Jacqueline, put on your wedding dress!"

"O incomprehensible abyss!"

"O Virgin Mary!"

"O infinity!"

"O Jesus."

There the two voices stopped. The ecstasy was the same on either side. A long silence followed.

Delighted by an enthusiasm that he had never felt before, Jacques Bonhomme judged, soundly, that in order to accomplish his destiny, he could do no better than to attach himself to the Enchanter's footsteps—with which the good Merlin agreed.

All Jacques asked was a day or two to inform his family and make his preparations. He found that easy because of the disappearance of his livestock, which had been stolen from him during his absence by a horde of long-haired Gaulish Franks. Jacques paid scarcely any attention to that occurrence, which would have overwhelmed him with despair at any other time. After having gathered up the few clothes he had left, he came back to the Enchanter, whom he found in the place where he had left him.

From that moment on, no one ever saw the sage Merlin without seeing Jacques Bonhomme close by, dazed by admiration—and thus this story is enriched by the character in question, at the very moment when his appearance might be most useful. Any sooner would have been premature; any later, and it would have been untimely. But everything has its place and its time in this story, as in nature itself.

BOOK EIGHT: PILGRIMAGES

I

And I too am following Merlin's fortunes at a slow pace. With him, I depart, without knowing where my journey will take me. Soon, I shall have lost sight of the most beloved things of my homeland. Here are the trees, the houses, the woods, the fields and the familiar mountains, still displayed to my gaze—but where are those who accompanied me at the outset? Some, I believe, are waving to me. Perhaps it's only an illusion. Their voices reach my ears, though...

Yes, it's them that I can hear, sad and grave, as at the moment when those that are loved leave forever. To their cry of adieu, repeated from shore to shore, I reply with a sigh, or rather by an exclamation of hope, an adieu of good omen.

Here commence Merlin's pilgrimages. He did not go, as other pilgrims do, to visit a relic or to accomplish a vow. Dolor drove him. He marched ahead, hoping to change his thoughts by changing horizons. Perhaps, too, he was not sorry to discover the exact extent to which he had conserved the gift of enchanting the earth.

It was, I think, on a cool and flowery Easter Monday morning that he started out on his voyages. He walked ahead, with Jacques Bonhomme behind him, unless the Enchanter called him in order to talk as they went along. They were both followed by their black dog.

That company had nothing imposing about it, but the greatest kings on earth bowed their heads when they encountered the powerful Merlin in their path. Nations passed before him; if he found them desolate, he groaned with them; or of they were asleep, he touched them with his hand to awaken them from their leaden slumber. Then he gave them laws: *Jura dabat populis*, says the chronicle that I am translating, without adding any reflection or idea to it, as any historian worthy of the name ought to do.[64]

Merlin was about to leave France by the Breton Sea. He only had one more step to take to cross the frontier. At that moment he stopped under the postern of Calais and darted a long glance around him.

"Adieu, honored France!" he said, with a sigh. "How many times will you crack, like the shiny ice, under the feet of the man who entrusts himself to your gleam? Shall my eyes ever see you again? Will this worm-eaten door ever reopen to me? At that thought my soul is troubled, as if I were descending to the

---

[64] The quotation from which the Latin phrase is taken, whose meaning is indicated in the previous phrase, is from Ovid's *Metamorphoses*, but it was frequently quoted out of context, especially in Biblical commentaries.

bottom of the sea of anguish. And yet, it's better not to see you again then to witness your troubles without being able to cure them. How many times have I worn out the strength of my heart for you, almost always in vain? It hurts so much! The thought of it is killing me. I'm going to search far and wide for a simple to heal your wounds. Dig me a tomb in advance under a talking stone, and put it in a place reserved for saviors to come."[65]

He asked the sailors what the weather was like and whether the wind was blowing from the north. The sea was placid; not a ripple disturbed it, although a leaden sky weighed upon it everywhere. Vessels were skimming the tranquil water, but the tempest was in the clouds. At the sight of that singular contrast, he said as he embarked:

"You too, when iniquity amasses over your head, remain calm and serene. What winged thoughts surge unexpectedly from your mind, as white as the sails that emerge at this moment from the bitter well of the Ocean."

That said, he set out, his heart a little less heavy.

The first country visited by Merlin was Great Britain. It was then called Albion. When he disembarked he was met at Dover, near the shore, by the three witches of the three islands, their eyes ablaze, their hair flowing over their shoulders. They showed him around the castle, which, at that time, had been reduced to a fragment of a crumbling tower. They visited the ruins.

"Woe, woe!" cried the prophet. "I breathe homicide here. Macbeth will be king; the three islands will acclaim him!"

"We know," said the seeresses, who were utterly ignorant of the fact, and they fell silent. But when they left that place, they went to post themselves on the heath and made the cry resound throughout the three islands: "Macbeth, you shall be king!"—which still resonates. They would thus have all the honor of the prophecy; they have retained it.

Merlin smiled at that fraud. He had known for a long time that prophets steal their prophecies from one another.

Without seeking that company any longer, he penetrated inland. The only individual with whom he had much communication, linking up on a whim, was the famous Robin Hood, a great poacher of that era, a great lover of crossroads, always hunting, always singing, something of a thief, something of a pirate, whom he taught to discover springs, to shear Scottish sheep, to fatten livestock, to dig mines, to burn coal and to work metals, and who paid his back with a few

---

[65] Hermione's notes repeat this paragraph in full, claiming that it relates to 11 December 1851, when Quinet's banishment began, but notes that before describing symbolically his actual exile in Belgium and then Switzerland, it recalls journeys had had made long before, in the 1820s.

ballads, some of which are still in favor today, including the most charming of all: "Do you know the poacher?"[66]

What Merlin admired unreservedly was the wide eyes of the women of the country. He compared them to primroses blooming under the snow. As for the men, he thought for a long time that they were the best in the world, beneath their flowery mannerisms. Unfortunately, he ended up convincing himself that most of them had a piratical soul.

Prodigal with enchantments, he spread them around in those days without keeping count. Age, reflection, and, I think, human ingratitude, was later to render him more circumspect.

Albion took advantage of his inexperience. At the sole request of a few lords, who emerged from their rotten boroughs and came to meet him what did he not do in a matter of days? Domesticating the dragons of Kylburn, planting the red rose in the gardens of York, the white rose in the groves of Lancaster, forging the crown of the Ocean with his own hands, sowing green Erin with emeralds, putting a sculpted bit in the mouths of the horses of the sea, building the tower of the City with exceedingly somber corridors, hidden redoubts, vaults, and padlocked doors to serve as hostelries for deposed kings and even their phantoms, preparing a place at table for Banquo's ghost...what else? A thousand other things—and all of it nobly and simply, without anyone begging him to do it.

When the inhabitants of Cambria saw themselves so easily replete, they conceived an ardent pride, mingled above all with a harshness and injustice for the rest of the world, because they attributed everything to themselves. Far from feeling the slightest gratitude to Merlin, they scarcely looked at him, with an arrogant expression in which conceit was all too easily visible.

True, if they saw him in a public place, at Hyde Park or in a square, they would shake his hand, but they did not invite him to their homes, to their houses or their cottages, much less their castles. They even disparaged his works. Forging the green crown of the Ocean? A good trick, in truth. Could he do the same, then, for the lords' lands. And then again, was he a gentleman?

These words, and other too, murmured in a hiss, were unfailingly reported to Merlin by Robin Hood, who was surprised at first, but also felt pity. That pity changed into indignation, however, when he was walking on the beach and discovered this:

On the highest cliff, in a very obvious place, the inhabitants set up a vast market, which was open day and night. They had a crier whose voice could be

---

[66] It is probably a coincidence that Thomas Love Peacock, the only English Romantic to write an Arthurian prose romance, in the *Misfortunes of Elphin* (1829)—in which Taliesin features much more prominently than Marrl—also wrote a prose romance featuring Robin Hood, *Maid Marian* (1822), which helped to formulate the modern version of the legend.

heard throughout the three islands, and beside that braggart there was a Bible, open by a crack. As soon as the watchman signaled the presence of some new people far away at sea, who were arriving full of hope, all sails hoisted and inflated, with the wind behind them, they sold those people to the highest bidder, and shared out the price.

"What do I see, Robin Hood?" cried Merlin, the first time he was introduced to that market. The human species is being sold here! Oh my friend, what traffic!" Did you know about this? Speak!"

Not knowing how to reply, Robin Hood started humming a tune, as was his custom.

That discovery added an almost infinite sadness to what Merlin felt. He sat down on the bank of the Thames on a large stone that I've seen with my own eyes at Westminster, and, thinking about that first misstep, made vain efforts to escape disenchantment and ennui, to the extent that spleen gripped him. The more hope he had invested in the people of Albion, for the liberty of others, the more desolate he was at having been do unworthily deceived.

Certainly, he could have taken back at a single stroke all the gifts he had made o those people, who were making such bad use of them. That thought occurred to him at once; he was about to put it into action when he reflected that it was perhaps unworthy of an enchanter to take back what he had once given.

Then he felt truly alone, and was horrified by his isolation. The faculties that remained to him only served to fathom his profound misery. He felt as powerful as a god and as impotent as an earthworm. He would have liked to die. All day long he wept, and the next day too. Nothing could console him for that first glimpse of iniquity.

Mysterious tears have been emerging for some time from the black vapors that besieged the hearts of the people of that land. Often, they become weary of living, and when they put an end to their days, it's doubtless because they're committing the suicide of which Merlin dreamed. Let them descend into the depths of their hearts; they will find the dolorous heritage of the prophet, at that point in his life. But where, alas, is his ingenuity, his simplicity, his innocence, his mildness and his candor? All of that has been worn away by time. What was in him the heart-rending cry of unslaked love, the thirst for justice, has too often become in them ennui and repletion.

With his head in his hands, Merlin sobbed. It was the first explosion of his dolor. Young, in a foreign society, nothing obliged him to contain it. His eyes, blinded by tears, could scarcely make out the objects around him.

That is why one hears so many sobs today in the rocks battered by the Breton Sea, and why a crown of black cares is eternally posed on the head of the three islands, veiling their sunlight.

152

II

To cap Merlin's desolation, the red-haired Saxons arrived in their black ships with curved prows; immediately the Britons, the sad sons of storms, were dispossessed of their fields, their mossy huts and their orchards of golden apples, planted by the Enchanter. The land of Arthus trembled beneath iron waves. The Angles joined the predators, so effectively that all souls were obliged to fall silent. Only wandering bards could any longer be seen, their hands empty, devoid of hope, requesting shelter of the tombs; all wisdom would have perished at a stroke if Merlin had not built a crystal vessel, more transparent than the sky, on which he embarked the best with him.

"Adieu," he said to Robin Hood. "I can't live here one day longer. Quit the poacher's life, my friend, I beg you. Above all, don't have any further traffic with the human species, if you desire to see me again someday."

No one accompanied him to the shore, no one waved to him, when he set off from Southampton. Having drunk his fill of bitterness, scornful of the proud, obliged to repent his benefits as a mistake, he turned round as he was about to climb aboard his little vessel, and that is when he pronounced what is still known today as the Bard's Curse.

"Although John Englishman is a vile traitor, worse than the rain and the winds, he will not tame my heart, so long as the Rock of Mael stands.[67]

"When evil days come, I shall return to this isle, the color of a swan's wing. I have cried: pity, truth, humanity, there is the white dwelling of justice, let us go sit down on those beaches.

"I came to their isle as to the rock of righteousness; I found it a den of iniquity.

"Oh, may they pay me dearly for the joy of sobbing in the face of the Breton Sea!

"How cold and arrogant their gazes are when they pass me by! How they have insulted my mourning, the mourning of justice! The young men with the

---

[67] Mael was a Welsh hermit, subsequently canonized, who concluded his life on the island of Bardsey [i.e. the Island of the Bards], off the Llyn peninsula in north Wales, which was an important place of Medieval pilgrimage, and one of the many claimants to be Arthur's place of burial. Quinet adds a longer note than usual to this passage, alleging that this "curse" is based on an old Breton popular song expressing the age-old French hatred of the English, but he hastens to add that it will not be Merlin's last word on the subject. Hermione, by contrast, suggests that it is an alloy of the feelings that Quinet experienced when visiting England in 1825 and his "bitter indignation" of 1854 at English support for Napoléon III—represented in the interlude of the curse, she claims, by "Hengist the Pagan."

hissing tongues have been harsher than the old, and the women with primrose eyes harsher than the men, and the people harsher than the barons.

"Those of whom I was most hopeful were the first to strike me; it was by them that the first wound was inflicted. Yes, it was from their yew-wood bows that the poisoned arrow departed.

"They have given me a taste for immortal death, those from whom I requested life.

"O you whom the Ocean insults with its mocking laughter, do not land here. Return to the storm. Better to die by the anger of the Ocean that purchase life by the pitiful homicide of John Englishman. Better to drink the mead of Hell drop by drop than the disdain and insults of the red-haired Saxon.

"How alone I was in the midst of the innumerable crowd! No one addressed a word to me. Oh, among them I almost forgot the sweet sound of the human voice.

"See them pass by, teeth clenched, among other peoples. Who has received a salute or an adieu from them? Who had ever seen their vitreous gaze blossom over the weak? Who had felt the clasp of their hand?

"Where are they going, strangers among men? What are they going to do to the gentle hearths of those who shelter them? Rain, frost and cold winds are less pitiless to the plaint of those who succumb under the most forceful law.

"Virgin of the bare wood, recognize your torturers. They will bind you on the pyre and the pyre will burn for five centuries. When it is extinguished, it will be them, the red-haired Saxons, who will relight it with their accursed breath."

While Merlin spoke thus in the storm and his boat skirted the coast, the inhabitants followed him with their eyes from the top of the cliff. Some said: "Who speaks of justice? It's for us alone that it's made?"

They tried to stone him, but the sea itself laughed at their impotence.

Meanwhile, they went to lick the feet of Hengist the Pagan, who was streaming with the carnage of the bards; they crawled beneath his chariot, eyes pious and hands clasped, and adored the murderer.

And they grew fat on the flesh of bulls; their cheeks reddened like those of sated men digesting the bloody wine of homicide.

Then, having climbed up to the highest rock, they cried out, in such a way as to be heard all over the world: "There is no justice; there is only gold."

And the Irish priest, cursing the bards, repeated after them: "There is no justice."

At these voices, coming from the midst of the people who seemed most sage, all other peoples paled simultaneously. They looked at one another as if the sea were about to swallow up the human conscience. Everyone felt momentarily stripped of his immortal soul.

At that moment, Merlin, looking at the three islands, recommenced the curse, and his voice covered those of the peoples and the tempests:

"I only knew love; why have they taught me to hate?

"I have seen bards, outlaws, outcasts, just men, whose cold indifference has taken away their reason. They laugh at the edge of the waves, and plunge into them simultaneously.

"No, I cannot pardon the insanity of the just man, provoked by the harshness of men of prey.

"Let it fall back on them, to their damnation, in tears, in anguish, terror and despair! In the midst of their dismasted vessels, let them wander upon the shore, bare-headed, shaking, lost, singing infantile ballads like their King Lear, deprived of his kingdom.

"Those are my vows for them; that is my mercy for their pity, for their humanity!

"I say this to you, red-haired Saxons: why have you provoked the roaring lion of justice? If the just are not powerful today, they will be tomorrow. Their reign will last forever.

"Why do you rip the hearts out of human beings to make them booty? The heart is immortal; it will cry out against you.

"Do you believe that the sheer coast will defend you eternally? The rock of Cambria wears away like the ox's horn; the vulture will peck away the summit of the rock.

"The patience of good people is long; its waits, it adjourns. In the end, it crumbles. On that day, do you believe that an angry god will not cross the Ocean with dry feet? Where will you flee then?

"Where is the unknown isle that will not nourish an avenger against you. Where is the reef, where is the strand that will not rise up against you?

"Name a people that you have not defrauded. If there is one, name it. Your mask has fallen; it had fallen into the abyss.

"Everyone can see you, everyone knows you, and everyone curses you.

"Where is the race, where is the people, where is the Christ whose scarlet-haired Judas Iscariot you have not been?

"Your own son will condemn you; his name will be Harold.

"Sons of tempests, you shelter behind the tempests and you say: 'No one can reach me; I laugh at Heaven and earth; I laugh above all at the good faith of men. The waves protect me,' Beware! The waves are beginning to weary.

"The sail-less and oar-less ships will come, and they will whinny like the horses of the sea. The breath of their nostrils will be so powerful that it will cover the green-tinted sea with vapors, and only the wind of justice will drive them away.

"The superb islands will tremble when they see that the girdle of the Ocean has disappeared, that the abyss separating Cornwall from Neustria has been filled in.

"And on that day, the eternal talion will weigh upon the homicidal island of the Lords."

The vessel that was carrying the prophet was already a long way from the coast; his last words resounded over the strand with the angry waves. Some of those who had tried to stone him at first began to repent their harshness toward the rest of humankind. Fear had gripped them. Some of those people went very pale; they still are today.

III

The boat has scarcely emerged from the port when a wagtail—which is a magical bird—arriving from overseas, fell on to the deck. Merlin picked it up and warmed it with his breath as it trebled. Struck by such a simple incident, the idea came to him to take advantage of it to send a letter that he had been planning to write for a long time, which he carried out in the following manner:

Merlin the Enchanter to Viviane

The sea is sad, the sky immense, the world empty; I am searching for you; can you hear me? If you are gazing at the shore of the profound sea, or if you are sitting in the corner of the forest, or collecting the golden herb, or reading in the magic book on the top of a mountain, or listening to the cricket on the hearth, remember Merlin. I'm calling out; answer me!

After having written those words, he folded them up and attached them to the wagtail's neck. The bird flew away in a straight line and disappeared.

What, you say? Could Merlin hope that a letter thus entrusted to hazard would ever reach Viviane? Is that evidence of wisdom?

And you, Reader, have you never thrown words to the winds? Have you never addressed a message to the evening star? Have you never confided an adieu, a regret, a greeting, or at least a sigh, to the distant sail of a ship whitening at the extremity of the horizon, hesitating on its way?

For myself, I've done it, not once but a hundred times.

Besides, what point is there in arguing? Anyway, to cut the matter short, the bird reappeared carrying the reply, and without getting weary, always flapping its wings, hardly allowing time to write, it went, came back and left again six times over, so long as there was a message to carry.

Viviane to Merlin

What is the cricket to me? I have no hearth. What is the magic book to me? Tears prevent me from reading. What is the profound sea to me? I scorn pearls. Come back, come back, Merlin. I have sighed. Heed me.

Merlin to Viviane

156

Come back, you say? I've reflected, Viviane, since my last message. Are you serious? How can I rely on your word? Have you not broken off everything between us? I can't forget that. Is it a further insult you're preparing?

Viviane to Merlin

You're right, Merlin, you're better off where you are. No, no, don't come back. I was wrong to ask you to come back. I only did it to soothe your pain, which seemed too great. Our characters are too different, and my godmother, to whom I confided your last letter, will never consent to our marriage. It's better for your glory to travel the world and sow benefits. It's a rigorous duty, in fact.

Merlin to Viviane

No, no, I need to see you again, to hold you in my arms, to expire on your lips. Do you understand, Viviane? Efface the words I wrote to you; I'm effacing them with my tears. Dolor has rendered me insane. In the combat with pride, you have emerged victorious.

Viviane to Merlin

Let's not play games like this, Merlin. Life is serious. Don't come back; I forbid it. If you're mad enough to reappear, you won't find me. You're the king of sages, and I've recognized your last resolution not to see me again. You've said it: it's irremediable. We're not made for one another. Let everything be finished between us, including this correspondence, well worthy, in fact, of being confided to all the caprices of the winds.

Merlin to Viviane

What, Viviane, you've sent back all that you have of me, even the magic ring given at the last moment and my sole heritage! What have I done, except love you too much? That's right, Viviane; no love, no amity, no humanity, no pity. Well, I forgive you. I was mistaken; your heart isn't wicked, it's just impotent. Here I am now, alone in the world, without knowing why, and no one can tell me what has become of you. The least earthworm is less miserable, less abandoned, than me. I suffer from the water I rink, the air that I breathe. Let the tempest come, then! It will be less implacable than you.[68]

---

[68] Hermione's notes make no specific reference to this correspondence, leaving it to the informed reader to wonder how closely it resembles Quinet's communication with Minna during the period of their separation between 1831 and 1834.

IV

After that letter, to which there was no reply, Merlin wandered sadly over the North Sea. Battered by the tempest that he had imprudently raised, his crystal vessel ran aground in Flanders, without breaking up. It returned to the open sea for a whole night, and then landed at high tide on the bare, eternally resounding beach that forms dunes between Ostend and Antwerp.

"Save me," Jacques shouted, "or I'll perish." Merlin had already gripped him by his woolen coat and put him in a safe place.

Venturing into the Low Countries, he was welcomed by Geneviève of Brabant,[69] who entertained him at first in her grotto, and served as his guide through the plain punctuated by marshes.

At the entrance to every village, the finches greeted him with an untiring song. He thought it was a concert organized to celebrate his arrival. How indignant he was, however, when he discovered that the singers were blind and that the inhabitants had treacherously put out their eyes in order to enjoy their chirping more.

"Poor Homers!" Merlin exclaimed, considered their little white eyelids lowered ne upon the other. "Isn't it enough that Thamyris, Orpheus, Amphion and the poet of the *Iliad* received the same price for their songs?[70] Who was made for the light if not you, since you're its messengers? Eyes closed by the wicked, salute the eternal dawn, since the dawn down here has been taken away from you!"

Turning then toward the people ruled by Geneviève of Brabant, he said: "O people, have you no shame, to take the light away from the children of light? To whom will you leave it, if you steal it from the dawn chorus?"

Then he added: "Men! This, then, is how you crush the true bards of cares and humiliations everywhere? You plunge them into the night of anguish, solely to draw more beautiful songs from them. If you put out the eyes of bards, what need have you of poets? Dread that they might no longer be born among you!"

---

[69] The heroine of a Medieval legend that offers one of many variants of the tale of a chaste wife unjustly accused and condemned. She lived in a cave for six years until the truth came out. By the time Quinet published his story the legend had formed the basis of a comic opera by Jacques Offenbach performed in Paris in 1859, but he must have written this passage before then.

[70] There does not seem to be any textual basis for the implication that Amphion, whose lyre moved the stones to build the walls of Thebes, was blinded, but it might be significant that Christopher Marlowe's *Doctor Faustus* couples Amphion with "blind Homer" in the course of Faust's invocations. Orpheus was not blinded ether, but did come to a sticky end.

This speech caused the people to reflect, who promised to reform at least on that point; but they did not keep their word.

Two days later, the Enchanter and his companion were going through a little Brabantine valley covered in wheat-fields and sheltered from the north wind by the forest of Soignes. Wearied by traveling they lay down in a furrow and went to sleep.

When they woke up Merlin said to Jacques: "Did you hear anything while we were asleep? It seems to me, my friend, that horrible chariots of war have passed this way and the ground is red with blood.

"I didn't hear or see anything," said Jacques.

"The ardor of the sun must have affected my head, then, and I had a terrible dream," Merlin said. "No, never did the ram of Cornwall colliding with the Gaulish wild boar, or the powerful Arthus at odds with the odious Saxons make such a racket. Can you imagine that I saw two mighty armies clash, and break up in the furrows of the very place where we were sleeping, and over there, on that hillock of red sand, where you can distinctly see a field of clover, a motionless phantom on a horse, whom I mistook at this distance for the discrowned king of tempests, was noisily slain."

"Who won the battle?" asked Jacques.

"The English."

"It's obvious that it was a dream."

"I think so too, but see how the wheat has been trampled down."

"Doubtless that's some kobold that has passed this way."

"It must be," said Merlin—and he got up from the depths of the furrow, which has remained hollowed out to this very day, to the point of taking on the form of an immense tomb, as can still be seen.

"Ask that shepherd for a little water, because I'm thirsty—and ask him the name of that village."

Jacques came back a few moments later.

"There's neither water nor wine, but the village is called Waterloo."

"That's good. Don't forget it, my son."

From these, wandering from Brabant to the Ardennes and the banks of the Escaut, they heard people boasting that they were according him hospitality. That made him turn red, because he always paid generously for his accommodation, either in money with Arthus' effigy or the inventions of his art, such as defensive walls for communes, keeps for beggars he held in particular honor and town houses, no vestige of which the people had possessed before him. He took the opportunity to give them a lesson in modesty.

"Don't make use so lightly of the holy word hospitality," he said to them. "The heart alone can set a price on it. Is it being hospitable not to cast back into the sea the victims of shipwrecks who land on your coast? Is it being hospitable only to let them breathe the air of the strand and contemplate the stormy sea, without hurling them into the abyss? Vultures do as much. Hospitalers by the same title, they too only butcher the dead."

Thus he spoke to the townsfolk and the people. Immediately fearing that he might be unjust, however, he turned to Jacques and said: "I foresee, by the sadness that grips me in this place, that it will become for you, my friend, not a place of pilgrimage but of exile. I don't know whether you'll leave your bones here, but I know for sure that you'll spend long days here, not by virtue of your own will but that of others. You'll remain chained in this place, because it will seem sweet at least to hear an echo of your native tongue. For what cause you'll be brought here I can't tell. At any rate, I'll make a sacred wall around your thoughts, and no one will be able to besiege you here."

"Will you be with me, Seigneur Merlin?"

"Yes, my son, I'll still be in the world."

"Then all will be well for me."

"Don't say that, my son. Nothing can replace the sweet air of the land where one is born, the shade of trees one has planted, the gossip of women who knew your mother; nothing, my son, can replace that—not even the powerful Merlin, who can move rocks. Only try not to be unjust to those in the midst of whom you'll live. They don't know you family or your birthplace. To them, you're a stranger who might leave the next day. Why should you expect them to give their heart to the bird that has not chosen its shelter, which the tempest has cast away on their shores, and who would like nothing more than to see the natal nest again? Content yourself with justice; don't ask for love. It's a great deal if they lend you a paving-stone on which to lay your head, and even that merits a recompense."

As evidence of this last remark, Merlin taught the people of the region, the Flemings, Batavians, Friesians and men of Bruges and Antwerp, to break the wrath of the ocean on their shores.

"Assemble little wicker sticks," he told them, and after having interwoven them, make a screen of them on which the impetuous waves will come to break."

The people of the region began to laugh. "What?" they said. "O king of sages, can we tame the sea by whipping it with willow-twigs?"

Merlin replied: "Great passions overwhelm great obstacles, but they are worn away by smaller ones, when they are repeated and leave no respite day or night. It will be the same with the fury of the ocean, if you do as I say."

Convinced by this speech, the Batavians followed Merlin's advice; thus they made, among the algae and the mollusk-shells, an invincible fatherland on the as-yet-stormy bed of the North Sea.

160

V

As they neared the grassy plains of Teutony, beyond Aix-la-Chapelle, Merlin gave ample instructions to Jacques, which he concluded thus:

"We're going to enter among people new to you, my son, of whom you have no conception. Until now we've been living nations of our own family. Henceforth you'll see other faces and other mores. Now is the time to use wisdom and circumspection. The people we're about to visit are very honest; they even have great generosity of heart when one approaches them in the right way, but it's necessary to know their language. I know it from having visited them in other times. I suppose them to be umbrageous, as befits people who have lived for a long time in the obscurity of sacred woods. I also think them bad-tempered, and not much inclined to laughter. Beware of sniggering among them; they'll imagine that you intend to insult them, and their natural forbearance will turn to venom."[71]

While speaking thus, they came to the banks of the green-tinted Rhine, the father of waters. Having hailed a boat that was going upriver, they got into it. Through the mist, Merlin pointed out to Jacques the prodigious number of castles built on the two banks; he showed him the hamlets sleeping at the foot of those high walls.

"Look at these people! They're happy; they're not making any noise. One might think that they were germinating in silence, like the meadow-grass."

"Don't they pay many taxes, then?" said Jacques Bonhomme.

"On the contrary, they pay a great many, but they're happy in spite of that, because enchanters have more credit hereabouts than anywhere else in the world, and if I'm not greatly mistaken, you'll soon see the proof of it."

Scarcely had he finished than many people appeared on the balconies and terraces of the old castles and on the esplanades of crenellated towers: an entire population of kings, hermits, minstrels, pilgrims, dwarfs and rhingraves, who, bowing low, showed the greatest respect for our hero. Sometimes a centenarian king with a white beard dropped his golden cup from a high balcony into the Rhine as he passed by. Sometimes an old harpist sitting on the top of a tower sang a ballad that the echo repeated three times. When he finished his song, he broke his harp.

A few peevish dwarfs, it's true, stood on tiptoe and, looking through a gap in the fortifications wondered: "Is that man really Teutonic? Are you certain?"

"No," other dwarfs replied, "he's French."

---

[71] Hermione's notes record that this chapter recalls the impressions of the German people that Quinet formed during his sojourn in Heidelberg in 1827-8; Faust represents German idealist philosophy, although Hermione expresses it, a trifle uncharitably, as "the obscurity of the German mind."

With that, a host of deformed dwarfs went back into their hovels, crying out in horror: "We're not celebrating! It's betraying blonde Germany to make a fuss of Merlin the Gaul."

All those whose height was not too far below average, however, laughed at the dwarfs' anger and took part in Merlin's triumph. Everywhere he stopped, young women as white as snow with long blonde hair tumbling over their shoulders brought him crowns of ivy. They took care to add a few slices of gilded bread, a few myrtle berries and a smoky wine in colored Bohemian crystal. Drawn by a sovereign force, the host of kings, hermits and pilgrims inhabiting the old manors came down from their retreats and went along both banks following Merlin's boat, which they had decked with hop-flowers. That crowd, which grew at every step, covered the land for some distance; it would have formed a cortege for him to the ends of the earth if he had not opposed it. A few deer from the woods even came into the river and swam after him. At Mayenne, Doctor Faust, emerging from the Thurmhaus, arrived in a small boat. He came to salute Merlin as his elder and his master—which would cause him a great deal of trouble, as we shall soon see.

Since time immemorial, the two banks had been inhabited by people who were very jealous of one another. They had always been ready to come to blows. While Merlin was passing by they called a truce on their age-old hatreds, subjugated by his mildness and his common sense. It was to be feared, however, that at the slightest opportunity, their opposed temperaments would cause them to fall out again and start fighting before the Enchanter's very eyes—which, alas, did not take long to happen. An imprudent word from Faust was the cause of it.

Scarcely had he finished speaking than some people started murmuring, saying: "Why is he being so humble? Why is he admitting Merlin's superiority? Why is he confessing that Mephistopheles, who is Teutonic, is a mere vassal and not the prince of Hell? There he goes, abandoning that honor to Beelzebub, who is French. Can that be tolerated?"

The dwarfs, hearing those comments, slipped out of their manors. They came to mingle their bile with the bitterness and envy that was already filling the hearts of the crowd. According to them, it was to humiliate the Teutons that Merlin had prepared this triumph. Was it not the ultimate insult to say that the king of Hell did not belong to the Teuton race? Only blood could wash away that shame. "There's nothing better than crushed Franco-Gallic bones to make the wheat grow," they added—so effectively that hatred replaced love almost everywhere.

Already, two armies were assembled on the two banks, opposed by race, tongue and genius. On the right bank, marching at the head, were Malvasius, king of Iceland, Grunvasius, king of the Orkneys, Lot, king of Norway, and

Holdinus, king of Ruthenia.[72] They had with them Thor, with his heavy hammer, Hildebrand, with his bow of steel, and Siegfried, who was carrying the recently-rediscovered Nibelung treasure in a chest. A rude, wild population was pressing on their heels, to the sound of buffalo horns.

At daybreak, on the summits of misty mountains on the left bank, knights with lowered visors filed past, hastening by Merlin's appeal. They were riding gray mares with saddles, leading their innumerable dogs of war on leashes, which they were about to unmuzzle. They were Arthus' people, proud of thought, lances held high, ready to strike. Their chief wore amber in the form of a twisted circle around his temples.

Several challenges had been shouted from both sides of the river. One more word, and the festival would end in carnage. Evil fate dictated that the spark be struck. Immediately, the two peoples precipitated themselves from both banks against one another. Within an instant, the great river, utterly impartial and philosophical as it was, took on the color of blood.

In the first moment of confusion, Faust took Merlin to a rock from which they could easily look down on the battle. With a mixture of excitement and coldness, he said: "What a sublime spectacle, Merlin! What an epic—not fantastic but real! Where can one see human power at grips with the supernatural better than here, pray? It's at such time as this that the energy of the soul appears in its epic grandeur. Thought shines here like a blade outside the scabbard; that's what's pleasing in this affair, because this is a matter of a clash of ideas, and as you know, nothing is rarer than to encounter similar ones. Men, I admit, have ended up hurling themselves into the battle, but take note that it was spirits who started the fight. Yes, it's a truly Homeric battle, such as one doesn't see any more, even in poems. Look over there, on that hillock, at Thor landing mighty blows of his hammer on Arthus' coat of mail. Hildebrand's steel bow is vibrating there, with a savage melody, in the midst of your paladins. Over that way on the left flank, the enchanted lances of your weepers are working marvels against Siegfried's buffalo-hide. In the distance, on both banks of the river, the plebeian iron men, nameless and devoid of glory, are shedding their skin like snakes in autumn."

Merlin interrupted Faust emotionally. "Faust, this spectacle had lasted too long. It's for us that they're fighting; the moment has come for us to intercede."

"Be very careful, Merlin," Faust replied. "To hide nothing from you, it's impossible for me to say which of these two peoples interests me. Which is the one that carried the most ideas with it? That's the question. That's all that it's necessary to know. Let's not disturb the course of events, then. Let's leave

---

[72] This list is slightly confused; the first sentence refers to kings supposedly beaten in battle by Arthur, according to Geoffrey of Monmouth, but in the *Historia* Lot is king of the Orkneys before becoming king of Norway; Grunvasius is not mentioned and the name appears to be original to Quinet.

things to develop with the masculine impartiality of destiny. Some advantageous truth always comes out of it, which we can turn to the advantage of our art."

At that very moment the valley was resounding with savage cries. No one was fleeing, everyone was striking out where he stood. The wounded dragged themselves on their bellies to the river. While they slaked their thirst their throats were cut by the dwarfs, who were almost equal in number in the two camps. Death was hastening everywhere on his pale palfrey.

Merlin could not stand such a horrific spectacle any longer.

"When blood flows in torrents," he cried, "I see nothing but blood."

He had not finished speaking when the beautiful Brunhild passed by, on her chariot harnessed to a team of swans. Her hair scattered, she was singing a death-song to the tempest, and pouring yellow mead for those who were thirsty.

Immediately, Merlin said: "You who are so beautiful, don't intoxicate them with your war-song.

But she drew away without having heard anything. The swans, their necks extended, hissed like snakes, and the vultures replied to them: "Ride, kings—your people are ours!"

The time had come, however, when even the most furious were weary of killing. Merlin seized the moment with an admirable presence of mind. At the risk of being pierced by a thousand thrusts, he came to place himself between the two peoples, and signaled to them that he wanted to speak.

The attitude and gesture of the lone man, who was unarmed—he had thrown his sword into the Rhine—struck everyone with astonishment. He spoke, he begged, he adjured; their weapons fell from their hands.

Not content with calming the people, Merlin dressed their wounds. He spread over the most envenomed the balm that he had obtained from Morgan le Breton.[73] He washed wounds with river water with his own hands. Above all, he promised to celebrate their reconciliation with a great feast that he would give for all of them, as soon as he had returned to French territory. He asked them to live in peace until then, as they were doing now, lying beside one another on the fresh grass, still stained with blood. Arthus' great sword, beautiful, sharp-edged and sharp-pointed, was sleeping in their midst. Already the stars were caressing their faces with golden says. Where the roar of the battle had been heard, only the murmur of the river interrupted the dreams of the drowsy nations. Merlin made sure that the dream was good, and only then did he consent to quit them.

Thus were reconciled the Teutons and the French. If only their descendants had followed their example!

---

[73] This might refer to the Arthurian enchantress Morgan le Fay, although she is referred to elsewhere in the text as Morgane, but there is also a subsequent reference to "Morgan, le médecin" [Morgan the physician], which suggests that there might be two different individuals.

VI

When night fell, Faust took Merlin to his dwelling, with a pointed roof, which was nearby. As soon as they were alone he said:

"What astonishes me most of all, Merlin, in what I've just seen, is that you were able to tame human pride. By that sign, I recognize your superiority. Another thing confuses me. In our land, enchanters only have power over the people of our race and our tongue. Outside of that circle, they have no credit. Your enchanters, it seems, have the same empire over foreigners as their compatriots. I've seen the humor of our Teutons tamed by your sweet talk. Explain that aspect of your art to me and give me your secret."

"I'd like that," said Merlin, glancing around him at the Teutonic enchanter's laboratory. But before anything else, Faust, I fear that you read too much."

"Too much?" queried Faust.

"Yes," Merlin replied. "Parchments, alembics, crucibles, retorts, dead men's skulls, the skins of owls—what a sad place this is! Why do you bury yourself alive in this dust? I couldn't live in it for a single day. For myself, I live in arbors, among spring flowers and bees."

"What! So scholarly, and you don't spend all day in your laboratory like us, the conscientious enchanters of the North?"

"Not at all. I read my best secrets on the wings of birds, iridescent butterflies and, it has to be admitted, in the dark or cheerful, caressant or indifferent gazes of young women—for that's a whole science."

"That's why, in spite of your power, people accuse you of being so frivolous?"

"They're wrong!" Merlin exclaimed. "Frivolous! A wish to God I were!"

And he told his story, which he concluded with the words: "Dear Faust, you're only looking at Merlin's shadow; I'm no longer more than half of myself."

Faust concluded that, in order to equal Merlin, he only needed to be in love.

"I shall be," he said. "I want to be."

Merlin replied that he would give everything that remained of his enchanter's empire for one of Viviane's smiles. On which the two friends, having exchanged rings, went to yield themselves to a sleep that was doubly necessary after such a busy day.

The next day, at the moment of parting, Faust gave his most recent book of magic to his guest. He accompanied him down the spiral stairway of the central tower to the arched doorway. There he suddenly stopped on the bottom step. His face illuminated with a livid light, as can happen to those who cannot help allowing a long-held secret to escape.

"Admit to me Merlin," he said to him, embracing him in order to bid him farewell, "That you don't exist. Admit that you don't have any reality, that you're nothing but an abstract idea."

Amazed, Merlin contained himself at first, and replied: "Is that your idea of an adieu, Faust? On what do you base your suspicion that I don't exist?"

"This is it, king of sages. Firstly, your works surpass my intelligence. Now, my intelligence is the measure of the possible. Secondly, you act, you think, you feel and you love as much as an entire people. Thus, you're not an individual, but the essential idea of that people. Make that confession—I'll keep your secret."

Merlin, who had had difficulty containing himself thus far, stepped out of character and replied with a vehemence for which he reproached himself later: "O most ingrate of men, you're accusing me of not existing—me, who has just informed you of the mystery of my art! You're accusing me of not existing! What, then, would you say about Viviane?"

At that point his voice broke; he burst into tears, because a frightful doubt crossed his mind; it was only a flash, but a lightning-flash in infernal darkness. He seemed to be searching within himself, interrogating himself silently; his entire person gave the impression of the most cruel laceration. Finally, unable to argue, he took Faust's cold hand and placed it over his heart.

"Can you feel it beating, Doctor? That's my response."

The German philosopher softened, in spite of his triple bronze. "You're weeping, Merlin," he said to him. "So you must exist—the consequence is reliable."

Emerging from a feverish aguish worse than death, Merlin gradually recovered his equilibrium. He overwhelmed with his angelic bounty the man who had thrust a dart into his bosom. But one word, which finally escaped him, proved that he was still suffering but that he had been able to master himself.

"After all," he said to the German enchanter, shaking his hand, "I know that I exist, myself, because I forgive you."

Merlin, judging that he had accomplished the task that had led him to that place, got ready to leave. Several matters were calling him to Italy, but as he already felt homesick, instead of taking the shortest route through the Grisons he made a detour and went through France.

He did not exercise such great diligence, however, that he did not pause for a few weeks in the Black Forest, on the banks of the Necker.

As he was gathering bilberries, a student came to ask him, in accordance with the local custom, to write something in his album. With a very good grace but in very poor handwriting, Merlin scribbled one of his tirades there. It began thus:

Behind every obscure word there is a slavery.

The student, unable to decipher it, went to interrogate his master, Albert the Great, who consulted someone wiser than he was. And to this very day, if you visit that enchanted place, through the thickness of the chestnut trees, among the meadows, the ruins of fallen towers, in the crannies of the ivy, you can see groups of old men, deep in thought, nobly trying to make good sense out of the page written by Merlin. They are the wisest and the happiest men on earth, for they are in perpetual commerce with him. Their eyes pause on his magic writing; they cover it with annotations; they fathom its depths; they divine its mystery, ignoring the rest of the world. It is a veritable paradise, although sometimes, for the sake of a comma or a missing full stop, they enter into holy wrath, which the generations transmit to one another; the peaceful city, full of the scent of new-mown hay, resounds with the warfare of pens, which will never have any truce.

And who can blame them? One letter more or less on a page of Merlin's writing would immediately change the earth and the heavens.

But let us leave those ancient rancors there. Let us forget them forever and adopt another tone. In any case, another voice is resonating out there, fresh and emotional, in the depths of the wood. What is it? Child, girl, woman or demon? Fortunately or unfortunately, I fear that it is going to crown the present book.

VII

Bring me flowers, but flowers of mourning. Bring me immortelles; I want to sow them on a tomb.

Merlin is advancing through the Black Forest, which has no exit. A young woman, abandoned by the world. is under the branches.

Her blonde, wavy hair, flowing over her shoulders—that's her cloak. Her strong, robust voice seems made of pure steel.

Her stature is petite, her determination great; its shines in her intrepid eyes. It's a soul of bronze in the body of a child.

"Are you lost?"

"A nation is marching after me, Seigneur."

"What is your country?"

"Carpathia."

"Your father?"

"The Danube."

"Your mother?"

"The Moldova."

"What are you looking for?"

"Eyes fixed on the land where the sun sets, I've been seeking the Enchanter everywhere."

Merlin has changed his route several times; she has followed him obstinately. He always found her in the morning, standing on his threshold when he was about to depart. The only thing she has ever asked of Merlin is to carry his book.

"Oh, Merlin, Merlin, I'm scared! The fays are jealous; the beauties of the woods will kill me, you'll see."

"Have no fear of the fays; have no fear of the beauties of the wood. They're my subjects; I can command them with a smile."

Pray to God that he might be telling the truth! Yesterday, in a dream, she has seen a beauty of the wood whose gaze pierced her like a dart.

By the description she has given, Merlin has recognized Viviane.

Since that moment, the young woman has been trembling in every limb; the accursed fever never quits her any longer; her teeth chatter as she speaks.

This morning, on emerging from his threshold, Merlin tripped over a dead body: the body of Florica.

He buried her himself; with his own hands, he has laid that child, who lived for one of his gazes, and whom Viviane's gaze has slain, in the ground.

Merlin, Merlin, will it be thus or everyone who loves you on earth?

Will young women die, and their eyes close, as soon as they raise them toward you?

Will the hawthorn be seen to pass, and the new grass to wither?

Bring me flowers, but flowers of mourning. Bring me immortelles; I want to sow them on a tomb.[74]

---

[74] Hermione's notes state, baldly, that "Florica is the portrait of a friend."

BOOK NINE: THE ROUND TABLE

I

Woe betide him who is forced to wander over the foreign earth! Men draw away from him, so fearful are they of the contagion of adversity. The world has not always been thus; beneath the rudest forms, there was a better heart once upon a time, as witness the pilgrimages that I am recounting at present. But what's the point of criticizing the world? Let's rather forgive it; even the most just anger will only harden it further.

At the moment when they left Germany and set foot in France, it seemed to our two travelers that they were emerging from the lands of dreams to enter that of reality. Merlin, on looking back, swung the door of dreams shut on its invisible hinges. The hinges barely grated. The sound died away in the islands of the Rhine, planted with poplars and alders.

Meanwhile, Jacques Bonhomme rubbed his eyes and whistled to his dog to prove that he was awake. He picked up his knapsack and took out a wine-skin that Faust's famulus had given him when they left. At the same time, he kissed the cheeks of a calf that was passing close by, which suddenly reminded him of his own livestock.

"Thank God we're out of the Sleeping Beauty's forest," he said. "Any longer and I'd have been sleeping the enchanted slumber like the others."

Merlin made no reply. They were both weary of having kept company for so long with pure spirits. They were in haste to get away from the realm of legends and finally rediscover men and animals of flesh and blood. So they willingly lingered at the door of even the most wretched hostelries, simply to exchange a few words with beings whose existence was not contested by anyone, such as carters, debauchees, donkey-drovers and manual laborers of all sorts. They did not go very far without some adventure throwing them back into the midst of the utterly real society for which they were avid, because they had been separated from it for some while.

In the Vosges pass, the path was strangled between two towers that overlooked the country.

Two sturdy squires wearing body armor fall upon them, and by way of a toll are about to deprive them of their lives—but wait! A hermit emerges from a cleft in the rock, a rosary in one hand and an immense rapier in the other. He runs, he shouts, he strikes; the predators fall, wounded. The hermit takes a trickle of water from a nearby spring in the hollow of his hand and hastens to baptize them; then, seeing that they are both dead and that their men are fleeing, he calmly puts his dagger back in its sheath.

Undoubtedly, Merlin could have defended himself with his power alone; nevertheless, he allowed himself to show gratitude to the man who lent him such generous help. He thanked him effusively, and then suddenly, after having looked at him more closely, he said:

"What do I see? Are you not the hermit I met on the bank of the Rhine on the day when Christ passed over on Christopher's shoulders?"

"The very same," the hermit replied. "I was holding the torch. I'm Turpin."

"Where do you come from, Turpin?"

"The Land of Legends."

"Then you're the one who will be Archbishop Turpin, the most celebrated of all by his Chronicles![75] You'll live for a long time—even longer than me. To you alone on the earth it will be given to see, in one lifetime, the court of Arthus and that of the emperor who will be called Charles the Great. Young under the first, you will be old under the second, but still sturdy enough to protect him with the sword, and you will thus hold both ends of the chain of the golden centuries. Thus, the weft of your years will be a tenacious thread that will resist the scissors, and that long life will make more than one envious. Come with me, Turpin. I will tell you more things you would be able to write on all the parchment in Gaul."

Turpin rejoiced internally at the long life that had been promised to him, for the humor that he had, prodigal to others of his time, was not of his era. Facile, enterprising, wholehearted and candid, he took everything—even killing—for the best. After his rapier and his rosary, what he liked best of all in the world was his writing-desk.

He was then in the full bloom of youth, being scarcely twenty-five years old—or so he believed—tall, strong and suntanned. His eyes were dark, his neck short and replete; he was ever-ready to sharpen his sword, pray or engross himself. He had his rapier and rosary on him, as we have seen. It would only have been necessary to look in his hole in the rock for his writing-desk, and there he marched at a military pace with Merlin. His whinnying horse emerged from a thicket and caught up with him in a few bounds.

---

[75] Tupin is the signature attached, apocryphally, to the *Historia Caroli Magni*, a twelfth-century document that pretends to have been written in the eighth century and to provide an account of the historical background to *La Chanson de Roland*, while actually being a scholarly fantasy derivative therefrom. It appropriates Turpin's name because he is named in the *Chanson* as one of Charlemagne's peers. The name also crops up, without any indication that it is referring to a similar character, in some versions of the story of Tristan and Iseult, thus forging a tenuous link to Arthuriana. There was an actual Archbishop of Reims with a similar name (Tiplin) in the 8th century, but Turpin is indeed a child of the Land of Legends, and a perfect candidate to become the symbolic representative of Medieval chroniclers in general.

The day was not over before the propriety of Merlin's action became evident. Why was he taking Turpin with him, who was not yet an archbishop and who only had his fine Gothic writing to distinguish him? You shall see.

It happened that in the first town where they stayed overnight, the ramparts were still reeking of the blood of the greater number of the inhabitants. Before consenting to set foot therein Merlin sought enlightenment as to the cause of that horror. He learned that a long war had been engaged between the bourgeois and the seigneurs; the was continuing because no one in the region knew his alphabet well enough to daft a peace treaty

Scarcely had he introduced himself than the victors and the vanquished pressed around him to implore him to compose that treaty.

"I'll dictate it to Turpin," Merlin replied, "and you'll be faithful to it, from father to son!"

"Forever!" replied the crowd.

With that, Turpin took the whitest page of parchment that could be found in France, sharpened his eagle's plume carefully, and wrote down what Merlin dictated in one breath:

From this day forward, the following has been agreed between the bourgeois and laborers of this region, the seigneurs and the king. From the hour of noon on this day, all those born on this cherished terrain, into which I have put my heart, will be completely free. They will be called French, which is to say that they will be free of all statute labor, obligations, vexations, hindrance, apprehension, anxiety, dolor or misery, in body and in soul, for the present and the future, it being understood that whoever will touch this soil or the attachments thereof, towns, villages, hamlets, woods, forests, watercourses and mills, and vain pasture, will have nothing to dread unless the sky should fall on the earth. No one shall have anything to envy in the flight of the bird who goes wherever he pleases, nor the fox in his earth; it being furthermore approved by everyone that the seigneur shall everywhere be like the pastor with his flock, and that the king or prince, always amicable, shall watch over them like the sheepdog. Furthermore, no miscreant or thief shall approach this place, not evildoers or the envious; all ducs, comtes and barons promising to remain humble of heart, and accepting, in receiving their duchies, counties and baronies, to protect the weak and nourish the orphan.

All dictated by the Enchanter Merlin, in faith of which have signed Turpin and made his mark Jacques Bonhomme, who has declared for himself and his heirs until the last generation, not knowing how to read or write.

"Is that what you promise and swear?" said Merlin to the people.

The people cheered.

"And you, sire king?"

"I swear it also!"

171

The Comtes made the same response. Jacques Bonhomme excused himself from having to stain the contract with ink, on the grounds that his penmanship was bad. The reply was made to him that he only had to make a cross, and everyone would be content—which was immediately done.

Scarcely had he made a cross with two strokes than he straightened up delightedly, looked at the assembly, and cried: "Now the whole world is happy! It's signed and marked." And he went to show everyone the parchment blackened with Turpin's square, massive writing. The latter had not failed to add to the edges two seals of red wax.

As soon as that news spread, all the towns entered into an extraordinary ferment. It was necessary for the good Merlin, assisted by his scribe, to go from place to place, and those who could not obtain a few lines of Turpin's writing were desperate. All the parchment in Gaul was promptly used up. But it is understandable now why the sage Merlin had made a detour in his journey, why he had gone into the ambush, and why he had said to the hermit: "Come with me, and don't forget your writing-desk."

II

Even if I had twenty tongues in my mouth and twenty scribes around me— of which the century still possesses a few—I would have difficulty recounting everything that Merlin did in traveling through France. One adventure will exemplify the wisdom that he manifested every day. The further he went into the land, the more he reproached himself for having neglected its provinces.

"Alas, my friend, it makes me blush," he said to Turpin. "How was I able to forget them to the extent that they're almost bare? I've done everything for Paris, and Paris has forgotten me. I've deserved that. Let's repair that injustice, if there's still time."

"But we'll still need a good opportunity," Turpin replied. "When will we find one?"

"Sooner than you think, friend. Remember everything you seen today; you'll write it tomorrow in my sacred book."

That was said under the skies of Provence, near Avignon and even nearer to the gorge of Vaucluse. Our voyagers, breathless under the oppression of the sun, were going upstream along the bed of the Sorgue, seeking its source. No man had ever penetrated into that wild region before. Immense rocks split, broken and jagged near the summit served as a barrier. In that season the torrent was dry, but the source, which no human gaze had yet reflected, was secretly amassed in the cleft flank of the mountain.[76]

---

[76] Quinet had no way of knowing that cave-divers would eventually recover coins from the Fontaine-de-Vaucluse—the biggest spring in France—dating back as far as the 1st century B.C. He would, however, have been familiar with

Our voyagers, being very thirsty, drank precipitately, one after the other, from the palms of their hands. When Merlin's turn came, as soon as he had approached his lips to the spring of Vaucluse, a prophetic shiver gripped him, and he immediately said to his companions:

"Either I've lost my science, or it's certain that this is a sacred water in which more than one soul will slake its thirst. Listen to the muffled sound of subterranean cascades, and follow those pigeons pursued by the kite through the air. Believe me: something extraordinary is in preparation hereabouts. It is not hazard alone that has led us here. What do you think I ought to do in this valley?"

Having observed what surrounded him, Turpin replied without hesitation: "This place was made throughout eternity in order that my abbey should be built here. Let's take possession of it. The source is made to serve as a fish-pond; here, along the rocks, the footfalls of monks can hollow out a slender path in order to walk at any hour, and the sun is not inconvenient in this low-lying place."

Jacques decided, on the contrary, that the place was ideal for the foundation of a commune. The mountains would serve as walls with battlements. The torrent would furnish the inhabitants with trout. Provided that was furnished with sufficient flour, it could hold firm, if necessary, against all the nobility of the region.

While they were talking, Merlin put down his traveling staff, which, having found a little fertile ground, put down roots and subsequently became the laurel that can still be seen. He also began to carve the banks of the spring with the edge of his sword, without paying any further attention to what his companions were saying.

"Good!" said Turpin. "One more thrust of the chisel, Merlin, and the spring at the foot of the mountain, will resemble a holy water stoup at the base of a cathedral pillar."

Merlin applied the thrust of the chisel. The immense stoup appeared, as it can be seen today. Turpin thought he could see the baptismal font of his abbey. Merlin exclaimed: "Yes, Turpin, believe me: more than one soul will be baptized in this spring."

"In the true faith?" asked Turpin.

"In mine," the Enchanter said, placing his golden bowl on the bank; then he added: "More than one pilgrim will visit this place, but they will be pilgrims

---

the legend that a hermit lived there in the Middle Ages who became Bishop of Cavaillon, and that the first monastery constructed there, ruined by the eleventh century, was replaced by another. Petrarch lived there in the 14th century, but the village was sacked not long after and returned to wilderness for hundreds of years. Hermione notes that Quinet had visited the spring in 1843.

of love, and one will come greater than the rest. From his mouth will flow a river more abundant than the Sorgue."

While they were talking, several travelers deviated from their route and came to ask the Enchanter for something to drink. He drew from the source and gave them what they required to slake their thirst with the amorous beverage. Then they went away, half-intoxicated and singing, in a language as musical as that of the swallow: "Remember the time of my suffering."[77]

Merlin did not want to withdraw until he had constructed a hut of foliage and contrived narrow paths in the rock. His companions helped him with a good grace.

"For whom are you making these paths?" they asked him.

"For Viviane. She will surely come to sit down here, if she has not come already, which is scarcely probable."

"But only the goats and the birds can reach these sheer peaks," said his companions.

"Viviane is lighter than a goat," Merlin replied, "and as light as a bird."

Then he started engraving in the rocks a host of verses that Petrarch would later find, and would content himself with translating, without ever naming the author. Merlin could not tear himself away from the place, but he needed to leave it, because there was a threat of rain. As he was leaving, he collected himself, and shouted with all his might: "Love!"

After a long silence, the rocks replied: "Love!"

They are still repeating it today.

It was thus that the spring of Vaucluse was enchanted forever. Visitor, don't take away the golden bowl that remains on the bank; it's a gift from Merlin.

III

Already they were approaching Lyon in order to go through the Romey valley into Switzerland and then to Lombardy. They could already see the steeple of Fourvières, he great aqueducts of Oullins festooned with wild vines and the place where the Rhône bears its excessively slow and timid company over its bed, when Merlin remembered that he had not yet asked the future archbishop Turpin how, having left him on the bank of the Rhine, he had found him armed from head to toe in a niche in the Vosges. Finding the leisure to do so in the plain, he asked him to clarify the matter.

---

[77] The line, slightly misprinted in the original text, is from Dante's *Purgatorio*; it was later to become a particular favorite of T. S. Eliot's; he quoted it in more than one of his poems.

174

Turpin had been expecting the question, and seized the opportunity, because, having remained in his solitary niche for a long time, he was burning with a natural desire to loosen his tongue.

"Everything in my life is linked," he said. "What I can tell you would be incomprehensible if I didn't begin the story with the day of my birth."

"That's just what I wanted," Merlin replied, who could probably have done without that introduction.

"It's necessary to satisfy you, then," replied Turpin. And expressed himself as follows, increasing his pace without Jacques who was following, missing a single word:

"I was born in the little town of La Tranclière, in the Lyonnais province. My parents, who had no other child but me, were very obscure peasants, even, if I dare admit it, a trifle pagan."

"Go on," Merlin put in. "Undoubtedly, they hadn't been appropriately enlightened."

"That's what I was about to tell you. My father had a hut and a field. We would have been able to live if a procurator had not come every month to take away the bread we ate for Caesar—that's what he called the master. I can still see him, his fat face, his flat black hair and his nose like an eagle's beak.

"Go on," said Merlin, who was already beginning to get impatient. "It would have been sufficient to say that he was a Roman."

"Forgive me, then or never was the time to give his description. He worked so well that, having stolen everything from us, he filled the huts of the garrison, all Romans like him. Having nothing to do, and seeing in me a thoughtful boy, apt for anything, they taught me a little Latin and religion, and as I had a singular inclination for reading and writing, they also amused themselves by teaching me their alphabet. I succeeded marvelously in that. In brief, without knowing how, I found myself one day tonsured as a priest.

"Our life was barely supportable when a host of barbarians fell upon our canton. They were Vandals, the worst of men, if they hadn't been followed by all those you know. They wanted to take two-thirds of our hut and our field and leave us the other third, but as we had only just enough to live on until then with our meager heritage, I leave you to imagine what became of us after that new arrangement.

"It's true that one of those vagabonds, with a moustache coated with sour butter, told me that I was ruled by Roman law, which consoled me at first and saved my vanity, for I thought that there was nothing finer than being a Roman. The same man also told me that it was no more than a horrible irony, and that to rise to the rank of our former masters was to fall into the vilest dust.

"All things considered, I could have adapted to my fate if it had been stable, but other bands arrived, and not only did my new masters steal the third that remained to me, but, as I was unfortunate enough to appear a capable fellow, they stole me. They took me from one place to another, far away, to the other side of the Rhine, into the heart of barbarity.

"You can imagine what I had to suffer in the course of that abduction—not that the barbarians were devoid of resources. When they had been pillaging or killing for the greater part of the day, in the evening they liked to laugh, play dice and listen to stories. The meals were interminable. I had my place there. As for my master, picture a tall blond man with only one hank of hair on the top of his head, who usually wore buffalo horns; for all that, he was a great lover of little Latin verses and subtleties. He even wanted me to teach him a little theology, in which I succeeded only too well.

"In return, he taught me how to handle a battle-axe and a broadsword.

"I knew most of the principal barbarians whose names and customs you have so strangely disfigured. It was then that I saw Etzel, whom you call—I don't know why—Attila,[78] who was an old man of a hundred and eight at the time, the gentlest and also the most pious of human beings, always having tears in his eyes, very assiduous in his religious observances, singing at matins in a voice still full and majestic, and in the meantime, a great horseman, who has certainly been calumniated.

"He wanted me to be his chaplain. I was. I would be still but for a circumstance that I shall soon specify.

"I also knew Dietrich of Bern, whom you call Theoderic of Verona,[79] as gallant a man as could be, less devoted than Attila but just as courteous—which didn't prevent him from being the involuntary cause of a great change in my destiny.

"One day he was playing dice with Etzel. Etzel was having a run of bad luck. 'I'll bet my chaplain,' he said, looking at me. He lost. Theoderic put a golden collar round my neck. I belonged to him. He took me away.

"That simple circumstance caused me to reflect, and, from the host of sentiments that assailed me, this was what emerged: first of all, a profound resentment at being treated as an item of booty; then homesickness, the ardent desire to see my home again, if it still existed, and to hear my own language. I've told you that I had a passion for writing on fine parchment, and no opportunity ever presented itself in those forests; in addition to which, I could never get used to barley-beer or mead, the only beverages, as you know, of the barbaric nations.

"Can that be?" said Jacques.

---

[78] The etymology of the name Attila is obscure, but Etzel, the name used in the *Nibelunglied*, is unlikely to have been its original form. Turpin is correct in his observation that all the surviving writings about him were inscribed by his enemies, and are undoubtedly heavily biased.

[79] Again, Dietrich von Bern was the name attributed in German legend to the 5th century Ostrogothic king Theoderic the Great, one of whose several residences was at Verona (Bern, in German).

"Yes," Turpin replied. "Give me a few drops of the wine of Provence from your wine-skin, Jacques, for the story is making me thirsty."

Having drunk moderately he resumed: "The idea of escaping from the midst of those barbarians and returning to my homeland had never occurred to me before, so difficult to achieve did it seem; however, as soon as I'd thought of it, it seemed to me to be the easiest thing in the world.

"My chaplain's habit concealed my coat of mail. I took possession one evening of the best horse in Dietrich's court. I added the weapons you see—sword, bow, arrows—and set off at nightfall. Everyone was asleep, in accordance with the barbarian habit. It's sufficient for you to know that I traveled thus every night; by day I took shelter in some cave or hermit's niche.

"How many rivers I crossed in a leather canoe—not to mention the Danube and the Dnieper! How many forests I traversed, where the eagles were perched more densely than the mosquitoes! Moldavian shepherds were the first to hide me in their huts at the foot of the Carpathians. In return I taught them Latin and helped them tend their flocks.

"For a queen they had a beauty of the woods named Dokia, with a heart as hard as ice, who made fun of my stories. She was found one morning on the highest summit of the Carpathians, changed into a rock, along with her flock of sheep. The sources of rivers water them eternally without being able to slake their thirst."[80]

At that point in the story Merlin smiled as if he had had some part in that marvel "Certainly," he said, that's a day that I envy you, because, to judge by all I've heard about the people who drink the water of the Bistritza, they seem to be good folk. Every day I regret not having visited them yet."

"There's no doubt about it, Merlin; they merit your visiting them one day, in addition to which the goatherds there speak the best Latin in Christendom, albeit with an Asiatic accent. Lying down in the shadow of the fir-trees, how many long days I spent listening to them sing their rustic Doinas, accompanied by the sampogne. After so many tribulations, the mildness of those good people seduced me. While war was raging all around us in the bloody woods, I wanted to become a beekeeper there. In the midst of the clash of armies, it seemed good to me to sow reseda and basil around the hives and hear them buzzing. The people offered me that responsibility, reserved by them to the prudence of centenarians. For three years I kept their bees, sheltering in a straw hut that resembled a hive itself.

"One day, one of my swarms flew away. I followed it, striking a bronze bowl with a bronze javelin. The swarm continued traveling, with me following

---

[80] Old Dokia, or Baba Dochia, is a character from Rumanian folklore, probably related to the Russian Baba Yaga.

it. Thus, from forest to forest, heath to heath, I was led on foot to the still-bloody walls of the superb Sicambria, the capital of the Empire of Legends.[81]

"Don't expect me to describe its marvels to you, Seigneur, nor those of Potentiana.[82] Alas, those queens of cities are under threat; soon they will no longer exist except in Turpin's memory. I received noble feasts there of horse-meat, consecrated by the priests, and above all, I saw the great fabric of nations. Through each of the gates of Sicambria, an incessant flux of people came who went forth to renew the world. They seemed to flow like inexhaustible rivers, each ripple of which was a man of iron. Something similar to the sound of threshing could be perpetually heard in the great square, and when I asked a passer-by what it was, he replied: 'Where have you come from? Don't you know that it's the flail of God?"

"In another place—it was a smoky forge—I heard the sound of a giant hammer. Again I risked asking what it was. Another passer-by replied: 'Where have you come from? That's the hammer of God in the hand of his worthy blacksmith.'"

Visibly emotional, Turpin paused momentarily, after which he finished his story in these terms:

"To get nearer to my beloved homeland, I set off through the green forests of Bohemia. I received hospitality there in Tchek's hut.[83] While hunting bustards he had just discovered an entire flat region, by which he was wonderstruck. He was a good man, although he still worshipped trees and hawks. He was then busy distributing the plains and mountains to his entire family, which did not prevent him from recommending me to Palemon, the Duke of Lithuania, who accompanied me to within sight of the Rhine, without me having anything to fear from the ambushes of Hagen the Teuton.

---

[81] The Sicambri were a Germanic people mentioned by Julius Caesar in his account of the Gallic Wars. The name was borrowed for application to the Salian Franks when they invaded Gaul in the sixth century, notably in a panegyric addressed by Saint Remigius to Clovis, who became the first of the Merovingian kings. In the imaginary history concocted in the anonymous 8th century *Liber Historiae Francorum*, refugees from Troy are reported to have founded a city called Sicambria, in order to link the Merovingians to Homeric mythology.

[82] St. Potentiana was one of the multitude of early Christian martyrs, somewhat distinguished because the name also crops up in the Norse sagas, as that of a beautiful princess.

[83] I have retained Quinet's spelling for the name of one of the three legendary brothers who founded three Slavic nations: Lech (Poland), Czech (the Czech republics) and Rus (Russia). Palemon is given similar credit in the Lithuanian Chronicles, while Hagen is now best-known by virtue of his appearance in the Nibelung saga as Siegfried's killer.

178

"You can now understand, Seigneur, how I found myself at sunrise at the entrance to the grotto when Christ was passing by. You didn't see either my horse, which was grazing nearby, or my weapons, hidden in the undergrowth. Know that I eventually arrived, sometimes riding and sometimes crawling, at the hill where my thatched cottage once stood; but know too that I found nothing there but a heap of fallen stones, and that was the greatest pain I ever felt.

"I searched for the hut, the roof, the walls, and found nothing but thick grass; I called out, but not a breath replied.

"Of what clay is the man formed who, after having been torn from his hearth, suddenly seeing the place again, can find nothing but dust and brambles, and look at it without weeping? Of what bronze, once again, is that man formed? That's what my mouth cannot say.

"I hastened to the nearby monastery; it had been sacked. I found nothing there by this writing desk and these quills. On searching more attentively, I discovered, scattered here and there, leaves of parchment in large number, covered to the edges with writing. I soon made a vast heap of them, which I wrapped in tree-bark, and I loaded all of it on to the back of my horse.

"From that moment on, fearing to risk my treasure, I scarcely made my abode among men. I continued to live on high crags, with the young of eagles and vultures. When daylight came, I unrolled my sacred parchments at the mouth of my cave and read them. Sometimes I drew birds and flowers in the margins. My science does not extend so far as to comprehend what those parchments contain; I'm content to gaze at them and to guard them, sword in hand. But what writing! It's not the men of our day who can do anything similar. You alone, Merlin, would be able to do likewise."

IV

Turpin thus gave our Enchanter the most fervent desire to see his treasure. There was a meadow beside the road that sloped away gently. Our voyagers stopped there.

Turpin took the scrolls of parchment from his saddle-bag and spread them out on the newly-mown grass. Merlin had scarcely gleaned at them than he threw his arms around Turpin and his eyes filled with tears.

"Turpin," he said, "your name will be famous throughout the centuries, for it is thanks to you that the works of the greatest enchanters who have lived among us have been preserved. Doubtless they would have resisted the fire, come through the flames, escaped the rage of those whom envy drive to attempt their destruction, but you have nevertheless acted sagely in sparing them that proof, and for as long as there are enchanters in the world your memory will be honored among them, even though it appears to me that you have sometimes mingled your writing with theirs, which was certainly a veritable profanation."

"That's true," Turpin replied. "I reproach myself for it—but it was when I had no parchment and my hand was avid to write. In any case, I didn't know that they were the works of enchanters."

"They are their works, as is signified by their names fully spelled out. Here is the most ancient of all and the most powerful of our family, the enchanter Homer, whose magic has not been surpassed and whose name I alone remember at the present moment. Look at that writing, which shines like a many enameled flowers. He alone possessed that kind of writing. Many have imitated it but none have equaled it.

"Here, in these uncial letters, is the hand of another of our brothers, the enchanter Virgil, less great than the first, but of whom the world has preserved a vague memory, like a shadow that has finished singing. It is high time that he reappeared on earth, for he knows how to draw tears, even from things that have no sentiment, and if I'm not mistaken, the time for weeping is close at hand.

"Look at this other parchment; one might think that the fays had written it in pure gold. Oh, I believe so! I recognize the handwriting of the most knowledgeable of enchanters. On your knees, Turpin and Jacques! You see here the magic book of the great enchanter Aristotle; he it was who taught us the secrets of stones and metals; whoever possesses his book holds the world in his hand."

Jacques and Turpin had fallen to their knees. Passing from one parchment to another, Merlin began to read the pages aloud as they came beneath his eyes. His voice rose and swelled, soon becoming as melodious as that of a nightingale in the woods of Colonna and as loud as the thunder on Mount Olympus.

It was the first time, for long centuries, that the words of the ancient enchanters had resounded on the earth. One might have thought that it recognized the empire of its past masters; all the winds fell silent, the air filled with an odor of violets and saffron, as in an Eleusinian temple. No dread was attached to that evocation; on the contrary, an unknown serenity shone in all things.

Jacques would have liked Merlin to explain some of the cadenced words that he read. Merlin anticipated that thought.

"Your hour has not yet come, Jacques. You need to visit the world in my company before you can profit from those I would gladly have chosen for my masters if I had been able to do so. But the day will come, my son, when you will read their minds as I do. You will thank me then for not having put into your hands sooner what you would not have the strength to carry.

"As for you, Turpin, see what power these enchanters have! I can assure you that those of today will never equal them, for, without understanding them, it has been sufficient for you to keep their sealed leaves close to you and to cast your eyes over them occasionally to retain your good humor in the midst of the savagery of our time. Having lived more often than not in the abode of bears and eagles, how could you not have become similar to them, if you had not had this talisman close at hand? Imagine, then, what you might have done if you had had ears to hear it."

The conclusion was that Turpin had saved what was to be the consolation of sages, and that he had would have guarded the common treasure even better if he had never added a line of his own thereto.

In recompense, Merlin promised him all the virgin parchment he needed, and the fact is that from that day on, he never once lacked it. Wherever he was, scarcely had he finished his meal than he copied and copied, whenever no one had need of his rapier—for he never refused his help to anyone.

V

Listen, good people! When Merlin found himself between Gascony and Brittany, between Ardennes and Broceliande, in the middle of hallowed France, he would have liked to surpass himself. After having passed from Gironde to Saint-Florentin, visited Saintonge, Tourane, Berry and Burgundy, wandered in the Beauce, the land of the Lorrains and the Francs-Comtois, lingered in wretched Champagne, dire Bresse and other places, when he had seen so many famished and starving nations, huddled shivering on the edge of the road, a great pity took possession of his heart. He made a vow to redeem them all, and for all eternity. The promise that he had made to the people on the eve of battle came back to him. Listen to how he kept his word.

Aided by Jacques and Turpin, see him erect a round table in the heart of France, between the woods and the wheat-fields.

In order that it would last forever, he made it of stone; but he made it round in order that all the hungry, either of body or of spirit, would be more comfortable there. The feet were made of granite; there were more than a thousand, extracted from quarries in Brittany. Where large stones were lacking there were pebbles. Where pebbles were lacking, the trunks of oak trees took their place. On those contrived feet, deeply rooted in the soil of France, the stone table-top extended, in mosaics artistically polished in large sections, vast and comfortable, open to all, almost infinite. Iron clamps forged by Merlin in Armorica connected the joints and side-pieces.

There was no table-cloth embroidered in lace, either from Bruges or Antwerp. Where would sufficient have been found? Jacques took charge of weaving mats out of wheat- or oat-straw. They would be for the kings; the people would do without. Large stone seats, some sounded in the back, most of them not shaped, arranged in circles, marked places for everyone.

King Arthus prepared for the day of the feast, along with his seneschal, his cup-bearers, his bread-porters and his negroes. Everyone was coming and going on caparisoned horses at a merry gallop. The cup-bearers carried silver-plated trays; ebony-hued negroes held hanaps, amphoras, finger-bowls and alabaster pitchers overflowing with foaming red wine. That was a gift from the people of Burgundy and Roussillon. Kay, the seneschal, placed cushions and footstools in the places of the kings.

A thousand fattened oxen, half white and half black, were lying on massive silver trays; around them, ten thousand wild boar, and as many roe deer, red deer stags and hinds, on silver-plated trays. The forests of the Ardennes and Broceliande had been almost depopulated.

When the great day came, Arthus took his place first in the middle of the table, on a seat of green rattan, under an awaking of gold leaves that hung down to the ground. Two red satin cushions were at his sides. Pensively, he waited, supporting his head on his elbow. He had already unbuckled his florid shield, unlaced his helmet and opened his visor as far as the noose-guard, desirous of eating.

Nine crowned kings arrived first; they were his faithful allies. Perceval followed them, with his son Lohengrin; after them came Odi the Frank, Tristan, then Hoel, King of Armorica, Lancelot, Geoffroy de Montbrun, Yvan and Yvanet, each with a falcon on the wrist for bird-hunting, Giffret, the petty king of Poitou, the good Mélian of Montpellier, cousin of the chief of the Burgundians, Brut le Truand, Giron le Courtois, Olivier de Verdun, Comte Ganekin de Boulogne-sur-Mer, Isaie le Triste, Hugon, Ermelin, Ysembart and many others.[84] They all apologized for being delayed, in the dark forest, the noisy valley, the plaintive mountain or the remote paths, by exhausted horses or great adventures, and even in distant lands, for more than one came from the far side of the world, one from Jutland, another from the sea of Syria; Titurel the Pious came from Grenada.

The kings and knights sat down, each on a stone stool, at distant intervals, leaving room between them for entire peoples. Behind them, planted in the earth, their lances unfurled pennants like tongues of fire over their heads. Each one was radiant beneath his crimson awning, like a kind of joyous sun in one of the twelve houses of the zodiac.

"Will have to wait much longer?" said Arthus. "I'm thirsty, Frenchmen."

"Here they are," the seneschal replied. "The long road has delayed them.

Seeing the foreign guests arriving in procession from the ends of the earth, Arthus stood up. He took three steps toward them, in order to welcome them. They dismounted: Germans, Saxons, Greeks from beyond the sea and Cappadocia, and the ports of Spain, Saracens from Gor and Armenia, Negroes from Nubia, men from Albania and Kent, kissed his hand, saluting in him the king of kings. To honor them, horns and trumpets sounded, and brazen buccinas.

---

[84] Few of these names actually come from Arthurian documents; some are borrowed from other legendary sources. Antar (Antarah ibn Shabbad) was a real 6th century poet, but his life was extensively mythologized. The deliberate mingling becomes explicit later in the passage, where contrasting mythologies are carefully juxtaposed. There are several references here and elsewhere in the chapter whose origins I cannot trace, some of which might be improvised or idiosyncratically derived from Welsh or other exotic sources.

Jacques led their breathless horses by the bridle to marble troughs full to the brim with oats and hay. He shod more than one. He took off their harness and gilded saddles.

Meanwhile, Merlin, with a gracious smile, let his guests by the hand and arranged them, not in order of their blazons but at his whim. All found that acceptable. As a good jeweler mingles amethysts in a pearl necklace, he mingled those who came from the North with those who came from the South, and the guests from the Orient with those from the Occident.

He sat pale Siegfried, his helm still quartered, to Arthus' right, and Rustem, the Shah of Persia, to his left; a little further away, Antar of the three Arabies. To each frowning Teuton he gave a cheerful Franco-Gaul as a table-companion: to Gontran of Worms, Lancelot du Lac; to the old prophet Gripir, Giron le Courtois; to the grim Hagen, still drunk on carnage, Tristan le Léonais, still fasting; to Hildebrand the Slayer, Gauthier d'Aquitaine, who came from beyond the Rhine.

Brunhild had Yseult of the white hands beside her, Chriemhild the blonde was beside Genièvre with the jet black hair, Gudrun the homicide beside Sanche the gracious, Hildegarde between Blanchefleur and Enide of the azure robe.

Where was Viviane? She had made garlands of cornflowers and ivy to crown the guests. The daughters of the land had to take her place. Even the Valkyries and Houris, mingling with the Undines brought roast meat accompanied by fruit preserves, and presented everyone with golden apples from Merlin's orchard. The Valkyries poured mead into aurochs horns, the Undines the wines of France into golden pitchers, staining the blue of carpets red. Kay the seneschal had many a joke with them.

And flowers were streaming everywhere, with gems and carbuncles; the wedding at Cana and that of the good master of Verona were eclipsed.

But where is Viviane? No one has seen her, not the kings, nor the queens, nor the barons, nor the poor people; she is all that the day is lacking.

When every king had taken his place, and all the barons were seated, many peoples arrived. Merlin took them all by the hand, and led them gently to their granite seats covered with rugs.

"Sit down, peoples," he said.

The peoples sat down—and that was the first time that they had appeared before the kings and the barons. But they dared not eat before the king, no matter how hungry they were.

"Eat," Merlin said to them. "Arthus grants you permission."

"That's true," said Arthus.

With that, they began to eat, without raising their eyes.

In the meadow, Merlin's dog was playing with Odin's two dogs, yielding bones to them. Around the table an entire population of singers was standing up; there were troubadours and minnesingers among them, and also Arabian singers who mingled prose with verse. Even Robin Hood whistled his tune, hidden in a group.

The French singers praised the heroes of Germany and Jutland, the land of mists, Odin, Baldur the Strong, and the Teuton gods born of the earth; the minnesingers lauded the sky of Provence, the sea of Brittany, honored France and holy Rome.

Thus, celebrating one another's heroes, all hearts were content. In addition, Merlin walked around the table, nourishing peace, concord and, most of all, good humor everywhere. If he saw a frown, he was there to prevent quarrels starting.

Arthus remained pensive, however, as if the table were empty; he still seemed to be fasting.

"I'm thirsty, Merlin," he shouted. "You wine doesn't slake the thirst. Do you hear me, Merlin? I'm hungry; your meats don't satisfy me."

The twelve peers frowned, adding: "The king has spoken. Your wine is not the best. The more we drink, the thirstier we become."

The people would also have said the same, but, not daring to do so, they began sighing.

Smiling, Merlin said: "Don't be annoyed. Here, Barons; this will content you better. Drink as much as you like; the thirst will pass."

At that moment, he made a sign to Turpin. The latter, coming out of the wine-store, was carrying a deep cup in both hands, jeweled and foaming, so much so that all eyes were dazzled. No one knew which sparkled more: the carbuncle embedded in the rim or the crimson liquid.

"The Grail—the Lord's cup!" they cried, in unison. "Who has found the cup?" And they were intoxicated in advance with joy.

Arthus said: "Frenchmen, I have ridden northwards, through the tenebrous forests, but in vain. I could not discover it."

And Perceval le Gallois said: "King, I have visited the Syrian Sea. With my bloody lance I have searched the desert, but I have not found the cup."

Everyone spoke thus, all adding: "Where did you find it, Merlin?"

"Tell them, you who know," replied the prophet, addressing himself to Turpin.

Then everyone fell silent. Turpin, placing himself in the middle of the kings and the peoples, spoke in this fashion, while each of his words was softly accompanied by a distant murmur of harps and viols, so that the angels seemed to be responding to every word.

"Yes, it is thus, as it is said:

"'This cup, great sires, was sculpted by shepherds and by kings, and given as a present to the Man-God wailing in the straw in the table in Bethlehem.'

"It is thus, as it is said:

"'When Jesus was on the cross, and he was thirsty, this cup slaked his thirst.'

184

"The worthy Joseph of Arimathea found it in the sepulcher and gave it to the Bretons.

"Rome pillaged the cup and was intoxicated by it.

"After Rome, the Goths drank from it at their leisure.

"After the Goths, the Huns, under good king Humbert.[85]

"Humbert gave it to me; I am giving it to Merlin."

"And I," Merlin put in, "am giving it to you all."

So saying, he approached it to Arthus' lips, who passed it to Siegfried; Siegfried passed it to Gauthier, Gauthier to Hildebrand, Hildebrand to Lancelot, Lancelot to the children of Lara, the children to Antar of Araby. Thus it made a circuit of the table, so that everyone found his thirst slaked and satisfied.

From the hands of the heroes Merlin took it back; he passed it to the people, including the most petty.

"How do you like it indigent peoples?"

"To our taste, Seigneur!"

"Don't get drunk."

And holy amity entered into the grimmest hearts. Already, Perceval was wiping his lance, which until then had remained stained by the blood of Calvary.

"How have we been able to tear one another apart?" asked Siegfried.

"I repent of it," said Arthus to his nephew Mogred.

"Grant us accord," said the crowd.

"It's done," murmured Jacques between his teeth, while he brought spices.

Everyone was delighted to meet at the table. Having come from so far away, had they ever hoped for that? Undoubtedly not. And yet, how many adventures would have remained inexplicable, without that denouement? Everyone recounted his own, modestly and hastily, impatient to hear those of others. Arthus spoke about the forest of Broceliande, Hagen the manor of Dragenfeld, Antar the desert of Africa, Rustem the sky of Persia strewn with rubies, Perceforest the crau of Bresse,[86] Hali-Hassan of Saracen towers; all of them understanding one another by implication, speaking in Old French, Christians and Saracens eating from the same plates.

At that moment, Golfin de Tours arrived, followed by his lion, which roared as it got near the meat, Frollon, of Paris, Ghérent, the son of Erbin, Mor-

---

[85] The forename Humbert is said to drive from "bright Hun" but its attribution of a Hun king is purely symbolic.

[86] Perceforest is the eponymous hero of a fourteenth-century prose romance, which recycles, transfigures and blends many of the elements of previous romances in a manner not unlike modern fantasy novels.

gan, the physician, and Gourdnei with the feline eyes who could see in the black night.[87]

"Are there any places left?" they asked, with one voice.

"At your pleasure," Merlin replied. "Sit down here, comfortably. Jacques, feed the lion."

Shortly thereafter came a host of nations, pale and exhausted, having missed their way.

"We're looking for the cup!" they cried, wiping away their sweat and their tears. "We were told that it was in the Sepulcher."

"Blind men!" said Merlin. "Here it is, on the table."

"But the table is full! How shall we get near it? There's no more room for us."

"Your seats are here, peoples; sit down."

The nations sat down, and the table was still growing. The peoples were growing too; for the first time, they were at their ease, which astonished them all, in view of the fact that their multitude was increasing from one hour to the next. Everyone admired Merlin's hospitality and swore privately to do likewise one day. Frankly, in comparison with his, what was the hospitality of kings and peoples? A veritable beggary. They had often begrudged their guests air, and above all light.

A wanderer also arrived, desperate, and walking alone. All the nations pointed at him as he came forward, and drew away from him.

"Poor Wandering Jew," said Merlin, who would have liked to embrace him, remembering that he had encountered him once before and had sheltered under his cloak. "Here, Ahasuerus, drink, as everyone is doing, from this cup. It's the cup of Calvary."

"Calvary!" cried Ahasuerus, recoiling in horror.

"Let him drink!" said the crowd.

"Is it," Ahasuerus asked, "a beverage to make one die?"

"No, it makes us immortal."

"Keep your odious present for yourselves, then."

He drew away. No insistence on the part of the peoples could bring him back to the table. Jacques devoured him with his eyes without daring to approach him. Turpin, having accosted him, tried in vain to bring him back. But at least he learned what would be written about him later, in the book of Ahasuerus.

"Let him drink from the cup!" shouted Arthus, Siegfried and Hildebrand, among whom hatred as beginning to weigh again.

"Yes," bayed the crowd. "If not, stone him."

---

[87] Gourdnei is otherwise known as Gwiawn Cat's Eye, and Ghérent as Geraint, while Frollon is cited in Geoffrey of Monmouth as an Armorican rebel killed by Arthur. Golfin de Tours and Morgan the physician remain elusive.

"Woe betide anyone who touches him," said Merlin. "Let him be, good people. He's the first one I was unable to cure. He is thirsty too, but of dolor, and wants a different cup. He will find it."

Those words appeased those who were already recovering a taste for hatred. The wanderer who had awakened it was far from their eyes. Everyone sat down on his stone seat. The gazes of the kings and peoples had only darkened momentarily.

Before separating, the reconciled guests, arranged by nations, exchanged presents, pledges and sacred promises of amity. If they ever broke them, the sky would fall on their heads—that was what they said.

Perceval gave his lance to Hildebrand; he received a beautiful steel bow in return, sharpened into a blade. Others did likewise. They all resumed the roads to their homelands.

Immediately, the cup-bearers cleared away the remains of the feast. Jacques had already taken away the king's part, and Turpin the flagons. Warned by Kay, the Seneschal, Merlin became angry. He ordered that everything be put back in place, and wanted the table to remain, day and night, eternally laid, in the same place, beneath the sky of France, laden with wine, meat and spices.

"Because," he said, "how do I know that there are not pilgrim peoples on earth, wandering, mendicant or sick, whose mouths lack bread at this moment. For them, it's important that the table always be set, in order that they can eat at leisure, whether they come from the north or the south. The cup must also remain full, within arm's reach."

Having said that, he confided the table to the French; he wanted the best of them to guard it, day and night, from father to son, sword in hand. Almost everyone had gone. They were called back by the sound of horns. Those who came back, Merlin placed as sentinels; there were some in every province of France; they promised to stand watch, from generation to generation, reliving one another in shifts.

"Watch, Frenchmen," he continued. "Watch for all, good men of Normandy and Gascony, Champagne, Brittany and Anjou. I entrust to you on this table the food and drink of worlds to come. Do not let anything be stolen therefrom, by day or by night, by any thief or gluttonous kind, excepting the birds of the sky, if they, like us, are also thirsty for God the Dispenser of Justice. Seneschal, you'll answer to me for that! You, Turpin, replace the flagons. You, Jacques, don't take away the king's part."

At these words, Jacques and Turpin, humiliated, each returned everything he had removed. Many naked swords, gilded shields and scarlet coats of mail glittered in the sunlight around the table; Arthus invited the world there every day, with his sword. The birds that passed overhead and untamed bulls drank from the cup.

The next day, without further delay, pale nations arrived, breathless, almost naked, dying for want of hope, and, finding the table laid in the heart of France, sat down in silenced and ate their fill.

After them, others came, hungrier still, and gorged themselves in their turn. The table, always growing, always had empty places.

"Who has prepared this eternal banquet for us?" said the mendicant peoples in shrill voices, shaking their ragged mantles, hardened by the winter.

"Merlin," replied the bread-porters.

And after them, I say this:

Fellow men what have you done with that round table? Peoples, you have tipped it over; kings, you have broken it; sages, you have laughed at it; madmen, you have forgotten it.

A few scattered stumps of it remain, under the brambles, in the crannies, in the ruts, under the thick bushes and in the pools where the reeds lament. Perhaps it could still be set up again, and for the rest of my life, I would gladly devote my two arms to gathering together the stones, patching the edges, carrying the mortar and standing up the granite seats.

But fellow men, those whom you loved, you no longer love. Those whom you honored, you now insult.

Peoples, you are thirsty; why have you broken the cup? Peoples, you are hungry; but it was you who tipped over the table.

What will you do tomorrow? Do you want to die, then?

BOOK TEN: MERLIN ENCHANTS THE ALPS AND THE GARDEN OF ITALY

I

When can I flee the noise of hatreds, the spiteful echo of venomous re-proaches, bloody words, the gnashing of teeth? I would climb to the grassy summit of Noirmont carpeted with fir-trees, or the jagged peak that looms up to close Lac Leman, and if my feet could take me there, I would envelop myself in the shadow trailing at the foot of the squat towers of Chillon.

Here,[88] in an age of stone, my conversation is with the rocks massed above my head. Alone, forgotten, buried, I have made friends with them. I have learned to understand their language; they understand mine. When my heart is near to murmuring, I gaze upon their immutable face. Shame grips me then, at feeling so fragile.

When my soul is unsteady, they sustain me with their soul of stone; they let fall upon me their unalterable thought, which has resisted, on foundations of granite, all the tempests of the sky. In a thousand sonorous voices escaped from their lairs, they say to me: "You are in your place as we are in ours. Let's stay where we are; be wary of looking for a better one."

Where would I go among human beings? How could I bend my tongue to their subtle thoughts? How could I fashion my visage and my heart to all their denials? I feel weak just thinking about it.

Here, in this enclosure, crenellated all the way to the sky, I receive a good message winging from every point of the expanse. Here, the pink summits smile at me at daybreak; none of them thinks on insulting me. Here, I contemplate, from the earliest hour, the high places to which no servile thought ever rises. Here, I draw from the serenity of limpid days in the blue cup of Lac Leman, which opens to give the Rhône a triumphant entrance.

With the dawn, I've seen a white veil emerge from the depths of the wa-ters; by its flags, I've recognized Merlin's boat. While it advances slowly, the Dent du Midi raises before it a tripod of snow prepared for his evocations. Where will he land? Will the two banks compete with one another to attract him? Which will he prefer? To his right, the mountains of the Oche allow silver ribbons of snow to unroll all the way to their feet, but to the left you can see

---

[88] Hermione's notes state that this passage is a depiction of Quinet's life in Veytaux, where he lived from 1858 until the events of 1870 caused him to has-ten back to besieged Paris.

Montreux, always bathed in spring sunlight, and the black collar of forests that twines around the summit of Cubli, so neatly that the others are jealous.

To celebrate my hero, the four seasons are assembled at the same time around me: spring with its soft ever-changing eyes of periwinkle-blue, violet and jonquil in the sheltered bed of the Verraye; summer in the fiery light of the morning that emerges from the gorge of Valais as from the mouth of a furnace; autumn in the crimson clusters of rowan-berries that hang from the leafless trees; winter with its ice on the faces of the Noirmont, the Jaman and the Naye. At their feet is the village where I signal to Merlin to land.

"Here it is, Master; it's here that you need to furl your sail forever. Come, prophet, under my roof, where I've prepared the morning meal for you. Bring us patience in the waiting, the victory of the just, the holy peace that follows it; also bring us the strength and health of oak trees."

But my voice doesn't reach him.

Standing in his boat, he contemplated the rocks of Meillerie sharpened into plowshares, Vevey, the nascent shadows of Clarens, the walls, then new and white, of Chillon, which served in those days as the palace of the Undines, the water-nymphs, as soon as dusk fell. At that sight, two streams of tears ran from his eyes; he would have liked to hide, for he was ashamed to weep in front of Turpin. Being unable to disguise it he said to him: "Have you never wept without knowing why, Turpin?"

"Never," Turpin replied, delivering a robust stroke of the oars.

Jacques claimed that it had happened to him two or three times in his life.

"Well," said Merlin, "I won't hide it from you, friends! As I consider these sacred places, these harsh rocks, this blue lake, and even those virgin vines that make a girdle from Vevey to Clarens, an invincible sadness invades me heart. If it's a weakness, excuse it. Why that painful melancholy? Don't ask me that. It seems to me that I can hear a soul in mortal lamentation. Tell me, can't you hear moans emerging from an oppressed breast? Oh, what if it were Viviane inhabiting the tower of Vevey where the ivy snakes? What if she had withdrawn to these unknown places? Can't you hear, on the other shore, an insensible sound, like an amorous soul leaning over a torrent?"

"I can only hear the cries of the eagles over the chalet of Chamosal," Turpin replied, "And the axes of woodcutters in the woods of Chillon. Do you want, Seigneur Merlin, to cast a spell over this part of the lake. For myself, thank God I can't see any subject of melancholy here: in the distance, green vines that promise a joyful vintage; everywhere, a salubrious air that fills the lungs. What reason is there to be sad? I've never been more disposed to rejoice in my life. Come on, drink from this pitcher with me, and drown these phantoms."

"I'd like to, my friend," Merlin replied, "but whatever I do, they reappear. Yes, yes, from both sides of the lake I can hear an amorous plaint emerging from the waters. Listen. It's Viviane who's calling. Let's hasten to where that voice is resounding."

All three went ashore at the place where the rocks of Meillerie where whitening. The traveled with the greatest care to the Chablais, drank the fantastic water of Evian, where Merlin cast a fortunate spell, interrogated the smugglers of Amphion, picked grapes with them, forgot themselves around the press, made friends with the basket-carrying Savoyards, friends of good people, picked hazelnuts and chestnuts freely. But nowhere did they find what they were looking for.

"I told you so," said Turpin.

"Was it a dream, then?" said Merlin, looking in turn at the water, the sky and the rocks.

"Believe me, Seigneur Merlin, give your brain a rest. The imaginations that pass through people's heads are will-o'-the-wisps or daughters of Hell. Woe betide anyone who trusts them!"

"Who knows?" said the prophet, sighing. And he went into the Valais by the gate of Scex, where he cured four goitrous tumors and a leper from the city of Aoste. He also cured souls merely by touching them with a glance.

Then, turning toward the Bernese mountains, the was the first to climb the virgin peaks, searching with his eyes, in the distance, for Viviane's white dwelling, fraying paths everywhere to torpid nations, collecting simples everywhere for unhealthy peoples. He passed the Furca, went down the Reuss, through the gap of Urseren, jumped over the Devil's Bridge, enchanted the Grutli, took the oath of three jurors in a meadow; from there he climbed the Righi, scaled the Titlis, drank from the cascades of the Hazli, wintered in the tower of Resti, went astray on an Alp of Linthal; and during those long days, not an hour as wasted, not a path along the edge of an abyss went untraced, there was not a chalet where justice, concord or at least sage advice did not enter with him. Ever chamois hunter marched in his footsteps thereafter.

The least of his works, in an old canton in Uri, was the arbalest that he carved out of maple-wood. Four times he tried it, standing the feet in the snow on the summit of the Titlis. With the first arrow he struck a black bear at Morgarten, the second at Sempach, the third at Granson and the fourth at Morat, and ten times further beyond the vast peaks. Finally, finding the arbalest to his taste, strong and gnarled, fitting it with a brazen string, he made a gift of it to a child named Tell, whom he found guarding goats and singing a *ranz des vaches* on the narrow road between Altdorf and Glaris.

II

Sublime Alps with teeth of ice and coats of snow, if it's true that I was born at the foot of the least and most humble of your steps—and it's for that reason, no doubt, that my heart so easily takes flight toward everything inaccessible hereabouts—tell me what engrossed thought, what intoxicated hope, drove

Merlin to traverse your summits, where and how, in order to descend into the garden of Italy.

For then, you were truly virgin, veiled since the morning of creation. No road had yet dishonored your summits, there was no hospice, no refuge and no Newfoundland dog bearing the salvation of travelers lost in the torment around their necks.

Eternally motionless, the spirits of the glaciers were the sole witnesses of Merlin's passage. They made an effort to approach him, when he followed the track of the chamois, but they were unable to descend from their summits, so tightly were they bound by their chains of crystal and diamond, glittering in the sunlight. Huddled under their white mantles, they tried to rouse themselves, but sleep was more powerful than curiosity.

Only the avalanche, always on the lookout, which the slightest noise awakens, precipitated itself in their midst, howling: "Who are you, the first to attempt this path?"

"I'm Merlin!" shouted the Enchanter, loudly enough to dominate the torment.

The avalanche passed by and fell into the gulf. Nothing remained but a damp vapor, with an explosion that faded away into a vague rumor in the abyss. Turpin, who was very courageous, had no difficulty admitting that he had been very frightened. Jacques asked, without blinking, whether such things happened often.

"We've taken the most difficult step, my son," Merlin said. "The rest is child's play. We're on the summits now."

Undoubtedly, if Merlin had wanted to be transported at his ease over the plains that then extended before his eyes, he would only have needed to issue the command. Among so many ever-ready dragons, wings deployed, there would certainly have been no lack of those who might have responded, in large numbers, to the diviner's slightest appeal; and, seated hindmost of three, on the bounding back of a winged bull, you would have seen him fly for some time over the garden of Lombardy, and then descend, slowly and majestically into the pines of a villa, where a crowd of people would have gathered to greet him—or, at least, a dogaressa, her neck laden with pearls, or the daughter of a podestat, since both of those dignitaries were already known on the other side of the mountains.

I will even say that he ought to have shown himself thus, in his pomp, inasmuch as people love to be struck by the marvelous; and even a little trickery in far from displeasing them at the start of things.

By depriving himself of those means of success, he exposed himself to being misunderstood even by the best. But if you have understood our hero, you will have seen that he much preferred simplicity, even though he has been greatly reproached for the contrary, and he had a particular horror of charlatanry.

That is why, unlike the majority of men of his art, he only ever employed the marvelous and the supernatural as a last resort.

It was by the soul that he produced his prodigies. He laughed—it was wrong of him to do so—at enchanted wands, necromantic bonnets, magic cauldrons, broomsticks, and even Medea's winged chariots, owls' tongues, toads' teeth, and the heritage of other enchanters: in a word, everything that was merely external appearance; masks, clothing, tricks of the trade and routine.

It was a capital error, the greatest of his life—which he realized, alas, when it was too late to correct it. What use was it then to know that it was in fact the mask that governs human beings?

It followed that Merlin preferred to all the monsters of the Apocalypse the most natural means and the simplest equipment. He descended from the Alps concisely. With Turpin's bow and arrows, interlaced with a few willow and rhododendron branches the three travelers formed a crude hurdle. Merlin and Turpin sat down on it. Jacques Bonhomme placed himself in front of them with a stick in each hand. When the preparations were complete, all three launched themselves perpendicularly into the abyss.

As rapid as lightning, they shaved the edges of the precipice, but instead of being engulfed therein it was sufficient, to swerve, for Jacques to lean on one of the two sticks, and the gulf was avoided. They turned over two or three times. Immediately they dug their arms into the soft fresh snow all the way to the elbow, and held themselves in suspension; then they crawled back to the hurdle, not without exchanging ingenuous, radiant bursts of laughter, which only the divinities of Homer had previously known, when they too traversed space in the blink of an eye.

More than the gods, however, Merlin and his companions had the sentiment of being human. As the moving abysses turned, hollowed out, were effaced and filled in before their eyes, all difficulty was forgotten in that serene intoxication. Merlin was obliged to admit that. He shared the joy of his companions and began to smile like them when they reached the bottom of the valley. That first mischievous smile of Merlin's is preserved intact at the place where they stopped. It's directly opposite the Lilliputian isles of Borromeo. Look at them! Everything smiles at you there with that whimsical joy, known only to the children of the gods, which Merlin rediscovered that day.

III

It happened that the gates of Italy were closed with iron bars, like a jail; the threshold was obstructed by an entire population of exiles who were forbidden to enter. A few were striking their heads against a bronze wall, others bending down to the opening of a ventilation shaft. In the crowd, thousands of voices were calling out, replying to one another, interrupting one another and overlapping, among which a few could be discerned.

"We're exiles from the pleasant fatherland, toward which even those unfamiliar with it turn their gaze."

"Like leaves torn from the lemon-trees and pines of Italy, which the tempest blows from place to place, we're traveling without knowing where; but we always return to this adored threshold, which it is no longer permissible for us to cross."

"Oh, how cruel the hour was when it was necessary for us to bid adieu to all that we loved! Today more than ever, it resounds with a funeral echo in our broken hearts!"

"Since that moment, not one joy has reached us. Strangers in a strange land, we have seen the days succeeding one another, and the feverish wait has consumed our souls. Now that everything has deceives us, we are still waiting."

"You who pass along this road, it you are permitted to enter, don't leave us moaning on the threshold."

"While hope still sustains this fragile flesh, labored by so many dolors, open the desired doors to us, for pity's sake! Perhaps we shall no longer be alive tomorrow; no one will find our bones, to carry them to the beloved soil that gave us birth."

They fell silent. Merlin paused momentarily to listen to the crowd of men with tanned faces and dark, hollow eyes in which the source of tears seemed to have dried up.

"They've certainly been waiting long enough," he said to his two companions. "It's too long to weep and moan. You, Jacques, get rid of this bolt that obstructs me; you, Turpin, the horizontal bar that keeps the gate so firmly closed upon the wretches. Do you hear me? Let's go, friends! Be bold! Be brave!"

And shaking the gate himself, he first made it screech on its age-old hinges; then he opened it wide to those who were moaning and dared not believe their eyes.

"Come home, good people!" he shouted.[89]

All of them immediately pressed upon his heels, and there was sufficient room for all of them. Having rediscovered their homeland, their fields, their enclosure, the stone stairways of their houses and their parents' graves, they sat down under the olive-trees and wept. For from the Brenta to the Arno and the Tessin to the Tiber, the local people had difficulty recognizing them, so many years had they been away. Their faces had changed, their hair had turned white; many of their best friends had died in their absence; they searched for them everywhere with their eyes; no one could tell them where their tombs were.

---

[89] As Hermione notes, one of the many political causes that Quinet embraced while in exile himself was that of Italian exiles forbidden to return to their homeland, to whose successful campaign he thought that he had made a useful contribution.

IV

Merlin took so much pleasure in the company of those just people that he forgot to drink and eat; he did not want to stop until he had reached Verona, where the worthy Romeo was waiting for him. One summer evening, as the Enchanter was entering the city through the French Gate, he found that the Teutonic emperor Max was entering triumphantly and emphatically through the German Gate. Max's pompous entourage contrasted with Merlin's modest one. On the one hand, there was nothing but men-at-arms with golden spears, prancing Mecklenburg horses richly harnessed with scarlet velvet saddle-cloths hanging down to the ground, strings of diamonds and amber around the necks of seneschals, undulating grouse feathers in Tyrolean hats; on the other hand you would only have seen simplicity, candor, a little embroidery on a short blue mantle.

The true royalty, however, was with Merlin; how could you doubt it? Scarcely had the emperor, who was about to take possession of Italy and have himself crowned in Rome, learned that my hero was in the suburbs of Verona than he sent him his golden orb, his sword, his baldric, his ax, his hand of justice and his leaden crown, with the instruction to have them enchanted and ensorcelled immediately, *without delay*. Such was the already-Gothic formula that the Teutonic lord was using.

Accustomed to seeing everyone bow down before him beyond the mountains, he did not doubt that our Enchanter would hasten to obey. Naturally, he attached a hundred times more importance to the popular consecration that answered to him for the love of the Italian people than to the ceremony in Rome.

Imagine, Readers, his fury and amazement when his messengers told him that Merlin had paid very little attention to them and their globe, and that he had obstinately refused to attach the slightest charm or the most wretched enchantment to the Teutonic crown.

At that news, the emperor felt shaken. Nevertheless, he put on a brave face, because of the Rhingraves surrounding him. Followed by the most important, he went on foot, bare-headed, unceremoniously, to the modest retreat where our Enchanter was staying. He found him eating figs. Although he was usually so polite, Merlin contented himself with greeting him with a curt nod of the head.

It was a terrible check for the pride of a sovereign habituated to having all of Italy under his feet. If he swallowed that insult, it was because he knew better than anyone everything that he had to gain or lose from Merlin's complaisance.

Caressing his long pale brown beard with his fingertips, the emperor said: "Do you alone want to resist me, Merlin? If you had followed me, you would know that this land is mine. I have it from Julius Caesar, who bequeathed it to me from father to son."

"Do you know Latin?" replied Merlin coldly.

"No, but I too am called Caesar."[90] Then, seeing that these words had no effect, the Emperor tried to win the Enchanter over with a little adulation, which caused him to add familiarly, in a low voice: "In spite of everything, just between us, I only believe that I'm half the emperor of this country while I lack the support of Merlin. A thrust of your hazel wand is worth more, in my eyes, than all the vain applause that welcomed me as I emerged from the Tyrol."

"You're right," Merlin replied, having decided to set aside all false modesty that day. "You know the art of command too well to be unaware that no scepter can do without Merlin's consecration."

"I know that. Every kingdom is dust if Merlin does not attach his charm to it."

"Don't hope, then, for peace in this garden of Italy," our Enchanter replied, proudly, "for know that as long as there's a Merlin on earth, Sire Emperor, that he will refuse you that homage."

"Render me my iron crown."

"It's mine; I'm the one who forged it."

"Assure me of Verona."

"Oh, no, fine sire! The worthy Romeo and Juliet have wept burning tears."

"But Venice?"

"It's me who nourished its marine lion; it only obeys me; I shall unleash it."

At this statement, the emperor quivered from head to toe. All the Germanic lords hesitated as to whether to implore Merlin or tear him to pieces. A few Italians mingled in the cortege felt their courage reborn.

Merlin did not leave anyone time to interrupt. His words flowed freely, like an Engadine torrent.

"Yes, Sire Emperor, there will be no lack of false diviners who, begging under your foot, will take lead for gold. They, with their thirsty throats, will acclaim the wan sun of Germany; they will legitimate the false heritage, and call you Caesar. But in the midst of their raucous acclamations, your heart will not enjoy a moment's repose, for Merlin, alone will be more powerful than all the false enchanters; he will ignite hatred even in the hearts of women, and they will give birth to justice. Don't pick, good sire, a single flower along your road; poi-

---

[90] More than one of the rulers of the tottering Western Empire had a name beginning "Max-" but this insistence on the title of Caesar is suggestive of Maximian, emperor from 286-305, who claimed that title with the permission of his superior co-emperor Diocletian, and subsequently began to term himself Augustus. This section of the text is, however, deliberately anachronistic, its subsequent references encompassing much later periods of time, based on Quinet's reflections when he visited Italy in 1832, and this confusion is foreshadowed by the fact that the syllable Max- also connects to the Germanic "Holy Roman Emperors" of the 15th century named Maximilian.

son will have been poured into it. Don't sit down on the grass of the meadows; it will hide the Lombard viper. And certainly, there will be no treason, since I have warned you. How many battles will be fought in these plains? How many tears will be shed to give you a crown that will always tremble on your head? Neither peace nor truce; not one mouth will open other than to curse you."

"If Merlin wished it, all would be changed to benedictions."

"Me, bless you? Great God! That would be to curse myself."

At that moment, he recognized in the emperor's entourage several individuals whom he had met in the valley of the Rhine, including the King of Thule. He addressed him: "What are these white mantles doing here? This is not their land. They offend the gaze like a fir-tree covered with frost in an orange garden."

Then descending to the most intimate details, he had the patience to show that the pretended testament of Caesar was false, and that the golden orb was bronze.

That convinced the courtiers that there was nothing they could do to obtain the complaisance of the Enchanter, and they turned in secret to Jacques, in the hope of winning him over. How many gifts they made him! Jacques had the indiscretion to accept them all, without thanking them. He was, for instance, given pebbles from the Rhine for emeralds, and some pieces of glassware that he took for the most precious jewels of India.

That tinsel dazzled him. Everything that shone in his eyes immediately blinded him. Already the reasoning of the Teutons seemed to him to be unanswerable, but Merlin fortunately perceived the maneuver in time; he interrupted the conversation with no regard for Teutonic etiquette—an abruptness that made him as many enemies as his refusal. Hagen the Mayencian disguised his hatred and his Germanic bile beneath a soft smile that allowed a glimpse of the gaps in his teeth.

From that moment on, Emperor Max felt the land of Italy trembling beneath his feet. He lost sleep over it and his sparse hair turned white. Everywhere, in the most secret things, he saw Merlin's hand. While hating him, however, he esteemed an enchanter who had been able to resist intrepidly caresses even more forceful than threats. His principal followers were already occupied with means of taking their revenge. As for the Italian people whose garden Merlin had defended, they conceived for him that day as much love as they had had dread, and did not take long to prove their gratitude to him, as you shall see in the next chapter.

V

Without taking any notice of the Germans' threats, or the traps that they might set for him, Merlin went further into Italy. The mere sight of the blue sky brought I don't know what mad hope into his heart; the further he walked, the more he felt his heart softening. As he descended from the Apennines, respiring the odor of lemon-trees and myrtles, he murmured: "I recognize Viviane's breath; surely she's living somewhere in this country."

And after those words, he formed a serious plan to search for her until he found her.

At that time, Leodegarius, the consul of Bologna,[91] was the podestat and gonfaloniere of Florence the Superb. As soon as Merlin had arrived in the city, and as he rested under the arcade of the *loggias*, the gonfaloniere brought him the great register of the major and minor arts and asked him how he ought to be recorded therein, and under what title.

"Enchanter," Merlin replied.

"I guessed as much!" exclaimed the gonfaloniere. "It's the foremost of the major arts. Poetry comes next."

Then he inscribed Merlin's name in golden letters at the head of the *Populani Grassi* and the *Popolo Minuto*.

That ceremony completed, our hero asked the five priors, the high council and all the common people assembled whether they had seen Viviane pass through the valley of the Arno. "Because," he took care to add, "there is hereabouts, in the most meager undergrowth, an embalmed scent that only her hair can exhale."

Their curiosity piqued, the five priors, clad in long red robes, asked him what Viviane looked like.

"Viviane resembles everything that is most delightful upon the earth. Her floating hair is like the agitated foliage of a sacred forest, her eyes like two sapphires newly emerged from the hands of a Florentine lapidary."

"You talk like a lover," said the priors and Leodegarius, with one voice. "Could you not paint her for us?"

"Gladly," said Merlin.

He took two brushes and a palette that happened to be in a corner of the Palazzo Vecchio and, going to a white wall, he sketched with a few rapid strokes a divine face that excited a murmur of admiration from the gaping crowd a long time before the image was complete.

"How beautiful she is!" the crowd said. "We've never seen anything similar, and God knows that Florentine women are beautiful!"

The aged priors confessed that they would like to begin their lives over, simply to meet such a ravishing person. Leodegarius expressed himself in very similar terms.

---

[91] Leodegarius, Count of Bologna, is one of the many fictitious European aristocrats cited by Geoffrey of Monmouth as contemporaries of Arthur, but one of very few who features in *Merlin l'enchanteur* as something moiré than a "spirit of the ruins."

"What would you say, then, if you had seen her in the flesh, and not this miserable sketch?" said Merlin.

And he went away, from place to place, painting the adored face, sometimes in a fresco, sometimes as a mosaic, but more often in simile pencil. I've seen one of those faces myself, as sketched by Merlin, in the church of San Miniato, to the right of the main altar at the back of the choir. When I think about it, a disturbance still grips me.

Although the people of our time would scarcely believe it, an entire people fell in love with the images painted by Merlin. There were no longer any men to be found but those who were gripped by passion for that unknown object, of whom the Enchanter had shown them, perhaps imprudently, the inferior portrait. There were thousands of painters who only breathed in order to reproduce some of Viviane's features. In truth, they were reduced to copying the model that Merlin had provided, but each of them hoped to discover a beauty hidden in that unknown model.

Merlin often took his kindness so far as personally to guide the hand of the painter or sculptor who had most success. To some he said: "Those really are her vermilion lips, but where is her smile and her kiss?" and to others: "I recognize her medallion nose here; that's almost the incorruptible line of her forehead and the slight arch of her eyebrow—but great God, how far that frail bust is from the truth!"

Merlin then corrected the faults of the imitation with his own hands. He added, he retrenched, he changed—but he left the glory to others.

The result was that Florence was soon covered with portraits of Viviane; churches, monasteries and palaces were all full of them. Even the hermits wanted to possess illuminated copies. The solitude of more than one shady Camaldolese retreat in the Apennine mountains was embellished by that image. It was the talk of the entire region. Everyone was interested in Merlin's amour. What am I saying? Everyone shared in it. "But after all, where is she? Who is she? Where does she live?" the common people frequently cried, in the very midst of their dazzlement.

One day, a young painter named Thaddeo,[92] none of whose attempts had been satisfactory, fell into discouragement. He began to hate his brushes. Full of bitterness and disgust, he went to find Merlin.

"Are you really sure that she exists, Master? Are you condemning us to pursue an imaginary, impossible resemblance? Look! I've squandered my days madly trying to paint her, without ever have seen her. Now I'm going to die. Oh, Merlin, you would be very guilty if you have deceived us!"

"Me, deceive you Thaddeo!" Merlin replied. "Oh, great God! If Viviane doesn't exist, I exist even less. If she's a dream, I'm no more than a shadow!"

---

[92] Suggestive of Taddeo Gaddi, a prolific painter of Madonnas who was placed at the head of a list of the most renowned Florentine painters in 1347.

At that moment the gonfaloniere announced that, having distributed Viviane's portrait throughout Italy, the living model had finally been discovered in Venice. She was, it is true, only a simple boatwoman, but in that nation, everyone was noble.

"What does it matter?" Merlin cried. "Nobility is in the heart. Let's go, Turpin."

They left that same day.

Nothing remarkable happened on the way, except that as they emerged from the outskirts of Ferrara, our voyagers found a hippogriff ready-saddled in a meadow. The bridle was hanging down from its neck, but the bit was not in its mouth, which permitted it to graze. Its two great red and gold wings were furled over its sides. It allowed itself to be approached to a distance of six paces; then it began to flap its wings, as if it were expecting someone and inviting him to depart. Turpin, always in quest of great adventures, seized the bridle. He was about to apply the bit to the hippogriff and mount it when Merlin stopped him.

"No, Turpin! Leave the hippogriff to graze here until the expected rider comes from Ferrara—for that rider with diamond spurs will come, and he'll look for his mount, and it will be a great misfortune if it's been stolen from him. All the more so as you could easily fall out of the saddle and perish without honor; instead of which its legitimate master will steer it, not without peril, across the plains of the atmosphere, and there won't be a point on earth or in the heavens that won't smile on seeing him pass by on the mount with extended wings. For us, until we've found Viviane, it befits our ill fortune to go modestly on foot."

Having received this reprimand, Turpin let go of the hippogriff's bridle and went back to the path that would take him to Venice.[93]

VI

When the Enchanter Merlin landed in Venice the Beautiful for the first time, neither its towers, nor its silver domes, nor its ducal palace, nor its golden-maned lion roaring in the bosom of the azure sea could yet be seen.

There were a hundred islets of arid sand, the dwelling of storm-birds, with a thatched cottage here and there, inhabited by poor folk; not a single keep and only a few boats moored on the beach by hempen cords.

The doge was a boatman. He lived in a fisherman's cottage with his daughter Nella, on the produce of his nets, and I suspect, a little piracy.

---

[93] Although a similar creature had been described by Virgil, the hippogriff was first named by Ariosto; one such mount is ridden in the *Orlando Furioso* by various enchanters and knights, including Astolpho, who flies to the moon thereon.

Nella was seventeen years old, perhaps less, but not more. The down was still on her cheeks. Her eyes were already shining like a star still steeped in the Ocean's tears.

A simple boatwoman! An ingenuous child, content with her lot, who sang joyful barcaroles on the shore!

She was not Viviane, but she resembled her, to the extent that anything earthly can resemble the celestial.

One evening, Merlin was sitting next to her on a wooden bench at the threshold of her hut. They were repairing the mesh of the same net together.

Twice Merlin looked up at Nella; twice he was astonished, in his heart, to find her so beautiful.

"Nella, Nella, how sad your lot is! Such a desert hearth! Such a small hut! Such a torn net! You're made for a better fate. Tell me what you desire; you have the word of a enchanter that I'll bring it about without delay."

"What do I lack, Seigneur? I don't know, in truth. My hut is small, but it's large enough for my father and me. My net is torn, but the mesh can be repaired."

"Nella, Nella, think about it more. Tell me, what do you want?"

"I'd like a light boat, Seigneur, with a steel prow to cut through the waves and the weeds of the lagoon."

"A boat? Nothing more. You shall have it, Nella."

The next day, Merlin attached to the threshold a gondola with a shining prow armed with a dozen teeth of polished steel, to bite the bristling mane of angry waves. On seeing it, the young woman smiled.

"Tell me, Nella, what else do you desire?"

"I'd like, Seigneur, a church with golden cupolas, in order to pray, and a tower a hundred feet high in order to see the hundred islands asleep at my feet."

"You shall have the church to pray in, and the hundred-foot tower."

And without adding anything, he built San Marco, with the campanile prostrate at the feet of the golden angel.

"Is that enough, Nella? Give me, in recompense, a smile."

"No, not yet, Seigneur."

"What! What else do you need, boatwoman?"

"I'd like an alabaster bridge, to walk over the profound sea."

"You shall have an alabaster bridge."

And immediately, groaning, he made the Bridge of Sighs.

"Well, Nella the boatwoman, are your wishes fulfilled?"

"Far from it," she replied, her eyes full of tears. "Won't you make me a fairy palace, embroidered with your hands, like Viviane's?"

Merlin made that palace; it is the Doge's palace.

"There you are; that's everything. Now give me that sprig of orange-blossom in your hair."

"Not yet," she said. "I'd like, to carry me over the shoreless sea, a flag-decked vessel that can carry an entire people."

"Oh boatwoman, how your desires have grown in so short a time! The vessel you shall have to cradle you on the shoreless sea."

Without further ado he fashioned the *Bucentaur*, decorated with gold, silver and silken flags.

"O boatwoman, you can desire nothing more. But as for me, my heart is desiccated by a strange thirst. I have not yet kissed your pink cheek once."

"One moment," she said. "I'd like the roaring lion that runs over the sand at my feet."

"Boatwoman, boatwoman, here's the lion with the thick mane. It's lying down at your feet. Already its roaring is causing Zante, Cerigo and Candia to tremble. Pay me now, with a kiss—yes, a long kiss from your lips."

"Wait, Seigneur—just one more thing. It will be the last. I'd like your magic ring."

"Take it," he said.

And Merlin removed his magic ring from his finger and gave it to her.

Laughing, Nella threw it into the bottomless sea—and now the Enchanter remains alone, deprived, weeping on the deserted shore.

He gazes at the vast palaces mirrored in the depths of the dormant waters. The mocking reeds insult him, whistling.

VII

Wise as he was, therefore, our hero could pile one fault atop another. Harsh experience had shown him that well enough. That discovery might have taken away his ancient pride, if that had been his inclination. In his confusion, he also lost his harp on the edge of the Lido, which brought his distress to a peak.

If, at least, he might be able to redeem his fall be some heroic enterprise…but where would he find the opportunity, in such lean times? It would come of its own accord to offer itself to him freely—heaven grant that he would be able to seize it!

It was in the Apennines beyond Bologna; one summer night, without a breath of wind or a murmur, stifling and stormy, still full of the inextinguishable fires of the day. At the zenith, bloody Cassiopeia was leaning toward Orion. From time to time, there was a rapid lightning-flash; then the horizon quivered, opened and closed, like a divine eyelid. To render the road narrower, black basalt rocks loomed up in smooth, tapering columns; you might have taken them for the dwelling of beautiful Italian dreams, especially when heavy nocturnal moths collided blindly with the clouds of fireflies by which the darkness was illuminated.

Merlin and his two companions had just climbed silently to the harshest crest. Two leagues still separated them from the little town of Taglia-Pietra; it was there that they would find their shelter. Suddenly, to their left, half way up, blue, red and violet flames, flowers of fire enameled with gold, sprang from the meager mountainside. An immense sigh was heard, slowly exhaled by a crater.

"Merlin! Merlin!" cried a voice that emerged from that lair, and everything fell silent again.

Prey to a thousand presentiments, he ordered his two companions to go ahead to Taglia-Pietra. Alone, he strode toward the place where his name had resounded. He reached it. At a corner of the rock, his eyes were dazzled by the crazy flames than ran over ashy fissures. A strange form was there. A seated man—was it really a man?—got up with a start as he approached.

"Don't deny your father," said the incubus. "Yes, it's really me—Satan, Belial, Beelzebub, whatever you care to call me; for I too am three in one, and I have three crowns. I reign in the night and I'd really like to initiate you in the increasing empire of darkness." In a hoarse voice, he added: "I'm getting old you see. You're now at an age to soothe me but it's urgent that you make a decision. Enough follies, Merlin. It's time to be wise."

So saying, he dug his foot into the ground, from which a fire-follet emerged. His composed face passed from menace to a smile. With the firm intention of making Merlin feel the yoke of paternal authority, he was fearful of terrifying him, and conserved in consequence a kind of bonhomie a hundred times more hideous than the outbursts of his fury.

As soon as he spoke, Merlin recognized the knight that he had so long honored as a father. There was no possible doubt. It really was the king of darkness, such as he had seen him during his descent Into Hell: the same swarthy face; the same ash-colored eyes; the same brazen collar. Merlin shivered; he would have liked to flee all the way to beyond Limbo. A secret power tied his feet and his tongue. All that he could say in reply was: "I recognize you." By virtue of a residue of infantile habit, he almost added: "Father." Fortunately, the word died on his lips, along with his breath.

"What kind of life is this, Merlin, I ask you?" the incubus continued, shaking his head authoritatively. "Where is my instruction, my advice? Was it for this that I watched so carefully over your cradle? Ingrate, why give me the trouble of engendering you myself, of my own blood? What have you been doing while you've been breathing? You've become infatuated with humans and peoples, you've listened to their whining with all the seriousness in the world. They have two ways open to them. You've done your best to teach them the better one, and you'd like to keep them bound to it. You know very well, though, that it doesn't lead anyone to me. You preach patience, mollify the violent, tempt the accursed with the bait of ridiculous virtues. Do you want, if you please, to ruin me, to dishonor me—me, your father?"

"Let me explain," Merlin put in, timidly raising his eyes.

"Let me finish," the incubus went on. "You can talk afterwards, at your ease, and above all, don't look at me like that. Yes, this is what you do for humans every day: you protect them; from what can you defend them? When they stagger, you sustain them; when they fall, you pick them up; when they're in rags, you clothe them; when they're damned, you pretend to save them. What a noble employment for a son of Hell! You give them all a taste for light and common sense. Are you mad, Merlin? No, you're just an unnatural son. It's out of hatred for your parents that you oppose us in everything. You're driving me to despair, and our plan, I can see, is to make me die of chagrin. Anyway, I've been disgusted with life for some time; this dirty trick you've played on me—you, my own flesh and blood, my everything—is truly too much. I can't stand it anymore."

Here the Devil burst into sobs, but it was impossible for him to weep. He hid his eyes with his clenched fists and put on a show of wiping away tears.

"You're crying?" said Merlin.

"As you can see! You've extracted my final tear. Oh, how cruel it is for a father to be rejected by his favorite son! Doubtless, in the preceding life, I merited this punishment. I accept it to my detriment! But it's more than I can take."

Incredibly enough, Merlin was moved by the distress of the incubus, which had begun with feigned tears and ended up with choked cries, on the brink of howling. To see the king of Hell crying was such a novel spectacle that the good Merlin burst into tears in his turn. I don't know what voice of blood still spoke within him, because he tried to console the monarch of the abyss, whom he saw then so tender and so humble.

Merlin's ingenuousness was immediately exploited advantageously by the incubus.

"Oh, my little Merlin," he continued, in a broken voice, "how I love you, how I love you still! For you're the very image of your mother Séraphine. How many times, in Brittany and in Bresse, on the threshold of the door, did I bounce you on my knees? Do you remember, child? That day, for instance, when you were playing knucklebones and I taught you to cheat! How that amused you! And that you promised me then to equal your father? And that other day, further back, when I taught you to bite your nurse's breast, laughing—do you remember that?"

"I have a vague memory of it," Merlin murmured.

"Well, if that's the case, my son, you won't want to crucify your father. Look, my friend, I'm speaking to you softly, when I could roar. In good faith, into what confusion have you fallen? Is it fitting, for the legitimate king of the abyss, to find his own son wandering on foot in the company of a hermit and a clown? Such as I see you, however, I could still give you a place of honor at my side."

"My destiny pleases me, because I've made it myself. I'm free—that's the most important thing of all."

"I advise you, my friend, not to boast about your destiny. What are these ridiculous prodigies, into which not the slightest devilry enters? What is this new pretention to give up wands and put the soul above matter? What are you trying to achieve in spreading the serenity of olden days around you? Silly, outmoded, threadbare ideas that no longer bring back what they cost. You live too much alone, you no longer comprehend your era; it surpasses you by a mile; it's ahead of you, my dear. Here you are regretting the light, wretch! What rubbish! Go on, at least give yourself the possibility, damn it. You don't know the new joys, the delights of the abysses newly discovered by me, nor the intoxication of those who nourish themselves on the latest fruits of darkness. You can't imagine the voluptuousness of being rocked in the bosom of the immaculate night, our common mother, of rolling from surprise to surprise, in gulfs that lead to other gulfs, of embracing, hollowing out, amplifying and perfecting nothingness, for Hell is making progress. We've added a great deal to it—entire galleries that overhang one another to infinity, lakes and seas of anguish that have no shores. The worm of the sepulcher has grown too; you'd no longer recognize him; and even that's only a beginning. But what am I saying? Admit that you now have a taste for the correct clarity. Just make me that confession."

"I admit it. I try to see clearly, at least within myself."

"Good! That extravagance is lacking in all the others. But what do you want, then, scatterbrain—to bring back Eden?"

"That's one of my thousand desires."

"Very good, Merlin! Bring back Eden! Oh look—the word alone has made my hair turn white. Dear son, fruit of my loins, by all that there is of the most powerful in the world, by your father's club-foot, by the boiling cauldron, by the sulfur of Gomorrah, by the foremost of vices, of false oaths, of murders, listen to the paternal voice, which has never deceived you! Be positive at last; search for the solid in everything; your youth is passing, or has passed, while we're talking. Leave illusions to defective minds. Say goodbye to stupid thoughts, and put on the virile robe of the strong. You lack worldliness, my dear; it's a question of propriety and good taste. Can't you be less bourgeois? A little flexibility—if not, you'll doom yourself and us with you. Pay attention, too, to the devotion that I ask of you for your cousins and your nephews. It's so easy to become a good man, a Roman, at the expense of one's own family!"

"I'd be irresponsible."

"What's that? What is the human species if not irresponsible? Head in the clouds and feet in the mud; it soars like the hawk but it crawls even better than a slug; it has the eyes of a lynx to count shooting stars, but for the rest it's as blind as a mole. Go on! All that there is of irresponsibility, of non-sense, shared between all beings, is found in its fullness in that masterpiece called humankind."

"Your words hurt me."

"And your actions crucify me. I no longer encounter anything here on the walls but mosaics and frescos, all representing a complete, albeit somewhat insipid, beauty. You know that nothing is more odious to me than beauty; even diabolical, it still seems to me to be a challenge and a reproach. And it's you—

yes, you—who has taught them to scribble those features on walls, the model of which they were incapable of inventing on their own. Do you want every expanse of wall to criticize me and blast me, then? Celestial, Edenic gazes, lighting up on wood, on stone, on bonze. Every one of them transpierces me; and the one who invented that torture for me, damn it, is my son!"

"If those features are divine, forgive me. I wasn't thinking about making a torment for you."

"What were you thinking about, torturer?"

"Viviane."

"Your future, that is?"

"The most beautiful of beauties."

"Yes, I understand—again some carpenter's ideal. For doubtless, poor fool, you still believe in the ideal. Truly, I thought you were more intelligent."

"All that I do, I do for love."

"What's that word you're pronouncing, Merlin?"

"I said that I only act out of love."

"Really?"

"Truly."

"So you, Merlin, whom I carried in my arms, you believe in love?"

"More than in myself."

"Very nice! Dare to repeat what you just said!"

"That's my faith."

"You believe in love! That word awakes all my hatred. Swear to me to hate what you love."

"Never."

"Come back to me. I'm the door of bronze that leads to everything. Even to enter into what is called good, it's necessary to go via me."

"You've always said that, but you've taught me that what one says ought always to be the opposite of what one thinks."

"So you're abusing my secret?"

"I'm taking advantage of it."

"You're using my weapons?"

"To defend myself."

"You're reasoning?"

"You were the one who taught me logic."

"Obey."

"One doesn't learn obedience in your school."

"You're denying your father?"

"As you denied yours."

"Treason! I'm the one who engendered it."

"You've engendered your own scourge."

"I disinherit you."

"Please do."

"I curse you."

"Your curse is my salvation."

"Marvelous, good man! At least I still have force."

"No, poor subterranean incubus, who exploits weak flesh."

"Enough. Inexorable powers of the gulf, black children of darkness! Kobolds, dwarfs armed with tridents, gnomes with sharp claws! Legion of the dead, spirits of the eternal night, with three eyelids and silken wings! Come, run, fly, seize the accursed, this parricidal child!"

"Spirits of the day with rosy hair! Amour that precedes the aurora! Mysterious god of the triads! You too, great king of Elves, immaculate Christ, protect me!"

"What a mixture you're making there, Merlin! Your evocation is worthless, it won't bring anyone. You're a heretic, my dear. You'll burn stupidly. But you'll be in the proletariat of the damned, when you could have been by my side. Come, then, kobolds, hydras, crawling tenebrions! How slow you are in coming!"

"Powers of the forests! Souls of centenarian oaks! Spirits that march in threes, armed with sickles! And you, first and last of spirits, Jesus of Nazareth, make haste! Come! Surround me!"

"Once again, my friend, you're confusing everything. You're confounding Olympus and Paradise. You don't know your Gospel. Come with me, and you'll learn it in letters of fire."

"*Vade retro, Satanas!*"

"What are you saying, my little Merlin? My child, my first-born son! Anything you wish, my Benjamin—but don't take that tone with me!"

"*Vade retro, Satanas!*"

"I beg you, don't talk Latin to me. I can't bear that language. It has the same effect on me as the clangor of bells. It drives away my ideas. Insult me—I don't mind that, provided that it's in French. In that language, I can bear anything."

"*Vade retro, Satanas!*"

"That's too much! I give in—but I curse you again! Merlin! It's you who are crucifying your father!"

With these words, the incubus plunged into the gulf. He disappeared, and the errant flames recommenced their magical dances, which are still going on. I saw them myself one starry night, in the same place, in testimony of what I've just related.

At the moment of Merlin's invocation, the jagged summits of the Apennines seemed to descend and hollow out into a funnel, like the circles of bronze in the plaintive city. The two seas that they separated, at Ravenna and Caprara, moved and whitened with foam. Thus, on a Sabbat night, two cauldrons, full to the brim with ensorcelled herbs boil in the witch's hearth.

Merlin had just sustained a struggle a hundred times worse than that between Jacob and the angel. Breathless, he went down the mountain and rejoined his two companions in Taglia-Pietra, whom anxiety had prevented from sleeping. Although they saw by his distressed expression that the night had not been tranquil for anyone, neither of them dared interrogate him. As for him, he did not reveal until a long time afterwards what had just happened to him.

BOOK ELEVEN: MERLIN'S PASSION

I

Herds of buffalo that dispute the Flaminian way with you, frightened horses running over the heath, clouds of dust that rise up—the dust of twenty peoples—a fiery sky, a terrain of darnel, with a solitary tower here and there that guards the desert, torrents buried under masses of mastic-bushes, broken aqueducts, white huts founded on black tombs; in the distance, a crumbling wall, a low gate with a death's head in an iron cage for an escutcheon—that is Rome. Our voyagers entered it by the People's Gate.

Already, each of them is hastening to where his inclination drives him. Turpin is going from church to church, cloister to cloister, from St. John Lateran to the Vatican. Jacques has heard the piping of the *pifferari*, which descends from the Sabine. Suspended on that rustic concert in the shadow of the Madonna, he has forgotten everything; he is swimming in ecstasy.

Merlin is visiting the sacred fountains, spurting in deserted squares at the foot of obelisks and ruins. He breathes, in the scent of the wallflowers of the Coliseum, the souls of the ancestors. For it seems to him, on arriving in this place, that it is enough for the living to walk over the dust of such great dead men.

Who knows how long that kind of life might have been prolonged, at the whim of our pilgrims, but for an incident easy to foresee? The voices that had been heard in the Apennines had resounded over the Tiber. The rumor spread around Rome that Merlin was a sorcerer devoted to all the practices of Hell.

As our Enchanter was picking daisies near the Baths of Caracalla, of the savage grandeur of which he was particularly fond, soldiers came to seize him. After having tied him up—for he let them do it—they took him to the Castel Sant'Angelo, a sepulcher that had become a prison.

Counting on Jacques' well-known weakness, the judges had him seized at the same time; it was him that they interrogated first. At the sight of the pincers and the braziers, Jacques felt his faith in his master wavering. When one of the doctors asked: "Are you not Merlin's servant?" he replied "Me, his servant? What are you talking about? I don't know the man."

Satisfied with that response, the doctors heaped him with caresses; that had an effect on him that terror could not have contrived. On the second day, when the judges asked him whether he had witnessed any infernal works, he replied: "I certainly think there's a little devilry in the man, and even a distant relationship with Satan."

On the third day, the same judge that had interrogated him told him that they needed two faggots of branches; he would render the tribunal the signal service of going to cut the necessary branches from Egeria's wood.

"Here, take this sickle, my friend, and go." At the same time, he indicated the route, so well that it was impossible to mistake it.

Jacques took the sickle, sharpened it and went to the indicated place; two hours later, he came back carrying two bundles of myrtle, orange and other odorant branches on his back, which he disposed in a small pyre in the Palazzo Sant-Angelo. At that moment Merlin was very pensive, leaning on his elbows at the window of his prison; he saw him pass by weighed down by his burden; he sighed, but as not astonished. It was at that moment that he said: *Sancta simplicitas!*

Before he had turned round, a hermit confessor with a hooded head and a girdle of rope had slipped into his prison, and was standing beside a prie-dieu.

"My son," he said, "Hell is still coming to you, since Heaven has abandoned you."

Merlin turned his head at that voice, having recognized his father disguised in monk's garb.

"Quickly, quickly, my son—I can still save you. Take my hand and follow me down this slope. My horses are whinnying in the courtyard. Come on, then, obstinate soul! There's not a moment to lose!"

"No, Father, it's not by you that I want to be saved."

"By whom, then?"

"Myself."

"So you're refusing me at this supreme moment?"

"Yes."

"Well, so be it. I'm at least curious to see how you'll redeem yourself by your own genius. Try, my child. Look, do you see the summit of that capital? That's where I'll perch. From there, I'll see everything, hidden under the stone mask of that tenebrion with three mouths crouching at the top of the colonnette. If you need me, I'll be there, my dear son, you hear."

"Once again, Father, I want to save or doom myself."

While the incubus when to sit down on top of the capital among the granite salamanders and ghouls, Merlin looked around or his harp, in order to fortify his heart at the approach of evil. It had never resounded in Rome. He thought that its echo would be more powerful here than anywhere else, in the circle of the seven hills, where the ashes of so many peoples would quiver at his voice. What would happen when the song of Arthus or that of Brut the Breton[94]—for he had both of them upon his lips—would enter into the tombs of Roma Vecchia? Brut would reawaken Brutus, the dust would be renewed; Marcus Tullius, Numa and

---

[94] The "song of Brut the Breton" is presumably Wace's verse rendering of the story told in Geoffrey's *Historia.*

the ancient sages would come under the cypress to hear the song of Merlin, which resuscitates the dead. But where was his harp, the consolation of the good? Someone had stolen it from him; perhaps it had even been broken by the wicked. Neither the jailer nor the watchmen he interrogated could tell him what had become of it. That was Merlin's first wound.

From the height of his prison he saw the vast distant horizon whiten under the radiant steps of the morning, and every time the dust rose up on the road beneath the sunburned arcades of the aqueducts, he thought that it was the peoples, arriving out of breath, coming to his aid. How many times, too, did he think he saw the sword and chain-mail of Arthus sparkling through the Italian pines, as the king, followed by his five hundred thousand knights, was coming to liberate him. Already, in thought, he must be lodging the twelve peers in the Pantheon. Every day, in the same place, he waited, looking in the direction of France, and, his heart going out to it, he said:

"O France! Sweet France, the hallowed, is it you appearing under that verdant tree? Hurry! Will you let me perish here, you whom I loved so much? Gird the sword that I have forged and place yourself beside me. Don't wait for the night to surround me, for death to descend upon my head and touch me with its wing; I yearn to see your flowery arbors, whose springs I have enchanted.

"Come, then, France the honored, with the handsome face and the iron breastplate; don't leave me any longer to be wounded by the wicked and insulted by goats. See how they are rising up here against me, and I'm alone in resisting them. Although I'm a captive, don't disdain me, for you would be disdaining yourself. It's not here that my tomb ought to be; it's beneath the shady forests of oaks strewn with sacred stones. If you free me, I promise to circle your head with the three crowns of Arthus.

"But if, on the contrary, you let me perish here, heartbroken, forgotten and consumed by waiting, walled up in this tomb with the specters of the Caesars, shame be upon you. From century to century your enemies will say: 'She has left her prophet to die, pitilessly.'"

It was thus that he spoke and prayed, but in vain. Only the dust of the dead stirred in the Roman countryside. That was Merlin's second wound.

The third was the deepest. As soon as the peoples had begun to suspect that he was not the strongest, they had become disdainful of him. As soon as they knew that he was a captive for their own cause, they believed him lost and rejected him. From all points of the horizon he saw coming against him not merely one Judas but entire populations of Judases, who were urging one another on, full of hatred, beneath the reddening sun, agitating their red hair across the plains. The human species took on, at that moment, over almost all of the earth, the face of Iscariot.

Merlin's father roared with joy.

"See, my son, how your people remain faithful to you!"

Heaven heard; it darkened, all the way to the region of the blessed.

Those whom Merlin had loved the most were the first to come to stone him with the debris of the round table on which he had nourished them. Others made the pilgrimage solely to mock him. They could be seen from afar swarming around their banners, on which was written: *Iterum crucifigi*.[95]

Sitting at the top of the tower in which he was imprisoned, their cries and mockeries rose up to him. They reproached him for the dew he had drunk and the wild fruits that he had eaten, as if he had starved the world. And the crowd said, in as many languages as here were on earth—for although they did not understand one another with regard to anything else, they understood one another enough to insult him:

"Can you see him?"

"I see him."

"Here?"

"No, there."

"How pale he is!"

"Bah! He's afraid of dying."

"Take aim with your arbalest, comrade!"

"Good shot! The bolt grazed his head."

"Aim lower, comrade—there, at the heart."

"Look, Merlin—here's my present!"

"Where are your enchantments, false enchanter! Come down then, if you dare!"

Saying that, they would have liked to spit in his face; they even tried, but the tower was too high. They consoled themselves, thinking that they would see him burned the next day, or dismembered, or crucified. Among them, Merlin made out some of those that he had favored most: Raoul de Cambrai, Yvain d'Avalon, the pious Titurel.[96] Fantasus was also among them, but curiosity seemed to be driving him even more than the fervor of repudiation.

In the rest of the world there was not one nation, or one creature, from which an insult did not reach him, like a poisoned dart. Forests of naked double-bladed swords marched against him. Among those swords he recognized those

---

[95] In the Latin version of the apocryphal *Acts of Saint Peter*, as Peter is fleeing Rome in fear of crucifixion he meets Jesus on the road and asks him "*Quo Vadis?*" [Where are you going], to which Jesus replies "*Romam vado iterum crucifigi*" [I'm going to Rome, to be crucified again]. The quotation was very well known even before the Polish writer Henryk Sienkiewicz wrote his international best-seller *Quo Vadis?* (1895).

[96] Raoul de Cambrai is a *chanson de geste* whose surviving versions date from the 13th-century, although almost certainly based on a 12th century original. Yvain is one of Chrétien de Troyes' heroes. Titurel is an invention of a 13th century work by Wolfram von Eschenbach, which has only survived in fragmentary form.

he had forged himself. That of France was the longest. It passed through the bars and he was heart-broken. Oh, how Durandal, Joyeuse and Hauteclaire were shivering to see themselves turned against the one who had forged them![97] At that sight, Merlin closed his eyes and thought about dying.

They believed that he was afraid. That was the signal for the greatest repudiation.

Some of them had, in fact, brought with them the cup of the Holy Grail, which he had given them, still half full of the sweat and blood of Calvary. They filled it with poison and put it to his lips; then, as he turned his head away, they threw it in his face, so that the blood of the Lord was once again shed upon the ground, which drank it avidly. The grass also drank, and withered in the distance. Hyssop commenced growing on the Janicule and the Palatine, as on Golgotha.

Meanwhile, they came to take him from his prison, and they wanted to make fun of him before putting him to death. That is why they led him, a halter round his neck, into the midst of the jeers, to the raised terrace of the Capitol, from which they hoped to show him in chains o the whole world.

"Triumph! Triumph to Merlin!" they cried. "Go on, Merlin, deny yourself as we have all done. This is your Sacred Path."

Merlin sensed that they were speaking and acting thus out of cowardice and meanness rather than black wickedness. He could not hate them.

The bells sounded a knell, and dusk began to fall. Then they dragged him toward the Tarpeian rock in order to throw him off it—but the rock was too low for their taste. From there they dragged him to the sewers of Tarquin, but he purified them with a breath. From there they took him to the Coliseum; they would have liked to throw him to the lions, but the lions were sated. Seeing that, they threw him into the catacombs, where they hoped that he would be buried alive, without there being any need to kill him with their own hands. Merlin found his way in the black labyrinth; he reappeared in the daylight before the baying mob of his enemies.

And from the garden of the Palatine Hill to the Janicule, from the Viminal to the Colline Gate, everywhere he directed his eyes, he saw a freshly-dug grave. Jacques had dug one himself, whistling, to flatter the gravediggers.

"It's too many," his master said to him as he passed by. "Those they had dug already ought to have contented you."

In every square he saw a blazing pyre, and Jacques had also lit one of those, larger than the others.

"For whom are all those pyres, when one alone ought to suffice?"

"For you, Merlin," replied the crowd. You have three lives. One pyre would not be enough for you."

---

[97] All three swords are from *La Chanson de Roland*, Joyeuse being Charlemagne's and Hauteclaire Olivier's.

At that response from the multitude, his father thought that his last hour had come; lost in the vast crowd, he drew close to him furtively.

"I'm still here, my son! I'm afraid for you. This is your last chance. Let's go, once and for all."

"I'm staying. I feel sorry for them!"

II

Meanwhile, the judges, doctors, sages, the great men of the continents and islands, all those who practiced the ancient art, Chaldean astrologers, Vortigern's diviners, necromancers from Toledo, were saddened that Merlin was still alive. Fearing that the anger of the peoples might be as vain as their love, they assembled and summoned Merlin to appear before them in the Coliseum. The peoples sat on the steps, the powerful on emerald thrones, all rejoicing in advance at seeing the defeat of Merlin by the sages and his crucifixion.

They chose to contest with him the most renowned of scholars and diviners; that was Blasius, whom time had magnified.[98] Without appearing to remember their old friendship, Blasius asked him where his instruments of sorcery were hidden, for no wanders or necromantic bonnets had been found in his lodgings, nor any of the things most indispensable to his art—except that the Enchanter was wearing a miter with three crowns that day.

Merlin struck his breast. "Don't search elsewhere," he said. "This is where the magic is."

"Merlin, false enchanter, tell us how you domesticated the lions of the islands?"

"With justice."

"On what did you nourish the dragons of Kylburn?"

"On light."

"How did you extinguish the blazing pyres?"

"With the dew of hymns."

"How did you shake the rocks of Cambria?"

"By thinking about them."

"What do you do to calm an angry sea?"

"I contain my anger."

"Why does that miter have three crowns?"

"Because I am the pilgrim of the three lives."

"For what do you live?"

---

[98] Quinet adds a note alleging that this contest is "in the tradition" [i.e. the *Prose Merlin*] and adds: "I could have borrowed a few more features from Latin prophecies, but they would perhaps have seemed excessive for our epoch so I abstained. The lines relating to the orchard of golden apples and Morgane are taken from Gallic songs."

214

"For liberty."

"And what else?"

"The future."

"Brave king of the future, what are you doing here?"

"Braving the present."

Then having seen the pincers that were there to torture him, Merlin finally interrupted himself in order to look at them more closely. He picked them and struck the cauldrons with them, which resounded under the colossal galleries and the vomitoria of the circus.

"Great God, what's this?" he said. "Doubtless they're your magic cauldrons. Show me one of your enchantments."

"As curious as Hell!" cried Blasius, who began an exorcism in these terms: *"Anima Abyssi, nomine Merlinus, retrogredere in Abyssum!"*[99]

At the same time, the members of the crowd, rising to their feet, waved their thousand banners. They said to the seven hills and the four winds: "Render to Hell its infernal Christ." And they burst out laughing.

The mockery of the peoples then did what their anger had not been able to do. That cold mockery cleaved Merlin's soul better than a blade. That was his blood-sweat. Weak and dying, he sought the prophet within him, and, no longer finding him under their jeering, he cried in agony:

"Weep for me, hills of darnel, uninhabited ruins, islands and bleak shores, since the eyes of men remain dry! My spirit abandons me. For century after century, the desert future offers me no shelter.

"Who am I to recount what is not yet, which perhaps will never be, other than in my dreams?

"Who assures me that I shall dwell in the resounding palaces of the future? Who has said to me: *Here are the keys; open; enter; they are yours*?

"The earth has not said it to me; and when has Heaven confided its secrets to me?

"Is this the day when I am born in Hell? Is it the one when I shall descend into the gulfs of the accursed?

"Have I learned the secret of justice with the damned, in the subterranean places where there is no hope?

"Abandoned by those who have loved me, I wander among the phantoms who do not know me; above me soar the homicidal vultures that bear a golden yoke."

On hearing him speak thus, all those who were there rejoiced. They murmured among themselves: "See how well it's going! He's discouraged, in despair. Now we'll defeat him easily."

Then Merlin said: "Where is the shadow of my orchard of golden apples in the Isles of the Blessed? How beautiful my sacred trees were, when the most

---

[99] Approximately, "Creature of Hell named Merlin, go back to Hell."

215

beautiful of the beautiful, with the long hair and pearl-white teeth watched over them and me!"

"Good," said the crowd. "Now he's prophesying. Who's that young woman with the pearly teeth he's talking about? Some gypsy, no doubt. Dolor has certainly taken away his reason. Yes, it's heartbreaking to see a great man raving. Listen! Listen! His mania's gripping him again!"

"Can you hear, kings and peoples, what the birds are singing in their radiant voices in the undulating treetops of the forests?

"They're saying: 'Has the mountain not shed its mantle of frost?

"'Has the hawthorn not donned its silvery florets again?'

"And me, I say after them: 'I want to hope against all hope. I want to believe, against Heaven and Hell united.'

"My prophetic song announces the advent of Justice in the midst of the resounding trumpets of Armorica and Cambria.

"I see Morgane bearing in her right hand the forest of Caledonia, and in her left the towers of Gaul.

"She will bring equity to the earth, and peace into my heart."

"Truly," said the crowd," he seems drunk on the wine of the future."

"Does he also intend to ensorcel us?" said Master Blasius. "He'll make a fine court jester. Laugh, then, peoples!"

The peoples the started laughing again, the stupid, hideous, servile jeering that is the prerogative of toothless skulls.

"Pity! Pity!" murmured Merlin.

"He's begging for mercy," the crowd replied. "No, no mercy."

"Woe betide you!" said Merlin, in whom indignation finished reawakening the prophet. "Peoples, you are laughing at yourselves and your own hope, for it was for you and not for me that I asked for pity.

"You are laughing at the sweet song of the birds that presage iridescent days.

"Listen, then, to the roar of the lion of justice; he is leaping out of the circus, disdainful of the dust of those who do not want to be reborn.

"Like dragons devouring one another in the ruins, despair and hope are colliding in my heart.

"But you who hate me, rejoice! Hope is the weaker today, and I feel it tottering; now, it has disappeared under your homicidal laughter.

"O men, how hard you are to me, and harder still to your posterity! Your children are born orphans of justice; they shall not see its sun; blindly, they will enter into a blind universe.

"But I, on the bank of springs, without them, without you, on my own, I shall deploy the azure tent where the good, the sage, the righteous, the irreproachable Arthus will come to sit down."

When the thunder rumbles in the sonorous forests, the great oaks are afraid. Trembling in every leaf, they whisper with the blades of grass and the pale heather lost at their feet. When Merlin had spoken, the kings bent down toward the peoples, the great toward the small; they all whispered among themselves. He completed their confusion with these words:

"If the power of charms is in my soul, if I have ever collected the mistletoe from the oak and drawn the dew of France from the golden basin, if Christ is of the family of enchanters, I order that these remain enclosed in this invisible circle."

And with his hand he traced a circle in the air, over the assembly of the judges, the doctors and the diviners.

Their heads inclined in spite of themselves beneath Merlin's yoke, like the bulls of the Sabine, which submit resentfully to the laborer's yoke. They felt imprisoned in a magic circle; since that moment, none of them has emerged from the invisible enclosure in which they are captive without even seeing the barrier. Their immobility became so profound that you might have thought them petrified if their lips had not continued to murmur speech that they no longer understood. The words that tumbled from their lips belonged to the language of the dead, and no living person could respond to them. The most frightening thing of all was the resounding void of their intelligence, by virtue of which nothing gave a better idea of the sepulcher of the mind.

The mages, the diviners, the ancients of the ages and the powers of the world looked at one another and went pale at the same time. Only Doctor Blasius would not confess that he was vanquished as yet. Addressing the crowd, he cried: "*Venite, populi!*" The words seemed strangled, and were not understood by anyone. He then had the idea of evoking some spirit enchained in the doctors' books. Several times he repeated the formula of invocation. The angry heavens remained closed to him. No spirit appeared, and terror seized him in his turn.

"Have no fear, Blasius," said Merlin. "I forgive you; but leave your ancient art and practice the new one."

With these words, he left. Without anger and without bile, he breathed on the pyres. The pyres went out. Carried by invisible wings, he skimmed the ground. As for those who wanted to block his way, they could not even crawl.

III

Meanwhile, on earth and in the heavens, all the spirits that were obedient to the Enchanter, wherever they were, had stirred at the same time to come to his aid, and, running or flying from the extremities of the world, a few even crawling, such as salamanders escaped from dolmens, they arrived in haste to make him a rampart. Water spirits came from the druidic forests of France, fire spirits from the gorges of Etna, those of the air from the heights of the Pennine Alps.

As they appeared they formed themselves into legions, camping on the Campo Vaccino, whose enclosure they had soon filled; then they overflowed into the gardens of the Palatine Hill, causing the gates to screech on their hinges. Gorgades with the faces of women and the bodies of goats formed two legions by themselves; then came after them the follet spirits, which formed more than a hundred; and they descended upon the maremma and the islands in the Tiber; then came the winged sylphs and the Scottish brownies; they sat on the steps of the Coliseum that were still empty and filed them to the top, as a swarm of bees fills a hive. The jinn also arrived from Persia; membranous wings extended, they soared momentarily over Merlin's head and went to alight in the Baths of Diocletian, making the air resonate with the sound of their gongs. Infinite numbers of gnomes also came, which divided up the Trastevere quarter and Monte Testaccio. As for the elves and farfadets, they occupied the Porta Salaria all the way to the Ponte Lamentano, where they bathed all night in fuming streams of sulfur and bitumen.

On the Antonine and Trajan columns and on the obelisks, the kobolds stood watch. The fays of Brittany chose to lodge in the Villa Borghese, the Villa Pamphili, the cypresses of Monte Mario, the stairway of the Trinita dei Monti, the Palazzo de Venezia and numerous cloisters with little twisted and fluted colonnades, where they took pleasure in riding in their nacreous chariots, looking at the old mosaics on the walls, gleaming gold, vermilion and carmine in the sunlight. As for the stryges and witches of France, England and Germany, some established themselves in the taverns, some in the hostelries; all of them, riding on their broomsticks, made the Sabbat dance around the seven hills.

In that way, the army covered the Roman landscape; the atmosphere was obscured. Turpin forgot himself trying to count them. There was nothing but the whispering and quarreling of strange voices; some cried, some brayed, some tried to roar. Hissing, mewling, yapping, croaking, squawking and shrieking could all be heard simultaneously, with human words; all of them seemed to be looking at Merlin and saying: "Woe betide anyone who touches him!"

The eagles that emerged from the rocks of Cambria and which had sharpened their beaks on Roman tombs, thought that the last day of Christ had arrived. Full of the anger with which they had nourished the bards, they soared above the seven hills, necks extended, and they said to their young:

"Come! It's not the flesh of dogs, ewes and pagans that you'll have today; it's Christian flesh."

They got ready to fall upon the mute city. Merlin felt pity for them, and shouted to them: "Birds of prey, what do you seek?"

"The cadaver of a god."

"It's too soon," the prophet replied. "When there's an old world to devour, have no fear; I'm the one who'll provide your fodder. I'll distribute it to you in equal shares. Until then, return to your aeries."

And they withdrew, confused, filling the air with their screeches, beyond the Apennines.

Then Merlin, turning to the innumerable legions of spirits that had come running to his defense from so many different worlds, filled them with astonishment by telling them that he had not evoked them, that he had no need of their support, and that he, and he alone, intended to stand up to the city and the world. He dismissed them with a gesture.

They all fled, by the thousand tortuous paths that they had taken to emerge from their retreats. Only the occasional chilly gnome from the North, suddenly infatuated with the Italian sun, remained hidden beneath the Arch of Titus.

Who had evoked them? Perhaps it was the patroness of the bards, Viviane. Several encountered her and took her for a reaper on the Sabine. Drawn in an ox-cart through the sheaves of wheat, she preceded and protected her bard. She saw him without being seen, for her head was crowned with ears of wheat. No one else opened the gates of the eternal city; but then she went up on to one of the towers isolated in the countryside; from there she seemed to be reigning in the desert.

The city and the world fell silent; the places that had thought they were seeing the reappearance of Attila's locusts did not know yet whether they ought to rejoice or cover themselves with ashes. Emperor Max was the first to break the silence, and, turning majestically toward a man of God named Euchariste, said: "Our blades are blunted by his heart of steel. He has tamed us without fighting us. What remains for us to do?"

"Become apostles again," said the saint. At the same time he bade the emperor farewell, took off his jewels, put down his golden cross, took up his wooden cross again and walked toward the tomb of Cecilia Metella, for he had chosen that place as his dwelling; having gone into it he became a simple hermit again, closing his door on the world forever.

As for Merlin, the disconcerted crowd dared not follow him. He left the eternal city, saying in his heart: "I shall return."

As soon as he had crossed the threshold the desert closed around him. He turned his head once more toward the seven hills, and, thinking that the nations had denied him seven times, he wept his most bitter tears. The countryside remained desolate and mute, to the extent that to this day, no ray of spring sunlight has ever been able to console it.

IV

In the meantime, what had become of Jacques in the midst of the crowd? He accused himself of being unworthy to live, although a residue of vanity prevented him from agreeing with that. Sadly and mechanically, without saying where he was going or taking his leave of anyone, agitated and sulky, forgetting Caesar and the Pope, not even asking which was the shortest route, he set off after his master—but after having found him, he dared not approach him, much less speak to him. They both marched around the city at a distance, maintaining the same silence.

Merlin had the magnanimity not to want to humiliate his servant in the presence of other people, or even of a gnome. But when, after having passed Saint Paul Outside the Walls, it was certain that no human ear could hear, and after having sent away the curious cicadas, he stopped at the most solitary place in the locality and said in a low voice, fearful that the earth might hear:

"What have you done, Jacques! You've been very prompt to deny me today. Oh, how weak you are, my friend! Did you too, then, want to crucify me in Rome?"

"Mercy!"

"Wait, my friend. I thought that your education was more advanced than it is in reality. Tell me, had you no shame in surrendering the man for whom you had promised so many times to live or die? What did it require for you to decide to make me a calvary here? Ask yourself that, nothing more."

"Calvary is in Judea."

"Today, my son, it's everywhere there's a sinner. It's you, Jacques, who dug my grave."

"I don't deny it," Jacques replied. "But who wouldn't have been deceived? Say the word and I'll go set fire to the four quarters of that accused city—although I won't touch the relics, of course."

"I'm not asking you for violence, Messire Jacques."

"Oh, the intention was good. What do you expect, Seigneur Merlin? The air goes to one's head here. Then too, the bells, the pilgrims, the old walls—everything has taken me outside myself. Is there not some magic in these buildings and these mountains of broken pots that one finds here everywhere? I suspect that they've put a spell on me."

"That's not improbable," replied the benevolent Merlin, casting glance at the Roma Vecchia. "One can believe that the ancient spirits that I've vanquished almost everywhere are lurking here in the crevices of these towers and these tombs, and emerge from these temples that you see scattered around for your instruction. I don't doubt, my friend, that if you struck these walls with your foot, the spirits of the past would rush out in a host in the form of owls and bats; you'd see them, bewildered by the light of the living, fluttering over your head with wild cries."

As he spoke, he taped a section of an old reticular wall in the Villa Adriani. An old magpie flew out, which went to perch on the arch of an aqueduct, crying out in a hoarse voice: "*Ave Caesar!*"

"Do you hear?" said Jacques, cocking an ear. "It speaks Latin!"

"It's true," said Merlin, "but that's no excuse. A good man can always resist a senile magpie, even if it's enchanted, as that one undoubtedly is. Haven't I taught you what it's necessary to do in such encounters?"

"I'd left your book of magic in the house, Seigneur Merlin. They must have taken the opportunity to cast a spell on me."

"False excuses again! I've told you, not once but a hundred times, that if you happen to be deprived of all the instructions of our art, one good thought or a single heartbeat will suffice, Jacques. I've taught you that; you've forgotten it."

"The fault is in the place, then, Seigneur Merlin?"

"Assuredly there's something here too powerful for your brain, which the slightest breath shakes in opposite directions, and I shouldn't be astonished that the spells employed here have disturbed your reason, but you can't deny that mine are more powerful still. In any case, it wasn't so difficult to remain the good man that I was pleased to believe that you were, until now." Hearing a howl behind him, he added: "Ah! There's my dog, Jacques, who remained faithful, while you surrendered me."

These last words, pronounced with generosity, put an end to Jacques' temporary hardening. He collapsed at his master's feet, weeping.

"Woe betide me! Who am I, to have handed over my benefactor? At least I didn't sell him for money."

"Don't even deceive yourself on that point, Jacques."

"No, Seigneur—I didn't receive the thirty pieces of silver."

"Were they offered to you?"

Those words broke Jacques' heart. He went on: "Well, yes, Seigneur Merlin: accuse me, judge me, condemn me; I deserve all that, and worse. It's only too true that you'll never make anything of me. I don't know what drives me to do bad things. I can see that there's nothing left to do but drown myself."

With that, the despairing Jacques ran to the Ponte Lamentano. He was about to leap into the Teverone when Merlin, quicker than lightning, pulled him back with a strong hand.

"Do you repent, poor Jacques? That's all I ask of you."

"Leave me alone, Seigneur. I'm a wretch, unworthy of seeing daylight; let me die. I no longer deserve to follow you."

"Your fall is great, to be sure, and it's not for me to hide that from you, but it's not without hope; Heaven forbid that it happens again!"

"Oh, for that, I swear, cross my heart!"

"Don't swear, even in patois, poor Jacques. Your fault has always been passing from extreme discouragement to extreme confidence."

"Well, I tell you, there's nothing left but drowning."

"No, Jacques, it remains to live as an honest man who remembers evil in order to practice good. Know then, my son, that I haven't adopted you to abandon you so soon. You'll have need of me for a long time yet, alas. But first, let's get out of these deserted, feverish places that aren't good for you, and where Viviane has never resided."

Jacques, with the facile changeability that was the basis of his character, had already wiped away his tears. Scarcely had he gone a league when he had opened his heart to boundless hopes. Merlin did not want to reduce him to tears again, and it was in silence that they traversed the Roman countryside and lost sight of St. Peter's city.

Everything was bleak on the vast horizon, where nothing had changed since the fatal hour. You would still think today that the Enchanter had only just left, so great is the stupor. In the distance, the land has remained deserted. The pale grass still cringes under the prophet's anger.

V

Readers who have followed the various incidents of this work thus far, if they have been paying the necessary attention, will render me the justice that I have remained scrupulously faithful to the text of the chronicles. See principally that of Monmouth, page 240, line 15 of the Halle edition. When I permit myself to add a detail or an ornament, or draw a conclusion, I have done so with the greatest reserve; it is, in any case, an indispensable liberty, without which it would be necessary to renounce the profession of historian, such as it has been exercised from the remotest antiquity to our own day. My plan is to enclose myself ever more narrowly in the sage limits that writers without restraint have too often crossed. The further I advance in life, the more I recognize that the imagination is the flail of the works of the intellect. That declaration must be made at the moment when I enter into the most historical part of my subject.

It is perfectly established today by science that in his pilgrimages, Merlin, as well as following his whims somewhat, had received a diplomatic mission from King Arthus to the Roman Emperor, who was then, if I'm not mistaken, Lucius;[100] to the members of the Senate and, to say everything, to each of the dynasties of Greece and the Orient, including Epistrophius, King of Greece; Aethion, Duke of Boeotia; Palamedes, King of Messenia; Evander, Duke of Syria; Hippolytus, Duke of Crete; Pericles, Duke of Athens; Sertorius, King of Libya; Xerxes, king of the Ithurians; Pandrasus, king of Egypt; Polyctetes, Duke of Bythinia; and Aschillius, king of Dacia. For it was then the most brilliant epoch of their reign.

---

[100] Lucius, sometimes named as Lucius Tiberius, is a fictitious Roman emperor cited in Geoffrey of Monmouth. He has no connection with the actual 2nd century Roman emperor Lucius Verus. Geoffrey claims that Arthur went to war against Lucius and his subservient (equally fictitious) kings, including Epistrophius of Greece and many of the others included in the list given below, which differs slightly but not significantly from Geoffrey's. The subsequent list of fictitious senators is also reproduced, again with slight variations, from the same passage in Geoffrey.

Inasmuch as it is possible to judge from the very rare documents of that embassy, which have been confided to me with admirable munificence, it was principally a matter of obtaining that all the empires and monarchs would promptly and unambiguously pay liege homage to the most powerful of kings, the wild boar of Gaul, Arthus of the round table; otherwise, war would be declared, the said sovereigns and princes dethroned and dispossessed, and their subjects treated as rebels. The ambassador could soften the terms, but that was the foundation and the substance of the letters that he had to transmit, while nevertheless maintaining propriety.

On arriving in Rome, Merlin had been careful not to neglect such important business. He had immediately asked about the Senate. Having been unable to discover it, however, he judged sanely that it would be better to look for it in the country; besides which, it was the hottest season of the year, the time when the great men went to shelter in their villas from the burning breath of midday.

After having traveled the Roman countryside in all directions without having seen a single human being, he ended up finding three shepherds clad in animal skins under an aqueduct, who were guarding a herd of buffalo. He approached them with precaution, because their dogs launched themselves toward him furiously—but they recalled them by whistling.

Then Merlin went up to them and said: "Here, take these few deniers and take me to the order of the Senate. You doubtless know where Caius Catellus, Marius Lepidus, Metellus Cotta and Quintus Carutius are living at present; you're their slaves."

"Us, their slaves!" relied one of the shepherds. "We're the very people you seek. I'm Caius Catellus, and these others you can see are Marius Lepidus and Metellus Cotta. As for Quintus Carutius, he's engaged for the harvest at two deniers a day."

Merlin, slightly disconcerted by his mistake, first excused himself on the grounds of simplicity, and then immediately continued: "You'll know what brings me here when you've shown me the emperor."

"We'll have to call him, then," said one of the shepherds, "because he's over there on a fragment of wall, playing his bagpipe in the midst of his buffaloes." Then he shouted in a loud voice.

The piper arrived, stood up proudly and looked at Merlin arrogantly.

"You're Lucius, procurator of the Republic?" said Merlin.

"Undoubtedly I am," replied the shepherd.

"In consequence, you know the great king Arthus. His glory has reached you."

"I've heard talk of him during late nights."

"Here are letters that he has instructed me to bring you. They begin with the words: *Lucio reipublicae procuratori Arthus rex Britanniae.*" And he presented the document, sealed with the seal of the round table.

The emperor Lucius excused himself from receiving them on the grounds that he could not read. Without manifesting any surprise, Merlin explained the context with an admirable clarity. They gave him sustained attention, but when he arrived at the article of liege homage, the emperor and the members of the Senate declared flatly that they would never recognize masters. They were too accustomed to command to be able to obey. They hoped, on the contrary, to reconquer Britain and Gaul and all of their northern provinces.

"What!" exclaimed Merlin, astonished. "You refuse homage to the wild boar of Gaul?"

"Yes, certainly," replied the mendicants, draping themselves in their rags.

"If that's the case, I anticipate terrible reprisals and interminable woes."

"Let it be thus," replied the shepherds, whistling. "Everyone knows that the world belongs to us."

That response did not prevent them from offering Merlin and his companion some curdled milk and a little black bread. That was all they possessed. After which, without adding another word, they withdrew to take a siesta in a tomb on the Roma-Vecchia.

Left alone, Merlin and Jacques lost themselves in reflections on the outcome of their embassy.

"Is it certain," said Jacques "that they really are the emperor and the order of the Senate?"

"Nothing is more certain," Merlin replied, displaying the open letters, which he was still holding in his hand.

"How, then, can an emperor who has been the master of the world be so poorly nourished?" Jacques added, as he finished eating his black bread.

"Never judge men and their condition by the manner of their nourishment. Know that the greatest men, and even a few demigods—Tages,[101] for example—have only ever eaten rye bread, which certainly isn't as good as this. Lift up your heart, Jacques; educate yourself. See how States lapse into idleness and superstition as empires finish. Reflect on what you encounter. It's not given to everyone, as it is to you now, to see the greatest of empires fall asleep in a sepulcher with three shepherds and a bagpiper. Profit from the errors of others. Think, Jacques think—if that's possible."

"I'll try, Monsieur."

"Also," our hero added, "I imagine that the dynasties of Greece won't give us a reception any different from these children of the she-wolf, for there's no denying that they've shown us the milk with which they nourish themselves. I'm in the greatest imaginable haste to hand my letters to Epistrophius, king of

---

[101] A diviner rumored to be a descendant of Jupiter cited by several Latin authors, including Ovid and Cicero, whose revelations were allegedly recorded in the *Etrusca Disciplina*, no copies of which survive and which might well be fictitious.

Greece. Make preparations for the voyage and let's set forth on the first vessel that we come across on the coast, provided that it's carrying good sail.

"I'll look out for one," Jacques replied, as they approached the port of Ostia, following the maremma.

VI

There was a little Levantine felucca in the harbor, which, after its cargo of olives had been sold at a reasonable price, was getting ready to return to the Estates of Epistrophius, king of Greece. Merlin and his companion made sure that they did not miss out on such a rare opportunity. The price of the passage having been fixed at sixty deniers—very moderate, given the extreme rarity of ships carrying the flag of Epistrophius—our voyagers embarked on a flat sea, with a mild north-western breeze, all sails unfurled except for the topgallant, which was kept in reserve by virtue of an excess of prudence. The course was set for the Duchy of Messenia.[102]

Save for a squall in the face of the roses of Paestum, the crossing was fortunate. Merlin took advantage of it to read his Homer all in one go, for before visiting a nation he informed himself exactly of its mores, the degree of its wealth and luxury, and the least of its customs. So, when the anchor was dropped in the immense harbor of Pylos, he was perfectly enlightened with regard to the institutions of the kingdoms that were about to be offered to him. He was not taking the risk of letting any surprise show, which is the sign of a lack of education, something blameworthy on the part of all people, and particularly risible and deadly in an ambassador.

Having disembarked on a sandy beach, they saw four men emerging from a cave, semi-clad in fustanellas, their waist surrounded by tattered girdles and sheepskins over their shoulders. It was Epistrophius, king of Greece, accompanied by his two best friends, Aethion, Duke of Boeotia and Hippolytus, Duke of Crete, and also, I believe, Auguselus, king of Albania. They were all smiling as they walked with a light step that left hardly any trace on the sand. They were murmuring a faint song, which they alone could hear.

Light, smiling, immortal dynasties, historians have allowed you to fall into oblivion; you are fortunate when they have not reproached you for being imaginary. They have not consecrated a single line to you, because you did not fill the earth with the blood of murders. Only the flowers that grow in the ruins, the bees of Candia, the nightingales of Colonna, the choirs of cicadas that reside at

---

[102] Hermione's notes observe that the journey described in the following section recalls Quinet's own expedition to Morea, as a member of a governmental commission, in 1829, in the course of which he encountered the copious debris of buildings and statues and suffered the consequences of the famine afflicting the region at the time.

Sunium or the foot of Mount Ithome, or in the heaths of Arcadia, know your annals. You have reigned without noise and without scandal, as the centenarian tree reigns in the forest.

Personally, I shall endeavor here to extract from forgetfulness at least one page of your past. What is a page, to be sure? Nothing, or almost nothing—but the authentic monuments have not permitted me to hear any more. The route that I am opening here, through regions where no human has penetrated before me, someone else will follow, in order to complete it. Whoever he might be, I salute him in advance.

As soon as Merlin had complimented the king, he told him his name and made him party to his message.

"My dear Merlin," Epistrophius replied, smiling. "If you're agreeable, we won't occupy ourselves with any serious business before I've shown you around my capital and my kingdom."

"I'm burning to see the noble Ithome," Merlin said, "for I've heard marvels said of it in my Homer."

"We call it Vourcano nowadays, and as for Messene, we have given it the name of Mavromati, which is certainly more agreeable to the ear than the former."[103]

"That's true, sire king," said Merlin, who had already become something of a courtier.

Such were the discussions in which they whiled away the time agreeably, while waiting for the horses that someone had gone to fetch from the marsh. They finally arrived. They were small, pale horses with long manes, with neither saddles nor bridles. On the other hand, they carried wooden pack-saddles, and two ropes serving as stirrups, not to mention a third, which, passed under the lower jaw, substituted for reins. These details are indispensable for an exact knowledge of mores, an objective of which I am not losing sight for a moment.

At a signal from the king, everyone, the Dukes, the Enchanter and the servants, mounted up and began to trot, sometimes along the sea shore, sometimes going up into the mountains dotted with arbutus, chaste trees and Indian figs with mud-colored leaves. In the split trunks of old oaks, shepherds stood like statues in ebony niches. A few tortoises crawled over the ground, accompanied by snakes had torn apart by eagles. I have made observations of the nature of the soil of Sparta and Athens; it is, in general, calcareous and friable; it is somewhat lacking in grease; the ashes of heroes, better tended, might have held

---

[103] Although these reminisces are based on memories of personal experience, parallel experiences are dutifully summarized by other hands in *Expédition scientifique de Morée: Relation, par M. Bory de Saint-Vincent* (1836), in which these changes of name are scrupulously observed, along with numerous other details contained in this chapter.

it together, but time flies and space expands before me, and I'm forced to abridge.

The first day they stopped at Coron, the second at Nisi, the third at Messene. As they dismounted, Epistrophius had a moment of legitimate pride. He said to Merlin: "My dear Merlin, you're doubtless delighted by the beauty of this capital. Well, know that my intention is to put at your disposal everything that it contains. Yes, I repeat, there is nothing here that is not yours. First, choose your palace, your temple."

Merlin, utterly astonished by what he heard, and even more so by what he saw, stood motionless his eyes attached to Epistrophius' domains. He perceived nothing but fallen columns and broken stumps hidden in the grass. Not one roof, not one building. That astonishment, and perhaps also the fear of giving displeasure, left him tongue-tied.

"Since discretion prevents you from replying," the king went on, "and night is drawing near, my servants will take you to rest in the most delightful palace I possess. Go, Merlin, you and your servant; the greatest joy for me is to give hospitality to those who pass by. What would I not do for the envoy of the noble Arthus?"

Merlin and Jacques followed the servants, who led them to a deserted field where two steps of a theater still rose above ground level not far from the fountain of the Clepsydra. A little stream bathed the ruins, murmuring like an actor rehearsing his role.

"Here," said the servants, "is the most noble palace in the land." At the same time they heaped up a little brushwood, with which they made a kind of mattress, which they placed on one of the steps.

"Lord," they said to Merlin, as they retired, "your bed is prepared. As for your servant's, we assume that it will be on the lower step. May the gods, if there are any, protect you from prowling wolves and jackals."

Soon, fatigue constrained Merlin and his servant to lie down on their marble beds, but it was impossible for them to sleep. Jacques, after having turned over a hundred times without being able to close an eyelid, was the first to break the silence.

"Alas, why have we quit the emperor Lucius and the order of the Senate? We'll perish here of hunger and lack of sleep."

"I confess," said Merlin gravely, "that everything I see here gives me a great deal to think about; without wanting to make a reckless judgment on the basis of a few words I've overheard, which appear to me to be true sophisms, I believe that we're voyaging here in the company of the spirits of ruins. I don't know whether you've noticed that our hosts have a muted tone of voice that fully befits debris, and the precise turn of thought—empty, subtle, sophisticated and Byzantine—that is generally attributed to the spirits of decadence. But if that's true, and we are, in fact, dealing with the spirits of ruins, you need to remember that they're no less veritable majesties, as legitimate as any others, worthy of your respect. Be careful of failing in that respect in any way, for these dynasties are all the more venerable for having fallen, especially when they support adversity with a smile, as we saw just now.

"Truly," Jacques replied, "all that I've remarked in these dynasties is that they neither eat nor drink. If King Epistrophius at least treated us as Emperor Lucius did, and gave us a little black bread, I wouldn't complain. But no! Without a few mulberries that I picked from the bushes, I'd have died miserably of starvation."

"I confess, friend, that I've done the same, but secretly and with more discretion. I'll even go so far as to say that I wouldn't be sorry to make a frugal meal at this advanced hour of the night."

"That's just what I was thinking," said Jacques.

"In that case, I advise you to get busy right away, while it's still dark, for if beings such as our hosts, assuming that they are immaterial, catch us eating and drinking, they might perhaps feel great pity for us, and will certainly find us quite ridiculous."

This advice was immediately followed by Jacques, who started searching the vicinity by moonlight. He soon brought back a lamb, watercress from the fountain of the Clepsydra and some almonds. The brushwood mattress served to light an ardent fire on which the meat did not take long to roast. A few moments later, our two voyagers began to eat, as if they had never done so before in their lives.

They had not finished when King Epistrophius appeared unexpectedly before them at daybreak, followed by his cortege.

On seeing them eating, he could not help bursting into laughter.

"Ah!" cried the king. "This is very pleasant! You suffer from hunger and thirst, then?"

"Sometimes," said Merlin, humiliated.

"Excuse me," said Epistrophius. "I should have thought of that. For ourselves, we scarcely live on anything but the blond rays on sunlight, and a little nocturnal dew—which is very abundant hereabouts, as you've been able to see."

"That's true," Merlin replied, showing his cloak dampened by the nocturnal humidity.

Epistrophius sent the troupe of his courtiers away then, and, having taken Merlin by the hand, talked to him with the utmost familiarity, for he knew that, as Merlin was only passing through, that familiarity would have no consequences for others.

"Tel me please, Sire," Merlin said to him, "by what secret you conserve such a magnanimous serenity in the midst of a State in ruins. I have not yet surprised a sigh on your lips, even in the time when we have been treading underfoot the debris and the dust of your empire. Undoubtedly, you conserve the hope of reviving these fallen walls and collapsed towers; in that case, the help of Merlin and his king will not be lacking. But tell me, I beg you, what remedies allow you to support such an immense adversity so lightly. For I confess, such a serenity is beyond even my wisdom."

"Your astonishment doesn't surprise me," King Epsitrophius relied. "Sage as you are, my dear Merlin, you're human, as I can see. You're yielding at this moment to human prejudice. Know then that, for being such as us, nothing is more scandalous and more odious than a new city. Without any exaggeration, we would stifle there. Every new edifice is a prison for us, unless it is falling apart. If we should happen to build, it's uniquely to have the pleasure of demolition.

"My joy, Merlin, is to march without obstacles over a plain strewn with nameless debris, even including a few bones whitening in the nettles. I sit down, I dream, I sense then that I reign in liberty over time itself, which becomes my subject, my workman, my slave. Assuredly, I have reason to be satisfied with my palaces at Mavromati, Sparta and Megalopolis. No fragment of wall interrupts, saddens or limits my gaze.

"However, I hear that my brother Evander, Duke of Syria, my father-in-law Micipsa, King of Babylon, and Polyctetes, Duke of Bythinia, are still better lodged than I am. The work in their homelands is more advanced, progress much more rapid, civilization more perfect. For the very trace of edifices has disappeared under the feet of goats, a result for which we are all ambitious, but which only a few of us have been able to attain."

"Is that what you call progress, Sire? Don't you fear that it's rather a decadence of your empire?"

"Decadence!" interjected Epistrophius, vehemently, with a hint of bitterness. "You talk about that very casually. Let's reason a little, if you please. It's very evident that States are made to be ruined; that's their goal; they hasten toward it. We should, therefore, be glad when they are reduced to an impalpable dust like that which whitens the wings of butterflies. Can you deny that?"

"As you wish, Sire," Merlin relied, bowing. "Nevertheless, I have a great desire to see your people flourish in abundance. I don't doubt that you'd gain a great deal by augmenting their numbers, for, if I dare confess it to you, your subjects appear to me to be starving, and already reduced to imperceptible numbers."

"Another error, good Merlin. Do you always measure others by yourself? Once, it's true, immense peoples, who were said to have been very beautiful, were abundant in these cities. But also, just Heaven, what a source of troubles and anxieties, what noise, what uncomfortable crowding, what anarchy! The clamor rose up to the clouds. Not a day without tumult, even the night full of tempests. Today, on the contrary, what truly sacred peace! What concord! What religious silence! There still remain for me to rule a few goat-herds, whom you can count from where we stand. They don't importune me with their rumors. I don't have to meditate on laws, nor fear violent revolutions. My empire is not disputed by anyone. The only event in my court is a falling stone, and I date the epochs by those falls. All the kings of my family do the same. We live as brothers, without wars or quarrels. But let's leave this profound conversation; let's go and rest on that lovely sarcophagus whitening over there beneath that clump of arbutus."

VII

Merlin judged that King Euphronius wanted to be alone. He parted from him and thought the moment propitious for visiting the surroundings. As he wandered through the countryside he encountered, lying in the grass, several statues that were all resplendent with an extraordinary beauty. The most marvelous thing was—would you believe it?—the faces, with the majesty, the naivety and even a little of the coldness of Viviane.

That encounter, so unexpected, threw our hero into an inexpressible perplexity. *What hands*, he thought, *what artists, have had the unique privilege of reproducing her features? Has Viviane been in this place, then? But when? On what occasion? Accompanied by whom? That's what escapees me entirely, for she never mentioned this distant voyage to me.*

Then, as he considered the statues strewing the ground more closely, the majority of which were mutilated, he thought: *Yes, those are, assuredly, her incorruptible features. Look how she wore her hair in tresses knotted behind the head in those days. Where was I? What was I doing? Why have I not seen her thus, crowned in that fashion?*

After a moment's silence, he went on, with a sigh: *All that's lacking here is an imponderable flame. It's easy to see that in those days, she had not yet loved. Doubtless her days were spent with her godmother, in a tranquil indifference. Who am I to complain about that?*

In that ecstasy of sorts, one thing filled him with both surprise and confusion. That was seeing that the statues of Viviane were, to tell the truth, as naked as a new-born child. The most veiled only had a light tunic that still seemed to be stirring.

How, continued our Enchanter, *was such inadvertence possible? It's very evident that Viviane would not have lent herself voluntarily to such an indiscreet art, unless, of course, someone abused her extreme innocence. It must be the case, therefore, that the artists, to whom nothing is sacred, had perceived her while she was bathing at dusk in some silvery stream, veiled by plane trees, as they are hereabouts, or perhaps while she was sleeping, as she was accustomed to do on warm night, under the guard of the stars, whose vigilance mutt have been deceived on that occasion. It's no less certain that that's her swan-like neck, her ivory shoulders. At any rate, I can't bear it that, under the pretext of art or divine beauty, Viviane should be delivered thus any longer to the indiscreet gazes of Epistrophius' subjects, and perhaps his own.*

The truth is that the sage Merlin ended up falling victim to a strange fit of jealousy, at the stones, which seemed to palpitate before his eyes. Without losing a moment, he hid them in the densest part of the woods. Not content with that, he even covered them with earth.

When he returned, the noble Epistrophius recognized by his distressed expression that he was emerging from a keen emotion; he asked him what had caused it. Merlin for whom nothing more uncomfortable than dissimulation, confessed what he had just done, even though he action might offend the king.

"Have no fear," Epistrophius replied. "Nothing is more in accordance with the intentions of my reign. I'll give orders to all my subjects that statues that resemble Viviane should be hidden from the gaze under ten or twenty feet of earth. Is that enough, Merlin? Trust my people to do the rest."

The order given by Epistrophius was immediately obeyed throughout his vast empire; Merlin saw to that personally. At the very most, the tip of a finger or a foot sometimes protruded from the ground—never anything more. Those who passed by were astonished no longer to see all the beauties that had once delighted hem.

"Doubtless the gods have taken them away."

The following day, they had forgotten them.

At least the good Merlin was satisfied; his jealousy had passed. Thus was conserved for posterity the face of Viviane in her early adolescence, even before she had fallen in love with our Enchanter.

VIII

Since it had become impossible for Merlin to doubt the character of Epistrophius' royalty, and he could see clearly that the society into which fate had thrown him was that of the spirits of ruins, his curiosity had only increased. He never lost an opportunity to observe such a strange people, and whether he was in the presence of Epistrophius or his courtiers, he informed himself incessantly about the institutions the laws, the customs, and principally the religion, of the spirits of the ruins.

"What do you believe? What is your faith?" Such was the question that returned incessantly to his lips. To which the good Epistrophius usually replied, in an indirect manner, with words such as these:

"That is, in truth, a delicate question. It requires a great deal of time; I fear that we don't have enough today, for we have to sow an entire field of heather in the confines of a temple."

"Precisely," Merlin said. "I'm asking what your religion is. Of what do your rites consist? Have you many dogmas? How do you speak to the imagination of the greatest number?"

"Listen, my dear Merlin, to the song of the owl that is waking," replied the king. "Let's not trouble its religious hymn. It is, as you know, our sacred bird. I'm going to bring its food."

With that, searching the Void, he left. The courtiers reminded our hero then that it was not permissible to interrogate the king.

"You, at least," Merlin said to them, "What is your dogma? Your sacred book? In what do your ceremonies consist?"

"Ceremonies!" replied the courtiers. "We have more of them than anyone else. Everything among us is ceremony, even sweeping the dust." Then they withdrew in their turn.

Left alone, Merlin was approached by a man who, to judge by his appearance, seemed to be a foreign slave of the people of the ruins. The man, seeing that his masters had gone, came to him and said hastily, in a convulsive voice:

"Don't listen to them, Merlin. They're deceiving you. They're all traitors, enemies of the plebeian. They pretend to want to knock everything down, to the level of the ground. Don't believe a word of it. If you knew them better you'd see that they each have the indignity of allowing something to subsist.—one the stump of a column to lean on while sleeping, another a fragment of wall, a third the debris of a tomb; this one a shard of pottery, that one…what do I know? Half a brick or a royal medallion. There's only me who values anything here, for I even resent the ash and dust of sepulchers.

"Are you envious, my friend?" said Merlin. "Don't take umbrage at a pinch of ash. It's our common lot, alas, we who are formed therefrom. They retain, you say, a little dust in the hollow of their hands? Be indulgent to that mania."

"What are you calling a mania?" said the slave of the spirits of the ruins. "Know that it's the most shocking privilege, and that I'm dying of rage just thinking about it."

"If you love your brothers…," Merlin replied. He was about to continue when he perceived that the person he was addressing was already some distance away.

A little time sufficed for him to discover that, in agriculture, the spirits of the ruins held darnel in the highest esteem; in iron, rust. Commerce was prohibited, with the exception of a little balm to embalm heroes. With regard to laws, they had a great many, which all contradicted one another.

Merlin asked to see the public libraries; they were shown to him; they were kept by a very short spirit named Griffopoulos, who showed him around with an inexhaustible complaisance. It was from him that he learned that the law forbade the expression of any clear and definite idea in a work, on any subject whatsoever, regarding them all as deadly.

"What! Even eulogizing ruins is forbidden?"

"Yes, if the eulogy is made in a certain tone. We fear to express that which might recall life. We're so glad to have lost the habit of it."

"Have you any philosophy?" asked Merlin.

"Of course," replied the librarian, presenting him with a scroll of extensively worm-eaten papyrus. "We have a national philosophy. We call it sophistic. It is reborn from one age to the next without ever running out."

"And your criticism?"

"Very rich. That's where we shine. We mock everything that doesn't amuse us."

Merlin opened a few volumes and perceived that they were effaced, from the first line to the last. "Are the others like this?"

"All of them."

"That's a strange literature, scratched out and erased from generation to generation!"

The librarian adopted a sober tone: "I've heard it said by our greatest minds that it's their torture. Whenever they've found some capital, bold truth, such as two and two make four, another generation arrives, which promptly effaces, in Indian ink, what they've done—and even intelligence itself is effaced. Then everything has to begin again, and there's never any lack of material for fine works—for it's necessary to be ingenious again, to compile, to analyze, to compromise oneself and one's family, to ruin oneself body and soul, to risk jail, exile, death, in order to demonstrate, but this time more modestly, that perhaps, if he ancients can be believed, but without too much assurance, nor wanting to offend anyone, everything in any case remaining to by decided by the powerful, that it might be the case that two and two make four."

"Oh, my friend, a strange torture for a mind that wishes to advance! A squirrel in its iron cage makes more progress in an hour than those in a lifetime. And your gods?"

"More often than not, our gods are ourselves."

That last response threw Merlin into the blackest melancholy. That society, deprived of Heaven, appeared to him in all its sadness. The very grace of the spirits of the ruins weighed more heavily on him every day. He felt a need to respire on sacred summits.

Without communicating his plan to anyone, he made a vow to go on a pilgrimage in search of the lost gods—which he executed the following day, taking advantage of the moment when Epistrophius was taking his siesta, as you will see in the next book, which commences with an inspiration that I drew from Mount Lykaon itself.

BOOK TWELVE: GODS CHANGED INTO DWARFS

I

A spark has sprung from the mountain through the bushy branches of an oak; the sun has risen—the sun of Greece. It dresses the columns of the temple with a golden tunic. In the distance, the pale mist amassed on the river-beds rises, snaking along the mountain-sides. A rain of flowers falls from the branches of the almond-tree that is shivering under Mount Ithome. A resin emerges from the split bark of pines, with an odor of incense.

Already the sea is bordered by a glittering line. An iridescent swarm of moths swirls in the valleys. The earth quivers like a tripod appealing to the god. The day has ignited. The eagle, the cicada, the torrent, the mountain, the plain, the forest, and the scarab with golden eyes, all demand the immortals in a fiery voice.

And I too, may I see once again with you the spring morning on the summit of Mount Lykaon on the threshold of the temple of Apollo the Smiling? I would like that first dawn to caress us both with its breath of jonquil, while the odor of wild thyme and virgin vines rises toward us from the wooded ravines of Phigalia.

May I also—if it's permissible too add another wish—when the supreme moment comes, with my hand in yours, exhale my serene soul with you in the serene temples, under the azure vault, at the same time as he nightingale sings in the valley of Ampellone and the isle of Zante flowers in the sea blossoming at our feet.[104]

Less fortunate, and yet worthy of envy, my hero follows the same steep slope and the same hour; he hears nothing at first but the cry of jackals and the solemn *hou-hou* of the sacred owls. But scarcely has he set foot in the cella of the temple than a murmur of winged voices resonates in his ears. In that concert, he disentangles words still steeped in a residue of ambrosia: *Andronte Theonte!*

It was an Olympian hymn to the morning that was about to blossom overhead. At the same moment he discovered, seated on the stumps of the ruins a host of dwarfs who all conserved a singular majesty in their appearance—and such was their pride that they seemed at first not to notice him.

---

[104] Hermione's notes repeat the last two paragraphs in full as an expression of Quinet's passionate Hellensim. She notes that his final thought, as he lay dying on 27 March 1875, was of Greece. She also relates that this Book was Jules Michelet's favorite, as an allegorical explanation of the origin of fairy tales.

Merlin advanced into the middle of the sanctuary. After having considered them, he said: "Who are you?"

"Your twelve great gods," replied the one who was nearest. What are mortals—for we assume by your appearance that you're mortal—thinking? What are they doing? Where are they? In the centuries we've been holding council here, no one has climbed to our summits. Have you brought us any nourishment? Without the drop of dew contained in the leaves of holly and arbutus that the cold has shriveled, we'd be in danger of dying."

Merlin's only response was to command Jacques to take the provisions he had brought out of his haversack. He servant obeyed, taking out of the bag ladyapples, walnuts, a few figs and slices of bread that was excellent, although very hard.

When those divine provisions were spread out in the cella of the temple, each of the gods lay down on the flagstones starred with anemones, reached out his tiny hands, and grabbed whatever was within reach. When they had all calmed their hunger, the principal one among them turned to Merlin and said:

"We too have been enchanters, and even gods. Now we're dwarfs! So changeable is the destiny that was thought to be immutable! But you, who, without being summoned, is mingling with our eternal council, tell us who you are."

"I'm Merlin, and the man beside me is my servant."

"Since you're an enchanter," the god with the ambrosial face continued, "Return our Olympus to us. Doubtless you've appeared in this place to restore our empire. Only let us enjoy the soft light of the morning, and we'll promise to rule the world better. Nothing will be done, Merlin, without your advice. Evoke us, with a powerful, magic word; it's high time that our reign recommenced."

At this point a small shrill voice pierced the clouds: "I'm Diana of Sicily, Viviane's godmother."

Those words struck Merlin's ears more violently than a thunderclap.

"Yes, my son, I'm your mother-in-law," the old lady went on, curbed down to the ground, leaning on a silver bow. "Give me back my huntress' arrows, lost at the foot of Mount Dicte, and I'll give you a hind every day."

Then she pointed to the light nets, like autumnal thread, that she had just extended over the meadows.

At this speech from Diana of Sicily, the gods started laughing; then they made the Enchanter similar promises.

"What! You're Viviane's godmother!" exclaimed Merlin, completely forgetting where he was. "You've carried her on your knees?"

"A hundred times."

"Tell me where she is. Shall I see her again soon? It's her that I seek in all things."

"I too, my son, have been looking for you," said the old huntress. "I have a message to give you. I do so in the presence of the gods. Let them bear witness, here, for my god-daughter and me, those who can read in the recesses of hearts."

Before she had finished speaking, Diana of Sicily had handed our hero a packet of letters, the majority formed from the wings of butterflies joined together.

Merlin covered the letters with kisses; he would have liked to unfold them and read them, without losing a moment, but he contained himself out of respect for the gods, although his heart was secretly devoured with sadness.

"Before anything else," Diana went on, "salute our king; commence with Jupiter."

"I'd like that," Merlin replied, "but show me Jupiter the Thunderer. Where is the powerful assembler of clouds about whom I've heard so much?"

At these words an elf a cubit high drew himself up to his full height and said: "Merlin, you're looking for Jupiter. Look, here I am. I still have the same eyebrows that made the vast skies tremble. Barbarian gods, the impious and the rebellious have dethroned me! Humans, will you consent to their reign being prolonged?"

"If humans have ceased to believe in you, Seigneur," Merlin said, "isn't that your fault?"

"Our fault?" repeated the dwarf god. "Can legitimate gods be mistaken?" And he looked around for his thunderbolt; he only found a sprig of rosemary, which he uprooted and hurled at the world.

"What do these barbarian gods do that we didn't?" added the assembler of clouds. "Do they also live in smoke?"

"They live primarily in people's tears."

Merlin then recounted the marvels of Arthus' court, Perceval's enchanted lance, the Lord's vase always full of blood, the converted peoples, the destroyed temples, the embroidered cathedrals, the knights, the ladies, the bards, the amours, the adventures of the bard voyaging around the lake of bones, the Hell visited by Saint Patrick, the Paradise by Saint Brendan, Attila recoiling before the word of Saint Paul, the nations passing like waves at the feet of Simon Stylites—all things that threw the gods into the greatest astonishment.

Each of them murmured like dry leaves at the foot of a centenarian oak.

Jupiter said: "What are the clouds at the summit of Ida doing, deprived of their chief? Who assembles them? Who disperses them? Can the thunderbolts still resound over Ithome when I'm no longer there to launch them?"

And Phoebus Apollo with the golden hair: "How, O Merlin, do the horses of the day drink in the Ocean since I've dropped the reins?"

And Mars: "Is it true that blood still flows, in combats, from the breasts of peoples, since I remain idle, empty-handed, out of the melee?"

And Saturn: "From whence emerge the new auroras, O Merlin. From what spring to the news days flow? How does time march while Saturn reposes?"

And Venus Aphrodite: "Is it true, O Merlin, that love still burns in human hearts?"

"There's no doubt about it," Merlin replied. "As witness Lancelot, Tristan, myself and many others I could name."

"How can that be?" asked the goddess with the gilded face. "Who, then, ignites hope in the hearts of young men today? Who causes virgins to pale and blush? Who parts rosy lips with the breath of insatiable desires? Who draws the bolts of doors and prevents the hinges from squeaking, at the moment when the young men once evoked me? Tell me, Merlin, if you know; for doubtless you can't imagine that these things happen of their own accord."

To that host of questions that overlapped and left no time for reflection, Merlin replied more often than not: "That's the secret of the barbarian gods."

"A little more time," Jupiter went on, "and they'll be finished; humans will miss us, Merlin." And, seeing a sign of incredulity on our hero's face, he went on: "Yes, Seigneur Merlin, just a little more time, and they'll regret our Hellenic heaven. They'll remember the lost security; for we were indulgent to humans. We made their lives light in an eternal azure. And for that, what did we ask? A little smoke. Was that too much to pay for our benefits? From all that we hear, they're plunged today in rainy darkness. Living in darkness, they've come to like it; but by this scepter, they'll emerge from it and climb toward Olympus again."

"I thought so for some time," Merlin replied. "Today, I no longer hope for that, because I see that they're capable of making gods themselves. Resign yourselves, great gods, to a condition that, although modest, is all the more sure and tranquil. Enjoy what remains to you. You've been left immortality. Is that so little? Take pleasure in your obscurity; it is, believe me, the foremost of possessions. Forget that you ever reigned over that inconstant universe. Let it suffice for you to reign here, over this resounding choir of cicadas, sacred musicians. Instead of the immense skies, content yourself with more humble retreats.

"Perhaps you can be more useful here. Help slaves and servants in huts to milk cows, churn milk into butter by night, refresh the litter of superb horses, comb their floating manes in the tempest, maintain the fire under the ashes, cause the water to boil and sing in the bronze cauldron, ignite the errant torches of glow-worms to light the way for belated travelers far from their dwellings at midnight. Those are noble occupations, still almost divine. You, who have carried the thunder, would lose little in becoming benevolent follets."

"Degenerate thus!" interjected the host of gods.

"It's necessary! Nothing is worse than dragging after oneself the ostentation of a pompous existence when one is not longer in a condition to sustain it."

Thus spoke Merlin; a great silence fell around him.

All those gods had a great deal of intelligence; the majority had genius. They understood immediately the common sense in the Enchanter's speech: better to surrender gracefully an empire that they no longer had the strength to maintain. They abdicated solemnly in his hands, offering him one after the other the liege homage of their persons, on condition that he would protect them—an engagement he willingly made, and observed in good faith, as future time would render testimony.

But how hard that change of fortune was to bear, at first! It would have been intolerable without the infinite consolations that Merlin was able to find, in his generosity. Nothing in the world inspired more pity in him than a fallen god. If he could have, he would have rendered them their empire.

More than once, the ancient pride nearly revolted, especially in the great gods. "Has one ruled the universe to become no more than a sylph, an oft-counterfeited dwarf? After having filled the skies, how, I ask you, does one shut oneself up in the corolla of a rose...?"

I'm abridging their speech—they never shut up.

And would you like to know what the worst thing of all was? It was that, sensing that their sacred costumes had become infinitely too large for their new stature, they felt truly lost in their ancient draperies. Their clasped mantles, falling from their shoulders, drowned them in red; their belts were also much too large for their diminished stature, and it was necessary to tighten them, even for Venus, whose guest assisted her without being asked. Their enormous sandals no longer clung to their dainty feet; they lost them at every step they took. Another annoyance was that that their heads disappeared into the hollow of their helmets all the way to their shoulders. Their shields covered them like prisons of steel. As for their divine swords, it was pitiful to see that crippling burden trailing along the ground, all rusty; they seemed to be chained to it by the baldric. In order to be soothed, did they have to be disarmed? It was necessary, though: another cause of tears.

An admirable thing! Merlin softened those hearts embittered by adversity. To the most superb he proved that greatness and smallness are only words invented by human mediocrity. "The infinite," he continued, "is entire within a dewdrop, as it is in the ample bosom of Homer's Ocean."

That put an end to the dethroned divinities' jealousies, resentments and bitter words; and from that day on, each one made it his ambition to take up as little space as possible in the world. Nothing seemed more divine than to be imperceptible. Neptune, being the first to take Merlin's words literally, wanted to reign over the tempests in a raindrop. Jupiter hollowed out his bronze sky in the cupel of an acorn. Venus Aphrodite hitched her chariot to two kites. Pallas Athena, the artisan with the glaucous eyes, made a buckler out of the umbel of a meadow daisy, and an aegis out of the shed armor of a cricket. She stole a bee's sting and made a spearhead out of it, brandishing it at the tip of a hawthorn spike. Most of their chariots were made out of seashells. As for reins, they were silvered and fabricated from autumnal spider-webs—and were rather becoming.

The bodies were small but the minds remained infinite. It takes a great deal to adapt to such a great change of fortune. There were gods who became so small that no human eye could any longer perceive them; it was necessary to divine their presence—and those were the proudest of all.

That was a new ambition that Merlin was obliged to restrain. "It's no bad thing, after all," he said, "for a god to allow himself at least to be glimpsed in something. Truly, he can only gain from it."

To win Jacques' heart, even that was unnecessary. From the first encounter, the familiar tone of the cheerful little gods subjugated him without difficulty. In their majesty there was nothing that could frighten him; he had never seen anything so mischievous, much less anything so ingenious. Most of all, the goddesses with the faces of fays conquered his love as soon as he saw them. Having noticed that they were all bare-headed, exposed to the sirocco, he immediately went down to the valley to pick bouquets of anemones, orchids, potentillas the color of mat silver, fumitories, blue scabiouses marked with black dots, and pink crocuses, to which he joined a few new pine-needles. He wove little hats of flowers, which he fitted as neatly as could be to their heads. He was careful to begin with Diana of Sicily, whom he already regarded as a member of the family.

In addition, he brought a blue bird, the color of time, in a wicker cage, which he had taken as a chick from the nest. He put it in the lap of the gods. Although still half-covered in down-feathers, the blue bird foraged the robes of Jupiter and Pallas Athena, whom he had soon consoled for the ingratitude of the voracious eagle and the myopic owl, both of which had casually abandoned them that same day.

Those were the most precious gifts they had received for many centuries; they rewarded Merlin and his servant with an Olympian smile—the last, I think, that shone on earth. Jupiter said that if he could, without offense, steal him from Merlin, he would gladly make another Ganymede of Jacques.

How, indeed, could so many benefits be recompensed?

"Nothing is easier," Merlin replied. "My servant likes fables; you know a great many. To listen to you, he'd follow you to the ends of the world. If, in repeating your tales, he alters them, if he puts your oracles into his patois, forgive him in advance."

II

Only one of the sacred troupe remained apart and shook his blond curls angrily. It is difficult to say whether it was pride or envy that held sway over him, to the point of preventing him from taking any part in the mild intoxication of the others. His clenched hand wandered over an old lyre soaked by dew, the metallic sound he drew from it suddenly obliging all eyes to turn to him.

Diana of Sicily took advantage of that to propose that Merlin engage with Phoebus Apollo—for it was him—in a singing contest.

"Measure myself against the king of hymns?" exclaimed Merlin, who had not expected such a challenge. "I've lost my harp."

Seeing, on these words that his modesty had gone to waste once again, however, and that an excessive pride was already reentering the hearts of the immortals, he signaled that he accepted the combat, not out of ambition for glory, but in order to please the omnipotent. Immediately, the gods and goddesses, arranged in a circle, sat down to judge the contest. The songs, alternating in the Olympian mode, commenced as follows:

Phoebus Apollo: "Io! Paean! Io! Io! Shall I sing the honeyed song of the sirens, or the one the muses sang on the day the universe was born?"

Merlin: "Shall I sing the song that cleaved the brazen heavens, or the song of paradise and that of the blue blade?"

Phoebus Apollo: "The serpent Python dared to raise its rampant head toward me; my arrow is steeped in its black venom. Io! Paean! Io! Io!"

Merlin: "More powerful than Python was the dragon of Kylburn in the heaths of Britain; my gaze alone crushed it, without my brows being soiled by its poison."

Phoebus Apollo: "The past belongs to me; it resonates my glory like my quiver on my shoulder."

Merlin: "The future worlds recount my actions, and the future runs from my lips."

Phoebus Apollo: "Nothing is more beautiful than the flock of Admetus, when, at dusk, conducted by a god, it drinks in the silvery spring of Dirce."

Merlin: "More beautiful are the herds of Arthus, when, under the guard of Merlin, they reply with their lowing to the green-tinted laughter of the Breton Sea.

Phoebus Apollo: "I love the blonde Delos cradled by the azure wave."

Merlin: "And I the rock of Cambria, where the vulture sharpens its beak."

Phoebus Apollo: "I am the father of smiling oracles."

Merlin: "And I the source of sacred tears. Never has Merlin's oracle lied."

Phoebus Apollo: "What are you saying, audacious one? Do you remember Marsyas? Be careful that your hide does not join his. His tanned skin is suspended from the tree of Delphi."

Merlin: "What can I have to fear? I have fought by night against my father, the father of eternal darkness; the grating of the gates of Hell has not shaken me."

Phoebus Apollo: "Fear at least the glare of the blazing sun, and my fiery horses, which will feed on your flesh."

Merlin: "Why should I, who am only eclipsed by the splendor of Christ, fear the fires of the blazing sun?"

Thus the songs continued, and neither of the combatants seemed vanquished. The gods had difficulty comprehending Merlin's language; sometimes they took him, secretly, for a barbarian, but they dared not say so. The more

240

Phoebus Apollo lost his serenity, the more Merlin felt his own increasing. That was the only sign that made his victory apparent.

"Cease the combat," cried Diana of Sicily. "Both deserve the prize." Secretly, however, she favored Merlin. Phoebus perceived that, and out of anger, was about to break his lyre when he was distracted by what was happened a short distance away.

In a ravelin shaded by chaste trees, carobs and arbutus, the domestic staff of the gods had assembled: fauns with twisted limbs, lamias and lemures emerged fearfully from tombs, along with gorgades, empusas armed with brazen bullroarers and tambours, tenebrions, Corycian spirits, Jupiter's harpies and dogs, dryads, centaurs, telchines, gluttonous satyrs with the ears and horns of oxen, and an entire population of pygmies. They all formed a circle around Jacques Bonhomme. From the top of a mound, Pan, the piper, threw pine-cones at him. Argus, the most curious of all, stared at him with his hundred eyes.

"Are you the valet of some god?" they asked him.

By way of reply, Jacques talked to them about his village. He told them, in the patois of Bresse, about the Bogeyman, Puss-in-Boots and Little Poucet, the Wandering Jew and the fay Dentu—in which the people with goat's legs took an incredible pleasure. The fauns, in particular, pricked up their hairy ears. Jacques taught them to dance the reel and the farandole. He even wanted to try Pan's pipes, which they lent to him willingly, and he played the latest tunes from his hamlet on the instrument of the oldest of the gods.

Success emboldened him; he dared to leap on to the back of a centaur that had moved close to him in order to listen to him—but the centaur, with a whinny of surprise, picked him up in his arms and threw him down on the lush grass, panting. At that spectacle, loud laughter burst forth, the echoes of which drowned out the polite murmur of the gods, to the extent that Merlin was obliged to call his servant back.

"Excuse him, great gods; he doesn't know you."

"Excuse him, Merlin? But why? We too like ingenuous joy. Does laughter offend your new gods?"

III

These exchanges and others cut the day short, which gods and men alike thought too rapidly elapsed.

One point remained to be settled: nourishment, about which the gods displayed considerable anxiety. Merlin promised to alleviate that concern. Every morning, they would find, in an easily recognizable location that he would designate to them, a little honey, myrtle berries, three or four olives, and even, on feast days, a grain of incense. That was for the great gods. The petty ones would have exactly half. That was the necessary; the superfluous would come later.

In recompense, the Enchanter only asked one thing of the fallen gods: to know that they would, blindly submissive, at the first signal, descend toward him in the quality of dwarfs, gnomes, elves, genies and follets, of which the least enchanter always has legions in his service. He promised, though, only to evoke them rarely—hardly ever, so to speak. And what would they have to do? To take Viviane a word, a plaint, a sigh, a dream, sometimes even less.

Thus was concluded, with neither trouble nor tumult, the greatest evolution that ever took place in the world. All the gods became genii, all the goddesses fays; and that infinite change did not cost a single drop of blood, not even a tear, either on earth or in the heavens.

Having thus settled the worship, the liturgy, the occupations and the status of the ancient gods, Merlin got ready to leave them in order to go back down to the dwellings of humans. The immortals followed him in procession to the foot of the mountain, armed with resounding whips, with which they spurred on their little chariot-teams. More than one turned over by virtue of excessive haste. It was a spectacle from which our hero would have been able to obtain some vanity: so many divinities, still beautiful, not wrinkled, marching in his footsteps.

A beautiful sunset illuminated their steps. The nightingale in the wood, the butterfly on the myrtle, the cicada beside the path, everything was in its place, except for the sacred things. Only the gods had changed; unfortunately, they perceived that in the mirror of streams. An unknown timidity slid into their hearts. When they reached the plain, they stopped. Their faces covered with blushes similar to that of a mulberry stung by a bee, and they said with a common voice:

"We'd gladly enter the dusty plain with you, Merlin, but we might perhaps encounter men, and we fear their mockery. For gods, there's nothing sadder than the fear of ridicule."

"O Heavens! Ridicule! Is that made for you, then? You're handsome, eloquent and ingenious. Your features, although diminished, are still worthy of marble. How, given that, can you fear irony?"

Then, turning in such a manner that Jacques could hear him, he continued: "Shame upon anyone who mocks the fallen gods! No, I don't know anything more cowardly than crawling beneath Jupiter so long as he wielded the thunder and jeering him when he's disarmed. Personally, I sometimes had occasion, in my youth, to provoke the gods. They were powerful gods, capable if they wished of striking me down with a glance, although sated with incense and flattery. But you who weep, poor immortals, when the entire earth is closed to you, still have a refuge in Merlin's heart; believe me, if I desire to see the reign of justice while I still live, it's in your interest alone."

"We believe you," Jupiter replied. "It's certain that at the sight of some iniquities, if they endure, Jupiter will no longer be able to believe in himself."

At these words, Merlin saluted the immortals one last time. He left them equally delighted with his politeness and his magnanimity, and while they went to hide under myrtle bushes, full of emotion, he took a narrow path bordered with planted trees, most often frequented by tortoises.

IV

"Is the good Prometheus still alive?" he shouted, turning back, confused by having been too late to address that question to the gods.

They heard him, however; the echo replied: "Still alive."

Merlin learned not only that the Titan was alive, but that his torture had only become worse, to the point that no one could foresee its end.

"Certainly," he thought, "I won't leave this place without having put an end to such a great evil."

And like a traveler who perceives too late that he has forgotten to pay his hosts their due, he retraced his steps in great haste and made the immortals blush at their rancor. Half-pleading and half-threatening, he extracted a pardon for Prometheus from Jupiter.

He did more than that; he filled Jupiter with the desire to free the Titan without delay, whom he depicted as one of the greatest doers of good, as well as a mortal enemy of pagans. Jacques equipped himself with a pair of files, pincers and a hammer, which his master let him bring, although he did not think that there would be any need. Thus armed, they both went from valley to valley toward Prometheus's rock, in the company of a hairy faun who served as their guide and knew the shortest route.

One evening, before climbing the accursed mountain, they heard roaring emerging from a marine cave.

"That's the sirens," said Merlin to his servant. "I expected to encounter them, but only a little further on. Be careful, friend, of allowing yourself to be seduced by their enacting voices. Imitate me and block your ears. This is the most perilous part of our enterprise."

Jacques obeyed—but from the corner of his eye he gazed at the entrance to the marine cave. He saw long oily bodies with bald heads emerge therefrom, dragging themselves on their bellies, which threw themselves one after another into the waves.

"Those aren't sirens, Master, but good fat sea-cows, by such indications as they have, like others, long stiff bristles on their muzzles."

"They're sirens, I tell you, and you're allowing yourself to be led astray by their trickery. Doubtless time, which corroded everything, has altered their divine features, and the bristles of which you speak are the proof of it, but be sure that their voices haven't changed; if they strike your ears again, I might not be able to protect you from all fascination, for I haven't yet tested my power against those enchantresses once. Be prudent, my son, and pass by without listening to their songs.

On the morning of the tenth day, they climbed Prometheus' calvary in silence. They often paused to see whether they could catch a glimpse of the Titan. More than once Jacques thought he could see him in the shape of a rockslide. But the mountain-side was fuming as the sun rose like the flanks of a horse steaming with sweat, and deceived their gaze.

Finally, they perceived him on the edge of a jutting rock—and how astonished and confused Merlin was on seeing that Prometheus was standing up, liberated, in front of two archangels armored with gold and diamond, who had just broken his irons, just as has been recounted more amply elsewhere.[105]

Merlin hastened his steps toward the Titan, and as soon as he was within voice range, he said, breathlessly: "See, O Prometheus, how everyone is hastening to your aid from all directions. I also pressed my pace in order to free you more quickly. I would certainly have liked that glory to belong to me; there is none that I'd have liked more. But since, thanks to their archangelic wings, these have been more prompt than me, I won't torment myself over it."

"Do you know them, you who arrive so late?" Prometheus replied, pointing at the two archangels, who had were just breaking the last iron ring.

"They're not of my legion," Merlin said, "but you can go without fear wherever they're in haste to take you. We're all working toward the same goal."

At these words the Titan drew away with long strides, following the two archangels over the summits; as they roe up, the latter deployed their wings, as if preparing to take off. Then from the height of the heavens, voices were heard singing *Gloria in excelsis*. At the same time, the sound of flapping wings agitated the air, as when a flock of cranes seeks a place to rest at dusk. Scarcely had they skimmed the ground than they departed tumultuously.

Doctors of law and saints crowned with aureoles, riding on clouds, leaned over to see the liberation of the Titan. They strewed celestial flowers, which fell like rain over the summated silvered by snow. A monastery bell could be heard, its ringing mingled with the *Ave regina coelorum* and the *Alleluia*. The Titan replied in a formidable voice with an Orphean hymn that made the sacred woods tremble.

Merlin, standing on the spot where the rock had been worn away by Prometheus' hips, replied in his turn to the cry of the earth and the heavens, with a druidic triad.

Meanwhile, at the sight of the archangels, Jacques had fallen face down on the ground. In a choked voice he repeated: "Jesus! Jesus!"

As soon as he dared to get up again, he saw Prometheus' eagle nearby, dragging its wing. He finished it off by throwing a stone at it, and, having torn out its bloody liver, he rubbed his limbs with it, which acquired an invincible strength by virtue of that charm. If only the same vigor had been communicated to his mind and heart! But that was not to be the case.

---

[105] In Quinet's epic poem "Prométhée" (1838).

244

V

When the Titan's liberation was consummated, there was a long silence over the whole earth. Merlin was the first to break it, with these words: "Is there still, in the world of the living, any noble spirit enchained to matter?"

The sobs that emerged from the depths of valleys told him that there were still several of that number, which filled him with astonishment and indignation. He then started searching for those enchained spirits, and wherever he found them, he freed them one after another. He attached himself principally to those who, by virtue of excessive audacity, had irritated the ancient gods.

"Because," he said, "they were my predecessors; I owe them my support."

With that thought in mind, the first he encountered was Tantalus, whom he found crouched beside a fetid pool.

"Why, poor Tantalus," he asked him, "do you persist in looking down at the mud swarming with reptiles and crabs, which flees from you and deceives you? Raise your eyes, for once, toward the spring on high; your thirst will be slaked."

And without waiting for a reply, he poured on to Tantalus' black and burning lips a few drops of water from the Holy Grail, the Gothic vase of which he was still carrying with him in his pilgrimages, in order to forearm himself against the frequent aridity of things, places and even humans.

As soon as Tantalus had felt the edge of the vessel taken from the noble Arthus' table touch his lips, he felt revivified.

"Permit me to follow you, Merlin," he exclaimed, "for I recognize in you the fount for which I was thirsty. I can finally slake my infinite thirst in the radiance of your eyes."

"I'd like that, Tantalus," Merlin said to him. "Follow me until you've drunk from the springs that never dry up."

In the same way, he freed the others that he found enchained in the bonds of matter, and they all followed him as their liberator, including Phaeton, whom he raised up, broken by his fall from the Empyrean. How astonished they were no longer to be enclosed in the ancient prison of things! They felt free for the first time.

Only one despaired for a long time of following the liberator, for that one was plunged waist-deep in a maremma, and cried incessantly: "Wings! Wings!" without trying to emerge from the sticky pool and clinging weeds in which he was buried. By his face, Merlin could not tell whether he was a god or a demigod, so much had the mire disfigured his features. On coming closer, however, much of his uncertainty disappeared.

"He's more than a man," he said, "but not a god."

"He's asking for wings, Master," Jacques replied. "Who could give them to him?"

"Me, if he's really who I think he is, and his name is Icarus."

"You're right," said the man at whom they were both looking pityingly. "I'm Icarus, and I'm weeping because I can't cross the abyss of terrestrial things, and have to remain eternally on this muddy shore in which you see me plunged, with no hope of getting out except with your aid."

"Worthy Icarus," Merlin replied, "Your tears do you honor. It's a noble pride that drives you, and the desire to cross the ancient abyss merited a better response from the ancient gods."

"Wing! Wings! Give me wings Merlin!"

"I'll give them to you but they won't be made of wax, and the jealous ardor of the sun won't be able to do anything against them. If you want to follow Merlin's science, the wings will drive your soul. You'll soar over things and the ocean of beings, without fear of falling into the gulf; you'll defy its soiling."

Instructed by dolor and his fall, the worthy Icarus understood those words. From that moment on he became Merlin's assiduous disciple, accompanying him for as long as the prophet remained in the region, and wings drove him every day; they grew so large that before the rainy season he was able to take off and traverse the immeasurable gulf without difficulty. It was child's play for him to soar over the quivering face of oceans and fly from the pillars of Hercules to Arthus' flag-decked threshold.

O seeing him so radiant, traveling the Empyrean, Jacques could not help feeling somewhat envious—that was his greatest fault—and from then on he too cried, day and night: "Wings, Master! Give me wings!"

Merlin replied: "They will propel you too, be sure of that, for I'm taking care of it personally, all the time—but it's not yet time. More modesty is appropriate today." And he added: "How we miss the sage Turpin now! Where did we leave him? Where is he forgotten? His pen would give immortality to all that's happened to us in recent days. You see, Jacques, how useful it is to know how to write nowadays! What beautiful stories you could eternalize, which risk falling into forgetfulness! Promise me, my friend, to learn the alphabet, as I've asked you to do so many times. For today, make a few notches in your hazel-branch, in order to remind you later, if not of everything, at least the principal circumstances of what you've seen of late."

That day, Jacques promised solemnly to read and write; for the first time, he felt the necessity of doing so. But times changed and he forgot what he had promised.

Seeing that, Merlin sighed, and said: "How rare men are, Jacques—even rarer than gods."

VI

"Shall I alone remain abandoned?"

246

These words escaped from a ruin that overlooked the shore; they were pronounced by a young woman who was obstinately searching for an object lost in the rubble of a palace. You might have thought that she was mad, so ardent and so vain as her search.

The beautiful searcher was naked, devoid of any veil.

Her beauty is her vestment," Merlin said to Jacques. "Stay behind here, since your eyes, still coarse, won't see the draperies that envelop her. I'll go to her on my own; I alone shall brave the gaze of Psyche, for that's certainly her, if I can trust my presentiments.

Psyche was standing on the mosaic paving of a crumbling stairway; she seemed to be listening, her head leaning forward, with a finger placed on her lips. Her other hand was still holding hr extinct lamp. Time had not diminished her beauty at all. There were still the same ingenuous eyes, the color of periwinkle, the same delicately-arched eyebrows, the same virginal cheeks tinted with their first down, the same vermilion lips, the same blonde wavy hair, falling loosely over the shoulders. Perhaps her face was a little paler; perhaps the blue veins of her temples were less swollen, les transparent; perhaps also, she was skimming the ground less slightly when she walked. In every other respect she seemed embellished; her bosom rose more frequently; longer sighs escaped her heart; a more vivid, more penetrating flame sprang from beneath her eyelids with ebony lashes. Her lips lightly parted, her mouth seemed ready to reveal a thousand secrets too long retained. You would have divined, above all, the yearning, the anguish and the melancholy engendered by hope too long disappointed and perennially reborn.

Around her, the Hours had paused at her beautiful hair, and were maintaining silence.

As he contemplated her thus, Merlin's heart shivered in its entirety, and went out to her. His tongue stuck to his palate. The place where he stood disappeared from view; he no longer saw anything but Psyche. To stay with her in this desolate place, among this rubble, to take the place of everything that she had lost, to built her a cabin with his own hands that would replace the ancient palace that had been destroyed, to espouse her before the gods—those ideas and a thousand others even stranger crossed his mind; but wisdom held sway over that heartfelt surprise; he had recovered mastery of his face, at least, when he stood before her.

He had trod upon and crushed beneath his feet little sea-shells encrusted in the sand. That slight sound awoke Psyche from her dream. She turned to him and uttered an exclamation.

"Do you know the one I'm looking for?"

"As well as you do, Psyche."

"Are you of his legion?"

"I'm its leader."

"Have you seen him?"

"A thousand times."

"With your eyes?"

"Yes, through my tears."

"What was he doing?"

"Everything and nothing at the same time, a world in a sigh."

"By that sign I recognize him. Is he still blind?"

"Still; and yet he sees what is impenetrable to all others."

"Has he mentioned me?"

"He doesn't dare."

"What has he said?"

"He remains silent, pale and weeping."

"Him, pale and weeping, without daring to say why! How he must have changed! Where is he, then?"

Here Merlin attempted to reply: "In me," but his lips stammered; he was troubled. His eyes filled with tears. For some time, he remained confused between desire and dread. Finally, he exclaimed: "O Psyche! O faithful soul! If only I had come to you before the one who inflicted your wound? I would not have recompensed you for so many sighs and such amorous curiosity with abandonment and forgetfulness."

"Only tell me where he is," said Psyche.

"Far from here. He's among the jousts and tourneys and the ambling palfreys in the resonant court of Arthus, with Tristan and Yseult, with King Mark, with Griselidis, with the worthy Lancelot, with the chatelaine de Vergy and the Sire de Coucy. They are the ones who, after me, know the most about love. Go find them, Psyche—they will tell you more. For myself, it's wiser to shut up. Viviane might be listening to us. But those horses will shorten our journey."

He had just perceived two unbridled horses grazing the weeds in the rubble, harnessed to a small chariot that had been forgotten in the desert.

Psyche ran to the ivory chariot and received, from Merlin's hand, the silken rains and a whip armed with silver knots. She did not want to be separated from her lamp. He handed it to her by its chain, and she placed it at her feet.

The he threw his own azure mantle over Psyche's bare, shivering shoulders.

How much, then, he wanted to sit down beside her and steer the team himself, all the more so because he feared a thousand dangers for her, and the uncertainty of the routes, often badly traced, in the new land she was about to traverse. But she did not give him time to change his mind. He remained motionless where he was, his arms extended, while Psyche, after having turned to look at him, was carried away toward the realm of Arthus, into the paradisal places where love was still alive.

He wanted to open his mouth, at last to say "Adieu!" but the word died on his lips. Then he searched with his eyes for the ruts of the chariot's wheels in the sand—but everything had already vanished: Psyche, the chariot and the tracks of the sparkling wheels over the evening dew.

BOOK THIRTEEN: THE MESSAGES

I

Why are you weeping? Is it true, then, that I can't dry up your tears?

Why are you sighing? Are you sure that the world is worth a sigh?

Why are you weeping? Can you not see that it's replying to you with laughter?

Why are you weeping? Because the country of your heart is far away? I can't give you what I've lost myself; but I can take you with me, crowned with that myrtle branch, into the cortege of the king of enchantments.

When the chariot had disappeared, Merlin felt the humiliating sadness that attaches itself to us after a splendid feast. As soon as it is over, we remember the ugliness that we bear within us and love to nourish. We feel miserable for having forgotten it, and it is revived by all that has been done to extinguish it.

That is what Merlin felt. Discontented with himself, with things, with Psyche, with the entire world, especially the gods, he took out the scroll of letters that he had received from Viviane's godmother. He crumpled it in his hands and almost tore it; then he moistened it with his tears.

To begin with, he only wanted to look again at the first line, then the second; after that, was it not necessary at least to scan the rest with his eyes? It was thus, with his heart squeezed, his eyes sometimes moist and sometimes burning, his breathing oppressed, walking back and forth, stopping, interrupting himself at every step, with a painful mixture of bitterness, joy, resentment, remorse and delight, that he reread the following, for the twentieth time.[106]

---

[106] Hermione's notes assert that there is much autobiography in this correspondence, conceding that Merlin's letters draw on letters that Quinet had written in 1931 prior to his marriage to Minna, but also asserting that the "poetry of nature" contained in Viviane's letters—wherein, she alleges, there is "no longer the distant echo of youth"—is hers, based on their life in Belgium and Switzerland. She does, however, point out that the earlier ones are supposedly dispatched from places where Quinet had lived in France, long before he met her. She goes into detail about the Swiss locations described in Viviane's later letters, but avoids any comment on Viviane's accusations of neglect and infidelity, and the surprising hostility and bitterness of some of Merlin's personal comments. The reader is free to suspect, however, that there is far more of Minna, and the anguish caused to Quinet by his separation from her (albeit more than twenty years after the fact), in the representations of the letters than there is of Hermione, from whom he was never separated.

II

Viviane to Merlin

The king's wood, month of the primrose.

You complain, Merlin, to the whole universe, of being abandoned, betrayed—what do I know? Ingrate! This is the hundredth letter I've written to you, and not a word in reply! Why this stony silence? My first letter was written on the wing of a butterfly iridescent with gold and azure, which served as the messenger itself; I told you about my pain and my insomnia since our separation. The messenger followed you for two days and you didn't even look at it. Finally, discouraged by so much scorn, it came back to me, dying of fatigue and hunger. After that, I sent you for messengers three companies of wild swans, two coveys of nightingales and three flocks of starlings, all bearing an embalmed letter. You did look at them, they said, when they passed your door.

I've done much more. I've written your name and mine, wedded together, in the calices of spring flowers, and I've instructed them to lean over and wait on the edges of paths where you were bound to pass by. There were daises and primroses, which had the patience to wait for entire months, day and night, on the highways of Germany, Italy and France; you didn't even deign to look down at them when you encountered them.

I had put into those flowers the perfume of the intoxicating bouquet that I had in my hand on the day—the sad day—of our departure; you breathed in that perfume without even remembering me. Is that what you had sworn to me?

Confess that you've encountered some young woman in your pilgrimages. I know you so well; first you wanted to make innocent use of your enchantments and then, without being aware of it, you'd be enchanted yourself. That's what has happened, isn't it? Merlin, Merlin, is it me that you think is trifling with you? Insensate is she who thinks she can retain you, when I could not do so myself!

You're going to escape me; I'd rather break it off.

Tell me, at least, what she's like, the one who holds your heart at present? Her eyes, her hair, her figure, her attitude, her homeland, her language: I want to know everything

Why did I fall in love with someone as frivolous as an enchanter? Oh, how cruelly you've punished me, Merlin! I was so calm, so cheerful, when I knew you! And how different everything is now!

Do you not see the sad mists rising like shrouds at the break of days that no longer have a dawn? Do you nor hear the moaning of the great waters in the forests? And does all that not tell you anything? Who, then has closed your eyes and hardened your ears? Can you not sense that I'm weeping? Can you see drops of water falling into a solitary pool without remembering me?

My godmother, Diana of Sicily, is the only person who can give me any consolation. Unfortunately, I see her too rarely; she's always hunting. Her life as a huntress has not hardened her, though; there is a great heart under that bronze visage. Speak to her, open up to her with all assurance. If there is still a future for us, it is to her that we shall owe it.

You have always dreamed of the wandering life of the enchanter, and you have wanted to experience it. Can you not soon feel its emptiness? I too have known it; alas, it is not even a distraction for someone in love.

But what am I saying? You only love glory and noise; you imagine your-self to be a martyr of love, when deep down you seek nothing but smoke. Who is preventing you from coming back to me? You have preferred—a sublime occupation!—giving laws to human societies. And what is poor Viviane, it must be admitted, by comparison with the court of the great Arthus, and even that of the noble Epistrophius, at which, however, I cannot help laughing? I humbly beg your pardon for that, for I assume you have become at least his chamberlain.

If you find this letter a little too jovial, it's necessary to attribute it to the violets and snowdrops that never cease to whisper in my ear and chat with the bullfinch while I'm writing.

You'll come back to me, Merlin, but will it not be too late? What will I be then? I'll write to you without fail at every opportunity that presents itself. Already the sacred green woodpecker is accompanying the flight of winter with its long jeers. The storks are preparing to return next week.

That would be an excellent opportunity for you, if you care to take advantage of their passage, for they're very reliable.

After they come, a month later, the starlings, and then the finches, and then the orioles will pass through the region where you are. Each of them might bring me something from you. It's said here that the wagtails will be very late this year. So much the better! Then we'll be in winter. But then, no more messages! O more news! Oh, what silence! What death, Merlin!

III

Viviane to Merlin

Ruins of Montmort, month of the flowering hawthorn.

My godmother with add this letter to all the others; she has promised me to put it in your own hand, even if she has to miss the hunting season. Every day I'm learning to know her better.

Yes, Merlin, I sense it, I shall survive in spite of you. My heart emits gusts of hope; the eternal springs that are gushing from the rock at this moment are nothing by comparison with the life of love that is accumulated in my heart. Oh, how thirsty I am for love! Do you still understand that word, O most savant of magicians?

A week ago, the bare trees were still trembling under a residue of dead foliage. All that I know of magic I employed to awaken them an hour earlier, and those great frozen skeletons have reanimated at your name. Already a light down envelops them; a slight aureole of verdure, the first gift of the reddening morning, is beginning to appear at the tip of ach branch.

The bud is buried in the brown hull. I arrive, I tear the shroud; the hidden soul appears; from the depths of its black sepulcher, a little green fay emerges, which smiles at me. Already she has made a robe of a folded, colored leaf, which she had fabricated and tailored herself. There it is, deployed! The white threads of silk that served for the weaving still trail on the edges.

Inconstant shadows from the depths of the forest pass beneath the frail embalmed arcades. Oh, there's a hawk swooping—woe to the bird whose song has betrayed it! But a woodlark, reassured by the sight of me, continues to draw out its shrill notes, like the rasp of a file. The wind inclines the crowns of the pines; they collide slowly and cry out like vessels in a harbor. Over there, a noise has resounded—a woodcutter's ax. The felled tree has fallen with a thunderous din. And silence again. Then the cooing of a turtle-dove, like whimpering; the perfume of resinous trees, mingled with the virgin breath of unknown flowers. No, Merlin, in spite of you, the wild roses won't die this year. Spring will have its garland once again.

I'm writing to you in the heart of a little wood, to the piping cry of a wren saluting the flowering hawthorn. The water-lilies with silver faces have surged forth from the depths of the waters like a brood of swans. How profound the solitude is here, now that the horse-drovers no longer come to disturb me! I have no companions but the cranes that come and go, alighting noisily on the edge of the large pond. When they pass overhead they form a great V. Ask them what I have said to them for you; they've sworn to me that they'll repeat it to you.

I've lent, or rather given, to the birds of the forest that winter has most deprived the silk dress that you like so much, which I was wearing the day I saw you for the first time. They've taken the threads one by one to their nests, and that work only took them two days. Their chicks will have never been so well accommodated as this year. It's a consolation to be loved by the little birds, at a time when enchanters are so ingrate.

This morning, while I was walking in the clearing, I found a butterfly numb and disabled in the dew. Its two white wings were already stuck together like a shroud; it was trembling. I took it in my hand and, after having warmed it with my breath, I carried it to a place where the sun caressed it with its first ray. The butterfly was reanimated and flew off.

I said to it: "You're looking for flowers; go to Merlin, then; he's the one who makes them bloom."

When you finally reply to me, Merlin, don't fail to let me know whether it kept its promise; it owes its life to me.

In spite of everything, I have a joyful heart; I can't encounter a hind without trying to bound like her. I'd also like to sing like the skylark. Why is that? In truth, I don't know. You'll think me frivolous, eccentric, insensate, won't you? Well, no. I can't die yet! You'd become too proud in consequence.

In any case, it's necessary to recognize that glory is arriving here from all directions; the ephemera, in particular, are making a great deal of noise. I've heard mosquitoes singing and publishing your praises until the middle of the dark night. I'm afraid that might go to your head and you'll no longer know me.

Seriously, no one at Arthus' court is talking about anything but Merlin's pilgrimages. Everyone, I tell you, is full of it. Am I the only one who doesn't know anything about so many great deeds? It's said they're a hundred times more marvelous than those of Ulysses. Tell me about them, these illustrious enterprises for which you've forgotten me. I promise not to smile at them. Can you repeat them to me one day, sitting under the flowering cherry trees in the ruins of the castle of Montmort!

In the place where I am, the odor of hay is so strong that it's going to my head, and I can hardly continue. But what a fête everywhere! Is the nightingale celebrating his wedding today? I've married the virgin vine, so long promised to the wild pear, and she immediately entwined her thousand embraces around him. Is it their epithalamium that the nightingale is singing?

Doubtless you want to know what I do every day? Alas, nothing is more monotonous. In the morning, I'm the first one in the house to get up. My godmother is still asleep when I'm already in the orchard. I see the sunlight spring forth through the branches, like showers of sparks from a blacksmith's anvil. A slight insensible breeze stirs the crowns of the poplars. Gradually, the mists rise from the valley, and I pursue he phantoms until they retreat into the caves, leaving behind them, on every bush, the shreds of their long white robes. There's always some idle bird slow to wake up, some bee that the night has surprised in the petals of a rose. I approach on tiptoe, and say to them: "Get up, it's daylight!"

Soon, I sit down at the crossroads, my distaff in my hand; there I spin, for two hours, the threads of spider-silk that pleased you in our happy days, and God knows what I think as I prolong that occupation, which pleases me more than any other. My fingers work, my thought is elsewhere, or rather, if it's necessary to be sincere, I don't think at all. I dream, I regret, I desire, I call...

Then I smile suddenly at those occupations in which I consume my days. To repeat a task that will be destroyed as soon as it's finished, spinning threads of spider-silk that the first passing fly will carry away; powdering flowers that pale and dry shortly afterwards—is that work worthy of a thinking creature?

Oh, Merlin, how you're going to despise me and believe that my soul is abandoned without mercy to these puerilities! Inventing arabesques, drawing them, paining them with colors moistened by dew on the wing of a butterfly or a damsel-fly that lives for an hour—that must appear very petty to you, O great Enchanter! Yes, doubtless, it would be a thousand times more worthwhile to write one of your triads.

Dusk is falling; I'm still on the edge of the big pond, rocking the branch of the almond-tree where there's a robin's nest with chicks. I listen to see whether one of them might still be awake, or whether the flowers are continuing to whisper among themselves. I sing in a low voice, the song that you know; and the birds, the flowers, the stars, the bees, the flock, the shepherd and even the dog all fall asleep at the same time.

If a leaf rustles, I turn round. It seems to me that it's you who is murmuring in the vale. The long shadows extend over the water, and I weep.

Laughing and weeping at the same time, that evokes your pity, Merlin. Oh, how many stranger things there are in the world that you'll never understand! Adieu!

IV

Viviane to Merlin

La Tranclière, month of the wild roses.

This, Merlin, is what has just happened near the village where Turpin was born, and which I wanted to visit because of him. It's absolutely as you foresaw.

The place being very rich in game, several noblemen and knights were forming a hunting party here with my godmother: very singular people, it's true, full of extravagant pretensions, who would be unbearable to me for that reason alone, if they weren't already by virtue of everything else about them. I suppose they're old ruined lords abusing the generosity of my godmother, Diana of Sicily, in order to slip into her entourage and devour her fortune, already much diminished.

Picture, among them, a knight already getting old, with curly golden hair, to the extent that he still has some; tall too, well-built, with a disdainful lip, always with a bow or a cythara in his hand, the most foppish of individuals; his name is Phoebus.

He takes advantage of it to say the most stupid things—for example, that he once guided the sun in a chariot of light, that he belongs to the family of the gods, that he has a temple, admittedly in ruins, on Lykaon, and a thousand other extravagances of that sort, to which I'm obliged to listen politely in order not to offend my godmother, whom I hold in high esteem and who allows herself to be easily deceived by that tinsel.

With a quavering voice he sings old songs about the gods at table, devoid of rhymes, and nonchalantly calls himself the king of hymns. I think he's utterly mad. I'm sure that his so-called temple is some hideous owl's-nest on Mount Lykaon. That, Merlin, is what you ought to investigate on the day when you pass that way. To hear him, his parents were at least gods. It would be good if you could bring down his truly Olympian conceit; immortals are all the same.

If he sees you somewhere, he'll propose, as is his custom, to compete with you for the singing prize. Accept, O Master! Without hesitation, oppose your sturdy harp to his old lyre. Show him what a difference there is between an inspired bard like you and a cold cythara-player like him. The whole universe will thank you for taking away his faded crown.

Such as I've just depicted him feature for feature, all would be well if the handsome knight in question hadn't had the audacity this morning to ask for my hand in marriage, convinced, by virtue of his fine manners, that a poor spinner, as he calls me in his wretched humor, would be only too happy with such a declaration. I couldn't help laughing in his face.

"If I ever marry," I added, "I'll only marry Merlin."

He went out furious, his bow still in his hand, sharpening a few old arrows that, fortunately, no longer have iron tips, and promising nevertheless to avenge himself. I'm warning you about all this; be careful. There's nothing more to fear from the gods, whom nullity has unmasked, but they'd like to avenge themselves on nature entire.

For me, the adventure is so odious that I'm thinking of leaving the country. There's no heather here, nor any branch of verbena, to retain me by the hem of my robe.

V

Viviane to Merlin

Field of the Crau, month of flowering heather.

Guess, if you can, what I've been doing with the days that remain before my departure? Well, yes, sublime Enchanter, while you're haunting courts, counseling kings and peoples. I been spending the twelve hours of the day inventing a new flower, which I've cut out an embroidered with a magisterial attention to detail that would make you smile if you could see me. It's a matter of little heather flowers with a hundred eyes, some white and others pink, with which I amuse myself carpeting the rocks where you sat with me on a similar day last year.

I've given them a hundred eyes in order to watch the road by which you ought to come back. I've set them on the hilltops in order that they'll see you from further away; I've laid them out in carpets in order for you to tread them underfoot. Into each of their eyes I've let one of my tears fall. But what am I saying? Why I am doing all that? What, alas, are my poor intentions to you, dazzled by the pearls, rings and earrings of the Venetians and the Neapolitans? One might think, however, that among their diamonds there are many whose litter is false. Beware of them!

It's the time when the threshers beat the ripe wheat. Everyone brings his sheaf and spreads it on the ground. But where is my sheaf? At the monotonous sound of the flails, and infinite thirst devours me. My soul, on which you heap so many insults, is consumed by an inconceivably languor. Look up at midnight at the stars of David's Chariot.[107] I'll look at them at the same moment. O stars! Carry me far from here in your sparkling chariots. Kiss the forehead of my beloved. Tell him that he doesn't know me, and take him this breath from my lips.

The great forests are spreading an acrid odor of burnt grass far and wide. Black shadows are quivering at sunset in the blue of the lakes. I've been trying to sleep. What sleep, Merlin! What dreams! You were beside me. Eternal lianas bound us to one another. I saw you enclosed with me in an impregnable tower, the key of which had been thrown into the abyss, and your lips were on my lips. I woke up with a start, but the dream pursued me. I woke up the woodpeckers, most of whom were asleep, and interrogated them. They all told me that they'd had an exactly similar dream. What does it mean? You won't have any difficulty explaining it to me, if it's true that you're the king of dreams.

VI

Viviane to Merlin

Field of the Crau.

I scarcely resemble myself, alas! Is it really me who wrote the letter you've just read? Where are the hopes, the invincible surges of the heart that the slightest breeze transported? Where are the burning gleams that lit up in the hot summer nights? On the edge of the stream I've seen a poplar that the lightning has enveloped without striking it. The bark has been torn away and dispersed. The calcined leaves have fallen in a fine, impalpable dust, which leaves no trace on the ground. It's the same, Merlin, with my works, my thoughts, my projects, my dreams: everything I undertake. The earth is stripped bare; it's strewn with debris; and I remain alone, a hundred times more deprived.

Insensate to have hoped for anything! I've been deceived by vain amusements; and those temporary amusements have been stripped away, when they were no longer necessary. Would you believe that I've been wearing mourning by turns for the daises, then the wild roses, then the violets, then the hyacinths, and then the heather? Finally, I've nothing more to weep for here but myself. All

---

[107] The constellation known in England as Charles's Wain, the Big Dipper or The Plough.

the shadows to which I attached myself have gone. And you, the vainest of all, the lightest, the most ephemeral, you, Merlin, were the first of those shadows to leave me, to dissipate in the eternal indifference.

O morning mists, heavy phantoms crawling over the earth, which I no longer have the strength to drive away, abysmal rains, bronze skies, coppery clouds beneath which I curb my head; murmurs of resinous firs; sinister splashing of banks, flights of frightened birds, more rapid than the clouds, funereal gleams in cavernous trunks, plaints and moans of the wind, solemn silences, yellowing leaves, livid suns, what are you telling me? Of what do you want to deprive me now?

When you were near me, Merlin, what did the fall of the leaves matter, or the rain resonating on the withered grass? All was joy and smiles. Did I perceive then that my works flowed away like water? I remade the same thing incessantly, and it was always new to me. But today, my occupations appear to me to be increasingly puerile. What's the point of beginning a task again that no longer has any purpose, since you're missing from everything? Discouragement, lassitude and ennui have taken hold of me. Sterile, incomplete, formless thoughts that I shall never even be able to express fill the emptiness of my days. A gray, leaden tint, expands from my eyes over the immense universe. I scarcely have the strength to chase away the dried leaves that fall in front of me. While I'm writing these words, my crown of verbena had just fallen from my head; I don't have the courage to bend down to pick it up again.

In front of me, the last rays of the sun are descending behind the mountain, from ridge to ridge, like so many staircases, and they seem to fall at every step. The opposite summits are reddened; they're reflected in the lake in quivering black pyramids, sustained her and there by twists of wavy snow at their points, of liquid fire, like the sepulchral pyre of some submarine god. What is stopping me from burying myself with him?

See, see, Merlin, what you have made of me, and at least enjoy your work. The radiant eye of the days of summer would be a mockery for me. It has been impossible for me to endure any longer the impassive song of the cicadas, which seemed to me an insult, so I tried to force them to be quiet. I wouldn't even be able to tolerate the rustic joy, the blossoming smile, surely inoffensive, of the meadow daisies. I've ordered them dryly to strip off their diadems in my presence and put on morning dress—which the innocent creatures immediately did, without complaint. Yes, mourning-dress, Merlin, that of Vivian. I don't know whether you believe a word of this. Beware, however, of weeping for me when it's too late.

Go on, bard and poet, be content with your works! I've retained only too well the sadness of your triads. I've learned their tearful rhythm; they come back to me at every hour of the day. From yellow thatch, from deserted heaths, from pale auroras, from streams that sob through fir-trees whitening with old age; from clouds with long pleats, laid out like a great damp sail over the nest of tempests; a stone standing in the forest, a dolmen, and then the eternal silence under the Oak of Mamre;[108] isn't it here that you instructed me?

Yes, I've become your worthy disciple. At this moment I'm attaching gray, silvery mosses to the black branches of the firs, in order that they'll resemble those old druids about whom you've told me so much! Around the rugged trunks of beeches, I unroll thin leaves, sparkling with silver, in order to write triads thereon.

Your triads! Oh, I've sung them on the edge of the Breton Sea, and the sea has covered itself in foam. I've sung them in the forests of Broceliande, and the forests have burst forth in groans. I've sung them to myself in the crau of Bresse, and intoxicated myself with crazed dolors that even you could no longer heal.

VII

Viviane to Merlin

Under the willows of Certines

During these miserable days, I wanted to see your mother's roof again, under which we were happy—yes, happy, whatever you say. I arrived treading on the moistened leaves through the little wood you know. I crossed the stream on the worm-eaten plank that splashed under my feet. When I emerged from the edge of the wood, I searched with my eyes for your enchanted palace. What did I find? Nettles and brambles. The fireplace can still be made out. Moss the color of ash, purple foxgloves, blue campanulas, broom and buttercups had climbed along the blackened wall, imitating the dying flames of a fire. That's what remains of our dwelling. I sat down on the stones, and, whatever you say, I found in myself a human breast. Only one of the trees that you planted on the isle of sacred apples remains; even the linden-trees have been uprooted.

A peasant woman came out of the ruins. Without being afraid of me, she asked: "Where is our master?" What could I reply? I remained silent. She took me to her hut, where she showed me your cradle. I wept. She did likewise. Such tears would bathe those ruins eternally.

Shortly afterwards I went into the little church, which I had never done before. I went through the cemetery, where almost all your childhood companions are buried, for people die quickly in that canton. The church was full of people

---

[108] The place near Hebron where Abraham is said in Old Testament mythology to have entertained three angels, revered by Jews and Christians for thousands of years. The tree on the site, rumoured to be five thousand years old, died in 1996, but it is unclear as yet whether the prophecy that that event would precede the advent of the Antichrist has been fulfilled.

because of the feast of the dead. The tolling of the bell, that old priest whom solitude has rendered almost mute, those astonishing prayers, the childish voices of the laborers, the incense burned by rustic hands, filled me with a terror that still pursues me.

But listen to the sequel:

At the crossroads, on a platform of wild roses in a niche carpeted with hawthorn, constructed by drovers, I found a young woman who seemed to be a queen. She was holding a child in her arms, crowned with a aureole, and a their feet, pipers were playing songs.

What is that blessed family? I launch myself toward it.

"Are you a fay?" I asked the one whose feet would gladly have kissed. "And who is that child's father? Why are you living, like the birds of the sky, under this roof of foliage? I'm the queen of flowers; let me cover you and give me a place for the night beneath your mantle."

But she looked at me with severity. "Have you come to dispute with me? It's me who is the queen of the flowers of heaven. Yours come from the earth, the sun withers them. Go away! Leave your garland there. You're already making the child cry."

At these words I withdrew, head bowed, without a garland; since that moment, the severe words of that divine mouth have accompanied me everywhere I have been.

Who, then, O king of sages, is this Christ that they invoke and whom you have never mentioned to me? Who is that enemy pursuing you? What are we, you and I? Once, such questions would have seemed insensate to me. As soon as my eyes saw you, I had an answer for everything. Today, the gaze of a child troubles me to the depths of my soul. Speak to me; sustain me. I love you, and yet I tremble, I'm afraid.

VIII

Viviane to Merlin

Stone of Fays, month of verbena.

How slowly this month advances! Shall I see the end of it? You'll accuse me once again, Merlin, of dreaming instead of thinking, like you. Listen, however, and pronounce.

I was at the foot of the brick tower of your castle of Montmort, the color of rust. I was looking at the stone horse that we saw together wallowing in the thick grass. The tempest arrived.

I look up at the sky; I think I see—yes, I can see, from behind, in astonishing majesty, borne by the clouds, an enchanter greater than you by a hundred cubits.

I could not perceive his face, which was turned away from me. He was enveloped in a mantle rolled around his hips, and with one of his bare feet he was treading the clouds, which were carrying him with the rapidity of eagles. In spite of myself, I threw myself on the ground in order that he would not see me.

When I got up again I met the little shepherds, and I asked them whether they had seen a great enchanter over their heads. They replied that they had seen him, and their fathers before them, and that they had always known him since they came into the world.

Those are not dreams, Merlin! How can it be that little children know things of which you and I are ignorant? What is it necessary to dread or expect of that encounter?

I have bent down at the edges of springs and shouted: "Merlin! Merlin!" But a voice stronger than yours replied, and since that moment I have been shivering. A falling leaf, a lamenting reed, a dry twig that moans as it breaks— everything consternates me. I remain motionless, a finger over my mouth. It seems to me that a great event, which will change everything, is arriving with giant strides.

Come back, come back, Merlin, if you want to see me again, or let me join you. I feel myself fainting and reviving a thousand times a day. If that is being fickle, as you claim, well, yes, I'm fickle. There are times when I run faster than a hind. I arrive before her at the top of the mountain to which hope has brought me; and immediately I feel more ponderous than a tortoise. I have the eyes of a lynx to discern the traces of my beloved; at the same time, I feel more blind than a corpse to everything that is not him.

Where are we going, my soul? You are so sad and the Alps are so near! Let us go up to the summits. Perhaps I shall be able to see my beloved!

IX

Viviane to Merlin

Vale of Maderan, month of the Alpine roses.

The black crows have announced the first funerals of the year. I have seen the Surene Alps cover themselves with their thick ermine mantle, and silver ribbons hanging down to their feet. They have chilled me with their breath. O proud summits of Clarides, why are you clad in diamond necklaces that sparkle beneath the livid daylight? Are you covering the footprints of me beloved on your heights? Virgins with hearts of ice, will you see him before me, through the fields that will be powdered by the lukewarm dawns of new days?

From pasturelands suspended from glaciers, bristling rocks whose folds resemble wrinkles of the face of a lion, forests that trail their tresses in the abyss: where now are the places that please me?

Most of all, I like to follow rivers upstream to their sources. I allow myself to be guided by the yellow-tinted snowy waters all the way to the entrance to the glacier. Their arched portals are constructed of pure sapphire. The transparent vaults of emerald serve my godmother simultaneously as a temple and a winter palace, when she passes through these remote regions. As the yet-dwarfish rivers gush over the threshold, I cast spells upon them, which they carry away furiously, from fall to fall, all the way to the depths of the valleys. Often, it is only a sprig of golden herb or verbena. I see it floating, without any tempest succeeding in dragging it under.

Meanwhile, the frowning mountains are colored in the dusk by pale pink and golden tints; they seem to be responding to signs glimpsed beyond the earth with gleams and reddened thoughts that they exchange with the heavens. O sage, tell me what hand it is that touches their faces like that! What sight, or what memory, covers the faces of those giant virgins with that sudden blush? Give me a frank answer to that question; above all, don't tell me that they're terrestrial gleams. It's a thought, I tell you, that forces them to blush. What is that thought? Do you know?

The marvel of this region, Merlin—is it necessary to tell you?—is the mountains covered in eternal snows, for they seem to be ruling over all the others like divinities. Often, they hide, and then suddenly appear, with a dazzling glare that my eyes can scarcely sustain. Then they hide again and envelop themselves in silence. Only their brown feet show themselves under the curtain of leaden rain, and it's thus that they excite by turns the admiration and the terror of the humans who glide tremulously in their shadows.

Be proud, Merlin, of having been the first to set foot on their immaculate summits. May I keep, like them, the whiteness of my soul!

It is certain, moreover, that all our enchantments are unworthy of those sacred mountains, and profane them. So I have not thought of exercising our art here. I have not even wanted to leave my footprints in those venerable snows, although I have written your name therein. It shines like a firebrand as soon as the sun rises.

What an ethereal peace there is on those peaks! Scarcely have I reached their roseate steps and I feel liberated from the earth—yes, my Master, even liberated from you. I say to myself: I'm free; his enchantments don't reach me. Dolor, regret and vain hope don't rise to that summit, where all existence stops, where the majestic fir trees, having become dwarfs, crawl miserably over the ground, cling desperately to the rock that cannot provide them with sap. A little higher up, even the thin grass disappears. There, Merlin, ceasing to live, I'm happy.

But those forms, those images are too great for us. I find myself immediately out of place there. That immeasurable grandeur terrifies me, and as soon as I reach the summit, I want to flee what I'm incapable of supporting without vertigo. How often, then, in the midst of those enormous forms, which cast me into stupor, I think lovingly about the smallest things! Never have I loved so much the humble florets that I find on the summit of the monstrous Wanguelé,[109] which gazes over the shoulder of Saint Gotthard himself.

I see the blade of grass, the ant, the dewdrop, and then I turn toward the inviolate summits. In the blink of an eye I pass from that smallness to that grandeur. I lose myself in the contemplation of the most paltry and the most colossal. But I always come back to that which is weakest, most imperceptible. I rest in that overwhelming sublimity; I recognize myself in the life of ephemera.

What do we have in common with these immutable mountains, whose impassive majesty consternates me? They give me the vertigo if grandeur after the vertigo of smallness. To contemplate them in safety, I would need to feel an imperturbable force in my heart, and that's what I lack the most. I suspect that it's from the utmost depths of what they call God that it's permissible to contemplate, without vertigo, the precipices that attract me.

But from the troubled, tottering depths of my soul, I can't struggle against the powers of the abysms. I don't know what can hold me or retain me. Delighted and consternated, I think I'm falling, infinitely, into the gulf that devours everything. O Master, where is your cherished hand to retain me on the slope?

What sculptor, O king of sages, has fabricated these colossal seats, whose feet bathe in the abysms and whose frost-covered heads are above the clouds? In the locale they're known as the Seven Margraves. Who has crowned them with those diadems of precious stones, atop their population of giants? Their silence, punctuated with the crackle of avalanches, frightens me. O cowbells, which alone mark the hour in these places from which time seems to have withdrawn, rise up to me! Goats guided by the herdsman's child, crickets of the chalet, where are you?

X

Viviane to Merlin

Cascades of Hazli, month of the anemones.

Who has carved, O Master, these stairways, of which each step is a mount to mount above the clouds? To what festival do they lead? Do you know?

Why are the cascades of Hazli in haste to fall? And why does their fury change to serenity as soon as they have touched the abyss?

Why are these rocks so pale when they lean over the gulf? Whence comes that sudden pallor? O Merlin, what can they see in the unfathomable?

---

[109] This name is unusual, but its location overlooking the St. Gotthard pass implies that the reference is probably to Pizzo Centrale.

Explain to me, above all, Master, why the ambush is extended here among the flowers. Tell me why the earth suddenly parts, all the way to Erebus, beneath the perfumed arbors of the Kirchet. I've hung on to the shaky trunk of a half-uprooted fir tree. Leaning over the precipice, I've seen the pale subterranean galleries over hanging one another. I thought I could hear the sinister Aar. But no; its roar, lost in the accursed gulf, couldn't reach me. Is that a vision of Hell? I only glimpsed it, but all my soul remains plunged therein. Help me get out.

XI

Viviane to Merlin

Castle of Resti, month of myrtles.

Without thought, without foresight, I live here in a continuous stupor that augments everything I discover. As I advance, the things I believed to be the most immutable change form. I suspend my hopes from these summits that even eagles never visit.

This is the season when all the livestock comes down from the Alpine heights to the chalets of the low valleys and shelter there for the winter. There isn't a rock that doesn't have its flock and its shepherd. I could believe that I'm seeing a celestial population emigrating from the clouds. The Alps are reddening with a crimson hue. You might think that scarlet carpets were extending beneath the feet of that divine people coming down the steps of the sky.

Among the shepherds is a young boy, Guillaume Tell, to whom you gave the arbalest that never misses its target. How dear that child is to me, among all the rest! I wanted to see him and adopt him. When I told him to come closer he was retained at first by a primitive timidity, and he bounded away, but I pronounced your name, Merlin; immediately, he advanced fearlessly, for he remembers you; he asks where you are.

Lacking in foresight, as usual, you forgot to give him an arrow; I've sharpened one for him. Thus, he's now endowed by both of us. His parents have promised me that the arbalest and the arrow will remain in the family until the last generation. May it be so, for their salvation and our glory!

After them, I remained alone in the high region that everyone is abandoning. In the icy desert of the Titlis, I encountered souls that float eternally in that abode of death, borne away by tempests that they cannot rule. Cheeks inflated, they blow out their cold breath perpetually. I asked them what keeps them in these places where nothing can live, and, pointing to the frozen tears stuck to their eyes, they replied: "The memory of our harshness when we were among humans."

Oh, Merlin, what a lesson for those who boast of knowing no pity!

As night approached, dwarfs who guard a herd of chamois offered to let me into their tower of ice; I refused. I preferred to go down to a chalet in Resti, the most charming dwelling you can image. It is also a mill, whose wheel is rotated by three cascades. The people who live here with me are the best on earth. Would you believe that they've never heard mention of you? Judge by that how extensive their holy ignorance of the world is.

No, no, Merlin, let's not hope to compete with the magic of this place. What can we do in the face of this perpetual prodigy? Forget our spells. They say in the locality, however, that an enchanter they call Manfred wanted to try his art on Lake Thun.[110] What a pity! There's an enchanter other than you, Merlin. I sense him, I see him, and I hear him in the muffled roar of the cascade in the depths of the valley. But where is he? Where does he live? Are you jealous, that you have never mentioned him to me?

While I was climbing the slopes of the Wetterhorn in order to go on to the green Alp, where I hoped finally to rejoin you, a gigantic chord was suddenly struck in the forest of firs. It quivered in the distance, and what has become of me? "That's Merlin's harp," I said to myself. "Only that could shake the granite heart of the snowy mountains!" I hastened my steps, but saw nothing except a shepherd applying his mouth to an Alpine horn. His instrument is made from the trunk of a young fir, interlaced with sonorous fibers. He rests the horn on the ground while he blows it, in such a way that its gigantic sound reaches all the way to the ears of the demons torpid in the glaciers.

So, Merlin, you take pleasure in playing with me. For it's not against your will that the shepherd had borrowed from you, even for a day, the power to shake the inexorable soul of the rocks of the Rosenlaui with a chord.

One last question, Merlin. Who is the king of the clouds here? Who ranges them in battle order at daybreak? Who dresses them in streamers at dusk, to shelter dreams? Who builds cities of gold and opal with them, from which tempests emerge through gates of flame?

They're so fantastic, Merlin, that I thought at first that you were commanding them. But they pour dew and joy over the earth, and you, Merlin, leave despair as you depart. No, you're not the chief of the clouds, although they resemble you in their vagabond spirit. They're constancy itself by comparison with you.

Who deploys their wings outside the nest of storms? Who parades their errant cities in the serene blue of the lake? How many times, alas, I've wanted to throw myself into it to earth for you in those humid crystal palaces!

Tell me, at least, whether I would have encountered you in those fugitive dwellings, and whether it's there that you dwell. They're worthy of you, lighter

---

[110] The reference is to Lord Bryon, here called "Manfred" after the title of one of the poems he wrote while staying in the Bernese alps.

than foam, more capricious than the waves. Answer, please, that last point; it's only in the interest of your science.

XII

Viviane to Merlin

Rosenlaui, month of the first snows.

Here I am in the abandoned chalet where you rested briefly. On the edge of the glacier, I've drawn forests of frost on the windows: eccentric landscapes engraved in the windows, in which I seek a more eccentric felicity—that, then, is my universe! What am I to seek my shelter in those icy lures?

Here's winter, frightful winter! What silence there is around me, Merlin! I shiver therein. Have you ever thought about death? I, who can't even believe in it, am suddenly enveloped by it. Shall I never see you again? What, already? What, so soon? The days, the eternal years that I promised you in our isle of Avalon, I see them being effaced one after another; in their place, tombs remain, covered by snow that no midday sun will dissipate. Are those giant tombs, where all joy is buried, my sepulcher and yours?

Where now are my godmother's noisy hunts, the tally-hos, the corteges of riders, the breathless packs and the whinnying horses galloping over the summits? Where are they? Will they ever return? Oh, if I could only perceive the dust fuming under the footsteps of my beloved! Why are you not waiting for me?

Why did you leave me, Merlin? I ordered you to, you say. What a reason!

Why let me die, when the violets and the snowdrops will be reborn tomorrow? They will see the light! They will lean over the fissures of the glaciers; and you will brush them with your feet, without remembering me.

As I've foreseen, there is no longer a single being here to which I can confide a message. Even the eagles and the vultures have left. The sapphire blue lakes are completed encased by their snowy shores. The desert of ice surrounds me. Only the avalanche remains, but who can command it? It's so capricious.

Adieu, Merlin, adieu. I'm cold.

XIII

Viviane to Merlin

Month of glaciers.

Ought I to rejoice? I'm still alive, but it's a miracle. Harassed, desperate, receiving nothing from you, not even expecting anything—for you're obstinate in not replying and you've been as hard s these rocks—I was sitting in the frost at the foot of the Wetterhorn, and the snow half-buried me. It seemed to me that I was on the threshold of a crystal palace lit by thousands of laps, and we had both been invited by Titania to a nocturnal feast. I only had to cross the threshold to rejoin you. Already I could discern the dance, and the round of the spirits, the very sound of their footfalls, half-stifled by the snowflakes.

I thought I could hear the distant barking of dogs. The cries redoubled; they were getting closer. It was my godmother's pack. She was following the hunt. On, I felt hands lifting me up and carrying me away. I woke up in the Castle of Resti, lying on a bed of straw, with my godmother in tears at my bedside.

"Have you sworn to die, then?" she asked me, as soon as she was able to speak. "What were you doing on the glacier at this hour?"

She did not add any reproach, but her tears said more than all her words.

I offered the excuses of my occupations, my duties. It was necessary to collect the golden herb that only grown on these peaks, to polish a few crystals, to sow diamond on the glaciers to remake their necklace.

"Cruel girl," she interrupted. "It's not enough, then, to want to die? You think you can deceive me?"

And she hugged me in her arms, stifling her tears. I couldn't hold back my own for long. I told her what she already knew, about my love for you, Merlin; how I had known you; the day, the hour, the place, our betrothal; how I had quit my father Dionas[111] for you; our oaths, even our disputes, the differences in our character, your poetic temperament; I didn't hide our caprices from her. But I didn't hide the fact that the ennui of living had griped me, that I'd toyed with death, that I'd half-entered it with terror mingled with indescribable delights.

"Poor children!" she cried, when I'd finished. "At least he still loves you?"

"He says so."

"We'll see," she said.

Since that moment she's thought of nothing but our marriage. She's taking responsibility for everything—letters, first of all; in a word, she's incessantly showing me a generosity than I've never known. It's been necessary to swear to her that I won't go up to the glaciers again, for as long as the season of frosts lasts. In return, I've demanded that the odious, ridiculous Phoebus be sent away forever.

That, Merlin, is a faithful record of the last few days. Do you believe, finally, that you're loved? Are you? Or is all this nothing but a dream? You'll doubtless judge that it's time to respond.

---

[111] Named as Viviane's father in the *Prose Merlin*, and her link to Diana the huntress, who prophesies in the text that Dionas' daughter will be loved by the most powerful magician in the world—hence becoming her "godmother," in Quinet's terminology.

XIV

Don't ask how many times Merlin put that last letter, in which he rediscovered Viviane in her entirety, to his lips. He affected, for several days, not to want to reply, hoping at every moment that another message might reach him, and finding an infernal pleasure in prolonging his beloved's despair. But, his calculation having been disappointed, he began to dread that she might be consoled, and had resigned herself to living without him. Then he took the decision to break the silence, which he did, after long monologues, in the following manner:

The Enchanter Merlin to Viviane

Kingdom of Epistrophius, month of myrtles.

Your messages, Viviane, were handed to me almost all at the same time, with the exception of the one you confided to a butterfly. Whatever it says, I haven't seen it, and I beg you not to employ it again. It's incapable of anything serious; it mingles with everything a frivolity that wounds me, because of you.

I've trembled on reading your letters. That winter night in the Alps! Don't you finally dread toying with destiny?

The contest between us is unequal, Viviane. What you're suffering, you have wished, blindly and pitilessly. Your will and pride are satisfied. But as for me, I wanted to be happy, and I was. All of this was accomplished against my will. You tore me out of my happiness fully alive. I cried like a baby, and you were deaf. Today, you're calling me back; how do I know that it isn't a further caprice? Do you want to return life to me in order to take it away again? Know that I no longer have the strength to suffer. I hate and abhor dolor, but you seek it out, you revel in it, at least in that which you claim to love.

Why are you talking to me about the Alpine glaciers? They are less cold that your final gaze. You never loved me for a single instant; who can tell whether you're capable of loving anything but yourself? My love was too hot for your heart, kneaded by the mountain snows. Don't you remember how you claimed that it consumed you as the sun consumes fresh snow? And I, insanely, when you pronounced those words, smiled at them foolishly. I even think I found them adorable, when it was a bald expression of the incapacity you have of feeling more.

What do you want? One doesn't change one's nature on a whim. I was wrong to expect from you what you can neither give nor share. Now I understand, too late, why you always begged me to love you as the flowers love one another, because, you said, the breath of my heart devoured you like the desert wind. And, stupid as I was, I saw that as a reason for inflaming myself further. I adored on your lips the immaculate breath of matinal roses, without seeing that your idle soul only demanded to vegetate. Oh, what combats of which you had

268

no idea! I called restraint, sanctity and virginity what was, in you, merely the impossibility of love.

Come on, Viviane! You can do many things; you can, I believe, write in the clouds; you can domesticate eagles, change the snigger of the Breton sea into a groan; but you'll never know what there was in a single beat of Merlin's heart, which you crushed under your feet.

After all, you were certainly right to praise the sentiments of flowers and offer them to me as models. I think they're much better fitted than I am to respond to the singular idea that you have adopted of felicity. They have, it's said, an incorruptible softness, mingled with a little banality, which doesn't seem to displease you. Their desires are as sage and temperate as dew. I assure you that their kisses won't burn your lips. Be happy, then, Viviane, as I sincerely desire you to be. Become infatuated with some beautiful lily, which will be able to satisfy everything that you seem to desire, and even to dream.

Believe me, there's nothing nobler and sweeter—I'm making use of our own words—than a love of that sort. And if, by chance, that isn't sufficient for you, if some grand and sublime passion has awakened in your heart, I can't see any reason why you shouldn't marry that Phoebus—who, by the way, didn't lie to you overmuch about his genealogy or his lyre; however, I obliged him to break it, after having defeated him publicly in a singing contest. That aside, he has, it seems to me, everything that is necessary to your happiness. He's handsome, you say...my God, I don't doubt it, and I can't pretend to compete with him in that regard.

Well, Viviane, marry him. Yes, the word is pronounced. Emerge from vain illusions; see yourself, finally, as you are. You think you love poetry; it's not true. What you love is emptiness. That Phoebus, already old, will suit you, I tell you. He won't overwhelm you with the inextinguishable flames of his heart. He'll let you cradle sleeping birds in peace and devote yourself to your other occupations. Marry him, then, if you wouldn't prefer to be a nun and go into a convent. But I'd prefer a thousand times more to know that you were married; I'd be far more tranquil myself.

In what blindness have I lived thus far! Finally, my eyes are open. I've awakened from the dreams that occupied me too much. Once again—I can't repeat it too often—your soul is made of the purest substance there is on earth, the soul of spring roses; I believe that; I recognize it; I'm ready to publish it; but in return, confess to me that it has nothing human about it. That confession is all I ask at this supreme moment.

Know also that I don't blame you; I'm not accusing you—no, I feel sorry for you, which is very different. We misunderstood one another, in thinking that we resembled one another, when everything separates us. Sooner or later, the split would have happened. It's surely better that it isn't longer delayed.

In my distress I thought I could warm up, with the fire that was burning me, your soul drawn from the eternal glaciers. And you—recognize it ingenuously—hoped to reduce my heart to that demi-slumber in which you delight, which you take for the highest virtue, but which is, I fear, only the sagacity and impotence of death. No, our souls are not made for one another; that's neither your fault not mine. You want a love outside human nature, which is only found in the convent or the lethargy of plants.

Is it my fault, then, if the blood of a man flows, drop by drop, through my veins? It would be better, I know, to feel the glorious sap of the most beautiful of lilies circulating there, as you incessantly said, to the point of making me stupidly jealous on several occasions.

Of love, Viviane, you only love the word; and I'm truly astonished that you aren't smitten with a dream. I have the misfortune to be entirely the opposite. A human being, I love in the manner of humans. Be a nun, Viviane; dream of the mystic lily; earthly love is veritably unworthy of you.

Shall I say one more word, Viviane? Know, then, that I have only had with you, and through you, a semblance of happiness. At the very moment when I seemed to you to be happiest, I sensed an abyss between us. I smiled, it's true, on the edge of that abyss; but I saw it and I thought that it would devour us both. That is how I lived. You know now, the explanation of my sighs, and even the tears of which you could not find the cause.

XV

Merlin to Viviane

Month of myrtles.

Well, yes, Viviane, I love glory. I would have liked to hear my name resonating nobly in the mouths of men. Do you know why? I shall be too unhappy if you can't deduce it.

It isn't me who can figure out whether you're talking seriously or ironically about my pilgrimages and the few works I've sown on the way. Far be it from me to have the pretention to compare my works with yours! The slightest embroidery woven by your hand on a flower or the wing of a butterfly is a thousand times beyond the best laws that I've been able to give to the peoples who asked me for them. The courts of Arthus and Epistrophius, too debased for you, are nothing compared to the redoubts of the honeysuckle that you deify with your presence. I shall always prefer—as you know only too well—a single beat of your heart to all the glory of empires, but in the end, after you so cruelly, so inhumanly chased me away, was it necessary to consume myself in sterile idleness? My works are derisory, agreed, but without them, I would have ceased to live a long time ago.

Alas, Viviane, my laws, my institutions, my royalties have not lasted as long as your flowers. While you were weaving illusory threads over the meadows, I have woven threads a thousand times more deceptive over the cradles of peoples. You mourn the instability of our works; they escape you, you say; they flee you; they seem futile, even risible. What, then, do you think of mine? Let's not talk about it, please. Confess that everything is vain and almost ridiculous, except the love that you broke—thoughtlessly, I believe.

Yes, men have asked me for laws, and I have given them some. More often than not, my heart wasn't in what I was doing. It requires a foundation of happiness to sow serenity around one; and for my part, I only knew trouble and anguish. How, then, could I have given them what I was so far from possessing myself? In spite of the pleasure that you take in disparaging me—a pleasure I've never understood—do you doubt that I can measure the true value of my enchantments? But it's necessary to die or to do something.

And if my works are imperfect, whose fault is it, Viviane? Yours. Is it generous to take away my reason, and to mock me afterwards regarding my glory? You make fun of the hymns of ephemera; I yield them to you. Do you believe, then, that you can dishearten me like a cicada? Disillusion yourself. I've obtained from my heart that it no longer bleeds from small wounds; there are enough large ones.

How bitter you are, when it's the world alone that ought to complain about me! If it had been able to read my heart, how distracted and indifferent it would have found me at the very moment when I seemed most occupied with it. Most of its evils have no other cause. It happens that peoples—and, without pride, I might say worlds—have put their fate in my hands. And during those times, I was pricking up my ears, listening for the sound of your footsteps. The innocent peoples, always dupes, thought that I was absorbed in the meditation of their future, and I, leaning over some stream, was following with my gaze a leaf that the current was carrying way, wondering if it might be carrying a message from you.

Where were you, Viviane, when I was sobbing on the strands of Brittany? And when the nations followed me to the banks of the Rhine? And when I invited the peoples to the Round Table? And the day when I heard the great breath of the volcano? And the other when I sat down on the shores of the Sicilian sea? Why have you waited until my heart has dried up with dolor? You have only begun to remember me when, indignant in my misery, I was ready to free myself from you. I knew that you were fickle, Viviane. Where and since when, in what school, have you learned calculation?

While traversing the Alps I heard a great sigh. I would have sworn that that sigh emerged from your breast and that you were hidden nearby, spying on me. Scarcely had I entered Lombardy than I recognized your breath in the myrtle bushes. Answer! Where were you hiding in that great garden they call Italy? Were you not in the crowd during the processions of the women of Tivoli and Albano? I often thought I recognized you. When that young woman of the Sabine brought me figs at the Tiber crossing, I cried in advance in my heart: Is it you? The same cry in Frascati on the threshold of a hostelry; the same delirium at the sight of a woman in the Roman countryside. I mistook them for you in our days of splendor and regal humor. It was the daughter of a *pifferare*.

What pleasure do you find, Viviane, in abusing me thus with vague dreams, in turning against me the enchantments that I taught you? A moment, a day, is forgivable—but an entire life employed in baiting, abusing someone else. Who could conceive of that!

You're doubtless not unaware that I taught those people to make your portrait. They succeeded in that better than I could have imagined. You know that I led their hands to rediscover your adored features in marble, on wood, on walls—and how you must have smiled at the master and the pupils! Don't hope, at least, to rob me of that image, on which I've set an entire people to work. Do you fear slander? I haven't said a single word that could trouble your renown. The majority here take me for a scholar, a doctor, a nephew of the Sibyl, who understands nothing of matters of love. Everyone, all the way to the hermits of the Camaldoli, is in love with you, for they know nothing about you but your beauty. Oh, if I had told them about the whims of your soul of stone!

But you, tell me whence came the host of your portraits, your statues, that I discover every day in Greece, in the domains of Epistrophius. Who made them? In what circumstances? To whom did you give them? Many questions, Viviane, to which you never reply! Why so many mysteries between us? I assume that those stone portraits were made during your early adolescence, when you lived in the palace of your godmother, Diana of Sicily. Why did she permit you to go about thus devoid of clothing and veils? Childhood and solitude are no excuses.

I'm jealous of those stones; I curse the goatherds who can look at them at their ease. It's true, then, that others have contemplated our beauty before me. Why, Viviane, was I not the first being that your eyes encountered? Your cold marble gaze would have been ignited by the fire of my gaze. Tell me that your lips of stone waited for my kisses to part. I remain in ecstasy before the tresses of your hair, knotted behind your head. That light tunic gives you a strange appearance that troubles me; it's you, there's no doubt about it. But it's you in your first adolescence, when you played with seashells and tortoises on the shore of the azure sea. Promise me, if we meet again, to resume that costume, even for a day. You owe me that long eternity, lost before knowing you.

XVI

Viviane to Merlin

I can't love, you say? Bear witness for me, then, sleepless nights, lukewarm dawns, burning days, agonizing tears that desiccate the flowers.

You certainly know how to profit, Merlin, from the advantages that I've allowed you to acquire over me! I crawl while you soar. My soul of ice cannot suffice for a soul of fire like yours. Have I repeated all your blasphemies, Merlin? I beg your pardon. Don't add another reproach, or, rather, console me in that abandonment of everything. I'm advancing, tremulously, toward desolate regions that you will never visit, where eternal silence reigns and where even your name finds no echo.

What, then, is the perpetual misunderstanding that separates us, Merlin? Are you, in fact, too superior to me for me to be able to understand you? Or are you jealous of my power? Oh, wretched power! I lay it at your feet. Be the strong individual who will protect me and explain me to myself. But let's not argue, my Master! I'm the reed; be the oak. If I've ever competed with you, that was very wrong—I see that now.

At least don't expect to relegate me with a word beneath the enchanted worlds, into the ranks of those dull creatures whose souls have not been warmed by the sun for a single day. Whatever you are, O prophet, bard, king, there's one thing that remains impossible to you. You shall not cast me back into the darkness of those who have never loved.

No, no. I won't become similar to those vagabond fays who, with empty hearts, devoid of regret and devoid of desire, parade their apathy from place to place, between life and death. Every time that I have had occasion to meet their like at crossroads in the woods, I have fled at a rapid pace. Their wrinkled antiquity will never attain me. I shall retain my immortal youth; for our souls are mingled, Merlin; the taste of your lips still remains on mine. No eternity can remove it.

Neither days not centuries can make me forget the scintillating nights when, your hand in mind, we counted the stars together. Did you accuse me then of sleeping the slumber of plants?

Whence comes this fury that drives you to tear me apart? But I was wrong, Merlin. Forgive me that word; it's better to weep. What! When your eyes paused upon my eyes, when we read the magic book together, when you gathered verbena that my feet had trodden, and you found me in the morning on opening our eyes and you cried "Felicity! Felicity!" you were not happy?

Can you not, then, forget or forgive one moment of—caprice, error, whim; I don't know myself what to call it? Is there no mercy in the hearts of enchanters? My godmother can tell you how changed she finds me; many people have difficulty recognizing me.

Shall we lose all the eternities because of a moment of misunderstanding? It's not astonishing, Merlin, that with such different habits and educations, that was an instant of difficulty between us—one alone. That happens to everyone. Today, when I know you better, it would be different, I swear. But it's too late, alas, and now it's your turn to be inflexible.

XVII

Merlin to Viviane

Nothing resembles your letters less than you, Viviane. You regard, while writing, certain caresses of language as a sweet music that has no precise significance and does not commit to anything the one who lets them fall romantically from her nightingale plume. For myself, I no longer believe in words; in my ears they all have the same meaning: dolor.

Once, in my life, the science I cultivate has been veritably useful to me. By that mans, I've discovered the source of my troubles. You and I do not belong to the same world, the same people, or the same race of beings. We don't speak the same language. The words that depart from my heart have no meaning for you. They emerge burning from my lips; they slide over our soul and freeze there without penetrating, like the water of the torrent of Ruti over a swan's wing.

Live then, since you prefer it, without enchantment, without impetus, without genius. Remake that which has been made a hundred times. Drag yourself along in imitation of the world. Avoid, like an impiety, any disobedience to the age-old routine. Regulate yourself in accordance with the noble advice of your godmother, her chamberlains and her courtiers. Let those experienced individuals tell you what is appropriate, and what is not in the passion of a courtier, and conform with their advice; for that is your calling, to be sage enough to deprive your heart of all magic. Have no scruples about anything, I suggest, except for my tears.

How right you were to say to me, the first time I saw you: "Don't love me; I can't reciprocate!"

In fact, since that moment, you have obliged me to desire immensely to obtain a drop of water. Your supreme ambition has been to discover how to give me the least possible happiness.

That coldness, which is a sort of continuous malady in you, renders dissimulation easier for you than others. You also find therein the advantage of watching, without flinching, tears or despair, the agony of the man you claim to adore.

At least it's certain that you adore me more when absent than present. Your heart fills up and is sated in a matter of days. You think you're happy; perhaps you are; and then you're your fatigued soul, extenuated by a smile, is suddenly enveloped by a mantle of ice, like the summits of the Alps that you excel in describing; under a serene sky, they're suddenly surrounded by a sulky mist—but they only ever engender tempests.

What do you want, then, Viviane? I have put your happiness in your hands, not once but a hundred times, and you've never had the strength to decide yes or no.

You're a frail creeper that needs an oak to sustain it. Poorly advised courtiers made you believe that it's you who is the oak; from that moment on, all was lost for us.

You know neither love nor hatred. You destroy with one hand what you've built with the other; afterwards, you cry: "I'm lost."

For myself, good or bad, I'm precisely the opposite. What I've wanted I want forever; what I've desired I desire forever; what I've loved I love forever; what I've hated I hate forever.

Are you going this year, as I believe you planned, to the valley of Kashmir, or are you not going there? Do one or the other, but at least do something. You've recently been talking about religion, Viviane; here's nothing more irreligious than that absence of determination.

After the ordeal I've undergone, I'd have to be insane still to believe in my power over you. Be, then, and continue to be, my sister. I should never have desired anything else, nor you anything more than to call me brother. Deep down, that's what you've always wanted; such a relationship is perhaps a honeyed paradise.

Recently, Viviane, you've adopted a pious verbiage that I never knew you to use before. To hear you, it's an unknown god, an all-powerful enchanter who is the author of my woes. No, once again. You alone have done the harm: your will, your harshness; your blindness.

On further consideration, I think I hate you, but the hatred does me no more harm than the love.

To what, Viviane, have you sacrificed me? To some futility? To some puerile fear? Sometimes to a curiously-inflated cloud that arrived hurriedly over your head, sometimes to a bad dream. Once you were retained by opinion of you held by the stupid reeds; another time, you said, by the sudden murmur of the wind that blew the door open, or even by the chatter of the magpies; and thus, perpetually adjourned, happiness never arrived for me. What will the cicadas think, what will they say? That was your great and serious anxiety in the woods. And if I said that there were no cicadas, you found some bee gone astray under the linden trees. How many times did that word spoil all my joy in our solitude, while I wasn't thinking about anything but intoxicating myself with your eternal kiss? You always had at your service some little maxim borrowed from your godmother's heart, and a rosy pleat on the lips to drive felicity itself to despair.

In spite of that, Viviane, if we ever seen one another again, I want it to be alone; the presence of any witness whatsoever, even a sylph or a kobold, would offend me like a suspicion unworthy of me. That's a subsidiary issue to you, though, like everything else. Adieu.

P.S. By way of conclusion, Viviane, you accumulate, as is your custom with respect to everything you encounter, question after question, at the risk of confusing them all. I'll at least satisfy you with regard to the principal one.

You ask why the snowy mountains redden with a mysterious light as the day declines, why the evening poses a red and gold crown on the white head of the grand old man of the Alps, and why the rest of the earth is in shadow when the Titlis still sparkles with diamonds attached to its brow.

If you had remembered my lessons, you'd be able to reply to yourself: "It's thus that the truth puts a charm on the white hair of a sage. When all is darkness around him, it crowns his head with the splendors of an invisible aurora. Full of light, he smiles at the approach of the night that will give birth to the new day."

Why, you ask, does the river hurl itself with so much fury into its cataracts? Why does it covet the abyss? Why, immediately after its fall, does it no longer recall its anger? Calmed between its two verdant banks, why has it forgotten the gulf so quickly? Response: The river precipitates itself to give the response to the sage: "If anger grips you at the approach of the wicked, let it only last a moment. If you are hurled into the abyss, collect yourself in peace. Let no sign reveal that you have traversed the cataracts of evil."

By these responses, Viviane, you can see that it's not difficult for science to dissipate the obscurities in which you take pleasure. Be careful, however, of too much interrogation; mistrust the mystical anxieties with which the soul disturbs itself, and in which it goes astray.

BOOK FOURTEEN: THE GAMES

I

Truly, Reader, you're right to complain about me; if it's not too late, I'll repair my fault right away. After all, what you want in an author is a slave, or at least a courtier who solicits your favor. Nothing is more legitimate. However, I haven't followed your whims and caressed your sovereign caprices, as I should have. On the contrary, more often than not, I've taken you where you had to desire to go. I, and I alone, have frayed my path in accordance with my whim, without consulting you or worrying about putting you off permanently, so sweet has liberty been to me! I would not have exchanged it for the throne of the world.

It's time to renounce overly lofty thoughts. I feel it, I confess, Reader. See my repentance; if it's belated, it's no less sincere. From this moment on, I'm shedding the old man; like you, I'll change color, sentiment, ideas and flags, and defer in everything to the slightest of your desires. Experience has changed you, you say? Me too. You converted yesterday? Me too. You're finally wise now? Me too. Do you want to change again? So be it. I conform in advance to each of your metamorphoses, even if they surpass those of Proteus. Fire, water, earth, I'll follow you easily under those various masks. There's only one thing that I beg you to spare me. It would be absolutely impossible for me to metamorphose into a reptile.

For all the rest, I give you now in a formal manner the government of my thought. Take it! Take the reins. Here's the silver bit that I invite you to tighten, and if, as I don't doubt, you want to make use of the whip, here are the new thongs. Be the Phaeton of this chariot, which is only half way through its course. Bring the overly ambitious four-in-hand back to the banal road. Choose the route, the subject, the characters. Speak! Command! Where would you like to go? Along the Milky Way? Or, as I suppose, through lower regions? It's for you to order, me to obey.

To prove to you that these aren't hypocritical words destined to lure you further, I shall enchain myself henceforth to the imitation of good models: Virgil, the fifth book of the Aeneid, and the epistle to the Pisos;[112] there, I think, is a

---

[112] The Fifth book of the *Aeneid* includes a description of funeral games, with prizes; Horace's "Epistle to the Pisos," [the addressees being Lucius Calpurnius Piso and his two sons] better known as *Ars Poetica* [Poetic Art] is an early work on literary theory, elaborating on themes in Aristotle's *Poetics*, itself cast in po-

safe path and names that will inspire you to want to know how the story continues.

Since Merlin's return, his somber sadness had not passed unnoticed by
Epistrophius. The noble king of the ruins attempted to dissipate it; when he saw
our Enchanter one day, his head bowed, more pensive than usual, he said to him:
"You want to study the mores of the spirits of the ruins, Merlin. Bless your star;
an incomparable opportunity is presenting itself to you. I've heard that the
Nemean Games will be celebrated in a few days. None of the great kings of our
family and their councilors would miss them. Our peoples will also be assembled there, like the dust one sweeps in the air. You can observe them entirely at
you ease."

"Games, Sire!" Merlin interjected, with a sigh. "They're not made for me.
I'd sadden them."

"Not at all. Ulysses, in spite of his desire to see Penelope again, never
failed to join in the cestus competition. Aeneas, in spite of his love for Dido,
took pleasure in the games of Evander's sons. Similarly, you..."

"Don't go on, Sire," Merlin said. "I'll be there. It's sufficient that you've
ordered it."

It was by the Arcadian Gate that they went out of superb Mavromati, in the
same order and with the same equipment that I have described above. Beyond
the marshes of Stenyclare, they began to climb one of the slopes of Lykaon by
means of narrow paths that had been traces by fauns.

A storm surprised them. They went astray. Fortunately, a centaur was just
passing, and he stopped to wipe away the rain that was dripping from his tufted
beard. Then, without waiting to be interrogated, he showed them the path, his
arm extended, with a whinny of savage joy to which the centauresses responded.
At the noise of those whinnies, Palamedes arrived, crowned with brambles. That
king conducted the travelers to the vast city of Lykosura.

There were still a few low fragments for which he apologized. It was not,
he said, idleness or lack or zeal if the ground had not been better cleared, but the
place was deserted, heavily wooded and the materials were rebellious. "After all,
of the immense walls of which the ancestors speak to us, only the few blocks
you see here remain. They serve as seats for my guests."

Epistrophius embraced him, consoled him, and even praised him. He replied that, far from having any reproach to address to him, what he saw surpassed his hopes.

They went to sleep beside a little fire of old stumps. Meanwhile, the
daughters of the noble Palamedes rocked the infants they were holding over the
fire, at the risk of blackening them with smoke, and in order to spread slumber
they sang in low voices, alternating soft hymns, as one might imagine of spirits

---

etic form, whose lessons were taken to heart by many French Classicist drama-
tists.

278

of ruins. To these hymns, the mewling of the jackals responded, dominated by the solemn appeals of the owls in the sonorous forests. Jacques found a teal nearby caught in a snare; he secretly made a meal of it for himself and his master.

As for the kind of food usual in that empire, they found, in addition to the handful of cress they had discovered in Messenia, a lettuce in Arcadia, five olives in the hollow of Lacedemon, a root in the flat country of the Tegeates, a water-chestnut in the home of the Mantineans, two onions in Megalopolis, a crab in Argoliode, three snails in Corinthia, not to mention a goat cheese forgotten by a Cyclops, probably Polyphemus, at the entrance to the vaults of Tyrinthe.

I shall not describe the rest of the journey. Know only that they tasted the same hospitality everywhere. But I shall not omit to say that in Sparta, they slept in the home of Hippolyte, Drunk of Crete, in a column carved into a drinking-trough; in Mantinea in the abode of Evander, Duke of Syria, in a marsh; and at Mycenae, on the threshold of a blazoned door, standing ajar, which led to the maremma.

From there it was no more than half a day's journey to reach the gorges of Nemea, which they did at a leisurely pace, following a steam in which a host of flame-colored flowers was bathing, like so many fire-follets. The name of the stream and the flowers escapes me momentarily—see Strabo, Book IV, Oxford edition.[113]

They had just reached the top of the mountain. At their feet, they perceived the innumerable multitude of the spirits and genii of the ruins crowded into the vale of Nemea. Imagine the form of a stadium at one extremity of which four or five columns of a temple still surged forth. Our travelers recognized with regret that the games had already begun.

Epistrophius could not help showing a little resentment at the fact that they had not waited for him.

What do you expect?" he said to Merlin. "They don't respect anything, even etiquette. But that fault is one of their qualities. Perhaps without it they'd be impotent."

As they descended into the valley he recognized the majority of the kings, princes and sovereigns he called his brothers, and pointed to them.

"Forget your chagrins, Merlin; fortune favors you, for you can see here a number of princes who aren't accustomed to come together. Look over there to my right. The one you can see sitting on a little mummy is Pandrasus, the King of Egypt, the most handsome and foremost of the genii of the ruins, a great slayer of peoples, robust in arms, famous for his probity—in a word, faultless, if he hadn't allowed the plague of Sodom to envelop him. The other next to him

---

[113] The Nemean games are mentioned, briefly, in Book VIII of Strabo, but there does not seem to be any mention in the relevant passage of a stream or a flower.

who's wearing the large miter sparkling with rubies and sapphires is Xerxes, king of the Itureans. His ancestors quarreled with ours, but time, which arranges everything, has extinguished our rancors. Consider that handsome old blind man with a rosary in his hand, whose signaling to me and has kept a place for me at his side. That's the powerful Teucer, King of Phrygia...

"But what am I saying? From the most distant regions of the globe, kings, our relatives or allies, come to meet up at our games. Who would have expect to encounter here, pell-mell, Feravis, King of Gor, Garamon of Cappadocia, and, I think, Alifantina, King of Spain.[114] The last is connected to us, no doubt, by the privilege of the poverty and nudity of his people. And yet, unless age has weakened my eyes. I recognize all three of them, over there by virtue of such signs as that the camels of the first two have started to graze the flowering grass in the cella of the temple. Am I mistaken?"

"Not at all, Sire," replied the foremost of the courtiers. "I too recognized the King of Spain's donkeys."

"Who's that one?" asked Merlin. "I could swear that I've met him before, without being able to say where."

"Which one?"

"The one with the jaundiced complexion and the evasive eyes. How heavily he hastens! Puffed up as he is, he seems to be visibly swelling further..."

"Pass by without looking again," replied Epistrophius. "He's a fine spirit of the ruins—a false enchanter who has sworn a terrible hatred against all true ones. He tried for a long time to remain a good man and make his way by his own merits, but, not being able to succeeded in anything by that path, he hastened to take his revenge with all the vices."

"How chagrined he seems!"

"That's true. In matters of conscience he still retains a hint of melancholy."

While the king was speaking, the sage Merlin allowed his eyes to wander over the crowd assembled in the narrow valley. A single glance sufficed to convince our hero that all the dynasties pressing in front of him were of the family of Epistrophius and possessed a similar genius. There was the same nudity everywhere, not only of body but of spirit.

I knew full well, he said to himself, *that the illustrious dynasties that fill the dark ages in which we live are not imaginary. It's nevertheless very useful that I've encountered them all in this place, in order that I can bear witness one day in favor of their existence.* Listening to the confused, discordant murmur that rose up from the floor of the valley, he added: *And truly, after all, I can't say that they're not making as much noise as the monarchies and empires more accredited in human history.*

---

[114] Alifantina is included in Geoffrey of Monmouth's list of kings, but not Feravis of Gor or Garamon of Cappadocia. A King of Gor is briefly mentioned in Macpherson's *Ossian*, but not named.

Our travelers having entered the enclosure of the games, there was a momentary silence. Epistrophius was taken to a fragment of a broken capital that was to serve as his throne. He sat down with his servants around him. Immediately, the national hymn emerged from all mouths.

Merlin made superhuman efforts to seize the name of the god they were invoking. At first, it was impossible for him to succeed, because the language of the spirits of the ruins was too new to him. He could scarcely stammer a few words of it, which he pronounced very badly, to the point of being unable to help blushing as he spoke. Soon, however, being assured that what he heard in the crowd was a hymn to hypocrisy, he freely translated it, in prose more faithful than verse, in the following manner:

"Hypocrisy, goddess of the spirit of the ruins, with carmine-painted eyelids, you are the most beautiful, the most fecund and the most helpful of immortals. Who has ever seen you twice with the same face?

"Neither the bird that sheds its winter plumage, nor the serpent that changes its skin in the spiny nopal bush, nor the rainbow that envelops the tearful face of day with its iridescent sash, can equal it.

"You are not enclosed at Delos or Egina between a single temple built in the waves of the sea. Everywhere, in every temple, you make your dwelling.

"Doors closed, by night, you penetrate into the sacred interior with the nocturnal bird. You crouch down in the sanctuary, on the marble parvis, and when the dawn awakens, you have preceded the god. If he arrived, it's too late; you expel him from his own temple.

"Your sighs, Hypocrisy, are heard further away than those of the wind in the devastated house of Aeolus.

"Your hymn in the loudest of all. It bursts forth like the ardent hammer on the anvils of the blacksmiths who wake the sleeping city."

What Merlin discerned even more clearly was the eulogy to withered flowers and darnel, to insult the wheat. Imitation was similarly preferred to invention, savoir-faire to genius, winter to spring and death to life. But nothing astonished him more than the nasal tone of the hymn. He could not help remarking to his closest neighbor, who happened to be Aethion, Duke of Boeotia: "Why does everyone here sing canticles to the divinity through his nose?"

"A fine question! Don't you know that that's the Byzantine mode? Nothing is more religious."

"But..."

"No, Aethion interrupted. "Don't talk to me about your young, fresh, giddy voices, which would be an insult in the face of ruins. We've adopted and organized the nasal chant because it has a senility that's perfectly suited to the decrepitude of our empires."

"I should have understood that," said Merlin

The dialogue was interrupted at the moment when a solemn offering of spider-webs was being made on the altar.

The hymn having finished, the games recommenced. There was no cestus, nor wrestling, nor the bow, nor running, not the discus, nor coarse pugilism, nor the smoking cart in the quarry. The first game consisted of tipping over a temple column. It had been previously raised by the rough hands of Good Faith.

Sertorius, king of Libya, was the first to present himself to compete for the prize. For a long time, one might have thought that the column was about to fall on him, and the faces of the spirits of the ruins were blossoming with pleasure. But his strength ran out; he withdrew, full of dolor, for he could hear a dull snigger that rose up in midst of the crowd.

While he went to hide his shame, Polictetes, Duke of Bythinia, climbed to the top of the column. Like a shepherd pursued by furious wolves emerged from the Hemus climbing from branch to branch to the top of a gnarled oak, from which he braves the gaping maws and bloody fangs of the pack, the Duke of Bythinia dominated the assembly. He began to demolish the edifice slowly, bit by bit; everyone admired or envied his good grace, while he detached the stones one after another. Soon, he had made the pride of the temple disappear. An immense applause went up everywhere. He received in recompense a crown of dead leaves and the mummy of an artistically-illuminated tortoise, which Pandrasus, king of Egypt, had brought from the banks of the Nile.

The emotion had scarcely calmed down when a herald asked the following question of the crowd: "What is the surest means of making a city or a State the abode of wolves and foxes?"

As soon as those words were pronounced, almost everyone got up precipitately to compete for the prize.

One often sees in autumn, in Burgundy or Bresse, a flock of crows, starlings or finches settle on the damp earth or bushes already stripped of berries; if one of them, perched apart, utters a cry, they all immediately depart in rapid flight, and the air is darkened by them. One alone, shrewder or more gluttonous, remains motionless and continues to gorge itself on nourishment.

In the same way, while everyone launched themselves forward inconsiderately, only Xerxes, the king of the Itureans, took the floor and said: "I know what leads the desert most rapidly into a city. It's fire, as witness the burning of the temple of Persepolis."

Having said that, he returned to silence.

With that, Sagremor, King of Byzantium, signaled that he knew the truth. Everyone fell silent to listen to him.

"It's not fire," he said, "but water that renders cities solitary and mute, as witness the deluge of Deucalion."

The spirits were thus divided, when Merlin went to Epistrophius and spoke to him in these terms:

"What about you, great king of ruins, aren't you going to speak? The shame would surely be great for you and our people if you allowed the prize to be stolen without a fight, pusillanimously."

"Assuredly, I'd like to speak, Merlin," Epistrophius replied, "but I don't really know what to think, and I fear provoking laughter."

The two of them conversed together for a few moments longer, after which Epistrophius, as if he had been carried away by a sudden inspiration, stood up on his remnant of a capital.

"King, monarchs, dynasties of ruins, all of you who can hear me, know that neither fire nor water, nor even iron, destroys cities. What makes them crumble is..."

"What?" interrupted the crowd, always to impatient.

"It's taking away liberty and justice," Epistrophius went on, calmly.

Merlin, who had whispered that reply, lowered his eyes. Everyone, or almost everyone, clapped their hands. The noise expanded all the way to the pine-woods of Derveni, which are five leagues away. Epistrophius was proclaimed king of the games. He was give the crown of parsley; he received, as an additional recompense, cracked urns still full of damp ashes—the last remains of the powerful people of the Itureans. Such were the games that took up the first day.

The next day, at daybreak, the ambition of the best was even more excited than the day before. They were due, during the morning hours, to contest the prize for sophism. It was a matter of proving that black is white, that yes is no, that it is night at noon—in brief, of playing with human consciousness and words as the excessively simple ancients played tennis, discus-throwing or knucklebones. The competitors were innumerable; it was the national industry.

Pericles, Duke of Athens, proved that it was night in broad daylight; Simonides, king of Pentapolis, that despotism is the father of liberty; Aschillius, King of Dacia, that evil is the author of all good; Helicanus, Lord of Tyre, that two and two make five; Hirtacius, King of Parthia, that to invade a country is to liberate it; Mustansar, king of the Africans, that to find the truth it is necessary to be stupid; Bocchus, King of the Medes, that God began with the Devil; Sangremor of Byzantium, that genius is a debauchery; Griffopoulos that Homer never existed, nor any other great man; Pandrasus the Pious that the height of human artistry is crawling; Ergoterion that the people of the ruins are never mistaken; Hocus-Pocus the Cunning that ideas make progress on their own without any person getting involved; and Tohu-Bohu, King of Assyria, that the truth is a lie.

There was a great uncertainty in the assembly when it was necessary to give the prize. Everyone had merited it in certain regards and claimed it with the same violence. Routine prevailed. It was given to the King of Byzantium because he had won it four years before at the Isthmian games. He received the crown of poppies and three Eginitic coins that had been recently discovered on the island.

After that, the assembled kings and peoples compete for the poetry prize. It was a matter of assembling the greatest possible number of sonorous words, without allowing a single thought to slip into them. In addition, it was necessary to avoid, at all costs, the fortunate sequence of long and short syllables from which antique melody was born. They counted the number of syllables on their fingers, impartially, after the performance, nothing more.

Aethion the Beotian was the one who most closely approached perfection. He succeeded very well in depreciating the language, but in the rest he failed. He was seen to pick up a sort of guzla with three strings, over which he drew a little bow. At first he had the sincere intention only to assemble words, but whether because the place, the circumstance or some fatality weighed upon him, he allowed himself to be drawn into pronouncing twenty lines in which there were a few ingenuous, or even energetic, images of severed heads conversing with golden-winged hawks, the whole forming an ensemble simultaneously full of inspiration and savage grandeur.

"Stop!" cried Polictetes, devoured by envy. "Stop! I glimpsed a thought and a sentiment in your verse."

Aethion defended himself indignantly. "I haven't had the slightest idea, I swear," he said. "I wasn't thinking about anything."

"If you haven't done it," retorted Polictetes, with even more bitterness, "you've at least let it be believed. It's too late to take it back."

"It was unintentional, then," said Aethion.

Many others tried after him. None was any more fortunate. Sometimes their voices rose up like the plaint of the wind in a field of asphodels, sometimes a sigh emerged from their breast, without them even being aware of it. On other occasions the words they pronounced, smiling, awoke distant echoes regardless. In brief, no one could rise to the perfect ideal of emptiness, sonorousness and preciosity that they were pursuing with so much zeal. The words, in spite of them, had a meaning in their mouths. So the competitors, full of shame, were obliged to withdraw amid the jeers of the crowd.

The day, already well advanced, was concluded by a solemn lecture in which Helicanus, Lord of Tyre, read the great history that he had composed of the dynasties of the ruins. It was perhaps the first time since Herodotus that Greece had witnessed such a feast of speech. Everyone crowded around the historian. He sat down on the etiolated grass and holding his vast volume on his lap, begun thus;

"In those days the nettles and the brambles were beginning to grow naturally in the ground of the temples; the thistles expanded over the faces of kingdoms, and there was universal rejoicing.

"The next year there were many reeds in the empire of Micipsa, and that prosperity filled everyone's heart with joy.

"The year that followed was more favorable still. The walls of cities crumbled with a harmonious sound.

"After that further progress, at which all good men rejoiced, instead of humans, foxes took up residence in Sparta. The Duke of Crete organized a great hunt in his citadel, which the old men still remember.

"Finally, civilization was brought to its peak. The vultures nested in Corinth and Sicyone. Sagremor, king of Byzantium, nourished hawks with golden wings in the rubble of the Parthenon, such as the men of our days can scarcely breed."

To conclude, the historian approved to the execration of posterity a few spirits that he called by name, who had attempted to interrupt the sage progress of ruins. He demonstrated by high-flown philosophy, how short-sighted human wisdom is, how the accomplished fact is always admirable, and what a calamity it would have been for the world if, instead of brambles, people were seen flourishing in the repaired enclosures of cities. The course of things would have been interrupted, fatality contradicted, nature violated, the majesty of ruins outraged...

"Where would we be now?" he cried, in an impulse that lifted all hearts.

After having offered a glimpse of the danger, he displayed salvation in the tutelary genius of Epistrophius and his principal counselors.

Thus spoke the historian. He had skillfully led the spirits from quietude to terror and from terror to security. An enthusiasm of which one would not have thought them capable had gripped the people of the ruins. Tears of pleasure were flowing from every eye. When the historian had finished, the transported assembly crowned him with parsley. More than one silent spirit stood aside, lost in profound contemplation—and it was not merely a base envy that agitated them, but rather a desire to attain a similar glory.

II

While the games caused the passing of the hours to be forgotten, Merlin nourished profound thoughts. He had expected that the lassitude of some, the resentment of others, and doubtless also the curiosity of all would produce a diversion in the spirits of which he could take advantage to raise the subject of his embassy. Epistrophius having signaled to him that the moment to speak had come, he said so in the following terms, not without having first invoked the unknown god whose name he had not been able to grasp.

"Powerful kings and magnificent lords, I have been sent by the king of kings, Arthus, to forge with each of you bonds of religion, politics, commerce and, above all, amity, for you cannot remain isolated in these deserts any longer.

"Regard me, if it suits your majesties, as the ambassador of the future; that title is the one that corresponds best to the instructions that I have received.

"No matter how spectacular your feasts are, you cannot be laboring under an entire illusion. There is among you a commencement of decadence, slight if you wish, imperceptible on the part of the majority, but which, nevertheless, shows through beneath the magnificence of your solemnities. Do not wait for the evil to get worse. We offer you an alliance with young, vivacious dynasties that no misfortune will ever curb."

He concluded by proposing that the assembled kings pay a small tribute; fundamentally, he would be content, as a homage, with a pinch of dust.

All eyes in the assembly immediately went to Micipsa, king of Babylon. He was reputedly the wisest. They waited for him to reply on behalf of them all. He contented himself with saying: "There is assuredly no one among us unaware of the glory of the great Arthus. Only tell us whether he possesses many ruins."

"He does not possess any," Merlin replies, ingenuously.

"What!" said Micipsa, who could not hide his scorn. "And you dare to call him the king of kings!"

"It's true that his cities are recently born. You will not find in his lands either crumbling buildings or rubble. It is an entirely new order, of which nothing can give any idea. Imagine a river enriched by a thousand streams. That is the image of his kingdom."

"What you are saying," murmured Micipsa, "inverts all known ideas. You are calling prosperity what everyone, thus far, has called desolation. But in the end, if Arthus is poor in ruins, at least I imagine that he has an abundance of the dust and ashes of ancient peoples?"

"No," said Merlin. "Everything in his realm is growing and developing. Where there was only a hamlet, the next day you see a town. Where there was only a town, the day after you find an empire."

"What a scandal! And that state of affairs is satisfactory! He tolerates it! There is no means of finding anything in common with such a kingdom! It ought be in fine disorder!"

"Posterity will judge that."

"Posterity, you say? We shall prevent it from being born."

As a sign of assent, the members of the crowd nodded their heads, and each was heard to say to his neighbor: "An empire without ruins!"

"Can you imagine that, pray?"

"But please, where is his strange monarch enthroned, then?"

Everything seemed to be broken with these words, and hearts were becoming increasingly acrimonious when the daughters of Epistrophius approached Merlin. Their names were Euphrosine, Theone and Thaïs. All three had shone in the dances that had served as intermediaries to the games. The eldest, Euphrosine, who was also the most serious, did not look as old as her eighteen years.[115]

"Before leaving us, Seigneur," she said to Merlin, "tell us about the young men of Arthus' court. Do they spend their time, like the sons of the spirits of the ruins, sleeping in the fields of heather? Are they as indifferent? Do they only

---

[115] Hermione, after a long and rather superfluous comment on the manner in which the games illustrate the author's disapproval of mendacity, hypocrisy and sophistry, notes that Euphrosine is another depiction drawn from life, as observed in Quinet's youth.

have eyes and ears for the owls and the foxes that they do not even hunt? In sum, do they consume their days in the most sullen apathy, without loving anything except for the sterile dust raised by their indolent feet? For such are, among us, the habits of young princes and all the sons of the spirits of the ruins."

"Nothing is more true," added Thaïs and Theone. "They no longer know either love or hatred."

"It's completely different among us," Merlin replied. "The young men there are always full of love; they steep their gazes in the eyes of young women, as witness Tristan, Lancelot and a host of others, whose entire life is nothing but a caress."

"Heavens! What a contrast with our fate," Euphrosine went on. "What you tell us, Seigneur, redoubles the bleak ennui that gnaws away at us in this fine place! But also, what implacable solitude! And above all, what monotony! Our life is consumed in watching the desert, fortunate when we can glimpse from the height of a ruin some sun-bronzed irate on the azure sea."

"You alone here have understood me, daughters of the desert. You are not without influence on the mind of your father Epistrophius. Help me to convince him there might be some good elsewhere than in the ruins."

"It will be difficult, Seigneur, but we'll try."

They kept their word, and partly succeeded. The body of the ruined dynasties declared the next day, it is true, that it could not yield any of its sacred principles, the religion of rubble, faith in the worm of the sepulcher, the innate horror of flourishing cities, and that there was, therefore, no possibility of an alliance such as the king of the future and his ambassador proposed; nevertheless, the relations established with Arthus for the import and export of rust and dust would not cease for that, and if some hero or simple enchanter presented himself, he would be offered the same hospitality as Merlin.

III

Before the assembly dispersed, the marriage of Euphrosine, the cherished daughter of Epistrophius, was celebrated, to the extreme contentment of our hero. He desired nothing more than discovering everything related to love, betrothal and marriage among the spirits of the ruins.

I have said that Euphrosine was then eighteen, although she looked no older than fifteen, with her small face and narrow nose, which seemed chipped at the tip—the trace of an accident in childhood. Her motionless eyes were a trifle lacking in soul, but they would have been a perfect model in a painter's studio. The slightly narrow head was admirably attached to a regal neck and a nascent bosom. She had an already-incredible pride, with a hint of dryness, and even harshness. At first glance, Merlin discovered her perfection through a bronzed complexion by which she was three-quarters buried. He pointed it out to others, and from then on, everyone exclaimed: "How beautiful she is! But then, she's the daughter of Epistrophius!"

All the princes and sovereigns of the ruins were invited to display the numerous riches they possessed in a field of asphodels. They formed little heaps of ash and sepulchral dust, covered with a few flecks of gold. Alifantina's heap was found to be the best-furnished, and it was Alifantina that Euphrosine chose for her spouse, without even looking at him. In fact, he was ugly of face, poor in heart and replete in years.

Merlin had no doubt that in that ceremony of the sepulchral ashes there was some ancient mystical religious meaning, which he counted on discovering by its sequel. He wanted most of all to know they story of the passion that had drawn the two fiancés irresistibly toward one another.

"How was this sacred love that has vanquished time born?" he asked them. "Where and when? Under some radiant star? Was it in the presence of the noble Epistrophius? What gaze, what speech or what silence first revealed you to one another? By what sign did you recognize the flame that is never extinguished?"

"This morning," Alifantina replied, "We did not even know one another by sight."

"There are examples of that impetuosity of two hearts that are precipitated toward one another," said Merlin. "Lightning is less rapid; the blink of a eye encloses a thousand lives."

"Let's speak rationally, Merlin. I already have three hundred wives. Only the propriety of fortune has led me to take another."

"It's true," Euphrosine added. "Propriety spoke; it is our sovereign, and doubtless yours too. Adieu, Merlin, keep your dreams; their time has passed for us."

After these distracted words to cortege began to move off. It was preceded by a troupe of young women who caused sacks of old rusty coins to resonate in the ears of the couple to be married by way of music.

"Good God!" cried Merlin. "What sordid harmony! Where are you going? Is this the way you marry one another, without disturbance, without joy, without passion, with neither preference nor love? Stop! What can emerge from this double avarice? What an impure generation I see born of these impure espousals! You're dooming in advance the future of the great people of the ruins. O profanation of the nuptial bed! The flesh revolts as well as the spirit. Never in my life did I suspect that this was possible."

"It is, however," Epistrophius put in, having overheard, "the immemorial custom established among all the spirits of the ruins that you have been able to visit."

"Can it be?" the good Merlin continued. "Such lightness combined with such covetousness! Among you, then, marriage is a calculation, an opportunity coldly grasped, an arrangement of fortunes?"

"Precisely; it's the most constant of our customs."

"What are you telling me, king of the ruins? I have forgiven you many things. I've accustomed myself to your royalties of ash. But a life without love—who can imagine that?"

"You're young and romantic, Merlin," Epistrophius replied, visibly piqued. "You've lived among us, but you don't understand us."

Merlin would have liked to reply: "I'm glorified by that," but restrained himself out of respect, and, placing himself behind Euphrosine in the cortege, he whispered in her ear: "Stop! There's still time. Surrender your near-divine charms for that pinch of dust? What are those displayed riches worth, compared to a single glance from you?"

The nuptial pomp paused momentarily in order that withered flowers could be strewn in front of the couple. He continued: "Do you know, then, what felicity would be reserved for you in a union chosen by the heart? Do you remember, Euphrosine, your winged dreams when you gazed at the clouds? I propose to realize them all."

The cortege resumed moving. Merlin went on: "Only wait, Euphrosine. On my word as an enchanter, I promise to discover the man that you ought to love: handsome, young, well-built, similar in all respects to you. What will it cost you to wait? Only yesterday, you were taking about love, and you spoke about it so well!"

"To speak in one sense and act in another is the first sign of a good education among us," Euphrosine replied, turning round with a touch of ill-humor. "Besides which, I feel that I'm getting old. I'm already eighteen!"

"Poetry is nothing to you but a kind of make-up, then? For me, it is life itself. How can we understand one another? However, if anyone ever weeps for you, it will be me."

At this point Merlin perceived that no one was listening any longer, and he resigned himself to keeping silent. The troupe of young women struck old pieces of silver found in the ruins against one another, in the guise of cymbals. The two spouses coldly exchanged fragile glass rings, and then crossed the threshold of the nuptial chamber with an excess of ennui that did not escape anyone's eyes. Everyone uttered the long, dry, forced snigger particular to the spirits of the ruins; it was confused with the noise of the dead leaves raised by the wind around the broken columns of the temple.

That vision of a world without love was so new and so extraordinary for Merlin that it completed his consternation, for he felt that he would never have any power over that singular people. *They're slaves*, he thought, bitterly, *incapable of love; only free people are capable of it.*

From that moment on, he found in everything in the kingdom of Epistrophius an insipid odor of catacombs that no perfume could dissimulate; he sought a pretext to distance himself from the court; the lassitude produced by the games offered itself of its own accord.

At the same time, the assembly of the spirits of the ruins broke up. Each king returned to his kingdom, but fortune did not favor them all equally. Polictetes, Duke of Bythinia, on the very day that he returned to his Estates, was pillaged by a horde that stole his crown of gorse. Pandrasus, after having been shipwrecked on Andros, wandered for ten years over the waves and found his realm occupied by a serpent and a lion. He succeeded nevertheless is regaining possession of his empire—but not without having received a thrust of a claw that was thought for a long time to be mortal and which never completely healed. As for the other dynasties, they regained their lands without incident, where they only had to clear away a little brushwood.

Such are the facts that I have been able to steal from the oblivion of history regarding the history of dynasties thought until now to be imaginary. It would be better if the facts had not been so sparse! At least I have applied a rigorous method to them, and if that method, the honor of our time, has not failed in my hands, I can commend myself for having raised a monument that will withstand the bites of an envious science.

BOOK FIFTEEN: MARINA

I

Already the games had been forgotten for several weeks. Weary of the constraint of grandeur, Merlin was impatient to get closer to nature again. With that intention he took his leave of kings and gods. Privately, he had made a vow. What was it? To retire for a season into the midst of what remained of the Homeric Greeks, among the Pallichares, people fallen back into complete barbarity, who were in complete contrast to the inhabitants of courts. That vow was sacred, and prevented him from sleeping.

"O women, women! How heavily ignorance and darkness must weigh upon these countries, once the chosen fatherland of pure enlightenment, since you no longer know how beautiful you are! It is appropriate that I teach you again, by means of a memorable example."

Thus, full of his recent memories, he talked to himself while traversing the Magoula in a field of Mistra, where he searched obstinately for traces of the house of Helen. In the middle of a stony furrow a young woman was marching slowly, harnessed by a rope to plow beside a donkey and the thin cow. The laborer had his whip raised over the ivory shoulders of the young Greek woman.

"Keep going!" he shouted.

Merlin saw that. To command the laborer to stop, to hurl himself upon the harness, to unfasten the young woman's yoke, was the work of a moment for him. He led her to the end of the furrow, and, having sat her down on a clump of buttercups, orchids, immortelles and euphorbias, he said to her: "How is it that you're dragging a plow here, in the very field of Helen, in company with that donkey and that ox, you who are the granddaughter of Miltiades, Leonidas and Epaminondas, or at least of Philopoemen?"

These words made no impression on the young woman. The glorious names pronounced by Merlin did not even seem to enter her ears.

"At least you know your own name?"

"Marina," she replied, in a tremulous voice.

"How can so much beauty be any longer profaned by that abominable yoke?" said Merlin. "That's something to which I can't consent without dishonoring myself; and if, in order to liberate you, I have to ignite with my own hands a war longer than the one your ancestors sustained in the fields of Troy to recover the beautiful Helen, who was assuredly less beautiful than you, I won't hesitate to give the signal."

Meanwhile, he wiped away the sweat that was running down the young Greek's face. At the sight of her moist eyes, sometimes black and sometimes blue, according to whether they were reflecting dolor or hope, he was dazzled. Already he was experiencing something akin to remorse for finding her so beautiful.

Her arms folded over her bosom, she was holding her head tilted like an anemone in the morning breeze. You might have thought at first that her entire person consisted merely of two eyes, so large, open, piercing, blooming and invasive were they, so much did they envelop you with flashes of splendor. After the initial dazzle, however, Merlin ended up discovering in those haloes of flame a proud, Arcadian head, silky hair that descended in curls over her neck, drinking the sweat of a moist, panting bosom; a slender figure, hugged by a woolen rag; and the expression of a virgin huntress searching her quiver for a javelin.

Such might Viviane's godmother have been at fifteen in the ravines of Etna or the forest of Erimanthus. Unfortunately, a recent sprain still swelled the blue veins of one of Marina's feet and prevented her from running, in the manner of goddesses, skimming over the tufts of wild thyme without treading them down. No one but the enchanter would have perceived all that.

"How," she said, finally, "would I dare to raise my eyes to look at my lord? Perhaps he mistakes me for a daughter of the ruins, emerged from Paloeo-Chorio. But they're beautiful. When they draw young men into the depths of forests, they enchant their hearts, so that they conceive a hatred of us."

"What!" said the Enchanter. "No one here speaks to you of love?"

"No," relied the young woman, gravely, tilting her head back to show that she had never heard that word. "Fortunate are the women of stone lying in the long grass! It's for them that magic words are made, for they too ensorcel men's hearts."

"Those stones," Merlin replied, "Are worthy of all admiration. They're the most faithful portraits I've encountered of Viviane. But the man is deceiving himself who disdains living creatures for inanimate stones, because of the imperfections he can discover in them."

Having said that, Merlin detached a little dagger from his own belt.

"Here, keep this in memory of me. It will serve to defend your honor."

II

Such was their conversation, in all sincerity. Not one word more or less— and who could find fault with a single word of it? These, however, were its consequences.

A few days later—three or four—Merlin was on the coast of Morea, ready to embark for the islands. He had just come down to Piada, which is a very unhealthy place sown with euphorbia. Ten paces from the shore, a distended leather sack was floating on the surface of the water. Merlin thought he perceived that the sack was agitated by somersaults: that convulsive movement sometimes brought it to the surface and sometimes, alas, plunged it into the depths.

Without deliberation, Merlin threw himself into the sea. The movement of the waves drove the palpitating sack under a low vault gaping at the foot of a sheer rock that opened in a vent at the steepest place. Merlin swam after it, entering into a marine cavern. Beneath a profound cupola, a narrow ledge was raised at the back, about a cubit wide, the only place where the swimmer could set foot. It was there that the leather sack had just run aground. Merlin seized it and deposited it on the rock. He hastened to open it.

O God in Heaven! The icy, inanimate body of Marina fell at his feet.

Why had he not left her in the middle of the furrow that she was helping to hollow out a few days before? She would still be full of life today. She would still be competing in purpurine coloration with the mulberries, the pomegranates, the carob flowers, the wild roses and even the incarnadine of the columbine, the most beautiful of flowers, which no sunlight can fade. And now, here she was, her face chilly, her lips violet, her hair soiled with sand, her eyes closed forever, breathless and unmoving. A last residue of warmth had not abandoned her heart, however.

Let us also say that, shaving the waves and penetrating through the narrow vent, the light tinted everything in the cave, including Marina's body, with a somber, violet-tinted, cadaverous light.

"What a frightful crime!" Merlin exclaimed, as soon as he could speak. "But it shall be avenged! No, never would the death of Malvina in Fingal's cave, nor that of Lucretia in Rome, nor the abduction of Helen, nor that of Briseis, not that of Yseult the blonde or Genièvre—for none was as beautiful!—have had such terrible consequences. Stamboul, you shall be shaken on your foundations!"

As he was proffering this speech, he rubbed the young woman's hands in his, in the hope of reviving a flicker of life, and even covered her with warm tears. He massaged her temples, her forehead and the nape of her neck; he made her breathe tufts of wild thyme and lavender, which were fortunately growing in abundance on the walls of the grotto. He even pricked her arms with the stems of nettles and wrack, which remained stained with droplets of blood. In addition, he did not forget to extend his cloak over her, folding it double—but all in vain.

It was then that the idea came to him of blowing his panting enchanter's soul gently over Marina's discolored lips.[116]

I have said, and I repeat, that all known means had been impotent: friction, penetrating odors, lotions of salt water. But when our Enchanter's lips touched Marina's lips—was it the work of magic or the effect of a specific whose em-

---

[116] Although this was written a hundred years before mouth-to-mouth ventilation entered conventional medical practice, the method had long been applied by midwives to help new-borns reluctant to take their first breath.

ployment ought to be recommended in similar cases?—the young woman's eyelids quivered and appeared to part momentarily.

What is that rapid hope? Almost immediately, her dying eyes close again, doubtless forever this time, for they are sealed beneath grains of sand adhering to the interstices of the eyelids. Merlin perceives the damp sand through the black lashes; he blows it away. Alas, the pupils remain closed.

He needs to know, however, whether the heart has recommenced beating; nothing is more urgent than to make sure of that. His ear attentive, glued to Marina's heart—the implacable sea itself falls silent—Merlin counts, to begin with, fifteen pulsations, slow, irregular, fluttering, scarcely perceptible. He fears that he might be mistaken; he begins again—and this time, he is able to count, distinctly, twenty, then thirty…and finally reaches sixty. Finally, it is life.

On reopening her eyes, Marina sees nothing around her but the azure of the vaults, the pillars, the deformed stalactites. Already she thinks that she is resident in heaven, and searches in a niche for the Panagia.[117] As for her savior, she mistakes him at first for Saint George—but that mistake only lasts a moment.

The sea having suddenly freshened under the mistral that makes itself felt in that region, the opening soon closed. Instead of the sapphire daylight, all was filled with impenetrable darkness. Marina thought she was dying for a second time.

"You're alive!" Merlin cried.

"Panagia! Panagia!" murmured the young Greek, raising herself up partly. Seeing that the exit was sealed by a mountain of water, she allowed herself to fall back on the prophet's heart.

A long silence followed; then, in a faint voice, she added: "I'm hungry."

Pronounced by an ingenuous mouth, those words, "I'm hungry," transpierce Merlin's heart. He measures the peril: no means of escape. He looks to see whether he still has any provisions about his person. One dry date, two bitter almonds, three grapes, but not a crumb of bread: that is all he can discover in a pouch at his belt—and frankly, what is that for two people buried alive in the equinoctial season, for it was September?

He gave it all to Marina.

Reader, you too truly have a heart of stone if this situation does not draw a sigh from you! For myself, I know it; I can describe it in detail by virtue of having experienced it.

They were no longer speaking; what would they have said? They both kept quiet, trying to see one another. But scarcely had they glimpsed one another than the dense, immense, humid darkness covered them again—and they lost one another, found one another, only to lose one another again, a hundred times over in an instant.

---

[117] A Panagia is an icon of the Madonna—such images are commonplace in the Greek Orthodox religion—or a name applied to Mary herself.

In the end, the obscurity took them; they felt walled up, in darkness, by the Ocean.

Meanwhile, they hugged one another tightly—and could they have done anything wiser, if they wanted to prevent the night, the waves and the cold separating them for all eternity?

Merlin utters a cry; the earth moves; an extraordinary sound rumbles overhead, as if all the herds of cattle in the country were responding to him with their lowing.

It was the waves, vomiting furiously from the mouth of the cavern. God knows what horrible echo that lowing found in their hearts!

Thus the day passed; more cruel, the night went by until the dawn, and Marina trembled under Merlin's cloak. He saw, not an aurora, but a shadow, a gleam, a pale dot—paler, surely, that the light that appeared to the Cyclops when his only eye was punctured and gushed forth a torrent of tears.

Twice the waves, in retiring through the vent, allow the daylight to slip in; twice they swallow it almost immediately. If our two castaways are to survive, they have to choose one of those brief moments when the back of the Ocean hollows out in a valley. Otherwise, how will they avoid being broken against the jagged vault of rock? But already, Merlin has seized the young woman by the rope that serves her as a belt. Taking advantage of the eddies of the waves, sometimes aiding himself with one arm, sometimes striking out with his feet, swallowing and spitting out salty water, he has enabled her to see daylight again. Beneath the vault of the sky, he has deposited her on the level beach, near a tortoise that is returning to its lair among the rushes and asphodels.

"Saint George!" Marina exclaims.

"Recognize me," said Merlin.

"Fortunate are the daughters of the ruins! For us, it costs too much to live!"

"If this land must be shaken to its foundations, things will change. But who committed the crime?"

"The Emir."

With these words, a man in a muslin turban appeared on the strand, his eyes sharp and his cheeks pale, vomiting frightful imprecations. So far as they could understand, he was complaining furiously that someone had opened the sack that he had sewed up with his own hands and confided to the discretion of the ocean. He was ready to do it all over again.

"What right do you have over this woman?" Merlin demanded.

"My eyes have encountered her—that's my right."

He launched himself forward to grab her.

Quicker than lightning, Merlin covers her with his body. Then a frightful struggle commences. Nothing similar has been seen since the combat between Jacob and the angel. The two adversaries' scimitars are broken at the hilt. Each of them still has a curved dagger stuck in his belt, but their arms clash without being able to make use of them. At the supreme moment, Merlin knocks the Saracen down and puts his knee of his breast.

"You love her furiously?" he said.

"The gaze of another has soiled her face; she must die!"

"That gaze is mine. Do you want to marry her, then?"

"By Allah, I can scarcely make her my slave. She's so thin!"

Indignant, Merlin thought of causing the Osmanli to pay for that last blasphemy with his life, but, changing his mind by virtue of a magnificent effort, he let him live.

"Go, you who blaspheme—be a living testament to the forbearance of Merlin. It's not in single combat that you ought to perish. Live, but become a Christian."

And the miscreant, who had shown such a cold barbarity, was to die a few weeks later, of wrath and impiety, in the convent of Vourcano.

III

Meanwhile, at the terrible cry that Merlin had uttered, the people of the vicinity had been moved, and they hastened to run to him. They came from the harsh crests of Arcadia, from the banks of the Coron shaded by mastic trees, from the snowy summits of the Acro-Corinth, from the grottoes of Souli, from the warrior isles of Hydra and Psara. They also came from Parga, Londari and the numerous foothills of the Taygete. They came from the Pinde and Roumelia, some coiffed in turbans, others in red skullcaps, almost all of them with shoulders clad in sheepskin.

As soon as they had assembled, Merlin tore the leather sack into shreds and distributed the various strips to all of them, to remind of the vengeance that they were to carry out. Then he said to them:

"If your ancestors fought for ten years for Helen, you won't hesitate to commence a bloodied war for this young woman"—he pointed to Marina—"whose beauty infinitely surpasses that of the wife of Menelaus. Prepare yourselves for battle, then. Only wait until I give you the signal.

"How shall we recognize, Lord, that the time has come?" asked the klepht Yorghi of Parga.

You'll easily recognize it by this: when the time is near, I'll send you as messengers two of my principal bards: René will be the first, and he'll come from France; Harold will be the second, and he'll come from Britain.[118] If the

---

[118] René Chateaubriand and Lord Byron, the latter again disguised by the name of one of his heroes, in this case Childe Harold. This entire section is, of course, heavy with symbolism regarding the plight of the Greeks under Ottoman rule, which excited such indignation among French Hellenists that that pacifist Quinet has actually allowed Merlin to use his sword, albeit not to kill.

victory is uncertain, I'll arrive myself. Don't fear then to attack the prophet Mohammed, for I too am a prophet. Listen."

The circle of the crowd tightened around Merlin and he continued:

"The prophecy of Merlin on Morea and the islands.

"O sacred soil, you are the tripod, I am the bard. I shall publish your victory in advance.

"Why was I not born on your summits? Never would sadness have approached me. When the winter wind blows over my roof, if your name alone is pronounced, I smile even in tears, even in fever, in the expectation of death. It is thus that an empty cup, if one fills it with the crimson wine of Corinth, smiles at cup-bearer.

"A cry will depart from the ruins of Caritene, and the entire land will awake with a start. The tombs of Mistra will give birth to klephts, whose arrows will be a hundred times more rapid than the arrows of Ulysses. The Nemean lion will roar; its voice will be heard in the cavern of Souli.

"The anemones of the mountains of Arcadia will be intoxicated by blood.

"Already I could pronounce the name of the warrior chiefs who will awaken the dust of the ancestors. I know their names in advance; they please my ear.

"I heard yesterday the dialogue of Olympe and Oeta. Both of them were recounting their victories to one another, in the quivering language of the oaks. Meanwhile, the birds with the brazen beaks were flying over the summit. They were pecking the head of the brave fallen in the ravines of Souli and Missolonghi.

"With my foot, I have struck the tombs of Paloeo-Chorios, and the dead have said to me: 'Here we are.'

"O land of bards, how have you allowed yourself to be stripped of your myrtle? Why have you preferred the wild brambles? I shall sow in your valleys and on your shores the golden herb that no tempest can uproot. By the power of my art, I shall attach here, in the odorous grass, in the olive groves, in the limpid waves, in the hard rock, in the lair of the echo, in the rapid footsteps of men, in the gazes of women, an enchantment that no magician will ever efface.

"At the bellowing of the bull of Missolonghi, the shores of France and Britain will shake. The vast kingdom of Arthus will ignite with love for the vulture of Souli.

"From the court of Mark of Cornwall and that of Arthus, sword-bearers and archers will rally to the battle-cry. Those who drink the water of the Seine will staunch their thirst in the maremma of Navarin.

"And the women with bright faces throughout Arthus' empire will lean over the balconies to ask for news from the sea of Messenia.

"And Harold, the king of bards, will pass over the sea in a winged vessel; landing at Missolonghi, the will sing his swan song on my brazen harp.

"And Zante, you will weep, like Albion, on learning of his death.

"Meanwhile, the land of flowering myrtle, the virgins of Morea, escaped from the yataghan, will dance, holding one another by the hand, on the flattened summit of the Ithome; a new people will surge forth from the dust in place of the old."

At Merlin's voice, Marina wept without knowing why. The others shuddered to the depths of their hearts; for the impatience of the distant future had gripped them all. They resembled men devoured by a burning thirst hastening toward crystalline springs, with the anxiety of being unable to reach them.

"With what will fight?" shouted a klepht from Souli. "We only have one yataghan between us."

"No matter!" Merlin replied. "I will furnish you with a thousand to begin with, and a thousand more the following day."

In testimony of these words, he gave them magic bullets as prompt as lightning, of which he fortunately had a supply. In addition, he taught them to make a hundred swords from a plowshare, ten yataghans from a sickle, and a dagger from a nail; to lay ambushes; to sleep standing up; to eat wild herbs; to construct fire-ships and set them alight, and to attach them by iron chains to the flanks of their own vessels.

After which he added, turning toward Marina, who could only sit up as yet on the mat on which she was lying: "As this young woman has been sowed into that leather sack and plunged into the sea, where she remained until my hands snatched her from the jaws of death, this Hellenic land, today sealed in slavery and plunged into the dormant abyss, will one day emerge from the profound waters.

"But then, no longer harness women to the yoke; even I could not absolve you of that."

Immediately, the Greeks withdrew by a hundred different paths, and each obeyed the orders he had received. Some sharpened their knives in secret, others prepared resinous torches. Other refloated the little vessels of Hydra and elongated them in the form of sea-swallows. Others preferred the forms of kingfishers and petrels. Others rediscovered Greek fire. The women made lint and murmured cantinelas of death in advance.

All of them, after Merlin had spoken, had but one thought and one soul, Already, with an ear to the ground, more than one was listening in the olive groves to see whether the Enchanter had yet given the signal.

IV

Meanwhile, Marina had been carried into the hut of old Father Dimitri. The interior comprised two compartments separated by a trellis of reeds. A few nets and a calabash were the whole of the furniture. There was also, however, a barrel half-full of olives in a dark corner.

Marina was lying in one of the rooms; the other had been reserved for Merlin, but he was more often in the first, and rarely left it except to collect centaury and other magical flowers from the nearby woods, with which he made a bitter beverage that ought to restore the rosy colors of life to Marina's cheeks.

He wanted to watch over her himself. In her hours of insomnia he was there to support her head, which he leaned upon his breast. If he found her asleep, with his arm or only his hand he pulled a goat's-wool blanket over her. If she uttered a moan, he responded with a sigh. If she dreamed about vampires he woke her up with a start. Twenty times an hour he went to her on tiptoe, one step after another, and leaned over, listening, and never withdrew without being assured that Marina had the calm of youthful respiration of a child.

It was the tenderness of a father, a mother, a brother and a sister all at once, and even something more.

As soon as she was able to walk, he wanted to teach her his triads; she could not remember a single word of them, nor of the hymns of Homer; she preferred her lively rustic airs, similar to the songs of the oriole and the sea-swallow; she showed no inclination to Greek history. After those various attempts, which only produced tears, he contented himself with teaching her to thread chaplets of aloe-wood or rose-leaves soaked and then hardened in the sun; to collect sea-shells; to embroider slippers; to smoke a narghile; to hunt tortoises; to nourish sparrows from her lips; to watch water flowing; to dance rounds on the edge of precipices; and to sharpen a dagger. Such was the education he gave her.

Did he tell her that he loved her? He did not say so even once; be certain of that; I'll answer for that as for myself.

He collected bunches of wild mulberries for her, it's true; he unearthed medallions for her, which he pierced in the middle and threaded in her black hair; he also helped her, like the most modest and most submissive of genies, to cream the milk in the bowls, to revive the fire under the ashes, to draw water in the pitcher, to light the lamp in front of the Panagia, to launch the caique into the sea, to ornament it with violets, to hoist the sail with the rope. He even went with her on Sunday to mass in the little church where a long-haired monk from Ligourio officiated behind a golden veil.

If she thought that he loved her, it's because she imagined it.

One night when everything in the cabin was asleep, a violent struggle erupted in the heart of our Enchanter. Should he continue his pilgrimages? Should he leave Marina? That was what was agitating in him.

"How can I leave her? I'm her protector. Dimitri is so old! He'll die when the leaves fall. What will she do without him? Anyway, she's become indispensable to my art. In eyes so limpid I can read presages better than anywhere else in the world. Her vermilion lips serve me as a talisman. In the beating of her heart, I measure the divine rhythm of the worlds."

Then, after a short silence, stirring the firebrands:

"Shall I be obstinate, then, in pursuing, in Viviane, an enchantress who, all too evidently, is toying with me? Is it wise to covet the impossible? Here, I shall find under this thatch, doubtless not felicity, which can only be encountered with Viviane, but repose, perhaps also forgetfulness. This country is frequented by the most illustrious female magicians, such as Medea, Canidia, Simoetha and the blonde Perimeda.[119] It's appropriate, surely, to remain here in order to perfect my art. Besides which, there are thousands of examples of enchanters who bind themselves with modest ties, as witness Faust, who was able to contract a misalliance with Marguerite without the world speaking ill of him in consequence."

Scarcely had these words emerged from his mouth, however, than a voice, which was that of his conscience, shouted at him in a forceful tone:

"Merlin, Merlin! Is it thus that you keep your oaths? Is it thus that you're faithful to Viviane? Do you remember what you wrote to her only yesterday? Coward that you are! Are you weary so soon of the pursuit of the ideal? Will you sell the glory of the world for two coral lips, which can't even pronounce your name exactly? You're blind, Merlin! You've enchanted yourself with magic words and gazes."

With that find statement, Merlin, making a desperate effort, broke the spell that was chaining him to that place. He stood up and got ready to leave. Nevertheless, he looked back one more time; one more time, he walked on tiptoe to the mat on which Marina was lying. It was to make sure that she was sleeping profoundly.

One last gleam of the fire, mingled with a ray of moonlight, illuminated the young woman, whose face was framed by tresses spangled with medallions. Beside her bed there was a little illuminated image of the Panagia, suspended from the wall. Merlin took the image down and he placed it beside Marina.

"May it protect you from vampires, wolves and ghouls! Personally, I need all my art to protect me from myself!"

Without adding anything, he went out of the hut. On the far side of the threshold he passed through a little flock of goats lying in the courtyard. The billy-goat recognized the Enchanter, and raising a silver beard toward him, bit the hem of his cloak in order to hold him back. It was in vain.

Dawn had not yet broken; the paling stars were letting their light fall through the clumps of olives and flowering almonds. Here and there, nightingales, drowsy and intoxicated by their songs, languidly repeated "Itys! Itys!" in the Palaio Chorio. There was a virginal peace in everything. Everything seemed to be saying: "See, at least, Merlin, what you're losing."

---

[119] Ancient Greek literature features numerous sorceresses, of which Jason's wife Medea is, after Circe, the most familiar. Canidia is featured in the *Epodes* of Horace. Simoetha is featured in Theocritus' *Idylls*, where she calls upon the aid of Perimeda, who is also mentioned by Propertius, as if her reputation ought to be familiar.

When daylight came, Marina sat down on the sandy shore to wait for the man she called her lord and master. She waited all the next day and the two following. By dint of looking at the blue of the sea, her eyes became the same color. More than one sailor, seeing her from a distance, thought that he was looking as a sculpted marble statue, so motionless was she. I too, passing along that coast, was duped by an illusion of the same sort.

Who can ever say what passed through Merlin's heart—whether it was the pure religion of beauty, the inspiration of the divine, or the surprise of the senses, or a cloud spread over his knowledge, or all of that together? Let's not try to discover what must remain hidden from us. The important thing for us is that he emerged victorious from that ordeal. Don't seek tasks in the sun. More amorous than Roland, my hero has been thus far, in reality if not in imagination, as wise as Aeneas. Don't ask any more.

Anyway, he explained himself overtly in the letter you're about to read.

V

Merlin to Viviane

They've told you about Marina, haven't they? And, in order to be more easily believed, they've slandered me. Don't you know that the earth and the heavens are full of venomous tongues, which soil the day-star if one listens to them: people incapable of understanding us, and who, to avenge themselves upon us, want us to despair?

The pure and simple truth is this, and only my numerous, even tumultuous, occupations have prevented me from telling you sooner. It's certain that I've made prodigious efforts myself to extract you from my heart. I'm not hiding or defending myself, Viviane.

Yes, to escape the damage you've inflicted upon me, I would have liked to numb and bewilder my soul, transpierced by a thousand blades. My most bitter complaint will always be that, in rendering me insensate, you've exposed me to the risk of becoming unworthy of you. In what miserable amusements I dragged the genius you admired such a short time ago! Nothing was beneath me, provided that I succeeded in drawing myself out of myself. I confess that I've been intoxicated by vain inextinguishable desires on the edge of volcanoes. The poplars of Italy, entwined with amorous vines, agitated at my feet like thyrses. The bell of the Camaldoli rang in the distance as if for the wedding of spring. The white veil espoused the blue wave. And what did I do then? What insensate desires were unleashed in my heart! Having come down from the mountain, I went to beg a smile from some beauty, or at least from a star; and scarcely had I obtained that smile than I fled at top speed, full of terror, as if I had awakened a serpent. That's the truth. You can see that I'm not hiding anything.

In the midst of that, two or three serene, straightforward, honest affections of which even you could not help of approving. Let's only talk today about Marina. No brother has a purer affection for his sister; there was never a word that you could not have heard; not a single caress except perhaps a fraternal kiss in seeing her again in the morning. Rude, practical occupations, a shrewd father, always present, no reveries, no sighs; once, a tear fell on her forehead, but she was on the point of dying. In brief, nothing was less similar to amour. Whoever says different is lying. And yet, I was abruptly seized by scruples. I left her, while she was asleep, like a thief.

I left her because of you, and also to avoid vile suspicions, slanders, or even the gossip of the cicadas, which, I know only too well, wouldn't fail to bring you such news. See, however, to what everything is reduced. Oh, how I hate the loquacious people, thirsty for lies, who blacken me to flatter you.

Now I'm alone in the world. I've broken a child's heart. I've caused divine tears to flow, and you won't give me any credit for it.

What should I tell you about the ruins of Italy and Greece and the many empires I've just visited? Personally, I'm a ruin in the midst of these ruins. I, who could once had lifted up that crumbling world so easily with a word—you were beside me then!—could only whistle with the winter wind, to disguise my embarrassment, among the heaped-up stones, as happened to me on the threshold of the partly-open door of Mycenae. I found the ashes of a shepherd's little fire in the tomb of Agamemnon—what an opportunity for a magician!—and in my confusion I couldn't even relight a spark under those white ashes, which the rain had, admittedly, soaked on the previous days. Several people, who came to me to hear the gravest conversation, or to ask me to resuscitate the dead cities— so easy to do!—were astonished, and even scandalized only to be able to extract from me a sigh and a name. So this period of my life has been the most sterile. My renown is fading away—well, what does it matter?

BOOK SIXTEEN: PARADISE REDISCOVERED

I

After having sent that letter by means of one of his usual messengers, Merlin went to embark at Epidaurus. On the marshy beach he found Mustensar, the king of the desert, and Alifantina, King of Spain, who were waiting for him while breathing the feverish exhalations of asphodels. Epistrophius had not neglected to offer him the aid of his fleet, formed of two of the most worm-eaten caiques that could be found in his Estates. Only one of the caiques had a complete crew; it consisted of two of the finest follets in the land; both of them, born in the tempests, were accustomed to laughing at them. The little craft emerged from the creek, skimming the waves with the rapidity of a petrel.

He only stopped to make landfall at a little Oriental port between Russicada and Mount Azara.

For a long time the king of the desert had been thinking about nothing but rendering Merlin favorable to the vast countries burned by the sun over which his empires extended.

"Don't be unjust to my kingdom," he said to him, as they touched the shore. "Although I can't offer you the same fêtes as King Epistrophius—because, except for the djerib,[120] the games here are held in mediocre esteem—it will perhaps be permissible for me to interest you in other spectacles." And, wanting to strike his mind with some great impression at the outset, he added: "Do you know Prester John, Merlin?"[121]

"Prester John!" exclaimed our hero, leaping out of the caique. "The marvel of the Orient! The enchanter of the land where the sun rises! The pearl of men of our art! My master, if I have one!"

"As you say," the king replied. "He lives in my Estates; I've made a vow to undertake a pilgrimage to see him, before even going to sleep under a roof of reeds."

"Prester John!" repeated Merlin, again. "I'd have made the voyage solely to hear mention of him."

"If you don't fear scandal, I can take you to him."

---

[120] A unit of distance, presumably cited here as the span of a race.

[121] The legend of Prester John—the ruler of a Christian realm lost somewhere in the Orient—was first popularized in the 12th century, although its origins in oral tradition might be earlier; he cropped up repeatedly in fanciful literary references, many of which credited him with possession of various magical devices, and some of which placed his residence close to the Earthly Paradise.

"Let's hasten, Sire."

Scarcely had they disembarked than they departed, without even being refreshed by the glass of water accompanied by candied fruits that an icoglan offered to them. They were all mounted on camels. Only Euphronius had chosen a white horse.

Having traveled for ten days through the highlands, they reached the abbey of Prester John in a desert area. From far away, the architecture struck Merlin with astonishment, for it featured was an incredible mixture of the pagoda, Greek and Roman temples, synagogue, mosque, basilica and cathedral, not to mention an almost innumerable host of marabouts, minarets, Byzantine and Gothic chapels, which gave the monastery the aspect of a modern pantheon open to all the religions of the world.

"Wait," said the king of the desert, who was enjoying Merlin's surprise. "Don't condemn this bizarre taste before having listened to me."

As they had drawn near enough to see the slightest details, they stopped on a small mound facing the portal. The king of the desert went on: "Every day of the week has its particular feast celebrated in that abbey. Monday is dedicated to Brahma, who is the most ancient, Tuesday to Buddha, Wednesday to Vishnu, Thursday to Jesus, Friday to Allah, Saturday to Jehovah; that's why you find here, in the same cloister, a pagoda, a synagogue, a mosque, a basilica and a cathedral. As for Sunday, Prester John then combines all the religions into one. On that day, he preaches peace and concord, in the name of the God of all."

"That's singular," said Merlin. "Is Prester John a pantheist?"

"Perhaps."

"You know that that's the most terrible accusation with which one can blacken a man in our misty land?"

"So I've been told," replied the king of the desert, who sought on every occasion to show his kingdom in the best possible light. "Just remember, Merlin, your promise not to be scandalized before having seen everything."

"I'll remember, O King!"

Then Merlin rang the bell at the door of the abbey with a firm hand. It rang twice in the silence of the desert. The door opened.

In the middle of the courtyard an august old man appeared, whose snowy beard hung down to his waist. On his head he was wearing a turban enriched by a sapphire cross. Around his neck hung a gold cross, and he was leaning on a white staff in the manner of a Brahmin. Three children were following him, each holding a book open over his breast. The first was the collection of the Vedas, the second the Bible, the third the Koran. At certain moments, Prester John—for it was him—paused, read a few lines from one of the sacred books, which always remained open before him. After which he continued his stroll, his eyes attached to the heavens.

He had just turned in the direction of the door when the strangers came in.

"They're pilgrims," he said. "Let's go see what they believe, and let each receive here the hospitality of his own God."

Then, with an imposing gravity, Prester John raised his hand to salute the voyagers.

"Be welcome here, all of you. Before we wash your feet, tell us which is your God, for it will doubtless please you to be treated in all things as he would wish."

The king replied first: "I am the king of this land, and my God is Brahma."

"That's good, my son," said Prester John.

Immediately, a troupe of Brahmins approached Mustensar and carried him away in a palanquin.

"As for me," said Alifantina, "my God is Allah, and Mohammed is my prophet."

"That's good," the worthy priest replied again.

Dervishes approached Alifantina and led him, dancing, toward the mosque.

Merlin kept quiet. Jacques did not wait to be questioned; his eyes on fire, he cried: "My God is Jesus, my church is in Rome!"

"That's good, my son," said Prester John for the third time.

Immediately, a procession of monks emerged from beneath the arcades of the courtyard with a banner similar to that of Jacques' village. His heart shivered when he recognized from far the great Saint Christopher painted in gold on an azure field, as he had seen him floating through the hawthorn in the quarries— but he was amazed when he saw that the man carrying the banner was none other than Turpin.

Jacques uttered an exclamation, and threw himself into his arms. Turpin recognized him in his turn. He called to his master. Merlin turned round...

That moment alone paid for all the fatigues of the route.

In the meantime, Prester John had fixed his eyes on Merlin. He ended up saying to him:

"Where are we to lead you, my son? What is your church? By what book do you swear? What name do you give to your God? Is it the unknown God? We adore him also; the pomp of his ceremonies loses nothing among us to the other religions."

"If you had not named him, perhaps I would have remained silent. But since you have anticipated my desires, I confess that the unknown God fills my soul."

"Don't be ashamed of that, Merlin. His church is very near here; you can see its marble roof whitening. No one but me will conduct you there."

During the voyagers' sojourn in the abbey, nothing was changed in the accustomed order. This is how the first hours of the day were organized. Before sunrise, a great fire of sandalwood, lit by the Brahmins, saluted the reawakening of Indra and perfumed the earth. By that sudden clarity, the chief of the dervishes climbed to the minaret and said the prayer of Allah, to which a Christian ce-

nobite, digging a ditch in his garden, responded: "Brother, it is necessary to die."
Then a hymn from the Rig-Vedas rose up languidly from the depths of the
courtyards, sung by silvery voices to which was soon added the guttural accent
of ulemas intoning a verse of the Koran. The whole concluded by fading away
into the majesty of the Roman *Te Deum*, sustained by Turpin's gigantic baritone.

After that a solemn silence fell in the abbey. Prester John showed himself
on a balcony, in the midst of a troupe armed with parasols; in a voice that resounded as far as the least corner of the desert, he pronounced the following
prayer:

"God who delights on the bank of the Ganges among the herds of russet
cattle harnessed to the chariot of the dawn; you who spring forth in the sacred
fire that comes to illuminate the parsees wandering in the vicinity of the naphtha
wells; whether you build your chosen temple at the exit from the desert with the
white stones of Sion, or prefer to repose in the refreshing shade of cathedrals, or
delight in staying awake on the towers of mosques, in the midst of angels armed
with golden arrows; or whether you are suckled by the white virgin in the desert
of Gobi, or the virgin of Judea, in the cradle of Nazareth, give us peace, light,
concord and love."

"Amen!" replied the crowd.

The walls of the different churches were covered with frescoes painted by
the Raphaels and Michelangelos that Prester John had formed. Particularly admired was a painting the decorated by the great cloister. In the foreground was
the little Buddha in the arms of the eternal virgin; he was playing with the infant
Jesus, and Mary, full of joy, seemed to be rediscovering a sister in the Indian
virgin and saying to her: "What! You too, my sister, have given birth to a god!"
A little further away, on the high place, Brahma was smiling at that spectacle;
cradled in a blossoming white nenuphar lily, he was landing in the Eden of Jehovah, who was holding out a hand to him and helping him to climb on to the
bank. Meanwhile, Allah was placing himself in their midst, and putting his
scimitar into its sheath forever, inviting both of them to rest under his tent, surmounted by a crescent whose shadow plunged into a transparent spring.

Every day the inhabitants of the abbey paused before that painting and others of the same genre. On seeing the union of their gods, they learned to remain
united themselves, and that was what attracted Merlin's admiration. For he had
noticed that, during his sojourn among men so different in origin and belief, no
brawl, misunderstanding, complaint, suspicion or resentful expression had saddened his eyes and mind for a single moment. On the contrary, there was behind
so many believers a singular competition to imitate what they called the reconciliation of the Eternal.

"How have you been able to establish this peace?" Merlin asked Prester
John every morning.

"By dint of patience, my son," the old man replied. Then he added: "The
Romans are the ones who gave me the greatest difficulty. For a long time I

thought I'd be obliged to expel them from the abbey. Many a time I threatened to do so. The complete abstinence to which I reduced them came to my aid. They had the habit of command. I was obliged to teach them to forget that they had reigned. All that wasn't the work of a day."

"Will you not come with me to the Occident, Father? People there have exceedingly false ideas in your regard."

"I know, Merlin. My time hasn't yet come. You will precede me there."

If Merlin admired the concord that reigned in the abbey, it was entirely different for Jacques. That profound peace scandalized him more every day. He could not help bursting forth on returning from a ceremony in which Prester John had personally explained the Vedas to the Brahmjins, the Izeds to the Sabaeans, the Koran to the Muslims, the Talmud to the Jews, the Gospel to the Christians and the catechism to the Romans.

"Horror!" he cried. "If the Christians here at least made war on the heretics! If they would only rush at one another, daggers in hand! But no: good companions, with neither worries nor resentments, they live as brothers, they officiate, they pray, they all worship together—isn't that the entrance to Hell? I don't know what restrains me from going to snatch his turban and staff away from Prester John, who'd certainly the Devil's priest."

"Don't you ever know anything but violence?" Merlin replied, softly. "Would you pay with a crime for the generous hospitality that we're receiving?"

"But what if that hospitality is Satan's?"

"Listen to me," his master went on. "Assuredly, many things are to be criticized among the spirits of the ruins, and you have been able to see that I said what I thought freely, at the risk of attracting the anger of the powerful monarch who reigns in those countries. But among so many faults, on which I have frankly explained myself, there are some qualities that we ought not to denigrate because they are buried in the dust. Such are their sobriety—may you always remember that, in order that it may serve you as an example!—their love of silence, of solitude, the small number of their needs, their scorn for luxury...you've seen what palaces their kings inhabit! Think about that when you complain about your thatched cottage. Those are true virtues, Jacques, although buried in the ash. But the one I esteem most, remember this well, is their tolerance, since they mingle all the ashes in the same sacred urn; and I would see nothing in this affair that is not praiseworthy if I did not suspect a little indifference, something of which I shall try to assure myself later."

This speech did not succeed in persuading Jacques. For love of the Enchanter, however, he consented not to set fire to the abbey. The mages offered him the gift of myrrh, the Brahmins that of coral, and the Muslims a rosary.

"I accept the coral and the rosary for my sister Jeanne," he said, "and the myrrh for the festival of the three kings."

At the moment when his guests took their leave of him, Prester John detached a small lamp suspended from the vault of the cloister and presented it to Merlin.

"Have you heard mention of the marvelous lamp?"

"A thousand times."

"Here it is, Merlin; I give it to you, since you're the king of enchanters."

At first Merlin wanted to refuse it out of modesty. The good priest embraced him and continued: "Take it Merlin, it's yours! It won't only help you to find treasures hidden in the earth, but even more so the virtues buried in the depths of human hearts. Go on—light it! Enlighten the earth; everywhere, in the slightest retreat, you'll find treasures."

Merlin received the marvelous lamp and handed it to Jacques, who could not avoid carrying it; but as he suspected that it came from Hell, he was careful only to light it when he could not do otherwise—which is to say, on the express orders of the Enchanter, who forgot it himself in various circumstances, as we shall see in due course.

Having saluted their host, our voyagers drew away, not without looking back several times to gaze at the abbey again.

"What do you think of Prester John?" asked the king of the desert.

"Sire," the prudent Merlin replied, perceiving that the djinn of the desert, all courtiers, were spying on him to see whether he was an atheist, "I'll give my opinion, but pantheistically!"

In the meantime, Turpin told his story. He related that, having perceived Merlin's departure too late, he had interrupted his reading to follow him. On the basis of public rumor, often very deceptive, he had searched for him for a long time, vainly, in the company of sages. At least he had been fortunate enough to find Merlin's harp in a harmonious pine-wood in Ravenna, and had brought it away intact, save for a few strings put out of tune by dew,[122] which would be easy to replace.

I leave it to you to imagine my hero's joy on seeing the sacred harp again, which he had thought lost forever. He received it from Turpin's hands weeping. How had it gone astray in the wood of Ravenna? Who had forgotten it? On what occasion? I know exactly how it happened, and I could explain it. But I can't suffice for everything, in a subject that opens the perspective of a new world at every step. It's up to the reader to make an effort of genius here; it's a good thing, after all, if you sometimes go toward the truth by means of your own conjectures.

Turpin's long story was only concluded when our voyagers arrived near the sources of the Euphrates, in the vicinity of the terrestrial paradise. At this

---

[122] There is an untranslatable pun here, the verb *détremper* meaning both "to soak" and "to put out of tune."

point, I yield the plume to Merlin. He alone can say how he alone, of all the human race, has rediscovered that location.

II

Merlin to Viviane

Eden, Palm Sunday

No, Viviane, that date-line is not mistaken. I am in the middle of Eden, in the famous garden that our first ancestors lost by their sin and I have just rediscovered. Next to me is the tree of good, further away the tree of evil; here, the first cradle, there, the four rivers of delights. But to the extent that the predicament I'm in permits. I want to give you a faithful account of a day unique among all the days of my life.

As I had just traversed the mount of Assyria between the towers of Seleucia and Thelassar, I was so close to Eden that I could not resist the desire to see it with my own eyes. No one wanted, or dared, to serve as my guide, for these peoples dare not approach that beneficent enclosure. They are held back by dread and its ancient renown.

Even my companions refused to go with me. I advanced alone, only taking my harp with me, to defend me from serpents and any evil spirits that might remain lurking in the dense brushwood with which the region is covered.

The surrounding barrier is still almost intact, except for a few places where the palisade has been devastated by the flaming word. As soon as I made out the entrance I was gripped by fear. I thought I could see a spirit armed with a sword coming to meet me. To preserve myself from his blows I drew from my harp one of the powerful chords with which you're familiar. The echo resounded in the sacred enclosure. But no guardian appeared over the wall.

I entered without encountering any obstacle, either because the archangel had quit the place at the same time as the first man, or because the lapse of centuries had occasioned some negligence, or, in sum, because the power of Merlin extends beyond Eden and can open its gates.

I crossed the threshold. To say what new emotions, unknown to enchanters and prophets, assailed me at that moment would be impossible. What struck me the most was the silence. Although there was a multitude of birds around me, none was making the slightest song heard. As if they were still frightened and stupefied by the memory of the things that had happened there, they seemed to be saying: *Are you the new Adam?*

Fruits were hanging down above my head. I dared not touch them, so fearful was I of eating, by chance, one that was already wiser than me.

Everything was tangled with creepers and virgin vines. Long grass had grown over the footprints of our ancestors. As I went into the dense shade, I found a flaming sword on the ground, abandoned there. I picked it up in order to clear a passage.

Astonishingly, the grass even covered the footprints of the Eternal, so well that I could hardly recognize them, although they were at least six cubits long. As soon as I had discovered the vestiges of the gigantic feet, I started to follow them, and trembled all the way to my bones. Under every verdant crown I feared and desired at the same time to see the divine host of the place appear! And what became of me when, through the rustle of leaves, I thought I heard a hissing tongue...?

That initial dread dissipated when I did not see anyone appear. The footprints led me to a lair that the lions had abandoned. The many wild beasts that passed close to me, astonished and mute, caused me less fear than the murmur of an invisible spirit would have done.

Thus the first day passed. I wandered without repose, and it was only toward dusk that I discovered the cradle of our first ancestors. I saw—yes, saw—the nuptial couch where the first son of man was engendered. It had not changed much; flowers had replaced other flowers there; the odorous masses had renewed themselves from era to era. That was the only place that bore no imprint of the insult of the years and the wrath of Heaven.

What thoughts I had, Viviane, on entering that sacred cradle! It seems made for you, waiting for your feet to repose there. We would visit the entire world without finding a place so worthy of being your nuptial chamber. For myself—witness my credulity—that idea assailed me with such great force that I could not help thinking that it was the blessed place where my eyes ought to find you again.

Fatigue having become overwhelming, I went to sleep on those virginal flowers; I was convinced that I would see you again when I woke up, next to me beneath the embalmed vaults. So, as soon as my eyes reopened, I extended my arms to take hold of you. I searched for you; I called out to you. What dolor only to find myself! It was the first I experienced in that place of delights!

When I had given up hope of encountering you in that blissful enclosure, the sentiment of eternal solitude filled me entirely. At the moment when I abandoned myself, two living beings appeared to my eyes. Oh, how the sight of them was both welcome and cruel! They were two old people laden with years—what am I saying?—laden with centuries, who had stopped, prostrated, before the entrance without daring to cross it. I soon arrived near them. As soon as they saw me they worshiped me, prostrating themselves, and said:

"Oh most fortunate of children of the earth, it is thus permitted to you alone to enter this cherished abode where we have known felicity, and from which we have been precipitated by a common fault."

"Who are you," I asked, "To regret with so much love this place where no one lives?"

"This place," replied the old man, "has not always been deserted. My name is known to you, my son, for, whoever you are, I am your father, and this is your mother Eve who is weeping by my side. Once a century we come on the same day to respire the perfume of Eden, without daring to cross the barrier. The perfume of ancient days gives us rebirth; we draw the strength therefrom to support our eternal labor."

Then the woman, who had maintained silence, broke it in her turn.

"Oh, my son," she said to me, "since you have penetrated into this place, which ought to be our heritage, tell me if you have found any trace of past felicity. Have you seen our first dwelling? Are flowers still wedded to flowers on the nuptial bed where I received the first speech of the man who accompanies me in dolor, having accompanied me in bliss? Does the resinous tree exhale the same odor of incense? Do cascades of delights still escape the basins in which I saw my face for the first time? Does the deadly tree with golden fruits, which I cannot name…?"

She was about to continue, but a sudden blush covered her face and, falling into her companion's arms, she hid her shame. Both were weeping at the same time, although their eyes seemed drained of tears.

At that sight, I hastened to reply: "O Eve, my mother, let me kiss your feet. I've visited Eden. The flowers there remember you; they have retained the memory of your felicity. The gazelles that you have nourished remember the names that you have given them. Come, follow me, my mother. Reenter the blessed enclosure with me."

At that moment I drew a chord from my harp. They were both shaken; they were about to follow me; but almost immediately, they shivered from head to toe and, drawing away from me, they said: "It's enough that we have heard the words of the man who has seen Eden; a greater joy is not intended for us."

And as if the mere thought of that beloved place had already filled their hearts with too much joy, they went away. As for me, I remained alone in the terrestrial paradise; neither the inhabitants of Heaven nor those of Hell attempted any longer to approach it.

Such was, Viviane, the meeting I had with our first ancestors. It has left my heart full of anguish, to the extent that I hesitate now to draw you toward this place, divine as it appears to me to be. Would the memory of such a great misfortune not follow us even into the arbors of Eden? Are we ingenuous enough for this ingenuous place? Would that spring-like life of our first ancestors be sufficient for us? What new needs and desires, alas, have entered into our hearts, which they did not know? What a torture, to sense oneself in Eden and find Hell there?

Already this horizon seems too narrow to me; it weighs upon me, oppresses me on all sides. A thousand flaming swords have ignited in my heart. Would you believe it? I'm in haste to get out of this place, which the unfortunate individuals I've just quit are burning to reenter at the price of a thousand lives.

It's true, then, the heart of an enchanter is insatiable. The terrestrial paradise is impotent to fill it!

Wretch! What was I about to do, when I nearly brought you here, Viviane? Is this world no more, then, than a trap beneath the feet of prophets? How can I fish what I still have to say, and what are you going to think of me?

As I came back toward the grove of delights, a serpent slid in front of me, its head raised, from beneath the honeysuckle. I set out in pursuit of it. I was about to strike it with the sword, but it turned toward me, and said to me in a soft, almost ironic voice: "Be careful my son; do you want to kill your father?"

With that, it disappeared.

Him, my father! Me, his posterity! What does it mean? What abysms are reopening before me?

Thus, it is in Eden that I have found Hell.

No, no, Viviane, I'll show you that I'm not his son.

III

Vivian to Merlin

Further on, further on, Merlin! What, you're stopping so soon? Can you think so? The happiness worthy of you is much further on, I tell you; it can only be found at the end of the earth.

In truth, your abandoned and devastated paradise scares me. What would we do there? Everything consternates me when I think about it. Have you really been able to desire momentarily to enclose yourself in the ruins of lost felicity? What! Recommence that vanished dream of Eden, and see, at the end, the same flaming sword, the same serpent, the same bronze door open and close forever. Would you like to make of me an accursed Eve, without ignorance of tomorrow? No, no; it's beyond that destroyed Eden that the edifice will be built of the unknown felicity for which your heart thirsts.

Continue your triumphant march, then. But be wary of returning to us, in the cold mists of Bresse and Brittany. A burning soul like yours needs a fiery sky.

Have you not heard mention, Merlin, of the valley of Kashmir and the gulf of Bengal, at the extremity of the realm of Cathay? It's there, it's said, in the shadow of cabbage-palms, that an amorous soul can content its infinite desires, without being troubled by any concern with the world. There, the roses have no thorns; the nights are voluptuous, all memory is embalmed. It is not yet the blue, starry palace of the ecliptic about which you have so often dreamed, but it is on the road to it. Suffer then that I give you a rendezvous at the place where the earth ends, on the beach, which the warm waves, as amorous as you, kiss day and night without ever wearying. There we shall exchange a few words, at the mouth of the Ganges; that moment will decide our future.

Go, then, Merlin, and come—or, rather, fly! But expect to find me very pale and changed by tears. You will recognize me at a distance by my long silken veil, which I shall wear down to my feet. I wish to Heaven that it had always been thus!

IV

Merlin to Viviane

Gulf of Bengal.

Sands, deserts, naphtha wells, antelopes, gazelles less prompt than you in fleeing toward the horizon; frowning mountains, devouring plains, abandoned cities, stone dragons standing in the ruins, mysterious inscriptions on spearheads, to which I've added your name; dances of dervishes, almas and bayaderes; caravans, camels laden with peris, houris, sun-tanned gods: how different this world is from the empire of Arthus! My eyes are dazzled, but my heart drains and dries up the further I go.

I am wandering like a pilgrim who no longer has an altar, without daring to gaze into the depths of my thoughts. I am like someone passing through the middle of a forest or a jungle. He turns his eyes to every thicket of kousa, afraid of seeing the head of a boa constrictor emerge therefrom.

From here I can contemplate the silvery peaks of the Himalaya, and I lose myself in that immensity.

I have been well received by the enchanters of this country, some of whom are so old that moss has covered parts of their visage; they have shown me in their stables those famous herds of russet cows that draw the chariot of the dawn here; I have formed numerous relationships with them that will be very useful to us, Viviane, when we are established, if that eventually happens.

In the midst of the twittering of bengalis[123] I have conversed with two god-infants eternally bathed in seas of milk. I talked to them about you. I promised them that you would bring them mulberries from the Crau, Normandy apples, medlars, water chestnuts and wild pears, of which they are all the fonder because they are unknown to them. In addition, what peace, what solitude, what inviolate repose! Everyone is astonished by my perpetual restlessness. How much more astonished they would be if they knew me better!

---

[123] In French, *bengali* is also the name of a kind of bird, known in English as a waxwing. I have retained the French term here and elsewhere because of the intended double meaning when it is used again.

Viviane, Viviane, what are we doing with our days? We pursue one another and flee from one another in a continual anguish. Will we ever know what we ought to desire? Our thoughts are consumed by momentary caprices. They, on the other hand, have the repose and endurance of the baobabs, which no storm can shake.

What would I do here with my enchantments? The idea of exercising them has not even occurred to me. You know, Viviane, that there is nothing more fatal in our art than to come after other enchanters. One wants to do better than them, or at least something different, and one falls into eccentricity. That's why, after mature reflection, I've made an irrevocable decision to do nothing at all here but dream about you, something to which the location is infinitely propitious.

I get up late, I go to bed at dusk. Cinghalese rock me in a hammock, while waving their peacock-plume fans over my face; it's an idleness full of you. I haven't yet despaired of encountering you unexpectedly, either in the vast forests of plumed sago-palms or on some desert summit; and that frail hope, which I don't have the strength o forbid myself, nourishes me, exalts me, depresses me, lifts me up and casting me down all at the same time.

Let's not lose happiness for the vain glory of pursuing it incessantly.

Tel me, what do you gain from this perpetual flight? Don't hope, at least, to weary my heart. I can't encounter here a queen, a sultana or even a bayadere, hidden beneath her veil, without enquiring of the camel-drivers as to whether it's not you, fleeing from me and calling to me at the same time: a curiosity full of difficulties, and even of dangers, in a country where lives are lost for the slightest indiscretion. I've sometimes traveled entire kingdoms thus, drawn by two eyes that bore some resemblance to yours. Can you imagine what I experienced when, after having followed the adored image from oasis to oasis, I suddenly saw it disappear into a harem or a slave-market, happy again when I could follow it there and buy it myself!

The peris and apsaras, which are very malicious in this land, are well aware of my distress; they abuse it cruelly, to the point of giving me vertigo. Not long ago, I encountered one while crossing a meadow bordered with malati flowers. The figure, the bearing, the gait...it was you! A familiar serpent, as blue as the sky, preceded her at a distance of fifteen paces. She was going toward the gulf of Golconda, singing in a low voice that tune you know so well: "Merlin! Merlin!"

I follow her, I approach. She draws away. I reach out my arm, I call out. Finally, I catch up. She lifts her veil. Great God! What a face, dazzling with all the fires of dawn! But it wasn't you.

She saw my mistake; she pursed her lips with chagrin, and avenged herself with a burst of laughter; after which she left me alone, lost in the forest of bamboo, cabbage-palms and prickly pears that separates the Euphrates from the Indus. Every day something similar happens to me.

From one lure to the next, here I am, relegated to the place where the world ends, on the edge of the sea of Bengal, where red-clad illusions make their abode in emerald grottoes beneath forests of coral. I've been vain enough to believe that you were waiting for me n this place, and it's certain that as soon as I'd come down to the shore I thought I saw your diamond necklace undone and scattered in the sands. Was it yours, in fact? I made a chaplet of it, which I wear around my waist. So, Viviane, you have played with me all the way to the edge of the world.

Where shall I go henceforth, unless to plunge myself into the unfathomable abyss from which so many crystalline voices are calling to me, echoing from reef to reef?

Retrace my steps? Go back over the same deceptive traces by which, this time, I'll no longer allow myself to be led astray? Everything is becoming insipid to me. The god-infants that I encounter here, everywhere, floating on lotus flowers, no longer interest me. I can't abide their eternal wailing; I've come to hate their stupid smiles.

How, Viviane, can I stifle this fire that is reborn of its own accord, in this poor soul that is devouring itself without being able to annihilate itself?

If you really are the virgin of the Alps, as you often say, chill my heart again with your breath.

Speak softly to me to send me to sleep, as you did in the heather of Brittany. I too am an uprooted spring of heather, which has never flowered.

If you wanted to, there would still be time. I recently visited a banana plantation—a veritable Eden—in a forest of sandalwood, near the garden of a young woman named Sacontala.[124] Say one word, just one, and I will build my cabin there, in the venerable shadow of the baobab where the foremost enchanter of this land, Valmiki,[125] wrote his gigantic works on bamboo bark. May I imitate him one day!

The Ganges rises in our domain. There are thousands of pearl-gray bengalis in this locale whose songs, petulance and sparkling eyes would please you immediately. Sacontala, in the midst of her antelopes and gazelles, would be our only company. For me, I would not want any other. She is waiting for you with great impatience, merely on the basis of the description of you that I have given her. You would do well, I think, to bring a few assorted fabrics from Lyon and Bruges for her, a thimble and a few packets of English needles, of which she is entirely deprived. She is taming a gazelle for you, and I know that she's preparing in secret a calabash and a rush mat, with which she wants to surprise you.

---

[124] Sacontala is one of many variant European spellings of the name of the heroine of one of the Sanskrit poems of the fifth century Indian writer Kalidasa, usually used as the title in translations into English and French.

[125] The Sanksrit poet identified in the text as the author of the epic *Ramayana*.

Here, we shall forget the overly agitated world of Arthus, and the concerns of courts. Soon, the world would forget us. Time would pass without encountering us in its paces. We would be like the recluses, of whom I know a great number here. When I ask them how old they are, they reply: "I'm the same age as the forest."

Once again, what prevents us from commencing eternity here? Why adjourn hour after hour what it would be so easy for us to grasp today? We'd have a favorite elephant that would kneel at your door, to receive you in a tower of ebony or ivory. It only requires one liana to lead it; it's the gentlest of creatures. When you pass along the bank of the Ganges, I can already see the king of rivers following you and bathing the soles of your feet, covering them with pearls.

We would only have one servant, a pariah, who cultivates kousa and whose hut is hidden in the jungle thickets. No enslavement, in any case, no constraint. Bananas and breadfruit in abundance. As for our clothes, you wouldn't even need to think about them. The bark of a mango-tree, or a coconut-palm, and a baobab leaf, would easily suffice for an entire season.

If this letter reaches you, of which I have no doubt, tell me exactly what you think of my establishment plan. Write to me at the Pillars of Hercules. It's a place that opportunities to reach are frequent. I'll be there in the month of tempests at the latest.

P.S. I waited for a long time on the Malabar shore for a valiant people, the Portuguese, who ought to arrived one day in order to connect by a magic chain the Tagus and the Indus. I expected at any moment to see their lateen sails on the horizon, but my patience ran out.

Adamastor, the spirit of the tempest—you know him—had sworn to bar the passage. I've ordered him to open the doors to the Orient to them himself, on their ruby hinges, and he's promised to obey.

Let them come, then, those sons of Lusus, to whom I extend my arms! Let them come! I respire in advance the glory of that fearless people, as one breathes at a distance the moist odor of the aquatic flowers of a continent long before seeing them emerge from the bosom of the warm oceanic plain.

Everything here has been prepared by my care for their hearts not to be afflicted by homesickness. I've suspended your necklace of precious stones and pearls on the embalmed shore, as the golden fleece once was, as the signal recompense for those new Argonauts. It's for them that the nutmeg-tree, the flowering sandalwood and the date-palms are crowned with wild lianas.

Not content with these gifts, I've engraved their eulogy in verse in the harmonious grotto of Goa. How astonished they will be, on seeing that the renown of their feats has preceded them to this extremity of the world and that the echo of the Maldives already resounds to the fanfares of Portuguese clarions! On that day, they'll be consoled for the absence of the cherished fatherland. They'll wonder what hand was able to write their history in this place before they had landed here. Perhaps a young Portuguese woman with moist eyes the color of wild mulberries will reply: "It's Merlin! Why was I not the one he loved?"

Such is the sole recompense I desire from those sons of the Occident, as the price of the sparkling realms of the dawn that I abandon to them as I leave.

BOOK SEVENTEEN: EL DORADO

I

O sweet serenity, patient virtue of ancient days, who can reanimate you among us? In those days, humans consumed the hours without counting them. The slightest odyssey lasted at least ten years. It never occurred to the crowd hanging on a story to say: "That's enough."

If I had lived in those days, what adventures might have been added to Merlin's pilgrimage! Doubtless I would have followed his ship beyond the Hesperides as far as the lost land of Atlantis with the golden apples.

Today, however, a feverish impatience agitates the human mind. The thirst for gold prevents them from lending more than an hour of attention to the narratives of story-tellers. It is necessary for me to abandon the rich matter that offers itself to me.

Like the navigator who sets a new course in the open sea, if he is suddenly gripped by homesickness, or even more so by the threat of an imminent bankruptcy, and bids adieu to the tempest. I shall furl my sails here and head for port.

In any case, at the end of the last chapter, I recognized the Pillars of Hercules decked with the colors of the King of Spain. Here, already, is white Cadiz, which resembles a seagull perched on the waves; a little further on is Seville. I can hear the crackling sound of the castanets, which, throughout the kingdom, are saluting the return of Alifantina and the Enchanter Merlin.

The evening was one of the most beautiful that had ever been seen on the coast of Andalusia. It had rained that morning, and whether it as the effect of the iridescent clouds, dispersed westwards, or an anticipated revelation of the yet-unknown continents of America, it is certain that landscapes of gold, opal and carmine were bordering the entire Occidental horizon.

Shortly before arriving in Cadiz, Merlin invited King Alifantina to return to the open sea, and said to him: "Sire, look at those magical kingdoms sparkling in the distance. They are the empires that we enchanters have called thus far Atlantis or the Fortunate Isles, but which ought to change their name when you possess them; for I invest you with them. Yes, Sire, I give them to you, and I'll gladly show you the way, on condition, however, that you promise me only to impose on those new peoples a yoke of flowers."

Alifantina burst out laughing.

"My dear Merlin, the joy of returning has rendered you blind, I think. For the kingdoms that you're showing me out there, heaped one atop another, are beautiful clouds that need no other pastor than the wind of Araby."

"Do you believe that I am an enchanter?"

"Yes, of course."

"If so," Merlin went on, "I repeat to you that those clouds are beautiful and lush realms where rivers and forests, abound, with mines of gold and rubies, and, most of all, the solitudes that you prefer."

"Indeed," stammered Alifantina, after having considered the spectacle offered to his eyes, "it seems to me that I perceive out there on that opal plain a golden throne with the thousand topaz steps. I would willingly believe that my ancient kingdom is nothing by comparison with the one you're showing me, provided that it's real. Anyway, it's a long way away; how can it be reached?"

"Whenever you wish, Sire, I shall be your pilot."

"What heading should we set?"

"Due west."

While he was speaking, Merlin threw into the water an oar, a scull, three clumps of nymphaeas that he had just uprooted, his old enchanter's staff and a pilgrim's gourd, and he blew on the face of the waters in the direction of the sunset.

"Now," he added, "the route is marked; let the pilgrim come!"

As one trains pigeons nowadays that carry in an hour, from Paris to London or Holland, not merely winged love-letters but heavy banknotes, Merlin had, in those days, trained nestlings that came and went incessantly between the most advanced promontories of Atlantis and the shores of Europe. All the time, they carried on their wings the messages of unknown solitudes, but no one paid the slightest attention to them. One of those flocks had just flown overhead.

"There, Sire, are your ambassadors," said Merlin.

The king was visibly shaken. It would not have taken much for him to give the order to follow the enchanter's advice; but one of his counselors, who was afraid of seasickness, came to him and whispered in his ear: "Sire, are you going to listen to these visionaries, these poets, the plague of States? Do you want people to say one day: 'The sage Alifantina left Spain to conquer a kingdom of vapor'?"

The king, who did not fear anything else in the world, was afraid of ridicule; the counselor's observation convinced him to return to Cadiz, not without having ordered that no mention should be made of what I have just recorded should be made in the crown archives deposited at Seville; thus, the discovery of America was postponed for several centuries.

At least Merlin's effort did not go entirely to waste; his oar, his scull, his pilgrim's gourd, and especially his enchanter's staff, continued to float and mark the route, Christopher Columbus would encounter them later, somewhat damaged and laden with moss, but still quite recognizable. Thanks to those floating sticks, he found America.

II

Bull-running, boleros and fandangos—nothing was lacking in the fêtes that followed the king's return. He had a large number of his people file past before Merlin. Our enchanter noticed that the population in question was mostly made up of donkey-drivers and muleteers, and that they were all singing ballads.

"What a lovely custom!" Merlin said, giving them a signal to stop in front of him. And he took the trouble to teach them the new ballads that he had learned in the Orient.

"Don't be mistaken on their account," Alifantina interjected. "I can't, it's true, offer you the same picturesque ruins as my brothers in Greece and the Orient; however, thanks to the poverty and nudity of my people, I believe I merit the honor of placing myself in the ranks of the worthy spirits of the ruins."

Then, pointing at the donkey-drivers who were filing past with a sovereign majesty, he added: "They sing, it's true—they have a superb range—but don't let appearances deceive you. I can assure you that under their mantles, they're almost as naked as the peoples assembled at Nemea. For sobriety, it's the same, save for a clove of garlic, which I've recently authorized in my Estates."

"Forgive me, Sire, but why does Your Majesty attribute it to his honor to be confused with the spirits of the ruins? Nature is opposed to it. What advantage do you find in imitating the decadence that is in them the work of fatality?"

"I'll admit to you, Merlin, that you're touching now on the most secret wound in my heart. In that desire to imitate the spirits of the ruins there might perhaps be some weakness. I want to be part of those venerable families that are enthroned in isolation on debris. That's what I covet with pride. I would think myself debased if they excluded me from their relationship. That's why, Merlin, I counterfeit as much as I can the decrepitude of the empires you've just visited. Not being able to equal them in the majesty of their cities in dust, I take my revenge, as you can see, on my peoples, whom I believe I have led to the shadowy slope."

Merlin refrained from contradicting the king overtly. He replied nevertheless with the arguments most appropriate to cure the king of such a strange mania. He said, in substance, that the imitation was inferior to the model: that Alifantina had too much genius to need to counterfeit anyone, even the just Epistrophius. Then he cleverly went on to a rapid sketch of Arthus' court, where the women, the knights, amorous talk, arms, bards, rendezvous and the outbursts of joy of nascent peoples filled the days so worthily.

"Confess, though, O sage," Alifantina concluded, "that nothing measures up to the eternal silence of the court of Epistrophius—with the exception of one accursed cicada that can't yet be made to shut up!"

"Sire, that thirsty cicada, which is still crying out, is justice!"

III

While traversing Seville, Merlin learned that a statue of the Commander had been erected in the cemetery, and he had the whim to visit it.[126] As he approached, the statue raised its marble arm toward the heavens and said in a thunderous voice: "Go back, Merlin! There is no other enchanter than God."

No one was less superstitious than our Enchanter, but the word "God" had never been pronounced without disturbing him; he took advantage of the circumstance-which was at least singular—to advise the king to found a church in commemoration of his fortunate voyage. The king consented, on the sole condition that Merlin built that *ex-voto* with his own hands, on the square in Cordova.

Our hero's tastes had changed during his travels; instead of a cathedral he built, distractedly, a mosque. Had he, then, become a miscreant? Was that the fruit that he had brought back from his distant voyages? God preserve me from thinking so. Had he, then, entirely lost the faith engraved on his heart by his mother Séraphine on her emergence from the convent?

I'm not saying that. And yet, take it as read that he had, at that time, a considerable weakness for the Koran. He liked its dazzling simplicity. The curved scimitar of Allah seduced him, and he would have liked to sharpen its edge. And to conceal nothing—for whence come the hidden agendas of men, even the best?—who can tell whether the promises of houris had not shaken his ancient belief? From all that, it followed that he built the church of Cordova on the Muslim plan of the palm forests he had recently visited.

Alifantina, however, was dying of impatience to see his wives again in the Alhambra, which was, as yet, merely a humble building. So they took the shortest route through the heather-striped mountains of Alcala la Real, even though it was said to be the lair of the leading bandits in the province. Picture a long bare gorge, armed with rocky teeth, which open here and there on lakes of dust and sand. That gorge leads in three days to the Vega de Grenada. If ever you follow that road, reader, don't forget provisions of food and drink, as I did.

As the voyage neared its end, Euphrosine had fallen into the blackest depression. She confided that to Merlin.

"Alas," she told him, "until now I've had the king's heart almost to myself, but the moment has come when I shall have to share it with three hundred, perhaps three hundred and fifty other women. How, Lord, shall I not weep?"

---

[126] Seville is the setting for Tirso de Molina's early 17th century play *El Burlador de Sevilla y convidado de piedra* [The Seducer of Seville and the Stone Guest], much better known as the source-text of Mozart's opera *Don Giovanni* (in which the "stone guest" is called Il Commendatore [The Commander]), in which the legend of Don Juan took on its definitive form.

Merlin replied: "Don't see all misfortunes at once, Madame. Many things might happen that will turn your sadness into joy. Once can only be happy with the strength of reason."

"You always fortify me, Merlin. At this moment, especially, I'd like to believe you."

One thing filled Alifantina with astonishment as they drew close to Grenada; none of his mutes came to meet him. The mystery was explained when he went into the Alhambra. The most beautiful of his wives, Carmen, Lindaraja and a few others, had been abducted a few night before, and the abductors had had the impudence to leave silken ladders hanging from the balconies of the windows. Euphrosine shed tears of joy.

Alifantina ordered all the inhabitants to be sown into leather sacks and thrown in the Darro, newly swollen by the autumn rains. Merlin dissuaded him. "Why drown an entire people in sacks? Stick to those who weave silken ladders." It was easy enough to prove that the best of them belonged to a young foreigner named Don Juan de Tenorio.[127] Anyway, what did the man who possessed Euphrosine have to regret?

Alifantina, appeased, agreed to everything. "But I shall renounce long voyages henceforth," he said. "It's here, in this place, that I'll spend my life."

He commanded Merlin to build him a pleasure palace where he could console himself for human fragility.

Taking inspiration from the sentiments of the King of Spain, Merlin built an initial enclosure of warrior towers, which spread terror around them, so menacing and jealous did they seem. In the interior, however, he assembled everything that he could imagine of the most voluptuous: marble rooms, alabaster vaults, murmuring jets of water in porphyry trenches, enameled flowers blooming on walls of jasper.

When the edifice was finished he said to the king: "Here's you palace, Sire. It's up to you to resemble it: on the outside, pride, power, jealousy and even holy wrath; on the inside, peace, softness, the inalterable serenity of the just and the divine scent that accompanies its paces."

Having thus lavished the resources of his art to enchant the place, Merlin abandoned himself entirely to its charm. He spent his days wandering from room to room, to the eternal sound of jets of water, as if he were already inhabiting the heaven of the houris. His soul was never in greater danger, and I don't know whether he might not have ended up converting to Mohammedanism, but for an incident that snatched him from his van hopes to hurl him fully back into reality.

---

[127] *Don Juan de Tenorio* is the title of the second major Spanish drama based on the legend, written by José Zorrilla in 1844 and explicitly associated with the Romantic Movement; it is far more morally ambiguous than its predecessors; Quinet probably saw a version of it in Paris before his expulsion from France.

He was in the Court of Lions, gilding their manes, when the shadow of a cloud passed over his feet. That cloud came from the east, perhaps from France; doubtless it had passed over Viviane's head. It required no more for him to decide to renew his correspondence, the sole positive monument that remains to us of those days of reverie and entire solitude.

Without these epistolary monuments, it would have been impossible for me, in spite of the most obstinate research, to recover the track of Merlin's pilgrimages, much less his thoughts. By an extraordinary good fortune, however, when the materials of this history were all lacking simultaneously, my heroes themselves bore witness.

IV

Merlin to Viviane

Alhambra, Vermilion Tower.

At the Pillars of Hercules, no message from you, Viviane, not even the simple word for which I had begged you. In spite of that, in spite of you, my head is in the clouds. I have a strength of hope that you will never tame.

At this moment, I'm living in the vermilion towers of the Alhambra. It's a palace that I've just constructed at the request of the king of the country. The truth is that I built it at my own whim for you and me, as if we were to be its sole inhabitants.

You know, Viviane, how soft the babble of the water is in the shade. I've placed jets of water in all the rooms, and I've ordered stone lions to pour embalmed springs from their mouths into silvery basins, night and day. I haven't forgotten, of course, the cool indolent alcoves of marble, so favorable to dreams, of which you once gave me the idea. You can also imagine that I haven't neglected the balconies and tocadors, from which you would be able to admire yourself at your ease in the torrential waters of the Darro. I've engraved the word *felicity* on all the walls in advance, in antique characters mingled with tulips and jasmines, because those are the flowers you like best. Judge by these preparations whether I only have ephemeral thoughts, as you have so often accused me.

Yes, I've constructed here, with my own hands, the palace of my felicity, in marble and granite; already I'm looking for you in that labyrinth of love. I call to you from hall to hall, from room to room, as if you were there to hear me. At the noise of my own footsteps I turn round and ask: "Is that you?"

The jasmines exhale an odor here that I've only smelled once before in my life. Where is the bouquet that you were holding in your hand when I encountered you in the heather, near the springs?

Let us therefore put all our power into not despairing of one another. Has our betrothal not lasted long enough? What's holding you back? What do you think the world is saying? It's astonished that our marriage has been so long deferred; if you listened to the gossip of the roses and the nightingales in your own gardens, here, under your windows, you wouldn't hesitate any longer to give them the necessary lie…at this very moment I've been obliged to interrupt myself in order to impose silence on them.

O delight, enchantment, sacred voluptuousness! Vermilion towers, open your doors to receive my beloved! Here she comes; I can already sense the perfume of her lips. Jets of water, spread your pearls and rubies before her steps. Lions, shake your flowing manes after her. Jealous walls, lift your battlements into the clouds to hide our first embraces. Houris, prostrate yourselves at your sovereign's feet. Stones of the threshold, paved with marble, alcoves of alabaster, cry out with one voice: "Felicity! Felicity!"

I swear to you, Viviane, that nowhere in the world is there a place better made than this to bear witness to our reconciliation, whether you only wish to celebrate our wedding here or whether, as I would prefer, to plan to make our eternal abode here. Reason, imagination, everything confirms what I say: pure air, salubrious nourishment, orange groves in open ground, but no simoom or sirocco; never a storm, at our feet a Vega in which the ballads of the Zegris resound;[128] lower down the Xeril, lower still the Darro; facing us, the white and rounded peaks of the Alpuxaras, striped with blue, violet, orange and purple. In addition, a people always in celebration, provided that I repeat our name to them; women with long eyelids, darting sharp glances like the fletched arrow launched by the bowstring. You could not ask for any more beautiful to form your cortege. What can I tell you, in sum? Fortunate Araby, sparkling in the shadow of Arthus' buckler.

I repeat to you that I have raised the walls of the Alhambra to make it your winter palace. I don't think I've forgotten a single one of the things you prefer. If, by chance, I've omitted one, it will be easy to procure it. Every stone, every inscription, every colonnette, if you interrogate it, will tell you at any time in the language of flowers and gemstones that you know so well: "See, Viviane, whether he has remained faithful to you!"

Perhaps this is the first time that my art serves to console me instead of making me suffer. I am the dupe myself of these crenellated walls, that I elevate so easily to an imaginary felicity; when I heap stone upon stone, it seems to me that I am giving a solid foundation to my dreams. I am building on granite the dreams of my heart. I believe them to be invulnerable, because I surround them with a blind fortress.

---

[128] The Zegris were one of the leading parties of the Grenadan Moors, whose feud with the Abencerrages is featured in the famous ballad known in different English translations as "The Zegris' Bride" or "The Zegri Maid."

V

Viviane to Merlin

Poor Merlin, you make me feel pity with your Alhambra. Is it with painted walls, with vermilion towers, hat you intend to dazzle me? Oh, why did I not find in your letter a single word—just one—in our language of old? You could have dispensed with raising to the clouds your marvelous towers, where I sense that I would lack air.

What has become of the time, Merlin, when you only had yourself? Your Alhambras, your giant towers, were in your heart then. How you would have laughed at the pretention of replacing a word, a smile, a silence, or a glance with a marble tower! Now you're like all the rest, indigent of heart, rich in ostentation, and infatuated with your misery!

Keep your Alhambra; I wouldn't like it. I'd dream about sultana, houris and Andalusians there, in our alabaster alcoves.

Just as I was about to set out for the Gulf of Bengal I suddenly changed my mind; that's a world too old for us, Merlin, too laden with relics and, in any case, on the banal path of all memories. I'd like, if there still is one, an entirely new place, surrounded by an uncrossable ocean, where we alone could land.

I'm assured that El Dorado, which is one of the Fortunate Isles, fulfills these conditions. The Fortunate Isles! I'm ready to embark on the strength of the name. Anyway, I desire no longer to see the stars that have deceived me; and I'm told that in those unnamed places, other and better stars would rise over my head and pour better fates upon it.

Such are, Merlin, the reasons that persuade me to summon you in the direction where the sun sets n the unknown sea. May they seem to you, as they do to me, unanswerable. If we find that fortunate island, let's not leave it again. I want the shore to be so high and the abyss so deep that no creature of the old earth can come to spy on us with its jealous gaze. Oh, that I might hold you tightly then, that my arms might envelop in a gentle eternal chain! But perhaps there are similar enclosures around two amorous souls in the world of the living. Where is the death in which it is necessary to seek that sacred isle? That's what we shall soon know, Merlin.

Think about it, I beg you. Don't play any longer with Heaven and earth. Think also that this pilgrimage might be the last.

VI

Merlin to Viviane

Pillars of Hercules.

Listen, Viviane! I have a great secret to tell you. Thus I am using, to send you this letter, little birds that have not yet carried messages. They're hummingbirds that I've just brought back from my excursion. They're so small that they'll easily escape curious eyes.

It was only a few months ago, on the beach at Cadiz, that I reread your last letter. I saw at my feet the smiling blue waves kissing and wearing away the Pillars of Hercules, rugged and cracked, kneaded by mollusks, so extensively that they're all shaky, and won't take long to crumble into the sea. It's thus, Viviane, that by your deceptive words you caress my robust hopes and destroy them at the same time.

Uncertain, I was saying all that to myself, and at the same moment I was thinking about the Fortunate Isles that are exactly opposite, of which all the world speaks, where no one has landed, not even you, who invite me to look for you there. As my gaze wandered over the horizon, I heard the sight of an awakening world on the far side of the Ocean. It was only a sigh at first, then a whisper of the waves, then a scarcely-articulate voice, warm with the perfumes of the virginal immensity.

It said: "Can you hear me?"

"Yes," I replied. "I can hear you, but infinity separates me from you."

"Come to me!" said the voice from the extremity of the universe, which I thought I recognized as yours."

"Are you in the Fortunate Isles?"

"Further away!"

"In Atlantis?"

"Further away, in a new world. Come, Merlin; I'm calling to you."

That conversation between two souls, across the Ocean, was only overheard by the abyss.

At the final word, I did not hesitate any longer to go and join you beyond all the known worlds. I made myself a small boat, poorly decked, furnished with two oars, speedy, on the model of the one we saw together in Gulliver's construction yard. Do you remember? As soon as it was ready I departed, my heart intoxicated by joy and hope, pushed by a land breeze, inflated with the breath of orange groves, which rose at that moment from the coast of Andalusia.

The route is very easy; it's sufficient to steer constantly westwards. Flocks of petrels, frigate-birds, ospreys, albatrosses and a few halcyons flying in front of me showed me the way, so well that it was impossible to make a mistake.

How many dreams, Viviane, assailed me during that solitary crossing? From time to time a whale appeared, like a reef, launching a column of water into the sky; sometimes, a little uprooted vegetation, or my floating staff, or a tree-trunk, announced land; then, again, the boundless immensity. Such is the spectacle that I had constantly before my eyes. Black waves swelled and rose up around me. I followed their profound valleys, breathing on the sea when the tempest was too strong, and the sea calmed down.

Meanwhile, I wondered why you weren't there with me in that little boat, and where it was true that the Fortunate Isles existed. "Doubtless," I shouted at myself, with a sigh, "it's one of the thousand lies with which humans cradle their sad lives. What would become of them if they did not deceive themselves?"

Then, with few other thoughts, two months to the day after I had embarked, one Monday, at five o'clock in the afternoon, I sighted an unknown land, low-lying and lush, which forms an entire new continent in itself. What a moment, Viviane! The sail as furled and I had lowered the oar, but the rising tide drove me toward a smooth beach. The sun rose.

Imagine another universe emerging before my eyes from the depths of the abyss as I came closer. Your breath alone can give an idea of the embalmed breath of that nascent world.

Perhaps it was the first day there has ever been on that paradisal continent, for the first dew had not yet been wiped away from the tresses of the vast forests, in spite of the warm morning breeze that was beginning to rise. I took possession of that land while pronouncing your name. As I plunged into the woods—which no man, I know, had yet penetrated—I imagined that you were the queen of that place, and at first I searched for your virginal throne in the midst of the inextricable lianas.

Also sleeping there, the slumber of chaos, were great condors and hummingbirds, beside one another on the same branch, their heads tucked under their wings. I called out, but I had had some difficulty waking them up, so deeply were they plunged in a profound dream. It was the same with the flowers I encountered. I was obliged to open their calices myself, and the iridescent curtains of a thousand colors that veiled the new day from them. They thanked me with their first smile.

In the silence of all things I stopped and collected myself momentarily in order better to understand the secret of that nascent world. Proud of being alone in knowing of its existence, I was impatient to talk to it about you.

You and I, Viviane, are, at this moment, the only beings in the old world who know that a new one exists. Let us keep that great secret to ourselves. I believe it would soil it to let it be known prematurely to the men of our era. For that, they would need to be more worthy than they are today.

Let the two of us, then, enjoy that universe together. You alone are worthy of treading it underfoot, because it resembles you: as serene as you, as innocent as you as immaculate as you. And then, it is a great bond between us to be the sole possessors of the mystery of an unknown world.

Since I have witnessed the birth of that other universe, it is difficult for me, Viviane, to say how worn out, withered and decrepit the old one seems, if I dare make that confession. I haven't able to help weaving here, in simple wicker, the cradles of numerous peoples, in the midst of numerous herds of buffaloes, vicunas, llamas, which watch me at work with an expression simultaneously confident and savage.

In this innocence of creation, I imagined that I was a new Adam, among the forests of another Eden. I set fire to vast savannahs, to prepare the abode of humans who might never know that I existed. I've given names to a host of animals, flowers and mountains. Already, the eagle and the ant know what the Chimborazo and Meschacebe are called.

The most difficult thing for me has been to understand the language of the flowers, which is very different from that of the flowers of our own lands. It's an idiom formed entirely from honeyed, flavorsome vowels, without any nasal consonants, as in Brittany. One might think that it was invented by magnolias and acacias; you'll learn it easily in one day. The tamarinds, the date-palms and the coconuts entwined with lianas were astonished, and murmured, on seeing an enchanter pass by their feet. They didn't even know what an enchanter is, so new is everything to them. They confessed to me that boredom was gnawing away at them in a solitude so profound, in which they never saw anyone pass by. "They will come here, under your shade," I told them, and they shivered with contentment at that, including their thick bark.

One singular thing: one does not encounter fays here, not spirits of any sort huddled in the hollows of old oaks. The solitude is all the more majestic for it. You know how beings of those sorts are often indiscreet and malevolent.

I've seen, it's true, a quantity of volcanoes on the flanks of the Cordilleras, but those volcanoes, which burn night and day, don't illuminate anyone. I've asked them who ignited them in the immense solitude where they are, but they weren't able to answer. I fear that they might become ingloriously extinct, for want of a spark, if no one is here to maintain their vast magic cauldrons. We'll be able to watch over them.

Here we shall be absolute masters of ourselves, a hundred times more so than in the old universe, full of jealousy, which only seeks to make us quarrel. If you fear the isolation, be reassured, I sense that I have love enough to fill the new immensity. Already I've regulated the employment of our days. We'll wake up to the calls of hummingbirds, which I've taught to repeat in their piercing little voices: "Viviane! Viviane!" The early hours will be spent domesticating vicunas and llamas, which will be eating from your hand after a few days.

We'll travel our domains. If we encounter a torrent, I'll make a bridge of lianas and see you pass over arcades of flowers. As for rivers, you'll traverse them in canoes made of cork-wood, which is, fortunately, abundant in these regions. Have no fear of wild beasts; the lions here have no manes and, if I can judge by appearances, you'll tame them with a glance. If necessary, we'll light a fire of aloe-wood.

To possess an entire world just for ourselves—and when I think about it, it's not too great for our love—to encounter no one but one another, to live far away from the slanders of the old world, to rejuvenate ourselves every day with the youth of things, no longer to expect anything from passers-by, to leave the old abyss of old magicians, to drink from the source of unknown auroras, to find everywhere the liberty that I love almost as much as love itself, to hear the Niagara precipitating in eternal flight in eternal repose, to eavesdrop on the dialogues of pearl and diamonds on the shore of the Fortunate Isles, to collect, in sum, the premises of a new earth—tell me, Viviane, does that project not transport you with joy?

For myself, I was immediately so full of it, so obsessed, that I did not hesitate to recross the sea in my canoe, in order to tell you about it. My boat had been destroyed some time before on the coast, by a furious hurricane, the sole scourge to be feared in that climate.

Do you not feel, as I do, the need to forget and be reborn? Let's not hope to succeed in that here. So long as we're in the old world, it will weigh upon us, crushing us with its eight. Let's quit the land of ruins, then, Viviane, and leave the dead their tombs. It's for old wrinkled genii to dwell in a wrinkled earth. The sight of ancient places reminds us too much of bad days. Souls as new as ours require a new universe.

Tell me, what are the isles of Alcina or Morgane, the palaces of Armida or Psyche,[129] by comparison with the countries to which I'm inviting you? What the visions of fever are compared to the creations of nature. The longer I live, the more disgusted I become with chimeras, in order to attach myself to a reality always more beautiful than invention. I'm so weary of dreaming, of imagining. I'm so impatient finally to savor a new joy in a new world.

Don't seek in me the Merlin who lived in vapors. The time of dreams is finished, Viviane. Let's enjoy the universe as it is. It's so beautiful!

The happiness that I demand today is a simple, idle, uniform happiness composed, above all, of common sense, and which is so easy to find: no more troubles; no tempests; an island or if you prefer, a shady continent, where one encounters none of the cares of the past; a vast pampas where we shall be masters and lords; a little boat on the Amazon; a few old books open in the virgin savannahs; a cabin in Peru, a pet snake; no gold mines, or, at the most, only one. All that must seem to you very miserable at the price of the ancient infinite domains of the enchanter you once knew.

What has become of the times when, for the least of our caprices, for a whim or for a frown, we were going to move heaven and earth? Today, I disdain the palaces of diamond with which, perhaps, we were once too prodigal. I've come back to the true, to nature. Accuse me, if you wish, of crawling in my turn. It's true; I've learned to limit myself. But tell me, Viviane—who broke my wings?

---

[129] Alcina is an enchantress in Ariosto's *Orlando Furioso*, while Armida plays a parallel role in Tasso's *Gerusalemme Liberata*.

If the very faithful description I've just given can finally convince you, let's leave forever the courts, the barons, the paladins, the Gothic ruins and even the Alhambra. Let's go far from human beings, whom we know too well, to bury our happiness under eternal lianas, at the foot of the Cordilleras. I'm sending you the seeds of coconuts, pineapples, vanilla plants, mangoes, sugar cane and maize. That last plant, cheerfully green, drawn over yellow, punctuated by nodes, with spearhead-like leaves, produces large ears covered in silky tufts, which blossom in orange or red plumes. Sow the seeds in the Crau, on the edge of dormant pools.

Don't tell anyone, not even your godmother, where these new plants come from. That is the price of our secret. I tremble now that an indiscretion or a stray messenger might divulge the secret of our Eden prematurely.

I nearly forgot to tell you that while searching that world I ended up finding human footprints in the and. How I shivered! They were the footprints of young Indian girl with whom I caught up. She seemed to me, like everything I've seen here, freshly emerged from the cradle of things. Her name is Omeania. Her hair, still damp with the breath of chaos, extended in smooth sheets over her shoulders; they have the hue of a raven's wing. Her figure is as supple as a liana; as for her eyes, you'll easily form an idea of them by looking into those of gazelles. She just appeared one day, and already she knows how to dance the dance of the eagle, the movement of which around its aerie she imitates very well, as well as handling a small stone hatchet with admirable dexterity.

"Where have you come from?" I asked her,

She did not know how to reply.

"Your parents?"

Same silence.

"Were you born on earth?"

She pointed at the sky.

I've given her a few glass beads; for that she wanted to worship me. I begged her not to.

With that, she led me to her hut and offered to share it with me, which I couldn't refuse, because the rainy season was approaching and is very redoubtable in that region. You'll find in that Indian, according to your wishes, a companion or a slave. It wouldn't be good for you to be entirely alone; I fear that you might be homesick.

On searching the continent further, at the other extremity, I discovered a man named Friday. I would have taken him into my service—for he appeared anxious to serve—if I had not already had Jacques Bonhomme to hand: a hard head who doesn't get on with everyone, and has caused me a thousand difficulties.

In conclusion, I'll add that I have the gravest reasons for avoiding the pursuits of my father. So widespread in the old world, he has not yet set foot in the veritably inviolate region that I have just discovered. In my eyes, that's a decisive consideration for us to establish ourselves there, sheltered from his love, which is worse for me than his hatred.

May you, Viviane, never know either of them.

BOOK EIGHTEEN: DOLORES

I

Merlin to Viviane

Hummingbird, hummingbird, carry his message! And may your wings be more rapid than the wings of the calumny that is flying after you!

On the day of Saint Isabella, the patron saint of Grenada, a student of the region, Lisardo, came to beg me to go to Cordova to a see young woman, Dolores, on whom evil spirits had cast a spell. Could I refuse the help of my art? No, of course not. Immediately, I set forth on the journey. The sierras of Grenada and Cordova delayed me by three days. I arrived under the colonnettes of a courtyard on the bank of the Guadalquivir. A veiled young woman was waiting for me there. As I approached she let a little dagger fall weakly from her hand. As there is frequent mention in those parts of veiled women and houris who drag you into stairways, and from stairways into tortuous streets, and turn out in the end to be frightful skeletons, I resolved o be very careful.

"What's the matter, Dolores? What do you want with me?"

"Lord Enchanter, ensure that I am loved, or I shall die."

"Gladly; but I can't do it if you don't lift your veil."

"I obey, Lord."

On that response, I expected to see the hideous face of a cadaver.

O splendor! Scarcely seventeen; a face almost as white as yours, if that's not a blasphemy; hair like yours, except blacker and not as silky; eyes that emit flashes; lips reminiscent of yours, except that they were trembling.

"Loved, Dolores? Loved, you? You shall be loved or my name's not Merlin. But by whom do you want to be loved?"

"By you, Lord Enchanter."

"At those words, I sensed that I had bound myself by excessive haste. What could I do, Viviane? The sacred word had been pronounced. That is how I was vanquished—but only by half. I explained forcefully that what she asked of me was almost impossible; my engagements, my promises, my diamond chains—there was nothing more solid in all the world. No, never...rather Heaven should...

Finally, I named you, Viviane. She did not take any notice, and did not hear me. Her burning eyes were fixed upon me; I was forced to lower mine, to look at her feet.

What she loves in me, she says, is not some quality or other, neither of my body nor my soul, but magic. That's why the evil is so profound. Her hands

332

trembled, her knees buckled; twice she fell in front of me on to the marble pavement; twice I took her in my arms and lifted her up, but I murmured immediately: "It's too late!"

"I must die, then!" she cried.

It's certain that since that moment she has tried six times in an hour to throw herself out of the window into the Guadalquivir—which, unfortunately, passes under her balcony. That has obliged me to put sculpted bars on all Andalusian windows. But my God, what's that?

Already her face in as pale as an alabaster vase through which a sacred lamp is shining. As soon as I go away, her screams can be heard from the depths of the patio, for she has a clear, silvery, slightly African voice. I'm teaching her to play the castanets. Then her dolor passes like one of the local storms—they're terrible, but they immediately give way to a radiant serenity.

Circuses, corridas, *toro embolados*: I accompany her everywhere. When I see her houri-like gaze feast on the majestic agony of bloodied bulls, while she agitates her fan over her bosom, I shudder.

I have also made the decision to accompany her to services—to benediction, to vespers, to the Angelus—in the immense mosque. What will happen if I quit her for a moment? I can't think about it.

P.S. It's too late to make a portrait of her today, although you've recommended me not to miss opportunities of that sort. Here, at least is a sketch. Her figure is supple, slender and tall—rare among Spanish women. She has the stride of a goddess skimming over roses. Her neck is snow-white, her throat always excited, like that of a frightened bird caught in a net. Small hands and feet—once all I could see except for her face. Her head, a trifle dainty for her height, makes her appear more gracious than beautiful. With that, a limpid, crystalline voice, which is indescribable, except by analogy with a honeycomb in which a bee has left its sting. Her only fault comes from the fact that she has always been surrounded by men submissive to the least of her glances. She cannot bear anyone adopting in her regard any other attitude than that of a courtier, or at least a supplicant. Her resentment then shows in a slight alteration of her voice.

II

Cordova

How poorly I knew her, and what an abyss there is in the human heart. I saw her again yesterday. It was in the orange grove and we were alone. Night was falling above our heads, and the golden spangles of the Guadalquivir were flowing at our feet. Never so many honeyed, caressant words, so many supplicant gazes. Citrus scents were also intoxicating me giddily. She noticed that and put her hand together in order to make me a plea. I took them in mine.

"Dear Merlin," she said, finally, in a low voice, "divine me without my speaking, you who can read hearts. What do you see out there in that star?" Her eyes were illuminated by the brightest ray of Cassiopeia.

"It's too much!" I said to her, momentarily vanquished by the magic that was falling from the sky on to the houri's forehead at that nocturnal hour and slipping with the dew into the ringlets of her hair. "In that star I read imminent felicity!"

And I took from her lips a myrtle twig that he was holding in her pearly teeth.

Immediately, however, she got up and changed her tone.

"Badly divined, handsome Enchanter. You're mistaken. Listen, then, since it's necessary to speak, and see in what I say the frankness of a Spanish soul. I no longer love you, since two days ago."

"Why is that, bounty of heaven?" I exclaimed, getting to my feet in my turn, with a start.

"Because the man I love is Don Juan de Tenorio. I met him at the bullfight yesterday. I'm counting, Merlin, on the grandeur of your soul. Procure me a silken ladder, a cloak of invisibility and two black horses, as rapid as the wind. Don Juan is going to abduct me tonight."

"Don Juan! Do you think so, Dolores. Do you know him?"

And I revealed to her all that I knew about that caballero: that he toys with all oaths; that he is the scandal of enchanters; that the Alhambra was full of his misdeeds; that he would cause her to die of shame.

"Die, Merlin! Precisely—I should like to die."

I reproached her for her conduct toward me. Was it a game, then, a caprice? Was it an artifice to make someone else jealous? My God, what ingratitude! For, after all, all of Spain had seen me complaisant and submissive. If she had at least made another choice, such as Lisardo! But Don Juan! And a thousand other things of the same sort, some quivering with indignation, others with a tender pity.

Her only response was to start playing the castanets. Angrily, I broke her fan. She danced a fandango. I wept. She burst out laughing. With that, I withdrew, speaking angry words that, I now fear, will rebound upon the face of Span, in such scourges as sterility, wars, famine and rains of blood—for the anger of an enchanter sterilizes all the places where it bursts forth.

Oh Viviane, how reduced an enchanter is, who has enchanted himself, by a word or a gesture, to a strange impotence! His wisdom promptly turns to madness and he becomes the plaything of young women! I sent the silken ladder, the cloak of invisibility and the two black horses faster than the wind to Dolores' door.

334

Viviane, Viviane, where are you? Eternal ideal, purity, stainless beauty devoid of caprice, from what a height you dominate all the beauties I encounter in this land and thought I have traveled thus far. You are their queen; they are not worthy to loosen your belt.

Heavens! Have I been able to say that Dolores bore the slightest resemblance to you? Have I said that, in fact? Were my eyes blind, then? Don't believe, at least, that there was the slightest spark of love in all that I have just recounted. Let's not profane that word, Viviane; your lips alone are worthy to pronounce it.

III

Seville.

I pursued the ravisher. It's in Seville that I've caught up with him, as he was going into the Alcazar. There I saw with my own eyes that illustrious enchanter Don Juan de Tenorio, who uses his art to seduce the most beautiful women and toy with amour. At first, only one name was able to emerge from my lips.

"Dolores! Dolores! Where is she? What have you done with her, curse you?

"Dolores? Ah, yes! I remember. I could scarcely tolerate her conversation half way to Alcala la Real."

"Don Juan, you surpass Cain! He merely killed; you soil, in order to kill more fully."

And in that tone I spoke, sometimes in the language of the ultimate judge, sometimes that of an indignant father, not forgetting the fact that his conduct was dishonoring our art.

"You alone, Merlin, can understand me," he replied, without anger. "You know what it is to love!"

"Yes, I know. I could teach you, Don Juan."

"What drives me, Seigneur"—as he pronounced these words he raised his eyes to the heavens with the expression of a devotee—"is not the vain pleasure of breaking hearts, even less a savage ardor of the senses. It's an infinite thirst for the ideal, which resembles divine love. I can't remain faithful to any woman, because none of them has the peak of divine perfection that I seek in everything. Only the mother of gods, I think, could satisfy me. If I were a pagan I would have wanted, like Ixion, to possess Jupiter's spouse."

"Enough, Don Juan! Enough blasphemy! Don't continue any longer with this hideous confusion of amour and theology, which is so fashionable today—a sure means of deceiving oneself and others."

"Seigneur Merlin, come to supper with me this evening. You'll learn more. It's a matter of magic; it will interest you."

335

"I'll be there, Don Juan, but as if remorse were sitting facing you."

"So be it, my dear Merlin." As he rose to his feet, he accompanied that remark with a smile that was, I must admit, irresistible.

I have just emerged from that memorable supper, of which all the centuries will converse. We had only just sat down and we were talking about you, Viviane. At your name, he dared to smile, with a conceit that put Hell into my bosom. But how quickly that smile changed into eternal tears! Someone knocked three times on the door. I opened it. A man of stone came in at a measured tread. I recognized in him the inexorable power of the abyss. He extended his marble hand to Don Juan. Don Juan gave him his. The man of stone dragged him away.

I remained alone, half-blinded by the paternal flames—and the black kobold that was stimulating them with his fang said to me: "Are you content, Merlin? See, cousin, what we do for you, and whether we're good relatives?"

That's what it costs, Viviane, to speak ill of you! What a lesson for inconstancy, with whatever name it adorns itself! One covers oneself with magic words—religion, martyrdom and heroism; the infinite and the ideal; generosity and devotion—and one wakes up plunged into Erebus. Our love, Viviane, does not resemble that. Thanks to you, I can finally see into myself clearly. I'm beginning to understand that you have always spoken to me the white wisdom of lilies.

IV

Cordova.

As I was passing over the bridge of Cordova on my return, I encountered a procession of revenants—something now infrequent in this region—and a long burning feminine sigh emerged from their midst.

"Who are you, errant souls?" I asked them.

"We're souls wounded by the love of Don Juan, and we're going in pilgrimage to the places where we first saw him. If you want to know more, speak to the one who is following us, whose heart is still lukewarm with the hot radiance of life."

I turned and recognized Dolores.

"You, here, in this sad chorus of the dead!" I said. "Perhaps I could bring you back to life, but that's the extreme of my art, and you'd have to aid me with an infinite desire."

"No, Merlin," the consumed soul replied, "I have no desire to live again; I shall march eternally in the tracks of Don Juan."

"You know, though, that he's in Hell?"

"I know."

"And you love him still, under the ashes?"

"More than under the sun of the living."

"But what of his cruel frivolity?"

"It only makes things worse."

"And his silken ladders?"

"He suspends them over the eternal gulf."

"What! He still sends you messages?"

"Yes—messages written with a red bitumen that burns Hell itself."

"And Hell hasn't been able to cure you?"

"My love has only increased with his crimes—that's my greatest torture." She added: "Come, Merlin, you who have loved me: I have a secret to tell you."

She walked ahead of me; I followed her.

Dark streets, resounding with the distant sound of dangers clashing in the shadows; mute hidalgos enveloped in their cloaks; mosques, chapels, large empty squares, funereal crosses nailed to walls, all accompanied by the dying sound of bells; and finally, a vast church that covers the ground for some distance. Dolores climbs the steps of the perron; she goes in, and closes the iron grille again, which grates lamentably on its hinges.

"Open it for me, Dolores!"

She stops; I glimpse a hideous skeleton.

"Further! Further on!" she says. "I promised you a secret; listen: this vast church, to which you have accompanied me by day, is about to collapse. Its walls are cracked. Flee! You only have a moment."

The immense edifice crumbles, with a din that frightens the dead. As they fall, the bells sound the knell of a world. I can no longer distinguish anything in the moonlight but a few fragments of the vault, which persist in order to show more clearly from what a height the edifice has crumbled.

I call out to Dolores once more.

Everything had disappeared.

What, then, Viviane, are the thoughts, the oaths and even the religions of human beings? They are built on sand, and how fragile everything is when we do not lay our hands on it!

How can Dolores' frivolity and lightness toward me be in accord with her inflexible constancy for an accursed enchanter like Don Juan? How many contradictions souls enclose, and how much darkness! Once again, you alone are light, beauty and incorruptible love.

Our two souls are eternally united. Although they seem to form two beings, in truth they only make one; and it is our destiny on earth to confound ourselves more intimately with one another, in order to live in Heaven, forming one radiance with our two lives. Tell me whether that isn't your belief?

Except that we have to make the education of one another before entering into that mysterious life of eternity in which we shall embrace inseparably forever. Do you not have, Viviane, complete confidence in that noble religion in which I live in retirement with you?

V

Diana of Sicily to the Enchanter Merlin

Know, Merlin, that I alone am still defending you. But for me my goddaughter would have sent back your letters.

Is it credible that you do not blush to have already given hr four or five rivals, all drawn from the lees of humankind—an Isaline, a Florica, a Nella, a Marina, a Dolores, even a savage, if I'm not mistaken—the best of whom would not by worthy to untie her shoelaces?

Everyone at my court is indignant; the men are polishing their weapons, he women are weeping. No more songs, no more hunts, even. Oberon's horn is scarcely heard at the crossroads once a month.

You dare to say, my son, that you have nothing for which to reproach yourself! You take Heaven as your witness. Well, personally, I believe you, because I know your candor combined with your science. But who else would believe you? And people's opinions are not negligible. Think, Merlin, that you're exposing me to the mockery of worlds.

In good faith, is that the life of an enchanter? Are you responding to the hopes that earth and Heaven have placed in you? Alas, Merlin, I still see many miseries and, if you'll permit the expression, many deserts around out. Why not fertilize them instead of counting Dolores' eyelashes? During the time you wasted with Marina alone you could easily have made Africa into a garden.

As for honored France, it would have cost you very little to dry up her tears, at least for three centuries. Tell me, have you done it? You keep quiet, Merlin; it would have been better to weep.

I'll leave the scandal there. It's great, my son, believe me.

And Viviane's chagrin and shame—don't they count for anything? I've seen her eyes hollow out; I've seen her cheeks pale, without her saying a word. To distract her, I've tried to take her hunting. Everything bores her, everything tires her. She lets the pack run off and remains in the depths of the forest all day, her head in her hands.

You talk to her about Omeania, and she blackens her hair like a Indian, with the juice of mulberries; about Dolores, and she makes a fan of flowers and shakes it over her burning face; of Marina, and she makes a crown of wild celery and laurels. I tell you this in confidence, my son. You know how proud she is. If she knew what I'd just told you, she would die of shame.

Truly, handsome pilgrim of love, it would be more appropriate for you to ask where she was when you were doing this, that and I don't know what, I don't know where. What, then, has saved you from so many ambushes into which you were about to fall at every step, head first? Is it your seven high sciences? No, Merlin, it's Viviane.

What, pray, assembled the kings around the round table and seated the honest folk? Is it your wisdom? Disillusion yourself, my friend; Viviane made the feast; you have reaped its glory.

What, tell me, prevented you from being crucified twenty times over in Rome? Is it your gracious face? Don't think so, Merlin. Without wanting to be seen, Viviane was there, charming your executioners.

Who then evoked the population of spirits to make a circle around you?

Who saved your harp, when a hundred felonious bards wanted to smash it?

Who snatched your divine cup from the lips of intoxicated nations and kept it safe, albeit cracked?

Who brought the good Turpin back to you, and rendered to you, along with him, treasures to which you are more devoted than to all of us?

Was that you, by your art? Oh, no, Merlin. Viviane has done everything, but Viviane wanted to hide everything from you.

For several days she has been more solitary than ever. She is pursuing a project, and attaching herself to it as she does to everything—which is to say, blindly. What can it be? I tremble to see her so taciturn.

The gazelles she nourishes from her hand perceive her melancholy, as I do, and follow her, weeping. The birds whisper in her ear: "Why are you so sad?" but she does not seem to hear them. Even I dare not interrupt her in that long monologue, which is not nearing its end. I know her; she will wake up from that depression—but by virtue of what thunderclap! May we not all perish therefrom!

Oh, Merlin, what have you done to this house, so serene until you came into it? The hours passed so quietly that one could not count them. You came, and the trouble and anguish began. Alas, it's me that I ought to blame. Should I not have opened Viviane's eyes to the flaws in your character, which you are, it appears, incapable of suppressing, or even correcting? On the contrary, however—it was me who supported your endeavors.

For once, my son, match your actions to your fine talk. It's less difficult to enchant worlds, which, you know as well as I do, are very easily duped. In any case, there are so many enchanters nowadays that it's hardly worth the trouble of being one. For myself, I'd never grant you my daughter if you had no other merit than that.

Listen to me Merlin; I have some experience. At my court, I've seen magicians, princes, powerful kings, and a few gods. I've lived in their intimacy, overheard their secrets, received their confidences. From all of that, I've drawn what I'm about to say to you: one day of legitimate happiness given to someone who loves us is worth more than all the glory in the world.

By dint of indiscretion you've compromised mu goddaughter in the eyes of almost all the world. An honest marriage might yet repair everything. Do you really want that? Give us a pledge, then. Prove to me that this need to wander, which is nothing other than that of fleeing your frivolity and your instability, will not grip you again when we have sealed the diamond knot. What regret, in fact, on both sides!

I tell you that my goddaughter could make a better alliance than yours—at least in terms of birth—today. Yours is not without inconvenience on the paternal side. Make that stain—for which I don't reproach you—invisible, by virtue of complaisance and good humor. It's no longer a matter of flitting from flower to flower, nor of stealing away to one abyss after another. Swear to me that you will tolerate, while smiling, the daily weight of domestic cares. What is sublime on a night of magic or a Sabbat on the summit of the Hartz or Etna, is, believe me, very small by the fireside in one's household. Nothing is more frequent than those spirits of which the entire world is amorous, but which are the surliest of beings in the evening, alone with their wives. I've known several of them; Heaven protect us from them!

How many quarrels and sulks have already spoiled the best of your days! She wanted to hide them from me; I divined them. Swear that they won't recommence. So many differences separate you, alas! She is so gentle, when everyone obeys her, you so angry! She is a dove; you are a lion. Both of you want to command. The thought of seeing you married would make anyone who loves you tremble.

Then children will come, Merlin. Have you thought about that? Your education is not what I would have desired for you. Is that what you will give them? I demand that they be brought up in my religion, which you know very well. If not, no consent. Finally, make your profession a solid means of earning your bread. Set aside, I beg you, a métier in which everything is pleasure, caprice, futility and smoke. Be useful, Merlin, to yourself and others.

No more of those enchanted swords, which dazzle the world and enslave it by blinding it. No more of those phantoms of chivalry with which you fill hearts. No more of those magic books that have cost you so many years yourself. In the name of Heaven, no more of those fiery messages, which make a young woman spend an entire day—and most of the next—dreaming on the wings of words in the depths of the woods.

Between the two of us, how much do you earn from that labor, in a good year and a bad one? Tears, I'm told, and often blasphemies. A well-regulated life, a little agriculture, commerce, prudent savings, a few bills of exchange— also a grimoire of sorts—no treasure, but an honest wage: that, Merlin, is what I expect from you.

I foresee a time when the profession of enchanter will no longer nourish anyone. What will you do then? It's necessary, however, that Viviane will not go out to beg for her bread. Do you know that an enchanter, emerged from Olympus, deprived of ambrosia, can very easily die of hunger, alone with his family? Alas, Merlin, I'm talking sense; you have to believe me.

I, Diana of Sicily, also believed in poetry once—and it was, not to displease you, on the faith of Phoebus Apollo. I believed in azure skies replete with

340

incense, inexhaustible flows of nectar, eternally game-rich hunts over the golden clouds—and I had a thousand good reasons for believing it. What has become of that beautiful dream of youth? Ask that first, Merlin, of that other enchanter, Homer—your colleague, I believe. What would I do today, pray, if I hadn't kept in my possession a few golden nails from my temple in Sicily, and as many from the one in Ionia? That's the foundation on which I live. I tell you that, my son—profit from it.

Let's get to the contract. I've drawn it up myself. Your wealth is very little, my dear friend, and between us, your father is eating up your heritage by the day. You have scarcely anything, Merlin, but your intellect—or, as it's said, your genius. Viviane's fortune is as clear and limpid as the sun.

You'll have for your portion, if you wish: pearls, diamonds, rubies and necklaces of dew; silk scarves of colors stripped from the rainbow; castles in Spain, cities and magical walls of opal and emerald constructed in the clouds; plus, all the streams, rivers and watercourses that shine in the desert; plus, after their deaths, the palaces of our relatives, Alcina, Titania and Oberon, with their furniture of crystal and amber; plus, the forests of silver planted on widows by frost in winter; plus, the sparkling gold massif of the sun on the face of the Alps, crowned with glaciers; plus, the entire domain of dreams, with its tenants, out-buildings, courtyards, ivory towers, bottomless wells, days of suffering, dried-up pools, clearings, orchards and hemp-fields; plus a herd of hippogriffs with bridles around their necks; the rest belonging, as it always has, to my said god-daughter and ward, Viviane of Sicily and of France, without your being able to acquire, retain or seize any of it by legal process, diversion, gift or any entitlement whatsoever.

Those are the conditions, Merlin; think about it at your ease. I wouldn't want you to make your decision lightly, for anything in the world. Know, however, that suitors are laying siege to me, and it's necessary to bring things to a conclusion.

If everything that I've indicated to you today had your approval, depart and come back. The marriage can take place without too much noise here in my castle. The celebrations won't last long. Everyone will keep quiet. I have very few courtiers and there is not a single musician in the woods for a hundred leagues around.

VI

Merlin to Diana of Sicily

Alhambra, Vermilion Towers.

Oh, be still my heart! Freeze! Don't allow your joy or your pain to over-flow.

A letter from you, Diana! I'll leave immediately. Peoples and kings will try in vain to stop me. I'm leaving in spite of them. What does the world matter to me?

I shall see her again; I shall squeeze her hand! Can it be, Diana? No, I'll die a hundred times before arriving.

Bounty and wisdom, that's your letter. Indulgent, because you're perfect, you foresee everything; I can only, alas, kiss your sacred feet.

Conditions, Diana? Conditions? A contract? Are those words made for us? With what magnificence you choose, in order to make me a gift of it, everything in the universe that is most agreeable to me! How were you able to recall so well everything that I love, everything that is in my tastes, my habits, and without which I would scarcely be able to live. Could my own mother have done any better?

But to possess something that isn't Viviane's, I can't lend myself. For example, the domain of dreams, the most beautiful of your possessions, can only have me for a master I having her for a mistress. Take back your decision, I beg you. Let it be common between us, in fact. That's enough for me to raise no opposition to the other articles, with which you heap my immeasurably.

Be reassured, Diana, with regard to the extravagances of my character. The change is complete, and, I can say, entirely to my advantage. A thousand witnesses, if necessary, can testify on my behalf. Interrogate—I invite you to do so—the nightingales that you encounter, the butterflies with a thousand eyes, the pearls on the sea-shore and the stars in the necklace of the night. They have all seen me; they have all been able to judge me, when I could not see myself. There is not a pearl in the sea or a star in the clouds that does not measure Merlin. Press them; force their confidence, when you are alone with them. Even interrogate dreams; let them speak freely, and judge me on their words.

You, Diana, would no longer recognize the Merlin you knew. No more fantasies; no more vacancy; still, perhaps, a little impatience. A sign from your hand, something negligible, raising your little finger, will correct me. Believe that voyages, time, absence, assiduous occupations, and pain most of all, have matured my heart. I'm bringing back to you, Diana, a mind quieted and tamed— at least partly—by so many ordeals.

Sometimes, ennui, solitude and despair have obliged me—as I've already confessed—to solicit here and there a smile, even from the stars of the firmament. A smile, Diana, do you hear me? Not more. Interrogate, I tell you, all your messengers—except for the lying cicadas. I have no fear of the testimony of worlds.

As for your happiness, I guarantee it. Don't worry about that any longer. I shall honor your old age appropriately. If you like hunting, you shall do it for pleasure, never out of need.

Think the same about almost everything else. We shall live under the same roof. In the evening, by the fireside, when you begin a sentence, I'll complete it.

I don't like courtiers, but in advance, I like yours.

Don't fear that I'll diminish the number of your guards, men-at-arms and halberdiers. They all please me; they're yours, and will be sacred to me.

I promise that no enchantment will ever be carried out without your advice; and to begin with, my first concern will be to find the stone that changes everything into gold. The smoke will be for me and the treasure for you.

The simplest possible wedding would also please me the most. A garland, a black cap that will sing overhead I the branches. No feasts, if you please, or noisy capers. I hate them for others, could I tolerate them for myself? A grave ceremony, however, which testifies for all.

I'll arrive with roses. Felicity! Felicity! That's all I can add today.

Your son and servant,

The Enchanter Merlin

P.S. I have proposed, by turns, to Viviane that we take up residence in the Gulf of Golconda, the Alhambra and Peru. I also have a domain in El Dorado, although it is still lying fallow. Decide as you wish; your choice will be mine.

If necessary, if all else fails, I could teach magic in Germany. With the knowledge I have of that country, we could live there entirely at our ease.

VII

Merlin to Viviane

One last word, Viviane; not a letter but a hymn; not a hymn but a triad, our epithalamium!

Who says that bards cannot sing of happy days? On the contrary; misfortune impoverishes the human heart. Nothing is more monotonous than the eternal plaint of the reeds on the strand.

Personally, I shall sing my felicity on your lips and build you a hymn that time will be unable to topple. The fortunate will repeat it from one age to the next, in the season of s[ring, until the earth itself bounds in the birth of a new day.

Go, publish this news, variegated flock of forest birds, who possess a treasure of sylvan songs in your throats, intoxicated by the morning dew! Say, publish far and wide: "Merlin is marrying Viviane today!"

Let all those who love rejoice in the depths of their hearts, and the consoled worlds forget the tears they have shed.

P.S. Come to meet me, Viviane, via the little path in the woods; it's there that I want to see you again.[130]

VIII

Scarcely had Alifantina been told about Merlin's plan to depart than he set everything to work to retain him. For the king appreciated our Enchanter more every day, and it would not have taken much for his to put the direction of the empire entirely in his hands. He had also recognized that Spain had never been so prosperous.

Sometimes, Merlin taught a Toledo cutler the art of tempering good curved blades in the Tagus, as he had done in Damascus. Sometimes, he taught a gardener of the Vega to hollow out a furrow, and it is obvious that his plan was to change Spain into a vast flower-bed, because he had drawn pathways and squares bordered with grass, tulip-trees and Judean trees, from Valencia to Cintra, passing through Murcia and Navarre. Most often, he taught new boleros and fandangos, and a quantity of dance tunes—for example, the Spanish Follies—not to mention several sword-thrusts still in use in bullfights.

In addition, he issued a host of decrees, laws and sovereign ordinances, which he thought it wise to write, not on parchment, but in the hearts of the people. For example, he wanted and ordered that all donkey-drivers and muleteers should be armed horsemen, so that no vagabond would encounter another without calling one another caballero. In addition, he enjoined and decreed that the castanets should be wedded to the guitar under the shady vaults of ever-open hostelries; that every window should have a sculpted balcony in order that beauties could come out on them to talk about love in the long summer nights, through jealousies, or listen to the dagger-thrusts resounding in the dark streets.

He also wanted the gazes of women to have a gleam resembling, as such as possible, the flash of precious stones, which he never failed to list in detail, such as rubies, sapphire, topazes, emeralds, amethysts and carbuncles.

As for the men, after perhaps a thousand trials to see what suited them best, he imposed on the Basques hair braided over the shoulders, the Valencians blankets in the guise of burnooses, The Catalans broad multicolored belts, the

---

[130] Of this entire exchange of correspondence, Hermione's notes have nothing to say, but it is hard to believe that the whimsically sarcastic letters from and to Diana of Sicily do not parody exchanges between Quinet and Minna's mother. At this point, however, the author might have written himself into a corner by excessive transfiguration of his autobiography—because, of course, Quinet did marry Minna, whereas Merlin, in spite of present appearances, cannot marry Viviane. Authors should sympathize, although ungenerous readers would probably expect and demand some ingenious narrative device to solve the problem, which Quinet might have done his utmost to provide—or maybe not.

Andalusians *alpargatas* embroidered with steel shoulder-knots, and to all of them the broad *navaja*, the guardian of their honor. Such were Merlin's laws, still obeyed today.

Don't be at all surprised, therefore, that Alifantina tried, by all the means at his disposal as an absolute ruler, to keep Merlin in his kingdom. He appointed him as his astrologer, and made him a Grandee of Spain—to which he added the plea, always so powerful in the mouth of a master:

"What will become of me, Merlin, when you've left me? I have been converted to your good genius. Every day I distance myself further from the spirit of the ruins. If you leave me, Merlin, given my admitted weakness, I fear being gripped again by habit and abandoning myself to the torrent. You have taught me to prefer cultivated fields to arid heathland. Gradually, I have acquired a taste for public prosperity. I have made it my own happiness. But my ideas are so new, so extraordinary, that I shall be unable even to admit to them when you're no longer here. My intimate counselors, I sense, will take me back to the desert."

The queen joined her pleas to those of the king.

"Who will explain the Alhambra to me, Merlin, when you're no longer here? What will translate the embalmed conversations of the roses and the jasmines beneath my tocador? Without you, Merlin, the palace will be like a dream without an interpreter. It seems to me, alas, that these alabaster walls are no more than an edifice of dreams, and that everything will undoubtedly crumble once you have crossed the threshold. You have made me enter into life—me, the daughter of the spirits of the ruins. I dread, if you leave me, that I might evaporate in the sunlight, like the vapor of those jets of water that the breeze stepped in the tears of the reseda carries away. Already I can see the sad heather taking root in the Vega in your stead."

All these speeches full of seduction and sagacity, these regal offers, regrets and tears, were futile. Merlin was obstinate in leaving.

When the day of his departure was decided, all the women of Spain dressed sadly in long black mantillas. "Why are you wearing mourning?" Merlin asked them.

"Because Merlin is leaving," they replied.

"Your beauty will lose nothing by that," he said. "You marble foreheads and your blazing eyes sparkle even more under those long black mantles."

"Without you, Merlin, we shall be unable to smile."

And it is a fact that, since Merlin's departure, the Spaniards have remained sad, to the point that it is difficult to recognize them. Everywhere there is heather, solitude and silence.

At Burgos he received the hospitality of the great Cid of Bivar and Chimène. They were both waiting for him on the threshold, near a small triumphal arch, on restive horses caparisoned in silk and gold. Fêted in their castle, which overlooked the platform, he repaid their hospitality by composing a few ballads eulogizing them, and put the stone diadem on the bald front of the tower of ancient Burgos.

When Merlin had reached the frontier of honored France he increased his pace further. The donkey-drivers and the muleteers, who made a cortege for him in large numbers, could not make up their minds to leave him.

"What will become of us?" they said. "Already ennui is afflicting us, for we're beginning to perceive that we're very miserable, and we had forgotten that on seeing you."

"I'll come back, señors."

"Is that a promise."

"Have no doubt of it."

"If you can't stay here, at least leave us your servant." And they pointed at Jacques Bonhomme.

Jacques refused to be separated even temporarily, from his master. All that he could do was offer to leave his black dog with the good people.

"He too knows a lot of magic," he said.

Seeing Jacques go away, the dog uttered such lamentable howls that the Pyrenees resounded with them, and he went to rejoin his master.

As for the donkey-drivers and muleteers, as soon as they saw that they were alone, they went back to Spain, bleak and silent, as if they had lost their father.

There Merlin's pilgrimages finished.

I alone possess the documents, maps, archives, letters and monuments that have permitted me to write this book. Whoever might attempt to add or remove a chapter from it, I declare that they can only be motivated by a deplorable cupidity or an envy more criminal still, and they will only succeed mutilating history, for a day at the most. In the end, the truth alone, without martyrs or champions, without defense or support, will shine sufficiently by its own light, as is always the case.

BOOK NINETEEN: THE ENCHANTER DISENCHANTED

I

To you, who suddenly discover in your heart a pain that you thought still hidden—what person does not have secret of that sort?—who sense a thorn beneath your garland, this last part is dedicated.

Come, imitate me: follow Merlin blindly. Above all, don't argue with him or criticize him; submit to him whatever judgment and reason you have left. That is the true means of profiting from his school. When sadness weighs upon me, I attach myself to his book, and hope revives in my heart. That is his greatest magic.

Let's see, where did we leave him? He is like the truth; nothing is more difficult than to pick up its vestiges when they have been abandoned. How many bad days I have passed through since I lost his enchanted trail! How much deep water has accumulated over my head! Am I not submerged? The wisdom of Merlin—although I have not hesitated to make his errors known as well—was, for me, the thread in the labyrinth of days. Since I have let that thread break, I have gone astray in the night without a dawn.

Once again, if you have found my hero, tell me. What has become of him? Who has seen him? Which way did he go? It seems to me that at the moment when we took our leave of him, he had just enchanted the land skimmed by the setting sun. At that signal, a comet had shaken its golden hair; it precipitated from the heights of David's Chariot, head first into the Ocean, while its starry, flamboyant robe was still trailing in the distance in the immense blue of the firmament. Do you remember?

At any rate, everything was serene in my heart and yours. We were young, you and I, or, at least, we passed for such. A circle of friends surrounded us, and not one of them denied us. Why has that changed? It was such a short time ago that things were like that.

The world is full, in the century in which we are living, of authors who want to steal the heroes that others have taken the trouble to disinter. I repeat to you—this is serious—that mine has been stolen. Who has taken him? Who has evoked him slyly while I was asleep? He was there, though, only a moment ago, also young, radiant with hope, standing on a summit in the Pyrenees, sowing joy and smiles all around. I arrive where I hid him myself.

O dolor! O treason! O ruin! I no longer find him there. To steal a hero confided to public good faith is a thousand times worse than stealing the treasure a man keeps in an old casket.

Believe me, the worst of evils is to be interrupted in an epic work like this one, which ought to have flowed out in one breath like a river swollen by melted snow. The grass grows over the footprints of your characters. The no longer know you and no longer respond to your voice. Everything has to be recommenced, as in a broken friendship; are those ever repaired?

If someone, alerted by my plaints, brings back my hero, or if I rediscover him in the melee of life, a hundred times more confused than the burning of Troy, where Aeneas lost old Creusa—assuming that he did not lose her voluntarily[131]—yes, if I ever catch up with our Enchanter, I swear an oath here not to separate myself from him again until he has finished dictating his story to me, all the way to the last line.[132]

II

The sage Merlin had completed his pilgrimages. From the Spanish gate he reentered the immense kingdom of Arthus, which then included England, France, Italy and the majority of the neighboring lands, not to mention the kingdom of dreams, of which he was the almost absolute master.

Someone who had seen our Enchanter pass by would have found him very similar to what he had been before his voyages: the same grace, the same smile, only his complexion somewhat sun-tanned, as was natural after having visited so many different climates.

---

[131] Creusa was Aeneas' wife, from whom he became separated while they were fleeing from Troy. When he goes back to look for her he only meets her ghost, who offers prophecies regarding his future but remains ungraspable. There is no hint in Virgil's text that Aeneas might have wanted to be rid of her.

[132] Hermione adds a long note to the text saying that everything in this section is "taken from life." The preceding chapters, she reports, had been written at Evian "in the midst of cheerful Savoyard grape-gatherers [with] the comet of 1858 shining over Lake Geneva," but that "the year that followed was troubled by illness, the war in Italy, and finally the [offer of] amnesty"—an offer that Quinet was inevitably tempted to accept, but eventually refused. "It was," she says, "after that interior conflict that he returned to his book, interrupted by other works." She then decodes the following chapters as a metaphorical representations of the phases of Quinet's exile, inevitably confused with the story of Arthus' sleep required by "the tradition." She claims, however, that Quinet's "immutable soul never knew disenchantment," even though circumstances condemned him to doubt the future. In effect, the narrative problem created at the end of the previous section is "solved" by a substitution of autobiographical infusion, moving that aspect of the text abruptly forward from the early 1830s to the aftermath of 1851.

Beneath that celebratory air, however, you would also have been able, with more attention to discover a profound change. After so much research, Merlin had not been able to find Viviane; he was beginning to despair of ever seeing her again. Then doubt was combined with despair.

"Isn't it a dream that I'm pursuing?" he said to himself, after having bid farewell to the donkey-drivers of Spain. "What journeys! What voyages! And what oblivion! Am I, then, more sage than all the other sages? Why be obstinate in this passion for a dream? I've been duped, alas! Is that a reason to continue to be forever?"

The most acute dolor had not annihilated Merlin's gift of enchantment. On the contrary, it had retempered his power, as we have seen in the course of his pilgrimages. As soon as the dread of being duped insinuated itself into his mind, however, every day deprived him of a part of his gift. He even reached the point of weakness at which he had commenced—which is to say, the point at which it would have been difficult for him to bend a blade of grass by his will alone.

It is true that the world was as yet unaware of the impotence to which our Enchanter gradually found himself reduced, and he had the weakness of living on his former renown, without daring to tell anyone that he was no longer in a condition to sustain it. Doubtless he would have done better to say to the world and its people: "I'm no longer the man you knew; look for another enchanter."

That would certainly have been more worthy, but he recoiled before that confession, which he thought both unnecessary and deadly. Thank God, his enchantments had been spread, without avarice, through the cradle of the nations. What need was there to begin again? Was it necessary, then, to tell the world that the charm had ceased? Where was the advantage? As for the inconvenience, that was sufficiently obvious. Would it not sadden earth and Heaven in vain?

Just remember, I beg you, how many people, and the best, were living in peace on the strength of his word alone! Who could tell what confusion would have been produced if the news were made explicit: Merlin is disenchanted! It is certain, at least, that all the things and people who were living on their faith in our Enchanter would be incontinently sunk, not only in Arthus' realm, but also the way to the confines of the habitable earth, and beyond.

Was that a circumstance for telling the truth without hesitation? Was not a little dissimulation preferable? One can live for a while on hope; and what was the great harm, I ask you? Hadn't the world lived well enough before Merlin? In any case—and this is conclusive—he did not resolve without combat and remorse to content himself with the appearance, he who had previously been all truth. To relate how that came about by degrees would be a long story. With the big book open in front of me, I've chosen one page.

III

The first indiscretions came from Merlin's own entourage. He was occupied in refreshing his soul with a profound sleep, and Jacques was fishing for frogs on the edge of the great pool of which legends speak. At that moment, follets appeared armed with phosphorescent torches, which mingled in their dances through the rushes near the bank, and this is the conversation that was established between them while they scarcely brushed the large floating water-lilies with their feet.

"My dear friends," said a little shrill voice that seemed to emerge from the reeds, "believe Farfarel.[133] Our master Merlin's fortune is evidently diminishing; he no longer has, I can assure you, the slightest credit over the elements and the stars. We, his former servants, would do well to quit him before he's entirely ruined. Personally, I've decided to disobey the first order he gives me tomorrow when he gets up. I'll be dismissed and expelled, I know—well, so much the better. On my honor, that's all I ask."

"That Merlin's declining," said Stem-of-Golden-Herb, "is perfectly obvious. He's a cracked ruin about to crumble. I'm going to look for another master."

"Agreed!" added Serpentine, relighting his torch. "Let's admit, though, that it's shameful to abandon a prophet like that because fate is no longer on his side. We'd dishonor ourselves!"

"Fine talk for a follet!" the first voice resumed. "Let's go, I tell you, and when he wakes up he won't even find an obliging gnome to collect a simple for him in the woods. Ha ha ha! Ho ho ho! Oh, my dear friends, mad laughter takes hold of me when I think about poor Merlin's face when he wakes up alone in the world! What chagrin! What anger! My God, though, he wasn't a wicked enchanter."

Shrill, whistling laughter, supported by jeers, ran around the desiccated pond; the voices recommenced:

"Let's clean house for a start. Let's take back, carry off and disperse all the enchantments that Merlin's stupidly spread over the world."

"That's a good idea, Serpentine," said Farfarel. "I'll take care of burgling Arthus' court personally, and the palaces and the cottages. Not a single love

---

[133] The same section of Dante's *Inferno* that names the demons Malacoda and Cagnazzo also cites Farfarello, but the name is probably generic, referring to a kind of goblin; it also crops up in plays written for the *Commedia dell'arte*, from which the French version might well derive, although French has its own equivalent term in *farfadet*. Quinet's consistent use of the term follet independently of its customary use in the term *feu follet* [will-o'-the-wisp] is probably also based on the Italian use of the term *folletto* [imp].

potion will remain in a single cup. No, no—I won't leave a drop that could satisfy a butterfly."

"And I'll rust all the armor, Cousin!" exclaimed Verbena-Flower, already brandishing a wisp of straw charged with dew.

"I'll erase all the sacred words in the hermits' books."

"I'll lift the charms from old towers crowned with ivy. I'll only leave the screech-owl there; he's our friend. Oh, if we could disenchant the amorous stars of spring nights as well! Look, they're smiling us and making fun of us. Be careful; they still have many dupes."

"Well end up reaching them," Farfarel replied, as he put out his lamp.

"Good! There's one star less already. It would be useful to disenchant Hell too, Believe me, there's more than one illusion left there."

"Don't worry, Serpentine," said Farfarel, who seemed to be the king of the follets. "I'll take responsibility for it, and remember what I say. To begin with, I'll get rid of the midnight revenants. I'll oblige them, with whiplashes, to go back honestly to their beds. I'll put stones over them."

With these words he went to stand in front of Jacques Bonhomme, and, prancing about, he added: "What about you, Jacques—are you coming with us?"

"Leave Seigneur Merlin!" replied the honest Jacques, who seemed to be familiar with the troupe of spirits. "What do you take me for?"

"Imbecile!" cried the host of follets. "Let's go find another enchanter, if there are any left in the world, and let's be the first to pay our court to him when he wakes up. Merlin's time is finished!"

Then they dispersed, sniggering, over all of Merlin's kingdoms, like the black clouds of locusts that settle on the oceans of wheat in Rumania and devour the ripe ears.

For a long time, Jacques followed the fugitives with his eyes. Nevertheless, he was not shaken that day. A few words of the spirits' conversation, spoken by Farfarel and Stem-of-Golden-Herb, were overhead by peasants in Ripes returning home from the harvest. Those words, mostly fragmentary, began to circulate through the world, but no one paid the slightest attention to them.

IV

Night had fallen; the wind, after having blown violently, had died away; the constellation of Orion, proud of its dust of stars, was putting Dionea,[134] who was producing gems, to shame. When Merlin, on returning from his pilgrimages, arrived at the frontier of France the praised, he thought he felt the earth tremble beneath his feet on seeing the places where he had once sown so many en-

---

[134] The goddess or Titan Dionea was sometimes referred to as one of the Pleiades; although her name is not conventionally used to name any of the seven major stars in that constellation, Quinet might be using it in that fashion here.

chantments. His heart palpitating, he paused for a moment to listen to the breath of the people.

No sound reached his ears. He said to himself: "That's all right. They're sleeping well, and dreaming. Let's go on. Tomorrow, at daybreak, I'll hear them in all their glory."

As it was midnight and the sunken road passed alongside a cemetery, he glimpsed a population of revenants on the level ground, escaped from the sepulcher, who were warming themselves up in the pale moonlight. Jacques saw them too, and wanted to flee as fast as his legs could carry him, but his master held him back and forced him to remain by his side, open-mouthed, in the company of the dead. "Stay!" he said to him. "No society is better for you."

In the middle of them, he had no difficulty in recognizing, on top of a Gothic terrace, Hamlet's father, who was reigning over the crowd that surrounded him, seemingly his courtiers. Among them was the knight who was still holding his fiancée Lenore on the rump of his sweating horse.[135] They all moved away slightly as Merlin approached, but Hamlet's father said: "What are you afraid of? It's Merlin; he's one of the family." On that, the dead remained where they were, and Merlin soon found himself in a circle that had formed around him.

"What are you doing here," he asked them, "gazing at these cold discolored rays? Speak to me of kings and peoples. What are the people of Arthus' kingdom doing? I don't know what's happened there since I've been rejected from it, and everything that isn't Arthus' land is a place of exile for me. Tell me about the many kings, my friends, and the many nations that you've doubtless known." He added, with the firm intention of softening their rigid faces: "It will be pleasant for me to learn from you what the living are doing, for the dead alone are not deceived."

"Answer for us," murmured the inconsolable population of specters, addressing Hamlet's father—after which he slowly pronounced these words:

"For the last time, we've come to show ourselves on the face of the earth. Until now, we've taken pleasure in warming ourselves by that star as pale and mute as we are. But the earth has become so sad, that we're renouncing visiting it forever. Our tombs are less icy than the hearts of men, our darkness less profound. A vain curiosity still attracts us toward the abode of the living. Always disappointed, that curiosity has wearied us. We're quitting our dwellings for the last time. Yes, Merlin, know that he earth has become so ugly since your depar-

---

[135] The reference is to Gottfried Bürger's enormously popular ballad *Lenore* (1773; sometimes translated as "Ellenore" or "Leonora"); it was composed in response to a specific request from Johann Herder, one of the fathers of German Romanticism, whose work Quinet translated into French, and which had a tremendous influence on his thought and work.

ture that we've sworn not to appear here again, even for the brief moments in which it was easy for us to lift the stones sealed over our heads."

"What he says is true," the crowd repeated. "Our nights are less sad than the daylight of the living." Then, shaking heads: "Adieu, disenchanted earth! Ruins, solitary walls, you shall not see us again!"

"What are you telling me?" Merlin interjected, refusing at first to believe what he was hearing. "Don't you know that I've enchanted the earth, especially this kingdom? I've put joy and smiles everywhere, personally. None of you will dare to deny it."

"Yes," replied Hamlet's father, forcing himself to soften his expression. "You spread serenity over the world. But your enchantments, poor Merlin, only last a day. That's what we've learned, now that you see us here face to face with eternal things. Everything you build in the morning crumbles in the evening. You build marvelous things, but they're dreams. You give out crowns; they wither. You summon smiles; they change into tears. Woe betide anyone who confides himself to your gifts."

Until that moment, Merlin had not seen any of the things that he had enchanted fall, so he had thought it certain that he was building for eternity. He had lived from day to day, without worrying about tomorrow. The idea that he had not created anything durable and that he would survive his works suddenly bit his heart for the first time. A blush rose to his face. He stammered at first, but then he replied:

"All of you who are murmuring," he said, "tell me whether my enchantments have not followed you into death."

"Another magician than you is necessary here now," the crowd replied.

"Are those that I have made kings no more? Are those who have learned magic from me forgotten, then? At least the beauties carry away my love potions with them."

"Your magic, poor Merlin, finishes here where death begins."

"But I have life on my side."

"There is only life in Heaven."

"But I still have the earth!"

"No, not even, not even the earth. Enter and pass. You shall see everything that you've edified fall: Arthus' kingdoms, the empire of knights, enchanted worlds, centuries of love, mystic towers. Beautiful soap bubbles! We've learned what Merlin's work weighs. No one will ever see us again, by the light of the moon, applauding with our resounding hands his vocations of smoke."

With these words, each of the revenants passed before him with a snigger that completed covering our Enchanter with confusion, for they pursued him with its echo all the way to their subterranean echoes:

"Adieu, Merlin, great king of dreams! We're going to tell the earthworms what your magic is worth."

And it is certain that from that day on, the specters ceased to appear in the greatest extent of the kingdoms traveled by our hero. If one of them failed in the formal resolution made by the great majority, he only did so by disguising himself and hiding beneath some ruined postern, and it was a disobedience that does not contradict what has just been related in the least.

V

To lose one's illusions! The most stupid and impertinent of all the phrases of our century. All too often, it has aided cowards to cover their desertion.

By his final words, Brutus has made an entire accursed people into plagiarists who say, in amplifying the master's testament: Love, poetry, magic, pearls of morning dew, virtue of evening breezes, *you are only words.*[136] And with that, empty of regrets, freed from remorse, they make use of that rusty phrase, not to stab themselves—a voluntary punishment that at least expiates the denial—but in order to go, head bowed, among the army's camp-followers, into the enemy camp.

It is entirely different when it is a matter of a disenchanted enchanter. That situation has not been depicted anywhere; and by virtue of its very novelty, how many almost-insurmountable difficulties it entails! No classic or model that I can take for a guide and a patron; an unknown, rocky road, full of potholes in which no human foot is revealed; on all sides, precipices that give vertigo.

If I had known in advance where my subject of predilection would lead me, I would surely have lacked the courage to begin it. But today it's too late to go back on it. Eight hundred pages already filled—that's no bagatelle! Let's continue, then, on the path that we're on, until we find an edit. With method, order and the art of dividing the subject into its various parts, and a sober style most of all—for nothing would be more perilous, above these abysms, than an intoxicated tongue—it's necessary not to despair of attaining a fortunate denouement.

As soon as Merlin had reentered Arthus' kingdom, his approach was announced by the sound of trumpets. The people scarcely recognized him, so forgotten as he, and very few voices murmured softly: "Merlin has come back!"

Meanwhile, it was near Caerleon that Arthus then had his court; before it flew, on the edge of a forest, anthropophagous vultures bearing a golden yoke.

"What's that?" Jacques asked.

"A sign of death," the prophet replied.

---

[136] The last words of Caesar's murderer, as reported by Plutarch and repeated, among others, by the 17th century French historian Pierre Bayle (but not by Shakespeare) were: "O wretched virtue, how I have been deceived in your service! I believed you were a real being, and I dedicated myself to you in that belief; but you were only a vain name, a chimera, the victim and slave of fortune."

354

Indeed, two bowshots from there, he saw a large crowd emerging from the palace, from which sighs and lamentations were escaping. He soon recognized the same court that he had left so triumphant on his departure. But where was Arthus himself? No one dared talk about him.

His relatives, who had each formed a dynasty, had lost their crowns. Bare-headed, without diadems, they were weeping as they walked, beneath a rain mingled with snow and frost.

There you would have seen, lashed by the horrible tempest, King Lear, bald, having gone mad, taking for his staff of old age Ossian, the king of the mists; after them, good Uther with the dragon's head, Arthus' stepbrother; his uncle, the king of the Orkneys; his foster-father Anthor; Owain, still followed by an army of crows. Who shall I name next? You, Claudas, king of the desert, with the green shield with three argent gules; you, Ban de Benoix, who reign in the forest of Briogne; and then again Rodarch of Cambria, Ambroise Aurele, Erec de Nantes, the sage Ulsius, the wisest of counselors: all covered in ashes, tearing their clothing.[137] The hermit Ogrin followed them, apart from the crowd, chanting: *Miserere! Miserere!*

As soon as he saw them from afar, Jacques cried: "Oh, God! What mourning, and what grief! Look at the kings weeping, and the queens in their mourning-dress."

"Let's go help them, if there's still time," Merlin replied, beginning to be gripped by anguish.

As soon as they had caught up the cortege, he stopped. The archbishop of Brice,[138] spoke on behalf of the dynasties that were following him, groaning.

"Merlin, blessed be the Man-God whom you lead by the hand. If not, it's all over for us and our kingdoms."

"Arthus will aid you!"

"He's dying."

"And my round table?"[139]

---

[137] Most of the names not previously are borrowed from the *Prose Merlin*, sometimes idiosyncratically varied; the usual form of Owain's name is used here rather than the Hersart-derived Owenn. Ogrin, however, is presumably the hermit Orgin featured in some versions of the story of Tristan and Iseult

[138] The Archbishop of Brice speaks at Arthur's supposed death-bed in the *Prose Merlin*; in Malory he is replaced by the Archbishop of Canterbury.

[139] Quinet adds a note here: "When I had the round table instituted by Merlin I did not know that legend had done so before me. It has often happened to me to invent incidents, details, even hazards, that I found subsequently in some twelfth-century work that it had been impossible for me to procure during my errant life. My thought thus went to join the poets of our origins without my knowing it. That coincidence, of which I have let more than one trace subsist, has proved to me that I remained in the intimate spirit of the legend in continu-

"Broken."

"By whom?"

"By the fault of all of us. Scarcely had you disappeared, Merlin, than Viviane said to the king: 'Arthus, your renown was great; it is lost. Merlin has gone, and with him, your joy, your fortune and your hope.'

"Immediately, in fact, the crowns of the kings began to tremble on their heads, and the tables to totter on their bronze feet. The people that you left so good-humored, sitting at our sides, drinking from our cup, entered into fury; hungry, they began by stoning us with the fragments of the round table. And if we asked: 'Why are you furious, stepsons?' they replied: 'Because Merlin no longer protects you.' O mourning greater than the mourning of Camlan! But their anger inspired them badly, and now melancholy is corroding them."

"Our own daughters have expelled us into the rain and snow," interjected King Lear. "Oh, how can they have hearts so hard, our daughters with the tender eyes of hinds? Merlin, little Merlin, help me, my friend. Don't leave my old head to crack like these crumbling keeps."

Merlin looked around. He only discovered, in fact, the ruins of keeps on the summits of hills. The towers that had not crumbled were all tottering; the best had at least lost their battlements.

The kings said: "Without you, Merlin, we're perishing. God knows who will replace us!"

Then the chatelaines began to weep. "What have we done," they said, "to be thus battered by the winds?"

Then the queens added: "What will it cost you to bring the people back to our feet? Less than a smile."

"You must have disobeyed one of my commandments," Merlin replied.

"Which?" retorted the crowd of kings, barons and chatelaines.

"I suspect that you have not loved one another, as I so often ordered you to do. But where are your peoples? And Arthus…?"

He was about to continue when a funeral knell resounded over the earth and froze the words on his lips.

VI

To arrive at Arthus' threshold it was necessary to traverse several nations that seemed moribund; they were extended or crouched in the sand like as many sphinxes at the gates of palaces, and each of them bore a mystery in its face. They were not weeping, nor sobbing, but they maintained a sepulchral silence.

---

ing it in the nineteenth century." It cannot have been easy for Quinet to find new twelfth-century sources while living in Switzerland, although he was undoubtedly in communication with Jules Michelet, and perhaps in correspondence with Hersart, privy to at least some of their research.

They were alive, however, to judge by the oppressed, panting respiration that elevated their breast. In every other respect, they seemed made of stone.

Yes, the bodies were alive, but the souls were dead, and each was wearing mourning for itself, sniggering.

No wound appeared on the surface of the bodies, but all the sores of Egypt would have counted for nothing by comparison with the invisible, tenacious ulcer that was devouring an entire world.

Don't talk any more about the plagues recounted by Thucydides and Boccaccio. What were they by comparison with this truly black plague extended over all Arthus' nations? A great evil, no doubt, but curable, since they was familiar; and besides, you could protect yourself from them by isolation—it was sufficient, to live in security, to refrain from touching bodies.

Here, by contrast, there is no shelter, no rampart, and no refuge. The venom is not only in the air, it is in a more subtle element, in the smile one encounters, in the speech one hears; it is in silence itself. From soul to soul it circulates without the contagion of bodies. It reaches you in the high places as well as the low. It flies with the gaze; songs and laughter carry it on their wings, tongues distil it, words dart it, phrases hawk it in a cloud, solitude nourishes it, the world entertains it, the void inflates it and exasperates it. Where can one flee? The bubo is in the heart?

And where is the remedy? Has Merlin brought the one simple that can heal the wound? No one knows, and no one cares to know.

They see the healer of souls pass by, and no one gets up to ask for assistance. They love their disease; it is, henceforth, their only love. Woe betide anyone who would like to cure it!

In the public squares, individuals and entire peoples were falling unconscious, but had no visible illness. They resembled fat specters sitting at an empty table. O Heaven, take that memory away from me! My heart fails just thinking about it.

As for decrepitude, it was taking possession of the youngest. They were those whose blood was the iciest. The children had the wrinkled faces and white hair of old men. The souls of young women had become as sordid as those of centenarians.

In the midst of them, some were dried out by a devouring thirst for what they called the future. They ran hither and yon, from one threshold to another, one temple to another, as if they were pricked by a sacred spur; then they fell exhausted on the sand that they had tainted with black blood, before having once slaked their hearts; for they were thirsty for the impossible, and were consuming themselves vainly in its pursuit. Others laughed on seeing their agony.

A strange thing: those people had forgotten the names of their ancestors, their relatives, their friends and their country. They did not remember the next day what they had done the day before, so indigent of heart that death could not take anything away from them.

More extraordinary still, they changed languages every day like clothes, and no one knew where they had learned those new, subtle, crawling, hissing languages, unless they had learned them from serpents with which they had contracted alliances in the dark.

Then again, you would have thought you were looking at peoples bitten in the heart, enveloped and stifled by a great reptile, like the sons of Laocoon, for they could not cry out. The soul of the reptile had passed into them and was snaking slowly through their livid veins. They had acquired its taciturnity, the oblique gait, the sticky and viscous face, everything except the sparkling gaze. If you touched their hearts, you felt cold. They could remain like that for a long time without beginning to be reborn and without completing their dying.

Their voices were as shrill as that of the wind in the desert; their breath poisoned the world.

Above them, in an open tower, there was a bell that sounded a knell night and day, and it was the knell of the world. But no one paid any heed to it, so accustomed were they to hearing it. Some took it for the ringing of the Angelus, at the hour when travelers seek shelter for the impending night.

For a long time Merlin contemplated the faces of those mute nations that had no desire to revive. A mortal cold seized him as he looked at them. He felt that if he stared any longer, the vertigo of death would afflict him, like a bird fascinated by a serpent's eye.

Without trying to talk to them—for he saw by their hardening how futile that would be—weeping and frightened, he hastened his steps toward the vestibule of Arthus' palace.

VII

It was a pale winter's day. The form of everything seemed to fade and vanish in a shroud of mist. The mountains, truncated at their summits by thick clouds, only showed their brown feet under the curtain that enveloped them with its pleats; there was no sound except the rattle of hailstones on the hardened ground. The mute and icy world seemed resigned to death.

As soon as the dogs that were guarding Arthus' threshold saw Merlin they got up and uttered long howls. Soon, they recognized him; lowering their heads they came to lick his hands and conduct him to their master's threshold.

Altered by their barking, the two porters, Drem of the strong hand and Kenon, son of Kledno,[140] got up in their turn from the bench on which they were sitting. Without speaking, both anguished and sighing, they opened the two battens of the oak door.

---

[140] These names are taken from one of the ballads in Hersart's *Barzaz Breiz*.

Arthus, the noble king of the future, was lying on his bed in the largest hall of his wooden palace, strewn with thin rushes. He was dying of the same disease as his peoples.

Queen Genièvre had just placed amulets on her husband's forehead; she was lying nearby on the bearskin extended at the foot of the royal bed.

Whence came Arthus' sickness?

Was it the satiety of wealth too easily acquired? Arthus admitted that he had not been sated by any cup, although he no longer had the same thirst for justice.

Was it old age? He had scarcely entered into mature age, but already felt all the chills of decrepitude.

Had he presumed too much of his time, and was he disgusted with life on seeing it so miserable? Had he been deceived by the generations that had promised to follow him, and which now denied him out of envy? Had that blow broken the strength and virtue of heroes within him?

Oh, how different it had been in the days, already distant, when, in the midst of a world intoxicated by joy, his head shaded by a plume, he had showed his smiling face to rejuvenated peoples who acclaimed hope in his person! Now he attached his gaze to his silver shield suspended above his head, but on seeing it tarnished as if by the breath of an impure century, he turned his eyes away and sighed.

When the year is about to die, the oak on the mountain murmurs as it sees its leaves fall one by one at its foot; it is envious of the sons of winter, the pine or the larch, which keep their green tresses entire, which no tempest can strip away. So Arthus, sensing that he was dying, gazed enviously at his companions, standing at the foot of his bed, who were retaining their green youth without withering.

It was at that moment that Merlin came in. When he drew close to the dying man he knelt down; then he took his hands, kissed them and said: "God save you, King Arthus! O father of all hopes, king of free souls, who has inflicted this wound on you?"

The king refused to answer that question, but he said: "Merlin, great healer of souls, it's too late! See how I lack breath, and how hope has been taken away from me. That is the knell announcing Arthus' funeral. May it please Heaven that it is not the knell of a world."

Then Merlin bent down to look for wounds, but he saw nothing except the increasingly livid face of Arthur, who went on, with the snigger that the precursor of death: "You don't see the wound, O wisest of men! It's there nonetheless, in the heart. But who inflicted it, in what manner, on what day, I shall never tell. It's gentler to die."

Without daring to respond, Merlin tried all the balms that he had collected during his pilgrimage, and which he thought infallible. He had brought them back from Prometheus' Caucasus, the isle of Philoctetes, the garden of Eden and the summit of Golgotha. After having steeped them in water that he had warmed up personally, he spread them over the monarch's limbs. None of them—not even the Promethean herb—appeased Arthus' pain.

At that moment, the nations that were lying down and torpid on the stone threshold made their snores heard, like the Eumenides lying on the paving stones of the temple of Delphi. That strange, muffled noise caused the king to shiver, whether with hope or dread it was impossible to tell; his tongue was already embarrassed; he was having difficulty speaking.

From the extremities of the limbs, the chill reached his heart. His eyes, rolling slowly in their bloody orbits, seemed to enclose all that remained to him of life. His clenched hands sought his sword. It was shown to him beside his bed; he made one more sign to indicate that it had been rusted by the poisoned breath of the wicked, and pressed it to his breast.

A few hours passed thus, alternating between stupor and disturbance. Finally, he wanted to get up one last time and die on his feet; his servants took him in their arms and sat him on his throne.

Having summoned the queen himself, he consoled her and forbade her to weep. Then he had his servants summoned; he thanked them for their loyal services and distributed to them the gifts that he had ordered to be prepared.

Then his crown was brought. He took it in his hands and said to Merlin: "I have no son. I don't know who will succeed me. Merlin, I confide my crown to you; it is that of the future; keep it for the most worthy."

Merlin promised that he would do everything as the king ordered; that put an end to his great anguish.

With every passing moment, however, his weakness increased, and the terror of death passed back and forth over his face. A few incoherent words fell from his lips: "All is lost...the future is just a word!" Almost immediately, he perceived that his mind was beginning to wander, and he extended his hands toward his friends, as if to beg them to forget what he had just said.

Then commenced the gurgling of death, to which the nations responded, and it seemed at each breath that he would choke. The vast windows of the hall were opened, but the air of the woods that carried life could not penetrate into Arthus' breast.

He asked to be replaced in his bed, and because his servants were too slow to arrive and he was in haste, he dragged himself there on his feet, leaning on their arms. There he had an instant's repose, but almost immediately, his head—that powerful, noble head—slumped on to his bosom and remained sealed there, as if it had been pushed forward by an invisible hand, against which resistance was futile. His eyes remained fixed, astonished by the first approach of eternal darkness.

A shrill cry departed from the hall and filled the palace.

"Arthus, King Arthus, is dead!"

Meanwhile, night had fallen, and for as long as the darkness covered the earth, Queen Genièvre prevented her dolor from bursting forth; she remained as cold and mute as the shift of one of the marble pillars that supported the hall. As soon as the shadow disappeared, however, despair was unleashed in her soul and death appeared to her for the first time without a veil.

On seeing the dawn recommencing to whiten, and the gentle light reappearing, for everyone except Arthus, and that he alone would no longer enjoy the gifts brought by daylight to the smallest creature, a sob, and then a lugubrious wail, and then an imprecation, emerged from Madame Genièvre's pious lips. That cry was repeated by her women, who were all sat around her on the floor, and the wooden palace was shaken by their hoarse lamentation.

"He has fallen, the king of the future, the one who brought hope to the earth!"

"The worm that crawls will see the light of day on emerging from the obscure mud, but Arthus will not see it again."

"The brute stone will be warmed by the dawn, but he will only feel the cold of death."

The grass of the fields will sense in advance the warm breath of spring and will rejoice beneath the snow, but Arthus, the sage, the good, the king of the just, will only respire the breath of the sepulcher."

"O God, where is your justice?"

"O Heaven, where is your light?"

"O Providence, where is your glory?"

"Mystic Rose, where is your perfume?"

"Ivory Tower, where is your whiteness?"

"Morning Star, where is your radiance?"

Merlin, who was transpierced by these clamors, stood up like a man inspired. He had Arthus' naked sword brought to him, and he put the blue-tinted blade to the king's icy lips. The edge of the blade was covered by a pale mist, like that the breath of morning leaves on a transparent window.

"Arthur is still alive! He's breathing! He's asleep!"

That word flew, more rapidly than lightning, from mouth to mouth; it stopped the tears, suspended the plaints. Long moans were succeeded by a silence of stupor and hope.

VIII

"There are, Seigneurs, several kinds of slumber," murmured Merlin's low voice, while he closed the king's eyes. "There is the slumber of ennui, which does not resemble this one at all; there is the slumber of death, which is much more similar; there is also the sacred slumber, populated by divine dreams. That is the one that the noble Arthus is experiencing at this moment. Let us make sure that nothing troubles his celestial dream."

Then, addressing the courtiers, he added: "Speak quietly"—which they immediately did, and have continued to speak in that tone until the present day.

The crowd dispersed at a measured pace, more silently than shadows. Sobs became sighs, sighs murmurs, murmurs whispers. Finally, the earth fell silent.

One of Arthur' counselors leaned toward Merlin's ear and said: "Is it so easy for a world to die?"

Merlin's only response was to place his finger over his lips.

All those who possessed a lute, a theorbo, a mandolin or even a bagpipe were enjoined to abstained from playing them if they would not rather break them. Even the bells were obliged to cease ringing. All of the living held their breath, for fear of troubling Arthus' pleasant dreams.

The castles that had once resounded with love songs were abandoned. No one knew what had become of their inhabitants. It was as if, within the enclosure of the ruins, hardly a single sprig of heather or a wild pear was tolerated, or a migratory bird permitted to alight with fearful wings—and if it began to sing, Merlin, sitting on the grass, would get up and say to it in its winged language: "Silence, blue bird, whoever you are. Arthus is having a beautiful dream, which I shall interpret in due course."

The bird fell silent immediately, and the entire world with it.[141]

Sometimes, a stone fell from the vault of the palace. As it was about to fall noisily, Jacques prepared a thick couch of leaves, which deadened the sound. By that means, the towers and the cracked walls fell gradually into ruin and were covered with vegetation without anyone hearing any din. Occasionally it happened that unwary people got up, barefoot, in the night, making a great racket, but the Enchanter only had to make them a sign. They all shut up immediately, like him, with a finger over the lips. Several generations passed thus without a sound, holding their breath, unshod, ears pricked, mute and choked, for fear of waking the sleeper.

Days also went by; nights succeeded days; and no notable change occurred. Jacques, standing watch, chased away the ants when they wandered over Arthus' forehead. He did not even let the cicadas approach. To pass the time, he sometimes sang a village song, in a whisper, but he soon gave up because Arthus had uttered a sigh. Sitting beside a brushwood fire, staring into the blaze, he polished and repolished the sleeper's sword; and every day it grew. Already the hilt was touching Scandinavia and the point the Pillars of Hercules.

---

[141] Hermione's notes suggest, improbably, that the scene of Arthur's death is a presentiment of Quinet's own, but also suggests, more plausibly, that his long sleep symbolizes the sensation of his long-drawn-out exile. Her note to the following section, however, offers the more obvious interpretation that it is a transfiguration of the history of France, seen as a progressive quest to reawaken something lost in the fictitious Golden Age already regarded nostalgically by its twelfth-century chroniclers.

Whenever Arthus woke up, he usually propped himself up on his elbow and asked for a drink. Immediately, Jacques Bonhomme informed Merlin, who hastened to arrive; he listened attentively to the account Arthus gave him of his dreams, and interpreted them immediately, almost always in the best light. When they contained a good augury, the world was informed without delay. On the contrary, when they announced bad times, plagues, famines, deaths, tyrannies and slaveries, Merlin kept the secret to himself, as much as he could, in order not afflict anyone. In either case, the king, appeased by the wisdom of the Enchanter, allowed his heavy head to fall back into the palm of his hand, and he went back to his long slumber.

Nearby, under the posterns, seven sleepers,[142] taller than all the others, were dozing in their iron armor and seemed to be giants; one might have thought that several of them were women hidden within masculine suits of armor. The first was named Francus, the second Polonius, the third Albion, surnamed Britannia, the fourth Lara of Castille, the fifth Ottavien the Lombard, the sixth Redbeard the Teuton, otherwise known as Teutonia, the seventh Pandeme, born in Esclavonia. Like good companions who have nothing to fear from one another, they extended their limbs on the thick grass, their eyelids closed and heavy, without suspicion, not even on the alert, all sown into the breastplates, clad in coats of mail, coiffed in iron helmets—but their swords were at their sides, espoused to them, dormant themselves, watching in their stead. Meanwhile, their unmuzzled dogs, good harriers, were also sleeping at their feet, along with strong hunting falcons.

Over their heads, the night sowed stars. The wan moon emerged from the clouds to gaze at those great torpid bodies, and took them for brothers of Endymion, or the seven conductors of David's Chariot. Many nocturnal moths played in their hair; many night-birds—barn owls, long-eared owls and ospreys—sheltered in their bosoms or their loose helmets. Then the daylight covered them with its incarnadine cloak, and dazzling sunlight was for them what darkness was.

Soon, nothing seemed so beautiful as to sleep the sacred slumber of the king. Everyone wanted to imitate him. The most beautiful women came to find Merlin; after Genièvre, there was Iseult of the white hands, Sigune, sister of Amfortes,[143] Brunissende and Orbance the angelic;[144] for fear of making too much noise, they had take care to remove their horses' iron shoes.

---

[142] Given the heavy symbolic loading of his passage, it is not irrelevant that *dormants* [sleepers], while clearly reminiscent of the legend of the seven sleepers of Ephesus, here transformed into symbols of European nations, has other meanings in French, with reference to architectural fixtures of various sorts and to heraldic figures.

[143] Sigune, sister of Amfortes, appears to be borrowed from a Provençal ballad collected in *Histoire de la Poésie Provençale* (1848) by Claude Fauriel.

"At least," they said to him, "you'll watch over us; if you give us our word, we truly won't be afraid."

"Sleep without fear," Merlin replied to them.

And Floramie, the fiancée of Titurel, Amide, nicknamed Héliabelle and unparalleled Hélène with the mournful heart[145] said: "We trust you, Seigneur. When the moment comes, wake us up faultless; we're very early risers."

"Word of an Enchanter! I'll wake you up at the propitious moment. Sleep your magic slumber."

And all those who had been esteemed the most charming at Arthus' court went to sleep under the stars, in caves, on the moss or on beds of leaves, in order to be ready more quickly when the morning call came. One had her hands clasped over her bosom, the other had them stuck to her body; this one had her head on a granite pillow that she molded at whim, that one preferred marble because of its virginal whiteness, another porphyry. All had taken thick scarlet shrouds because of the nocturnal wind, against which no roof protected them.

Thus, although Merlin had not done exactly what he wanted, he nevertheless conserved his worldly renown as an enchanter. "After all," he said to himself, "are not dreams worth as much as life? I can't, it's true, in spite of my good will, preserve Arthus' real empire, but I have given him the empire of dreams in its stead. Who knows whether that might not be the true one?"

Those reflections were only an artifice on the Enchanter's part to conceal his impotence from himself. How far he was from the ingenuity of his early years! He was beginning to pay himself with empty words. For the first time, he failed to be honest with himself, instead of recognizing that he was no longer what he had been. What irreparable consequences that first failure has had, alas!

---

[144] Brunissende is the beloved of the eponymous hero of *Jaufre* [Jaufry], the only surviving Arthurian romance written in Occitan, also discussed by Fauriel. Orbance is cited by Fauriel in the synopsis of a work in which she the wife of Feravis, there represented as the son of Perceval and brother of Lohengrin,

[145] Floramie is, once again, mentioned by Fauriel in connection with Titurel, but Amide, alias Heliabelle, is not to be found there and remains enigmatic; Hélène is too common a name to permit specific identification.

BOOK TWENTY: THE BRAZEN SLEEP

I

You who pass by, don't wake King Arthus. Don't see the fortunate crime; don't hear his fanfares; don't see the smile of his slaves; don't hear the hiss of serpents; don't breathe the incense that burns the feet of the wicked—that's happiness. That's what Arthus is savoring in his sacred sleep. May I never be stone or ice like him!

Several seasons having passed, the lethargy being still as profound, Merlin decided to wake the monarch up abruptly, at the risk of overturning feudal etiquette. He approached him, and, tugging on the hem of his fleur-de-lysed cloak, said to him: "Great king of the future, it's daylight. Out there, in the flowering orchard, the leaves of the wild roses are quivering in the hedge; the blackbird is singing; the waves are sparkling, the meadow daisies and the sweet marjoram have wiped away their tears of dew, and the cock has crowd three times: "Here comes the day!"

But Arthus was content, as was his custom, to sigh deeply; and, turning on to his other side, appeared to become marble once again. Seeing that, Merlin was gripped by a great fear, as if he had committed a murder, and he did not know what to think by way of self-defense, for he said to himself:

"Have my enchantments become enchantments of death, then? Now it's impossible for me to extract the greatest of kings from the torpor into which I plunged him—and with him, an entire world, the one that I knew in my youth, has fallen into the same stony slumber."

For old men, sleep is all very well, but he was conscious of having put into the long slumber, in the prime of life, so many charming women, mostly betrothed and promised, or scarcely married, who had trusted his word and had taken the shroud as one dons a bridal gown. That he could succeed in waking them was something he could not doubt, but when would the moment come? Today, tomorrow, or later? That was what he could not affirm. It might last a year, perhaps more. It did not require any more to trouble an honest enchanter as scrupulous as ours.

In that anguish, he went to stir up several new peoples, iron races, and commanded them to rise up with a great racket—which they did very willingly, for they all liked noise, which they easily mistook for glory. So they arrived, armed with the most sonorous instruments they had been able to find, and they struck iron and bronze, like holiday-makers, reminiscent of a swarm of bees flying out of a hive. Many a time they filed passed King Arthus' bed with the barons; they even fought various homicidal combats against one another, in which they filled the ravines with their dead, taking the further precaution of uttering furious cries that rose to the skies, trampling the bloody mud and striking and hammering the vanquished with a bronze flail.

"Why are you making so much noise?" the mothers and the maidens asked them.

"To wake the noble Arthus," the peoples immediately replied, in a breathless voice.

But even that was futile. The sleeper's torpor was uninterrupted by the tumult of so many nations at odds, which believed that the noise of their fall would reach the stars. Once, and only once, during the collapse of an empire, two kingdoms and six grand duchies, he said in a low voice to Jacques, who had to lean over his lips to hear him: "Make those chattering magpies shut up; they're disturbing me."

Then he went back to sleep.

When the nations in tumult heard those words, their confusion was unequaled. As for Merlin, he saw clearly that it was all over with the world; he put on mourning and lost the serenity and cheerfulness he had conserved until then.

Forgetting himself, far from cities, nourished on acorns, with wolves for companions, he no longer took pleasure in any society but that of phantoms. *Fit silvester Homo!*[146]

II

A few days later, lamentations resounded in the king's great wood, to which Merlin had retired, not far from the Charterhouse of Seillons. They emanated from the chief of hermits, Brother Ogrin, who had lived an exceedingly solitary life until that day, his forehead incessantly tilted over his sacred book. He had just perceived that all the divine words in his Bible had been dexterously erased during the night. In despair, he tore out the hairs on his head and in his beard, which had previously been very thick.

Then, having followed Merlin's tracks, he said to him: "Look, O sage, at what has happened last night," and showed him the sacred book. "What can be done? There's certainly no one but you, in all the world, who can recover the words erased by the evil spirits."

Already Merlin had seized the book; he saw with amazement that all the places where the name of God appeared had been torn and lacerated, as well as those where one could read the names of the angels, the archangels and, in sum, all the heavenly spirits. All that remained were the names of inferior spirits of

---

[146] This phrase, found in Geoffrey of Monmouth when describing Merlin's retreat to live wild in the woods—this reconciling his story with that of Myrddin Wyllt—is repeated in more than one romance.

the lowest rank. The miracles had also been removed, or, at least, crossed out with a red, corrosive ink that had burned, yellowed and eaten away the paper.

"I know no one but Farfarel or my father who could have had the audacity to work a spell of this kind."

"If you know this Farfarel," said Ogrin, "punish him—but first, Merlin, return the sacred lines, without which the holiest of books has lost its virtue."

"Gladly, Master Ogrin; I know them by heart."

With these words, he picked up a pen in order to reestablish in the text all the words that had been treacherously stolen, but, to his amazement, he had forgotten the holy names, or, at least, only knew them inexactly. Where *Jehovah* had been, he put *Nature*, less by virtue of conviction than the fear of letting the ignorance into which he had fallen show. In that way, he perceived clearly that the gift of enchantment was almost lost to him. If only that which remained to him had disappeared without leaving vestiges!

As for the hermit, he received his corrected book gratefully. By the time he perceived the changes he had returned to the depths of his solitude. Gradually, he familiarized himself with the new lessons: it was even said that he no longer swore by anyone but Merlin.

III

Scarcely had Master Ogrin taken his leave of our Enchanter than another desperate individual appeared before him. At first, he had some difficulty in recognizing that newcomer as the poet Fantasus, to whom he had once given good advice.

How Fantasus had changed, in fact! The face was still handsome, and even more noble and expressive, but it as furrowed by profound wrinkles, except for the forehead, which remained unalterably pure and immaculate, like a white slab of sacred marble that lightning has not dared to strike, and which still rises over debris. He was no longer the proud man of old who scarcely designed to tread on the earth, and walked on the clouds. He was a tremulous old man, tottering at every step. He was not blind, but he was limping on two shaky crutches, not even having a child with him to serve as his guide and sustain him.

"What do I see?" said Merlin. "Is that really you, Fantasus?"

"No, Master," replied the latter, "it's the shadow of Fantasus, and the evils that you see are nothing in comparison with those I would like to hide. The breath has gone, inspiration is lacking in me, O prophet! I seek and I no longer find. That's the greatest evil of all. Hunger, thirst and frost are nothing by comparison with that; it gives me a taste for death. Speak to me, Merlin, reply to me. Let me contemplate more closely the king of bards and the inspired race. I shall draw from your eyes in flame that I dread having lost."

That naïve hope on the part of the aged poet embarrassed Merlin more than a reproach, for he sensed that the source of eternal beauty had dried up in his disenchanted heart, at least for a time that he could not measure, and he was ashamed to let it appear. So he wanted at first to reject the eulogy that Fantasus had addressed to him.

"No, poet, Merlin is not the only source of the most beautiful songs."

"You are and you remain, Master, our sacred fount. It's on you alone that we live. We poets only amplify the word of Merlin; that is the limitation of our work."

"Speak without exaltation, Fantasus. Overly ardent words make the worst of evils more violent. Only tell me how you have lived until now."

"I have forgotten to live. No wife, nor children, nor relatives, nor friends have brightened my threshold. I have scorned the real; I have only found the ideal."

"Have you at least found glory in the game that so often leads to death?"

"Glory! I seek it still, when I no longer hope for it."

"What have you done, then?"

"Everything has passed through my head."

"And what do you sense now beneath the forehead, which still burns?"

"Something extraordinary. Cathedrals no longer speak to me, as they were accustomed to do, nor old suits of armor when they clashed against Gothic arches, nor keeps with pointed roofs, nor turrets clad in ivy. Once, those powers interrogated me with their colossal voice, I replied to them and everything flowed from the source. Today, everything is dead. No more complaisant echoes in people or in things. Where, Master, are the enchanted beings who haunted my mind? Where are the winged symphonies, vagabond and triumphant, that resonated beneath my feet in the depths of the solitary woods? I had more than a hundred ballads in the workshop, and as many sonnets and mysteries, not to mention a poem about the round table, which was to immortalize the society that you had formed with your hands. I can no longer extract from that brain even a grain of gold dust, as it was once so easy to do—and what completes my misery, I no longer dare say."

"You make me tremble, Fantasus. What, then, is this ultimate misfortune of Job? Speak—I'm listening."

"At least it's to you alone that I'm confiding that incurable wound."

"Come on, speak."

"Well, Master, the demon of beautiful verse has quit me; it has fled my house, alas. Shall I ever see it again?"

"The demon of beautiful verse, you say? Oh yes, trust in that one. I know him well, and have also had him in my service. Fine-Ear, also known as Golden-Tongue—that's his name, isn't it? Good God, what a head, what a brain, what an arid conscience! The tricks he played on me are incredible. I'll wager that he's now in the mad company of Stem-of-Golden-Herb, Verbena-Flower, Serpentine: a crowd of follets, the most fickle, the most capricious, the most vagabond and the most indolent spirits I've ever known. I've done everything to attach them to me seriously. What trickery! They'd sell me a hundred times in a day for the floating seed of a thistle, for a pretty spring of thyme, for a trill of an hautboy artistically cadenced in the forest. I pity you for having to deal with them. I've dismissed them; they're taking advantage of it to get drunk on dew, God knows where, in some ill-famed corner of the universe."

"Tell me, Master, is my genius lost forever, then? Am I getting old? Is the world?"

"Between us, Fantasus. I fear, not without reason, that the world might be dead."

"What's that?"

"Yes, my friend, dead—and by my fault." As if he were afraid of giving himself away, he added: "For as long as Arthus of the powerful breath sleeps, I foresee that the times will be bad for poets."

Far from appeasing the ulcerated poet, however, that last remark merely revived his torments, and he astonished Merlin with a cry of anguish, which subsequently became known, in all languages, as *The Lamentations of Fantasus*:

"O Master, take away from me the sterile old age of the bard and the poet.

"I have seen several of them, heads shaky, sitting in their desert hearth, still seeking a vain sound that flees from them. Without echo, without friends, without posterity, they survive on their works, like a wrinkled hollow tree-trunk filled with nocturnal birds, rising up among the withered leaves, amassed at its feet during sixty winters.

"Is that the fate that awaits me, Merlin? Shall I also see my works, fallen from the tree, strewing the ground around me far and wide?

"Cain the murderer has only been condemned to cultivate fertile fields in which crops called delight grow for him every year. He carries his sheaves into granaries that are still overflowing with last year's produce. Why, Merlin, am I condemned to cultivate the sterile field of the mind, where I harvest nothing but brambles and hemlock, after a glimmer of hope that is always disappointed? Am I more accursed than Cain the accursed?

"Tell me why the labor of thought has been imposed on me, which cannot even give me daily bread. I alone in all the world sow but do not reap.

"Oh, if youth remained to me, I would strike with my forehead once again that brazen Heaven which refuses me its radiance. But today, the outcome has too often disappointed my desire, and as once I sought noise, now I seek silence.

"How many times, Master I have sworn to myself not to think any longer, and not to dream any longer. In the middle of the night, however, when all the noises have died down, my thoughts awake with a start, and in spite of myself—for I have lost the strength to apply the brake to them—and attempt to climb to the accustomed summits. Until daybreak, insomnia devours me. My head, where a thousand ancient songs are ringing, aches in seeking new ones, but when daylight appears, everything flies away and vanishes in its glare.

"Old men are surrounded by the sons of their sons, arranged in a circle close by; shall I only see around me my dead works, cold specters, to make my cortege?

"When life commenced for me, I said to myself: I shall tame their coldness and indifference with the force of inspiration, and I shall amass works and songs around me without counting them.

"Oh, if the sympathy of men had then been added to my strength, nothing, Master, would have been difficult for me. But what the thousand teeth of adversity could not do, indifference has done. It has insinuated its ice into my veins.

"Now, I am like a man who has only one arrow left in his quiver. Woe betide me if I miss the target just once more! It will be the last, and eternal oblivion will gather over my name.

"Teach me, Master, that final song, that supreme swan song, which will tame their hearts and open their hardened ears to me. Tell me the words, if any such exist, that can still touch this age of bronze, for all those that have emerged from my lips have fallen impotent upon their ironclad minds.

"Show me the road to petrified souls, before old age, worse than death, renders even me deaf to your lessons. Already infirmities, harbingers of the tomb, have taken away my smile. Tell me what language it is necessary to use to enter into hearts of stone."

"Soften the hearts of men today!" Merlin interjected. "What are you asking of me? I've tried, and could not succeed myself. Hearts no longer respond to the heart, nor voices to the voice. You can pour your soul at their feet, like water; they will not look at it."

"I am, then," Fantasus cried, "the refuse of the universe—I, who thought I was its master! Fallen from Heaven to earth..."

"That is the fate of Phaeton; you have tried to rule the sun."

"Why not? I felt courage enough to create worlds."

"Now, resign yourself to prose."

"Never."

"Live, I tell you, a prosaic life."

"Never."

"Well then, die."

"So be it. But before I die, give me, of king of hymns, one last fecund thought, a flash of wit, a delight of intelligence, and I'm saved again. I win the hand in the great game of immortality; I brave the years, old age, future centuries, and the wrinkled earth that is already opening up to bury me. Give me, I tell you, one inspiration, a motif, a chord, a rhyme, a ray of light—less than that, a magic word—and I can enchain the universe at my feet, at yours."

"An inspiration, you say? Poor Fantasus! It would be easier for me to give you a kingdom."

"What use are kingdoms to me, Merlin? I despise them all, Give me, Master, the charm that, with a word, ravishes the heavens themselves, or tear out of my heart this thirst for beautiful things that dries up my lips."

At this point, Merlin, whose mind was at bay, doubtless harassed by too keen a commiseration, replied: "Your woes are great, Fantasus; they're the torments of a soul excessively amorous of poetry in an age of prose. I know them by virtue of having experienced them, at least the greater number of them. Pity is drawing from me the secret I shall tell you, after having promised myself not to confide it to anyone.

"The secret is this: renounce all ideas, since they will cost you too much henceforth to find them. Words can take their place when they're well-framed. The rattle of certain syllables throws off sparks, and they suffice to dazzle the human eye. There are also bloated words, hollow within and crested without, which I can teach you, and which resonate of their own accord, like Memnon's statue. You can try them out."

"Can it be?"

"Nothing is more certain."

"I would not like, however, to comprise at the end of my career the renown I have acquired."

"Do as I tell you, poet, and the whole world will approve."

With that, he sent the dazzled Fantasus away; but secretly, the Enchanter felt that he was dying of shame.

Fantasus, almost bewildered by astonishment, dolor, isolation, and most of all by old age and misery, went away, in quest of crested words, finding rhymes that he repeated with a complaisance that ought to have drawn stars from those who encountered him.

But the cruel crowd looked at him without seeing him. No one gave him the alms of a smile; no one remembered his splendid youth and ancient poet's crowns. Only the children took pleasure in hearing him, when, having returned to his cabin open to all the winds, he sat down in the ashes and murmured his redoubled rhymes, henceforth deprived of meaning.

The best said, as they passed his threshold: "What a pity it is that such a great man has gone mad. But did he need to distinguish himself more than us?"

IV

Who could depict Merlin's dolor? His eyes beheld nothing around him but mourning, disenchantment and decline, and yet that was nothing by comparison with the poisonous hydras reborn in his heart, where he felt a world perishing. The necessity of dissimulation, or, to put it more accurately, of playing the tragi-comedy with the majority of creatures, was what cost him the most. If only the entire universe could have been duped! Humans, accustomed to being fooled, could still be fooled; they saw everything magnified, with an uncertain gaze. But no! There were always, beneath his feet, a thousand tiny gazes of perpetually wakeful insects, which pierced him by daylight. He was a creator watching his creation die. Except for the poets among us, it is difficult for us to form an idea of such a cruel punishment.

And don't forget that in the midst of this ruination, Merlin had promised and instructed himself to smile, in order at least to save appearances. Alas, what use was that mask? The crickets, the flowers and the birds that knew his secret mocked him cruelly while he wandered over the rubble of some old keep.

The wallflowers scattered in the ruins said: "There he is, the great enchanter! Where are the fêtes, the tourneys, the words of love, the ornate standards, in the deserted halls?"

Then the mocking birds, perched on the solitary tree, took up the refrain: "The castle is deserted on the mountain; the tower has collapsed; but Merlin's heart is sadder than the tower; Merlin's genius is emptier than the ruined castle."

On hearing these words emerge from the dense branches, Merlin put on a semblance of a smile, but deep down, his heart was corroded; and, seeing that the smallest worm knew his secret, he no longer knew where to go. If he returned to the company of humans, he would hear their sighs too close at hand; if he withdrew to solitude, there was not a single wren that would not make a game out of laughing at his dolor.

V

This is my testament, he wrote to Viviane. *I confide it to the vultures and the eagles.*

Since I no longer believe in you, I no longer believe in anything, not even my father. In any case he no longer gives me any sign of life. If I could at least see his tracks, I might perhaps have something of which to take hold. But what am I saying? If I saw him there, standing before me, sniggering or roaring, I would not believe my eyes. I would say to him, as to everything: "Go away, Father: you don't exist."

The peoples that I have loved I am tempted to curse, for those to which I gave the most have been the first to forget me. How many times they have encountered me, and they have all forgotten my name! So light of heart, so avid for gain, so idolatrous of tinsel, so vain in nothingness, so demanding when they are given something, so craven when everything is refused to them; oh, Viviane, chimera of chimeras, should I be as disappointed on their account?

They know that I'm still alive, but none of them any longer turns his head in my direction. I nurtured them on justice, and they want to lick the feet of all my enemies. Is it necessary to despise what I adored? Is it not better to die?

The worst of misfortunes for a prophet is no longer to be able to prophesy, and that is what has happened to me. Once, as you know, I unfurled the future like a book. The more it hid from others, the more it showed to my discovery. I

372

possessed it much more than the present. I enjoyed its treasures in advance and made others enjoy them. How many times we amused ourselves spreading out a young oak leaf, folded and verdant under the hard winter bark! It was thus that future things appeared to me: young and flourishing beneath the rigid face of the present.

Today, my eyes seek in vain to pierce the shroud that holds me enclosed in the vale of anguish. Future things escape me. For the hearts of humans, and ours, from which I drew my presages, are covered with an envelope so hard that it is impossible for me to discern anything through the thick leaden mantle, and I cannot tell whether humans will soon climb again toward the limpid light, or whether they will continue to fall, with increasing rapidity, into the inexorable Hades.

When the future is thus veiled from the eyes of prophets, it is time for them to die; death alone can render them the clairvoyance that reads in the dark.

Come, then, supreme night! I shall see starry verities glowing in the clarity of the sepulcher, which flee me now in the withered splendor of terrestrial daylight. Come, propitious hour of the tomb; in the meanders of the Milky Way I shall savor at leisure the nourishment of unfathomable wisdom.

VI

Such was Merlin's distress. Seeing all things being effaced, how he would have liked to be a mystic! He tried, in good faith; adoring his suffering, deifying his tears, he sought Viviane all the way to the ivory tower of the virgin of Judea. How many time he tried to scale the world of dreams on Jacob's ladder! But scarcely had he set foot thereon than his reason could not extirpate his reason. He fell back heavily to earth, dragged down by his common sense, and in that effort to extinguish the white visions, his distress was only increased.

Veritably, it was brought to its peak by the arrival of Turpin. The face alone of the future archbishop, pale and distressed, said more than any words. His beard tangled, his eyes haggard, clad in the tatters of a cloak, he was on foot and unaccompanied.

"Have you also come, Turpin, to break this miserable heart?" the prophet said to him, welcoming him with his old bounty. "Have you found what I seek?"

"No, prophet."

Merlin heard him; he went pale and replied: "God have mercy! What has become of the gilded land of legends? You've come from one; it's yours. I wish to God that I had never emerged therefrom. Your life has been spent in magical empires, you have left all the government and burden of the real to me. Tell me about the fortunate worlds that I no longer know, populated by fays, genies, sylphs, dwarfs and necromants, which live lightly. Console me for what I suffer here, among base kingdoms and peoples from which the positive spirit has expelled all others."

"Prepare yourself for the most dismal news."

"What are you announcing to me?"

"The death of the spirits."

"I expected that."

"I don't know, Master," Turpin said, "what tempests have blown over the worlds of the fays. There too, there is revolt. The best-founded capitals of the fays, the vast cities of the land of legends, Potentiana and Sicambria, with walls of gold and crystal, where I spent my best days, and so many others that you have built of emeralds, have risen up against the light scepter of the sylphs. Who would have believed it? I have counseled, warned, harangued, prophesied, all in vain; the enchanted peoples no longer want to support a yoke of flowers."

"If that's so, woe betide them. I'm the one who wove it; they'll have a yoke of bronze. I gave them Titania for a queen; no one had a lighter hand in wielding the scepter. Clement to the wicked, protective of the good, hardly living, have they also dispossessed her? If they have, they have rejected felicity itself."

Turpin had just witnessed the dethronement of the fays, and then their funerals; he was still very moved by them, especially Titania's. So he recounted it in the minutest detail. Lying in a bier of nacre encrusted with golden nails, he had seen Merlin's own valets, Serpentine, Oat-Stem, Golden-Tongue and Lavender-Eye carrying Titania's corpse on their shoulders through the flowering tree-stumps. She had been buried under the sacred stone in the middle of the Crau. Good God, what a crowd of dwarfs, gnomes, and especially genii! What plaintive murmurs of ephemera in the thick branches. Everyone had been stunned by it. The weepers marched in the lead, after them the princes of the fays, Octavian, Zerbino, the king of Yvetot, all in mourning cloaks, all weeping hot tears.[147]

Merlin would dearly have liked to ask whether there was any news of Isaline, Nella or Marina, but he abstained, foreseeing the worst in everything.

"But the spirits of the ruins?" he exclaimed, after a long silence. "They, at least, still remain to me; they're long lived."

"No, Merlin, they were the first to die. I saw the race of the last fauns become extinct with my own eyes."

"How is that?"

"I was passing close to the isle of Pantellaria, the ultimate frontier of the realm of Epistrophius, in your crystal vessel, in order to search for you. A di-

---

[147] The King of Yvetot is a character in a humorous French ballad; Zerbino is the name of a character in the Orlando Furioso, but the juxtaposition of that name with Octavian in a list of fay princes might have been prompted by the fact that the German Romantic writer Ludwig Tieck, author of the classic "Die Elfen" [The Elves] used both names in the titles of other works.

sheveled woman clad in animal skins, running along the strand, sent us signals of distress. We landed to pick her up, and this is what she told us:

"'Three years ago, Lords, I was shipwrecked on this rock. At first I thought it was deserted, but from the promontory you can see from here, a faun emerged, hopping from rock to rock. It called to me in a barbaric voice, and brought me figs and hazelnuts. I tried to flee. It redoubled its cries. Fearfully, I followed it into its grotto, where I found two goats and dry cheeses in wicker cages. It appeased my hunger first; then, sitting on the threshold of the cavern, it began to play the pipe.

"'Three years passed thus. I tried to teach it to pronounce a few words of a human language. I gave up on hearing the clucking that emerged from the faun's throat. Every time I thought about what my companion was, I was afraid for myself; but when the sight of your vessel reminded me of the gentle family of humans, I forgot the creature, which I left behind me, and only thought of fleeing.'

"As she finished speaking, the faun, attracted by the sound of the oars, emerged from the rocks and ran toward the shore, carrying a hairy infant in its arms. It extended its arms toward us despairingly. Several times, it made an effort to speak, but its tongue refused to pronounce human words. Then, seeing that the vessel was continuing on its route, it did something of which the memory will remain eternally before my eyes. It walked into the sea until it was waist deep. Then, topping abruptly, it seized the infant by the foot and, brandishing it like a sling, it tore it to pieces and threw the palpitating shreds into the wake of the ship—after which it threw itself into the waves and disappeared.

"Such was, Merlin, the end of the last of the fauns. Don't hope to find another ever to draw you back to the sacred mountains."

"Let's leave the pagans. Rather speak to me of Geneviève de Brabant. She was my hostess. Does she remember me?"

"I found her very old, scarcely recognizable, with her centenarian stag. All she was able who say to me was: 'Are you still alive, then?'"

"Friend, we are perishing with regard to the women. Nothing sucks any longer at the teat. But Oberon, so gracious in his youth, so youthful still in maturity—what were his adieux?"

"Oh, yes, Oberon! The reception he gave me was, in every respect, incredible. He sensed that he was dying—he, the beloved of the fays—and that rendered him furious. He was veritably foaming with rage when her servants announced me; when I finally appeared before him, he was no longer in possession of himself; he started trampling the pearls of dew, and muttered; 'In truth, Turpin, I can't imagine what more you want from a spirit who is on his way out!'

"Oh, Master, what a spectacle is the agony of an old sylph who had never interested himself in any living cause. What aridity! What a death devoid of majesty! That sight will pursue me to my dying day."

"But at least my old friend Robin Hood has remained as he was? Is he still singing between his teeth, as in the time when I knew him?"

"If only he could! He has the spleen. Tanned, bronzed, curbed at the edge of his waves, he only had one breath left to him, and that was to whistle over the Ocean. He called me; I ran to him. 'Go tell Merlin that I'm laughing at his prophecy,' he said, and threw himself into the Ocean head first."

"Desperate words," Merlin replied. "Don't hold them against him. I confess myself that my malediction against Albion has rebounded on me. I've always reproached myself for it, and willingly retract it today, when more experience has enlightened me. The three isles had provoked me, and we prophets also give way to anger sometimes. We are fortunate when we can bless what we have cursed! Peace, then, to the red-haired Saxon and the Angles! If they have not always respected others, they have at least respected themselves. Besides which, the king of Thule pleads for them; the best of the daughters of King Lear, all of Ossian's, and the blonde sirens of Scotland have come to my threshold. To appease my anger, they have made me the gifts that delighted me the most; they have poured into my alabaster cups the mead of Harold's hymns, which sages drink. Let the Angles and the Saxons plow the sea in liberty, then, and let their isle be honey; I would like that. But let them not forget any longer to take justice with them at the prow, and to seat it on unknown shores, from the Hebrides to Coromandel. At that price, I will be their pilot. Go tell them that!"

VII

Dolor is sometimes so mute in the depths of the soul that one does not sense it on the surface. It does its work, night and day, at times when one is thinking about it least. Such was the effect of the news of the death of the spirits. Merlin thought at first that he had accepted it with self-composure, but it pierced his heart, dully, like a drill, and he never ceased repeating: "Titania! Oberon! Robin Hood! Perhaps the best beings that I knew in my youth! It's me who sustained them with my breath; they're perishing with me!"

Turpin, hearing him moaning, approached his bed of leaves.

"Recover your courage, Merlin," he said to him. "If you let yourself die, Turpin will not survive you by an hour. What! So many magic empires founded by you on the immutable rock of justice will vanish without return? What! The wind will whistle in the palaces with ruby columns, into which you personally introduced the Erl-King, Queen Alcina, Queen Urganda,[148] the Toothed Fay,

---

[148] An enchantress in the Spanish romance *Amadis de Gaula*, which is known to have existed in the 14th century by virtue of secondary references, although the surviving manuscripts are later; it probably originated from an earlier 13th century Portuguese text, and it became one of the most popular of all Medieval romances.

who all owe their scepters to you—which I have tried a thousand times a day to remind them, their families, their people and their courtiers."

"Calm down, Turpin. The moments are too precious to waste the in reproaches. Don't forget, my friend, that when I founded those beautiful magical empires on diamond rocks, they were promised to decline. Nothing escapes it, alas, not even dreams. The day has come. Only great task remains for you to fulfill, for them, and for me, who gave them their laws."

"What's that?" Turpin interjected, having difficulty holding back his tears.

"To write in an illuminated book all that you have learned, by means of your own eyes or those of others—provided that he reports be faithful—about their existence in the times when they were most flourishing, of course, Turpin. Know that by that means, you will ensure them an eternal existence in human memory, and me a veritable consolation in the thought that perhaps the best of my works has been saved from oblivion."

"I'll do that, then, Merlin, while it is still fresh in my memory. Only tell me, I beg you, to begin."

"So be it, my son. And when I'm in the tomb, don't stop, but continue writing; you'll make a marvelous book, which humans lack, your monument and mine, which the goatish teeth of lying centuries will be unable to chew up. On the contrary; you'll draw from it a glory like that of Joseph of Arimathea, who took Jesus down all bloody from the cross. And when the great Charles comes, he'll make you an archbishop to reward you."

With that, Merlin guided Turpin to a place in the forest where he domesticated bears and rode stags. He found numerous scrolls of parchment there, with ink and pens carved from eagle feathers. Turpin immediately set to work to write what he remembered having seen of the legendary kingdoms. A swarm of bees had made its hive in a corner of the grove. Without distracting him, their buzzing mingled with the scratching of the pen. All that remained on earth of blue or marvelous birds came in turn to perch on the nearby tree branches, and in their ingenuous voices they recounted conscientiously and simply, without wanting to shine at the expense of the truth, what they had seen or heard, whether in the Fortunate Isles or the lands of the fays. From those murmurs, buzzings and chirpings, checked one against another, Turpin formed the pure weave of his tale.

Thus were written, to the very last line, his gilded chronicles, the nourishment of sages, to which is owed the source of everything veridical and profitable that has been said in the world. My book is its faithful shadow, or rather its literal copy.

Not long before those chronicles were completed, Merlin took Turpin's hand, kissed it and said: "Now I'm content! I can die. Without you, the existence of so many enchanted peoples that I have nourished on the pure wheat of justice—as you have witnessed more a hundred times—might have been denied. I've personally taught the eagles and the crows that come every morning to obtain their food without any need to sow or to reap; my project was to do as much for the other nations, if the wicked had not risen against me."

"As witness," Turpin put in, "Attila's bird, which carried newly-hatched cities in its beak. Its name was Turul."[149]

"The witnesses are everywhere; don't forget the smallest and the most modest, such as the warblers and the robins, which I've often sent as messengers to the hearths of nations, when they consulted me."

"Those good times will return. Prophet, you will live great days with us again!"

"Blind man that you are! Don't you see, then, how they are all sleeping a leaden slumber?"

"Patience, Master! It's during sleep that the soul, the good seamstress, is busiest. It often happens to me that I lie down searching for a word, a name, or a date that I've forgotten. I go to sleep dutifully, and I find it when I wake up on the tip of my tongue. It's the same with humans. They've forgotten the name of justice, but they'll find it when they open their eyes again."

"No, no," said Merlin, ending the conversation. "No longer, hope, my friend, to make me believe that. I no longer walk over anything but ruins; those ruins are also deserted, and I have a presentiment that a further blow, coming from I know not where, has yet to strike me in the heart."

At a signal, Turpin retired, and the prophet remained alone.

VIII

What could that new blow be with which our hero was menaced? And how could his heart, torn apart so many times, give any further purchase to misfortune? The story is so simple that my author has excused himself from relating it. Nevertheless, here it is.

A troupe of acrobats, tightrope-walkers, and other fairground performers, all subjects of the King of Bohemia, made its entrance to the nearby town to the sound of twenty trumpets, and Jacques, a lover of entertainments of that sort, obtained an entire day's leave from his master in order to take it in at his ease. The decorations, the cavalcades and the songs had their usual effect on him; then the marionettes tickled agreeably the infantile soul beneath his Polyphemus face. But what bowled him over completely were the feats of arms of the fairground performers, punctuate by fanfares, at the moment when the most beautiful of the Amazons, armed with an ax, defeated the king of the Moors, all intermingled with the explanation of tableaux suspended in the wind, which represented the battle of the giants, Bluebeard washing his old rusty dagger, the king of

---

[149] The Turul bird is the legendary divine messenger of the Magyars, whose image is still preserved in Hungarian emblems.

Maurienne, and Tristan and Iseult surprised on the bed of leaves where they were separated by the great sword, the witness to their innocence.

Jacques uttered a cry of admiration that attracted attention to him. One of the tightrope-walkers, descending from the stage, struck up a conversation with him.

Did he really dare to compare the life of the enchanter and bard with that of an acrobat? Great God, what a difference! Everywhere, red coats decorated with gold braid, ostrich plumes, crimson velvet tapestries fringed with virgin silk; always welcome in every abode, pampered and caressed. How, I ask you, could that paradise be compared to the rude métier of the prophet?

He only had to decide to accept the wealth that was being offered to him. The troupe lacked a bread-porter to King Thierry of Maurienne; the costume was all ready, in scarlet, adorned with turquoises and carbuncles; it would be given to him; the rest would come later: a feathered cap, a garnished purse, a curved Damascus saber and a walking-horse.

Anyway, what was his present salary? Apparently very miserable. It would easily be doubled, perhaps more, not counting the good food: at daybreak, a good mouthful and claret wine; at midday, meat in plenty and Gascony wine; for a snack, chicken; in the evening, at supper, fresh seasoned hash with crepes, to procure a long sleep.

In brief, they dazzled him. Fascinated and stunned rather than convinced, Jacques did not betray his master; he had also forgotten the king confided to his guard. He did not come back the next day, nor the one after. Open-mouthed, he followed the acrobats, without knowing where.

Oh, if someone had pronounced in front of him the name of his beloved master, no doubt he would have dissolved in tears; he would have rejected the costume in which he had been dressed; perhaps, in his initial fury, he would ever have turned his bread-porter's saber against his seducers. But no one alerted him, even by a sign. No one reawakened his numbed thought.

Alas, let us allow him to follow is destiny wherever it might take him; let us return to his master.

As soon as he realized that he had been abandoned by his last servant. Merlin was seized by a misanthropy that he had not yet experienced, and his plaint was exhaled before the only friend who remained faithful to him.

"Would you believe it, Turpin? Jacques, whom I have nourished on the bread of the strong, has denied me for the hundredth time. He's been ambushed by some king of Bohemia, who will have captured him by means of his weakness for tinsel. He's left me without saying farewell, for he doubtless did not dare to look me in the face."

"Accursed vagabond!" exclaimed Turpin, in an initial surge of anger. "You've spoiled him, Seigneur." He soon softened, though. "Trust me, Prophet; I'll bring him back to you humble and repentant."

"And when will that be? How can I believe him henceforth? How can I confide myself to him for a single day? I've forgiven him too often; perhaps it was necessary to make him feel the rod, but that's odious to me."

"Yes, the oak rod or the bullwhip. I'll take charge of that."

"At least, if that happens, let it not draw blood!"

"No—a simple flagellation."

"Oh, my friend, mercy! Mercy! Spare him. I can hear his heat-rending cries in advance. He has a loud and clear voice."

"Don't worry, Merlin. I've wielded God's flail more than once. I know how to make use of it."

With these words, Turpin went to search his personal effects. He drew out a long-handled scourge in a leather sheath, very flexible, with knotted thongs and bronze tips.

"What's that?" cried the prophet.

"God's flail," replied the future archbishop. "It's the one with which David chastised the Amalekites. From David it passed into the hands of Scipio Africanus, who found it in the Syrtes, from Scipio the Just to the emperor Dorotheus,[150] who left it to his sons, from them to Attila, from Attila to Dietrich of Bern, who gave it to me one day after the Benedictus. It still lacks a few thongs; that will be remedied."

The good Merlin turned his eyes away in order not to see the flail, but Turpin, after considering it proudly, struck the ground around him to test it, like a thresher in a barn when he commences his task. At each blow the earth trembled. Tears, stifled cries and sobs, like those of flagellated people, emerged from who knows where, and the furious thresher redoubled his efforts. The sound was heard of towers crumbling in the distance, under the rhythmic blows.

"Stop!" cried the prophet. "What, then, is your crop? I can hear human voices moaning, as if criminal nations were attained by your flail."

"You're right, Master—as yet, though, they only sense its approach. How will they wail when the good bronze tips strike their shoulders? As for Jacques, I'll hardly have any need to touch him. The sight of the thresher will suffice, I hope. Let's go—the wheat is ripe! Let me do it—I'll thresh the corn; you'll collect the good grain."

"Wait. Don't avenge me—put down your flail. Events will avenge me well enough. Just Heaven, what times I foresee! Write this, Turpin: *First will come the goat with the golden honors and silver beard. The breath of his nostrils will be so strong that he will cover the whole surface of the isles with thick vapors. Women will walk like serpents and all their paces will be filled with pride. Then*

---

[150] There was no emperor Dorotheus, but there was a Saint Dorotheus who was a chamberlain to the emperor Diocletian and perished during his bloody persecution of Christians at the beginning of the 4th century, and it is probably Diocletian that Turpin has in mind as the sometime custodian of the symbolic scourge.

they will charge with chains the necks of those who roar, and they will cut out
the tongues of untamed bulls. O crime of crimes! To bind like an ox the man that
the author of the world created in liberty! Woe to you, Neustria, because the
brain of the lion will expand over your meadows. And they will give to soldiers
that which is due to the poor! The owl of Gloucester will roost in the walls of
Lutèce, and the viper will be engendered in his nest. Gaul will be soaked by noc-
turnal tears; the brutes will have peace between them, and humankind will en-
dure torture. The Germanic worm will be crowned; the forest will tremble; it
will cry out in a human voice: 'Arrive, Cambria! Bind Cornwall to your side,
and say to Guintonhi: The Earth will be swallowed up!'"[151]

After a moment of stupor, he added: "Those, Turpin, are a few of the evils
that I foresee, and which trouble my soul like that of Saul; I foresee them, and
cannot prevent them."

Even Turpin's heart of bronze seemed broken by those last words, and, letting his flail escape his hands momentarily, he replied: "Master, if the evil is
without remedy, if the world crumbles, if the real peoples are betraying you,
let's go, let's flee, let's return to the magic kingdoms. There, at least, you'll sit
down on diamond ruins. One can still console oneself and spend good days in
the debris of an emerald palace."

"I know," Merlin said, with a pensive expression. "Thank God, there are
still grateful beings on the earth, and I have no doubt that if you and I were to go
to the imaginary countries of which you speak, we'd be welcomed there with
honor. More than one king of Faery, escaped from ruination, would remember
that he owes his diadem to me. But know, Turpin, the full extent of the sadness
of my soul. I dread, my friend, that I would wear my mourning in those places
and sadden them with my presence.

"Yes, if there remains a single enchanted place in the world—which I
sometimes doubt—it requires, in order to enjoy it, a simplicity of heart that I
fear that I have lost in commerce with real peoples. I would sadden those happy
kingdoms—if there are any left on earth—and they would not give me their joy.
What would I do alone, without Viviane, without love, under the tree of the
fays? A profound ennui would grip me, my friend; I would seek out the abyss in
order to precipitate myself into it. There is nothing worse, believe me, than the
power of enchantments when it turns against the enchanter."

"Patience, Master! The centuries will render you justice."

---

[151] Quinet adds a note crediting his version of this quotation to his own translation of Geoffrey of Monmouth's *Prophetiae Merlini*. He had originally published it in the *Revue de Paris* in 1831 and Jules Michelet had reproduced it in
his *Histoire de France* (1841). The term "Guintonhi" does not seem to exist
anywhere else but this translation, and its meaning is enigmatic. The version of
the prophecy reproduced in the *Historia* does not contain a parallel sentence that
might cast some light on the matter.

"It's better to learn to do without it. Do you know that the dead themselves emerge from tombs to mock me? But there is another pain: you might perhaps smile; on reflection you will weep. The young women no longer love me, Turpin. They no longer seek my conversation; my presence no longer makes them dream, nor pale, nor blush; they no longer turn their heads toward me when I pass. 'It's an old enchanter,' they say. Worse than that: they no longer perceive that I exist. Those are signs, I think. Have I aged, then, Turpin? Admit it!"

"Do you think so? True age is in the heart."

"My God, don't say that! Has my hair turned white, then?"

"No."

"Do I have wrinkles?"

"No."

"Then what has happened?"

"Since you don't believe me, ask the flowers, the woodland daisies; they're sincere; they render you a striking testimony when you pass by."

"The flowers!" retorted Merlin, bitterly. "How little you know them! I would never have thought them so spiteful and rancorous. They, who only live for a morning, will never forgive me for having praised before them in a trial the durance of centenarian oaks. Since that day, they look at me with an irony that transpierces me. They could offer me the royalty of roses and I would not accept."

"Oh, Master, for such great evils, is there no remedy?"

"There is one, Turpin, but I hesitate to employ it. To govern the world, I perceive, my friend, it is necessary above all to despise it, and that is what I have difficulty deciding to do. I could, if necessary, scheme, warp, lie and cheat, as so many enchanters do routinely with profit, but I have difficulty accustoming myself to that; if my reign had to continue at that price, I'd rather die. Certainly, I would not have disdained a veritable glory, which every flower of the fields would proclaim every morning in rising with the sun. So many works have had for their objective, along with human happiness, that solid glory—but if I were to obtain only a vain, temporary fame, maintained by the gross tricks of sylphs; if it were necessary to capture, by dint of complaisance, the meager applause of gnomes...if the name of Merlin does not resound of its own accord throughout the realm of Arthus, let that name never be pronounced."

As Merlin concluded this speech, the King of Sophists, followed by the entire race of the disabused, passed by. His eye was keen and gleaming, and he was enthroned in the void. An entire blind people formed his cortege. He proved to those surrounding him that nothing is more beautiful than a world in which one dies. That was something to make all times envious. At that spectacle, Merlin felt, more than ever, the desire to die.

"There's my Antichrist," he said to Turpin. "I recognize him without ever having seen him; where he reigns, I perish. You, who love me, don't let him come any closer. I couldn't bear that triumph of the blind."

He raised his eyes toward the veiled stars. "Men tear me apart and the vultures spare me, while covering me with their wings. The peoples refuse me their threshold, and the wolves cede their dwellings to me. O devouring nature, whence comes your pity, when the good, the honest, the pure and the charitable have banished all pity? Come, death! Of all enchantments that is, I believe, the best."

Excited by the prophet's words, Turpin had taken up the bronze-tipped flail again; he had advanced with his hand raised; those who saw him from afar thought: *Who is that thresher carrying that flail? Has the season of the harvest come already? And where has he made his threshing-floor?* Before they had finished speaking, Turpin struck the earth; the accursed peoples, stunned, strewed the ground like wheat-sheaves crushed beneath the thresher's flail.

Meanwhile, in the distance, Merlin, having become misanthropic, lost himself in the depths of the forest. There, he did not have to fear encountering a human face, or hearing any voices other than those of torrents.

At intervals, through the murmurs of the foliage, a chorus of voices rose, which repeated, in the manner of the ephemera, the ancient refrain of happy days:

All is divine!
Love will commence!

And others concluded, with the magnifying noise of distant waterfalls:

Then comes decline;
Death or dementia.[152]

Let us leave Wild Merlin plunging into the depths of the words. May he go, alone, where the gaze of a deceitful soul cannot arrive, where perfidy cannot slide beneath a caressant face, nor false speech intrude the point of its blade, so high is the rock, so dense and thorny the undergrowth.

Do not pity Wild Merlin; he is already far away, in the rain, in the snow, under the fury of the winds, but he is sheltered from lies. Do you know what the cruelest thing of all is in profound exile, the desert of wandering? It is not the deprivation of the native land, of the cradle, of the tomb, of all those beloved things. It is that, uprooted and wandering, you lend yourself to every smile you encounter as if it were a refuge, and often, it is an ambush.

Woe! Woe! Without having the time to examine, or to choose, or to know—for you must hasten—your poor soul, stripped, naked and dying, gives itself to anyone on the road who gives you the alms of a kind word; often, thus

---

[152] Unfortunately, the substitution of *demence* [dementia] for the earlier *immense* does not allow the rhyme to be preserved in English.

you fall prey to denial, to lies, to perfidious grace, without being able to recover the serene soil where verity grows in love.

The friend no longer knows you pierces you to the depths of your heart if he encounters you. There is the evil; all the others are honey and ambrosia by comparison.

All is divine!
Love will commence!
Then comes decline;
Dolor immense,
Death or dementia.

BOOK TWENTY-ONE: LOVE IN DEATH

I

Fortunate is the man who guides the plow in the field where battle has re-sounded! Fortunate too is the man who makes his dwelling there. Beneath my window snakes the river where battalions have passed in the rain of iron and lead. There is the wood of firs and maples through which the heroes frayed a path. There, where tumult and fury were, peace and silence now reign. Laden with clusters of grapes, the vine awaits the last radiance of summer. The crows remain, and they remember the feast. In the evening I go to sleep to their cries; in the morning, they circle overhead, demanding their bloody fodder; but before them, the nightingale has awakened in the night. It is here, it is here, that it is necessary to talk about felicity under that flowering linden tree, from which un-leashed war was unable to expel the nightingales.[153]

Until this moment, the reader will render me the justice that all the events of this history—or almost all of them, at least—could be explained by purely natural causes. Search and scrutinize the events; you will easily find the causes in the accomplished facts that preceded them. I hold it to be assured that logic has been scrupulously respected, and that progress has been realized without interruption, even for an instant.

In what I am going to recount, that logic is less evident; but one is very strong when one has on one's side history herself, the instructress of peoples and kings. Is it for me, anyway, to change the course of events? God forbid! To ob-serve them, to record them, nothing more and nothing less: that is my mission. No obstacle shall prevent me from carrying it through to the end.

The last page of Turpin's chronicles was complete. He had just got up from his seat, carrying the book closed by its golden clasp. The birds of every species that had dictated his story, hidden in the braches and loosening their tongues, chirping with all their might, seemed to be saying: "I too figure in the chroni-cles!"

Merlin, remaining alone in the depths of the forest, nourished himself on the blackest misanthropy; it was even more profound that day than all the others.

It is important to specify the moment; unfortunately, I cannot fix the date rigorously. It was in the month when the hawthorn comes into bud, as indicated

---

[153] Quinet adds a note identifying this passage as a reference to the site of the Battle of Zurich on the banks of the river Limmat—the second of that name, in which French forces defeated a Russian and Austrian army in September 1799.

by a hawthorn that shaded the Enchanter's head. It was, therefore, no longer winter; however, it was not yet spring, for ribbons of snow still silvered the edges of the beds of the torrents. It was not night, but nor was it the dazzling light of midday. It was one of those hours that resemble dawn as much as dusk. Ah! There's a warbler diving into the dense hawthorn bush; after a final twitter, it hides its head under its wing, stands on one foot, tucks up the other and goes to sleep. It was, therefore, evening, not morning.

Yes, it was evening, but the sun was still darting a few of its last dying rays over the purple-tinted crowns of the trees. The forest, like that of Soignes, immense and solitary, seemed a temple with innumerable columns, where belated colored shadows were passing and disappearing into the obscure distance of clumps of beeches.

Among the centenarian trees there was a wrinkled, fissured oak bearded with white moss, thunderstruck at the top, the domain of eagles and ants; it was the old man and father of the forest. Cavernous voices emerged from its trunk, mingled with the humming of bees.[154]

"I am Merlin's oak," said that implacable voice. "It is on my stem that the first bird reposed, on the first day of the world.

"It was me who covered Cain's crime and drank Abel's blood.

"It was me who stiffened my arm to denounce the first murderer.

"From my bark the first buckler as made, and from my branch the first lance.

"It was from my branches that Absalom remained suspended by his bloody black hair.

"From my branch was woven the first mural crown.

"I taught wisdom to the first of the Druids, and nourished him with my sap.

"It was from my wood that the savior's cross was made.

---

[154] Quinet adds a note saying that this tree is based on a "memory of an oak in the Ardennes in Belgium." He does not say why, but Hermione's notes to this section points out that this is where Merlin meets Viviane again—in effect, where Viviane ceases to be a reflection of Minna and becomes a reflection of Hermione—and it was in Belgium that Quinet and Hermione forged their relationship. "The imagination," Hermione writes," especially the heart, was able to magnify the scope of this book, but in reality, it is a depiction of our intimate life in the profound solitude in which the exile lived from 1858 to 1870. We called our residence in Veytaux 'Merlin's green mound.' It was there, in spite of the absolute isolation, that the fortunate days of Merlin and Viviane recommenced; they ended up forgetting that time was marching, so much were they retrenched from the living and absorbed by eternal thoughts." If Hermione realized that, in the context of the narrative, the Hermione-based Viviane is a pale shadow of the Minna-based Viviane (and how could she have failed to do so?) she did not see fit to mention it.

"It was in my crown that Jupiter's bird nested for the last time.

"I have plunged my roots into the profound earth to discover what the abyss hides. I have raised my crown into the clouds to discover what is glorified in the sky.

"The ant has found its abode in me, but I do not refuse my shelter to the vultures and vagabond wolves.

"Armies have clashed in my shade; they have fattened me with their funerals, and I alone know their name for I have taken everything, including their glory.

"Caesar has sheltered his bald head at my feet, and the last of the Brutuses confided his blade to me.

"I have covered the good and the wicked by turns with my shadow, the just and the unjust, the sage and the insensate. That is why I have made the rude bark that you see. Even iron could not cut into it.

"I know what appeared at the emergence from chaos. I possess all the secrets of those who have sat down in my shadow."

"Do you know where Viviane is?" Merlin interjected.

"I know. She comes every day to stand where you are, and converse with me. I see her playing with the young roe deer whose mother has been killed by hunters. At other times she fills the cup of an acorn with dew and takes it for the thirsty cicadas to drink under the thatch.

At these words Merlin tilted his head and cocked his ear. Soon he fell into a reverie so profound that he seemed to be asleep. Lying on the ground, his head leaning on his elbow, although his eyes were open, he stared without seeing; he listened without hearing the last sacred whispers of the old oak with a hundred branches.

Now, will you believe it or not? Viviane, walking over the moss, suddenly arrives near the flowering bush. Can you see her? Personally, I can see her distinctly, leaning slightly forward, holding her breath, her hair moist with dew. But where has she come from? Why is she so belated? Why this moment rather than another? Is it credible that she could fray her path without any voice, not even a cricket, greeting her or betraying her approach? I repeat once again that that reasoning intelligence is the contrary of history. If it were necessary to answer every question, no story would any longer be possible. Let us not mix up, please, history and philosophy.

I'll go on.

As soon as Viviane was close to Merlin, she pushed aside the hawthorn and suddenly appeared before him.

He turned round and saw her.

"Where am I? Is that you? Is it you?"

In the first moment, he felt nothing but pain.

"Are you a shadow?" he went on. "A vision, like so many I've encountered in this fragile life?"

Then he threw himself at her feet, and kissed them, as well as her knees and the moss on which she trod. He thanked Heaven and earth for having returned her to him.

Sobs, interrupted questions, reproaches, bitter kisses, blinding tears, stifled cries that no words ought to try to describe, filled the first hour. When he finally collected himself, he saw that a profound sadness had paled Viviane's cheeks and prevented her replying to him. The more effort she made to overcome her dolor, the more she allowed it to show.

"Why are you sad, dear soul?" he said to her.

"Me, sad! I'm not," Vivian replied, with a smile in which all the bitterness on earth was assembled.

"That smile pierces my heart, my dear life. Better to cry. Tell me what is hurting you."

"Is it necessary to say it?"

"Yes, speak."

"No, I won't speak; it's nothing."

"Oh! Speak, or I'll die."

"Well, Merlin, I'm sad because I'm afraid of losing you again. So long as you know things that I don't, I feel separated from you by magical worlds. That's what's hurting me."

"Only that?"

"Nothing else. I weep because I don't have your science."

"And which is it of all my sciences, that you envy?"

"I'd like, dear friend, to know what it's necessary to do to imprison a man, without bonds or chains or walls, in such a way that he can't escape. Teach me that art, Merlin, the only one of your seven sciences I lack, and I'll be happy, as you want me to be."

On hearing these words, Merlin groaned profoundly.

"Why are you sad in your turn?" asked Viviane. "What's making you sigh?"

"I'm groaning because I can see what you want to do, and because it's impossible for me to refuse you anything."

With these words, Viviane flung her arms around his neck. She kissed him, and spoke to him softly, leaning on his shoulder. "Of what are you afraid, my beloved? Can you not confide yourself entirely to me, then, as I am entirely yours? Have I not quit my father and mother for you? My desires, my thoughts, and my entire soul are in you. There is no joy, nor wealth, nor hope where you are not. When I love thus, are my wishes not yours? In doing what I ask, are you not doing that which pleases you?"

"You're right; I'm ready to obey. What is it, then, that you desire?"

"I desire that we build an indestructible enchanted retreat, where we can live together, communing with one another, without ever being troubled by the rest of the world."

"Is that what you want? Be happy, then! I'll build you that dwelling."

"No, dear soul; I want to build it myself, to my own whim, in order that it shall be entirely in my power."

"So be it," said Merlin. And he taught her the magic required to operate an enchantment of that sort. As he spoke, he regretted every word that emerged from his lips, but love was stronger than he was; he did not stop until he had revealed his secret in its entirety.

As soon as he had finished and Viviane had understood, she showed so much joy that he was consoled for having spoken. He even felt glad that he had no secret that was not shared with her, certain that she would not make use of it without consulting him at least once more.

II

Both of them were locked in an embrace on the thick fresh grass near the flowering bush. They had exchanged a thousand caresses amid a thousand twittering speeches. More than one tear of happiness had trickled from their eyes. Merlin rested his head on his beloved's bosom. She cradled it and played with the curls of his hair, so soothingly that he seemed to be asleep and dreaming.

Being assured that he is dreaming of love, she stands up quietly, takes her long veil and envelops the branch under which the Enchanter is lying. Nine times she walks around the circle she has traced; nine times she repeats the magic words that he has taught her; then she comes back into the circle, sits down again on the flowers, and replaces her beloved's head on her palpitating bosom.

Finally, he wakes up, opens his eyes—and at first it seems to him that he is walled up in a high tower, crenellated at the top, without doors through which to exit or steps up which to climb; and he sees himself lying in the depths of a marble alcove, on a bed of silk and gold.

"What have you done, insensate? Is this the promised marriage? Why have you only waited until absence and dolor had killed me?"

Viviane looks at Merlin, smiling. Who would believe it? At that smile, my hero's resentment fades away. He scarcely contrives one more reproach.

Stuck to her lips, he only said, between each kiss: "At least don't leave me again, Viviane."

And Viviane replied: "Never."

"But why, cruel woman, have you abandoned me once?"

"To test you."

"What!"

"I was jealous."

"Of whom?"

"Of stones, flowers, stars, Isaline, Psyche, all the Beauties; for all of them loved you amorously, and you also loved them. Now, Merlin, no more pilgrimages, no more absences. You belong to me alone. I shall see you all the time; you shall only see me."

"Yes," Merlin exclaimed, "there is only you, in all the world, who can release me from this tower."

"Not even me, my sweet friend; you're here for all your lives."

And she told him that she had turned his strongest enchantments against him, that the door of the tower was walled up, and that she had thrown the key into the gulf of gulfs.

"But my dear soul, you've buried me, then?"

"I've buried myself with you."

"Am I dead or alive?" Merlin asked.

"What does it matter?"

"That's true. I've found you again. I can see you again. What does all the rest matter?"

"Don't worry. I'll often be in your arms."

III

In the meantime, two townsmen who were passing through the vicinity had seen what had just happened; they were talking about it.

"I've always predicted, colleague, that it would end like this."

"Me too," the other replied.

"When I saw Merlin pass by in the market-place, I said to him: 'My son, you're going to come a cropper.'"

"I told him so a hundred times, for my part, when he was little. But there you go! No judgment at all in that gilded head!"

"It's true that he always erred with regard to judiciousness. Glamour, glitter, false gold, that's all."

"Letting himself by buried alive!"

"Taking a tomb for a marriage bed!"

"What a pity!"

"What stupidity! That's how all these imaginative men end up."

"It's not us, colleague, who'd be taken in like that!"

"Thank God! We're positive, shrewd individuals, from father to son, and we know how to keep a firm hold on the strength and weakness of things."

"When such things happen, though, you know it's a sign of the black death?"

"Indeed?"

"And the rain of blood and war."

"Really? I've heard it said."

"And pillage."

"Uh oh! I agree with you. Pillage, you say? Let's go bury our Spanish ducats."

"And count our spices."

"In truth, there's not a moment to lose."

"Hurry up! We're nearly at the postern. Do you hear that bell? Ssh! Yes, it's ringing an alarm. We'll never get there in time to save our possessions. Get a move on, colleague!"

IV

Love in death, that's something no one has described since humans invented the art of saying everything. Who can I invoke to assist me in that narrative? No one can serve as my guide. I'm the first to march along that path, where even the witnesses who have accompanied me thus far are abandoning me.

Merlin's tomb—it's necessary to admit that it was a tomb—did not resemble those in which you bury your dead every day. On the outside, it was an immense tumulus surmounted by an ivory tower, like a snowy peak on a verdant mountain in the Alps. The door, it's true, was frightful, bare and inexorable. A hand of justice had been engraved above the vault and showed passers-by the inevitable road where all paths end. But beyond that threshold, what a palace, sustained by crystal pillars, what marble courtyards paved with mosaics, what alcoves eternally refreshed by jets of water! The walls were embroidered with arabesques, with no inscription. It was like a blank page abandoned to the imagination of our Enchanter; you will see in due course that he was able to take advantage of that circumstance.

Add, if you please, balconies without number, suspended over rivers whose murmur is scarcely audible, over cataracts from which rise to fall back the iridescent vapors of the abyss; at the summit of the steep shore, latticed pavilions of citrus-wood, where Viviane went to comb her long hair; no cypresses nor funerary trees, and yet vast forests; under their shade, in the background, a few residual puddles of stagnant water, where, it's true, frogs escaped from the marshes of the Styx are croaking. But with the slightest effort, those puddles would find their outflow and form little waterfalls—that would certainly be child's play for Merlin.

Here and there, an ambrosian odor exhaled by every flower sculpted on the walls—there are certainly a few nettles and pale asphodels in the corners of the courtyard, but they'll be extirpated; alongside the palace, a rustic habitation even more appropriate to meditation; everywhere, terraces, trilobate arcades, sixty ogival windows where the Enchanter could place himself at will over the tenebrous gulf, to contemplate the living from afar and converse with them through the sepulcher.

As for its extent, in its surface area, Merlin's tomb initially protruded into the kingdom of Arthus, France and Spain, a romantic realm, like a beautiful subterranean kingdom, well-furnished with defenses and bastions, well enclosed by moats, well garnished with keeps and ventilation towers; from there, still invisible, hollowed out in the entrails of the earth, it snaked into Italy as far as Calabria, and under Mount Gibel and Etna, from which it went via long submarine corridors to join Greece, Poland, Hungary and Rumania, not to mention Germany, high and low, through which it circled tenebrously; which comprised a space apparently very habitable for the mind most intolerant of any kind of frontier. Furthermore, one enjoyed the most various climates there; but peace, the companion of eternal silence, was everywhere the same.

In that immense sepulcher, three things were found that only hazard could have brought together: I mean Merlin's harp, attached to the vault by a golden chain; the marvelous lamp that Prester John had given to him; and finally, if it's necessary to name everything, a chessboard and pieces. The lamp illuminated that invisible world. The harp resonated to the slightest breath of Merlin and Viviane. As for the chessboard; it was placed on a marble table, the pieces, made of pure diamond, already aligned, doubtless to deflect the first moment of lassitude, ennui or caprice that might grip the two lovers in their eternal intimacy.

As you can imagine, my hero had never thought about taking his chessboard into his tomb; too many other thoughts filled his mind—but when he perceived the castles and knights on the checkerboard, and the population of pawns grouped around the gem king, who bore a bizarre resemblance to Arthus, he could not resist the desire to play a game, doubtless to mock the sepulcher. Viviane gladly lent herself to it. Sitting facing one another, in the silence of things, forehead supported by hands, hands on the stone table, they moved their diamond people forward or back.

As they were never pressed by any of the occupations of the world, they meditated at leisure, without either of them experiencing impatience, and above the castles and the emerald knights their quivering lips sometimes met. Eventually, Merlin, feeling that he was close to winning, stood up, mixed up the pieces and said: "There is no checkmate but death."

Then, casting a first glance over his new abode and not yet knowing whether they were alone, he said: "What have you done, Viviane, with the indiscreet troupe of my servants? Have the follets that escorted me most of the time whether I liked it or not followed me into this place?"

"No," said Viviane. "I didn't want anyone here but you. You're the master and the servant."

"Thank God!" cried the joyful Merlin. "I'm rid of them at last. More often than not, they only served to compromise me."

Here Merlin's fortunate days recommenced, for the lost serenity reentered his heart almost immediately. Thanks to the glare of the lamp, the difference between days and nights was scarcely perceptible, and yet, that continuous splendor did not offend the eye. It was a perpetually radiant aurora that never wearied, any more than Viviane's gaze, springing forth between her ebony lashes.

When Merlin was not holding her enlaced in his arms, they visited their vast domains together. "Until now," the happiest of the inhabitants of the sepulcher never tired of repeating, "I've known nothing but anguish. What, then, were our best days under the desiccating sun of the loving?" Then he detached his harp from the wall to sing his felicity, and the entire earth resonated to that harmony of the tomb.

After that he took the lamp in his hand and set off with Viviane to search the most obscure corners of the tenebrous realm. With her, he went all the way to the places where the mysterious seeds of things are in preparation. Everything appeared to him in its native splendor.

"But where, then, have I lived thus far?" he cried. "What was my darkness?"

At that moment, Viviane's eyes lit up with a sacred flame.

The only instants in which he remembered the former suffering were those when she left him, principally in spring, when she went to visit the flowers and the new-born birds whose patron and queen she was. The first time that happened, as soon as Merlin felt that he was alone, he uttered a groan that resounded in all the invisible worlds, for he thought he had been abandoned again, forever. And what would he do in eternal solitude? Viviane, who had heard his plaint, did not take long to reappear.

"You don't want me to leave the roses to die, and the birds in their nests?" she said.

In spite of those words, Merlin begged her, with his hands joined not to leave him again; she agreed to his willingly, and that year, all the flowers and almost all the broods of chicks died, for both had the greatest need to feel, at least once, Viviane's amorous breath.

At that news, Merlin promised that he would not hold her back again. Knowing that she was only absenting herself out of necessity and to watch over the immaculate realm of the flowers, he summoned reason and universal justice to his aid. Was it necessary to sacrifice the roses to his own felicity? Thanks to that reflection, sustained by much wisdom, he rediscovered and was able to retain his former peace, even when he was alone.

From that moment on, it can be said that no suffering approached Merlin's heart.

Was he alive or dead? That is for you to decide. It's certain that he was attached to Viviane's lips for long hours, or rather, that those hours could not be counted. He had conversations with her, punctuated by murmurs, and sometimes mingled with bursts of laughter. Are they, yes or no, signs of life?

He also liked the long silences, full of indescribable reveries; at the same time, he never experienced a single fit of impatience, ill-humor or melancholy. As for disquiet and anger, they were far from him. He knew neither jealousy nor rivalry. Are those signs of death?

When thirsty, he drank in his cup from the source of the great Oceanic river. When hungry, he nourished himself on sacred apples from his orchard. If, by chance, he felt cold, he lit a fire of brushwood from the tree of knowledge. If he felt drowsy, he went to sleep on Viviane's quivering shoulder. If the silence inspired him, he played the harp; if ennui threatened, he played chess. Are they or are they not signs of life?

Like Ulysses, he had hollowed out his own nuptial bed in the trunk of an ebony tree.

A starry veil hid the inexhaustible delights that ran in his veins, so well that tears fell from his eyes in the midst of sacred voluptuousness, as if too much happiness were oppressing is soul. Is that a sign of life or not?

Sometimes, when he went for a stroll, a ray from the lamp suddenly escaped through one of the fissures of the tomb and immediately illuminated the earth. But Viviane said to him: "Hide your lamp, Merlin; your light is blinding them."

Merlin obeyed without protest; he covered the brightness of the lamp with the palm of his hand. The earth immediately darkened from pole to pole; but Viviane's face had been lit up in its entirety; she appeared more beautiful. When you see the hearts of men darken, and night falls in broad daylight over the peoples, say with certainty: "Merlin is hiding his lamp with his hand."

There were a few herds of unicorns and aurochs that occupied them briefly every day. Those herds, handsome and sturdy, where guarded by a centaur who obtained milk and fleece from them. The well-stocked poultry-yard was overflowing with ibises and phoenixes, which were fed on grain,

In the beginning, a huge clock at the summit of the tower marked the hours exactly. Its pendulum was often the only sound that could be heard, along with the lowing of the funereal herds as they emerged from the stable or returned to it twice a day, udders trailing. Merlin forget to wind the clock once, after that, they no longer differentiated the hours. At any rate, they never asked one another "What time is it?" and never even thought about it. They ended up forgetting that time passed, on seeing the black hand always in the same place on the marble dial.

Twice or three times, Merlin asked: "Why are you so pale, Viviane?" but immediately took it back. "Nothing suits you as much as pallor. How often I cursed the sun that tanned your cheeks!"

And Viviane replied: "It's by the light of that lamp that I discovered Merlin's beauty. I scarcely perceived it in the white light of days that scarcely lasted a moment."

One day—perhaps it was night for us—Merlin heard drops of water falling into the depths of the abyss. He imagined that they were Viviane's tears, and, taking her in his arms, said: "You've been weeping, Viviane! Don't hide it from me. I can still see a tear bathing your long lashes."

"It's true, Merlin, I weep when I think that I've imprisoned you in this invisible, subterranean, inexorable world, deprived of the dazzling eye of day. In vain I'd like to help you recross the barriers that I've closed. I could never reopen it. Meanwhile, you regret the amorous earth and the stars of night. That thought poisons all joy for me in our tenebrous abode."

To those words the good Merlin relied with a burst of ingenuous, expansive laughter, which made the vaults resonate in the distance, and then he closed Viviane's lips with a kiss. "There! That's my response."

Almost immediately, however, he felt that it was necessary to talk seriously, and, detaching his harp from the four delicate golden chains that held it suspended, he added: "Listen."

Sitting under the arcade, Viviane raised her eyes toward her beloved. He drew a first chord from his harp; the long, somber corridors resounded; the echo was prolonged from kingdom to kingdom, over the entire surface of the earth. And the first people to wake with a start said: "Did you hear Merlin's harp?"

"Yes," said the others. "We recognized it. We've been searching everywhere without being able to find it. Let's go to the place where the harp is resounding."

Open-mouthed, they turned in the direction of Merlin's tomb. And this is what the peoples heard:

V

The First Song of Merlin in the Sepulcher

"Worlds, rejoice! Merlin has recovered his joy and his smile. Console yourselves, disenchanted peoples. Merlin has recovered his enchantments on Viviane's lips.

"It is from the tomb that the good news comes today. I am contemplating serene forms here in the eyes of my beloved. With her I roam the profound forests full of the scent of oaks. I read the veins of metal the paradisal book of eternal wisdom. I live in the marvelous tower of the King of Enchanters.

"Let his be heard by God and man! Let this be clearly understood by young and old. I have chosen silence, the world has chosen tumult; I have chosen justice, the world iniquity. I have preferred liberty, the world has preferred slavery. I have loved the light, and the world darkness. I have loved the truth, the world the lie. It is just, it is good and it is wise that we love on two opposite shores; the world in what it calls celebration, me in what it calls mourning; the world in what it calls life, me in what it calls death.

"In this tower, I fear no ambush by nocturnal humans drunk on mead. I see from afar their army assembling and dispersing, like the deceptive mist on my threshold. Neither azured lances, nor blue-tinted swords, nor poisoned arrows, can pierce me here. My high tower is built on the rock of justice. Who could shake it?

"Like vain vapors that prowl over ruins, the generations range around me. Oh, how quickly the gaze of morning has dissipated them!

"Dust of a day, you say: 'The Enchanter lied; his words are merely illusions; his enchantments have perished with him.'

"And I say to you: 'The Enchanter is upstanding, and trampling you underfoot; poor reeds, who made you so fragile?'

"Young women, what has become of your pride? How many times you have refused me even a smile, thinking: *He's no longer young; he's an old enchanter*.

"And you adopted the gait of serpents, while I went, heavy-hearted, to sit down by myself, on the edge of pools, far from the fête. What have you done with your pride? I've found mine again.

"Roses of the woods, flowers of spring, you sniggered when I passed by and you said: 'His crown has fallen, his perfume is withered.' Tell me: what have you done with your spring? Mine is recommencing.

"Cups that circulate in the banquet at the festival of the sword, you said to yourselves: 'We're still full to the brim, and his days are dried up.' Fragile cups, what has become of your intoxication? The wine of the Eternal still inebriates my cup.

"Harps that resound under the fingers of bards, what have you done with your chords? Where are your echoes in the deserted hall? My harp resonates here; it is you who have fallen silent.

"I know a song to make the skies split with envy and the great sea shiver."

With these words of the prophet, the sea began to laugh and all its waves were green with anger. "What is this song?" they said, as they beat the threshold and covered it with foam.

"I can see here," Merlin replied, "an ocean next to which you are but a drop of water in the sand of Syria."

"Can you see anything more beautiful than us?" cried the stars.

"I can see a sky next to which you are but sparks under the ashes of a shepherd's fire."

At that moment, the world having fallen silent again, the Enchanter resumed with greater force:

"Let this be heard by God and man! Let it be heard by young and old alike!

"I defy the tomb; it shall not chill my heart. That which I hated, I hate twice as much. That which I despised, I despise a hundred times as much. That which I loved, I love a thousand times as much.

"I defy the night; it shall not cast darkness around me.

"I defy the voracious eagles and vultures that feed on the flesh and blood of the dead. The eagles and vultures have come to me, wings spread, to ask me for their rightful nourishment, as of all the others who have died; I have refused them, and they have fled with shrill cries into the solitude, to the bare summit of the rock.

"I defy the earthworm; it shall not feed on me.

"I defy the evening wind, charged with rain in autumn; it shall not enter sadness into my heart.

"I defy the memory of things past; it shall not put a wrinkle on my brow.

"I defy the poisoned word of my enemies; it shall fall at my feet without wounding me.

"I defy the serpent and the immense tortuous viper, in the woods and within the bounds of cities; their fangs shall be pulled.

"I defy laughter; it shall not transpierce my bones.

"I defy tears; they shall not consume my eyes.

"I defy exile; it shall not take way my hearth.

"I defy forgetfulness; it shall not devour me.

"I defy iniquity; it shall not crush me.

"I defy Hell; it shall not swallow me.

"When, every morning, the sun reappears above their heads and everything begins to shine, they swell with pride, and they rejoice, and they all cry: 'Here comes the day, dazzling son of morning. We are escaping the shadow; woe betide the man who is in the night.'

"And I reply: 'Where is the night? Who has made it? I do not know it, nor the shadow that marches after it.'

"Let this be heard by God and man:

"I laugh at dolor; it is already passed. I laugh at death; it has come and I have buried it. Yes, it is me who has put the shroud upon it from which it will not emerge.

"I laugh at the day that passes after having risen in its glory. Oh, let it be ashamed to flee so quickly the first shiver of the leaves of the ash-tree, under the nocturnal tears of the hundred isles.

"I laugh at the cypress that withers like the rose, the star that is extinguished, worlds that are lost, temples that totter, gods who only live for a moment."

Thus Merlin was intoxicated by the pride of the tomb—but that only lasted a moment, for the nearest peoples, whose sleep had been troubled by his songs, unable to go back to sleep, approached the base of his tomb, and cried:

"Who reposes here under this green mound? Is it you, Seigneur Merlin?"

"Yes, it's me!"

"What! Is it from the tomb that your songs emerge today? You are singing in the sepulcher, Merlin, while the living groan!"

"It's true, and if only I could send you my joy! But answer me truthfully: are baseness, ingratitude and cowardice still your three patrons?"

"Alas, yes."

"Do you still know how to crawl like serpents?"

"We have not forgotten—but we still excel in combat."

"In combat! Yes, that's a glory that you must share with bulldogs. Do you still know how to bite the hand that frees you and lick the one that enchains you?"

"We have not forgotten."

"If it is thus, stay where you are, and I shall stay where I am. It would cost me too much to see the noble human face descend into bestiality."

"But Seigneur, will you not come back among us?" said the peoples, weeping.

"That depends entirely on you," Merlin replied. "Unless you reform yourselves greatly, I shall have the greatest difficulty in the world in living near you even for a single day; for, to speak frankly, I have always felt—I don't know why—something of a stranger in the midst of your cities, and even your rural regions. What I despise, you adore. Besides, which I was never able to do before, I can breathe here, with full lungs, justice, truth, liberty, peace and, above all, love. I would have difficulty losing the habit, and would doubtless stifle among you."

"It's said, Master, that you're our friend."

"Speak, shout, roar—your words will be wind until you have ballasted them with justice."

In speaking thus, rudely, the Enchanter hoped to spur the hearts of men; which did not fail to happen, since the crowd immediately replied: "Don't despise us too much, Seigneur Merlin."

"That's my greatest desire, but the tomb is no courtier."

"To see Merlin among us again, there is nothing we would not do. Only leave us the hope."

That word began to soften the Enchanter. Without thinking about it, he picked up his harp again, mechanically, and replied with a hint of excitement, after having run his fingers over the lowest strings:

"Has the noble Arthus with the snow-white beard not awakened?"

"No, Seigneur."

"That astonishes me, good people; but he will wake up soon in his power, although the truth is more belated than I was able to foresee. He will come back, I tell you, on his horse the color of a swan; the pommel of his sword will be resplendent in Scandinavia, and the point will be sharpened on the Pillars of Hercules. When that happens, don't fail to run to him promptly and kiss the hem of his garments and his magic buckler, which I forged with my own hands. That will be the signal for a great joy over almost all the earth."

"By what signs shall we recognize that the moment is near?" asked the nations.

"I will tell you," Merlin replied. "The teeth of wolves will be broken then. The very stones will speak and cry out, from France to England and from England to the Hesperides. The human heart will quiver like an overflowing lake.

Winged thoughts will soar overhead. Dead pity will be reborn in the bosoms of women; they will rediscover tears in their eyes to weep for those at whom they laugh today, poor orphans of justice. Then Orion, after having drawn his sword, will put it back in the scabbard."[155]

Among the peoples who interrogated Merlin there were men of all nations, all languages and all races. He spoke to each one in his native tongue, as was his custom, in order to persuade them all that he knew their veritable interests, better than they did themselves. To the inhabitants of the isles he spoke of the fay Alcina, to the French, the fay Morgane of Avalon, to the Germans the women of the waters of the Erl-King; to the African of the giant of the tempests, Adamastor; to the Spaniards of Don Juan de Tenorio; to the English of Robin Hood; to the Italians of the Hippogriff of Ferrara, on which he lavish the greatest praise; to the Rumanians of Dokia; to the Dalmatians of vampires; to the Serbs of Marko.[156]

If he was dealing with hunters, he talked about Oberon's horn; if to pastors, of farfadets; if to laborers and cattle-drovers of gnomes; if to fishermen and fish-eaters, of follets and undines; if to miners, of kobolds. In brief, he was able to accommodate himself to the customs, mores and industry of whoever addressed themselves to him. All were astonished to find him so knowledgeable as to their ancestry, their needs, their laws and their ways of life; they were filled with hope.

So," they said to him, "the fatherlands still means something to you, Seigneur Merlin. Even in the high spheres where you have acquired the habit of living, you have not forgotten the homelands?"

"At the word "homeland" Merlin's excitement suddenly died away. His heart burst, and then melted like wax. The prophet divested himself of the man of bronze he had donned, and, dropping his harp on to the ground, changed his tone and replied: "Tell me, good people, about sweet France, although she has been hard to me alone. I've seen many fatherlands, but that is the one, after all, that still pleases me the most, although she has denied me more than once."

"Forgive us," said the peoples, "but we are witnesses to the fact that she has never denied her enchanter Merlin."

"So be it!" Merlin said, "I would like to think so. Her children, it's said, have hearts that have changed to stone; the splendor of gold has dazzled and blinded them. Outrages, calumnies, villainies, banishments—that's the news I most often receive of them, but I'd willingly forgive them, because they call themselves French, and in spite of everything, I persevere in believing that the

---

[155] Quinet adds a note identifying this paragraph as a passage from his translation of the *Prophetiae Merlini*.

[156] Hermione's notes allege that legend dictates that people should come in pilgrimage to Merlin's green mound, but the source she cites is the *Orlando Furioso*, which hardly qualifies as legend.

sons of their sons will be better than their fathers, for they'll remember me. May I see them again, if only for a single day, with Viviane, in the company of the noble Arthus."

"It shall be," replied the crowd.

The Interred wiped a few tears from his eyes, and then he asked, with a simplicity that won all hearts, about his mother's tomb, the little field of his heritage, his house and his garden: whether it was true that the house was in ruins, whether a few stones remained, at least—and from there, passing on to other objects, he wanted to know whether Jacques had returned to his village and was prospering there, which peasants and cowherds were married, which widowed, which orphaned; whether the lower marches had been drained; whether there were many people trembling with the fever; whether the rye-field of the Crau had yielded well that year; whether the swallows were nesting in his window; whether the apple-tree he had planted in the garden of bees had borne fruit, and of what variety.

In sum, he did not forget anything in the world that could show that a good part of his heart still remained in the village: all things to which he received satisfactory responses. They admire the fact that that he could so easily change his tone, and that, even after having traveled the universe and the constellations, he was still familiar with the careers of the hamlet and the hemp-field. As he pronounced his final words, his voice trembled and his heart shivered. He would have liked to launch himself toward those who were listening—but in the blink of an eye, he changed his mind. Then, taking his leave of the multitude, he added:

"Go, good people. My only pain, believe me, is to see you leave in such great distress. May it not last long."

That said, the peoples withdrew; each felt fortified by Merlin's words, as if nourished on the marrow of oaks and lions.

VI

And know that the desolation of the Syrian and Egyptian people, when they had lost Adonis and Osiris, was nothing by comparison with the initial desolation of the peoples immediately after Merlin's disappearance. For a long time, nothing was seen but wandering kings, fallen princes, crowds in mourning, people beating their breasts, not in ceremonial grief, as at Egyptian festivals, but in real and agonizing dolor.

Everywhere, there were plaints of rusty armor, tearful moans, empires turned to dust; you might have thought it the death of a demigod.

Then you would not have recognized the vagabond nations that went in search of the Enchanter. If they had, at least, found one of his dispersed limbs, they would certainly have thought themselves saved, like an Egyptian on rediscovering the body, the head or the arm of Osiris. But of that, what appearance? No news, no vestige!

"What will become of us?" the nations had said to one another. "Where can he be buried? He was our joy, our support. Certainly, we shall die, to the last man, if he does not reappear."

Such had been the cry of human beings for a long time. You could easily believe, therefore, that the first reverberation of Merlin's harp was heard with delight all over the world; and, to be sure, there was no being, however petty or paltry, who did not rejoice in his soul, as for his own felicity. The bird-chicks in the depths of the woods peeps over the edges of their nests and said to one another: "Did you hear Merlin's harp?"—with which, all the nightingales began to sing, which they had not done for centuries.

Their soft spring-like voices arrived in the tenebrous orchard where Merlin and Viviane were at that moment.

"Listen, listen," she said to him. "They're there, over our heads."

Then, having taken the harp in her turn, she made it quiver under her fingers. To that which the nightingales heard, they responded as best they could, competing in seeking to duplicate it. And it was thus that they learned a quantity of songs that they have never forgotten since.

It is also necessary to know that Merlin, no longer differentiating between days and nights, had taken up his harp in the middle of the profound night, and that is the reason why nightingales love to sing their sweetest songs—those that they learned from Merlin and Viviane—at midnight, when all other beings are in repose.

BOOK TWENTY-TWO: FELICITY! FELICITY!

I

As he took possession of his sepulcher, Merlin made his joyous reentry even into the remotest provinces of that subterranean realm. He imposed upon himself the task of commencing the day by visiting his mute companions, the dead; and he maintained them in a radiant serenity that might have excited the jealousy of the living.

They're my guests, he thought. *I'm their guardian; they're confided to me. Who will take care of them, if not me?*

And like a host anxious for the slightest concerns of those sleeping under his roof, who does not rely on his servants, Merlin maintained the dead in flourishing health, by excavating vast galleries over their heads through which the matinal air of eternal auroras was engulfed; he brought crystalline, bubbling waters near to them, which bathed them perpetually with the silvery eco of uncreated springs.

If one of them had an open wound, he cured it incontinently by means of a balm that he cultivated himself in his funereal garden; and the injury, even if it was in the heart, closed without the sleeper waking up.

By I don't know what—the visage, the countenance, the attitude—he recognized those whose heads were still burdened by terrestrial cares; he raised them up in his own hands and replaced them, appeased on beds of moss.

To those who woke up exclaiming; "Where am I?" he replied: "Under my guard. You've woken up too soon. Great Arthus is still asleep."

If one of the dead began, by chance, to doubt his immortality, our Enchanter scolded him roundly. To remind him of it, he set down next to him a cup full to the brim, which was never drained, along with a crown of carbuncles that shone in the darkness. And all of their faces took on a majestic peace that they had never known, and were also more beautiful, with a beauty more correct than that in the visible world.

At the same place in the sepulcher there were also entire nations prematurely buried, of which he took the greatest care. Each of them reposed on an elevated platform, paneled with gold and perfumed with the scents of his orchard. Sparkling diamonds expelled the darkness from those regions. Neither decline nor corruption approached Merlin's guests. The worm of the sepulcher never entered into those dwellings.

Next to the buried peoples he had placed perfumed garments of linen and silk, some of them red, in accordance with habits, tastes and national costumes of each, in order that at the first signal they would be able to get dressed, and that none of them would be stopped by the fear of confronting the sun in the nudity of body and spirit.

There were even black horses in vast stables paved with mosaics, with smooth manes hanging down to their knees, all caparisoned in gold and scarlet, and chariots prepared in order that the nations, their leaders and their good servants could launch themselves forward more rapidly on the great day of awakening.

Sometimes, though, they mistook the dawn. In the utmost depths of their brazen sleep, can you see peoples getting up slowly and sadly, their eyes open and staring, charged with a leaden veil, like somnambulists? Look! There they go, emerging wanly from their couches. Can you see them putting on coats of mail, lacing spurs, setting baldric around their waists, brandishing swords, beating their shields, causing banners to flutter? Where are they now? Blades in hand in the darkness, they are going to mount up; they bump into one another. Their eyes are open and staring, but cannot see.

No cry emerges from their mouths; no clarion has sounded. The obscurity augments their fury. What subterranean combats they deliver, far from the daylight, blind, unknown, fratricidal, of which no poet has ever sung!

Visors lowered to augment the darkness, heart-sick, they do not hear the clash of their moist blades. Woe! Weep, my eyes, your cruelest tears. They slip in their vermilion blood; their eyes are open, but cannot see!

From no matter how far away he hears them, Merlin hastens. He has raised his hazel-branch. Immediately, breathless, they all return to their couches beneath their tombstones. Again, the night and the silence extend around them, and the truce of the dead is no longer broken by anyone. Weep, my eyes, your cruelest tears. Their eyelids are closed now.

II

In the labyrinth of the subterranean kingdom, can you hear a muffled groaning, like a man buried alive, whimpering? The man who lets that plaint escape is lying on his back; his breast rises and lowers alternately; with it trembles Mount Etna, which is crushing him and serves as his sepulchral stone.

As soon as the noise of Merlin's footsteps reaches him, he holds his breath momentarily in order to listen more carefully; then, turning his head effortfully in the direction from which help is coming, he says in a cavernous voice:

"You who seem to be the master of these subterranean regions—so many roads are known to you—and who, doubtless, have never seen those whom the sun illuminates, tell me whether the name of Enceladus has ever reached your ears, or whether they have succeeded in burying it with me. See how I am crushed unjustly beneath this ardent mountain. Meanwhile, above my head, on the summit shaded by pines, among the torrents of cooled lava, the Cyclops of Sicily, in order to mock me, is making his song and his pipe resonate night and day, all the way to the depths of the sea.; and the bounding flocks, and the sonorous forests, agitate their tresses; the cities of men fill up with sound, without a care for my pain—me, who carries all of them in my panting breast!"

"Be patient, good Enceladus," Merlin replied to him. "I recognize you by the mountain that is crushing you. I too carry in my breast mountains of dolor and forgetfulness. I have overturned them all by a great effort of my heart, so effectively that I'm free, as you see, in his subterranean empire, which is my heritage; it will be the same for you, if you maintain serene hope."

At these words, the worthy Enceladus felt consoled. Viviane wiped his brow, streaming with the sweat of the dead. Twice, he shook his head, and it shook the hills, the blue-tinted promontories, and the cities seated on his knees. His entire face lit up with a somber gleam of joy, as in the morning of his combat against the great gods. At the same time, he made a signal with his eyes and eyebrows, to indicate in the distance one of his companions.

Without interrogating him, Merlin raised his lamp in that direction; he perceived, at the place where its radiance was reflected, as the darkness fled, a man standing up, immobile—except that his shoulders and head were curbed, like those of men unloading a ship in the port of Marseilles. Blood was gushing from his forehead under the burden that was crushing him, and that dew was falling like rain all around him. With more impatience than his companion, he started shouting in an oppressed voice: "Hurry, if you're coming to relieve the shoulders of Atlas. I'm weary of carrying the world. It wouldn't take much for me to let it fall at my feet, even if Nemesis were to lash me eternally with his whip."

"Atlas," Merlin said to him, "I will take your burden on my shoulders, but only for an hour. In fact, you're maintaining the equilibrium poorly. Too many tilting States are going to collapse, if I don't come to your aid. See how you're inclining to that side, and how unsteady your foot is. Poor colossus, get your breath back for a while, and slake your thirst from this cup; it was given to me by Arthus, and it's full of the same wine that intoxicated Lancelot."

The sad Titan who was carrying the old world smiled, and his eyes devoured the beverage in advance. After having held out his silver-plated cup to him, Merlin took the world from Atlas' shoulders and placed it on his own. But he was not oppressed by it and would not consent to be bowed down. His head, especially, remained straight, raised toward the heavens, so that he resembled a joyful grape-gatherer who, after having filled his basket, is carrying his provision of grapes to the press. Even then he was a hundred times more carefree than grape-gatherers usually are.

"You see, friend," he said to Atlas, who was still holding the cup to his lips, long after having emptied it, "it's with the mind that I'm carrying the world, not with the body, so that my shoulders are not overburdened; neither the muscles nor the tendons of the arms are fatigued in any way, and the stance of the feet is controlled. Do the same in your turn, and the burden of the universe will certainly be lighter. But above all, debonair Titan, prevent from falling the peoples that you almost tipped over by holding them so low, faces to the ground. Here, imitate me, and stop whining."

"I'll try, Merlin," Atlas replied, that brief moment's respite having restored his strength—for he had sat down, his body curled up, on one of the boundary-markers of chaos, which chanced to be covered with moss in that place.

Having taken some nourishment and slaked his thirst, sufficiently rested, restored in his speech and relieved in his heart, with his head straighter and his feet steadier, his knees better braced, his arms tauter, his hands firmer and, above all, his mind clearer, his soul more determined, his hope renewed and his imagination enriched, he took the world once again on his broad shoulders; and you would have thought that he had never carried it for a single day, so fresh was his vigor.

In fact, the whole earth felt the Titan's encouragement and pleasure. Those who had felt closest to the abyss were encouraged, without knowing why. Many of those who were on the brink fell irrevocably into the gulf, and equilibrium was thus restored.

For as long as Merlin was within sight of Atlas he turned round continually to inform and encourage him.

"Good, Atlas! Courage, my Titan! You're leaning back a little too much. A little further forward, I tell you. Come on, then, old giant! Oh, now you're falling back into your old error..."

Already, however, these objurgations were lost in the distance of the sepulcher. Atlas, left alone, could no longer hear them.

III

That is how Merlin consoled the disenchanted worlds from the depths of the tomb, with the result that the sepulcher, which had previously been the scarecrow of humans, became their support and their joy. So pilgrimages, whether of entire peoples or mere individuals, were only to be expected. It even happened, many a time, that the Enchanter was importuned by the indiscreet appeals of the living—for he was then snatched from a reverie into which his entire soul was plunged, or a stroll beneath the sacred shade, or his chess game, which he no longer had any scruple about winning, since Viviane's brow had settled into eternal serenity.

He never preferred his pleasure to the repose of the living, however, and never made them wait when their voices appealed to him. As you can imagine, because of that, he never knew in his sepulcher the ennui or monotony that trail idleness after them. After having been interrupted by the petty passions, the common bonds, the malicious gossip and even by the sincere or exaggerated dolors of the living, he came back, with a new felicity, to the place where his beloved was waiting.

Theirs was not, therefore—understand this—an indolent existence. That is what it is necessary not to forget; otherwise, the entire moral of my story might be lost. Consoling worlds is not an unimportant occupation, and that was my hero's employment. Only afterwards came the long relaxations on the banks of springs, the semi-slumbers, the amorous whispers—in sum, everything that Mohammed has falsely promised his believers and that Merlin alone has tasted thus far, because he alone has merited it.

From the height of his balcony, between the eighth and twelfth hour, he regularly proffered his prophecies to the Eagle. He had the feeling that he was doing good, but in secret, it must be said, he quietly enjoyed his superiority over the living. As for other beings, he did not see any who could command him. That solitary joy had turned to pride.

It was interrupted, but only for one day. This is how it happened.

Viviane was spinning at her window, and dropped her spindle, which it amused her to hold and move back and forth over the abyss. She was gazing, at that moment, at black shadows that were reflected in the ripples of deep waters. When she hauled in the thread, she no longer found the spindle. Who had taken it? She leaned further over, and thought she saw a being with extended wings gliding over the somber lake. Perhaps it was Merlin's father passing by chance through that remote region in search of his son, tracing long circles, like a hawk in quest of its prey.

Imagine, if you can, Viviane's amazement, alarm and terror. Until then she had believed that she was alone with Merlin in his immense tomb; she had never seen a winged angel, a seraph, or any of the inferior beings that populate the Christian heavens. She lowered her long veil over her head and withdrew from the balcony. Unsteady on her feet, she went to rejoin her companion, and I swear to you that the warbler that has just perceived a merlin with its wings spread, and hides in the hedge of an orchard, would give a very feeble idea of Viviane's fear when she hid her face in Merlin's bosom.

"What's happened?" he exclaimed. "Who has been able to offend or threaten you, my better half? If you haven't found immutable peace here, where can we go in search of it?"

Viviane told him what she had just discovered. Immediately, he thought of his father, and felt gripped by terror himself at the idea that the King of Hell had found a way into his retreat.

"It might be an angel gone astray, trying to find a way out."

"What is an angel?" asked Viviane.

He told her. Again she exclaimed: "So we're not alone, even in the sepulcher! Where can we flee?"

"Beyond death. I sense that I have the power."

And, seeing Viviane's fear increasing, he feigned a confidence that he did not feel. Doubtless the stranger had not perceived her, withdrawn into the shadows of the tomb. Why, then, be frightened? They would not take a single step outside the marble hall of the funereal tower. Who would dare to attack them in that redoubt? Not even the prince of terrors.

In spite of these words, and others of the same sort, anxiety had entered into their dwelling. A vague terror was mingled with their sweetest joys. At the slightest breath of wind that blew in the courtyards or the alabaster alcoves, Viviane turned round and shivered. She thought she heard a rustle of silken wings. But what they feared did not arrive, and they ceased to think about it; and forgetfulness restored their former serenity, so much improvidence is there among human beings, even among enchanters.

IV

As soon as people had learned that it was possible to converse with Merlin through the tomb, adulations, venal promises, devious offerings, overt seductions, disguised gifts and smiles were all put to use to tempt and persuade him to return to the earth.

When the initial crowd had dissipated slightly he glimpsed, confusedly, a courtier named Gauvain,[157] who had been delegated to approach him by all that still remained of the old world.

"Can you hear me, Master Merlin?" asked the knight, making his sours resonate at the base of the tower.

"Very clearly, Messire Gauvain."

"And I can perceive your ceremonially embroidered mantle."

"Men of the court, will you never see anything but appearances?"

"How, then, were you, the wisest of men, able to fall into this ambush?"

"Because, Gauvain, I was foolish enough to love someone other than myself."

"Is it necessary to despair of seeing you again in the vast halls of King Arthus?"

"I am retained here by a bond that I would not break even if I could."

"What happiness can you have in that tomb?"

"My happiness, Gauvain, is greater than you think. It is that of struggling against injustice, of being submerged in Erebus and never crying: 'Pity!'"

---

[157] Gauvain [Gawain in Malory] has a slightly peculiar situation in the Arthurian documents because he is abundantly featured in the fragmentary manuscripts that Chrétien de Troyes left behind at his death, which were bundled together for copying, with the result that an incomplete account of the adventures of Gauvain was appended to the later and markedly different allegorical account of Perceval's encounter with the Fisher King, and thus features in published versions of the *Conte du graal*, even though it is perfectly plain to anyone but a scholar that it does not belong there.

"But what will become of the knights, the barons and the people of the court without Merlin?"

"Let them sleep. I can do nothing for them."

The knight Gauvain carried this response to the small number of barons who remained awake and standing in the tottering ruins of their castles.

As soon as the messenger was perceived in the distance the barons and courtiers called out from the height of the towers: "Is Merlin coming back?"

"He can't come back," the messenger replied.

All of them shed torrents of tears.

"We can clearly see," they murmured, "that our hour has come. We should have understood that when the noble Arthus fell into his magical slumber."

On which each of them withdrew; the courtyards became deserted, and even the ruins disappeared. All that remained anywhere was the occasional palace porter to say to passers-by: "Look! This is all that remains of noble Arthus. Everything finished thus when the powerful Merlin disappeared."

V

The news that Merlin's harp had resounded reached Jacques' ears on the fairground performers' stage. Although he was a trifle deaf, or at least hard of hearing, he distinctly heard the strings resonate himself at the moment when, after having buckled on his bread-porter's sword, he went running in response to the screams of Sister Anne to assault Bluebeard.

The blood rose to his face again. Without telling anyone, he left his companions there; drawn by the desire to hear his master's voice again, he hastened his steps to arrive at the foot of the funereal tower—but he dared not present himself until he was sure that the last courtiers had gone and that he would be alone, face to face, with the Interred.

Although he had not said anything yet, Merlin had already shivered at the approach of his servant, and, forgiving him for the thousandth time, magnanimous tears flooded his eyes, he had resolved in advance to keep quiet about Jacques final infidelity, fearing in his infinite bounty that the merited reproaches might be too bitter if they emerged from the tomb.

"Darn it! My master ensepulchered!" cried Jacques, sobbing.

"What, Messire Jacques," replied Merlin, gently. "Are you still talking in patois?"

"Where are you, my dear Master?"

"Here."

"I can't see you."

"Don't try, my friend; content yourself with hearing me."

"Speak louder," Jacques replied, cupping his hand around his ear.

"Know, friend, that my sole displeasure in this place is having to abandon you to your own sagacity. Your education, which I had attempted, is scarcely begun. Mistrust false enchanters, Jacques; they will come in large number, my son, and seek to exploit your weaknesses. They will promise to nourish you better than I did, but it will only be a lure. If you often had a hard life and bitter bread with me, it was because the times were bad. But I loved you from the bottom of my heart, and with a little patience, you would have seen better days. Oh, how I tremble to see you delivered to your own resources. At least, my son, don't fail to come to consult me here, every time your occupations permit. Don't attempt anything in the world without seeking my advice. You'll always find me as you've known me; the tomb, my dear friend, hasn't changed me at all. Provided that you follow my advice exactly, point by point, there's no need to despair of your self-sufficiency."

"Master," Jacques replied, "what kind of life can you lead in this tomb? Is it not too narrow for you?"

"Not at all. I've never been so free in all my life."

"Are you not lying on a hard surface there?"

"Not at all; my bed is soft and better prepared than when you made it yourself."

"Are you not suffering there from cold and ice?"

"No."

"Or heat?"

"Even less."

"And mosquitoes?"

"Not at all."

"Do you endure thirst there?"

"None."

"But hunger?"

"On the contrary; I'm fully sated. Don't ever believe, my friends, that hunger and thirst are the principal occupations of the dead, as they are of the living. There will be too much risk of our never seeing one another again if you don't keep a firmer hold on the information and, if I dare say so, the examples that I gave you in the kingdoms of Spain, not to mention elsewhere. You've often seen me nourish myself on nothing but mulberries and a few other berries, and I was happy. If I could do that when I was with you on earth, what can I not tolerate today? Don't worry any more, my friend, about my nourishment; it would even content you."

As he was speaking, Turpin and Prester John arrived; they knelt down, and Merlin saluted them with his hand; without interrupting himself, he recommended his servant to them tenderly: "There he is, friends; I bequeath him to you, for your share of the heritage. Sustain him. He's so weak, in spite of his vigorous muscles. Above all, enlighten him. He's so short-sighted that I fear that he might become completely blind."

Both swore that they would do their best to assist Jacques, still orphaned.

"We can't replace you, Merlin," they said. "To hope so would be vanity. Don't worry, though. We possess nothing that is not his, in the spiritual as well as the material sense. Adieu! And may peace be with you in your sepulcher!"

With these words, Prester John stood up in order to bless the immense tomb. Turpin, on both knees, said his prayers.

After that farewell, Jacques, his heart slightly less anguished, returned to take his place at Arthus' bedside. What was his astonishment to see that the king had disappeared!

"Where has he gone?" he said. He reproached himself a thousand times over for not having appointed a watchman to guard him.

Doubtless, he thought, *unless the wolves have devoured him, King Arthus has awakened; he's asked for something to eat or drink and, not finding anyone to serve him, has got up. God knows where he'll have gone in search of subsistence.*

With that he set out to look for him the surrounding area, searching the meadows, the ravines, the vicinity of the ponds and marshes, and the ground, not neglecting woods, thickets, hedges, ditches, orchards, clearings and tree-stumps beating the bushes and peering into everything.

He eventually discovered the monarch, on the sacred isle of Avalon, more deeply asleep than before, at the entrance to a grotto from which a spring emerged, suddenly swollen my snow-melt. The king of kings had encountered that obstacle and had not been able to get over it.

It was there that Jacques resumed his long vigil. But of all those who went past that place on their way to work, there were few who did not turn round to mock him. They said to him: "What are you doing, poor Jacques? What are you waiting for there? Have you lost your mind, watching over a dead man?"

"He's not dead," the good man replied. "He's going to wake up one day."

The mockery of rustics and townspeople took away his courage to say any more; without knowing what to add, he began to weep. Those solitary tears, viewed from Heaven, redeemed his infidelities.

VI

When the world had finished drawing away, Merlin started to reflect; and every day, in his tomb, he grew in wisdom. "Even in the bosom of love," he said to himself, "A regular occupation is necessary; if not, the heart devours itself, and the flame is consumed by flame." That was especially necessary at the times when Viviane crossed the threshold that he could not cross. What could he do during those mortal hours of isolation?

The idea occurred to him of writing in his sepulcher. And, in fact, it was thus that he became for the French what the sage Hermes had been for the Egyptians. For he composed in his tomb the sketch and the plan of all the famous books for which French authors would later attributed the merit to themselves.

The walls of his tomb were marble and granite; he covered those vast walls with his writing, and if many authors have acquired an immortal glory, let us confess that their difficulty has not been great, since the best of them had only to copy the works of Merlin, silently engraved by him on the rock that served him as a tomb.

Let us also recognize, here, the character of our Enchanter. Although he could hardly imagine that any human eye would ever see those works buried with him, he nevertheless devoted the greatest care to them, as if they had been made for submission to the judgment of humans. The truth is that he worked for the satisfaction of his own conscience, not out of vanity.

In any case, finding great difficulty in contenting himself, when one of his works was finished, he took Viviane into the room in which he had written it, in beautiful cuneiform characters, somewhat similar to those at Persepolis, if not better molded. There he made her read it slowly, weighing every word, and every syllable, ever ready to defer to her advice.

Before she had spoken, he was the most modest and the most submissive of beings. Once Viviane had approved the work, nothing in the world could have led Merlin to change a single line.

"I don't know," he said, whether these works will ever be perceived by humans. I've written them for you by the light of the enchanted lamp, sand truly, I haven't spared the oil. If they've amused Viviane for a single instant; if they've made her forget the abode of death, Merlin is abundantly recompensed."

Then, the next day, if it rained or snowed—for that sometimes happened, but without any breath of wind—or if he were alone, he began again to engrave another work, so determinedly that all the columns of the vaults, the florid pinnacles, the door-panels and the plinths ended up being filed—and it was thus, and not otherwise, that all the works about which the French boast to other nations were composed, in an eternal serenity.

Good authors, full of submission to the enchanter, had only to copy and transcribe, on parchment or on paper, what Merlin had written on stone; and the only reproach that I have to address to them is that of having disguised the larceny more than is perhaps appropriate. In the end, though, the earth reveals its secrets.

Bad authors, on the contrary, carried away by a puerile pride, have wanted to do otherwise than the Enchanter, being men of noise and smoke, who would have thought themselves dishonored if they had only been my hero's copyists. And although they have certainly had knowledge of his works—I don't know how; perhaps by virtue of some infidelity on Jacques' part—they have mixed so many inventions of their own heads into them that they have succeeded in spoiling the original, with the result that their vanity has doomed them.

At any rate, every time you find an immortal page, say boldly: "That's pillaged from Merlin." Every time you find a work that is affected, or ridiculous, or simply insipid, also say: "That's what comes of wanting to correct the Enchanter."

The first work that he attempted, as soon as his eyes had got used to the dazzling light of his lamp, was in verse. He filled three hundred and forty-five rooms with it, from the floor to the vault. It was a great poem in which he related, with a relaxed head, everything that he remembered about Arthus' court and his knights. He wrote those poems in the morning, in a single breath, without crossing anything out. Viviane, who wanted to encourage him, refrained from telling him that they were a trifle overlong.

"It's a rough draft," Merlin said, adding. "I'll develop it..."

"Others," he resumed, perhaps with too much conceit, "will be praised more highly than me for detached pieces; their versification will be more applauded than mine. Yet others will carry off the prizes for songs and odes, although I too have occasionally knocked on the door of hymns, closed since the worthy Pindar, but they will find it difficult to refuse me the honor of having taken on great subjects, composed vast ensembles, followed the threads of immense labyrinths, borne the burden of bold inventions—in sum, attempted the paths that demanded not a momentary Pindaric flutter but an indefatigable wing, to travel without wearying the whole epic field. All that I fear, Viviane, on reflection, is that our French people have little taste for vast and noble compositions—in truth the most difficult aspect of our art—in which earth and heaven are mingled. Their windswept brains have difficulty embracing such vast horizons, and if my works are revealed to them some day, I foresee that these poems will be the ones they esteem the least, or even that they will let all the honor of them be stolen by other peoples, for whom, on my word, I have not intended them."

And you will notice here that none of Merlin's presentiments have been more fully confirmed, since the French, while possessing Merlin's poems of chivalry in stone and in tablets of granite, have allowed the best of them to be stolen, under their noses, by Ariosto and Cervantes, an Italian and a Spaniard, without the slightest desire for reprisals.[158]

The thought that his best works would be misunderstood by his own people, by his nearest and dearest, almost saddened Merlin's soul more than once.

---

[158] Perhaps Malory, as a Briton/Breton, is exempted from this charge of theft, having some presumed entitlement to the materials; it is, however, slightly odd that the parodist Cervantes is cited rather than the works to which he was reacting, as Quinet was certainly not unaware of *Amadis de Gaula*, the best-known of the imitative epic romances of the 14th century, even though he only mentions one character therefrom, and none at all from its companion-piece *Palmerin de Inglaterra* [Palmerin of England]. Perhaps he thought that they had no right to set their imitative fictions in Gaul and Britain.

But he would have judged himself unworthy even of one of Viviane's smiles if he had given access in his heart to sadness engendered by vanity.

"I'm not writing," he whispered to himself in subterranean places, "to make a noise, or even for renown. Otherwise, I ask you, what would have prevented me from doing it before the light of the sun was taken away from me? I'm writing for the truth; it can see me in this gulf and judge me. Let's continue, then, as if we had the applause of worlds in our favor."

With that, Merlin, indefatigably, got back to work, smiling; and you can take it for granted that he quite forgot that he was buried.

When that work was finished, he started on two others that were to chase away the melancholy of his tomb forever. That day, the Enchanter was perfectly joyful. Everything succeeded as he wished. He wanted to call those two works *Gargantua* and *Pantagruel*.[159]

"Why those names?" Viviane asked.

"In memory of two good companions I left on the earth."

Furthermore, those two individuals had grown prodigiously, as happened naturally to all the shadows that passed through his sepulcher. Their laughter resounded like that of a Cyclops in a cavern, or like the whinnying of a centaur drunk on wild grapes; and it is a fact that, during the composition of that work, the centaur guarding his herds came several time to ask: "What are you making there, Seigneur Merlin?" and that Merlin replied: "A book to rejoice the human heart," on which the centaur said, with a plaintive whinny: "Put in a good word too for the centaurs and the poor monsters eaten away by melancholy in the depths of solitudes," to which Merlin replied: "Don't worry—I won't forget anyone; just bring me a bunch of those ripe grapes reddening there on the vine."

And I beg you to believe that in that lapidary work, in which all creation is gripped by mad laughter, there was then none of that monkish ordure that has been added subsequently, by the hand of the living, to *Gargantua* and *Pantagruel*. It was then the drunkenness of a sage purified by the sepulcher.

In any case, even if he had wanted it, Viviane would have been opposed to anything deceptive, begging for human applause by flattering their impurities and ignominies. "Imitate the ingenuity of the Cyclops by all means," she said, "but don't descend to the level of the gluttonous monk." Then their naïve laughter resonated all the way to the center of the globe. Even Hell heard that laughter several times, without knowing where it was coming from.

On another occasion, it happened that an ant got into the tomb. Those creatures are curious. It was followed by a bee with a beautiful golden corsage, and the Enchanter heard them distinctly conversing between themselves.

---

[159] Hersart's *Myrdhinn* also has a long quasi-narrative section featuring these Rabelaisian characters, whose connections to the Arthurian mythos he exaggerates somewhat.

"Isn't it a great injustice that the age Merlin is only occupied with humans? Is there only wisdom among them?"

Such were their bitter comments. Those simple words caused Merlin to reflect at length. He profited from everything; he felt the spur. The tiniest insects, with ruby yes, instructed him in his art.

"They're right," he admitted, privately. "It's high time to repair such injustice."

That simple circumstance, which someone else would not even have noticed, caused him immediately to compose and write a first book of fables.

Never, it must be admitted, had his verses been more subtle or more natural, not to mention that they did not recoil before any stride. Sometimes they were grandiose, as if they spanned the whole world, and suddenly they were marching as if on the feet of ants or crane-flies, or launching themselves upwards and perching, as if on the membranous wings of cicadas. Sometimes there was a breath of spring, like that of the great forests in the month of May, sometimes a brief, impetuous note like that of a quavering blue-tit on the edge of its nest.

In brief, Merlin became the inventor of a fortunate mixture of great and small verses that dispelled monotony, marvelously imitating the harmonious confusion of all beings: the eternal dialogue of the elephant and the mite, the star and the pearl.

"What do I hear?" exclaimed Viviane, who arrived just as they reached the conclusion. "It's for me, most amorous of sages, that these verses are made? Repeat them, friend. Murmur them again. Confess that you were thinking about me while engraving them around that colonnette." And she kissed Merlin on the lips.

It must be admitted that Merlin, true poet as he was, had only been thinking about his subject. He was entirely penetrated by the honeyed scent of flowers, the sagacity of ants. That's what he was celebrating at that moment—but he did not have the courage to disillusion Viviane, nor to lie overtly. Without replying, they looked at her with an expression that meant: *All my thoughts are inclined toward you.*

He never obtained more pleasure from anything than from those little works, which were born without difficulty and almost without reflection beneath his fingers. He had soon composed a hundred books of them. And there was an unprecedented joy, in almost all the worlds, when the beings who were the most unknown and the most ungraspable, by virtue of their smallness, and the most unnamed, learned by chance that they had their poet.

"We too shall finally have our immortality, then," said the ephemera.

"Do you know," said the butterflies, "that that glory, of a hundred colors and a thousand eyes, was really due to us?"

"I'd almost despaired, for having waited so long," replied a gnat. "I've worn away one of my two wings."

"I've almost lost my voice," replied a melancholy bullfinch.

"Itys! Itys! Itys!" added the nightingales. "Something told us that winged genius would finally have its day. That's why we never lost courage, even in the middle of the night, when no one was listening to us and the whole world seemed to be asleep."

Thus, that work of Merlin's received the applause of all the worlds, with the exception of a few serpents with necks swollen with envy, who insulted it with their hisses. Our La Fontaine had the intelligence to copy Merlin word for word and to cite him. I believe, however, that in the Enchanter's work humans did not appear so frequently, and every creature had retained its native language more accurately. I believe it, I said—I wouldn't swear to it.

The season having changed, Merlin invented a host of other works. When the thought of his father suddenly came back to him in dark and stormy days, he composed vast tragedies and declaimed them in a sinister voice that was further swelled by the echoes of the sepulcher. The French extracted a few tirades therefrom, but they left the greater and more pathetic part, the part in which death itself seemed to reveal its secrets; none of them dared follow Merlin into that abyss. And that was where they were greatly mistaken, for they only took, so to speak, half of Merlin into their tragedy. That is why it still seems lame among them, no matter what effort they once made to reconcile themselves on that point with the Enchanter, so true is it that wanting to correct him is the most imprudent of human vanities.

Perhaps because of the distance there was between him and the living, only any longer able to glimpse him through ostentatious deaths, he also exaggerated the truth in the tragic slightly. But he grasped the natural again in the comic, to the point of surpassing himself; not being able, either, to tolerate virtue being duped. While he loved humans, he saw better than anyone else in the world how perfectly ridiculous they are.

"Their ridiculousness," he was accustomed to saying, "is so obvious, so blatant, that it's impossible to forget it once one has caught a glimpse of them."

He amused himself innocently, therefore, in counterfeiting the vices of the living, their grotesque ugliness, their intolerable hypocrisies, their vile avarice, their hatred, their comical inability to enjoy any possession, their risible self-importance and, most of all, their pretentions.

"My God!" he cried. "How glad we are only to be able to see all that now from the distance of the tomb!"

Playfully, he made, in that fashion, an almost complete representation of human life, at least such as he remembered it. Make no mistake; you would have thought you were witnessing the reality. He even wanted to have his works performed, and built for that purpose a little stage lit by artificial light. For his part, though, he did not want a mask.

Never were such masterpieces seen, with the sole reservation that the declamation left something to be desired; Merlin's was a trifle muffled, and Viviane's a little eccentric. One sensed that death alone could have divine and published thus all the mysteries of life; and no less astonishing, after having laughed at the vices of the living, one was more inclined to pity them than hate them.

All those plays were engraved in granite, with predilection, by Merlin's own hand, which also drew large masks on the capstones ornamenting the pillars, in order to give a better idea of the characters. It was there that Molière rediscovered them, all speaking, and he did not take the trouble to change anything about them, save for a few names and costumes, in order better to disguise the larceny.

In any case, it required nothing less than our Enchanter's experience to unveil the secrets that humans were most skilled in hiding. Anyone else would certainly have failed, and without the oil that he renewed more than three times in the marvelous lamp, it would probably have been impossible for him to read, in the depths of hearts, so naturally were they filled with shadow of duplicity.

Meanwhile, Merlin had become pensive. He was afraid of becoming too serious; he relaxed in lighter works, frivolous in tone, among which were fairy tales, and *Zadig*, which he once engraved on a cameo of Viviane. What, *Zadig*? Yes, *Zadig!* Have I not said that Merlin was the son of the Incubus? How could his genius not have retained something of the paternal blood? It's here that his genealogy was betrayed, with evidence. It's even said that he subsequently borrowed his father's claw to write *Candide*.

Admire, in that regard, my hero's modesty, which never sought its recompense other than in the eyes of his heart's beloved. As we have said, he wrote all these works in the shadows, leaving the glory of them to others, without claiming his share. He was very different in that regard from Hermes, who also composed, single-handedly, the works of the Egyptians, but who collected all their fruits, since no one on the banks of the Nile would have dared to steal his renown by copying his works and attributing the honor to himself—in contrast to what is done among us routinely and with impunity. The most intrepid thieves and plagiarists—the Rabelais, the Poquelins,[160] the Voltaires and many others who only love in the marrow and substance of Merlin—are the most honored among us. Something assuredly as punishable as it is scandalous! What have they done, those illustrious authors, who have brazenly transcribed the writing of Merlin, being careful never to name him or cite him? Nothing that we could not do ourselves, in our turn—and I certainly see no greater shame for our nation and nothing that better demonstrates, as others say, its vanity and frivolity.

Furthermore, I suspect that even in this century, among our contemporaries, that depredation of Merlin's works is continuing, without encountering any obstacles. I'm ready to denounce our men of prey pitilessly, unless they confess the plagiarism in advance and disarm justice by means of a prompt and generous confession. Even you, my brother, who are repairing the old tapestry of the his-

---

[160] Poquelin was Molière's patronymic.

tory of France, I will not spare, unless you declare that, in the dead of night, entering like a hawk into Merlin's sepulcher, you have stolen his finest thoughts.[161]

Many names celebrated until now would perish. I know that, but what does it matter? Even I—yes, even I—have often been tempted to steal from my own hero. I declare it; I admit it. It would have been easy for me, so frequent were my opportunities. What didn't I do it? Because I feared being discovered pillaging a tomb. In consequence, a little timidity, and doubtless more than one error, as you, dear reader, have been able to perceive. That's my confession. Make your own, I beg you, in good faith.

Why, anyway, be astonished that those works have easily delighted the world? A great marvel, in truth! First of all, they came from a professional enchanter. Consider that Merlin never had any lack of time; that meditation was much easier for him than for us; that he never worked for love of money or the need to make a living; that, in that regard, he had absolutely nothing to fear. So many favorable circumstances for weighing one's ideas and one's syllables at leisure! When will such favorable circumstances present themselves again? Probably never.

In addition, no need to flatter the taste, the depravity and the caprice of a reader—you, Reader, are the only exception—who might well never be encountered in such a remote place. He did not court generations who would, I dare say, seem somewhat ephemeral to him. He towered over his audience, or rather, never gave it a thought. Had he finished a work? No rest! He composed another, in an entirely different genre, glad a thousand times over of it had been able to disconcert Viviane, but maintaining her in perpetual surprise. And all that without effort, as a game. For what he feared most of all was the pedantic. Not to mention that so many magnificent or gracious works, which still nourish all the peoples today—an aliment that often replaces bread—have been put into the world in the midst of the most perfect serenity, like a gauntlet thrown down to the threat of the tomb.

Whoever you are, have no doubt that there still remains a great deal to pillage in that sepulcher. I can affirm it, having seen with my own eyes that quantity of works that I have been too conscientious to steal. But since the world gives me so little credit for that reserve, curse it! In future, I shall be less discreet—for age, it's said, removes scruples—and I warn you now, honestly and solemnly, in order that, if necessary, you can post guards, spies, men-at-arms, bailiffs, policemen and halberdiers, if you still have any, to stand watch around the tomb.

---

[161] Michelet, to whom this sentence is addressed, did prompt someone to say of him that no historian had ever cared less for accuracy, and said of himself that "I have drunk too deep of the black blood of the dead." If that is not tantamount to an admission, what is?

If you so much as ask me irritating questions, I will even confess that the present work is entirely copied from one of Merlin's columns, situated at the back of the peristyle, on the left as you enter the sanctuary. You'll recognize it by the fact that it's made of pure, flawless emerald. That confession, of course, shouldn't be used against me. I've given an example here of a veracity that will, I fear, have far too few imitators.

Will plagiarists ever exhaust the profundities of that sepulcher? Will the day come when all the beauties it contains have been pillaged, to the very last line? I doubt it, having scanned at my ease the innumerable pages, stuck to one another in the most orderly fashion, like sheets of slate in the bosom of mountains. I estimate that all the scribes and pen-wielders in the land—they are, merciful God, more numerous nowadays than the grains of sand in the desert—working eighteen hours a day for twenty centuries would scarcely exhaust three quarters of the text, and that's only the prose. "Is that credible?" you might say. I don't know, but it's a fact, and that's enough for me. Do you see, then, what a single vision of love can accomplish in a tomb?

VII

Meanwhile, Turpin had retired to a bare mountain scattered with hyssop flowers, into the ruins of an old castle of rust-colored bricks, of which he had made a dwelling quite suitable for a man like him, accustomed, as I've said, to living amid foxes and eagles. He rarely went out of that refuge, and was beginning to feel a great pity for the world.

New generations passed rapidly at his feet, as dry and light and icy as winter leaves, about which he did not want to know anything. More often than not he did not even ask their names, or only did so in order to disfigure it at his whim when inscribing it in his illuminated book. So he hardly ever took the trouble to go down the spiral path to see their faces at close range. He knew that his master's prophecies were being accomplished, slowly and irresistibly, and that was sufficient for him. As patient as before, but curbed by age, he wrote at distant intervals, in the same Gothic script, the little that he learned from the migratory birds, increasingly frightened by the collapse of peoples and things.

His ennui increasing and his hand trembling, he wrote entirely in abbreviations. For the death of a nation he put a cross, for that of an empire a dash, for that of a hero, such as the great Charles or Roland, a large dot. Often, he even erased that when people became too proud. Then nothing remain of an entire mutinous people but an ink-smudge.

Every day, at sunrise, Jacques brought him a bowl of milk, a little brown bread, and then chatted for a few minutes while searching the dew with the recluse.

"What news?" Turpin asked.

418

If Jacques had heard a leaf tremble or quiver in the wood, or the piping and tender voice of a goldfinch, iridescent on a black larch, he replied: "I've heard Arthus' footsteps on a leaf. He's going to wake up! He'll come back tomorrow, accompanied by Merlin and Madame Viviane."

When the next day arrived, Jacques reappeared with another item of news of the same kind.

Turpin refrained from dissuading him. "Let's hope so," he replied. "I know now that hope is more necessary to a man than bread."

"And even more than ink," added Jacques, putting water in the colossal inkwell.

"That's true, my son. I'd never have believed it!"

In the meantime, the world became increasingly dull and morose.

VIII

In the same era, or shortly afterwards, Viviane gave birth to a child, who proved to be the most beautiful that had ever been seen, for he was more beautiful than the son of a summer dream. What should they call him? Twenty names were alternately proposed and defended: Formose, because of his beauty; Lazare, because of the sepulcher; and also the pet name of Almus, by which he had been saluted while still in his mother's womb. It was the first quarrel in the sepulcher, neither of them wanting at first to give way to the other. Finally, they both yielded at the same time. They called him Merlin, after his father.

Then the nightingales that had nested in the tomb in order to hear Merlin's harp at closer range began to sing next to the cradle, and these were the notes that they varied infinitely:

"Merlin's child is born! Flowers and stars rejoice! He will be greater than his father!

"Leave him to grow in solitude; that is where his silvery voice will resound most clearly.

"He will be greater than his father. But we, faithful troupe, will always remember Merlin the Enchanter."

He was the first infant born in a tomb, so I shall leave you to imagine how his parents made a fuss of him, in such a manner as to spare him all the bad impressions that a sepulchral environment might impart. Certainly, there was never so much joy under the open sky as appeared then in that subterranean place, the mere thought of which makes people shiver.

The good Merlin was radiant, and I have no need to say that he forgot his books and his harp in order only to occupy himself with the new-born. He took him on his knees, kissed him and said to him aloud, while rocking him: "Since I've been so easily able to accustom myself to the light of the tomb, I who saw the sun in all its glory, what will this child born in the sepulcher do? Assuredly, he'll never regret what he has never seen."

And it was an admirable thing to see that child growing older in the midst of the shadows of death, not even suspecting that there might be another world and another light.

At the first cry he uttered, humans were greatly astonished to hear an infant's wails coming from underground. They gathered together and, summoning Merlin with the blast of a trumpet, said to him: "Seigneur Merlin, since when has the tomb given birth?"

Merlin replied: "Since I've been living in it." Picking up his nursling, he carried him on to his balcony, from which he showed him to the people.

They could not see him, but they could hear his whimpering, similar to that of a fox-cub emerging from his den for the first time by night, and going to seek nourishment in a dovecot. They did not know whether to smile or be afraid.

Merlin, waving the rattle with which he appeased the new-born's tears, reassured the timid. "Come on, good people, rejoice and have no fear! Can't you hear the rattle? Since the child, who is barely two days old, can laugh and amuse himself in the tomb, must the place not be a hundred times more pleasant than you think?"

"It must be," the replied, and sounded their bagpipes, their buffalo-horns and their sambucas. They struck their shields and rang all the bells. The noise of the corybants at the birth of Jupiter in the cavern in Crete was merely a cicada's song by comparison.

Soon, Turpin came down from his mountain. "Is it true that the tomb has given birth?"

"Nothing is truer," Merlin replied, for a second time. "See for yourself."

"Have you baptized him?"

"Yes, of course."

"Where?"

"In the river Ocean, which emerges from the earth before my threshold."

In the meantime, Jacques had gone to fetch a few small birds that he nourished in a cage: blue-tits, linnets, yellowhammers, greenfinches, bullfinches and chaffinches. He offered them to the new-born and introduced them easily through a crack in the sepulcher. Merlin took them gently by the two wings and placed them at the child's feet, who smiled his first smile at those bewildered creatures, unknown in the world where he was; and take my word for it that not a single day passed without there being a celebration in Merlin's tomb.

IX

If my hero's education had been mixed, I dare say that his son's was accomplished, but circumstances contributed to that. Is not education in the tomb the best of systems? No deadly examples to keep away, no imprudent speech or coarse language on the part of a crowd that cannot always be avoided; a silence that commands respect; hours that are slightly monotonous but nevertheless well filled. Perhaps a little too much curiosity with regard to invisible things; that's the only inconvenience.

And it was a spectacle that would have delighted you, to see Viviane sitting on the ground, suckling that son of the tomb, hanging on to her teats. The good Merlin, standing next to her, looked at both of them with an infinite ecstasy. "That one, at least," he said, "will escape the false enchanters. He won't be stopped by the obstacles that have shackled me at every step, and which I've only half-vanquished. If my paternal instinct hasn't blinded me strangely, he'll go further than me, and without much difficulty; for after all, even though my career hasn't been all that it promised to be, my works can't fail to be useful to one who must bear my name. It's always useful to have a father who has cleared a path for you. The future is infinitely easier."

On hearing these words, Viviane could not help smiling, and that smile illuminated everything around her.

Veritably, Merlin would have liked his son never to hear mention of humans, or at least to delay it as long as possible. But how could that painful subject be avoided? When he conversed with the living, he could not entirely hide it from the child, who once asked him: "Father, who are you talking to?"

"With humans."

"And what are humans?"

"Nasty shadows that pass by the foot of the wall and whisper for a moment, before disappearing."

Another time, the child heard Viviane mention the sun. "What's the sun?" he asked.

His father explained to him, awkwardly, that it was a small lamp that remained suspended for a few moments over the heads of humans.

"What! Their lamp doesn't light them all the time, like ours?"

"No, my son. Half the time, it hides."

"Oh Father, how sad that world must be!"

"That's truer than you can imagine, my son."

By means of that conversation and a few others of the same sort, he had no difficulty in giving Formose the saddest idea of the world of the living. Formose could scarcely imagine humans in any other way than by analogy with the bats that he had occasionally glimpsed fluttering and swooping around the enchanted lamp.

How profitable it would have been for you to listen to all the instruction that chills received from his parents! Soon, Merlin was able to wander with him in the forest. He had the centaur go with them, and the two of them taught the child to draw a bow and play the lyre, in which he succeeded marvelously. Then Viviane appeared unexpectedly, she taught him to collect the simples that cure wounds.

"What wounds?" asked the child.

"The wounds that cause death, my dear son."

"Death! What's that?"

"Immediately, Viviane and Merlin perceived that they had retained the language of the old world. They composed another, richer and more sonorous, and especially more winged. But often, whatever they did, they fell back into the old one, whose purest accent they had preserved. And thus they gave their beloved son a few vague obsolete ideas that they would have done better to hide from him forever."

Meanwhile, the nightingales sang, in the silence of the sepulcher:

"Merlin's child is born. Flowers and stars rejoice.

"Precious stones, sparkle in the necklace of the night.

"The child will be greater than his father; but we, faithful troupe, will always remember Merlin the Enchanter."

BOOK TWENTY-THREE: THE CONVERSION OF HELL

I

One day, Viviane was sowing fields of narcissi and wild strawberries on the edge of the forest. A rustling in the leaves became audible, and she shivered to see emerging from a clump of oaks the being that she had already seen once before. He was disguised, at the moment, as an old prince, who seemed to have gone astray while hunting. In one hand he held a heavy pike, and in the other a spindle.

She would have liked to run away, but she did not have time. She called Merlin's name, but speech expired on her lips.

"Is this beautiful golden spindle yours?" said the stranger, as he approached. "I found it over there in the valley, under that weeping ash-tree."

"Thank you, Monseigneur, it's mine."

"Where am I, my beautiful child?"

"In Merlin's tomb."

"It seems to me, Mignonne, that I've met you once or twice in the moonlight, at Oberon's court."

"I beg your pardon, Seigneur," said Viviane, not daring to contradict the stranger overtly.

"Was it in the company of Titania or Morgane, then?"

"Neither. I've only seen a court in the home of my godmother, Diana of Sicily."

"That's it! I have it!" exclaimed Beelzebub. "But what does it matter? So young, so beautiful, and already in a tomb?"

"This tomb is Merlin's."

"Look at yourself, my beauty, in the mirror of this lake. Have you never seen yourself?"

"A hundred times," Viviane replied.

"It's a throne you need, not a sepulcher. Follow me, both of you; I'll make you both kings."

"We're kings here, Seigneur."

"Well, then, you'll be gods!"

At these words, Viviane took the stranger for some prince who had gone mad, and fled like a hind toward Merlin.

The king of Hell followed her, clicking his teeth, and talking to himself: "It's one last proof. What does it mean? I'm no longer obeyed by my own. My gaze would no long even fascinate a kobold's Eve or the fiancée of a gnome in the paradise of the fays. So, gee-up to my son's house! I'm old. Who respects old age? I no longer create; I no longer invent. I imitate; I copy. All that I've just said I said, word for word and a hundred times better, in Eden, at the beginning of things. And how I was obeyed then, at the slightest glance, without talking! There's nothing sadder than an old disenchanted demon. Mocked today all the way to the sepulcher, and doubtless by the earthworms. Come on, it's too much! Hell is on the way out!"

II

As soon as Viviane had rejoined Merlin and shown him the stranger who was trailing after her, the Enchanter exclaimed: "It's my father! Something told me it wouldn't be long before he appeared. Oh, how curbed and changed he is! Pity grips me on seeing him so defeated. Can I refuse him my threshold? Let's go down and see what he wants."

"Oh, my son," said the Ancestor, "it's true, then, that you haven't disowned me? You're the sole being nowadays who looks at me kindly..."

"Let's forget how we parted, Father," Merlin said. "The tomb has enlightened me. I see things with more impartiality today."

"Good! I no longer hold a grudge, my son, and don't have anything against you. Just play your harp for me a little, as long as it doesn't resemble David's melodies. If you knew how long it's been since I heard music! Good! More! Play that tune again! Truly, I'm getting better listening to it."

Although there was perhaps a little irony in those last words, the good Merlin did not fail to draw the best chords from his instrument, principally the most touching he could find.

Let's give him that pleasure, he thought. *He's so unhappy.*

"I'm thirsty," said the father of the damned. "No one, thus far, has wanted to give me a glass of water."

Immediately, Viviane went to draw fresh water from the edge of the torrent, and presented it to her guest in a bronze urn. He slaked his thirst with a feverish ardor. After that she went to prepare a meal like those customarily prepared for the Feast of the Dead. Merlin and his father were left alone.

"Is it true, then, my son, that one can be happy?" asked the master of Hell.

"As you see, Father."

"Indeed! But assuredly, you're the only happy being in creation. I've traveled it in its entirety; I've found no one but you who praises your fate."

"Mine is felicity itself."

"You'll make me jealous, my son. How, then, do you conserve this inalterable repose? Undoubtedly, my son, you owe it, in great measure, to being retrenched from the mass of the living. It's so long since I've slept, my poor Merlin! Sleep! Oh, what bliss! I'd give an empire for an hour's sleep. It's those infernal insomnias that have hollowed out my cheeks, you see. Give me a herb to help me sleep. I alone, in the entire universe, am always awake. The gods often sleep."

As he finished speaking he wiped away the burning sweat that was streaming over his brow. In the meantime, little Formose, who had been frightened at first, gradually drew nearer. In his hands he was carrying a small nest of birds of paradise; he put them in the Ancestor's hands. The Ancestor accepted them; he had a momentary temptation to stifle them, but—a singular thing!—he dared not do it. He returned them to the child with a smile like that of a Cyclops who has just discovered a warblers' nest in the depths of the woods.

"This is your son!" he said.

"Yes," replied Merlin.

"He resembles his grandfather. Certainly, these family joys aren't to be disdained. When I was very small, I had hair like him, that beautiful red-tinted golden blond. Does he already like poking the fire, and making a toy out of a witch's broom?"

"He'd do nothing else if I let him."

"Good! I recognize my blood there. Why oppose him?"

"Why don't you come, Father, and share this family life with us? If you want, we can live together?"

With that, the good Merlin, with an expansion that did more honor to his heart than his perspicacity, waxed lyrical on the subject of the merits of the family. It alone soothed all ills; it even tamed monsters. Cacus, Polyphemus and Caliban had yielded to its gentleness. What has prevented the demon from doing likewise? Far from humans, his hatreds would calm down. Forgetting the wickedness of creatures, he would forget his wrath, for, undoubtedly, the evil that he had done or tried to do was only an exaggeration of good.

There was such a great desire on Merlin to be reconciled with his father that he permitted himself this sophism: "After all," he concluded, "why not try a little of our kind of life, Father? You won't have any shortage of space here. If you want, you'll have the whole of that great wood of fig-trees to hide your meditations. A family, your own, who will be devoted to you all the time—wouldn't that soothe your chagrins?"

"Since you're taking that tone, I'll talk to you as to my true son. Know, then, that the life I've freely embraced is beginning to weigh upon me. But keep my secret. Don't say anything to the tomb; it's too full of echoes. Who knows that better than you?"

"That's the truth, Father, Go on."

The chief of darkness resumed, lowering his vice: "Is it certain that no one's listening to us here? Death is curious—where is she?"

"Far from here."

"I was afraid that she might be listening to us.[162] It's just that no being, great or small, celestial or infernal, can boast of having surprised my secret on my lips. Not one even suspects what I'm going to tell you. All of them believe me triumphant; all of them would swear that I'm as hard as rock, and I've certainly done nothing to dissuade them. Before all, let's preserve honor. But you, my son, know that the rock has been worn away by the water drops that fall eternally from the vault of heaven; know than beneath this tanned mask there is—how shall I put it?—a soul, yes, in truth, a pitiable soul that cries and laments. Finally, to say everything, I'm bored, my son. I no longer sense within me that masculine resolution, that rigid will, which once composed a kind of infernal happiness for me. Something has withered inside me. I doubt, I totter, my son. A little more, and I'll succumb."

"I've always thought that it would finish like that."

"Even in Hell, my child, I have more than one disgust to swallow. Beneath that royalty, which seems so absolute, there are miseries that only I know."

"What?" Merlin put in, timidly. "I thought that in the abyss, at least, everything went as you wish."

"Not at all, not at all. Make no mistake, my son. If you're to succeed me some day, I owe you the naked truth. Once, I reigned in the midst of fallen archangels; their sins had some grandeur; at least pride was satisfied. Energetic, aristocratic souls, which had refused to bend the knee, I could reign over them without any misalliance. Today they've unearthed, I don't know where, vices so servile, crimes so petty and leprous, that they even disgust me. No more trace of the old pride that made Hell a worthy rival of Heaven. No! Not one among them dares raise his head any longer. Not one has the courage to bear his sins. The wretches! They deny themselves! They've become hypocrites, they practice, my dear! I can no longer take a step in that simpering, degenerate Hell without hearing their *oremus*, for they also speak Latin. They've learned to strike their breasts, kneel and chant; they oblige the serpent to intone the *Gloria*. What do I know? They've become a hundred times more devout, more wheedling, than anyone in Heaven. Yes! That hypocritical Hell is more odious to me than Eden. I wasn't made to reign over cowards."

"Father, your words fill me with joy. Your crown has become too heavy. Perhaps it would be wise to renounce your reign."

"Well done!" cried the king of Hell. "You've anticipated my thought. For a long time, dearest, I've been thinking about abdicating, but to your advantage. I'm old and tired. You, Merlin, are still young enough to repair and rehabilitate Hell. If I've held on to that royalty it has been, on my honor, to leave it to you. Do you think that I've been working for myself? Get away! On my word, I've

---

[162] *Mort* is a feminine noun in French, so the natural translation of the pronoun used here is "she," but it is worth noting that Quinet had elaborately developed a female personification of Death in *Ahasvérus*, as the old crone Mob.

426

done nothing except for you. 'He'll succeed me,' I said to myself. 'He'll honor his old father. I'll give him good advice from the depths of my retreat.' Those, my son, are the projects with which I sustained my ennui. Come on, Merlin—I'll leave you the empire! Only assure me of an honorable retreat, appropriate to one who had carried the scepter of the abyss."

"Thank you, but my tastes are too different."

"You'll allow yourself to be guided by my advice. It's no longer necessary to imagine the government as too difficult. They're so limited, no stupid in their vile debaucheries. They catch themselves so easily in their cowardly nets. Provided that you oppress them, they'll believe you to be a genius. Lying and more lying—that's the whole secret. My long career has taught me that the crudest, grossest lie, is that which best suits their coarse nature. It seems that that's the element best adapted to their organs. They savor it with delight; it's their nectar and their ambrosia."

"One thing disturbs me in what you're saying, Father."

"What's that?"

"Can souls of mud by immortal?"

"Why not? We have mud in Hell, too, and it's indelible. Don't worry, my son! You'll carry it off marvelously. Succeed me."

"No, Father. That's not my vocation. I can't accept that crown; I'd lose it."

"Well, my dear, that's what takes away all my courage. So long as I saw before me the future of my son, of my race, of my dynasty, I devoured all difficulties. But if I can no longer have an heir of my blood, what point is there is so much eternal labor in the abyss? I, too, wouldn't be sorry to breathe for a while on the edge of a spring. I'm weary of that eternal exile. Yes, if I could hide this white head in forgetfulness! Ignorant of demons and humans—the difference is trivial—if I could only be ignored by them!"

"It seems to me that it would be more dignified, Father, to publish your change of life to the face of the worlds."

Those imprudent words awoke Satan's genius with a start. His eyes threw off flames. He replied, roaring: "Gently! You're going too quickly, Merlin. Can you think that? Belie myself? Me? Confess that I was mistaken! What remain to us, to demons, is character. Take that away, and we're no longer anything. Between the two of us, I can recognize a few errors, but to deny myself, to belie my past, to bury myself stupidly in a ridiculous contrition—don't ask that of me!"

Have you ever, while walking in the Bernese Alps, come across a dry stone wall on the edge of a field of barley, which is smiling at you at harvest time? It confines a meadow of about two arpents, strewn with primroses, gentians, scabiouses, anemones, in which a dairy cow is ruminating, half-hidden in the flowers. From there, a pretty path attracts you, winding under stands of maples, dwarf oaks and sorb-trees, carpeted with myrtles, whose little fruits, bitter but refreshing pierce the silvered emerald of the moss like black pupils.

Stop!

If you take one step more, the abyss is there! It opens. The gaping earth disappears beneath your feet. The vertical galleries of the gulf overhang, from stage to stage, and the pale walls of rock plunge vertically into the edifice of the void. To the cavernous sound of the seething of the Aar, which trickles invisibly, your gaze is lost in a blue-tinted crevasse, without finding anywhere to stop. Your knees tremble as in a dream. For you have had the vision of infernal regions. Can you not retain yourself by means of your hands, clenched on that young branchless larch lying on the ground? But it's uprooted. You recoil in horror, crawling, over the damp edge of the precipice.

Thus, beneath his father's complaisant smile, Merlin discovered the genius of Hell. He saw that, by virtue of an excess of zeal, he had lacked prudence; and, backtracking on what had escaped him, he resumed in these terms:

"After all, Father, there's no need to publish indiscreetly your change of life, if it suits you, for example, to imitate ours. Here, in this walled enclosure, far from the gazes of the curious, you could make a hermitage, and the universe would know nothing about it."

"Bah! You're mistaken, O sagest of enchanters. I'm too important a mechanism in the arrangement of things to disappear without the worlds knowing and talking about it among themselves. Know a little more, great dreamer, about these worlds that you claim to enchant. They curse me because of my sins, they say. Fundamentally, each of those sins is imposed. They see them as a proof of cunning. If I mended my ways, those same people who stone me today with their maledictions would accuse me of weakness. If I persist, they execrate me; if I change, they scorn me. That, my dear, is the difficulty.

"Set down the fiery crown, you say? That's easy; but it's necessary to envisage the consequences. Let's think it through. If I reenter the host of beings, as a simple homunculus, do you think that there is one among them who would not come to reproach me for his fall or his crime? Yes, there would not be a single man or reptile who, seeing my disarmed, would not assassinate me with his bravado. They're such cowards?

"Certainly I have pride enough to scorn their insults. Perhaps it would dignify my character to offer myself, disarmed, to their mockery. It would not be devoid of grandeur to say: 'Here is the king of Hell. He has taken off his crown himself, out of ennui. Come to your damnation; run, perverse race; he was weary of your obsequiousness; so much servitude wearied him He wants to test your fury. Once again, come! He's is here, unmasked and bare-breasted, exposed to your vengeance.'

"How's that Merlin? What do you think of a speech like that, addressed to creation? Would it not be a brilliant theatrical gesture? Would it not be glorious to rid myself thus of a royalty of which, believe me, I've exhausted all the ostentation? Come on, quickly—your opinion?"

"Undoubtedly, that would be true grandeur."

"And I would find thus a glory that I have conspicuously lacked?"

"Precisely, Father; let's profit from this fortunate moment when pure light has entered into your genius. Let's finish it."

"Finish it, my dear Merlin? That's what unbearable to me. You're in too much of a hurry today, as always. And then, my dear, there's another difficulty. If I reconcile myself with the universe; if, in addition, I take that great humiliating step, who, I beg you, will believe my word? Can't you hear in advance the sniggering of all the beings who will pursue me—me, a poor night-bird, harried by the birds of the day? Who will want to believe in my sincerity? 'It's a new hypocrisy! Now he's old, he's become a hermit!' You know how they talk.

"In that immensity of worlds, beings creatures, angels, humans, demons and fays, can you find me one single individual who will want to trust me, even for a moment? Even you, Merlin, with all your ingenuity, which I've mocked so many rimes—come on! Would you entrust little Formose there to me for a single minute? Would you confide his education to me for the blink of an eye?"

Merlin's only response was to call his child. He lifted him from the ground and put him in Satan's arms.

"This is your grandfather," he said. "Don't be afraid."

The child did not know whether he ought to laugh or cry, and it was a terrible thing to see that ingenuous infant in the arms of the king of Hell. Even I accuse Merlin here of having given too precious a pledge, but he always made the error of overconfidence.

At least he was not mistaken on this occasion.

"Good," said Satan, putting down the child, who was no longer afraid. "That's something I would never have believed possible, either on your part or mine. The temptation was great; the proof was strong. Perhaps today won't be a waste of time. That's your Abrahamic sacrifice; here, take back your Isaac."

And with that, he drew away, very pensively. Sitting on the summit of a rock that overlooked the region, he lost himself in meditation on what he had just seen and heard.

III

"Abdicate!" said the king of Hell to himself, shaking his head. "Certainly, I'm capable of it, since no one but me could replace me...and who would dare? I can be tranquil. Poor pygmies, I know their measure. None of them would retain that empire of evil for an hour, which I've contained, conserved and magnified until today. I alone was able to govern it. If I disappeared even for a moment, I'd bequeath them a beautiful chaos, the chaos of Hell...

"To defy creation, when the smallest and most insignificant of insects would be able to rise against me without peril—that would be my pride! I would sit down on this same rock. I would summon all beings around me, ready to settle my account with each of them. Sulla, Diocletian—those are examples with

429

which I can authorize myself. I too could cultivate in peace my garden of Salone;[163] I could live here with my lettuces. Am I not like them, having drained the cup a hundred times over? Does a single illusion remain to me? Do I not know that darkness has limits and that one wearies of everything, even Hell?

"It's certain that I no longer feel the confidence in myself that sustained me in my youth. Shall I wait until I'm vanquished, or should I take away from defeat the opportunity to strike me? Which is the cleverer?"

As he was speaking to himself in that fashion, his foot detached a block of stone, which rolled into the gulf. The abyss responded with a roar. At the same time, Merlin appeared by his side.

"Be careful of falling, Father. This place is one of the most unreliable. Let's go sit under that clump of trees instead."

"Listen," replied the Ancestor, leaning on his son's arm. "You're a great enchanter. I think, in truth, that you've ensorcelled me."

Soon, they found themselves far from the edge of the precipice, in a more rural location. The funeral herds were grazing tranquilly. Their guardian, the centaur, was on watch lying in the grass, from which he raised his venerable head.

"Once again," said Satan, "I'm not insensible to this rustic life. Come to get back to it after such devouring days—that's the question. Let's see—what's your doctrine? Your church? Your *Credo*? Speak frankly. To what church do you want to convert me?"

Merlin had not expected that question. He had only prepared a certain number of scenes, of encounters, of pictures of life in the fields, on which he was counting to bring peace back to Satan's burning soul. He hoped that the sacred freshness of his sepulcher would insinuate itself into the heart of the leader of the wretched. When he heard him ask such a direct question, his embarrassment was visible. Without giving himself time to reflect, he replied a trifle inconsiderately: "The surest means would be to make your peace with Heaven."

"Very nice! That's rather vague. Which Heaven do you mean? There are so many kinds!"

"But...the Heaven from which you fell," Merlin went on, increasingly troubled.

"Say Paradise then, if you dare!" his father replied, in a thunderous voice.

"Yes, Paradise."

At these words, Satan got up, with a gaze in which the pride of ancient days reappeared unalloyed. "Very good, wise Merlin! That's all of your science?

---

[163] The emperor Diocletian was said, in many French sources, including a famous passage in Chateaubriand, to have boasted of preferring to cultivate "the lettuces of his garden at Salone" to continuing to rule the empire, as he handed it over—under duress—to his successor Galerius.

I suspected as much, my dear. The catechism, isn't it? Life has taught you nothing, nor the tomb. Still bogged down and bewitched by dreams. Well, so be it. Remain buried alive forever in your plastered mummeries."

And he made as if to leave.

"Know, then," he added, turning round, "that centuries of centuries can accumulate on your father's head, but he will never be reconciled with the angels; they've been too superb. I'll even tell you that I respire here a vague odor of figs, which reminds me of Adam and Eve in Eden—and that resemblance alone, even if it were only a fantasy, would make me flee to the other extremity of the world. Would you be their imitator, by chance? Adieu, Merlin. If that's what you have to say to me, it's all over."

Often, on a beautiful day in April, the joy of those who had hoped for a better season in suddenly deceived. Over a blue, limpid sky one first sees a grayish mist extend. Slowly, quietly, snow covers the embalmed ground. Everything that had blossomed prematurely is gripped by an icy hand. The reddening buds of the wild plum tree are crowned with a down of frost. The cups of the anemones fill to the brim with snowflakes and hailstones, instead of the dew they were expecting. The surprised birds, who had sensed the breath of spring, taken back to yesterday, try to sing to disarm the old winter—but in vain. After a few hesitant notes, they are constrained to remain silent. How they regret then having quit too soon their leafy houses beneath a more indulgent sky.

It was thus that Merlin repented, for the second time, of having hoped too soon for his father's conversion. He regretted his premature joy and felt vanquished by one more powerful than himself. Before renouncing his greatest hope, however, he made a supreme effort.

"Wait, Father! There's some misunderstanding here, I assure you. You know that in youth, one brings too absolute a judgment to everything. Let's reread the Bible together with a calmer mind. I swear in advance that you'll savor its beauties. A mind as great and just as yours can't allow itself to be governed by an ill-considered hatred."

"Ill-considered! Don't ask anything that's incompatible with my dignity. I'll never consent to another blow. Since you've reminded me of the accursed days, all the ancient evil has reawakened in me."

Seeing his father hardening, already blocking his ears, Merlin hazarded to say: "You might at least convert to philosophy."

At that suggestion, Satan softened slightly, and muttered between his teeth: "I've always thought that it might be possible to reach an understanding on that terrain. Go on, then—talk! Explain yourself."

"My dear Father, have you read *The Philosophy of Nature* by the celebrated doctor and enchanter Benedict?"[164]

---

[164] The title *La Philosophie de la nature* is most famously attributed to a translation of a book by G. W. F. Hegel, although it is also employed by Jean Deslisle

"Yes, I scanned it one evening, by the light of my furnaces. I'm talking about the first edition, because I'm told that the second is completely changed since the author became a counselor."

"And how did it seem to you? It proves that God began by being the Devil."

"I liked that very passage; it was good. On that basis, I can, without dishonor, reconcile myself with philosophy. I couldn't with the Church, without letting myself down." In a more bitter tone, striking the earth with his foot, he went on: "Tell me, my son, between us, do you know the great Pan, with the hairy heart and a club-foot like mine. It's him I'd rather deal with, not his people. Go find him. After you, he's the only one I can trust."

"It's a long time since I saw him last, Father. I've heard that he's dead."

"Dead! Great Pan! Get away! He'll bury both of us."

Merlin, with a foresight that marked his wisdom better than words would have done, had composed an abstract of the principal philosophies of nature. He had written that book on a beautiful virgin parchment, embellished with drawings depicting intermingled flowers and birds in almost infinite number. Taking the volume from beneath his cloak, he offered it to his father.

The latter received it complaisantly, and from that moment on, not a day passed when you would not have been able to encounter him on the edge of a precipice, his eyes fixed on one of the pages of the volume. He only closed it to meditate; when, by chance, he opened his mouth, it was always to cry: "No, no, no!" until he ran out of breath.

Then Hell shivered, and many demons said: "What is our leader thinking about, then? Truly, he reads too much. He'll betray us too, you'll see."

Meanwhile, darkness enveloped him and shadows marched by his side. Like an immense, confused, nameless crowd pressing around a traveler at the gate of a city, the shadows hampered him at every step. From that multitude, a confused murmur emerged:

"Where is he going?"

"What does he want?"

"He's stopping!"

"Is he deaf?"

"Is he going to disown us?"

---

de Sales. Neither argues specifically that God began as the Devil. The attribution to "Benedict" recalls the fact that Merlin called the future spirit of Spinoza by that name in Limbo, and Spinoza did, indeed, adopt it late in life, but the description does not fit Spinoza's *Ethica* either. The Bibliothèque Nationale catalogue has a book by the Swedenborgian surgeon Bénédict Chastanier entitled *Le Livre de nature* (1788), but that is unlikely to be the intended referent, which is probably generic rather than specific, the name Benedict (that of the founder of monasticism) being employed to mean meditative scholarship.

"He's going away."

"He's coming back."

"Let's crawl toward him."

"Let's darken his heart."

"This way!"

"No, further on!"

"There he is!"

"Leave me alone," said their king.

"What, leave you!" replied the darkness, in chorus. "Are we not your counselors? Your soul, you know, is made in our image, your thoughts are full of us. O King, you borrowed almost everything from us. We live in a crowd in the utmost depths of your heart. How, then, can we separate ourselves from you? Thanks to our faithful troop, whom you torture, you've never seen the horror of that abyss. Oh, if you had looked it in the face, like us, would you be able to live there?"

"Leave me alone," the sovereign of the darkness replied, again. "Go away! Let me gaze just once, alone with it, into the depths of the gulf."

At these words, the flocks of shadows withdrew. They fled heavily, confusedly, crawling, looking back continually, because they still hoped that their master might recall them. He did nothing of the sort.

For the first time, he saw, without a veil, face to face, the abyss in which he lived. He was frightened by it.

IV

"Come back, Merlin, come back! I'm afraid!" howled the king of Hell.

Merlin ran to his father. He found him foaming, mouth agape, trembling in every limb.

"The darkness knows where I am, my son. Its shadows will denounce me. Do you now a place more deserted than this one? I'll retire to it."

"There is none, except for the abbey of Prester John."

"Precisely. A hundred times over, I've had the desire to cloister myself there for a season. Only prejudice has stopped me."

The conclusion was that Satan would go to make his retreat far from evil tongues, in the abbey that he was obstinate in calling a Pantheon. During that time, the worlds would lose track of him. He would finally be able to realize the project of solitude that had become dearer to him every day.

Satan left. He went to ring at the door of the monastery, to which the most opposed roads led. He was received without ceremony, without astonishment, as was the custom with regard to all pilgrims. In addition, there was no sordid haste. No one even asked him who his god was. He was taken to a cell where everything had been prepared for him in advance.

"You're doubtless the pilgrim that Merlin told me to expect a long time ago?" said Prester John.

"The same."

"That's sufficient, my brother. Go in."

Without adding anything, Prester John bowed and withdrew.

Left alone, Merlin's father opened the window. Half way down the mountain, a waterfall made a chamois leap to reach the opposite bank. Its noise, deadened by the narrow funnel, faded into a dull, stifled sound at the foot of rocks stacked up into towers, ruins and black peaks, overlaid with a network of snowfields that had not yet melted.

"How cool this place is!" said the pilgrim of Hell, filling his lungs with the humid balsamic breath of the valley. "Above all, what tolerance! Merlin didn't deceive me."

The next day, and the following days, he was astonished to live as he wished in the abbey without anyone ever asking him what he thought, much less what he believed. It was dispute that had exasperated him most of all. His ancient arguments with the angels and the seraphim had irritated him to the point that he had thrown himself into the most opposed opinions. As Heaven had thundered, he had roared in Hell, and that eternal dispute had resulted in embittering him to the point of denaturing him. Left to himself, far from the world, when he saw that he was unknown in this place where no one opposed him, he could not help reflecting; and as he had a powerful intelligence, that first reflection had an immense influence on the projects he formed. Every day he felt his hatred decrease, as the opportunities to exercise it were increasingly lacking.

Certainly, he did not become an ideal of virtue, abnegation and sanctity. I would be wrong to say so. But his humor became gradually milder; that is undeniable.

In any case, he thought, *I'm given space here. People don't take much notice of my existence, it's true, but at least they don't contest with me. Have I ever demanded anything else?*

Sometimes, it must be admitted, at the fall of dusk, and especially during the night, the appetite for darkness came back to him with an inexpressible violence. He tossed and turned furiously in his bed. The solitude that he had desired so much weighed upon him now. He would have liked to fill the universe again. He was afraid of being forgotten, and was already accusing the world of ingratitude. Then he summoned the darkness. Immediately, its shadows pressed around him, and conversations took place between them and him that woke the brothers of the abbey with a start.

"What's wrong, Brother?" they said, gathering at the door. "Are you having a bad dream? We'll sit up with you if you like."

"It's up to me to keep vigil," said Prester John. He sat down then at the pilgrim's bedside and waited with him until dawn appeared.

434

As soon as the bells began to ring, a frisson gripped the new brother. He was close to yielding to the desire to plunge himself back into Hell.

"I'd only have to want it! I'd find myself on the throne of darkness again. I'd reign again...but over whom?"

That last thought calmed him down. The assurance of being able to grip the world again, whenever he wanted to, took away the desire to do it.

Certainly, it was a terrible things for him to hear, every morning, the prayers of the monks. His entire being shivered; but as their antiphons mingled with the verses of the Koran, the Zend-Avesta and the Vedas, he breathed more easily. The Mohammedans consoled him for the Christians, the Parsees for the Mohammedans, the Brahmins for the Parsees. Each religion gave him relief from the others. Deep down, his old personal hatred of Jehovah was soothed. He delighted in the enjoyment of seeing that he had so many rivals.

"As long as he doesn't rule alone, without division and without trouble, I'm content," he murmured.

That sentiment was not the best; it was the lassitude of evil rather than the love of good.

He was seen more than once fishing in the torrent with a net or a line, with the other brothers, so much had peace become welcome to him day by day. He also cultivated a little garden enclosed by horns, which he filled with lettuces. More often than not, his hood was pushed back from his face. He spoke rarely, with discretion, only when he was asked a question, which almost never happened.

One day, he had the whim of celebrating his funeral. He lay down in a coffin and the inhabitants of the abbey filed past him in procession, singing the mass for the dead; after which he sat up and said: "Fortunate are those who can die."

Another day, in the cloister, as darkness was falling, he was walking with Prester John.

"Excuse me, Father," he said. "Are you not great Pan? It's strange how you resemble him."

"What folly, my brother! You think too much. Be careful; you'll catch a fever."

"Show me your feet under the robe, that I might kiss them."

"No, my brother; that's excessive humility."

V

In the corner of the tomb there was an obscure, misty place cluttered with pale creepers and nocturnal flowers, where Merlin felt more buried than anywhere else. At first he only approached it with horror, but, having familiarized him with the vapors of the sepulcher, he visited that place every time he wanted to collect himself more intimately in death.

In spite of his frequent retreats into that place, he had never noticed a vast, massive door, as if intended for a giant, so narrowly sealed was it into the living rock. One evening, however, he saw it, and a dazzling light insinuating itself through the crack at the height of the vault. When he had pushed the door, it opened of its own accord, noisily, as if thunder were rumbling over its hinges, and he found himself in the realm of the Lightning.

He called out and asked: "Who is living so close to me in my tomb?"

A voice emerged from the bowels of the earth, replying: "ME! I'm the hidden god. When you passed over the earth, I was in the clouds. I was on the heights of Lebanon while you were in the valley. I was seated on the ecliptic when you contemplated the stars. Now that you're in the tomb, I live beyond death."

Merlin fell prostrate to the ground. He veiled his eyes and cried out: "Spare me, Lord. Don't trample the worm. I've searched for you among the living, but among too many other thoughts, and I only glimpsed you from afar, in the twilight, obliquely, when your mantle was trailing in the clouds. Often, your voice called to me. 'Come back, come back!' said the echo. But I closed my ears, fearing that you were setting an ambush for me. And the hypocrite who always had your name in his mouth caused me to flee far away from you. Finally, I discover you alone in the depths of the sepulcher. It's not too late, Lord."

God replied: "It's now in the sepulcher that I please myself, and there isn't one where I'm not resident. The universe is profaned; I've withdrawn from it. I no longer reside outside in the tottering heavens, nor on human lips. I've renounced all the tents deployed at the entrance to the desert and the pavilions erected in the clouds. But everywhere there's something secret, I live in its greatest secrecy; if there were one more remote than death. I'd like to reside there."

Thus Merlin learned that he had become the host of the Eternal, and he conversed with him, without dreading the noise of drowsy thunder. A sacred familiarity had banished terror. It was no longer the formidable voice of the Elohim. It was, beside subterranean springs, the murmur of the hidden God, which let its secret escape into the wisest ear of all.

Merlin's guest went on:

"Do you know Behemoth and Leviathan? Did you encounter them on earth? What were they doing? I'm content to have formed them with my hands; they remain faithful to me, celebrating my immutable power.

"Surely Behemoth is amusing himself today in the damp places that I instructed him to inhabit; he won't want to change them. Is Leviathan thinking about emerging from the depths of the sea, where I placed him with my hand, and wandering in the waterless deserts?

"Have you encountered the wild ox in Armorica? Can he no longer make use of his cloven feet or ruminate, lying down in the oak forest?

"Have you seen the horse insult his flanks and covet the vulture's wings?

"Have you seen the vulture envying the skinny scales that I gave the crocodile, on the day when I placed him in the river?

"No, they haven't spoken ill of me when you passed by. If that's not the case, say so! Speak! Repeat their accusations; I'll listen to them and do them justice.

"Have you visited the eagle on the mountain? Surely that one hasn't wearied of chasing his booty, wings outstretched, since the first hour, and he isn't saying: 'Why isn't my prey prepared for me in my shelter, without my having to pursue it and tear it apart with my beak?'

"Speak! Talk! Have you found yourself face to face with the lion, in the early morning, when he quits his lair, mouth bloody? Assuredly that one hasn't denied me. He's roared as I taught him to roar; he calls me by my name, as in the days of Moses, in the cave of Horeb.

"Have you encountered the elephant as he moves like a hill of clay? Has he forgotten how to make use of the trunk I gave him to uproot oaks and trample reeds? No! You've seen him. He doesn't criticize me; he remembers my commandment.

"Have you walked in the narrow path of the scarab? Has he looked up at you? Does he no longer remember his borer, with which to dig in the soil and bark impregnated with morning dew?

"Ephemera—have you conversed with the population of the ephemera? What do they say? Have they complained about me? But no, your eyes weren't able to see them, because they're so small. But I can see them from here, with the same magnitude as Leviathan. Not one of them, in retreat in its abysm of pettiness, has spoken ill of the one who made them invisible.

"All of them remember my laws; my speech still resounds in their ears, so well that none of them speaks ill of it or tries to avoid it. I rejoice in having extracted them from nothingness.

"But human beings have not done what I told them to do. They have forgotten my ways. I repent of having created them and of having extended the earth beneath their feet.

"I attached their heads vertically on their shoulders in order that they could look at higher things. Why do they conduct themselves in the manner of the crawling beasts, forgetting to address themselves to the heavens?

"I've shaped the arches of their brows in order that they might set the seal of innocence upon it, and they've made it the dwelling of pride. I've engraved my thought in the membranes of their brain, like a scribe writing on virgin parchment. Why have they erased what I've written in the marrow of their bones?

"I've put my intelligence on their lips in order that they might expand in joy, and they've turned it to jeering and homicide.

"Have I not freed their tongues in order that they might publish the truth? They've published lies.

"I've given them two eyes that see inside, in order that they might perceive justice; they've gazed at iniquity.

"That's why I repent of ever having given my breath to their nostrils. Why didn't I consign them to oblivion as soon as they appeared on the face of the earth? Their mouths wouldn't given birth to lies. Their false promises wouldn't have been able to soil the aurora, which I made so pure. They wouldn't have saddened the dusk, by conceiving crime, and the night, by carrying it out. Now, where can I descend to the earth? It's stained everywhere by Abel's blood.

"If I descend into the gulf, hypocrisy is already seated there in my place. I'm tired of seeing it deified everywhere instead of what is due to me. I, who made them with my own hands, am thinking about unmaking them."

Merlin replied: "Before that day comes, Lord, grant me my father's pardon."

God continued: "His eternal torment was due to me, and you're the only one who has dared to plead for him. Only let him repent."

Then Merlin withdrew, searching his heart to discover how he could complete his father's conversion. He carried away a radiance on his brow, and said to everything he encountered in his sepulcher: "Oh, how good it is to reside here. The Eternal is my guest."

Enough! Enough, my book! It's here that it's necessary to finish. I can't smile anymore; and what's the use of talking to a deaf, enemy world that stops its ears? Let's expel the hope that has amassed in my heart, in spite of me, and wants to burst forth. Let's put a triple seal here. Let's shut up...

Yes, if another word escapes me, let it at least be the last!

BOOK TWENTY-FOUR: TRIUMPH! O TRIUMPH!

I

They're finished, the voyages of the three lives. Others will travel the same path, but not me. It's necessary for me to say goodbye here to all the serene things that have given me peace.

Friends, I replace in your hands the hazel-branch that has enabled me to penetrate into the land of Merlin without fear of going astray. Hang on—here are the keys to the enchanted worlds. Open them in your turn. You know now how easy the route is through the innumerable halls of the house of justice.

At the place where I stopped, you'll find other horizons, which I've been obliged to abandon. They'll belong to you as soon as you set foot there.

Let your intelligence take wing. When you've found those new places, you'll think to yourselves: "These places please us, they promise to be very beautiful. But he's the one who opened them to us."

For myself, I'm stopping; and I'm doing so like those who separate from an old friend who has retained them for a long time under his roof, and whom they despair of ever seeing again. They hasten their farewell, in order not to give the tears time to arrive.[165]

II

What became of Hell, though, deprived of its chief?

Hell, having been liberated, devoid of a guardian and master, devoured itself.

Until then, Merlin's father had maintained in the abyss an order that rendered it habitable to the accursed. No one had dared to infringe a single one of is commandments. His will reigned supreme; that was the law of all. Everyone knew what his legitimate torture was, and remained attached to it. Everyone rendered to dolor exactly what he owed to dolor. There was no usurpation in the eternal fall. There was a regulation in despair.

When the chief of the abyss had disappeared, to begin with, all the accursed searched for him, for a long time, because they were accustomed to his au-

---

[165] Hermione's notes observe that the text from here onwards is no longer personal. What has concluded, in fact, is not the text *per se* (obviously) but its quasi-autobiographical component. It is, if not Quinet's prophecy, at least his wish-list.

thority, and they did not believe that they could live for a moment without the one who filled the vast inferno with his thought.

"Where is he?" said the accursed to the darkness. "When will he return?"

And the shadows of darkness replied: "We don't know where he is."

"Keep searching," said the demons. "You're his counselors."

"We've searched," the darkness replied.[166] "We haven't been able to find him."

Then a flash of joy passed through Hell, for each of the accursed began to hope that he might replace the chief of the abyss. All of them looked simultaneously, with an oblique gaze, in the direction of the funereal throne, and, seeing it empty for the first time, each of them promised himself to sit down there, in the place of the one who had disappeared.

Immediately, the one who was closest to the infernal throne climbed its steps and shouted: "Console yourselves! I'll replace the one you have lost, and will be a veritable father to you, which he has never been. In spite of appearances, I'm full of kindness. Only obey me as you obeyed him. All will be well. I'm a partisan of progress. I'll carry out reforms."

That was what he said. But know that there was not a single power in the abyss, no matter how petty, that did not enter into fury at those words. The smallest and the greatest alike all wanted, equally and with the same frenzy, to be the King of Hell; and each one roared: "Be careful! There are angels in disguise here!"

There was then an uninterrupted succession of tyrants of the abyss who passed over the throne that none of them could hold for more than a moment. Scarcely had one of them occupied it than he was overturned and torn apart by the crowd. Even though it was only for a moment, however, each one took advantage of it to change the old established order of tortures, with the result that the evil was revived hour after hour; it changed and was renewed, rotating like the wheel of a chariot drawn by winged horses. Tortures succeeded one another with a prodigious rapidity—or, rather, were inflicted all at once, at the same time, on every one of the damned. A long scream went up. All the wretched said: "Where is the old king of dolors? His reign was more just."

And nothing in the world can give any idea of the force of Hell turned against Hell. It set about destroying itself with a hundred times more fury than it had ever put into destroying the work of Heaven, for it was the dupe of all its own traps; the grossest were those that pleased it the most. It fell infallibly into all its ambushes.

---

[166] In French, *ténèbres* [darkness] is plural; hence the use of "we." Translation thus creates occasional difficulties, which I have overcome in part by sometimes substituting "the shadows."

Then Malacoda, the most paltry, the most impotent of demons, always crawling, always sniggering, shouted in his high-pitched voice: "It's me who ought to reign."

"No," replied Taillecosse,[167] "it's me."

"Rather than let him reign," howled a third voice, "let Hell perish!"

That voice was that of Merlin's father, who had heard the frantic cries of the accursed resounding in his heart.

He arrives; he is carrying in his iron belt the rusty keys of the abyss. He alone knows what a twisted column supports that entire edifice, so terrible and so fragile, which he was charged with repairing and sustaining while time undermined it.

He draws near to it.

"I shall perish, but they will perish with me."

As he finishes those words, he topples the column of his temple, already worn away at the base. The prodigious vaults that form the basilica of Hell all collapse together. Immense mountain plateaux slide into the valley. They leave behind them bare, eroded slopes that the accursed populations resident at their feet can to longer climb.

So the herdsmen of Goldau were surprised in the night by the collapse of the natal mountain. They were sleeping in their chalets, lying on the litter of dead leaves, after having marked the herds that they had to conduct the next day to the pastures of the verdant alp, because the season had arrived. The alp slid from the summit with the monstrous moraines; it collapsed over the pastures before the heifers and the bull could be untied in the stable. The stripped rock retained an immense wound on its face that no century could efface. Zug, you have howled your wrath there; and you, Uri, you are still uttering roars![168]

In the same way, the pastors of souls who lived on tortures were taken by surprise. The funereal sun, which illuminated them dimly, is veiled and extinguished. The sea of fire flows away and dried up. In the distance, one last red wave fades way in the sands.

The ramparts of fire have fallen, and the chains are broken. But the imprisoned souls, accustomed to torture, dare not seize liberty. The immense servile proletariat remains lying and crawling in the ditches of dolor. They do not have the courage to escape the cowardly torments that have become life itself. Nourished by serpents, the greater number has acquired a taste for the inferno. How could they dream of rising from the depths of their extinct sepulchers? Seeing it devour itself, they wait, stupidly, for a new inferno to emerge from new darkness.

---

[167] This name is improvised, and is presumably intended to suggest a scorpion.

[168] Zug and Uri are cantons in Switzerland, where Goldau is a mountain subject to avalanches

In that human sea, only a few souls dared to stand upright in the face of eternal dolor, and they saw it disappear. They appeared from a distance like the white sail of a vessel on a boundless Ocean. Among them surged forth the most ancient of the damned, who preceded all the others in evil and in punishment. Centuries of torture did not seem to have wearied him.

"Get up, Brothers!" said Cain to the troop of humans. "Out of here! Hell is finished!"

These words were repeated by those who had dared to raise their heads. Then the trembling souls emerged one after another from their torture beds, and, seeing that Hell was indeed collapsing, started to flee like people emerging hastily by night from a town shaken by an earthquake.

They fled, and none of the demons thought of pursuing them, so intent were they on destroying one another. In the anarchy of Hell, they had even forgotten to close the gates of the city of mourning. The souls exempted from torment hastened toward that gate; they passed through it; they saw the light again. Thus was realized Merlin's prophecy: "The dust of the ancestors will be renewed."

III

At the din of Hell's collapse, Merlin felt the sepulcher shaking. His father, deprived of shelter, astonished to survive, disinherited and proscribed, had wanted to remain in the ruins of the empire of dolors. The two of them met in that vast abyss. They both searched for the effaced frontiers of the accursed realms.

Anyone who has climbed to the summit of Vesuvius or Etna at midnight in warm ash over trembling ground, cut by rivers of fire, from which the heavy respiration of giants exhales, can imagine the calcined road along which the last two pilgrims of Hell were walking.

As they went forward, Satan recognized the places that were most familiar to him.

"What a strange thing memory is!" he said. "I like seeing once again these places where all the wrath of Heaven was used up upon my head."

And he pointed out the debris of his throne to his companion. They both sat down on the extinct ashes; they listened for some time. Instead of the gnashing of teeth that had filled the place, no sound could be heard. Only an occasional breath passed over the ashes, raising them in swirls. No living being had remained in that tenebrous immensity.

"We're alone," said Satan. "Everything passes. Even Hell has passed. Will it be thus with Heaven?"

That word case a shadow into Merlin's soul; he dared not analyze it at first, but he thought secretly about his Guest, and recovered peace.

"At least it's me who wanted it," his father went on. "If I had consented to it, Hell would be triumphant still. Now, where is it? I can't rediscover it in me."

"Glory to you!"

"O sagest of sages, tell me where the countless multitudes of plaintive souls that once filled these valleys can have taken shelter?"

"In the mercy of Heaven."

That said, they got up and eventually arrived at the gates, which were still open. At the sight of the inscription in letters of fire: *Abandon all hope, ye who enter here*, the Enchanter stopped; he would gladly have effaced that motto written by eternal despair, but he did not know whether that was in his power, and he hesitated.

"Let me do it, child—these gates know me."

And the Accursed lifted them on his shoulders. After having removed them from their hinges, he hurled them into the depths of the pool of tears.

A little further on, he perceived brands that were reigniting; he extinguished them with his hot foot. An immense sigh was heard in the depths of the gulfs.

"That's the death-rattle of Hell. Listen." Then, after a pause: "Once again, Merlin, I and I alone destroyed the inferno. My punishment, I inflicted upon myself."

"I'm witness to that."

"I alone have delivered the world from that which was its terror, and the world will mock me for it. I'm already repenting of it, as a suicide—but the evil I've destroyed, I could remake."

"Don't regret it, Father. From all that I can see, the time of reconciliation has come. The best day of my life will be the one when I announce that to the world."

"All well and good, my son. That's precisely what costs me the most. I've been able to overturn Hell, but to confess it to the world is truly beyond my strength."

"It would be the simplest ceremony."

"At least don't invite, as you too often have the habit of doing, worlds, spheres, comets and—what do I know?—the Milky Way as witnesses. If the thing has to be done, let it at least be done without a fuss. I've acquired a taste for simplicity. Let it be a family affair, then. Two or three witnesses sufficed, I believed for the creation. It would be materially impossible for me to bear, as before, the mocking gaze of all the assembled suns."

"Choose your own witnesses."

"Well, let's see: your most intimate friends, Jacques, Archbishop Turpin and Prester John."

"So be it!" replied Merlin, whose heart was overflowing with joy.

He carefully refrained from contradicting his father on one detail when, by dint of precaution, he had been victorious in almost all the rest.

"You, and you alone will be my tutelary demon," he went on.

While these things were happening, the smallest of the spirits of evil, Farfadel, thanks to that vey smallness, had succeeded in escaping the destruction of Hell. He was meditating in isolation on that great ruin, and saying to himself: "That's what it costs to counterfeit Heaven! We wanted to be too fine, too clever. We're the ones who created Merlin, and its Merlin who has doomed us. Hell has been the dupe of Hell; it always will be."

He fell silent, hoping than eye would perceive him in the ruins. A voice became audible in the distance, clear, high-pitched and silvery. Farfadel was afraid of being caught. He hid his head under his wing and covered up his ears with both hands, for that voice was saying from the depths of Heaven:

"Come back, Merlin, Merlin! There is no other enchanter but God!"

IV

The great day of reconciliation had come. Without Merlin having let his secret escape, the entire universe had divined it, so no more radiant sun had ever risen. There was not a bird that was not singing on its branch. The flowers from the height of their stems, seemed to be awaiting a visitor. Only the peoples had no presentiment of what was in preparation. They are sometimes much less well-informed of great secrets than the birds and the flowers; often, they are even deaf to the trumpets of the archangels and blind to the light of the midday sun.

At the hour marked by Merlin, a veiled pilgrim was seen to appear at the entrance to his tomb; he was accompanied by Prester John, Turpin and Jacques.

"What do you want?" Merlin asked.

"Peace."

"I give it to you, Father; speak. Who are you?"

"The King of Hell," replied the pilgrim, raising his hood.

At these words, his three companions recoiled in horror. They were about to run away; Merlin recalled them hastily.

"He's my father," he said to them. "My true father, in flesh and blood. He asks for peace. Friends, will you refuse it to him?"

"Kneel!" said Turpin. "Let him fall to his knees!"

"That's not necessary," put in Prester John.

"At least let him confess!" said Turpin.

"Peace! Listen. And you, world, be quiet."

"I confess," said the pilgrim, "to the torrent, to the unleashed tempest, to the sand of the Syrian sea, to the flowers of the forest, to the volcano that still burns."

"Why those?" asked Turpin.

"Because," the pilgrim replied, "my heart is more impetuous than the torrent, my soul more arid than the sand, my thoughts stormier than the tempest

444

and more burning than the volcano, and because my works are more fragile than the woodland flowers."

"Is that your *Confiteor*?"

"Don't get into an argument with him," Prester John put in.

"But what guarantee of his change has he given?"

"The destruction of Hell," replied the king of Hell.

"Write that down," said Merlin to Archbishop Turpin. "It ought to suffice."

Turpin wrote down what he had just heard and seen.

The Enchanter ought to have many reflections to make on what had just happened, and his companions lent their ears in advance, but he feared more than anything else the impatience of his father, who was already showing a few signs of it. That is why he abbreviated the ceremony and contented himself with saying: "You are witnesses to the conversion of Satan. Go spread the news of it. It is, incontrovertibly, the greatest of my prodigies."

For a long time, humans refused all credence to that news. When Jacques went to spread it in the cities, they closed his mouth. He had remained so credulous and had so little in his external appearance that his testimony had no authority. Turpin inspired more respect, but it was said that he had more imagination than intelligence and more intelligence than judgment. As for Prester John, he passed for a heretic. So the crowd assembled in front of Merlin's tomb said, with a common voice: "How can we believe in the conversion of Satan? Undoubtedly, that's just one lie more. Who will be his guarantor?"

"Me," replied the tomb.

"You, Merlin?"

"In person."

And with that, Merlin closed the vent of his sepulcher, which trembled and almost collapsed for a second time.

V

Meanwhile, at the splash as the gates of Hell were precipitated into the pool of tears by Merlin's father, King Arthus had sighed; then he had extended his arms, felt his couch, bitten his lips and opened his eyes. Finally, he had raised himself up on his elbow. Jacques had hastened to present him with a cup of mead and a bottle of extravagant wine, sure that the sleeper as about to go to sleep again, as had so often happened.

Nothing of the sort—on the contrary, Arthus stood up, buckled on his sword and rubbed his eyes. He met Jacques' gaze.

"My cup-bearer must have given me poppy, for it seems to me that my sleep has been longer and heavier than usual."

Jacques excused himself without difficulty for that beverage, and to demonstrate his innocence, drank what remained in the cup. But as he feared reproaches, and had never had any exact notion of time anyway, he contented himself with replying: "The night has been long and rainy. The best thing was to sleep. Have you had a dream, sire?"

"Several, and all more strange than pleasant," replied Arthus, in slightly Gothic language, in which the rust of time was detectable. "Remember what I say; this was the main one. I would have sworn that many centuries were devouring one another like unmuzzled bloodhounds, that many kingdoms were collapsing, that peoples were succeeding one another hastily, generations passing, like flowers or shadows, battles ranging; and, incredibly, languages were changing, along with laws and customs. Have you heard anything similar, you who have remained awake?"

"Something like that."

"Furthermore, I heard peoples panting, like wild boar tracked to the lair."

"Exactly."

"And more than one altar was poorly incensed; the very face of the heavens changed."

"As witness David's chariot, which has lost its helm."

"There were also kings without heads and queens who sat down on the ground and wept."

"That's been seen, sire."

"After every one of these changes, I always found you again, Jacques, warming yourself at the same fire, half-extinct and half-flamboyant; and you were always more deceived and more miserable than before."

"That's the truth, good King!"

"It seemed to me, too, that the desolate earth was calling me to its rescue, and I made a prodigious effort to arrive in time—but can you imagine that a quantity of dwarfs was holding me villainously, one by the foot, another by the arm, some by the hair, some by my baldric; and thanks to that host of gnomes, a good number of which were wearing crowns or miters, I couldn't take a single step forward! Rancor and felony! That was the time, or never, to assist me, Jacques; you didn't do anything. In the end, a loud noise, like a door being torn from its hinges, woke me up. What noise might that have been?"

"Seigneur Merlin will explain everything," Jacques replied.

"But where is he?"

"Nearby, in his sepulcher."

"What! He's dead! Weep, peoples! When shall we ever see another sage like him?"

"He's buried, but his wisdom is twice as great."

"Let's go visit him then."

VI

At that moment, the sun, emerging from the edge of a black cloud, poured a cascade of flame over Arthus' white armor; the horizon was dazzled by it.

By that sign, Merlin recognized the Monarch of Virtues, who was advancing slowly, in his glory, surrounded by his trusty friends. For the first time, the tomb weighed upon him. He would have liked to launch himself out of the funereal tower to meet the man who, alive or dead, he had always loved as his legitimate King. Too impatient, he shook the bronze doors that separated him from the living on their hinges; but his efforts were futile. He groaned dully, under the ground.

Then he resolved to give the King the best welcome he could in the enclosure of death. For that, he instructed Viviane and his son to weave garlands in haste, with which he crowned the twenty ventilation shafts of his dwelling. He released a number of birds with double eyelids, all of which bore this motto around their necks:

Death has remained faithful to sleep.

At the same time, he hoisted his tumulary banner, clouded with the brightest colors, fringed with gold, which blazed in the early morning light, so vividly that it was mistaken from afar for a joyous rainbow. How he would have liked be the first to offer King of the Future the bread and wine of honor, and the keys to his dwelling! But he could not think of any way to do it. All that he could imagine was to renew the oil in the enchanted lamp, tune his harp, alert the dead and make the subterranean regions resonate to the fanfares of the sepulcher—with the result that the flag-decked tomb was filed with a joy so profound that it radiated fully outside.

When these preparations were complete, the expected king was very near, and Merlin, with his family beside him, greeted him with these words:

"I salute you, great King Arthus! Come, come, great king of justice. Everything here among us is yours: yours the tomb, yours also the Interred. Many kings, sire, have passed over the earth, handsome, young, long-haired, amorous of battles. They came, triumphant, to ask my advice for the sake of appearances, fundamentally deaf, impatient to disobey me; they went away in mourning, bald, wrinkled, limping, and curbed by the years. You alone, Sire, have retained your youthful vigor. How little you have changed! Time has been impotent against you. Such as I left you in Lutèce, in the most beautiful days of my life, I see you again."

At these words, Viviane and Merlin's son let fall in front of the King, by way of homage, a white rain of apple-blossom, in which he rejoiced more than any other gift.

Touched by that welcome, the King graciously held out his hand to the Enchanter; if he had dared, he would have allowed his tears to flow. "Yes, it's me, Merlin! My God protect you in joy! Your fidelity pleases me, and does not astonish me. Your honor has been preserved without stain in that sepulcher. I wish to Heaven that no one had erred more than you!"

"Thank you, sire. Since the day I saw your crown, I have not saluted any other."

"O antique fidelity!" Arthur replied. "Heart of gold! Pillar of my house! How sweet it is for a king to rediscover a friend whom neither adversity nor time, not even the tomb, has been able to change!"

"A hundred times," said Merlin, "I feared that I would never see you again. I begged death very quietly not to close my eyes until I had had that joy. 'Implacable Death,' I said, 'sacred Death, enable me to see him one day, if only for an hour, in this place, at the base of this tower, and I will not dispute with you the portion of myself that remains to me.' That, Sire, is how I spoke to her. She has been kind, and I thank her. My only pain, today, is not to be able to place in your hands the homage-liege of my sepulcher. If, Sire, I could offer hospitality here at least for a day, in my hall of honor, to you and your knights, your friends and Madame Genièvre, and your nephew Tristan, and all your people and their horses, whose proud whinnies I can hear from here, the memory of it would be eternal. Forgive me, great King of the just. It is neither ill-will nor avarice of the heart."

And the good Merlin wept.

"Console yourself, friend," Arthus replied. "I know that you possess nothing in that tenebrous place that is not your King's. But you can still serve me, with a loyal heart, in the tomb where you are lying—to emerge one day, to our honor. Explain my dreams to me."

"You have only to interrogate," the Enchanter replied.

"Listen. In that night without dusk or dawn, have I dreamed everything, then?"

"There was also something real, Sire. Every time that your majesty shifted on side, the world turned over from top to bottom."

"Did that happen to me often?"

"Enough."

"How many times in the night?"

"Twenty or thirty."

"And if I moved my head, what happened?"

"France shook her head."

"And if I moved my arm?"

"Rome fell."

"If the feet?"

"The Lombard snake reared up and bit the German worm. It announced its presence to its young with long hisses."

"If the legs?"

"The marches of Germany began to tremble."

"When I propped myself up on my elbow?"

"The Gaulish boar sharpened its teeth on the rock."

"When I sat up?"

"Brittany, Germany and Sicambria threw off the bit fabricated in Italy."

"And if I sighed?"

448

"Vesuvius and Sicily trembled."

"And if I cried out?"

"The lion of justice roared, and its roars shook the towers of Gaul."

Thus Merlin explained King Arthus' dreams to him; the latter showed his contentment. At the same time as the monarch, his knights, his cavaliers and his courtiers stood at the base of the funereal tower and said, one after another: "It's true, then, Merlin, that you didn't deceive us in promising us an awakening?"

"Hard-hearted people, you can believe me now. Are you awake or asleep?"

"Awake, to be sure—but in the name of Heaven, let us not sleep the long slumber again. The dreams are too heavy."

Here Jacques, after having hesitated for a long time, dared to interrupt he courtiers, for a muted desire as gnawing him, and he could not contain himself any longer. "I see here many barons, knights and men of the court," he said, "but where are my companions of the plow that I left dormant in the stables? Where are the drowsy serfs? Why have they been forgotten? I'll go myself to wake them up and sing their songs—or is the good awakening for barons alone?"

Then Arthus, seeing that jealousy was making him speak, smiled the smile of justice and replied: "Peace, friend! Look in this direction with me and cease to be envious. Do you know those who are following me?"

Jacques looked behind him. He saw the great populations of serfs who were emerging in a swarm from the glebe, all awake like the king, bewildered, their eyes wide. They seemed never to have been sleeping the brazen slumber. At that sight, he repented of having shown so much envy, and swore that he would correct himself.

The earth also emerged from its torpor; the flowers were ashamed of appearing drowsy, the butterflies quit their cocoons, and the serpents shed their skin.

That ensured that Merlin's renown was then at its peak. He recovered at that moment all the favor he had lost on earth and in Heaven. People reproached themselves or having doubted him.

"Great God, what injustice!" was murmured on all sides. "It's true, then, that the best are always the most misunderstood."

That sudden return of the world toward Merlin also profited Jacques. He was no longer regarded with pity when he passed by, like a simple soul. Far from it; he was admired for having been alone in conserving a vague hope for so long, in spite of appearances. His past credulity appeared as an advertisement of Heaven. Even then, however, he still remained incredulous, as will be seen in one of the subsequent chapters, in which we shall also learn how difficult it was for the dead nations to be resuscitated.

VII

Walking in the woods, Jacques found the Sleeping Beauty at the food of an ivy-clad tower; her head on her arm, she was dreaming about love. By her side, on the same virgin grass, also asleep, was a person that the gods had once plunged into a similar divine sleep. It was the handsome Endymion.

At the noise of Jacques' clogs on the stony path, they both raised their eye-lids slightly and turned over. Without being aware of it, they wrapped their arms around one another while dreaming, like the elm and the vine. Jacques saw them: it annoyed him. He shook them, the one by her ducal mantle of sable fur and her cape, the other by his tunic of Tyrian purple.

Eventually, both of them opened their eyes. They both sat up, and then rose to their feet. They were both astonished to find one another so beautiful; they were also astonished to have been lying down for such a long time and sleeping beside one another. The Beauty blushed, still full of an amorous languor that increased her beauty.

"I was dreaming about you," Endymion said to her.

"And I, Seigneur, saw you in a dream, in my Gothic manor."

"Are you not Cynthia, the moon with the moist silver face?"

"Me, Cynthia? You're still dreaming, Monseigneur. Are you not my fian-cé, the Prince des Ardennes?"

"Me, the Prince des Ardennes! Open your eyes. I'm Endymion."

"Don't play that game, Seigneur. What would the barons say? Come on, let's go back to the old château. I've already lingered too long in his shady wood."

Let's go instead to my grotto in Latmos, carpeted with hyacinths. It's too long since I've watered my goats; they'll perish of thirst."

"Listen, Monseigneur. Here the sound of bells. The chaplain is calling us, to marry us at the altar in the gilded chapel."

"Listen to the bagpipe! The nymphs are calling us to my cavern to sing: 'Hymen! O Hymen!'"

"Are you a pagan then, my sweet seigneur? Since when and how? But what does it matter? Come, I'll convert you!"

While they were speaking thus, Jacques, without listening to them, led them directly to Madame Viviane, who invited the Sleeping Beauty to climb up next to her, under a ruby awning.

"Where is my lover, then?" she said, as she said down.

"Have patience, Madame. Your lover is on the threshold; he's putting on his carmine suit."

"And my courtiers?"

"They'll come, Madame; they're putting on their livery."

"And my morning gifts?"

"Here they are, Madame," Viviane replied, offering her a casket filled with pearls of dew and, laughing with surprise, she entertained both of them thus for as long as the dawn lasted.

VIII

Arthur having awoken, Merlin immediately sought information regarding the dead nations buried alongside him in his own tomb. He sent his servant to take his message outside and call them by their names, to the powerful sound of the Alpine horn. Jacques, not receiving any response, thought of singing to them in his loudest voice, dragging out each syllable, the three verses of the following aubade:

Now the star is paling;
And the singing swallow awakes,
Sleeping peoples, get out of bed!
The silver dawn is smiling!

What says the watchman on the tower?
He says: shame on those who sleep!
Get up, peoples it's daytime
The silvery dawn is paling.

Crowned with gold and jasmine,
Day is ablaze in the orchard,
What azure field appears out there?
Get up, peoples, there's your road!

Hardened as they were, however, the nations refused to put any trust in Jacques' aubades. After having jeered at him to the point of drawing more than one tear, they went back to sleeping the slumber of the dead.

It was, therefore, necessary for Merlin himself to come to them, indignantly, and he shouted, in a voice that broke his sepulcher:

"Idle nations, get up! Arthus has woken up!"

At the same time, he armed himself with a whip, which he caused to resound in the subterranean world; and the quadrigas, impatient to see the daylight again, stirred beneath the vast porticos hollowed out in the tomb.

At that noise, new for them, the dead nations awoke; they groped around them searching for the festival garments that had been prepared for them; then, clad in luminous red, they climbed into their chariots and reappeared in the daylight, young and bright, so that they seemed as many new, autumnal dawns fleeing the domain of darkness.

Which was the one that reappeared in the light first and rendered to the world a part of the lost ancient joy? Is that you, Italy, that I see hastening so rapidly from the scarcely-open tomb? Oh, be careful of the unproven path that skirts the mountains on the edge of the Adige. Have the prophet climb into your chariot in order that he might guide your horses intoxicated by the sun. If you were precipitated once again into the bloody waves of the Tiber or the Oglio, no one could save you.

Is that you passing by, Poland? You glide over the hardened snow without leaving the imprint of your rapid course therein. The false aurora is blinding you. Mistrust that which you have loved too much; that road leads to the sepulcher.

Is that you pulling ahead of the others, Hungary, whose frightened horses are still respiring death? Take pity on those you have trampled for too long, and see that they are still ready to hate you. Don't make them repent of having wept for you.

Is that you, Rumania, the most deeply buried?

Is that you, O most beloved...?

But the dust rises us beneath their feet and prevents me from discerning which is the first to emerge from the sepulcher. I only see that the gentle light of lost and rediscovered day has intoxicated them with a blind joy; already they would be lost a second time, and would already have taken the road to death again, if the prophet, without consulting them, had not climbed on to their chariots.

He guided them himself, by the best road, over the open threshold of the sepulcher, until they had accustomed themselves again to the dazzling light of the living. Then he reclosed the door of his tomb behind them and placed a large stone there that none of them could lift.

In vain lassitude, custom, indolence of heart and fear of the morrow rendered them, at moments, a taste for the sepulcher; they found it sealed; they could not get back in.

The first thing the conductor of peoples enjoined them to do, as soon as they had quit the threshold of the tomb, was to go to the noble Arthus. He welcomed them with a cheerful countenance, with the serene majesty that he had brought back from the vestibule of death; they confided mutually what dreams they had had during the night that had amassed over them; all of them, finding themselves better, without too much glory, no longer insulted anything but the darkness.

Arthur was astonished that his profound wound was closed; he would have liked to ask how it was that his blood had ceased to flow. The most heartbroken peoples also put their hands on their wounds. They consulted one another as to what had happened to them. Was it a sudden faint? Was it slumber, a dream? Was it death?

All of them looked at their nearest funeral companions and were astonished to find them alive. All of them sensed that Merlin had accomplished the
prodigy while they were buried, but none of them dared to say of their wound:
"Will it ever reopen?" Merely to think it would have been to die a second time.

IX

With things thus ordered, Merlin went to sit down on the threshold of his
tomb; and, whip in hand, he chased away the nations as they reappeared, ready
to plunge into it again. Seeing that several of them had avoided his surveillance,
and that a number of people were coldly advising them to go and repose in
death, he took the wisest course: that of destroying his sepulcher—which was
already considerably worm-eaten and undermined, almost collapsing—with his
own hands; it could only serve any longer as a dangerous refuge from night and
rapine.

With the aid of his companions, the number of which was swelled by all
the men of good will he could find, he patiently demolished his sepulcher, inside
and out—but not without warning passers-by in advance when the great walls
fell. He left one rock standing, similar to the Tourmagne of Nîmes; but soon,
that still seemed too much; he only left one stone, on which he came to sit at
dusk, having also planted around it a few bushy trees: walnut-trees, sycamores,
plane-trees, chestnut-trees, tulip-trees and Judas trees with fiery red clusters of
flowers. He had brought back from the tomb a love of beautiful shade: the only
thing by which you would have recognized that he had been buried.

In that favorite place, he liked to tread on his tombstone, and to remember
what he had said and done in the sepulcher. It was there that he arranged to meet
his friends and most enjoyed working in peace; for he had no need to speak—to
those who came to seek some hope, the location, the brute stone, spoke sufficiently for him.

He liked nothing better than the naïve surprise of good people who passed
close by; there was not one who did not ask: "Where, then, is Merlin's tomb?
The entrance was here, and it extended a long way into the surrounding region,
but we can no longer see any trace of it. Has Merlin taken his sepulcher away,
like a tent or the caravan of some shepherd?"

Then they were afraid and began to flee. Soon, they turned their heads and
changed their minds; and then, discovering Merlin in the sparkling evening
light, sitting and smiling on the debris of his tombstone, between Viviane and
his son, the reawakened people joined hands and formed an immense round
dance around him.

To the poorest, he always gave some of the savings that he had accumulated in death. It was some cloak, some still-virgin diamond, or a provision of food,
or a cordial to revive the dead. All were received with pleasure.

453

And everyone was delighted to see how easy it is for a free soul to wear away and abolish its tomb.

X

"Are you, then, a God or a son of God?" said Jacques to Merlin as soon as they found themselves alone. He would have liked to worship him and make him a fourth person in his Credo. He even made him a little *ex-voto* in secret, a simulacrum of lead that represented the sage Merlin—rather crudely, it's true—as a little rustic, sylvan divinity; and he suspended that amulet in the debris of an ancient chapel, once consecrated to nymphs. Having lit two clay lamps, he put two grains of incense next to it.

Merlin, who soon perceived that crude worship, did everything possible to oblige Jacques to renounce it. He could not abide his servant taking him for a god, and he explained in a tone that permitted no resistance:

"Will you always confuse me with the Invisible, with the only true wisdom, the only true greatness? If I have a spark of him, am I, like him, eternal light? Oh, how far I am from that, my friend! I know full well that by means of that *ex-voto*—you ought, in all conscience, have sculpted it a little less crudely—you think that you're honoring me, but, apart from the fact that the material is vile and the work barbaric, know, and may I never have to say it again, that you're only humiliating me by confusing me with all the fairground spirits that have deceived your good faith.

"You want to honor me, you say, but you don't see that you're crucifying me with that image of lead, as if I had stolen from the only sage, the only worthy individual, the only seer, compared with whom you and I are only dust. The things that I do astonish you, my son, but there's no need to be a god to do them. One day, if you follow my advice, you'll do them yourself, perhaps better than me. Magic isn't always necessary. But what is necessary, I admit, is more courage than is commonly shown, even nowadays."

Having spoken thus, he put out the two lamps, and returned the incense to the earth.

XI

In the meantime, Jacques wanted nothing more than to return to his village; he received leave to do that; and his heart almost failed him when, arriving in the evening. He saw the thatched roofs fuming above the wood bordering the Crau. He looked for the shortest path, but the long grass had covered it long ago.

Informed of his return, his best friends came to meet him on the other side of the stream. The first he perceived, coming out of the thickets, were the blond Polonius, Jonathan the Yankee, John the Englishman, with whom he was reconciled, Gauthier of Gascogny, Gustin the Bressan, still in clogs, Pancho the Araucanian, Tobie the Black, Herrman the Teuton, Zerbino the Lombard, Stefan the Rumanian, Marko the Serb and many others. They were the first who kissed his cheeks.

After them, entire peoples said that they were his family. They had him pass under arcades of flowers to where a feast had been set up. All together, you would have thought that they were brothers.

Everyone in the region, shepherds, carters, players of pipes and bagpipes, had assembled and were singing carols.

Where was his hut and his thatched roof? The thatch had been dispersed and the hut was in ruins, but everyone wanted to help him rebuild it; there was no one from far around who did not bring him at least a stone. They put a slate roof on it, and two spiral stairways at the sides, and two shady acacias nearby.

But he, visiting it sadly, said: "Where is my mother? Where are my sisters? What have you done with all my brothers?" And, not seeing them, he wept. A door opened. He saw them all come in, having seemingly just woken up, and his joy was so great that he thought he might die of it.

His dog came out of the thicket too, and came to lick his feet. It did not die, like good Ulysses' dog, on seeing its master again; on the contrary, it was rejuvenated, and followed him to work many a time.

They felt his garments, without worrying about appearances. Great God, was it really him? They had thought for such a long time that he was dead, or lost, or at least buried. Everyone wanted to know what Arthus and Merlin had said to him while they had disappeared from the world, and he told them, not in the dialect of Bretagne, Bresse or Savoy, but in Parisian French, which they all understood.

And his old companions said: "Jacques! Is that you, Jacques? Have you come back from Hell? You talk better than a king."

XII

It is true that, informed by so many adventures, by his periodic conversations with Arthus, and by the sight of Merlin escaped from the tomb, Jacques' education was better than sketchy. You would have had difficulty recognizing him.

Although he had not lived in the sepulcher, he had seen its shadow, and had contracted something of the clear sight of sages. His eyes, once myopic, always half-closed and blinking, had finally opened to the light of day, and as they were naturally large, wide and well-shaped, his physiognomy had changed completely, to his advantage. As well as his forehead being more serene, his cheeks were better nourished, his hair tidier and his beard less bushy; which, combined with his more assured stride and his tall stature—of which he had not lost an inch—made him a new man, who no longer had anything in common, except with his old probity, with the man or homunculus he had been for so long.

During Arthus' lethargy he had more than once, when he had nothing else to do, tried the crown on his head; he had accustomed himself to carrying it easily and simply, like a shepherd's hat. Often, he had kept it on his head while doing his work, sometimes even while sleeping; no one took any notice of it, so much, thanks to habit and the lapse of time, did it seem to suit him.

Utterly disgusted with men of war, he did not forgive them for having dazzled him for such a long time and almost blinded him with the flash of the sword.

As for envy, he no longer had any. Of what could he have been envious? He had all that he wanted, basing his satisfaction on the happiness of others. Content with his peasantry, as with his Frenchness, he no longer denied his ancestors, He blushed to have pretended for a while to be a gentleman.

Certainly, he would have liked to avenge the noble Arthur against all those who had insulted his slumber; he proposed to himself that he do it right away; already he was holding in his hand the blade named *Blue Death*.[169] But Arthus assured him that it would afflict him by drawing it from its scabbard. His glory would be diminished by it; his royal heart was weary of hatred; to forgive would be paying court to him. And those reasons, which would once have made Jacques leap with anger, entered into his heart; so much was it already purified, and penetrated in advance, by the rain of justice that then impregnated the earth, day and night.

XIII

The next day, at daybreak, he visited his field, which he found fallow and much diminished—but before he had even thought of complaining, it had been increased by a vast area that Hell had left as it retreated, and he found that the new portion was marvelously fertile because of the great abundance of ashes of Gomorrah, mingled with tears, with which it was covered.

Sometimes, while working it, he found beneath the soil a fang, a trident, a broken fork, or a rusty and twisted ring from the infernal chain. His plowshare sometimes ran into a calcined fragment of the furnace, and the abyss resonated beneath the plow. Then, the valiant oxen stopped, frightened by a whiff of sulfur. He took a step back himself. He contemplated the abyss, and was astonished that such a great evil could be destroyed. Then he spurred his oxen, in order to drive them across the uncrossable boundary.

And he sowed the next crop in the furrow of the accursed. He rejoiced to see his crop growing green in the mouth of Hell.

---

[169] The phrase is derived from Homer, who sometimes calls the death that closes human eyes blue for the sake of scansion.

Already he could heard blackbirds whistling where demons had whistled; he saw bullfinches nesting in the debris of Satan's worm-eaten throne.

Where the circle of the lukewarm had been, he planted his cold-sensitive vines; where the icy region of the gnashing of teeth had been, he grew winter-friendly larches and firs; but in the ditches of bitumen he assembled orange trees, lemon trees and sacred apple trees.

If a smoky lair still remained anywhere, a crevasse or a well of dolor, that was where he set up his press, and the rubicund demon of the vintage, surprised, bound, moaning, tortured and crushed under the stone poured torrents of crimson blood into the vat.

Meanwhile, at the end of a furrow, Merlin's father lay on the ground in the new grass; he raised his white head through the darnel, and seeing, in the vast plain, still accursed the day before, trees budding, vines flourishing, crops yellowing and the earth amorous beneath garlands of green, he repeated: "Behold my punishment, Jacques! I'm inflicting it on myself."

XIV

Jacques got married, not to increase the size of his property, but because Jonathan's daughter pleased him. During the marriage ceremony, a chaffinch, hidden in the foliage, sang so loudly that it would not have taken much more to drown out the spouses' *ouis*. The heavens heard it, and Jacques has several sons, all fair of face and great in heart, courage and audacity. He taught them to read Merlin's book himself.

At the end of the day, he loved to sit down on the edge of the sea of Brittany, on the cape nearest to the sunset, and there he conversed, beyond the Atlantic, with his friend Jonathan the Yankee, sitting opposite him in the savannahs on the far side of the great Ocean. In the blink of an eye, their words traversed the profound sea. Were they borne by the albatrosses, the dolphins or the winds? Without raising the voice, they were heard from one world to the other.

They talked about the daily work, the crop or the haymaking, sometimes a little business. They enquired after their families and their grandchildren. What new-born peoples, still wailing, could be heard in the cradle? What great breath from on high was passing over their heads? What dreams, good or bad, had they had last night? If assistance was necessary, a word sufficed. If death rose up between them, they aided one another with a sigh.

By that means, the prophecy of Merlin's book was realized: "Man will converse with man and the two opposite sides of the immense Ocean."

The days went by in that fashion, similar to one another, the time of Merlin's triumph having finally come. When everything was prepared, Jacques went in quest of the horses with bronze shoes that with grazing among the pools. For three days he made their litter of magic herbs and verbena; then, having fed them well on fresh gilded barley, he harnessed them to Merlin's chariot.

457

XV

And neither the triumph of Bacchus, who had been believed lost and dead in India, nor that of Osiris swallowed by Typhon, nor that of Adonis devoured by the boar's teeth, was anything by comparison with the return of Merlin, escaped from the long pilgrimage of death.

His joy on seeing so many old friends again was so great that he almost fainted. He spotted in the crowd some he thought returned to dust, and waved to them. All those who had loved him acclaimed him on the threshold, where they had come to welcome him. All now recognized his power, his wisdom and his generosity.

"Is that really him?" cried the crowd.

Then he felt such a disturbance in his soul that he thought he might die. But at that moment, the doors opened to hymns, and the echo was so powerful that the sources of life were reborn in his heart.

First came the liberated peoples, who were marching, heads erect, as if they had never been bowed down.

Then came Arthus covered by his white shield, in which the sun of justice was mirrored.

Then came the chariots clad in scarlet and crimson, laden with the tributes of the tomb.

Then came Merlin, Viviane and their child, in front of Jacques, who was carrying the harp.

After them, the legions of spirits, with Turpin marching at their head.

After them, the population of exiles—and for that day, they had recovered their robust youth.

In that place, the cortege had formed of all those who had known Merlin and who figure in this story, all those to whom he attached his thought or his gaze momentarily, and all those who had denied, insulted or hated him. Only the indifferent were excluded.

After them came, as in the Olympic fields, fuming quadrigas; they were laden with insignia drawn from Hell.

And, as in Naples on funeral days, a multitude advanced carrying banners; on every floating banner could be read:

Hell is vanquished!

Then, behind Merlin's chariot, came the spirits of Hell, heads bowed, as prisoners, mute, covered in sweat and in despair, for they believed that they were going to be immolated. From their midst emerged a dull roar, which was that of the abyss. Their hands were not tied behind their backs; they were enchained by their own terror. At their head marched their King, who contained them with a glance. Without speaking, he mastered them, seemingly saying: *Follow him! He's my son!*

458

Momentarily uncertain, the infernal troupe hastened to follow the banner-carriers. But their legion was confused; they marched sightlessly, so dazzled were they by the light of day. They resembled night-birds surprised by the summer sun at the foot of Minerva's white house.

As they passed by, the nations went pale, fearing that they might break their bonds; but, seeing that they were tamed and prisoners, they resumed following the cortege.

Then came the birds of the woods, with iridescent plumage; they flew, soaring and singing, over the cortege, shading it with their wings.

After them was seen the troupe of bards, poets and all those able to sing hymns. Their voices rise up above the clouds. They looked at one another while they sang: "Triumph! O Triumph!"

Then came the spirits of air, water and fire; they were brandishing thyrses and formed an innumerable multitude; then those who had never emerged from veins of metal and precious stones, but found themselves free that day; those who inhabited the cold Alpine glaciers from which they never descended, which no sun of ancient days had been able to warm; those who lived petrified in the heart of rocks; those who made their abode in the Milky Way and disdained to descend therefrom; those who had never had names in any language and had never been evoked; those who hid in the souls of the just; those who lived in inexorable reclusiveness in the brazen skies, or vegetated dormant in the depths of ages of silver and bronze; and those who hid in hardened breasts closed to pity.

All of them emerged pell-mell from their retreats for the first time, and they too advanced, crying: "Triumph! O Triumph!"

And the skies of bronze and lead commenced to stir; those who had never wept shed tears of joy that could not be stemmed.

Even the seraphim and the cherubim, lost in the ultimate confines of the Empyrean, felt delight; cheeks inflated, they cried out to the four winds: "Alleluia! Glory to God!"

And those who were sculpted in stone in the porches of cathedrals suddenly opened their mouths of granite and porphyry. And all those voices—pagan or Christian, human or titanic, angelic or demonic, repeated: "Triumph! O Triumph! Hell is vanquished."

Then came, crowned with myrtle, the twelve great gods; and all those who were along the road left their dwellings to swell that legion. Many had the feet of goats, or bulls, some of antelopes, hopping as they marched. Prometheus drove them before him like a shepherd pressing his flock; whenever they stopped he threatened them with the debris of his chains.

They were followed by Death on her pale, emaciated, breathless horse. She was covered with iron armor, but followed at a considerable distance, and also seemed to be among the vanquished.

And the cortege went all the way around the world!

Where the sea commenced, vessels were found, which carried them to the other shore. Those vessels whinnied like sea-horses, and black vapor emerged from their nostrils. Then came the dragons and the winged bulls that had carried Isaiah, Daniel and the ancient prophets. Breathless now, they took the new prophet on their wings and carried him across the abyss.

When they passed by, the isles quivered with hope. The continents lost in the vast seas emerged from the depths of the waters, on columns of coral, as the king of justice approached. The errant humans who feed on the marrow of palms, those who live in bamboo huts, those who have not yet discovered fire, those who wear loincloths and dress in sarongs, and those who eat the flesh and hearts of humans climbed to the summits of rocks and thought to themselves: *Is that the Great Spirit passing by?*

And there was not a single island, gulf, desert or cleft in the ground from which a voice did not merge, saying: "Triumph! O Triumph! Hell is vanquished."

SF & FANTASY

Adolphe Alhaiza. *Cybele*
Alphonse Allais. *The Adventures of Captain Cap*
Henri Allorge. *The Great Cataclysm*
Guy d'Armen. *Doc Ardan: The City of Gold and Lepers*
G.-J. Arnaud. *The Ice Company*
Charles Asselineau. *The Double Life*
Henri Austruy. *The Eupantophone; The Olotelepan; The Petitpaon Era*
Cyprien Bérard. *The Vampire Lord Ruthwen*
S. Henry Berthoud. *Martyrs of Science*
Aloysius Bertrand. *Gaspard de la Nuit*
Richard Bessière. *The Gardens of the Apocalypse*
Albert Bleunard. *Ever Smaller*
Félix Bodin. *The Novel of the Future*
Louis Boussenard. *Monsieur Synthesis*
Alphonse Brown. *City of Glass; The Conquest of the Air*
Emile Calvet. *In a Thousand Years*
André Caroff. *The Terror of Madame Atomos; Miss Atomos; The Return of Madame Atomos; The Mistake of Madame Atomos; The Monsters of Madame Atomos; The Revenge of Madame Atomos; The Resurrection of Madame Atomos; The Mark of Madame Atomos; The Spheres of Madame Atomos*
Félicien Champsaur. *The Human Arrow; Ouha, King of the Apes; Pharaoh's Wife*
Didier de Chousy. *Ignis*
Jules Clarétie. *Obsession*
Michel Corday. *The Eternal Flame*
André Couvreur. *The Necessary Evil; Caresco, Superman; The Exploits of Professor Tornada* (3 vols.)
Captain Danrit. *Undersea Odyssey*
C. I. Defontenay. *Star (Psi Cassiopeia)*
Charles Derennes. *The People of the Pole*
Georges Dodds (anthologist). *The Missing Link*
Harry Dickson. *The Heir of Dracula*
Jules Dornay. *Lord Ruthven Begins*
Alfred Driou. *The Adventures of a Parisian Aeronaut*
Sâr Dubnotal *vs. Jack the Ripper*
Alexandre Dumas. *The Return of Lord Ruthven*
Renée Dunan. *Baal*
J.-C. Dunyach. *The Night Orchid; The Thieves of Silence*
Henri Duvernois. *The Man Who Found Himself*
Achille Eyraud. *Voyage to Venus*
Henri Falk. *The Age of Lead*
Paul Féval. *Anne of the Isles; Knightshade; Revenants; Vampire City; The Vampire Countess; The Wandering Jew's Daughter*
Paul Féval, *fils. Felifax, the Tiger-Man*
Charles de Fieux. *Lamékis*
Louis Forest. *Someone is Stealing Children in Paris*

Arnould Galopin. *Doctor Omega; Doctor Omega and the Shadowmen* (anthology)
Judith Gautier. *Isoline and the Serpent-Flower*
H. Gayar. *The Marvelous Adventures of Serge Myrandhal on Mars*
Léon Gozlan. *The Vampire of the Val-de-Grâce*
G.L. Gick. *Harry Dickson and the Werewolf of Rutherford Grange*
Edmond Haraucourt. *Illusions of Immortality*
Nathalie Henneberg. *The Green Gods*
V. Hugo, P. Foucher & P. Meurice. *The Hunchback of Notre-Dame*
Romain d'Huissier. *Hexagon: Dark Matter*
Jules Janin. *The Magnetized Corpse*
Michel Jeury. *Chronolysis*
Gustave Kahn. *The Tale of Gold and Silence*
Gérard Klein. *The Mote in Time's Eye*
Fernand Kolney. *Love in 5000 Years*
Paul Lacroix. *Danse Macabre*
Louis-Guillaume de La Follie. *The Unpretentious Philosopher*
Jean de La Hire. *Enter the Nyctalope; The Nyctalope on Mars; The Nyctalope vs. Lucifer; The Nyctalope Steps In; Night of the Nyctalope; Return of the Nyctalope; The Fiery Wheel*
Etienne-Léon de Lamothe-Langon. *The Virgin Vampire*
André Laurie. *Spiridon*
Gabriel de Lautrec. *The Vengeance of the Oval Portrait*
Alain le Drimeur. *The Future City*
Georges Le Faure & Henri de Graffigny. *The Extraordinary Adventures of a Russian Scientist Across the Solar System* (2 vols.)
Gustave Le Rouge. *The Mysterious Doctor Cornelius* (3 vols.); *The Vampires of Mars; The Dominion of the World* (w/Gustave Guitton) (4 vols.)
Jules Lermina. *Mysteryville; Panic in Paris; To-Ho and the Gold Destroyers; The Secret of Zippelius*
André Lichtenberger. *The Centaurs; The Children of the Crab*
Jean-Marc & Randy Lofficier. *Edgar Allan Poe on Mars; The Katrina Protocol; Pacifica; Robonocchio; Return of the Nyctalope;* (anthologists) *Tales of the Shadowmen 1-10*
Xavier Mauméjean. *The League of Heroes*
Joseph Méry. *The Tower of Destiny*
Hippolyte Mettais. *The Year 5865*
Louise Michel. *The Human Microbes; The New World*
Tony Moilin. *Paris in the Year 2000*
José Moselli. *Illa's End*
John-Antoine Nau. *Enemy Force*
Marie Nizet. *Captain Vampire*
C. Nodier, A. Beraud & Toussaint-Merle. *Frankenstein*
Henri de Parville. *An Inhabitant of the Planet Mars*
Gaston de Pawlowski. *Journey to the Land of the 4th Dimension*
Georges Pellerin. *The World in 2000 Years*
Ernest Pérochon. *The Frenetic People*
Pierre Pelot. *The Child Who Walked on the Sky*
J. Polidori, C. Nodier, E. Scribe. *Lord Ruthven the Vampire*
P.-A. Ponson du Terrail. *The Vampire and the Devil's Son; The Immortal Woman*

Edgar Quinet. *Ahasuerus*
Henri de Régnier. *A Surfeit of Mirrors*
Maurice Renard. *The Blue Peril; Doctor Lerne; The Doctored Man; A Man Among the Microbes; The Master of Light*
Jean Richepin. *The Wing; The Crazy Corner*
Albert Robida. *The Adventures of Saturnin Farandoul; The Clock of the Centuries; Chalet in the Sky; The Electric Life*
J.-H. Rosny Aîné. *Helgvor of the Blue River; The Givreuse Enigma; The Mysterious Force; The Navigators of Space; Vamireh; The World of the Variants; The Young Vampire*
Marcel Rouff. *Journey to the Inverted World*
Han Ryner. *The Superhumans*
Angelo de Sorr. *The Vampires of London*
Brian Stableford. *The New Faust at the Tragicomique;The Empire of the Necromancers (The Shadow of Frankenstein; Frankenstein and the Vampire Countess; Frankenstein in London); Sherlock Holmes & The Vampires of Eternity; The Stones of Camelot; The Wayward Muse.* (anthologist) *News from the Moon; The Germans on Venus; The Supreme Progress; The World Above the World; Nemoville; Investigations of the Future; The Conqueror of Death*
Jacques Spitz. *The Eye of Purgatory*
Kurt Steiner. *Ortog*
Eugène Thébault. *Radio-Terror*
C.-F. Tiphaigne de La Roche. *Amilec*
Louis Ulbach. *Prince Bonifacio*
Théo Varlet. *The Golden Rock. The Xenobiotic Invasion; The Castaways of Eros; Timeslip Troopers* (w/André Blandin); *The Martian Epic* (w/Octave Joncquel)
Paul Vibert. *The Mysterious Fluid*
Villiers de l'Isle-Adam. *The Scaffold; The Vampire Soul*
Philippe Ward. *Artahe*
Philippe Ward & Sylvie Miller. *The Song of Montségur*

www.ingramcontent.com/pod-product-compliance
Lightning Source LLC
Chambersburg PA
CBHW030927020726
47498CB00001B/142